PENGUIN BOOKS

THE RAPSTONE CHRONICLES

John Mortimer is a playwright, novelist and former practising barrister. During the war he worked with the Crown Film Unit and published a number of novels before turning to the theatre with such plays as *The Dock Brief*, *The Wrong Side of the Park* and *A Voyage Round My Father*. He has written many film scripts and radio and television plays including six plays on the life of Shakespeare, the Rumpole plays, which won him the British Academy Writer of the Year Award, and the adaptation of Evelyn Waugh's *Brideshead Revisited*. His translations of Feydeau have been performed at the National Theatre and are published in Penguin as *Three Boulevard Farces*.

Penguin publishes his collections of stories: *Rumpole of the Bailey*, *The Trials of Rumpole*, *Rumpole's Return*, *Rumpole for the Defence*, *Rumpole and the Golden Thread*, *Rumpole's Last Case*, *Rumpole and the Age of Miracles*, *Rumpole à la Carte* and *Rumpole on Trial*, as well as *The First Rumpole Omnibus* and *The Second Rumpole Omnibus*. Penguin also publishes two volumes of John Mortimer's plays, his acclaimed autobiography *Clinging to the Wreckage*, which won the *Yorkshire Post* Book of the Year Award, *In Character* and *Character Parts*, which contain interviews with some of the most famous men and women of our time, and his bestselling novels, *Charade*, *Like Men Betrayed*, *The Narrowing Stream*, *Paradise Postponed*, its sequel *Titmuss Regained*, *Summer's Lease* and *Dunster*. *Paradise Postponed*, *Summer's Lease*, *Titmuss Regained* and all the Rumpole books have been made into successful television series. John Mortimer lives with his wife and their two daughters in what was once his father's house in the Chilterns.

JOHN MORTIMER

THE RAPSTONE CHRONICLES

PARADISE POSTPONED
TITMUSS REGAINED

PENGUIN BOOKS

PENGUIN BOOKS

Published by the Penguin Group
Penguin Books Ltd, 27 Wrights Lane, London W8 5TZ, England
Penguin Books USA Inc., 375 Hudson Street, New York, New York 10014, USA
Penguin Books Australia Ltd, Ringwood, Victoria, Australia
Penguin Books Canada Ltd, 10 Alcorn Avenue, Toronto, Ontario, Canada M4V 3B2
Penguin Books (NZ) Ltd, 182–190 Wairau Road, Auckland 10, New Zealand

Penguin Books Ltd, Registered Offices: Harmondsworth, Middlesex, England

Paradise Postponed first published 1985
Titmuss Regained first published 1990
This omnibus edition first published by Viking 1991
Published in Penguin Books 1992
3 5 7 9 10 8 6 4 2

Printed in England by Clays Ltd, St Ives plc

CONTENTS

Introduction

Is this the twilight of Titmuss? Is the Hartscombe boy who rose without trace (as a senior member of his party said at the time) to occupy a number of important Cabinet posts in the last ten years, and now presides over H.E.A.P. (the key Ministry of Housing, Ecological Affairs and Planning), about to become as much a creature of the past as the landowning Conservative grandee, the 1960s flower-child and the 1970s all-powerful Trades Union boss? Are we, in truth, in the Götterdämmerung of the Titmuss years? If so, it is perhaps a good moment to consider what Titmuss has done for England, and what, indeed, England has done for Titmuss. Whatever the future holds in store, shall we look on his like again?

The public face of Titmuss is well known, and has been almost too uncritically reproduced in *Leslie Titmuss, the People's Conservative* by Timothy Warboys (Fortress Press, £14.95). He has become known as a sardonic wit, a card and a man who gives honest utterance to the feelings of ordinary citizens, one who doesn't give a damn for what liberal intellectuals think. Liberal intellectuals are, after all, in the Titmuss view responsible for most of the ills of the modern world, from drug abuse to the B.B.C. Some of his phrases have become part of the language, as when he called the Welfare State 'the Scroungers' Charter', or the Opposition 'ageing hippies' because their principal concern seemed to be free hip replacements to a population continually growing older. 'One chap's plastic hip,' Titmuss was fond of saying when he was at Health, 'is another chap's crippling taxation.' The politician who referred to barristers as 'wallies in wigs, wrapped in the tattered gowns of class privilege', and called the unemployed 'ladies and gentlemen of leisure', has always been sure of a headline or a place on any chat show. It has been his proud boast that he has moved the Conservative Party 'from White's Club to the Pig and Whistle', although perhaps his most enthusiastic supporters are not in the Public Bar but the middle-management canteen and the local Rotary Club. However that may be, the England that came of age politically in the eighties grew up in the image of Leslie Titmuss.

Born fifty-four years ago in 'The Spruces', Skurfield, a small village in the Rapstone Valley outside Hartscombe, Titmuss has always spoken with pride of his working-class origins. In fact his father, George Titmuss, was a clerk in the local brewery, Simcox Ales, although his mother Elsie had worked as a cook in one of the local stately homes. The 'People's Conservative' often refers to the fact that he earned his pocket-money by 'cutting nettles' in the Rector's garden. It is perhaps ironic that the Rector of Rapstone who helped support the young Titmuss was the Rev. Simeon Simcox (sometimes known as the Red Rector of Rapstone), whose tall figure and flying grey hair were seen at so many C.N.D. marches and all-night vigils against apartheid. Titmuss told reporters when Simeon Simcox died that he 'had an immense regard for the old man', who had 'taught me a lot'. Later he was always at pains to point out that the old Red Rector 'could afford to be a Socialist because of his large shareholding in Simcox Ales, the family business'. He has also frequently quoted the saying that Simeon Simcox and his wife Dorothy, who were both on the board of the *New Statesman* and frequent speakers at Fabian weekends, 'wanted the working classes to rule the country but had no desire to ask any of them to tea'. This remark has always been found particularly wounding by the more mandarin type of well-heeled left-winger; perhaps because of the unpalatable truth it contains.

Politically this may be one of Titmuss's greatest achievements. He has made the left-wing intellectuals seem privileged, paternalistic and old-fashioned hypocrites, who preach about the evils of materialism to a new, ambitious working class who are only interested in buying their council houses, getting a second car and taking holidays in Bangkok. He has been quick to deride the Red Rector's sermons about social equality and the fair division of wealth, being composed, as they were, in the comfort of an eight-bedroomed rectory supported by a considerable private income. Later he was able to make Simeon Simcox's followers, with their concern for such matters as education and the preservation of the countryside, seem like woolly-minded conservative Canutes trying to order back the rising tide of history. Socialists – and this is a real Titmuss achievement – have been made to seem like Conservatives with a very small 'c'.

Titmuss's first struggle, however, was not against the left but against the traditional elements in his own party, whom he has called 'the Old Etonian eggheads and the Hooray Henrys from Harrow'. And here again his career has not been without its contradictions. At the start of the Titmuss rise to fame the chairman of the Hartscombe party was Sir Nicholas Fanner whose family had occupied Rapstone Manor since the Middle Ages. Sir Nicholas was a typical Knight of the Shires, concerned about the welfare of his tenants, to whom he personally delivered blankets, pounds of tea and boxes of biscuits at Christmas, a sympathetic J.P. and a great builder of 'workmen's cottages'. 'He was one of the dear old dinosaurs of the Tory Party,' Titmuss has said of him, 'and absolutely ripe for extinction.' However that may have been, Leslie Titmuss married Charlotte, the only daughter of the 'dear old dinosaur', and became, by a distinct irony of fate, the owner of the beautiful and much restored Rapstone Manor.

Titmuss's career undoubtedly began when he made his speech, as an aspiring candidate, to the Hartscombe Conservative Selection Committee. There are still members of the party who remember the deathly pale and deeply intense young Titmuss claiming the party for the 'true Conservatives like my father, who knows the value of money because he never had any, and saved up for five years to get our first Ford Prefect without a penny on the Never-Never'. These were the sort of supporters the party needed to win over, he said, and not 'the chaps in the City or the folks from the stately homes who'll vote for us anyway'. Needless to say Titmuss won the adoption contest against the Old Harrovian Christopher Kempenflatt (of Kempenflatts the builders); he went on to win the election and has sat for Hartscombe and Worsfield South ever since.

After a brief and successful career in the City (his partners came near to bankruptcy but Titmuss emerged with a fortune far greater than any dreamt of by Simeon Simcox, which enabled him to devote the rest of his life to politics) he set about changing the face of England. There are now few, except for the Royal Family and the Church of England, who haven't adopted, to a greater or lesser degree, the Titmuss attitudes. These are said by most people, and particularly by Leslie Titmuss himself, to be a great dependence on hard work, thrift, common sense, self-interest, market forces and a refusal to suffer fools, or even idealists, gladly. As a result the 'People's Conservative' has claimed in his many speeches and in his recent Adam Smith lecture that England is now a more efficient, slimmed-down, hard-working and admirable place than ever it was in the soft and soppy days of Wilson or Callaghan state Socialism. Doubts have been expressed, of course, and murmurings were heard even at the high point of the Titmuss era, the year of the Big Bang on the Stock Exchange and before the Docklands development fell into decline. Had England become a country that no longer produced anything of any value to anyone? A collection of service industries doing nothing but serve each other, with a population of brokers and bankers and P.R. men and people in advertising – in fact a nation of hairdressers? 'Nothing wrong with a nation of hairdressers,' Titmuss said in his speech to Allied Cosmetics, 'provided all the hairdressers vote Tory.' Other questions came to be asked, such as, is it absolutely necessary for so many of us to be sleeping in cardboard boxes? 'If a man prefers living in a cigarette carton to going out and finding a job of work,' Titmuss said on a recent *Any Questions?* programme, 'who am I to interfere with the liberty of the subject?' That universities and schools are starved of funds is a frequently heard complaint, but 'I never heard that a close study of medieval poetry did much for the balance of payments,' Titmuss said on receiving an honorary degree in Political Science at Worsfield University.

Sometimes it seems that the Titmuss vision of prosperity and hard work is a sort of dream kept alive by a few pungent phrases and a great deal of North Sea oil. But politics, like beauty, is more often than not in the eye of the beholder, and there is no doubt that a large number of people, for a considerable amount of time, felt more secure with Titmuss and his like at the helm. And it would only be fair to say that England has become a less snobbish place, perhaps on the American or Australian model, since the voice of the Titmuss was heard in the land.

So what has happened? Why has the potent dream faded? How can we speak, today, of the twilight of Titmuss? At least one of the answers, I think, must be 'Greenery', and to understand the term and its effect we should perhaps take another brief look at the life of the Minister of State which has, once again, such a curious way of reflecting the political events.

After the death of his first wife (in a somewhat mysterious road accident at Worsfield Heath) Titmuss recently married the young widow of Professor Anthony Sidonia, an Oxford history don with as impeccable Socialist mandarin credentials as those of the Rev. Simeon Simcox. He has also acquired Rapstone Manor, but it, and the valley over which it stands, are threatened by a new development, financed by Kempenflatts, of some ten thousand houses, to be known as Fallowfield Country Town. So, as head of the Ministry concerned with planning, Titmuss has come up against the problem of the English countryside and, in particular, that part of the countryside in which his own back garden is situated.

Leslie Titmuss's attitude to the preservers of rural England, of whom his late father-in-law Sir Nicholas Fanner was a leading light, was simply derisory. 'I would say this to the whingers and whiners in their tweed hats and green wellies who come and lecture me about England's green and pleasant land,' he said in a speech to the United Construction and Developers Association, 'I would say my old father had a name for you, "Dogs in the Manger". And I would say that while I'm at H.E.A.P. there can be no "No Go" areas in the free-market economy. After all, if we'd spent all our time worrying about the wind warbler and the lesser spotted toadstool, we'd never have built Manchester!'

Later, however, and perhaps as the threat of Fallowfield Country Town grew more imminent, the Titmuss utterances took on a slightly greenish tinge. Addressing the Birmingham Chamber of Commerce he spoke in laudatory terms of the whale. At a Southampton Trade Fair the black rhino came in for a favourable mention, as did bottle banks and lead-free petrol. There were distinct signs that Titmuss was becoming ozone-friendly. And not long ago he told a meeting of the Bow Group which was discussing planning that 'We shouldn't despise the green-welly brigade of rural preservationists. They've got votes, haven't they, and we should be careful not to lose them.' And he has said to the Countryside Association, 'I should know all about England's green and pleasant land. I walked home from school through the woods and often picked a bunch of bluebells for my mother, who's still alive, bless her.'

The discovery that has struck the Titmuss philosophy and left it badly holed is that caring for the environment is quite inconsistent with the free-market economy. Green and true-blue are colours that don't, unfortunately, mix. Preserving the countryside, protecting the woodlands, concern for the ozone layer, all demand levels of government intervention unthinkable in the heady days of victory over the miners and the Falklands War.

Introduction

The high spring of *laissez-faire* economics is over, the bloom is gone and, such is the nature of politics, with the bloom goes Titmuss.

Who will take his place? It seems likely that Conservatism in the Titmuss mould is now out of style, and his successors may be those prepared to revert to the old consensus days of Butler and Harold Wilson. But what of the left? If free-market Toryism has taken a beating it's as nothing to what recent events in Europe have done to the hazier dreams of the Rev. Simeon Simcox. The Labour Party seems to have achieved its huge rise in the opinion polls by freeing itself from what are seen as the tentacles of a Socialist octopus. So what is the new, up-and-coming Labour M.P. going to be like? No doubt he will have extinguished the dear old Trades Union dinosaur. Unquestionably he will be outspoken, quick-witted, with a talent for P.R. and a complete freedom from class distinctions. He will, of course, be wearing a blue suit with a discreet tie, own a car phone and a word processor and believe in free enterprise in a mixed economy. Is the stage set, after the next election, for the emergence of the first Labour Titmuss? Whatever happens, of one thing there is no doubt, British politics will remain a fertile ground for comedy.

John Mortimer, 1991

The Rt Hon. Leslie Titmuss, O.B.E., M.P.

12 October 1936   Born only son of George and Elsie Titmuss of 'The Spruces', Skurfield, nr Hartscombe. Educated Hartscombe Grammar. Studies bookkeeping and accountancy at Worsfield Polytechnic.

1954   Joins the Hartscombe Young Conservatives. Becomes their Secretary. Starts a career working for various City property developers.

1962   Marries Charlotte Fanner, only daughter of Sir Nicholas and Lady Fanner of Rapstone Manor, Rapstone, nr Hartscombe. Joins Kempenflatts, builders and property developers, becomes a director.

1966   Enters Parliament as Member for Hartscombe and Worsfield South.

1970   Only son Nicholas George Titmuss born. Becomes P.P.S. at the Ministry of Technology in Mr Heath's government. Later Junior Minister at Communications.

1975   Leaves Kempenflatts, having sold his shares for a profit, alleged to be around £4 million.

1979   Made Minister of Technology in Mrs Thatcher's new

Conservative government. Subsequent posts: Communications, Domestic Policy, Law and Order, Privatization, etc.

1983   Charlotte Titmuss (née Fanner) killed in an accident at Worsfield Heath. Titmuss insists, 'She was never a member of C.N.D.'

1984   Becomes Minister of Housing, Ecological Affairs and Planning (H.E.A.P.).

1989   Lady Fanner dies and Titmuss takes possession of Rapstone Manor. Marries Jenny, widow of the late Tony Sidonia, Miller Professor of Ecclesiastical History and Fellow of St Joseph's College, Oxford.

Paradise Postponed

For Penny, Emily and Rosamond

Acknowledgement is gratefully made by the author and publishers to the following:

Faber & Faber for kind permission to reproduce lines from *Look Stranger*, XXX in W. H. Auden's *Collected Poems*, edited by Edward Mendelson, copyright 1937, renewed 1965, by W. H. Auden, and for the same extract to Random House, Inc.

The National Trust for Places of Historic Interest and Natural Beauty and Macmillan London Ltd for kind permission to reproduce an extract from 'The Gods of the Copybook Headings' in *The Definitive Edition of Rudyard Kipling's Verse*, copyright 1919 by Rudyard Kipling, and for the same extract to the National Trust and Doubleday & Co., Inc.

The Literary Trustees of Walter de la Mare and The Society of Authors as their representative for kind permission to reproduce lines from 'The Listeners' by Walter de la Mare.

Chappell Music Ltd London for kind permission to reproduce lines from 'Twilight Time', lyrics by Buck Ram, music by Morty Nevins and Al Nevins, copyright © 1944 by Campbell Porgie, Inc. and by Duchess Music Corporation. Copyright renewed 1972 and assigned to Devon Music, Inc. N.Y. for U.S.A. Rights in Canada administered by Manitou Music (Canada), a division of M.C.A. Canada Ltd. Used by permission. All rights reserved.

Mills Music, Inc. for kind permission to reproduce lines from 'Ain't Misbehavin'', copyright © 1929 by Mills Music, Inc. and renewed. All rights reserved.

Frank Music Corporation for kind permission to reproduce lines from 'On a Slow Boat to China' by Frank Loesser, copyright © 1948 by Frank Music Corporation. Renewed 1976. All rights reserved.

Belwin Mills Music Ltd for kind permission to reproduce lines from 'St James Infirmary' by Joe Primrose.

CONTENTS

Part One

In the houses
The little pianos are closed, and a clock strikes.
And all sway forward on the dangerous flood
Of history, that never sleeps or dies,
And, held one moment, burns the hand.

from *Look Stranger*, XXX
W. H. Auden

Chapter One

DEATH OF A SAINT

'I had a disagreeable dream,' the old man said.

'What?'

'I thought we'd grown out of all that in first-year theology.' He looked bewildered. 'God on a cloud, a sort of pink electric light bulb behind his head. He was actually busying himself,' he clearly found the conduct he had to describe unsympathetic, 'judging people! Parting the sheep from the goats. That sort of thing.'

'Don't worry.'

'He was surrounded with cherubim. Your mother would find them dreadfully vulgar. She wouldn't give them shelf room in porcelain.'

'It's not true,' the younger man said.

'I suppose not. I shan't have to wait very long to find out.'

The old man was wearing striped flannel pyjamas and lying on a bed on which sunlight was falling. He was tall and thin, looks which gave him, in the course of his lifetime, the appearance of a rather bothered eagle. Now, white-haired and thinner than ever at the age of eighty, he was almost beautiful. His name was Simeon Simcox, and he was Rector of the village of Rapstone Fanner.

There was nothing ecclesiastical, however, about the Rectory bedroom. There was no crucifix, or prayer-book by the bed. Like the rest of the house it was furnished in austere taste, betraying a nervous embarrassment at the idea of ornament or

9

ostentation, with only a few discreet china objects, a William Morris chest and a Paul Nash landscape by way of decoration. There was about the room rather more comfort than might be bought on the stipend of a Church of England clergyman.

On the dressing-table, beside the Rector's silver-backed hair-brushes, were some framed family photographs: his two boys in long shorts and short haircuts in the Rectory garden; Simeon Simcox and his wife, Dorothy, at the time of their wedding, standing outside Rapstone village church, he in a dog-collar and tweed suit, she in a silk dress that was deliberately unbridal, looking gently amused and vaguely 'artistic'. There was also a yellowing Victorian group showing members of his family and a selection of loyal workers standing outside the Brewery in the local town, over the gate of which, an entrance for dray horses and loads of barrels, the gilded sign read 'Simcox Ales'.

The other occupant of the room was in his late forties, a doctor who was there as a son. Fred Simcox lived alone in a flat above his surgery, played the drums and listened to old jazz records in much of his spare time. Looking at his father he felt a wave of affection for the old man, who seemed to be approaching death, like most of the other events in his long life, with a puzzled goodwill under which lay a certain dogged persistence. He thought, almost for the first time, that he could understand what his father was saying and it made him smile. But the joke, if it were a joke, came too late, like something shouted from a train window, after the last awkward and prolonged goodbyes have been said and after, to everyone's relief, the guard has blown his whistle. All the same, he sat now, by his father's bed, and showed an interest.

'The ridiculous thing was . . .' Perhaps it wasn't a joke. Simeon seemed genuinely perturbed. 'He bore a remarkable resemblance to Dr Salter. Salter's an unbeliever, of course, and he hasn't even got a beard. You'd think he'd be nothing whatever like God but the resemblance was quite striking.'

'You say he was parting the sheep and the goats?'

'There was some sort of judgement going on.' Simeon Simcox frowned unhappily.

'You shouldn't worry about that.'

'Shouldn't I?'

'Of course not.'

'Judgement!' The Rector turned his head to look at his younger son and spoke with a fading urgency. 'I should like you to know that it hasn't been so simple.' And then his voice came from further away, as though the train were already drawing out of the station. 'Not half so straightforward as it might have looked.'

The Rapstone Valley is only some two hours' drive to the west of London but its inhabitants have been spared, no doubt for longer than they deserve, the slow but inexorable march of civilization. At the head of the valley the road divides, one way leading south to Rapstone Fanner, the other north to the villages of Skurfield and Picton Principal. Standing by the signpost and looking down at the landscape spread out below you can see beech woods, thick hedgerows and fields of corn, with an occasional tiled roof over a flint and brick building, a group of barns and the distant tower of Rapstone Church. After a deeper acquaintance with the place you may realize that the flint cottages have been converted to house a pop star or a couple in advertising and the roof of what looks like a farm-building now covers an indoor swimming-pool with sauna attached in which guests flop like woozy porpoises after Sunday lunch. Such matters are discreetly arranged. The first sight of the Rapstone Valley is of something unexpectedly isolated and uninterruptedly rural; a solitary jogger is the only outward sign of urban pollution.

As with the countryside the changes in Rapstone village are behind the walls, which have been carefully preserved to placate the planners. It is true that what was once a shop has been turned, skilfully and expensively, into a weekend cottage with a B.M.W. parked in front of the aubretia-covered garden wall. What was once the school, which still has a bell in a little turret on top of it, has been taken over by two ladies with grey hair and booming voices who illustrate children's books. In fact the only institutional buildings left unchanged are the church, with its Norman tower, its ornate seventeenth-century tomb and Victorian additions, and the Rectory, approached through an open gateway, past the dark and dusty laurels of a short driveway and entered, under a pointed, neo-Gothic porch, through a front door which is never locked. There were an unusual number of cars parked in front of the Rectory and round the churchyard, and there was a small clutch of reporters and a couple of press photographers on the day of the Rector's funeral, for Simeon Simcox had, in his lifetime, achieved a fame, some would say a notoriety, which stretched far beyond the boundaries of his parish.

'We brought nothing into this world, and it is certain we can carry nothing out,' said the Reverend Kevin Bulstrode, Vicar of Skurfield, conducting the service in the unavoidable absence of the Rector of Rapstone.

'*Naked* came I out of my mother's womb, and naked *shall* I return thither,' a furious and gravelly whisper came from the congregation. The Vicar of Skurfield, who would shortly take over Rapstone also when the parishes were amalgamated under a new scheme of 'rationalization', did his best to ignore the interruption. 'The Lord gives and the Lord takes away, blessed be the name of the Lord,' he continued bravely.

For a moment the interrupter was quiet. He was a tall, thickening fifty-year-old, whose red hair was now flecked with grey but to whom watery blue eyes and a look of perpetual discontent gave the appearance of an irate, retired sea captain. He wore a thick tweed suit in spite of the late summer weather, with a heavy gold watch-chain, and a bright silk handkerchief lolled from his breast-pocket. When Henry Simcox, the late Rector's eldest son, published his first novel his name had been connected with a group of angry young men; now he was a grumpy, late-middle-aged man. Once his political ideas had been thought as red as his hair; now he gave many warnings on the menace of the Left and wrote articles for the Sunday papers on the moral disintegration of life in Britain today. In these contributions he never failed to denounce the abandonment, by the Church of England, of the King James Bible and the older forms of prayer, although his knowledge of these matters was sometimes unreliable.

'Shush, Henry,' his wife Lonnie, sitting beside him, had whispered nervously when he interrupted the Vicar, but Henry grumbled to himself, 'Why should the Rev. Trendy Kev get away with castrating the prayer-book?'

Lorna (Lonnie) Simcox was not only concerned on account of her husband's liturgical complaints. She looked behind her from time to time during the prayers. She was conscious that she was, as she would say, Mrs Henry Simcox Mark Two, the Numero Due, and the Numero Uno was seated a couple of rows behind her gazing at her, as she imagined it, with studied contempt.

In fact Agnes Simcox, Henry's first wife, née Salter and the only daughter of that late Dr Salter whom the Rector had, in one of his last dreams, so strangely confused with the Almighty, was not seeing anything but a blur, as she had left her glasses in the car. Short-sightedness added to her habitual expression of ironic contempt, so that she looked as though she were watching a theatrical performance which she had decided not to enjoy. She was huddled into a raincoat with a fur collar, dressed for the damp and draughty inside of the church rather than for the bright sunshine of the day outside. She was in her late forties, but when a shaft of light from a clear window struck her face it was only a moderately unkind blow; her beauty was, on the whole, less ravaged by the passage of time than she had the right to expect. Agnes was thinking a little of her past, her long knowledge of the Simcox family and the days of her childhood, but mainly she was longing for a cigarette. She heard the Vicar say, 'I'm sure that neither death, nor life, nor angels . . .' and 'I am *persuaded* that neither death . . .' she heard Henry Simcox, her ex-husband, correct him gloomily.

So the Reverend Simeon Simcox lay enclosed in a long box, surrounded by these people and other local inhabitants. There sat Lady Fanner, with a face dead-white and powdered, a head apparently held up by a choker of pearls and a mouth like a small wound. The Simcox family solicitor, Jackson Cantellow, joined in the prayers which he knew as well as his forms of conveyancing, and the Rural Dean was there to represent the Bishop. Also in the congregation were some of the wives of Rapstone Fanner, comparatively new arrivals whose husbands were busy in London offices, large, healthy women who called their children 'The Young' and drank brandy at coffee mornings because they were bored with being left alone in the country. There were a few, only a few, men and women from those cottages which hadn't yet been turned into commuter houses; among them old Percy Bigwell, known as 'Peasticks' because of his splayed legs and two walking-sticks which had brought him, in a slow crablike motion, across the village green to pay his last tribute to the Rector. Among these people sat strangers to the village with familiar faces, some ageing Labour politicians, journalists, broadcasters and representatives of the various groups and movements connected with peace, political prisoners and racial equality for which Simeon Simcox had been known for many years as a constant campaigner.

Shortly after the service began a large, official Rover, with a lady chauffeur at the wheel, passed the signpost at the head of the valley and descended quickly on Rapstone. Sitting alone in the back was a man of obvious importance, wearing a dark suit and a black tie. In contrast to the 'progressive' politicians already assembled round the late Rector's coffin, the Rt Hon. Leslie Titmuss, M.P., was a power in the Conservative administration. He was a pale man with inquisitive, almost colourless eyes who, in spite of his receding hairline and gaunt features, had preserved, since his childhood in the Rapstone Valley, an expression of simple, boyish cunning. He sat forward on his seat as though late for an appointment and, as the car stopped outside the church, he opened the door and hopped out in the eager way of a man ever anxious to appear energetic to photographers. On his way to the lychgate he was waylaid by a loitering reporter and he switched on an instant smile.

'Minister!' The reporter fluttered a notebook. 'We hardly expected to see you at the funeral of a left-wing cleric.'

'Certain things transcend political differences. Simeon Simcox was a great man. He was an old family friend and a tremendous influence on my life. Thank you, gentlemen.' Having given his quote Leslie Titmuss turned off his smile and hurried into the church.

Fred Simcox and his mother were whispering together as the Reverend Kevin Bulstrode climbed into the pulpit. Dorothy Simcox looked pained. Her hair, which like her elder son's had been copper but had become grey, was gently out of control. The silk scarf she wore round her neck seemed to float away and she was staring with fierce concentration at a particular floral tribute which lay on her husband's coffin. It was a huge and expensive affair, a great circle of dark twisted leaves pierced by the white military trumpets of lilies and spears of gladioli; the sort of thing which some ostentatious Head of State might lay on the tomb of his unknown soldier.

'It's appalling!' Dorothy Simcox complained.

'It's only a wreath, Mother.'

'Your father would have hated it.'

'Perhaps he wouldn't have minded.'

'Where could it possibly have come from?'

Fred didn't answer his mother. His head had turned at the sound of the church door opening and footsteps on the flagstones. The Rt Hon. Leslie Titmuss had joined the congregation.

'For Simeon Simcox,' Bulstrode was saying, 'the Church of England wasn't the Establishment at prayer, it was the force of progress on the march. One of the many obituaries in the national press suggests he may have been a bit of a saint. If so, he was a saint smoking a pipe, dressed in that old tweed jacket with leather patches we came to love and know so well, a very caring sort of saint, be it at the Worsfield Missile Base or leading us in prayer outside the South African High Commission.'

Dorothy was still gazing in incredulous horror at the wreath, hardly hearing the well-meant words from the pulpit above her. 'One of his parishioners, our old friend "Peasticks" Bigwell, must have the last word. "He were a smasher, our old Rector, weren't he?" Peasticks said to me. Well, perhaps it wasn't the description we'd all use.'

'Hardly,' Henry whispered to Lonnie, 'for a dedicated pacifist.'

'But, you know, I think Simeon would have understood. Today we are gathered together to say goodbye to a "smasher".'

After the funeral service many of the congregation, some starting to chatter, others lighting cigarettes, all relieved that the worst was over, crowded into the Rectory to be met by Dorothy with a look of considerable dismay. Henry Simcox, turning away from the crowd for which his mother had clearly made no sort of preparation, went to the cupboard in a corner by the french windows and found it almost bare. 'It'd need a miracle,' he told Lonnie, 'to divide one bottle of strictly non-South African, anti-apartheid sherry among all those thirsty mourners. I don't suppose *he*'d've managed it. My father wasn't much of a man for miracles.' Then he saw another dusty bottle behind a row of glasses, took it and held it up to the light. 'There's a drop of brandy, left over from the Christmas pudding.'

'Agnes shouldn't've come!' Lonnie was looking across the room at the Numero Uno. 'Not after all that's happened.'

'Agnes enjoys anything at all tragic.' Henry poured himself a brandy. 'It was summer holidays she found so terribly harrowing.'

'It's embarrassing for you!' Lonnie was always more concerned for her husband than he was for himself.

'Don't exaggerate, Lonnie.'

'And for your mother.'

16

'The Simcoxes don't embarrass as easily as that.'

As Henry raised his glass he looked out of the french windows and did not drink. He could see, across the unweeded garden, his younger brother Fred standing, alone and in silence, by his father's grave. The sight seemed to cause Henry Simcox some displeasure.

'I'd say Kevin Bulstrode did us a very fair service.' Jackson Cantellow, the family solicitor, was talking to Agnes. She inhaled a Silk Cut greedily, pushed one clenched fist into her jacket pocket and coughed with deep satisfaction. 'I'm not really an expert on funerals.'

'Have to be in our job,' Cantellow told her. 'A family solicitor has to be. Has its compensations, of course. I think I gained my taste for sacred music at clients' funerals. We don't always get a legacy but we do occasionally get the Parry. They used to do an absolutely super Stanford in G when old Bagstead was at Hartscombe. Now of course it's all this taped stuff. Not the same thing at all, I'm afraid. We had "Going My Way" from a cassette at Bill Backstay's cremation in Worsfield.'

'So long as it wasn't "Smoke Gets in Your Eyes".' Agnes looked round the room, feeling trapped and wondering how long it would be before Henry produced the sherry.

'What did you say?'

'Nothing. I said absolutely nothing.' She was relieved to see Dorothy moving towards her.

'No sort of will surfaced yet.' Cantellow tried to get down to business with the widow. 'I was always pestering Simeon to make one. Well, once we've got over this we'll make our searches.'

'Agnes, I'm glad you came.' Dorothy ignored her lawyer. 'Simeon would have been so glad.'

'Would he?'

'He liked you. You know, he always regarded you as a challenge.'

'I think I'm rather tired of being regarded as a challenge.'

'I know you don't like discussing business' – Cantellow was insistent – 'but some time, Mrs Simcox. Some time soon.'

'Not now,' Dorothy said. Dismissed, Cantellow gave a little bow of resignation and moved away. Dorothy looked round the room and hoped that the crowd assembled wouldn't expect to eat anything. As though in answer to her unspoken thoughts, Lonnie came bustling by on her way to the kitchen.

'I thought I'd just put out some biscuits,' she told them.

'Oh, Lonnie! What a wonderful little brick you are.' Agnes gave one of her weariest smiles and Numero Due almost hissed back at her, 'I do think it's embarrassing of you to come. I know Henry's embarrassed.'

'Why on earth should he be?' Agnes spoke quite loudly. 'It's not *his* funeral, is it?'

'I'll go and put out those biscuits.' Lonnie went on her way with her face set and Dorothy looked as though she hadn't been listening.

The Rural Dean was doing his best, on the minute glass of sherry provided, to make the party go. He said how impressive it was to have the Cabinet represented in the shape of Mr Leslie Titmuss. He recalled how very famous Simeon Simcox had been. 'Not a conventional clergyman, of course. The Bishop had to haul him over the coals when he was getting too deeply into politics. Saints are never the easiest people to get along with. You put that across jolly well, Kevin.'

'Thank you.' Bulstrode was gratified. 'I think we managed to strike just the right note of reverent informality.' Unfortunately he was within earshot of Henry, who came delightedly in on the cue.

'I think you struck a perfectly ghastly note. That castrated edition of the prayer-book may be perfectly suitable to bless the union of a couple of crimpers in a unisex hairdo establishment. It's got no place in the Christian burial of a priest of the Church of England.'

'May I suggest' – Bulstrode was tentative – 'that we've got to make things clear to the common man?'

'However common the man he could understand the old prayer-book perfectly well. Ask the Right Honourable Leslie Titmuss.' But then Henry saw his younger brother coming in through the french windows and moved away.

'Powerful turn of phrase!' Bulstrode told the Dean admiringly. 'No wonder he's always off to America.'

'What were you doing?' Henry asked when he met Fred by the corner cupboard.

'Saying goodbye.'

'With a certain amount of quiet ostentation?'

'I'm sorry you thought that.' Fred had discovered that the Christmas brandy bottle was empty. He took the sherry from Henry and poured himself the last half glass.

'I was away,' Henry said, 'when it happened.'

'Yes.'

'I had to go to the Coast.'

'The coast of what?' Fred asked, although he knew perfectly well.

'You know. Hollywood. The suburbia of the soul.' Henry made a habit of abusing what was still a considerable source of his income. 'You were with him, though. At the end?'

'Yes, I was with him.'

'Did he say anything in particular?' Henry asked the question as though it had no great importance and Fred finished his sherry.

'Not . . . so far as I remember.'

'I don't suppose he would.'

'What?'

'Say anything in particular to you.'

'He seemed to be frightened.' Fred moved away, wondering why, on this of all days, meeting his brother was like another round in a contest which had been going on as long as either of them could remember.

There was a pervasive smell of face-powder and Chanel Number Five and Fred found himself looking down into the ravaged face of Lady Fanner, who had once been beautiful. 'So many funerals! We've had Elspeth Fairhazel and the "Contessa" and old Uncle Cecil. I'm quite exhausted.'

'I'm sorry, Grace. My father should have consulted your engagements.'

'Now that's naughty of you, Fred. I was devoted to your father, even though he sometimes looked at me as though he disapproved of my not being black. Well, I get discriminated against too. I told him that so often. That horrible little man in the fish shop in Hartscombe absolutely declines to serve me.'

'My mother's been cornered by Leslie Titmuss.' Fred looked across the room.

'Poor woman. Well, do go and rescue her then.'

When Fred arrived at his mother's side she was telling the Cabinet Minister how strange it was to be at a service in Rapstone Church and not to hear Simeon's voice and he, in turn, was apologizing for having arrived late at the ceremony. 'When the P.M. calls a breakfast meeting you really can't say "no". But nothing would have made me miss the old man's funeral.'

'Why ever not, Leslie?' Dorothy seemed not to understand his having felt the burying of her husband to be such an important occasion.

'I remember how good he was to me, when I was a young lad. How good you all were.'

'Is that what you remember?' Dorothy was still puzzled.

'Sad occasion, of course. But beautifully done.'

'Except for that wreath!' Dorothy told him and went on regardless of Fred, who muttered a warning 'Mother!' 'Whoever could have sent that perfectly appalling object?' She gave out a small, mirthless laugh. 'They must have pinched it off the Cenotaph!'

'Please, Mother!'

'My secretary ordered it actually,' Leslie admitted. 'He's got an uncle in the business.'

'Oh dear!' But Dorothy's disarray was only momentary. After Fred had praised the kindness of the thought, she went on firmly,

'You shouldn't've done it, Leslie! It's the way you used to carry on when you were a little boy. You really mustn't spend your money on such foolish objects.'

It was with relief that the Minister then caught sight of his uniformed lady chauffeur, standing in the garden, waving silently. 'I think I can see my driver making a signal. Respects to all the family. Sorry I've got to rush. Working lunch with the C.B.I.' And then he assured them both, 'I'll always be grateful.'

When Leslie Titmuss was on his way out through the french windows, Henry joined his mother and brother and they all three looked at the retreating dark-suited figure of the man who was now one of their rulers.

'I wonder what he'll always be grateful for, exactly?' Dorothy appeared to find the question amusing. 'I remember he used to bring us presents. So embarrassing! Things he'd saved up for.'

'Or things he'd nicked from Woolworths.' Then Henry turned to his brother. 'You said just now that our father was frightened. Of what exactly?'

Fred thought for a moment before he answered, 'Heaven.'

Chapter Two

CHILDREN AT THE RECTORY

'It's Leslie, Simeon. Leslie Titmuss.'

'Welcome, Leslie! Have we no cake or any such thing?'

'I think he's come to do a job,' Dorothy said firmly.

A long war, widely thought to have defeated the forces of tyranny and injustice and ushered in the age of the Common Man, whoever he was, had been over for three years. The British had dismissed Mr Churchill and installed a Labour Government, an event which caused Simeon to choose, as a frequent text, Revelation chapter 21, verse 1, 'And I saw a new heaven and a new earth; for the first heaven and earth had passed away.' His sermons at the time often referred to the New Jerusalem in a way which may have been unclear to his congregation, who were being told by the Government to pull in their belts and who found, despite their undoubted victory, that everything was still on coupons.

After a cold spring and early summer the weather became exceptionally fine and hot, as it was on the day that the twelve-year-old Leslie Titmuss stood in the Rectory garden, wearing long shorts and grey socks which fell like a couple of woollen concertinas over his dusty shoes. In honour of his visit to the Rector and his wife he had slicked his hair down with brilliantine ('Anzora masters the hair') and it was as flat and shiny as patent leather, apart from a little crest which stood up stiffly on the crown of his head, giving him an eager and birdlike appearance. His arrival had interrupted Simeon's dictation of letters of protest to the Bishop on the Church's lack of leadership on the question of apartheid in South Africa, and worried Dorothy, who was afraid that, if left to his own devices, Leslie might dig up her most tender plants.

'Why, Leslie,' Simeon said. 'Whatever's that?' The child had in his hands a small statuette of a lady in a bright red bathing-suit standing on a rock. She was leaning slightly forward, one hand stretched out behind her, the other with a finger laid lightly on her cherry-coloured lips. Her eyes were open very wide, her expression could only be described as 'roguish', and the base of the statue bore, in gilt letters, the legend 'A Present from Cleethorpes'.

'It's for you, Mrs Simcox.' Leslie held out the trophy towards Dorothy, who retreated slightly.

'Dear me. Where *did* you get it?'

'I got it for you,' Leslie said, not quite answering the question.

'Leslie! You must learn not to do things like that.' Dorothy sounded severe but her husband interrupted her. 'Leslie Titmuss comes bearing gifts! How exciting. Do let me see.' To his wife's despair he took the object.

'It's a present, Mr Simcox.'

'It's a beautiful object.' Simeon sounded almost convinced. 'My dear, isn't that a most beautiful object? Wasn't it kind and thoughtful of Leslie?'

'Leslie. As you're here,' Dorothy said firmly, 'I was thinking about the nettles.'

'The nettles by the old croquet lawn?' The boy sounded eager.

'Yes, Leslie. Those nettles.'

'We shall treasure this, Leslie. We shall keep it on our mantel-piece,' said Simeon, who was left holding the gift as young Titmuss marched off to get a hook for the execution of the nettles.

'Shall we have to?' Dorothy said, when he was out of earshot.

'Of course.'

'But the thing's hideous!'

'Hideous things are something we have to put up with,' her husband explained patiently. 'We can't shut our eyes to them. That wouldn't be right.'

'I can shut my eyes to a present from Cleethorpes any day of the week. Simeon! You're not going to put it next to my little bit of Spode?'

'We really can't offend the boy.'

'I don't see why not. He's such a particularly disagreeable child.'

'That's not a very Christian thing to say.' Simeon looked at his wife sadly.

'Why not? Perhaps God made people like Leslie Titmuss so we can find out who's nice. Freddie!' As she said the last word Dorothy looked upwards and sighed. In his bedroom her younger son was accompanying a record on the second-hand drum set they had allowed him to save up for at Christmas. She went upstairs to Fred's room, knowing that her husband had a busy afternoon ahead. She switched off the gramophone and 'My Very Good Friend the Milkman' was cut off in mid-flow. The accompaniment also fell silent. 'Your father's working,' she said. 'He's trying to write letters to the Bishop.'

'What about?'

'About what they're doing to the black men in Africa, if you must know.' Fred was gently swishing on a drum with a wire-brush. 'Fats Waller's black,' he said, 'and you switched him off.'

'Try not to be childish, Freddie,' his mother advised him.

In the end she had her way about the present from Clee-thorpes. It didn't disturb the Spode in the living-room. It landed up on the mantelpiece in Simeon's study, along with a number of invitations to lecture, a clock that kept poor time, a wood carving of a pregnant woman he had brought back from a visit to an Anglican bishop in Nigeria and a small bust of Karl Marx.

Although the summer holidays seemed endless the boys were

never bored. There was always too much to do at home. Fred played his records and practised from manuals with such titles as *Jazz Drumming for Beginners*, for which he sent away. Henry was writing a long novel in a number of school notebooks which he kept hidden in his sock drawer and was secretly hurt that Fred had never asked to read them. When it was hot they bicycled down to Hartscombe, the local riverside town, and took out a dinghy. They quarrelled about the efficiency of each other's rowing (Henry always steered them out to mid-stream and Fred got their heads scraped by overhanging willows near the bank) and pulled up past the lock where they swam in the river. The water was dark and brackish, filled with rasping reeds, and, if your foot touched the bottom, black mud oozed between your toes. Sometimes they had wished on them the company of Agnes Salter, whose father was their doctor and a family friend. They seemed to quarrel less when Agnes was with them. She dived better and more neatly than they did and showed no terror when Henry deliberately rowed towards the churning, yellowish water of the weir. When she was in her black one-piece Jansen bathing-suit Fred would avoid looking at her, afraid he might find her beautiful. When he was alone he thought mainly about Betty Grable.

Dorothy was busy gardening, preserving, making jam and potting meat, seeking refuge in such occupations from too much contact with her husband's parish. She had been an Oxford professor's daughter, brought up on Boar's Hill in a small house where the garden was filled after lunch on Sundays with high-pitched, excitable voices discussing the reviews in the *New Statesman* and Fabian Socialism. Such an upbringing didn't equip her for running white elephant stalls at local fêtes, or afternoons with the Women's Institute. She believed that, in an ideal world, the working classes would rule the country, but she had no particular desire to ask any of them to tea.

Simeon pursued his political interests more doggedly. He sat for long hours at the desk in his study, among a clutter of pipe-racks, walking-sticks, pamphlets, Left Book Club volumes, Penguins and blue papers, cuttings from *Tribune* and the *News Chronicle*, haphazard shelves supporting the works of Engels and R. H. Tawney, H. G. Wells and Bernard Shaw, the Webbs and Bertrand Russell. He went regularly to meetings, committees, protests and deputations in London. During such absences Henry sat in his father's chair and became quite intolerably bossy.

On the whole they were a closely knit group and, like all parsons' or policemen's families, set apart from their neighbours. When Simeon had an evening away from his correspondence they played bridge. Henry overbid outrageously and quickly lost interest. Fred underbid but played his hand with determination. Dorothy joined in with her mind elsewhere and Simeon had an unexpectedly good memory for the cards and took a great pleasure in winning. Once, when he went to the lavatory during a deal, Henry contrived to present him with all the hearts. When Simeon picked up his hand he was bubbling with triumph and a kind of childish glee, until he realized that he'd been deceived and became disappointed and sad.

Often the boys decided to get up plays, but openings were postponed because they couldn't agree. On one remarkable occasion Simeon offered to accompany them in scenes from Shakespeare given to the single audience of Dorothy. As he had played Lady Macbeth at school their father undertook the 'Letter Scene' again, his tall, bony figure fitted into one of the old black evening-dresses Dorothy was about to send away as jumble, and a sort of lace mantilla. Inappropriately, considering the climate at Glamis, he carried a fan. While waiting in the hallway to make an entrance Simeon heard the front door bell ring and unthinkingly opened it to a young couple who'd come to be prepared for marriage. Seeing what they took to be the Rector *en travesti*, they backed away into the darkness. Much was to be made of this incident in the distant future, but such extraordinary events were rare. Most of the time life at the Rectory was quiet, as it was on the summer afternoon when Leslie Titmuss hacked at the nettles on the edge of the old croquet lawn, and Henry lay on his stomach in the long grass with an open exercise book in front of him, chewing a pencil.

'What are you doing?' Leslie paused in his work to ask.

'Just writing a novel.'

'What's a novel?'

'It's a picture of our society, from top to bottom. A human story.' Henry began to write again, as if to deter conversation.

'Got any bits about girls in it, has it?' Leslie fell upon the nettles again, slaughtering them wildly.

'Yes. But you wouldn't understand them.'

'Is it difficult? Writing that, I mean.'

'For some people.'

'I bet it's not as hard as getting rid of these old nettles.'

Henry looked up at Leslie, as though at some specimen whose activities he was about to record in a nature notebook. 'What're you doing that for?'

'Your mum gives me half a crown.' Leslie didn't stop hacking.

'My parents exploit you! It's the beer money.'

'I don't get any beer money.'

'They do,' Henry explained patiently. 'Out of Simcox Ales. The Brewery in Hartscombe keeps our family going, so they can exploit the workers.'

'They're all right. I brought your dad a present, a statue. He was delighted with it.'

'It's because you live in Skurfield,' Henry told the worker. 'My parents think everyone who lives in Skurfield's there to be exploited. They don't ask *me* to cut down the nettles.'

'Your mum says she's asked you. But you don't ever do it.'

Henry started to write again. 'When the revolution comes,' he said, 'they'll be the first to go.'

'Where?'

Henry was busy and didn't answer.

'*Where* will they be the first to go?'

'Never you mind.'

Leslie stopped hacking and pushed back his sticky hair. 'Where will *you* be, Henry? When the revolution comes?'

'Probably in charge.'

Fred said, 'Leslie Titmuss is going to Hartscombe Grammar.'

'Leslie's done well. He's got his wits about him.'

'I'd like to go to Hartscombe Grammar.'

'I suppose none of us can have everything they want in this world.'

Fred was with his father in the church vestry, with its smell of mice and old prayer-books, among the choir surplices and bleeding hassocks in need of repair. He was pumping away at a harmonium, playing the chorus of 'My Very Good Friend the Milkman', which he could do because he had an ear for music. Simeon was at a table, cutting bread into small cubes for the Communion service. Both the boys had been to a preparatory day school not far away. Now the plan was to send them to a public school, Knuckleberries, on the Norfolk coast. Simeon had himself been to this remote establishment, and his brother, Pym Simcox, who was Chairman of the Brewery (Pym later shot himself in the hop loft for some unfathomable reason), spent his schooldays there. This period of Uncle Pym's life, wretchedly unhappy at the time, later became a source of mysterious and almost mystical pride to him. Pym always, even at the moment of death, wore the O.K. tie, and regularly reported his unchanging circumstances in the *Knuckleberrian*. It seemed to Fred that he and Henry were being mercilessly dispatched to this mysterious institution as some sort of compensation for Uncle Pym Simcox's untimely death.

'Why do I *have* to go to Knuckleberries?' Fred stopped playing and asked, not for the first time that summer. 'I mean, I thought you believed in everyone being equal. Don't you believe in everyone going to Hartscombe Grammar?'

'I suppose things aren't always so simple.'

'Why aren't they?'

'I respect that in you, Frederick,' Simeon assured him. 'I respect you for asking questions.'

'So will you tell me why I have to go to Knuckleberries?'

'Perhaps it's the will of God.' Simeon spoke in a somewhat offhanded manner of the Divine Plan and then pulled a wristwatch with a broken strap out of the pocket of his cassock. 'Good heavens. Parish meeting! Couldn't you do the rest for me?'

Fred got up and went reluctantly to the table and fiddled with the knife. 'Does it turn into flesh, during the service?' he asked, looking at the bread.

'Freddie! You know it doesn't.' Simeon looked as though his son had expressed a literal belief in Santa Claus.

'It might do. One day it might surprise you. I don't suppose you can be certain. Well, if it doesn't do anything interesting, why do you have it in the service?'

'To celebrate the basic things of life, Frederick,' Simeon explained patiently. 'The bread that's made simply. Kneaded and put to rise in the oven.'

'It's a sliced loaf, isn't it? Doesn't it get made in a factory?' Fred looked up at his father surprised, for when he said that Simeon appeared, on his way out of the vestry, to be laughing.

That afternoon Fred went to the village shop with his mother and he asked her, 'Is it the will of God, Henry and me going to Knuckleberries?'

'It may not be the will of God,' Dorothy said. 'It's something that's been arranged.'

'Did Dad arrange it?'

'Well, no. He doesn't always arrange things. You know he's so busy.'

'What's he so busy at, exactly?'

'Good heavens, you know! The Labour Party and the Worsfield Mission and the United Nations and the Peace Pledge Union and South Africa . . .'

'*You* arranged it!' Fred's voice was accusing.

'It's much better for you and Henry to be away at school. Anyway, you know your Uncle Pym went to Knuckleberries.'

'So you arranged for us to go there too?'

'I suppose I did.'

'So it's the will of God?' Fred took an apple out of the shopping-basket and bit into it. He felt that he was powerless in the hands of fate. His mother, he knew, was an implacable, unpersuadable force. She looked at him, smiling vaguely, and said, 'Poor Freddie! You do come out with some strange ideas.'

Chapter Three

KNUCKLEBERRIES AND AFTER

What Fred hated was the dormitory. He longed for his small maid's bedroom in the Rectory with its dormer window, his drums and records and pinned-up pages from the *Picturegoer*. He wanted to be alone, with his milk and biscuits, to read *The History of the Blues* in peace. The dormitory was a long, dark, bare, barrack-like room with iron bedsteads and icy draughts which blew in through the compulsorily opened windows direct from Siberia with no intervening mountain range. It was also the scene of sudden outbreaks of violence, the selection of victims and lightning shifts in popularity from which, it must be said, Henry always emerged unscathed and Fred only occasionally suffered.

One night he was sitting up in bed in his dressing-gown, pyjamas and socks before lights out. Parted from his drums he had a tin chamber-pot inverted on his lap and, with a pair of wire-brushes, he was swishing out the rhythm of 'Slow Boat to China', a recent hit. Around him some boys were on their knees, some were throwing slippers at those praying, others were taking advantage of a last chance to clean their teeth before the water froze. Henry was pacing the deck looking masterful, taking advantage of his privileged position as dorm leader to be wearing a long woollen muffler and a cap with his dressing-gown and pyjamas. That night's victim, a boy called Arthur Nubble, had been satisfactorily reduced to a sobbing, blanket-covered lump in the corner.

Most of the boys in the dormitory thought of the war as a rare treat which they had missed and which would never be on offer again. One tall, red-faced boy with a premature five o'clock shadow, a great masturbator named Maybrick, told them stories of his father's exploits in the Navy. 'Six days in an open boat, my dad was,' he said, not for the first time. 'One of the ratings went raving mad!' 'My father did commando landings in North Africa.' This was Pusey, a minute boy in the corner, lying hopelessly. 'One of the young sailors in the open boat just couldn't take it.' Maybrick ignored the interruption. 'My father cradled him in his arms all night.'

'I saw that film.' Henry looked at Maybrick, who stared back at him red-faced and angry. The dormitory fell silent; only Fred sang quietly to his own wire-brush accompaniment:

> 'Get you and keep you
> In my arms evermore,
> Leave all your lovers
> Weeping on the faraway shore.'

'That film had Richard Attenborough in it.' Henry was determined to shut Maybrick up. 'I saw it at our local Odeon in Hartscombe.'

'So that was your bloody war service, Simcox Major.' Maybrick was clearly planning to start a slipper-throwing, anti-Henry landslide. 'Watching flicks in your local Odeon.'

'And what did you do for Britain, challenge the German High Command at pocket billiards?' It was an easy laugh, not typical of Henry at his best, Fred thought, and Maybrick came back with a dangerous question, 'What was *your* father in the war anyway?' The answer 'a parson' was too awful for Fred to contemplate, and he waited for the attack on both of them, the flailing towels, hurled bodies and flung slippers, which it was bound to provoke. 'Secret Service,' Henry said with great authority.

'What?'

'He did Secret Service disguised as a parson,' Henry said to end all further argument. 'And now I'm going to see if anyone's unthawed the bogs.'

There was an awed silence after he had left, until Maybrick asked quietly, 'Simcox Mi. Why does your brother tell such amazing lies?' During a sickening pause Fred again felt that public opinion might be about to turn against him. Happily a diversion was caused by Pusey hopping out of bed to pull the blanket off the sobbing heap in the corner.

'What's the matter with Nubble, has he got the screaming habdabs?' The small boy looked down with clinical interest at the cowering bulk. 'Of course he has,' Fred told them when he was sure no one was listening. 'Haven't you noticed? This dorm's just like being adrift in an open boat. Thirteen weeks among the ice-floes.'

In the afternoons, even if they were not down to play in any particular game, the boys at Knuckleberries were ordered to 'take exercise'. For Fred this meant changing into football clothes and running shoes and hiding in the sour-smelling 'bogs' or sprinting off to a neighbouring spinney where he would crouch in the bushes to read the *Picturegoer* or those novels, which Henry told him were an essential part of his education, by Aldous Huxley, D. H. Lawrence and Norman Mailer. He kept these works stuffed up his football shirt and he was pounding along one afternoon looking vaguely pregnant when he heard a stirring in the undergrowth and stopped to discover Arthur Nubble, also in full running-gear, taking cover. Nubble looked up at Fred with plaintive, soft brown eyes; he had full lips and curling dark brown hair and was not so much fat as inappropriately overweight for a schoolboy, like an Italian tenor who has to squeeze into the costume to play a romantic lead.

'What on earth are you doing?'

'Hiding from your brother.' Nubble spoke in an accent which Fred's mother would have described as 'slightly off'. 'He's meant to be in charge of exercise. I seem to spend most of the time at Knuckleberries hiding from people. Bloody awful place, isn't it?'

'Pretty terrible, yes,' Fred agreed.

'My dad told me it'd be bloody awful. Ghastly grub and I'd be homesick and miss our mum's cooking, but he said it was worth it all because I'd meet useful friends. You look like a nice sort of friend for me to meet, Simcox Minor.'

'I'm not all that useful, really,' Fred assured him.

'Why?' Nubble sounded disappointed. 'What do you do then?'

'I turn on people.'

'You *what?*'

'I lead people on to trust me and then I turn on them. I'm well known for being treacherous.' Fred thought of his habitual behaviour in the dormitory.

'Couldn't you be a useful friend for me, just until you start being treacherous?'

'We'd better get moving.' Fred started to walk on, deeper into the wood, and Arthur Nubble trotted after him, panting, 'Fond of a bit of brawn, are you?'

'What?' Fred began to run slowly and Arthur lolloped behind him, talking incessantly. 'Ox tongue, peaches in a decent white wine syrup, chicken in aspic, liqueur chocolates off coupons. My dad says it's shocking the rationing we've still got in England. He says for all we won the war, we might as well be bloody Germans. He puts it all down to us having a Labour Government. He says it's ridiculous, us not being able to get a bit of brawn if we've got a fancy for it.' Arthur Nubble stopped then, and looked at Fred appealingly. 'Look, as long as we're friends, let's go down the music huts.'

'Why the music huts?' Fred stopped too. He hadn't, after all, come out in exercise clothes to run.

'Because,' Arthur muttered darkly, 'nobody here learns the double bass.'

Music did not have a great following at Knuckleberries, which specialized in Latin, mathematics and rugby football. The music huts were long, low, prefabricated buildings at the foot of the kitchen gardens from which scales and arpeggios were infrequently heard. The cubicles containing pianos or other instruments became places of hiding for nervous boys or shelters for solitary love affairs inflamed by illicit copies of *Reveille* or *Titbits*. In one such room, furnished with broken chairs and rusty music-stands, Arthur Nubble showed Fred an old double-bass case which opened like a cupboard to reveal various tins of food. The two boys, still in their running clothes, sat on the floor and hungrily consumed sweets and savouries, serving themselves with Nubble's pocket-knife, a weapon usefully equipped with a tin-opener and a corkscrew. Post-war austerity and the indifference of the school cooking left Fred permanently hungry. He tucked into the exotic fare with fierce concentration.

'My dad knows why there's no brawn available,' Arthur Nubble told him in a knowing way. 'It's because of that Attlee and Ernie Bevin and Sir Stifford Crapps. They keep all the brawn and peaches and white wine to themselves. And the same goes for the liqueur chocolates when they can get their sticky fingers on them. Like ox tongue, do you? Better than the muck you get here, eh?' As he watched Fred eat, Arthur Nubble had all the pride of a society hostess laying on an elaborate dinner party. 'Our headmaster ought to get himself in the Cabinet. Bet your father says the same thing about the Labour Government?'

'He doesn't,' Fred told him between mouthfuls.

'Doesn't he?'

'My father's a Socialist.'

'Sorry.' Arthur clapped a hand over his mouth. 'Dropped a brick.'

'That's all right.'

'No, I'm sorry. You must be bloody poor, if you're a Socialist. Come here on a charity place? Well, we can still be friends. You'll probably depend on me for a bite to eat.'

'I thought you said Socialists were rich.' Fred was working on a tin of marrons glacés.

'Not *Socialists*,' Arthur explained. 'Not the rank and file. Just the Cabinet. The Cabinet get all the tinned stuff off points. The rank and file'd be better off as Germans.'

'My father's not especially poor,' Fred admitted.

'He's not?'

'In fact I think he owns most of a brewery. Simcox Ales. You know. All that sort of nonsense.'

'He owns best part of a brewery and he's a *Socialist*?' Arthur Nubble was laughing as he passed the chocolates. 'Have a Tia Maria centre. He must be bloody *crackers*!'

Nubble didn't have long to wait before he had more material on which to judge Simeon Simcox's sanity. As an old boy and a priest who often got his name in the papers, the Rector of Rapstone was invited by the Headmaster to preach at Knuckleberries, and to his sons' horror he accepted. Fred sat, his nails dug into his palms, his fists clenched with embarrassment, and Henry listened stony-faced, giving nothing away in the icy, sham-Gothic school chapel. As soon as he heard the text, Revelation, chapter 21, verse 2, Fred's heart sank, feeling sure that his father was going to preach about the Labour Government. 'And I John saw the Holy City, New Jerusalem, come down from God out of heaven, prepared as a bride adorned for her husband.' A few of the smaller boys giggled at the word 'bride', but Simeon beamed down upon them all. 'What's the great virtue of an English public school?' he asked them. 'What did I, for instance, get out of Knuckleberries? A great deal. I mean, it's no use having a *sensible* education. No. What we all need is something to rebel against. The ridiculous importance attached to football, the absurd rules about which side of Coppers Piece you can walk down after two years with your hands in your pockets, the Armistice Day sermons I've heard from this very pulpit about the Christian virtues of blowing each other up, wonderful stuff; thank God it all made a revolutionary of me! I mean, if Our Lord hadn't heard a lot of rubbish preached by the Pharisees, he'd never have been driven to write the Sermon on the Mount.' There was a sharp intake of breath from the Headmaster, but Simeon continued undeterred. 'Perhaps my belief in a Just City, a New Jerusalem, an equal society, was born out of intense boredom on the playing-fields of Knuckleberries. Really I have only this advice for you all. Be rebels when you're young or what on earth will you have left for your old age?' No one answered his question, and Arthur Nubble, hunched against one of the few radiators at the back of the chapel, bit into a liqueur choco-late.

Sunday evening was always a bad time in the dormitory and Fred went upstairs with dread. He was not surprised to find a hostile crowd round Henry and to be greeted by a low murmur of mistrust.

'Was *that* your father, Simcox?'

'Of course.' Henry was perfectly calm. 'He's keeping up the disguise. The war's not really over, you know. We've still got lots of enemies.'

'What's he need a disguise for?'

'Perhaps for when he goes to Russia.' Henry sighed, as though having to explain himself to idiots. 'He needs *some* sort of cover, doesn't he?'

The boys looked puzzled but they slunk away and later threw their slippers at a boy called Catchpole, who wore shiny pyjamas. He made a change from Nubble.

It clouded over after lunch on the day of Simeon's funeral. Fred and Henry and Henry's second wife were drinking coffee in the living-room of the Rectory when Lonnie said that she thought it was coming on to rain. To check his wife's forecast Henry went over to the barometer on the wall and found that there was nothing to tap. When Dorothy came into the room with a note in her hand he looked at her with suspicion.

'It's gone,' he said. 'Father's old barometer's gone.'

'She must have taken it,' Dorothy answered vaguely, and asked, 'Did you see her?'

'Who on earth are you talking about?'

'Francesca. Your Frankie.'

Lonnie winced slightly at the name, as though she had taken a mouthful of ice-cream and awakened a dormant toothache. She had tried, she often told herself that no one could have tried harder, to get on with Francesca, Henry's daughter by his first wife, the child of Numero Uno. She had been quite prepared to take Francesca on. It was clearly no life for the girl in a poky flat down the wrong end of the Fulham Road, having to put up with Agnes's smoking and great flashes of gloom. But since the age of six Francesca had, she thought, whenever the child was compelled by the terms of the divorce settlement to come for the weekend, consistently disapproved of her. So Lonnie pursed her lips when she heard who was responsible for the theft, as though she had suspected it all along.

'Francesca took my father's old barometer?' Henry made it sound an unnatural crime, like patricide.

'Well, I gave it to her.'

'You *what*?'

'I said she could have it.'

At this Lonnie thought it right to intervene, purely in the interests of justice and her husband. 'I think Simeon would have liked Henry to have the barometer. As the eldest son I think he's entitled to have it.'

'Why?' Fred asked. 'Is Henry starting out on a career as a weatherman?'

'Henry was always to have the barometer and the clock,' Lonnie answered with dignity, 'and as the only writer in the family he has to be entitled to the desk. That was to be Henry's.'

'She left a note when they took the things.' Dorothy put on her glasses and read without expression from the paper she was carrying, '"Darling Gran. Came this morning for the stuff. Didn't want to disturb you but it was the only day we could get the van."'

'Came this morning when we were *what*?' Henry's voice rose in outrage.

'Well we were in church, weren't we? I think she must have forgotten the date. I mean, she says she didn't realize until she got here and by then, of course, it was too late.'

'Not too late to loot the place. Who did she come with?'

'Oh, I think Peter,' Dorothy told him.

'So my daughter and her boyfriend raided the Rectory during my father's funeral and took away his furniture!'

'Only the desk and the barometer. Oh, and the little kitchen clock.'

'What on earth did they want the little kitchen clock for?'

'How about telling the time?' Fred suggested, it seemed unhelpfully, because his brother glared at him and started his tirade. 'Brutes! Robbers! Barbarians! Francesca the Hun!'

'I'd told her she could,' Dorothy assured him. 'And they're young.'

'Young and with all the tact and delicacy of a crowd of drunken mercenaries.'

'It's appalling,' Lonnie chipped in. 'You'll have to speak to her, Henry.'

'Just a few things' – Dorothy was understanding – 'so she can remember Simeon.'

'A barometer!' Henry was working himself up into a thoroughly enjoyable rage. 'What do they want a barometer for? They don't *have* weather in Tufnell Park.'

'The young have no sort of consideration,' Lonnie agreed.

'Consideration! All Francesca's consideration's reserved for South American guerrillas, under-privileged Eskimos and one-parent lame lesbian families living in Greater Manchester.' Listening to him Fred began to think how remarkably his brother had inherited their father's habit of preaching. 'Oh, I forgot,' Henry went on. 'And whales! Huge bloody whales swimming about in the sea, spouting and suckling their young and never even realizing that all the concern that normal girls lavish on their parents, all the reverence that decent-minded daughters might feel for a death in the family, is entirely concentrated on their bloated, inarticulate, blubbery bodies. We were never like that.' He looked at Fred and added, less certainly, 'Were we?'

*

Having his brother at school seemed no sort of advantage to Fred. Henry's presence reminded him of home but offered none of its consolations and as Henry moved steadily up the school, driven by an ambition Fred could not understand to be head boy, he chose different friends and became contemptuous of his younger brother's association with Arthur Nubble. 'Do stop hanging around with that fat spiv.' Henry knew nothing of the feasts in the music huts. 'Can't you see you're letting the family down?'

Separated at school the boys remained apart during the holidays. Henry wrote in his notebooks, went to stay with school friends and joined the village cricket team. Fred went on solitary bicycle rides. On one of these he made a discovery and a friend who was to prove, it seemed, as much of a let-down to his family as Arthur Nubble.

He was riding down a path in the woods when he heard a pheasant calling – the sound seemed near to him and close to the ground. He got off his bicycle, dropped it, left it ticking in the leaves and went to investigate. A little away from the path he found a cage in which the calling bird was imprisoned. He knelt down and had some idea of liberating the cock pheasant from the trap when he heard a voice behind him.

'You let him be. He's happy enough in there.'

'What's he doing?'

'Calling out to all the ladies in the neighbourhood. With a bit of luck they'll all be round to see him shortly, they find his voice very attractive.' The man was fat, dressed in an old flannel vest and shapeless trousers; he had a sharp nose, bright eyes and an expression of considerable glee, particularly when he was carrying, as he was at that moment, a shot-gun under his arm. 'Aren't you the Rector's boy?'

Fred admitted it.

'Grown, haven't you?'

Fred admitted that also.

'Tom Nowt. Used to come up and see your father a bit in the

old days, used to bring him rabbits. Mother keeping well, is she?'

Fred supposed his mother was well.

'All right then. I'll make you a cup of tea.'

The man set off through the bushes and down a rutted cart-track until they reached a haphazard sort of building that looked as though it had been cobbled together in odd moments out of old planks, bits of hardboard, asbestos and corrugated iron. Inside it was warm, damp and stuffy. There was a paraffin stove and as the man made tea, sweetened with sugar and condensed milk, for both of them, Fred looked round and saw an old brass bed, assorted chairs, a broken sofa leaking horsehair and another shot-gun and a rifle in the corner. Deer skulls hung among the pin-ups on the walls, fleshless heads with dark eye-sockets and proud antlers. It was the first of many visits he was to pay to Tom Nowt's hut.

In time it became the first place he would make for when he came home for the holidays. He came to know more about Tom, that he lived in a cottage at the edge of the wood with his wife, Dora, and a number of children, that his hut was merely his shooting-lodge, and that he was mistrusted in the village since a tree he was felling had dropped wrongly and permanently injured old Percy Bigwell's legs. Although he undertook casual farm labour it was said that his real occupation was the secret shooting of deer that, having escaped from the Fanners' park at Rapstone Manor, bred freely in the woods. He also took pheasants by various means and shot over other people's land. None of this mattered to Fred, who sat, when he had got to know Tom Nowt better, nursing yet another warm mug of tea and condensed milk and said, 'How did all those die, Tom?'

'Some say they was got quietly by cross-bow bolts,' Tom told him solemnly. 'Some say they was dazed in an old car's headlights and a rifle did them. Those particular ones, I am prepared to take my oath, passed over peaceful, in their sleep.'

Fred had been suppressing laughter. Now it erupted. 'Been eating a lot of venison have you lately, Tom?'

'Breakfast, dinner *and* tea.' Tom sat down beside Fred and gulped tea. 'Nothing better than a deer's brains on toast for breakfast. How they been treating you, Fred?'

'Oh. Badly, Tom. Terribly badly.' Fred chose to look pathetic.

'What do they do to you, boy?'

'At school? Half starve us, make us sleep in a dormitory where the bogs freeze, hit us quite often for silly reasons, teach us Latin poetry so slowly you can't ever understand what it's about. And do cross-country runs where you have to break the ice and wade through streams. I cut my legs on the ice this term.'

'You're part of the privileged classes, of course.'

'Is that what we are?' Fred looked at a brace of unplucked birds hanging by the door. 'Been a bad year for pheasants, has it?'

'Has for the Stroves up Picton House. Some says it's due to a nasty outbreak of raisins soaked in brandy put on fish-hooks.'

Fred bubbled with laughter again. 'But you wouldn't know anything about that, Tom, would you?'

Next morning in the Rectory Fred asked, 'Why don't we ever have deer's brains on toast?' He was dipping soldiers into a boiled egg, a childish habit of which he was trying to break himself.

Simeon was reading an article on himself, topped by a Vicky cartoon, in the *New Statesman*. '"Unbelievers can see the benefit of no beggars, no hungry children, no one out of work. It's harder for Christians. We seem to find starving children rather useful, I mean there has to be someone to receive the collection. I tell you,"' he read his own words with a certain satisfaction, '"it's easier for a camel to go through the eye of a needle than for a Christian to enter the Kingdom of God." It's rather good,' he told Dorothy and held up the magazine.

'I do wish you'd try and keep out of the *New Statesman*.' His wife looked genuinely distressed. 'It's so embarrassing. What were you talking about, Fred?'

'I believe deer's brains make a smashing breakfast.'

'Could you try and not be quite so disgusting,' Henry said wearily. 'Watching you eat a boiled egg is revolting enough. Try not to put us *completely* off our food.'

'Tom Nowt has deer's brains every morning. Of course, he doesn't dazzle them in his headlights and shoot them out of his old banger with a point 22 rifle. Oh no!'

'Simcox Minor!' Henry used his Knuckleberries voice. 'Do shut up!'

'And would he put raisins on fish-hooks to catch all the Strove pheasants round Picton Principal? Raisins soaked in brandy? Tom Nowt wouldn't do that now, would he?'

'Where ever have you been, Fred?' Dorothy refilled his cup.

'Oh, I was down at Tom's old hut, in Hanging Wood.' And then he looked down the table and saw what he had never seen before, his father angry.

'Well, you're not to go there again.'

'What do you mean?'

'I don't think that was a particularly obscure remark. I don't want you to go there again.'

'Why ever shouldn't I?' Fred was trying to keep his end up but Simeon, collecting his letters and *New Statesman*, spoke with unusual severity.

'Because I'm telling you not to. For once in your life.'

'But *why* are you?'

Simeon stood up; he seemed to Fred to look suddenly very tall. 'Don't always be asking questions!' he said and banged the dining-room door behind him as he left.

So, before the holidays ended, Fred went down to say goodbye to Tom Nowt. He didn't go into the hut although invited but stood with his bicycle among the fallen leaves. 'My father doesn't want me to come down here any more.'

'Not when you get back from school?'

'Not ever. Why do you think that is?'

'He's got his reasons, I expect. Wouldn't he tell you?'

'No.'

'Well, then. I don't suppose he would.'

Back at Knuckleberries Fred noticed a change in Henry. His brother actively sought out his company, and that of Nubble. This was a mystery to Fred until he discovered that what Henry wanted to do was to read passages of his novel aloud to someone, and he had more sense than to choose his immediate friends and contemporaries, those who might become his fellow prefects, as a preview audience. After a good many hints and half-promises Henry met Fred and Nubble outside the old games pavilion carrying his notebook. He led them inside and they sat, on a damp Sunday afternoon, on the lockers while he read out the title, '*A Tale Told by an Idiot: A Novel by Henry Simcox*. What on earth's eating you?' for Nubble was having a fit of the giggles.

'Isn't it by you, Simcox?'

'Yes, of course it's by me.'

'Well, are you the . . .' Nubble didn't quite dare to say it.

'God! Are you completely illiterate?'

'Almost completely,' Nubble admitted.

'It's a quotation from Shakespeare. *Macbeth*.' At that stage in his literary career Henry didn't realize that his title wasn't entirely original. '". . . a tale told by an idiot, Full of sound and fury".'

'Well. How were we to know?'

'Really there's no point in reading it to you now.' Henry closed his notebook, although Arthur Nubble begged him not to.

'Go on,' Fred urged his brother wearily. 'We've been asking you to read it for ages.'

'Well, it's not finished. It's only a first draft.'

'Read it to us when you've finished it then.' Fred stood up and prepared to leave.

'So you *don't* want to hear it!' Henry sounded almost triumphant.

'I said read it to us when it's finished. I'm going to Ma Price's to get an egg and chips.'

'Apparently everyone wants me to read my novel except my own brother!'

'I didn't say that.'

'We all have to sit for hours while you murder "Slow Boat to China" on those old scratch drums.'

'You mean you want to read it now? All right then.' Fred sat down again and waited patiently.

'Well, apparently Nubble's been looking forward to it.'

'Oh yes, Simcox! I've been looking forward to it immensely.'

'Don't let's disappoint Nubble,' Fred agreed.

' "*Told by an Idiot*",' Henry started again.

'Good title, that,' Arthur said eagerly. 'Isn't it, Simcox?'

'Chapter one,' Henry went on firmly. ' "You'll hardly believe this, Alan," said Lady Cynthia Plumley, wrinkling her small retroussé nose and raising her plucked eyebrows, 'but I've never actually made love in a punt before." '

'That's good. The first sentence gets you,' Arthur Nubble told them. Henry had hit on a technique which he would discover was known in the film world as 'coming in on the middle of a scene'. He went on reading. ' "But then, thought Alan Podgson, neither have I." ' Henry was getting into his stride. ' "As the son of a brewery worker Alan had never been able to afford such luxuries. In a way he felt ashamed, he was betraying his class, and his mates at work, by falling so much in love with Lady Cynthia, the owner's daughter. He felt even more ashamed of his heavy boots and his baggy Aertex underpants." '

'Can you say "underpants" in a book?' Arthur wondered.

'Don't be ridiculous, Nubble. You can nowadays.' And Henry read on. ' "Alan started to make love in the expert way he had learnt with the girl workers in the bottling department. Cynthia felt small, delicate kisses land like butterflies on the backs of her knees, the inside of her elbows. Slowly and cunningly she was raised to a purring fever of excitement." '

A master in sports clothes pulled open the door and looked at them with disapproval. 'I thought you fellows were meant to be taking exercise.'

'We've taken it, Sir,' Arthur Nubble chirped up respectfully. 'Simcox was just reading us his history essay. It's jolly interesting.'

'Oh, is it?' The master put out his hand for the exercise book. 'Let's have a look.'

'Oh, you couldn't read it, Sir.' Arthur seemed to have taken charge of the situation.

'Why ever not?'

'Simcox has got such awful handwriting, he's going to copy it out neatly later.'

'Really?'

'It's terribly interesting, Sir. All about the relations between capital and labour in industrial England.'

'Not my subject, that. Hope you all show as much keenness on your geography. All right, you fellows. Carry on with the prep.' The master loped away and was soon lost in the mists of autumn.

'You know what, Nubble?' Henry said. 'You're not quite so terribly unintelligent as you look.'

A week later disaster struck. Arthur Nubble came up to Fred during a break between Latin and yet more Latin. He was in a state of advanced panic and deathly pale, bearing ghastly news about a new chap called Strove.

'I know him,' Fred reassured him. 'He lives near us.'

'Well, I was talking to him and he said he had to go. He was late for his music lesson. Oh, Simcox Mi, what do you think he's learning?'

Fred didn't wait to be told. As of one mind the boys started running towards the music huts. As they did so Fred asked breathlessly, 'Nubble! What did you do with the actual instrument?'

He didn't have to wait long to find out. When they got to the prefabricated huts Nubble pointed to the dark space between the floor and the ground. There in the shadows, hidden from the world like some lurking jungle beast, lay the inert form of a huge double bass. And when they peered for a moment into the usually empty room they saw the music master with his back to them, seated at the piano. They watched with horror as Magnus Strove, a rather pretty, curly-haired boy with an astute financial sense, opened the tall, standing, double-bass container out of which poured, as from some mythical cornucopia, what appeared to be the entire tinned food department of Fortnum and Mason.

'Cheerio, Nubble!' Fred took to his heels then and didn't stop running until he had arrived, five minutes early, for the next Latin lesson.

'Nubble's going to be sacked,' Fred told Henry later in the dormitory. Arthur had been isolated in the sanatorium although suffering from no known disease.

'Has he been jumping rather too low in the leap-frog?' Henry used the usual Knuckleberries euphemism.

'Not that. Running a black-market food stall in the music huts.'

'Quite right then. You can't have spivs at Knuckleberries.'

'You're not serious?'

'Aren't I?'

'I mean, I thought you were all for the revolution, blowing up Knuckleberries or something.'

'Of course I am. But while it's *here*, well, it's far better to keep the spivs out of it.'

Only Fred paid a brief tribute to the departed. 'Poor old Nubble. I don't suppose we'll ever see him again.'

Chapter Four

A GAME OF MURDER

In the spring of the next year Simeon Simcox got a dose of flu and sat shivering by his study fire wearing a dressing-gown and a muffler, occasionally coughing as he read a large number of pamphlets on global concerns. Dr Salter was shown by Dorothy into his presence. Agnes Salter's father was a short, broad-shouldered man with close-cropped greying hair, strong hands and stubby fingers. Dressed in a check hacking-jacket and still wearing breeches after his morning ride, he looked more like a hard-bitten horse-dealer than Hartscombe's leading G.P.

'He gets this wretched chest,' Dorothy explained. 'And his voice is going.'

'Cut down on the sermons, I'm sure the congregation'll be delighted. And,' the Doctor asked, 'I don't suppose you've got a spot of brandy left over from Christmas?'

Dorothy looked at Simeon, who nodded his permission, and she went off to find it. When she had gone the Doctor pulled up an armchair, stretched his boots to the fire and lit a thin, aromatic cheroot which made Simeon cough. 'Well,' the Rector said plaintively, 'surely you'll take my temperature?'

'I doubt if that's going to do you much good.'

'Dorothy thought we should call you in.'

'Can't imagine why.' The Doctor blew out a perfect smoke-ring which floated up towards Karl Marx. 'Surely a man of your persuasion ought to be grateful for a touch of spring flu. Don't want to hang about in this vale of tears, do you? Fellows like you ought to get in the queue for heaven as quickly as possible. You want me to tinker with divine providence with a couple of aspirins and a bottle of cough mixture?'

'For a doctor you have a remarkably simple-minded view of the Christian religion.' Simeon couldn't see why he should be expected to die of flu just because he was a clergyman.

'Christian religion? I thought it was based on the extreme desirability of death.' Dr Salter leaned back comfortably in his chair. 'It's a lesson I wish my patients would all learn. Duty of the sick, in my opinion, to get out of the way and make room for a few healthy breeders. But you take the Bishop of Worsfield, never knew a fellow so remarkably coy about meeting his Maker!' Dorothy returned to them with a small liqueur glass about half full of brandy. 'Is the Bishop not well?' Simeon was concerned to know.

'That's amazingly generous of you, Dorothy.' Dr Salter took the brandy, squinted at it like someone assessing a microscopic specimen, and finished it at a gulp. 'The good Bishop has never been quite the same since you made him take part in an all-night vigil in his draughty great cathedral to protest about the South African Government.'

'You can't blame me for that.' Simeon was troubled. As though to cheer him up Dr Salter slapped his jacket pockets, produced a pad and pencil and started to scribble a prescription.

'Of course it was remarkably effective! Soon as the dear old Boers heard that you and the Bishop had gone without a night's sleep they decided to elect a Blackamoor as prime minister. Or isn't that what happened?' The Doctor laughed, a short splutter of rapid gun-fire, and handed the prescription to Dorothy. 'Get that made up for him in Hartscombe if you like,' he said. 'It can't do him any particular harm.'

Dorothy, taking it, smiled unexpectedly. 'We've missed you lately,' she said.

'Simeon doesn't have to get sick for me to visit. In fact I avoid ill people as much as possible.'

'One of the great mysteries of life,' Simeon brooded with his head down, 'is why you ever chose to become a doctor.'

'Why did you choose to become a parson? Only one reason. Neither of us could hold down a decent job in a biscuit factory.'

Since his wife had died Agnes's father often took her on his rounds with him during her school holidays. In fact she was outside the Rectory now, sitting in the passenger seat of the Doctor's beautifully polished old Alvis coupé. And from nowhere in particular Fred emerged and stood by the car, scuffling his shoe in the gravel of the drive. He started, tentatively at first, to engage her in conversation, while indoors his mother was confiding her anxieties to Agnes's father. 'I'm worried about Simeon,' she told him. 'He gets so tired, and all these little colds of his. Is there nothing you recommend?'

'Take up hunting.' At which Simeon, a paid-up member of any society against blood sports, was seen to shiver in his chair and murmur, 'Hardly!'

'Not for killing foxes. That's not the point,' the Doctor explained. 'They do you a wonderful death on the hunting-field! One minute you're up there, sun in your face, fresh air in your nostrils, giving a brush hedge a clean pair of heels, and then you'll come smack on the hard ground – break your neck and it's over in a second! To hell with bed-pans and the cottage hospital. I plan to finish up on a long run round Picton Principal.'

There was a silence then. Dorothy wandered to the window. 'Your Agnes home from school, is she? Do let her come in.'

'No. I don't think so. She's like her father. Can't stand the sight of illness.'

But as she sat in the Alvis, Agnes was telling Fred that it was a shame and that she'd like to go in and look after the old people. In fact she wanted to be a nurse but her father wouldn t allow it. 'He says wanting to be a nurse just shows an unhealthy interest in disease. Fathers!'

'Yes. I know.' There was a long silence between them and then Fred went on, 'What're you doing for the holidays?'

'Sitting out in the car. I told you.'

'I thought of going on the river.'

'In a rowing-boat?'

'Yes. A boat on the river.'

Agnes shivered at the idea of the river in March. 'Have you got any better at guiding it?'

'I've always been rather good at navigation.' Fred was nettled.

'I don't know. Just as long as you don't get us suddenly out in the middle of the river and then want to *go* urgently.'

'Oh.' Fred sounded disappointed. 'You remember that.'

'Did you think I wouldn't?'

There was another prolonged silence, and then he asked, 'Are you going to Charlie Fanner's party, at Rapstone Manor?'

'Everyone's going to Charlie Fanner's. They've asked *everybody*,' Agnes said. 'They like doing that, don't they? Inviting the tenants.'

'I know,' Fred agreed. 'It's a sort of national event! They've even asked Leslie Titmuss.'

Rapstone Manor is an old house on a hill a little way out of the village and has been, since Edward IV rewarded a steward with a sense of humour with the gift of a manor and the estates of Rapstone, the home of the Fanner family. The house was begun in the middle ages, added to under the Tudors and extended at the Restoration, when the Fanners received their reward for continued loyalty to the Royalist cause. An eighteenth-century Fanner built a new façade and added a folly in the shape of a Gothic tower in the park, and a Victorian Fanner put on the ostentatious portico which gives the house the disconsolate air of a small city railway station set down in the middle of the countryside, with no trains. It's a house shaded by large trees, approached up a long drive, set in a park where the deer are constantly on the look-out for ways of escape from death at the hands of Tom Nowt.

The countryside was much divided during the Civil War. The

Fanners at Rapstone were Royalists, the Stroves of Picton Principal, which then incorporated the entire village of Skurfield, supported Parliament. The Fanners were known as good landlords, usually cheerful and, perhaps because of their origins in the medieval catering business, fond of feasting the tenants on all occasions. The Stroves of Picton House were private people, often of a gloomy and withdrawn disposition, and much given to hanging their tenants from the boughs of the old yew tree by Skurfield Pond. When the young heir, Nicholas Fanner, was celebrating his twenty-first birthday at Rapstone in the usual manner with ox-roasting, bonfires, Morris dancing and a quite exceptional amount of feasting, the then Doughty Strove sent a number of Skurfield villagers to the party secretly carrying crowbars and reaping-hooks. These invaders fell upon the Rapstone tenants, Doughty rode in with a troop of Parliament men and Rapstone Manor was captured for the Puritan cause. Young Sir Nicholas was arrested, certain women of the household were raped, the barns burned and crops commandeered. During the Protectorate Rapstone Manor suffered a further series of violations.

At the Restoration the Stroves were deprived of much of their land, including the village of Skurfield itself, which was added to the Rapstone estate. These events naturally encouraged the gloomy and solitary nature of the Stroves. They became addicted to such private pursuits as spiritualism, social credit and studying the dimensions of the Great Pyramid. The lands they were left with deteriorated. They took to financing impractical schemes for reclaiming parts of Central Australia, or building garden suburbs in Matabeleland. Magnus Strove (died 1917) improved matters a good deal by buying up slum property in Worsfield at a time when the biscuit factories were expanding and inadequate housing was needed there for cheap labour. However, his son Doughty lacked his father's remorseless energy and spent a great deal of time sunk in gloom, when he was not trying to convert his long-isolated valley to growing sunflower seeds for cosmetics or prospecting, without any particular optimism, for various mineral deposits. Doughty's son, Magnus, however, had more of his grandfather's business sense. In his first year at Knuckleberries he cornered the market in horror comics, which he sold at a wide profit-margin, and started an insurance scheme for those likely to be beaten. He had considerable charm and a quick head for figures.

Although rewarded on the restoration of the monarchy, the Fanners, like their neighbours, the Stroves, declined at the end of the eighteenth century. A succession of Sir Nicholas Fanners, although continuing to feast the tenantry, spent most of their nights at the gaming-tables and one Sir Nicholas contrived to lose the villages of Cragmire and Hulton Bathsheba by a single throw at hazard. During his time a wing fell into ruin, the grape house collapsed, dry rot overtook the folly and the squire spent his days, when he could no longer show his face at Boodles, laying wagers with his butler, Garthwaite, about the number of flies which might be caught in the spiders' webs which festooned the dining-room ceiling. (The family fortunes having been founded on a friendship between a royal person and his steward, the Fanners were always most at their ease in the master-servant relationship, particularly now they had become masters.) On his death it was discovered that Garthwaite was owed £1,000 from gambling on spiders, a debt of honour which the next Sir Nicholas paid honourably, enabling the servant to open the grocery and provision shop in Hartscombe (Garthwaites) which survived for many years. In the latter half of the nineteenth century the Fanners sobered up considerably, went into politics and became fairly undistinguished parliamentary secretaries and junior ministers in a number of unmemorable Conservative administrations. They remained popular landlords and great organizers of garden fêtes, firework displays and children's parties. The ruined part of the house was pulled down and tidied up, the greenhouses let out to a market gardener and Rentokil has done its best with the folly.

The presiding Sir Nicholas Fanner, at the time of this eventful birthday party, had just turned fifty. He was a tall, comfortable and amiable man who believed in buying his trousers large and loose enough to admit of their being hoisted on with the braces fixed ready and without the necessity of undoing any of the buttons. He was A.D.C. to a general who translated Horace during the war, and then became Chairman of the local Conservative Party (where he was criticized for a lack of determined hostility to the Attlee Government), and President of the All England Begonia Society. It had come as a surprise to many people, including Nicholas, when he married Grace Oliver. Everyone knew Grace; she was at every party, race-meeting and country-house weekend, although her father Tommy Oliver had decamped and left her mother in a state of penurious confusion. Grace borrowed clothes from her friends, did a succession of odd-jobs 'helping-out' interior decorators, charity organizers and Great Hostesses. She was known to be beautiful and thought to be impossible, but she was an asset at a party. Her tireless activity was felt to be in search of a great and glittering marriage and her final acceptance of the dullish Nicholas Fanner was widely held to be something of a defeat.

Charlotte (Charlie) Fanner was their only child. On her eighth birthday she was a puddingy girl who lacked her mother's startling good looks and Nicholas's comfortable ease of manner. A throw-back through history, he thought, who looked most like that Charles Fanner who earned the friendship of Edward IV, she had the same pale face, colourless hair and small eyes, but she was without the jokes which had endeared his old servant to the King.

Late in the afternoon of Charlie's party, Grace, wrapped in a silk kimono and not yet fully made-up, looked out of her bedroom window and saw Leslie Titmuss, stiffly dressed in his best Sunday shorts and jacket, belted mac and Hartscombe Grammar cap, being regarded dubiously by Wyebrow, the Fanners' manservant, a lugubrious fellow who had been Nicholas's batman during the recent war.

When Leslie had been admitted, after some hesitation on the part of Wyebrow, Grace turned discontentedly into her bedroom, which contained a curtained four-poster, many photographs of minor royal persons and of Grace when young and beautiful taken by Cecil Beaton, drawings of her by Cocteau and Augustus John and, less pleasing to her at that moment, her husband Nicholas standing, almost apologetically, in his loose-fitting suit in the centre of a faded, rose-coloured carpet.

'Please come down. Charlie wouldn't like you to miss her party.'

'I look terrible.' Grace flinched at her reflection in the mirror.

'To me you look beautiful.'

'You always *say* that. You'll say it when I'm old and covered with tramlines and my teeth have fallen out.' Grace was displeased by the compliment.

'Charlie would hate it, if you missed her party.'

'It doesn't mean anything to you, telling me I look beautiful. It's something to say, like "How're the crops?" or "Good planting weather". I can't face all those people.'

'They're only children.'

Grace moved away from the mirror and faced her husband with contempt. 'Charlie's party! Our great social event.'

'We've got all the children from the cottages. Rapstone *and* Skurfield.'

'How terrifically exciting! What do you want me to do? Slip into an evening-dress so you and I can play sardines? Look at me. I'll scream if you tell me I'm beautiful!'

'Charlie's all tricked out.' Nicholas's words came tiptoeing carefully out, as though crossing a minefield. 'In her party dress and so on.'

'I hope you didn't tell *her* she looked beautiful.' Grace moved to the bed and flopped down on it, her long, chalk-white legs protruding extensively from her kimono. 'It was never so boring during the war. At least there were the Americans. And we even got the odd bomb that missed Worsfield.'

'I'm sorry . . .' Her husband moved to the door.

'What're you sorry about now?'

'I'm sorry we couldn't keep the war going to entertain you a little longer,' Nicholas found the courage to say, before he left her.

'Go on, Miss Charlie. Your mother told you. You're to make an entrance.' Charlotte Fanner, miserably shy and lumpy in her party dress, which stuck out round her like bright orange chicken-wire, was being pushed from the darkness of the bedroom corridor to the top of the stairs by Bridget Bigwell, a small, agitated woman, who had been in service at the Manor for thirty-five of her fifty years.

'Mummy's not here.' Charlie peered down the staircase in the way that someone contemplating a suicidal leap off the top of a building might look from the dark height to the brightly lit and crowded street below. In fact the hall was full of milling children and from under the big chandelier her father called up, a blood-chilling cry of 'Pray silence, everyone, for the birthday Queen!'

With tears blurring her vision Charlie stumbled down to the crowd as they sang 'Happy Birthday' in what seemed to her a tone of menace. She knew hardly any of the children from the cottages and she liked none of the girls from the convent school in Hartscombe where she went daily. She particularly dreaded an encounter with Magnus Strove, who called her 'Apple Charlotte' and pulled her hair. She decided to pretend that it wasn't her at all, that she was still safely up in her bedroom and it was all happening to someone else, someone she didn't like, perhaps to a girl at school called Rachel Bosey whom she hated and had never spoken to at all. 'Happy birthday, dear Rachel' – she clenched her fists and sang savagely to herself – 'happy birthday to you!'

In this state of non-participation Charlotte was swept into the sitting-room and thrust into a game of musical chairs. Wyebrow was operating the wind-up gramophone, playing the family's old records, including the version of 'You're the Top!' made specially for her mother (including the lines 'You're the top! You can trump the A – ace, You're the top! You're the Lady Gra – ace'). One by one the children dropped out and sat stuffing themselves with such cakes as sugar rationing would allow. At the end Charlie found herself lolloping round a single remaining chair with a flushed and bright-eyed Leslie Titmuss, who seemed to scent victory. However Wyebrow, with a rare loyalty to the family, stopped the record when Charlie's bottom was hovering nearest and Leslie departed sniffing with disappointment.

'What on earth's the matter with you?' said Henry, who met him on his way out of the room. 'You didn't ever think you were meant to win, did you?' To the company in general he said, 'Come on. We're going to play a decent game of murder.' So, taking instructions from Henry, the children found an old opera hat, property of Nicholas, and drew from it many folded-up bits of paper. 'There's one for the detective,' Henry told them, 'and one for the murderer. All the others are blank, get it?' When Fred opened his message it told him that he was the detective.

Simeon Simcox arrived rather too early to collect the boys, stood by the front door and waited for Wyebrow to open it. He heard the sounds of laughter and stooped to peer through the letter-box. When he had done so he saw the lit hall and a crowd of children picking bits of paper out of a hat. He thought of a way of amusing them and of a dramatic entrance. Accordingly he went down on his hands and knees on the doormat and, swinging one arm as a trunk in front of him and the other as a tail behind, was ready for the front door to open. When at last it did so he entered Rapstone Manor on his knees, trumpeting like an elephant, but the children had vanished in search of a murder and he found himself looking up at the startled faces of Wyebrow, Nicholas and Dr Salter, who had also arrived early, apparently to collect his child. Slowly, and in the circumstances with some dignity, the Rector rose to his feet. This, also, was an incident which would be remembered.

Fred had wandered upstairs and was walking along a corridor, not at all clear what his duties were in detecting a murder which hadn't yet happened. He found the door of a chilly spare bedroom a little open and, looking in, saw Agnes hiding from the party, lying on the quilt reading a pile of old *Vogue*s and *Tatler*s which were kept on the bedside table. She didn't look up as he plonked himself on the bed beside her. He thought that she looked pretty in her party dress and she smelt of Wright's coal-tar soap and, more faintly, of strawberries.

'You know who that is?' Agnes showed him the photograph of a beautiful fair-haired young woman enjoying a joke at a party in the Casino at Cannes.

'She's wearing pyjamas.' Fred observed the picture closely.

'Of course.'

'Pyjamas in public!'

'Poor Charlie.'

'Why?'

'To have a mother who was once so beautiful. For heaven's sake, Fred, what on earth are you doing?'

For Fred had suddenly noticed Agnes's sprawling legs and the slender white backs of her knees. Some memory of Henry's book stung him and he leant down and started to plant what he hoped were small, delicate kisses on that part of her body.

'Butterfly kisses,' Fred explained. 'Don't they rouse you to a purring pitch of passion at all?'

'It feels like having insects crawling all over you!'

Leslie Titmuss, whose paper had been blank, was walking down a dark, ill-decorated passage that led from the hall to the kitchens at the back of the Manor. Since being pipped in the finals of musical chairs he hadn't enjoyed the party. Among the crowd he was as lonely as Charlie, his hostess, but they hadn't spoken to each other. He had no clear idea of how this game of murder would turn out but he suspected it would be alarming and that he would be made to look foolish in front of the other children. As he walked he heard footsteps on the stone flags behind him. Leslie didn't turn his head but pulled open the first door he came to and went in.

He found himself in a big, untidy cloakroom, littered with gumboots, shooting-sticks, raincoats, fishing-rods and a shepherd's crook. There was a lavatory in a corner, beside which was a yellowing pile of *Country Life*s. Leslie sat disconsolately on the large mahogany seat, merely for a place of rest, and looked fearfully about him.

Upstairs Bridget Bigwell walked along the corridor to turn down beds. She was opening the door of Grace's bedroom when Henry, having found the main switch somewhere outside Wyebrow's pantry, pulled it down and extinguished the lights. Bridget stepped into darkness and a mouthful of abuse from her Ladyship for what might, if the room had been illuminated, have been an even more unwelcome interruption.

Sitting on the loo seat Leslie was expecting something horrible to happen. When the lights went out he didn't scream. He sat on breathless, motionless, listening, but he heard nothing until a pair of young hands came out of the darkness and fastened round his neck. Then he screamed fit to blow the roof off, giving out huge echoing yells, remarkable for a boy of his size, with which he further terrified himself.

It couldn't have been very long before the lights came on again. Children came out of doors and clattered downstairs. Wyebrow, Bridget and Nicholas all made for the downstairs passage. When they reached it Dr Salter was already there, as was the Rector. The Doctor opened the door and they found Leslie Titmuss alone, lying huddled on the floor, still screaming.

'Cheer up, young fellow! You're not dead yet,' the Doctor told him. Behind him the children were gathering, looking down with interest at the small, yelling victim on the floor, but it was Simeon who knelt by the boy and put his arms about him and comforted him until the screaming turned to a low sobbing and then died away.

Chapter Five

THE WILL

Not long after Charlie's party a tall, doleful-looking man came to call on Simeon at the Rectory. 'Ah, Titmuss.' Simeon rose from behind his desk where he had been drafting a letter of protest to the Bishop on the Church's complacency about sub-standard housing in Worsfield. 'This won't take long, it's about my boy.' Mr Titmuss didn't sit. He was a man who had spent twenty years as a clerk in the Simcox Brewery in Hartscombe and he regarded the Rector, in spite of everything, as part of the management.

'Young Leslie.' Simeon fumbled for a pipe. 'Extremely helpful lad. He lends a hand with our nettles here occasionally.'

'Not any more,' said Mr Titmuss. 'I'm afraid all that must be put an end to. It won't suit, you see.' He spoke in a deliberate and extremely boring voice, which caused his utterances to be dreaded at the meetings of the Parish Council. He was, undoubtedly, a direct descendant of one of those dedicated Skurfield Puritans who attacked Rapstone Manor with crowbars and reaping-hooks during the Civil War.

'It won't suit?' Simeon frowned. 'I'm sorry. I don't understand.'

'I suppose you know what tricks your family has been playing?'

'Tricks?'

'Your boy playing games. Near scared my lad to death. We've had to have Dr Salter to him.'

'Oh, yes. I was there. I'm sorry.'

'It's his mixing with people as he didn't ought to mix with.'

'Surely not.'

'Coming up here puts thoughts in the boy's head which is more than he can contend with.'

'Leslie's not in any sort of trouble, surely?' The Rector frowned anxiously.

'Not if he keeps to himself. But it's all this play-acting and helping with the nettles, and listening to books being written and stupid games at the Manor. That's not going to be any help to my boy. You ought to know that.'

'Surely you'd like him to widen his horizons?'

'I would not.' Mr Titmuss was quite firm about that.

'No?'

'I would like him to stay at home in Skurfield when he's back from school and mind his own business. Minding your own business is what I set great store by, Rector, as I'm continually trying to point out in Parish Council meetings. Them as chooses to live in South Africa can take care of themselves.'

'Well. Perhaps not entirely . . .'

But Mr Titmuss was looking at the florid lady-bather, the present from Cleethorpes, beside Karl Marx on the Rector's mantelpiece. 'You had that ornament long, have you?' he asked deliberately.

'Not . . . not very long. No.' Simeon hesitated and no doubt sounded guilty.

'May I ask you a personal question, Rector?' Mr Titmuss said, after a long pause.

'Please. Please do.'

'Have you ever, in actual fact, *been* to Cleethorpes?'

'Now you mention it, I can't say I have.' The Rector was doing his best to sound casual.

'Well, I have visited that resort. And I bought a memento, a keepsake to mark the occasion. It was very like this lady-bather here. Unfortunately it has gone missing.'

'I'm sorry to hear that, of course.'

Mr Titmuss took the statuette in his hand and stood looking at it with deep suspicion. 'Rector,' he said, 'can I ask you to explain the presence of this ornament on your mantelpiece?'

At this point Simeon became entirely vague. 'No, I don't think I should. That is to say . . . I don't think I can at all. It's a matter of confidence,' he said, and felt that he had explained nothing.

'Then you would have no objection to my removing this from your possession?' Mr Titmuss, without waiting for further permission, put the statuette into his pocket.

'No objection in the world.' Simeon laughed a little. 'In fact its removal might come as a considerable relief to my wife.'

'Would it indeed?'

'Oh, yes. I dare say it would.'

'Then I'll say goodbye to you, Rector. From now on it will be formal communication only on the business of our joint Parish Council.' He went to the door. 'Fine words on the subject of Socialism may come to you very easy, but they hardly excuse the acquisition of the other person's little ornaments.'

Simeon was left looking at the closed door in surprise and bewilderment.

After his father's funeral Fred returned to the practice he carried on in the old house in Hartscombe, which had once belonged to Dr Salter. It was a busy time, for which he was grateful, and he avoided thoughts of the past, failing to return a number of calls he had from Jackson Cantellow, the family solicitor. Driven to desperation by this conduct Cantellow called at the surgery, where Miss Margaret Thorne, Fred's strict, grey-haired receptionist, made him sit for a while in a row of sick people, reading back numbers of *Punch* and *Good Housekeeping* or staring into space. 'I'm not ill,' he protested, 'it's a matter of urgent business!', when a staggering four-year-old offered to show him her colouring book. At last Miss Thorne relented and said, 'Doctor will see you now, Mr Cantellow.'

'I've got to talk to one of you, and I can't get a word of sense out of your mother.' Fred looked up at the red face hovering over him above a purple bow-tie and wondered if he should suggest taking the patient's blood pressure. 'A word of sense about what?'

'The position! You realize of course why the Rector could afford to be so independent, why he could cock so many fine liberal snooks at the Bishop and Synod and the Parish Council? The stipend at the Rectory could hardly have kept him in pipe tobacco or bought your mother's little pieces of china. It was his share in Simcox Ales, that's what Dorothy might have expected to depend on.'

'*Might* have?'

'I've been trying to explain it to her. Of course it pains your mother to talk about money and you can live a pure and unselfish existence writing out chitties for days off work and tending to the slightest whims of your National Health patients.' Jackson Cantellow, a pillar of the Worsfield Choral Society, was accustomed to give way to such arias. 'Oh, it's all very fine and elevated, no doubt, to be perfectly uninterested in money when you've got plenty of it. But you haven't now, Dr Frederick. Your family hasn't.'

'I never expected any.'

'Never?'

'I supposed Simeon would leave it all to Mother.'

'Well, let me tell you what's happened.' Cantellow sat down and went on with the relish of a man who has bad news to impart. 'For years I'd been urging your father to make a will, but he never gave me instructions. Now I hear from a little firm in Worsfield who do police court business, that sort of thing, and it seems . . .' Jackson Cantellow looked deeply shocked. 'It seems that your father went to them entirely without my knowledge and made a will, quite recently. He left none of the Brewery shares, which must be worth about two million nicker, if I know anything about it, to your mother, or to you, or to your brother, Henry.'

'Well, who did he leave them to?' Fred was growing bored, as he sometimes did with a long list of patients' aches and pains.

'He left the whole bloody shooting-match' – Jackson Cantellow came to the point at last – 'to the Right Honourable Leslie Titmuss, M.P., absolutely and forever.'

On the day after this meeting Henry and his second wife, Lonnie, drove down to the Rectory and saw Fred and Dorothy in what the older brother called a 'Council of War'. 'Of course we're going to fight it!' Henry said, pacing the study in considerable anger.

'I don't see why "of course".'

'Oh no, Fred. You wouldn't. You never fought anything. You never even cared about winning when we played games.'

'I always thought that life was rather too short to care about losing to you at ping-pong.'

'Then you'll be a great help in defeating the abominable Titmuss!'

'Such an unattractive child,' Dorothy remembered. 'I always thought that must have been very hard for him to bear. As a boy he always smelled, as I remember it, of lead pencils. I pitied him for it.'

'Well, no need to pity him any longer,' Lonnie said. 'He's got all our money.'

'*Mother's* money,' Fred corrected her, and Henry gave him an unfriendly look. 'Such an extraordinary thing for your father to do!' Lonnie went on undeterred. 'Do you think he meant it as some sort of joke?'

'Did he mean many things as a joke?' Dorothy asked.

'Perhaps only his profession.' Fred smiled, but Henry looked extremely serious. 'Our father, perhaps you need reminding, was a priest of the Church of England.'

'Exactly.'

'I don't know. He never told me he thought being a parson was funny. He never said it in so many words.' Dorothy started to collect their teacups.

'Well, I'm going to fight it if nobody else is,' Henry told them. 'Quite clearly our father was out of his head.'

'He was a saint,' Fred reminded him.

'What?'

'You heard what Kev the Rev. said at the funeral. We have lived in the presence of a saint.'

'Or a complete raving lunatic?' Henry asked, and answered, 'That's what we're going to have to prove.'

After Henry and Lonnie had gone back to London, Fred left his mother and drove into Hartscombe. He saw the sights of his childhood, the bridge and the broad river made for pleasure, the moored punts and canoes and white launches, the willows and pubs by the water. He passed the long, red-brick brewery buildings and the sign of 'Simcox Ales'. He came to the rather shabby Victorian house where he lived and worked and parked his car in the space marked 'Doctor'.

The working day was over. He looked in on Miss Thorne, who was putting away the patients' cards, and went up to the top floor. His room was untidy, it was a bachelor's living-room with piles of books, records and his old drum set. He found a 78, wiped the dust off it and put it on the record-player. Then he gathered up the plate and cup and saucer which he had used at breakfast and carried them out to the kitchen as Benny Goodman started to play 'Slow Boat to China'. He sat at the drums and began to accompany the record, singing softly also,

> 'Get you and keep you
> In my arms evermore,
> Leave all your lovers
> Weeping on the faraway shore.
> Out on the briny,
> With a moon big and shiny,
> Melting your heart of stone,
> I'd love to get you
> On a slow boat to China,
> All to myself alone . . .'

As he played the years vanished. He thought of nothing very much, except, for some reason, the sound of wire-brushes on an upturned chamber-pot, and wondered, not for the first time, why their father had sent them so far away from home.

Part Two

Let's be frank about it. Most of our people have never had it so good. Go round the country, go to the industrial towns, go to the farms, and you will see a state of prosperity such as we have never had in my lifetime – nor indeed ever in the history of this country.

Harold Macmillan
Bedford, July 1957

Chapter Six

THE DESERTER

Fred had seen them again on a yellowing newspaper photograph he found in an old tea-chest of Simeon's belongings which he was going through after his father's death. There was the Rector marching along as proud as a field marshal, swinging the stick he took out on country walks and smiling for the camera beneath a huge black banner which proclaimed 'March from Aldermaston, Easter 1958'. Beside him was Ben Leverett, once the Labour M.P. for Hartscombe, and his wife, Joanie. Behind them young men and women marched with the seriousness and dedication of soldiers in a war they had missed. Many of them held up circular C.N.D. signs or slogans such as 'Ban the Bomb or the Human Race'. Behind the leaders the trailing procession included men with caps and macs, for it was a miserably wet Easter, playing trumpets, trombones and penny whistles. And among them Fred saw, looking absurdly young, the faces of himself and Henry. His elder brother was frowning, clearly taking the matter extremely seriously. It seemed as though Fred had made a joke and Henry hadn't laughed.

'Peaceful demonstrations!' Henry said that Easter as they trudged out of London. 'I mean, what peaceful demonstration ever altered the course of history? Do you honestly imagine that the October Revolution could have been brought about by a few people tootling on penny whistles and a couple of vicar's sons carrying sandwiches?'

'There are more people here today.' They had started off as a few hundred from Trafalgar Square and had lunch by the Albert Memorial. Even then a number of their better-dressed supporters had defected at Turnham Green and taken the tube home. As they marched along the Great West Road there was a flurry of snow and somewhere a man had run out of his house to tell them that Cambridge had won the Boat Race. Somewhere a woman advised them to get back to Moscow, but there were new recruits, men carrying rolls of blankets and sleeping-bags for the nights they were to spend in churches or village halls, and mothers pushing prams. In one section the marchers played and sang protest songs, they were those whom critics of the enterprise would call the 'beards and weirds'. It was the first of such expeditions, the small start of a period which would be marked by an uncontrollable escalation in bombs and demonstrations.

'Do you really think,' Henry asked, 'that Marie Antoinette would have gone scooting out of Versailles at the approach of a few students strumming guitars and a couple of overweight M.P.s? The idea's ridiculous.'

'Why are you here then?'

'Well, I think, in my position, I should stand up and be counted,' Henry said in all modesty.

'I'll count you then.' Fred looked at his brother and said, after some calculation, 'One!'

'Oh, really! At times you are excessively childish.'

But they were children no more. Fred was then twenty-three and had done his National Service, unheroically in the Pay Corps. He was still at Cambridge, Simeon's old university, where he found himself reading politics and economics with a growing lack of interest. Henry was twenty-six, his National Service had taken him to Malaya, so he had a travelled and somewhat world-weary air. He read English at King's, joined the university Labour Party, had three of his plays acted by undergraduates, engaged in several notable love-affairs and was the subject of a profile in *Granta*. When he came down he got a job in a publishing firm where he wrote scathing reports on the novels of middle-aged and established authors.

'Will you see your children die?
Men and women, stand together,
Do not heed the Men of War!
Make your mind up – now or never,
Ban the bomb for ever more . . .'

The song, taken up and then let go around them, drifted away over the wet hedgerows and soggy fields. Some sang full-throatedly, and quickly gave up with the effort of marching; others, adopting the more professional nasal whine of the trans-atlantic protest singer, kept it up longer. The children joined in, guessing at the words or breaking into giggles when a group of adults changed it to 'Ban the bum'.

'What *is* your position, anyway?' Fred asked.

'Well, with the book just coming out,' Henry explained patiently, 'it's obvious that an artist should take a stand.'

Henry's first novel, *The Greasy Pole*, had just been accepted for publication by a rival and more go-ahead firm than his own and he was nervously awaiting disaster or life-long fame. In fact the book was to get some good notices and moderate sales. Although *The Greasy Pole* might have appeared as the latest word in the new style of comic, social and sexual realism intro-duced some years earlier, it was about the tenth re-write of the work which Henry read to Fred and Arthur Nubble by the playing-fields at Knuckleberries.

'Which artist?' Fred asked, a question so foolish that Henry did not bother to answer it. By the time they had stopped for lunch Fred had decided that, although he was prepared to take all reasonable steps to save mankind from self-immolation, sleep-ing with his brother on the floor of a church again was an act over and above the call of duty. A plan began to form itself in his mind, but he knew himself well enough to doubt whether he would ever have the courage to put it into operation. They sat outside a pub. Ben Leverett, who made a good thing out of journalism and liked more than an occasional glass of champagne, a tipple which it was his avowed intention to spread evenly among the labouring classes, was panting and wiping his forehead with a red-and-white spotted handkerchief. His wife, Joanie, made of sterner stuff, was still singing, 'Ban, ban, *ban* the bloody H Bomb!' to the tune of 'John Brown's Body' with a group of Worsfield women. Simeon reacted with smiling detachment to a request for prayer from a group of Christian Pacifists. It was when he said, 'I think at the moment I'd rather have a pint of wallop,' and 'Today we're praying with our feet,' that Fred felt driven to go into the saloon bar and make a telephone call. His hands were hot and smelled of the pennies he had been clutching; he waited as the number rang and had almost decided to go back to the marchers when the ringing stopped and he heard a voice say, 'Yes? Who is it?' As usual she sounded desperate, as though the house had caught fire and she was trapped at the head of a blazing staircase with no possibility of escape.

'Agnes!' He had pressed Button A and now he was committed to at least try for an adventure.

'Where on earth are you?' She asked the question as though she felt no real need to know the answer.

'By a road somewhere. I'm doing something with my father,' he insisted on telling her, 'but I might be able to get away this evening. I mean, would you like to do something? Or something,' he ended lamely.

'I wanted to go to Worsfield tonight.' Agnes was standing in the hall of the Doctor's house in Hartscombe. Down the passage the living-room door was open and she spoke quietly, not wishing to be overheard. 'To go dancing,' she told Fred. 'Is that an extraordinary thing to want to do?'

'I don't suppose so. Where?'

'There's an absolutely horrible club where they have the most repulsive food. I thought that might be a good place to go.'

'Oh. All right then.' It had to be better than the night with

Henry in the church and he now felt that if he didn't take her out he would be a failure in Agnes's eyes for ever.

'I can get over in my father's car, but not if you don't want to. How will you get over?'

'Oh, I'll hitch a lift or something. What's it called?'

'What's what called?'

'The awful place.'

'Oh. The Barrel of Biscuits, isn't it ghastly? It's in West Street, so far as I can remember. But honestly don't bother.'

'Yes. I want to. You know I want to. About eight o'clock?'

'Just don't expect anything much.' When Agnes put the telephone down she walked along the passage, past the half-open sitting-room door. She didn't go in as her father was there with a lady. She was Mrs Dorothy Simcox, Fred's mother, for whom he was pouring a second glass of lunchtime sherry.

'Guilt,' Dr Salter was saying, as he often did, 'is a most malignant disease.'

Fred wasn't discouraged by Agnes's description. That afternoon he told Henry he was going to march with the musicians; he was doing so, he hinted, out of professional interest. So he fell behind his father and his brother, and when the guitar players passed him he loitered behind them also. When the whole procession had vanished up the road he thumbed a lift from a passing lorry.

Worsfield, home of the biscuit and an ailing furniture industry, is a place which seems like a grim northern town set down unexpectedly in a south-west riverside landscape. Its cathedral is a barrack-like red-brick 1930s building, its university a series of concrete blocks specializing in engineering and its streets glum and ill-favoured. Fred arrived there about two hours early for his meeting with Agnes. He went into the Railway Hotel lavatory and washed with liquid soap and wondered if he needed a shave. As he saw no way of getting one he brushed his clothes, cleaned his shoes on the machine provided and checked, without any particular optimism, the continued presence of a single french letter in the corner of his wallet. When he thought about it sanely he couldn't imagine that Agnes who, although beautiful, had not a good word to say for all the other pleasures in life, would have much time for sex.

He had no difficulty in finding the Barrel of Biscuits, a converted warehouse in West Street, and no difficulty at all in becoming a life member. As he sat at the bar and waited, drinking slowly to preserve his money, Fred began to tell himself that Agnes wouldn't have wanted to meet him unless . . . Well, after all, it had been entirely her suggestion. He'd been dragged away from a most important protest march at her insistence and what else could that mean? When he got out a pound note to pay the barman he felt the circular ridge in the inner pocket of his wallet and thought it might come in useful after a long period of inactivity. And then she was half an hour late and he decided she wasn't coming at all. Well, perhaps it was all for the best. He looked towards the dance floor, at the girls in huge circular skirts, rustling petticoats and ankle socks. They seemed to be totally unaware, he thought, of the coming destruction of mankind.

'Aren't you hungry?' He looked round and Agnes was there. She'd changed into a tight-fitting skirt and wore a cardigan improbably buttoned down the back. 'I've kept you waiting.' She sat on a stool at the bar beside him and picked up a menu. She lowered her head and he saw her thin neck and the ridge of her backbone vanishing under the cardigan buttons.

'I didn't mind.' A group of boys in drainpipes and duck's-arse hair-do's, laughing and punching each other's arms, invaded the dance floor. A waitress who looked about fifteen appeared to take their food orders. 'Curry and chips,' Agnes told her. 'And draught bitter. A pint.'

'Yes. All right.' Fred had no other ideas.

'Curry and chips twice. And two pints of Simcox.'

'Is that the best?' Fred asked when the waitress had left them.

'The worst.' Agnes sounded pleased. 'The curry smells of the monkey house.'

'Why do you like that so?' he was bold enough to ask.

'Like what?'

'Things that are really ghastly.' He felt angered by her expression of sad superiority. She looked as though she had been through experiences she was afraid he would never live up to and didn't deserve to share. However she smiled now, almost timidly, and seemed to take him into her confidence.

'I don't know,' she said. 'My mother liked everything nice.'

'You never talk about her.'

'Oh, she was a great beauty. Anyway, you know she snuffed it. When I was ten.' Fred had heard the story from his parents. The beautiful Mrs Salter saved up her coupons and went up to London to buy a dress in the sales and a stray buzz bomb caught her. It was a chance in a million of course but there were people in Hartscombe who still felt it showed a sad streak of flippancy to die for a new frock in Oxford Street.

'Your father had to bring you up?'

'We brought up each other.' The curry came and Agnes pursued it gently round her plate with the back of the fork. 'It was a shock for him.'

'Is that why he doesn't seem . . . well . . .'

'Well, what?' She took a few mouthfuls and then pushed the plate away with a look of gratified disgust. Fred was eating almost with pleasure. 'Why he doesn't always seem tremendously keen on curing people like my father.'

'That's what he *says*.'

'Doesn't he mean it?'

'Does *your* father mean what he says?'

'Yes. Yes, I quite honestly think so.'

'A new heaven and a new earth? My father says that's what yours is always talking about.'

'He wants things to be better, yes. Not like before the war. Not with unemployment and dole queues and hard-faced business men in charge of everything. Nothing particularly wrong with that, is there?'

She didn't answer, indeed she appeared to have lost all interest, not only in the conversation, but in him. He stumbled on, not caring if he was boring her. 'You don't want an H bomb dropping on Worsfield, do you?'

'Worsfield?' Agnes seemed to be thinking it over. 'Well. Perhaps now if you'd said Hartscombe or Rapstone Fanner . . . Anyway, what's he doing to stop it? What *can* he do?'

'He's marching. At least he believes in it enough to march.'

'Shouldn't we dance to the rotten music?' As Agnes said it he thought she was giving him a last chance to stop being a bore. They finished their beer and as he followed her towards the spot-lit floor he thought he was going out for a test but felt confident that he could dance rhythmically and rather well. Agnes did a creditable imitation of the pony-tailed girls twirling round them. It had its own expertise but it was a parody of something she half envied, half thought ridiculous. She raised her eyebrows in mock admiration as Fred went through his repertoire of steps, collected her and sent her gyrating away from him like a yo-yo and then pulled her resolutely back again.

'You're quite good at this,' she shouted at him.

'Surprised?'

The music changed, quietened, began to pour out of the juke-box like treacle. He decided to hold Agnes and dance closely to her. She didn't move away and he felt that her breasts were not at all supercilious and her thighs made no effort to patronize him. Suddenly elated by this discovery, and by the pints of Simcox Special that he had drunk with the curry, he began to sing along with the Platters,

> 'Heavenly shades of night are falling,
> It's twilight time,
> Out of the mist your voice is calling . . .'

'You must be better at dancing than you are at marching.' Agnes's voice was unexpectedly close to his ear.

'I didn't want to march especially.'

'Why?'

'I could think of better things to do.'

She stood still then, looking at him. 'I think I'd like another drink.'

'Are you sorry,' he asked her when they got back to the bar, 'that I'm quite good at dancing? I mean, would you feel better if I fell about and stood on your feet?'

'I don't know. I haven't made up my mind yet.'

The beer, when it came, slopped over the pint mugs, drowning the change. Fred decided that he could cope with Agnes best if he were either drunk or dancing, preferably both.

When they left the Barrel of Biscuits a good many pints later, Fred put out his hand for the Doctor's car keys. 'I'll drive,' he said.

'Are you good at that too? How appalling!' But Agnes got into the passenger seat and he drove her out of Worsfield. They hadn't met often since he went away to Cambridge and she went to Worsfield university, but they had gone out on a few occasions to pubs or the Hartscombe Odeon. The first time she had kissed him non-committally on parting and, as he went home alone to the Rectory, he had decided that he was in love with her and that his success or failure with Agnes was a test on which the whole of his life would be judged. He put off any decisive attempt however because he wanted to postpone failure. But the night he deserted from the march he had decided was the time for winning or losing everything. Driving her home he knew that he had lost and that he had been unentertaining. Even his small skill at dancing would be held against him.

They drove to Rapstone first, where he would leave her, and parked beside the lychgate which led into the churchyard. He was about to give her the driving seat and to go home and pretend that the evening had been more eventful than it was. He might hint at great happenings and even lie about it to himself. Fred knew that he had a capacity for self-deception which could cushion many disappointments. He kissed her, as he had done after their other meetings, a tentative and token 'good-night', and was astonished at the strength, almost the desperation of her reaction. He felt himself dragged down, below the level of the windows, and was conscious of the taste of her mouth, a vague worry about villagers peering out from behind lace curtains and the inconvenience of a gear-stick in the groin.

After what seemed a long while Agnes surfaced for air. Fred looked at her, with a new sort of assurance.

'What do you think?' he asked her.

'It beats butterfly kisses.'

'So you remember Charlie's party?' He was pleased.

'No,' Agnes said decidedly. 'I don't remember.' Then she kissed him again, it seemed endlessly. When she came up for the second time she said, 'What do you call this then?'

'Heavy petting?' Fred suggested. 'Seventy per cent of fifteen-year-old Americans pet to climax-point two to five times a week.'

'How on earth do you know that?' She was looking at him with disapproval.

'A boy called Arthur Nubble smuggled the Kinsey Report into school.'

'How absolutely disgusting!'

'Yes,' he had to agree with her.

'I hate heavy petting,' Agnes now decided, pushing him away from her. 'It's *Yank*.'

'Is it?' Fred asked, feeling in a confused way that he was being blamed for the embarrassing researches of Dr Kinsey, and that the evening was over.

'Terribly Yank. Let's get out of the car at least.'

Fred looked out of the window. A thin rain was blurring the moonlight. 'Isn't it a bit wet?'

'Oh, for God's sake!' Agnes was losing her patience. 'You didn't mind marching in it!'

The pews in the church had been pushed aside and the marchers slept on the floor. Simeon was stretched out in a sleeping-bag, reading *Human Society in Ethics and Politics* by Bertrand Russell. He remembered that he had not seen Fred for a long time.

'There's a lot of beards and weirds with guitars about the place.' Henry unstrapped his blanket and his sleeping-bag in an efficient and military sort of way. 'Fred must be with them.'

'I suppose so.'

'Trust young Fred to get himself lost. He'll never get himself round to banning anything.'

In the graveyard, where he would come to stand over his dead father, in a dark corner under the wall, Fred lay on Agnes. Her clothes were pulled up, her long white legs were wrapped round him. He felt a great sense of triumph. It was a victory over Henry, although he would never tell him of his undoubted and unlooked-for success.

Later Agnes and Fred, more or less composed, were standing hand in hand by the car. They spoke in whispers. Agnes had to drive back to Hartscombe and, confident now that he could do anything, Fred insisted on turning the car round for her. He reversed in a fine arc and backed into the wall by the lychgate, producing a bang which might have wakened the long buried inhabitants of Rapstone and the sleeping Fanners in the nave of the church. He stood with Agnes and examined the dented bumper.

'What will your father say?'

'Nothing much. I'll drive it now.' She got into the car and left him standing.

'Shall we go dancing again?' he called after her.

'Possibly.' She let in the clutch and drove away from him.

After she'd gone, Fred let himself into the Rectory. The light was still shining under his mother's bedroom door but he went silently, with his shoes off and still feeling triumphant, into his own bedroom. He was delighted with himself the next morning also when he left the Rectory before his mother was awake and walked up the long road to the signpost which pointed to Rapstone in one direction and Skurfield in the other. Then he thumbed a lift from an early morning farmer's van which came rattling out of the mist. Another young man was bicycling up the road from Skurfield to get on to the Hartscombe road; he was wearing a cheap, dark, gent's suiting, bicycle clips, and a row of pens in his breast-pocket. He was Leslie Titmuss and he saw Fred board the van, but Fred didn't see him.

The newspapers had ridiculed the well-known supporters of C.N.D. for not turning out on the march, so a number of journalists and politicians, some of whom would live to attend Simeon's funeral, joined on the last stage as did a lot of less well-known faces, so the numbers were swollen to thousands. Fred found them on the heathland of gorse and pines round Aldermaston and he saw a crowd listening to Simeon, who was making a speech by the high wire fence round the atomic research establishment. 'Peace through fear! God had a similar idea once . . . Goodness through the fear of hell fire . . . Not one of his most brilliant notions.' Fred heard his father's words blow away across the waste-ground, projected towards the anonymous huts behind the wire. 'I can't remember the fear of hell stopping much slaughter . . .'

'I've been looking for you,' Fred told his brother when he found him.

'Where've you been?'

'With a band. We found an old van to sleep in.'

'Dear little Freddie.' Henry looked at him, almost with kindness. 'You're such a hopeless liar!'

'I've taken counsel's opinion,' Henry said.

'What about?'

'You know what about. Our father's alleged will.'

Some months after their father's death the two brothers, one just on the wrong, the other still on the right side of fifty, were having dinner together in Henry's club. The Sheridan is a meeting-place for lawyers, actors, writers, publishers and the more presentable type of advertising agent. Its premises are somewhat dusty, its carpets worn but its pictures of past novelists, vanished players and dead judges are famous and its brand of nursery food (overdone roasts, mashed potato and jam roly-poly) is very popular with the sort of Englishman who has never totally recovered from an emotional relationship with his nanny. Henry was proposed for membership of the Sheridan by his second publisher, having left the firm who had accepted *The Greasy Pole* because of what he thought were disappointing sales.

'"Alleged"?' Fred asked. He was already regretting the rare visit to London and the meeting which his brother had told him was of such urgent and secret importance.

'Well, it's not his real will, is it?' Henry explained with carefully simulated patience, as though Fred were still in his first term at Knuckleberries and needed instruction on the harsh rules about undoing buttons. 'Simeon couldn't have meant to ignore his entire family in favour of that jumped-up little sod Leslie Titmuss.'

'I always found it difficult to discover what he really meant, quite honestly.'

'The thing's perfectly obvious!' Henry was visibly allowing his patience to wear thin. 'That ridiculous will's either a forgery . . .'

'A forgery by a cabinet minister?'

'It's been known. Or Titmuss leaned on our father in some way. Blackmailed him, I mean. Or the old man had simply gone stark-staring mad, which to judge from his behaviour is, in our barrister's opinion, by far the most likely explanation.'

'*Our* barrister's?' Fred had never met this adviser.

'Of course, I'm protecting your interests as well, Fred. We're all in the same boat, you know. As a family we sink or swim together.'

'Simcox!' Henry had been hailed by a tall, florid-faced old man with white hair, a dark suit and a Sheridan club tie, who was ambling past the table. He was a judge, Mr Justice Mervyn Haliburton, who sat in the Chancery Division and happened to be expert on the trying of will cases. Knowing this, Henry rose in his seat with exaggerated respect. After having directed him to sit down the Judge said, in that tone of mild self-congratulation which people always use to an author whose work they have endured, 'Saw that old film of yours last night on my telly-box.'

Henry waited for judgement. Instead Haliburton explained to him, in case he might have forgotten, what the work was about. 'It was the one where the lad from the Brewery rogers the girl in the punt.'

'*The Greasy Pole*.'

'Oh, I dare say. I liked the snaps of the countryside. I don't suppose you took the snaps, did you? I suppose they have special fellows for that.' Henry made no comment. Fred was pleased and a little surprised, that his brother took no credit for the camera-work. The Judge said, 'You haven't introduced me to your guest.'

'I'm sorry. My brother, Frederick. Mr Justice Haliburton.'

Fred didn't rise. He wanted no part of this sudden involvement with the legal profession. The Judge was looking curiously at

Henry, as though he not only needed telling his own plots but was inexplicably forgetful of his closest relations.

'We don't hear about your brother, Simcox. Never read about any brother in those thumbnail sketches of you we always get in the Sunday supplements. Perhaps your *brother* doesn't like to get himself into the papers.'

'I'm a country doctor,' Fred explained.

'Oh well. I suppose that might account for it. Do carry on. Don't let me stop you having food.' The Judge wandered off, beaming as though he had trapped an unwary witness, and Henry laughed, Fred thought, a little nervously.

'There's nothing like the Sheridan,' Henry told his brother, who wished he were far away, in the Badger at Skurfield, playing a session with a middle-aged jazz group who were still tolerated at occasional gigs. 'You meet actors, judges as you can see, wonderful old characters, and the occasional bishop.'

'Just a typical cross-section of British society in the eighties?'

'You do agree, don't you?'

'Oh yes. It's fascinating.' Fred only wanted to stop his brother talking. He longed for the company of the ageing trumpet-player from the Imperial Wine stores in Hartscombe with whom he could exchange quotations from old Louis Armstrong records they both knew by heart.

'You do agree that the conduct of our father' – Henry persisted – 'over the years, showed every sign of complete insanity?'

'He was credulous. He believed in causes.'

'That hardly explains his entering other people's houses on his hands and knees, trumpeting like an elephant.'

'There was a reason for that.'

'You'd find a reason for everything! I don't know why you should make excuses for him. He cut you out of his will too.'

'Perhaps he didn't think I needed the money.' Fred stole a glance at his watch. It was still lamentably early.

'Don't be ridiculous!' Henry looked hard at his brother. 'You never quarrelled with him, did you?'

'No,' Fred answered quickly, not giving himself time to wonder if he were telling the truth.

'Never. On any occasion?'

'No. Never.'

'May I come in?' Fred stopped helping out King Oliver on the drums as his father came into his room after they were all back from Aldermaston. 'Is it the noise, are you trying to write a sermon?'

'Are you expecting one?' Simeon moved a pile of records and sat on the end of the bed. 'Odd, this need people seem to feel for sermons. I could never understand it. You know, often on Sundays, I look down at those upturned faces and I feel an irresistible urge to say, "Oh, for heaven's sake go home to lunch. Don't flatter yourselves by feeling that you've sinned." What do you want a sermon about?'

'Nothing.' Fred tapped his drums impatiently. 'I don't want a sermon at all.'

'About the march . . .' Simeon began, but his son interrupted him. 'Don't tell me I made the slightest difference to the march. No one could've noticed whether I was there or not.'

'Don't be modest, Fred, don't feel you're grand enough to be modest. I expect you think all that marching is quite futile. Perhaps the good it does is to those who take part in it, it makes them feel they're not simply leading dull, materialistic lives, perhaps . . .'

'It all sounds extremely self-indulgent.' Fred was longing to be left alone, to play his drums and think about Agnes.

'I'm sorry we're not pure enough for you,' Simeon smiled.

Fred continued his attack. 'Perhaps you can achieve the same result with Simcox's Best Bitter, and it's not half so hard on the feet, or with any inexpensive pleasures like . . .'

'Like what?'

'Oh, never mind. How did you find out I left the march, did Henry tell you?'

'No. No it wasn't your brother.' The question apparently caused Simeon some embarrassment. He fumbled for a pipe and started to fill it clumsily, dropping shreds of tobacco on the carpet. 'It was Leslie who told me.' He seemed apologetic.

'Leslie?' Fred enjoyed sounding incredulous.

'Young Titmuss.'

'*What* did he tell you?' Fred was now able to feel betrayed and was surprised at how defensive his father had become.

'He saw you getting a lift, early in the morning.'

'Leslie Titmuss! I can't believe it.'

'You know he works at the Brewery now,' the Rector said, as though it explained something. 'Well, he bicycles in early even at weekends. He's studying for a degree in advanced accountancy, his father told me that. I believe he's anxious to take up some sort of public service.'

'Like spying on my movements?'

'That's not charitable, Fred. Leslie's had absolutely none of your advantages. He wants to make something of his life.'

'And something of mine too?'

At lunchtime Simeon asked Dorothy if she had been away from the house on the last day of the march and she said that she had been in the garden all day and at home in the evening. She had seen nothing at all of Fred. Her husband held a green apple in one bony hand and, with the other, he peeled it carefully. Not for the first time he felt the simplicity of the great issues, he knew exactly what should be done about South Africa and urban poverty and the bomb. It was the small events, those nearer home, that seemed to him forever shrouded in mystery. He bit into the apple with sudden determination and a small wince of courage, like a swimmer who plunges briskly into the sea on a cold day.

Leslie Titmuss would have stayed in the office at lunchtime, with the sandwiches and Thermos his mother had prepared for him, if he hadn't had some business to attend to. He never liked crossing the Brewery yard; the wide expanse smelled of sour beer and horse shit from the four great stamping Suffolk Punches Simcox's still kept to advertise the Brewery and enter for the County Show. Huge lorries were always backing in and out of the gates and he had an irrational feeling that the barrels which were rolled on to them might bound away out of control, trundle across the yard like huge cannonballs and snap his thin legs like matchsticks. As he picked his way across this danger zone in his dark suit and white detachable collar, older men in aprons, enjoying their free beer in the shadows under shed roofs, would call out at him, asking him questions about his uneventful sex life, which he pretended not to hear.

That day he had got safely to the gates without being shouted at or coming to any harm. He was about to set out on his mission when he heard his name called in a peremptory, not to say hostile manner and turned to see Fred standing in the road outside the Brewery entrance, waiting for him.

'Mr Frederick.' Leslie meant to appear casually surprised. He was conscious that his voice sounded startled and ingratiating.

'Oh, for God's sake, Leslie. Don't bother about the "Mr Frederick". You've been speaking to my father.'

'Yes. He lets me. I'm very grateful.'

'*Why*, for God's sake?'

'Shouldn't one speak to the Rector?' Leslie spoke in a hushed, almost reverent tone which Fred would have found funny if he hadn't been so incensed. 'If one has spiritual problems?'

'Am I one of your spiritual problems?'

'No, "Fred", of course you aren't.' Leslie tried another cautious smile. 'I just happened to mention I saw you up early. I thought your father'd like to know that.'

'When I ought to have been with him, banning the bomb?'

'I don't agree with that, exactly.' Leslie Titmuss was quick to state his position.

'Oh, don't you?'

'We need the bomb.' Leslie looked nervously back at the

Brewery yard, as though he were thinking of his personal protection.

'*You* might need it,' Fred told him with some contempt. 'It might come in frightfully handy for you in the accounts department at Simcox Brewery. It may be absolutely vital for your daily cycling to work from Skurfield. But I don't know why anyone else has the slightest need for it.'

'Think of England.' Fred was surprised to find Leslie looking at him with a kind of pitying sincerity.

'What?'

'Think of England, "Fred", and the defence of freedom.' This came out in such a new, carefully modulated and confidential voice, so far removed from the squeaky and complaining tones of the old Leslie Titmuss, that Fred asked, 'What on earth's happened to you?'

'You should learn about that.'

'About what?'

'About the defence of freedom. You going to be at the Swan's Nest on Saturday night, are you?' The question seemed so irrelevant to the cause of freedom that Fred was at a loss for an answer. 'Dinner dance of the Young Conservatives,' Leslie told him. 'Dress is formal.' And as Fred stood looking at him Leslie started to retreat hastily, saying as he went, 'You want to join the Y.C.s, Mr Frederick. You want to make something of yourself.'

Fred might have followed Leslie Titmuss in order to protest further, or to make an appropriate reply to his invitation to join the Young Conservatives, but he was himself summoned to account by an insistent voice calling him from the other side of the road.

'Come here, young Fred!'

Dr Salter had emerged from a terraced house where he had been visiting one of that class of people whom he considered pampered and overprivileged, the sick. He was clearly glad to be out of the bedroom and was gulping in fresh air mixed with smells from the Brewery and standing beside his cherished antique sports car, which Fred couldn't help noticing, as he approached it guiltily, had a buckled bumper and a dented rear-end.

'I positively approve of your battering down Rapstone Church,' Dr Salter said, 'but I would be obliged if your lust for destruction stopped short at the backside of my old Alvis.'

'Oh,' Fred affected surprise, 'is it damaged at all?'

'Get in,' said Dr Salter, and opened the car door.

Faced with the crop-headed, unsmiling, square-shouldered Doctor, Fred felt like those characters in the gangster-movies he most enjoyed who were hustled into cars by mobsters with bulging pockets and taken to a cement overcoat in the East River. 'I'll buy you a couple of pints in the Badger at Skurfield. Dora Nowt's just about to drop her fifth. She's a reasonably cooperative patient, usually manages to pull it off before lunch. Agnes has gone up to London,' the Doctor went on, interrupting Fred, who seemed about to make some excuse, 'so don't pretend you've got anything better to do.' They drove for a while in silence, but when they reached the place where the road divided at the signpost which pointed one way to Rapstone and the other way to Skurfield, Fred, who hadn't stopped thinking about it, asked, 'Where did you say Agnes had gone?'

'To London. She went to stay with her Aunt Molly. Wanted to admire the holes in the latest exhibition of stone carving, some such fascinating occupation.'

'She's gone to the Henry Moores?' Fred felt reassured.

'If that's the fellow's name. At least, that's what she told me,' Dr Salter, said, not being reassuring at all.

So they drove on and into Skurfield, an entirely different sort of village from Rapstone Fanner. Although only three miles distant it has a different climate; it's higher, colder, and even when the sun shines on the brick and flint cottages of Rapstone there seems to be a continual dark cloud over its concrete out-buildings and pebble-dash walls. Skurfield is a great place for corrugated-iron sheds, greyish washing flapping in the wind and chickens roosting in the abandoned and rusting bodies of Austin Sevens through which nettles and willow herb are growing. The front gardens of Skurfield cottages are unweeded dumps which accommodate prams, bicycles, motor-bikes under constant repair and defunct paraffin stoves. Flowers are rare and seem to have seeded themselves by accident and in spite of their surroundings. The village exists shortly on either side of a fairly wide road which looks determined to go on to Worsfield as rapidly as possible.

At the end of the last century a simple-minded Nowt, who had hitherto spent most of his life sitting at his cottage's gate on an old kitchen chair paring his nails with a pocket-knife and muttering to himself, considered he was suddenly crossed in love, poured a gallon or two of lamp oil into the vestry cupboards of the old parish church and set fire to the building. What remained of the early English structure was restored by old Magnus Strove, ever a parsimonious landlord, with a strict eye to economy. The result was said by the then Sir Nicholas Fanner to look like a public urinal built for a community lost to God. The outside has yellowish bricks and a slate roof, the interior, echoing like an old fives court, is ornamented only with a stained-glass window in which Magnus Strove, wearing a frock-coat and surrounded by pallid cherubs, is to be seen receiving the freedom of the City of Worsfield, and a white marble plaque on which are written the names of the depressingly large number of local inhabitants who fell in two world wars. 'Sons of Skurfield', reads the inscription above it, 'Not lost but gone before'.

Such cheer as there was at that time in Skurfield was dispensed by Ned Gower, the usually surly landlord of the Badger. However, the Simcox Extra was as good there as it was at Rapstone and in the evening a particularly brutal game of bar billiards was played by the regulars for minimal stakes in the white glare of a hissing kerosene lamp. Licensing hours were elastic in Ned Gower's time and the Hartscombe police avoided the Badger with studied disdain. The village also boasted a small shop with a fly-blown window which displayed a sleeping tom cat, a few tins of corned beef, boxes of biscuits and yellowing knitting patterns. The shop had been run by an elderly couple who entered into a suicide pact and died in a state of desperate confusion because they were unable to cope with the system of sweet rationing during the war. There was, however, one small house in Skurfield which stood out like a gleaming porcelain crown in a mouth full of crumbling and nicotine-stained teeth. It guarded the entrance to the village from the Rapstone crossroads, a neat red and white box, striped like bacon and built by a local jobbing builder in the thirties. 'The Spruces' had a trim, low privet hedge, a tirelessly mown patch of front lawn and never, in any circumstances, displayed washing – articles of great privacy which Mrs Elsie Titmuss, Leslie's mother, dried on a clothes-horse in the kitchen. Net curtains kept all prying eyes away from the windows of 'The Spruces' and such precautions were wise because, with both male Titmusses employed in the accounts department at the Brewery, there was certainly property inside, a refrigerator, a handsome electric clock, a set of china ornaments kept in a glass-fronted cupboard, which would have excited the envy and possibly the greed of the Skurfield inhabitants. There was also a small garage, heavily padlocked, which contained the meticulously polished Titmuss runabout, a Ford Prefect, kept only for Sunday driving and 'days out' during the summer holidays.

Admiring the Skurfield landscape was all Fred had to do as he sat in the passenger seat of the Alvis outside Tom and Dora Nowt's cottage. Agnes's father had forbidden him to go in ('You'll only faint or something unhelpful'), but the punctuality he had predicted was fulfilled. There was a faint cry behind the sealed-up, curtained windows, and when the Doctor emerged, accompanied by a respectful grandmother wiping her hands on her apron, he opened the car door and said, 'All right. Let's go over to the Badger. I don't suppose you're any bloody good at darts.'

'Success?' Fred asked him.

'Who knows? The nipper may turn out to be an unmitigated disaster. Most people are.'

During the same lunchtime, in Hartscombe, the young Magnus Strove, by then a good-looking but still boyish twenty-two, whose curling hair and soft, candid eyes concealed the fact that he was as tough as old boots and had a strongly developed money sense, came out of the bank with a giggling cousin, a not-too-distant neighbour called Jennifer Battley, and five pound notes which he was tucking into his wallet. Magnus was constantly aware of what he called his 'cash-flow situation', which meant that he carried as little money as possible and relied on his Oxford friends and Hartscombe neighbours to pick up the bills for his drinks and dinners. Jennifer, who was very stuck on him, usually agreed to 'go Dutch' anyway, which meant that she paid, because at a vital moment at the end of dinner Magnus would slap his pockets in a fruitless search for his cheque book, which he kept always under lock and key in Picton House with all the counterfoils neatly filled in.

So Magnus and Jennifer, arm in arm, went off down the street and, for not much reason, Magnus stopped at the dusty window of a small local outfitter called Henry Pyecroft – 'Ladies and Gents Bespoke and Ready-made – Evening-Wear for Hire by the Occasion at Reasonable Prices – All Garments Impeccably Clean'. He pulled Jennifer to a stop and they looked in. What they saw was Leslie Titmuss being fitted for a hired dinner-suit. Mr Pyecroft, in his shirt-sleeves with a tape-measure round his neck, looked with irritation at the giggling young couple on the other side of the window. Leslie was too busy admiring the images of the fine, sombre suiting with glistening lapels and a wide trouser stripe in the long, tarnished mirror to notice, and in a moment, Magnus and Jennifer had gone laughing on their way.

'I'm sorry. About the car, I mean.'

'Well, if that's all the damage you've done.' Fred and the Doctor were sitting in the draughty interior of the Badger, demolishing Simcox bitter with bread and cheese and breathing in the smell of wet dog.

'Of course, I expect to pay.'

'With your father's money? It'd be a miracle.'

'If you could take instalments.'

'Getting a bit of ready cash out of a wealthy Socialist in a dog-collar would require the talents of Moses striking the rock in the desert,' Dr Salter said, ignoring his offer. 'Charity, according to your reverend father, begins in other people's homes.'

'I don't think that's very fair.'

'You want to argue with me?' The Doctor looked at Fred, his blue eyes cold and his face set.

'Not really.'

'Pity. It's becoming a damn dull lunch.' Dr Salter sounded disappointed. He stood up, collected a handful of darts and took aim. Saying, 'Middle for diddle,' without the hint of a smile, he threw a dart plumb into the centre of the board. 'Did Agnes tell you?' Fred stood up and collected some darts. He had no confidence in his ability to score against the Doctor.

'Tell me? Tell me what?' The Doctor pulled out his dart and then threw again.

'About the car.'

'Oh, about the car. Of course. She told me all about the car.' He removed his darts and chalked up his substantial score.

Fred started to play, unable to get a double or throw a dart into the centre of the board. 'Everyone seems to tell everyone everything.' He sounded resentful and younger than his years.

'Only secrets. The only things people tell are secrets. Foolish to have them. Your family are rather given to secrecy though.'

'My family?'

'Must be the religion that does it.' Agnes's father threw again, scored satisfactorily and scrawled his figures on the board, as illegibly as though they were on a prescription. 'Secret sort of business religion. All that whispering to God behind other people's backs. Damn funny though! Old Simeon leading the multitude into the promised land of peace and all that sort of nonsense and you playing truant in order to bust up my motor.'

'Do you think he's wrong?' Away from home Fred always felt protective about his father.

'I don't deal in right and wrong. I deal in collywobbles and housemaid's knee.'

'Do you think he was mistaken, though, to go on the march?' Fred threw and started his game modestly. Dr Salter stood watching him, his legs apart, as though sizing up some not particularly promising piece of horse-flesh. 'You can't change people. You know that. You can't make them stop hating each other, or longing to blow up the world, not by walking through the rain and singing to a small guitar. Most you can do for them is pull them out of the womb, thump them on the backside and let them get on with it. Isn't that enough?' He threw a dart and asked, 'You love my daughter, don't you. It's really not my business what else you get up to. It might be healthier, if you didn't fall in love.'

It was Fred's turn. His shot went hopelessly wide, struck a tankard on a shelf and knocked it to the ground with a clang which echoed in the empty bar.

'I knew it!' Dr Salter was laughing. 'I knew you'd turn out to be a bloody awful darts player!'

Before his game with Dr Salter Fred had felt his love-affair with Agnes to be a sort of protection, an insurance of privilege and pleasure which kept him apart from less fortunate beings. Now it became a mysterious complaint which brought the familiar ache of doom into the pit of his stomach. It also made him quite unable to think of anything but why she had gone to London. He looked in *The Times* and found that there was an exhibition of Henry Moore's sculpture. This comforted him for a while, until he realized that she couldn't be spending twenty-four hours a day gazing at faceless and reclining people. He rang her number two or three times but she wasn't back from London and her father answered him shortly, as though afraid Fred might start telling him the symptoms of his disease and expect a visit.

About a week later he was having a lonely lunchtime beer in the Baptist's Head in Rapstone and talking to Ted Lawless, the landlord and former Battle of Britain pilot, who kept his bar hung with photographs of Spitfires, parties in the mess and himself with his thumbs up as he climbed into the cockpit. Ted and his wife, Ivy, were starting to make 'improvements' in the saloon with checked tablecloths, knives and forks wrapped in paper napkins and chicken or scampi in the basket at lunchtime. Fred was listening, not for the first time, to Ted's account of a New Year's Eve party at R.A.F. Worsfield when he and Ivy, then a succulent W.A.A.F., had been having it away in the back of an old transport plane which suddenly took off on a night flight to Dundee. Then the saloon door opened and Agnes walked in wearing trousers and a military-looking mac.

'Where on earth have you been?' she said. 'I've been looking for you for days.'

Fred bought her a drink and thought he did so too eagerly. He couldn't imagine why he felt guilty, as though he were the one who had disappeared and left her no word. In a little while she said she wanted to go for a walk, a thing he'd never known her to do before, and he was afraid that she might want to use the occasion for a serious talk, to tell him that it had all been a mistake, an ill-considered moment which he must never expect to repeat. They walked across Rapstone Park in silence and he didn't know what to expect when Agnes took his arm and led him towards the folly, a place which, because of its rotting staircase and bramble-covered approach, was always sure to be deserted.

It was a stunted Gothic tower meant to give the casual visitor to Rapstone Park the deluded impression that he could see all the way to Worsfield Cathedral. Now Fred and Agnes heard the scuttle of birds nesting in the rafters and climbed unsteadily towards a patch of daylight, the open door on to the roof.

'You told your father!' She had said nothing about her visit to London and Fred needed to prove himself hard done by so he accused her.

'What did I tell him?'

'About us.'

'What is there to tell?'

'I should have thought, something.'

'Would you?'

'You told him about the car.'

'Oh, about that!' She seemed in no mood to take him seriously.

'Everyone seems to tell about everything,' Fred grumbled.

'I'm not accustomed to lie to my own father.' She had reached the top of the staircase and stepped out on to the roof of the tower. 'Why're we coming up here?'

'Because it's Rapstone folly.' Fred followed her out.

'I suppose so.' She was looking out over the parkland, the trees each surrounded with a protective palisade, the herd of deer dappled in the shadows and the drive curving up to the house. Fred went on asking questions, as though the last week were a constant itch he couldn't help scratching.

'How was Henry Moore?'

'Who?' With Agnes, it seemed, the name rang no bell.

'The sculptor,' he reminded her.

'So far as I know he's perfectly all right. What ridiculous questions you do ask.'

'And how's Aunt Molly?'

'Almost as well as Henry Moore, I suppose.' She was laughing at him now.

'What did you do in London?'

'Oh, London? Hung about, went round the coffee bars in Soho; that sort of thing.'

'Who did you stay with then?' He thought he was mad to ask her the question and hoped she wouldn't answer it.

'Oh, just some people.'

'*People?*'

'People I was at college with, that's all.'

'Where do they live, these people?'

'Well, aren't you quite extraordinarily nosy?' She was frowning now, no longer laughing.

'You told your father you were staying with your Aunt Molly. I thought you never told lies. To your father.'

'Well, honestly! No one could ever accuse you of not telling lies to *your* father.'

'When you were in London . . .' Fred started again patiently, but Agnes interrupted him, lifting up her arms and joining her hands behind his neck.

'When I was in London I wasn't here, was I? Now I'm here. Why don't we try and make the best of it?'

When she kissed him her eyes were closed. His were open and he looked past her, over the park to the driveway where he could see the minute figure of his father walking purposefully towards the house on some private errand or visit.

Chapter Eight

THE PASTORAL VISIT

The manservant Wyebrow opened the front door, gave a quick look to assure himself that the Rector was not on all fours, and crossed the hall to knock on the drawing-room door and so produced a sound which was lost in the mounting crescendo of screams which came from the other side of the door, an outcry which had been audible in the driveway and had sent the rooks clattering out of the trees on the other side of the kitchen garden.

When he went into the drawing-room Simeon found Grace was seated at a small, photograph-laden desk writing letters, apparently unconcerned. She lifted her head from the scrawled handwriting on mauve crested paper and nodded wearily towards the hearthrug where eighteen-year-old Charlie stood, her hair awry, her eyes closed, her face purple with indignation, her clenched fists beating against her tweed-covered thighs, kicking up this extraordinary hullabaloo. The effect might have been weirdly comic, like the sight of a fully grown comedian acting the part of a baby screaming in its pram, if the anger behind the outcry had not been so obvious. The Rector only glanced at the mother and approached the deafening girl. He took her arm and said, 'Now then, Charlie. Isn't it time I took you up?'

There was a moment's silence and then the girl, with another howl, tried to shake Simeon off, but the laying-on of hands had been accompanied by unexpected strength. She found herself gripped firmly by the Rector, who had apparently been sent for to perform a miraculous cure, or at least minister to her spiritual needs, and propelled to the door, through which she went still screaming. She was still doing so when Wyebrow came out of his pantry and, looking up from the well of the stairs, saw the ill-assorted couple disappear into Charlie's bedroom. Bridget Bigwell, sweeping the upstairs corridor, saw it too, paused, clicked her tongue in mild disapproval and then continued her work with renewed determination.

The bedroom door closed; the intervals between the screams increased in length. Then the cries died away, turned to low irregular sobs and finally to silence. Wyebrow returned to his pantry and continued with his letter to an old wartime friend, now an officer in the New York City police. 'Dear Chuck,' he wrote. 'Thrilled to bits to hear about your new leisure-wear and wish I could see you in it. I haven't bought anything exciting in the way of trousers lately owing to the shops in this part of rural England being distinctly below par.' Grace also sent her pen scurrying across the paper, writing to those distant members of her husband's family she suspected might be divorcing, or sick, or even dead, always avid for news to relieve the heavy monotony of life in Rapstone Park.

Charlie lay silent, fully dressed under the warmth of the eiderdown. Her sensible shoes had been removed and put side by side in front of the fireplace. Her face was red, her eyes swollen but she was silent now, gently sucking the knuckle of her first left-hand finger as the Rector turned to the bookshelf. From among her childhood favourites including *The Scarlet Pimpernel*, *Little Women* and *Five Go Adventuring* he selected one from which he started to read to soothe her anger. '"A propeller, set behind two exposed seats, revolved slowly."' Simeon used the voice he kept for the lessons. '"Beside it stood a tall, thin man in flying-kit; his leather flying-coat, which was filthy beyond description with oil stains, flapped open, exposing an equally dirty tunic, on the breast of which a device in the form of a small pair of wings could just be seen. Under them was a tiny strip of the violet-and-white ribbon of the Military Cross. 'You one of the fellows on the new course?' he asked shortly. 'Er – er – er yes, sir,' was the startled reply. 'Ever been in the air?' 'No, sir.' 'What's your name?' 'Bigglesworth, sir. I'm afraid it's a bit of a mouthful, but that isn't my fault. Most people call me Biggles for short.' A slow smile spread over the face of the instructor. 'Sensible idea,' he said.'''

'''All right, Biggles, get in.''' Charlie supplied the words, quite calm now.

'What did you say to her!' Simeon was angry by the time he got downstairs to Charlie's mother.

'Nothing very much. I mean, nothing to cause all that fuss. I think I was saying that at her age all my friends were thinking of parties and dances, being presented at Court. It was just the time when we were all being "brought out". "But with you, Charlie," I told her, "there's nothing at all to bring."'

'How did you *expect* her to react?' He spoke with some contempt.

'Oh, I don't know. When I was Charlie's age we didn't have a brass farthing. Daddy had pushed off and taken most of his miserable army pension with him. I used to fill my handbag with bits I scrounged from cocktail parties. That was my lunch.'

'How the poor live!'

'All the same I managed to not wear the same party frock too often.' Grace was looking in a succession of alabaster and mother-of-pearl boxes for a cigarette. 'I was typing letters for old Lady Naboth's dreadful charities and dancing until three o'clock most mornings. Can you see any of your precious trades union members working hours like that?'

'Their night-shift probably doesn't entail much dancing.'

'You're angry just because I tell Charlie what I think! Don't you want me to be honest with her?'

'It might be better to be kind, or at least take an interest in her?'

'Oh, you think everyone's interesting. That's because you're a

Red. I don't. I believe that quite a lot of people were just manufactured when God was thinking of something else.'

'Like the next cocktail party.' Simeon seemed to despair of the woman, and she also looked at him with genuine disapproval. 'Don't be blasphemous, Simeon,' she said piously. 'Please, do try not to be blasphemous!'

That afternoon Nicholas Fanner had also been out visiting. Percy Bigwell had been a skilled and expert woodman and an elegant dancer and so won the love of Bridget Bigwell, then only one of the Fanners' housemaids, when they were both in their teens. In middle age Percy still worked in the woods, felling trees and sawing them into lengths suitable to be taken into the furniture factories in Worsfield. A few months before, Tom Nowt, felling an old elm in a brutal and inexpert manner (all his skills were for shooting), caused the accident in which Percy's legs were broken. After this incident Tom Nowt was rightly blamed, shunned and became more isolated in the village and spent more time in his hut in the woods.

Nicholas, with his comfortable, well-meaning smile and his baggy clothes, wandered into the stuffy back room of Percy's cottage and urged the crippled man not to get up. He was sure that Percy would soon be out again, beating on the next shoot that Nicholas shared with Doughty Strove of Picton Principal. Percy told him that Dr Salter didn't hold out much hope for that and added, 'And Doctor says the worst of it is, I'll probably last like this another thirty years. I'll be a creaking gate, he reckons, and they goes swinging on forever.'

'Dr Salter never has been terribly keen on keeping his patients alive,' Nicholas admitted. 'He's a bit of a gloom merchant, quite honestly, Bigwell. No need for us to listen to all that doom and gloom now we've got rid of the Socialists.' He rose to go on his cheerful way. 'We'll be together again this autumn, you'll see. You putting up the birds with your old ash stick and me and Mr Strove bagging them high on the wing. You get well, old man. We can't do without you.' As he went Nicholas decided to send

Bridget home with a box of biscuits for Percy. He didn't know, because they had never told him, that the Bigwells didn't like Worsfield biscuits and had a cupboard full of Mrs Bigwell's employer's presents.

When he got home Nicholas found that the Rector had come to tea and that Charlie was upstairs resting. Grace told him that she had sent for Simeon because of another of the girl's ridiculous tantrums. 'It's the excitement, I expect,' Nicholas said, noticing that Simeon had polished off all the buttered toast. 'She's excited about the Young Conservatives dinner dance. Well, Charlie doesn't have many treats.'

'Take sex, for instance.'

'What do you want me to do with it?'

'Try to be serious for a moment. Take the sex life of our father.'

Dinner at the Sheridan club was over and Fred was hoping that the meeting with his brother, and another indignant and frustrating discussion of the Rector's will, would soon be over also. He thought of the last time he had seen his father, an old, dying man in pyjamas who smelled faintly of the inside of linen cupboards. Even after a couple of brandies he felt extremely reluctant to discuss sex and his father. 'It's something I'd rather not think about,' he said. 'We all come into existence as a result of a momentary embrace by our parents which we find impossible to imagine.'

'You talk exactly like he did.' Henry was impatient.

'We all assume we're the result of our own particular immaculate conception. You mean, I talk like our father?'

'No. I mean like Dr Salter. My dear Frederick, that ludicrous will can't have been an isolated incident of complete irresponsibility. Our barrister wants further examples of eccentric behaviour.'

'Is sex eccentric behaviour?'

'If you happen to be a vicar. I'll have to ask Mother.'

'I don't think you should do that.' Fred became serious.

'I'll have to.'

'I don't believe that those are the sort of questions our mother would care to answer.'

'I'll have to make systematic inquiries.'

'Why? Are you such an expert?' Fred resented his brother adopting the role of detective.

'On sex?'

'No.' Fred looked at his brother. 'On fidelity.'

Henry let the accusation go by, as though it were a sneaky and underhand ball thrown at him which it would be beneath his dignity to touch. He sipped his brandy and said, 'Another thought occurs to me.'

'Does it?'

'Of course you know our father was a Commie.' Henry said it as though he were stating the obvious. 'A raving Red, quite clearly. I mean, suppose he was spying for the Soviets and Leslie Titmuss got wind of it. Suppose it was a simple case of black-mail!'

'My God, Henry!' Fred laughed. 'You mean he was selling the secrets of the Parish Council to Russia? Brilliant! Good enough for one of your movie scripts.'

'Seriously. What do you think?'

'I think you've got to a dangerous age.' Fred stood up. His brother looked up at him inquiringly, no doubt thinking their conversation was again going to concern itself with sex. 'The age when you sit in the Sheridan club drinking too much brandy and dreaming about spies.'

On his way out Fred passed a telephone in a glass box by the front door. He lifted it and dialled a number. The voice which answered him sounded, as usual, as though it was trapped in a burning building with no possibility of escape.

'Agnes? It's Fred. Freddie Simcox. Well, could I come round and talk to you for a moment?' When she asked him what he wanted to talk about he said, 'Well, of all things, Leslie Titmuss.'

Fred found Agnes in her rent-controlled flat at the far end of the Fulham Road. She had turned herself, since her divorce from Henry, into a one-woman organization called the Flying Kitchen and cooked, alone or with occasional help from unemployed actresses, for dinner parties, directors' lunches and such-like functions, work which she carried out efficiently but without many smiles. As she spent so much of her time cooking she had knocked her kitchen and living-room together, the resulting space being a dark but workmanlike cavern with a lot of shelves, wooden surfaces, cookery books, yellowing recipes pinned to the walls, pots and pans well scoured, bunches of herbs hanging up to dry. Agnes was wearing trousers and canvas shoes, smoking industriously and with a litre bottle of red wine beside the old rocking-chair in which she had been sitting.

'You should have rung earlier. You could've had the remains of an oxtail I had left over from a ghastly dinner party I cooked in Highgate last night.' She shuddered at the memory and poured him a glass of wine. 'Rag trade!'

In the dim light the shape of her face seemed unaltered; for all her cooking she had remained thin. Her smile was, as always, one of rueful courage against enormous odds. Fred thought that what he had loved was her unhappiness, although it was a quality which made him feel uneasily inferior to her. He had thought she knew of great cosmic causes for discontent of which he, in his mundane way, was cheerfully unaware. This unhappiness, which she gave off like a rich and potent smell, had been, for the years, the decades he had known her, the secret of her sexual attraction.

'Are you doing a lot of cooking?' He knew it seemed a trivial question in the face of so much heroically borne grief.

'Henry doesn't like me doing it. He's dead scared of showing up at some film mogul's house with La Lonnie and finding me slaving away in the kitchen.'

'Look. About Leslie . . .' Fred started when they were sitting beside her small but genuine and smouldering fireplace.

'Leslie Titmuss!' Agnes refilled her glass and, because she was used to living alone, forgot his. 'He's a cabinet minister and his mother was a cook. My father was a doctor and I'm a cook. Perhaps I passed him on the way down, or did he pass me on the way up?'

'About the will.' Fred felt it necessary to explain his visit.

'I never knew your father had such a sense of humour.'

'Well, about the will. I want you to stop Henry.'

'What?'

'Stop him blundering about, trying to unearth secrets, attacking everyone. He's coming out with the most ridiculous ideas about my father.'

'What makes you think I've got the slightest influence on him?'

There was a silence. He wondered how he was going to control his rogue brother. 'Has Lonnie any influence?' he asked.

'Of course not. He married her for her remarkable talent for agreeing with absolutely everything he says.'

'Francesca? Would he take any notice of your daughter?'

'Strangely enough, I think he's afraid of Francesca. She's young, you see. Young people alarm him now.'

'You see her?'

'Sometimes.' She smiled and this made her look unhappier than usual. 'She was coming tonight, actually. I was going to cook her supper.'

'What happened?'

'She chucked me.'

Fred got up, refilled his glass and wandered round the room. He smelled herbs and spices and started to read about how to make a simple, classic *blanquette de veau*. It was like a tone-deaf person reading a musical score. 'Are you comfortable here?'

'Quite.'

'Not lonely?'

'No. Are you?'

'No.' Fred put away the recipe book he'd taken from the shelf. 'Sometimes I wonder why not.'

'You've got all those ill people to keep you company.' She said it seriously, not as a joke, as her father would have said it. Then she asked, 'What are you going to do now?' and gave him no hint as to whether it was a general inquiry about his remaining years or an invitation to stay the night.

'I suppose . . .' Fred found the question difficult. She gave him no help. 'I suppose I shall drive back to Hartscombe.'

'Well. That's that then.' She stood up and threw her cigarette end at the fireplace in a business-like sort of way.

'Yes.' He moved to the door. 'Thanks for the wine.'

'Any time.' But before he went she said thoughtfully, 'Leslie Titmuss! I wonder what on earth your father really liked about him.'

Chapter Nine

A FORMAL OCCASION

Elsie Titmuss was a maid at Picton House, in the employment of Doughty Strove, when George Titmuss, already a clerk in the Brewery, met her at a Skurfield church-outing and they entered into a prolonged engagement and a ferocious programme of saving money. This culminated in marriage and the birth of their only child, the young hopeful, Leslie. Elsie was a surprisingly beautiful young woman with a calm and untroubled expression which survived her long and demanding life as a wife and mother in the Titmuss household. On the evening of the Young Conservatives dinner dance she was fussing round her son with obvious pride, dabbing at him with a clothes-brush and arranging a white handkerchief in his top pocket, as he stood in his hired dinner-jacket in front of the mirror over their sitting-room mantelpiece, his hair neatly combed and slicked down with brilliantine, his face industriously shaved and lightly dusted with his mother's talc.

'You use the handkerchief for display purposes only, Leslie,' his mother instructed him. 'Don't go and blow your nose on it, will you?'

'Mother. I do know.'

'Stop finicking with the boy, Elsie.' George Titmuss sat under a relentless overhead light at the dinner table, his jacket hung on the back of his chair, and he wore sleeve-grips to keep his cuffs high and his bony wrists free. The green velvet cloth was spread with files and papers. He was working late on the Simcox Brewery accounts.

'Or you can have it in your sleeve.' Elsie took the handkerchief from her son's top pocket. 'When I was in service a lot of the gentlemen carried the white dinnertime handkerchief in the cuff.'

'I'll have it in the display pocket.' Leslie, who was always firm with his mother, returned the handkerchief to its previous position.

'I don't know why the boy has to be sent out looking like a tailor's dummy,' George grumbled as he added up a column of figures.

'When I was in service with Mr Doughty Strove at Picton House. Pre-war, when I was in service . . .'

'Yes, Elsie,' George said. 'I think we've all had our fill of when you were in service.' Neither of the men in her life wished to hear about Elsie's past in the Stroves' kitchen.

'It was dress for dinner every night,' Elsie continued happily. 'Except Sundays. Sundays it was casual dress and cold cuts, naturally, with beetroot and a lettuce salad. But any other day of the week it was one gong for dressing and then half an hour later the second gong for dinner.'

'Yes, Elsie. We do know all about it.'

'Can I borrow the Prefect?' Leslie asked his father over his mother's head.

'Oh, go on, George. All the other Young Conservatives'll be there with their own transport.' As always Mrs Titmuss supported her son.

'I suppose it'll stop people talking.' Mr Titmuss gave the matter the careful consideration he bestowed on the agenda at the Parish Council. 'At least you won't be hanging round the bus stop dressed like a waiter.'

'He looks handsome.' Elsie stood back in admiration. 'Doesn't our Leslie look handsome, George?'

'I'd rather see him looking handsome at eight-thirty in the

morning when we've got our annual audit at the Brewery,' George grumbled.

Elsie, giving the collar of her son's jacket a final brush, noticed his ready-made bow-tie clipped on to the front of his starched white collar. With the knowledge she had gained in service she was shocked. 'Oh, Leslie. They didn't give you one of them!'

'One of what?'

'Ready made! They ought to have given you a tie-your-own. They always wore tie-your-owns when I was in service.'

'It doesn't matter.' Not for the first time Leslie found his mother irritating. 'No one's going to know, are they?'

'I suppose not.' Elsie was doubtful.

'I bet it cost enough, whatever sort of tie it is.' George was still muttering over his columns of figures.

'Well, you didn't have to pay. I said, you didn't have to pay, did you, George?' Elsie asked as she gave the spotless dinner-jacket its last brush.

'You're always spending out your money on the boy.'

'Well, you ought to be grateful. I put by enough for all his little bits and pieces. You ought to be grateful for what I put by.'

A twisted gilt and china clock on the mantelpiece struck metal-lically. Leslie escaped from his mother's clothes-brush. 'I'm going to be late. It's seven for seven-thirty.' He went to the present from Cleethorpes and found the car key under it. As he went out into the hall his mother called after him, 'Goodbye, Leslie. It looks so well on you.' But he was gone in silence and his parents heard the front door slam. Elsie looked at her husband and smiled happily. 'Don't you feel proud of him, George, seeing him go off like that?'

Mr Titmuss looked up from his figures. They were clear signs of a steady increase in the consumption of beer, but he wasn't smiling. 'Why should I feel proud?' he asked.

Fred was also on his way to the dinner dance, as part of the band. It was almost a year since he went to a Chris Barber concert in Worsfield and met Joe Sneeping, who worked at the off-licence in Hartscombe market place and devoted his spare time to the trumpet and the work of the New Orleans musicians recorded in Chicago during the prohibition era. Fred also knew Terry Fawcett, who worked at Marmaduke's garage and had played the clarinet since his schooldays, and through Joe he met Den Kitson from the Brewery, who could double on banjo and guitar and even play the bass when one was available. Together they formed the Riverside Stompers and they'd played in pubs up and down the river. They owed their present gig to Fred, who had cashed in on his old acquaintance with Magnus Strove. At least, he had said, they'd be cheaper than the Swinging Romeos from Worsfield. Joe had agreed to sully the purity of the group with dance-hall numbers, Terry had got hold of a saxophone to double on and they had rehearsed 'Always' and fallen about laughing.

The Swan's Nest at Hartscombe is a pleasant, low, brick and weather-boarded building by the river. Its untended garden stretches down to the water, where a few punts and rowing-boats are moored for the pleasure of visitors, and swans glide in a ghostly fashion over the dark water. In the twenties and thirties the name of the Swan's Nest was synonymous with adultery and illicit weekends. It figured in society divorce-cases and it achieved that somewhat raffish reputation which it cannot quite shake off, although the Guards officers and debutantes, the dubious foreign Counts and undependable married ladies no longer trail their fingers in the water from its punts or order champagne in its bedrooms. At the end of the 1950s it was a respectable, rather down-at-heel hotel living, like Grace Fanner, on memories of more eventful days. In the course of time it would be taken over by a motel chain, re-christened Ye Olde Swan's Nest and given piped music, colour T.V.s in every bedroom, Teasmades instead of discreet rustic chambermaids in black bombazine, an enlarged car park and the Old Father Thames Carvery.

When Leslie Titmuss went there for his first formal occasion he caught the hotel between its notorious past and its bleak future. Up to the end of dinner the occasion was uneventful. Prawn cocktail, chicken, ice-cream and pineapple slices had been served. The carafe wine had been supplemented by those Young Conservatives prepared to pay for their own drinks, and the buzz of their voices had risen to a pitch of excitement which had more to do with extra bottles of champagne and brandy than the immediate prospect of a few words from Sir Nicholas Fanner in his role as Chairman of the Hartscombe and District Conservative Association.

At the top table the Chairman beamed about him with his usual amiability. He was sitting next to Doughty Strove, then the Hartscombe M.P., who was known as a dependable Party member and had greatly assisted the proceedings in Parliament by rarely opening his mouth. So far as his political opinions went he was known to be in favour of capital punishment, corporal punishment and large subsidies for those landlords who were doing their best to grow sunflower seed in bulk. He was also greatly in favour of severing diplomatic ties with France, a country which he regarded with particular horror and suspicion. At Doughty's right hand sat Grace, who made no secret of the fact that she thought him both unattractive and dull; indeed she was flirting outrageously with the Young Conservative President on her left, a serious-minded junior stockbroker, who was finding the fluttering of Grace's middle-aged eyelashes unnerving, her jewelled hand on his sleeve alarming and her low, gravelly purr inaudible. Charlie was sitting on the other side of her father and was wearing a green dress made of some shiny material which did nothing for her. She was frowning and the fact that she did not scream or burst into tears was of little help to the nervous Young Conservative beside her who had vainly tried to arouse her interest in cricket and the idea of a European Free Trade Association. In time he gave up and concentrated on the toothy girl to his right.

The President beat on the tablecloth with a spoon. Nicholas rose slowly to his feet and began a low-key, somewhat inaudible address which was more like random jottings from the diary of a Conservative gentleman of the old school than a speech.

'I look around this room at you,' he began, 'and I see young, some very young, *Conservatives*. You know, there was a time when to be young meant that you were sure to have one of those sort of red tweed ties. Do you remember what I mean?' The question was clearly rhetorical, and no one answered it. 'If you were young you wore a corduroy jacket and you were,' his voice was shrill in comic and pretended fear – '*a Red! a revolutionary!*'

Around him the Young Conservatives, most of whom belonged to the organization for the same reason that they joined the Hartscombe Amateur Operatic Society, to meet each other and fall in love, smiled faintly. There were a few more serious faces. Leslie Titmuss looked pale and intent, concentrating fiercely on Nicholas's ramblings as though the way to the future might be revealed in them. He was sitting, by some quirk of the placement, next to Jennifer Battley, who was not delighted to have him as a dinner companion. At a table opposite them young Magnus Strove was sitting with a party of pink-faced young men and braying girls, the junior members of the Hartscombe Hunt who had brought their own drinks and cigars. Prominent among the group was one who looked plumper and even more prosperous than the rest. His name was Christopher Kempenflatt, heir to the Kempenflatt family building firm, a young man whose eyes always seemed to be popping with carefully simulated surprise and whose moist lips were now open to admit a large Monte Cristo cigar. He was responsible for the fact that the group around him were mopping up more old brandy than the rest of the Young Conservatives and getting more rapidly out of control.

'Looking round this fine old room' – Nicholas looked around it – 'and after a dinner well up to the Swan's Nest's high standards . . .'

'Kitty Kat and soggy potatoes!' Kempenflatt had unplugged his cigar, and was greeted by a salvo of giggles from the girls around him.

'It wasn't so bad,' Magnus Strove told them. 'I actually found a prawn in my cocktail.'

'Probably got in there to die,' was Kempenflatt's opinion.

'Looking around me,' Nicholas went on, 'I see that to be young is to be Conservative. To be on . . . on the "other side" is, if I may say so, distinctly "old hat".'

'Well, he should know about old hats,' Kempenflatt told the girls.

'You mean that amazing tweed thing he wears with the flies in it?' Magnus increased their helpless laughter.

'There was a moment of aberration' – Nicholas seemed not the least disconcerted by the hunt members – 'some of you may be old enough to remember, when Hartscombe itself went Socialist. That was as unfortunate as the time when Oliver Cromwell's levelling soldiery occupied Rapstone Manor!'

'Some of us may be old enough to remember that!' Kempenflatt raised his glass to the Chairman.

'But now England has come to its senses.' Nicholas beamed at them all in a mildly congratulatory manner.

'Charles the Second's back!' Magnus announced.

'Boffing the girls.' Christopher Kempenflatt filled in the details. Leslie Titmuss looked angrily at the claque opposite him and led a scattered volley of clapping.

'And my old friend Doughty Strove is back where he should be' – Nicholas continued with the good news – 'in the House of Commons. Thanks to your tireless canvassing.'

'Hear! Hear! Give your dad a hand, Magnus.' Kempenflatt was puffing out smoke and clapping with his cigar in his mouth.

'Good old Dad! The silent member for Hartscombe.' Magnus was not applauding. 'I don't know why they don't replace him with a cardboard cut-out.'

'But you've heard enough from me,' Nicholas said and got,

from the Kempenflatt table, the warmest applause of the evening. 'Unlike the doom merchants of the Socialist Party we can enjoy ourselves. There will be dancing too . . . Who will there be dancing to?' He stooped to hear the Secretary whisper to him, 'Joe Sneeping and his Riverside Orpheans.' The Secretary whispered again, Nicholas again bowed his head and came up smiling. 'Oh, Riverside Stompers,' he said. 'I stand corrected. And the bar will remain open until midnight.' The Secretary whispered again. 'I understand it's a question of "buy your own" from now on. "Let joy be unconfined; No sleep till morn, when Youth and Pleasure meet".'

'I do wish Nicholas wouldn't do that,' Grace said to the Young Conservative President. 'He does make such a fool of himself when he quotes poetry.' Nicholas sank back into his seat to the apparent relief of everyone including himself. The Stompers began to play the music that the Young Conservatives liked to dance to, selections from *South Pacific*. They were parodying 'Bali Hi, They Call It', grinning at each other over their instruments and raising their eyebrows in despair at each syrupy swoop of the music. Then they did their own jazzed-up version of 'I'm Going to Wash That Man Right Out of My Hair' and felt more at ease. Den Kitson, wearing a tartan dinner-jacket he had borrowed for the occasion, slapped the bass and wondered what the chances were of picking up a bit of Conservative crumpet. Joe and Terry both wore dark suits with black bow-ties and Fred the dinner-jacket he had spent out on in his first term at Cambridge. None of the guests seemed to look at the band, and neither Leslie nor Charlie had shown him a flicker of recognition. Nicholas and Grace were both unaware of his presence. He began to enjoy being overlooked, a pleasure which would grow on him in the years to come.

'You know Doughty Strove, of course?' Leslie Titmuss broke a long silence to ask his neighbour, Jennifer Battley, this unenlivening question. He looked with a certain awe to where the square-faced member for Hartscombe, deserted by his neighbours in favour of the dance floor, sat nodding out of time with the music.

'Oh, yes. He's my uncle.'

'I say. Is he really?'

'His son Magnus is over there. He's my cousin, actually. Do you know Magnus?'

Leslie looked to where Magnus Strove and Christopher Kempenflatt, surrounded by girls, were enjoying a joke.

'Well, *I* don't really know him,' Leslie admitted. 'Of course, my people know the family.'

'Your people?'

'My mother.'

'Oh, really?' Jennifer was laughing at the sympathetic yawns Magnus was performing for her at the table opposite. Leslie, who hadn't seen Magnus's mime, asked her, 'Do you know who puts up the nominations for the Y.C. Committee? Does Mr Doughty Strove have a voice in these decisions, in your view, Miss Battley? Just the General Committee, you understand. I'm not looking as far as the F. and G.P yet. It's early days, of course, that's understood. Or would Sir Nicholas, the Chairman, be the fellow to contact?'

At which point a crusty bread roll, thrown by Magnus, whizzed past Leslie Titmuss's right ear.

'He's such a fool!'

'Sir Nicholas?' Leslie was puzzled.

'No, Magnus, you idiot! He's my boyfriend, you know. Such a cretin! I say, are you going to eat that roll?' Jennifer seized it without waiting for his answer and, with a strong throw learned on the cricket field at Benenden, hit Christopher Kempenflatt on the forehead.

'Of course,' Leslie said, paying no attention to the fusillade but looking at the guests on the top table, 'that's Sir Nicholas's daughter, Charlotte. You know her? I must say she looks awfully left out.'

'Oh, bull's eye!' Jennifer couldn't help clapping as another bread roll, hurled by Magnus, got Leslie on the cheek. He stood up quickly, looking very pale. 'I say.' Jennifer tried to stop laughing. 'You're not miffed, are you?'

'No. Not at all. Of course not. It's terrifically good fun. Would you mind excusing me a moment?'

'Of course not. Take all the time you want,' Jennifer told him and Leslie was still smiling as he set off towards the top table, and continued to do so when another roll struck him on the back.

Charlie was sitting alone. Her neighbour had gone to dance with the girl on his other side. Nicholas and Doughty Strove had joined a group at the bar, and Grace had suggested a dance to the President of the Young Conservatives, an offer which he had not felt able to refuse. So Charlie was bored to despair, sitting alone and talking to no one. She kept her head down and stared at the pattern she was making with fork lines on the white tablecloth, wanting at all costs to avoid catching a glimpse of her mother steering an apprehensive young man round the floor with relentless charm. She didn't raise her head when Leslie glided up to her and spoke. 'Frightfully jolly party, isn't it?'

'You think so?'

'Rather! You wouldn't care to dance, would you?'

'No, I wouldn't care to.'

'Then shall we?'

She looked up at him and saw a look of extraordinary determination. Astonished and a little alarmed by his pale intensity she put down her fork and stood up, her arms held out in what looked like an attitude of self-defence rather than an embrace. He put a hand on her waist and manoeuvred her towards the floor where they moved awkwardly, self-consciously and without great skill or enthusiasm. Fred tried to embark on an ambitious drum roll, met a warning look from Joe Sneeping and returned obediently to the straightforward rendering of 'Some Enchanted Evening'.

'Good fun, these do's, aren't they?' Although he found that it required great concentration to talk and dance at the same time, Leslie felt that Charlie looked so ill at ease that he was bound to divert her. His hand at her waist felt very warm, as though he were touching a radiator. When she didn't answer he repeated, 'I said these do's are pretty good fun.' And added, 'Of course, there's a serious point behind them. I mean, I don't suppose I'd be here at all if I didn't want to get on in the Party.' He danced on in silence, waiting for a comment that never came. Christopher Kempenflatt hove up behind them, shunting a tall girl backwards. Magnus was in front, dancing with Jennifer.

'I say, Titmuss. I say, old boy,' Kempenflatt shouted as he approached. 'Who's your tailor?'

'Like your tie, old fellow.' Magnus steered alongside. 'Bet it took simply hours to get such a perfect butterfly.'

Leslie looked at them, puzzled. Holding the solid, embarrassed Charlie he came to a slow halt as Magnus's hand snatched the clip-on tie from his collar. He gazed after it and saw it settle, a black bow in Jennifer's hair.

'You old cheater!' Magnus's voice was high-pitched, accusing. Leslie seemed to be surrounded by young men, healthy-faced, loud-voiced, and Charlie had abandoned him as the music stopped.

'Where did you get that suit, Titmuss?' Kempenflatt asked, and Magnus was pulling open Leslie's jacket, searching for the label. 'Savile Row, is it? Huntsmans?'

'Better than that,' Magnus announced. 'Please see this garment is returned to Henry Pyecroft, Gents Outfitter, River Street, Hartscombe.'

'Lovely bit of schmutter, isn't it?' Kempenflatt said in a stage-Jewish accent, feeling the cloth between his finger and thumb, and Magnus went on reading the label to announce, '"All clothing impeccably clean". Ugh!'

'Look here. I know it's just a bit of fun but . . .' Leslie smiled round at the strange faces, anxious to enjoy the joke. As he did so he felt a jerk behind him and Kempenflatt was pulling off the jacket. Magnus was saying persuasively, 'Take it off, Titmuss.

You don't know where it's been.' Leslie began to panic, wondering where this unsolicited undressing was going to end.

'"Impeccably clean"! Strong smell of mothballs.' When it was off, Kempenflatt sniffed the jacket and chucked it to Magnus, who said, 'As last worn at the Municipal Sewerage Workers Ball,' and did a quick pass to Jennifer, who held it uncertainly in front of her in a dark bundle.

As they stared at him Leslie said, 'Can I have it back, please?' After that the silence seemed endless and then Fred, who had been watching with interest from behind his drum set, started to whistle and tap out the rhythm of 'Always'. The other Stompers joined in. Jennifer looked at Magnus and then handed the jacket back to Leslie. He thanked her and turned away towards the glass doors that opened on to the hotel garden, walking as quickly as he could, but he still heard Kempenflatt boom, 'I say, Magnus. Do you actually *know* that fellow?' And the answer, 'Of course I know him. His mother was our skivvy.'

When they had begun to gather round her partner and attack his clothing, Charlie had gone out into the garden. It was still early in the summer and the night wind soothed her burningly embarrassed skin. She crossed the grass and stood on the old landing-stage, looking down at the moored punts which had been put out during the Easter holidays. The water rattled the boats at their moorings, dangerous-looking swans glided by about their business and she heard Leslie say, 'It was all good fun.' He was still smiling, wearing his jacket now, but not his tie.

'Was it?' She couldn't accept his description of an evening which had come so close to making her scream.

'They're all right really,' he told her. 'Just excited.'

'My mother wouldn't have let them behave like that.'

'No.'

'My mother would've given them one look and they'd all have knelt down and kissed her hand.' She spoke with contempt. 'Like slaves! They all fell in love with her at dances. They'd have obeyed her breathlessly.'

'I expect she was very beautiful.'

'That's what she keeps telling me. You've lost your tie.' She seemed to notice it for the first time.

'Yes.'

'My mother hates me, because I'm not beautiful. I don't suppose she cares very much for you either.'

'But your father?' Leslie, who wasn't in the least interested in Grace, asked anxiously.

'My father's sorry for me. You know what he's president of, apart from the Conservatives? The All England Begonia Society. And you know why he chose begonias?'

'No. I don't know.'

'He says they're such ugly little flowers. He feels sorry for them.'

'Sorry for begonias?' Leslie Titmuss was out of his depth.

'Such ugly and vulgar little things! He says somebody has to look after them.'

There was a silence, and then Leslie tried to cheer his partner up. 'I think you look jolly nice in that dress.' It wasn't a remark calculated to give offence, but Charlie was offended.

'Isn't it horrible? Please. Tell me it's horrible. *She* made me wear it.'

Further down the landing-stage Leslie saw Young Conservatives and their girlfriends climbing into punts, shouting, laughing, pushing away from the bank.

'Look. Would you like to have a go on the river? It might be a bit of fun.'

Charlie didn't say anything, but after the boat containing Leslie's tormentors had got clear, and the splashing and laughter had died away in the darkness, she allowed him to help her into a punt. He stood up stiffly and remembered the lessons in poling the Simcox boys had given him once, long ago, when they all went on the river. He was cautious at first but soon gained confidence and threw up the pole between his hands and steered them away from the willows which overhung the bank. Charlie sat on a cushionless seat, trailing a hand in the welcome chill of the water, wondering what she thought she was doing, but glad to be away from the dance floor and to hear the music of the Stompers fade as they drifted away from the hotel. She would have been quite calm if Leslie hadn't felt the need to pay her compliments.

'You've got nice hair, too. That was the first thing I noticed about you this evening. The niceness of your hair.'

'Don't say that!' She thought his voice had sounded extraordinarily loud, echoing across the water and alarming the swans.

'I never noticed your hair. Not when we were kids.'

'Please. Don't say things like that to me.'

Then they heard the shouting and the laughter again. The punt paddled by Christopher Kempenflatt and a crew of girls had turned and was being driven fast towards them. Magnus Strove was standing in the prow holding the huge pole like a lance at a medieval tilt-yard. He gave a wild cry of triumph as his weapon struck Leslie Titmuss in the chest and sent him and his dinner-jacket, with his arms and legs waving helplessly, into the dark, brackish water of the Thames.

George Titmuss worked on his accounts and Elsie sat up knitting, determined not to go to bed until Leslie was safely home. They had the wireless on, playing late-night dance music, and she thought of her son, so immaculate and debonair, floating round the dance floor with a girl in a white dress who was smiling up at him. Then she heard the car arrive and the garage door shut. She went into the hall to meet him.

She heard his step on the gravel and opened the front door. He was still soaking wet, the starch gone out of his shirt and his brilliantined hair standing up in spikes because he had tried to rub it dry with his handkerchief. He stepped into the hallway, leaving a small puddle on the linoleum, and came very near to his mother to whisper, 'Bastards!'

Chapter Ten

THE TEMPTATION OF HENRY SIMCOX

After her visit to London Fred never felt entirely secure with Agnes, but that was nothing compared with the rising panic he felt at the thought of being without her. He had left Cambridge with no clear idea of what he wanted to do: except that he was certain that he wouldn't be a parson. Agnes was finishing her course at Worsfield University and spent her weeks in a hall of residence and her weekends at home. Fred found that he thought about her always and when they weren't together he was spending more and more time with her father.

His habit of joining Dr Salter on his rounds, which had started with the birth of Dora Nowt's fifth, grew as Fred tried to fill his uneventful days, waiting to see Agnes at weekends or on occasional evenings. He took to going into the cottages the Doctor visited and learned to change a dressing or turn an old woman in bed. Dr Salter's methods were a continual source of amazement to him. He could quieten a child with a broken arm or a woman with a crushed finger by producing what he called 'a special pain-killing pill flown in to me from America' which he kept in a small paper in his waistcoat pocket. When Fred asked him what it was he said, 'It's a rare drug known as an Extra-Strong Mint.'

'You're an old fraud,' Fred told him.

'Of course, I'm just like your father. It's faith, that's what we're both after.'

Dr Salter told Fred that when he was a young man he also had joined an old doctor on his rounds. 'Alfie Dawlish. Invented all sorts of imaginary ailments for the family at the Manor so he could rob them and treat the village for nothing. It was his primitive version of the Health Service. Finally old Lady Fanner, Nicholas's mother, sacked him for giving her an uncalled-for enema and charging ten quid. She didn't mind the money but she couldn't look Alfie in the face again. After that infant mortality in Skurfield rose considerably. I was a bit like you in those days. You know what Alfie Dawlish called me? The Sorcerer's Apprentice.'

Simeon, although far too liberal to do anything about it, didn't approve of the hours that Fred spent with Dr Salter and this disapproval did nothing but increase his son's respect for the medical profession. After all, he argued with relief, doctors weren't concerned with the reform of the world, or spiritual values, or protests about some faraway injustice it was impossible to remedy. A doctor's concern was entirely practical and had nothing whatever to do with the patient's soul. When Fred asked Agnes's father if that was why he had wanted to become a doctor he got a short answer. 'Balls! I had no choice. I couldn't pass the bloody exams to be a vet.'

But Fred had chosen his profession. When he told Agnes she looked at him quite nervously and said, 'Not because of me! Don't do it because of me, I couldn't take the responsibility.' He told her that of course it wasn't because of her, but he wasn't altogether telling the truth. The house in which Agnes was the only woman, the fact that she had become, apparently so easily, his lover, and her father who laughed at ideals, wished to die on the hunting-field, approved of backing into church gates and showed so little concern for his patients except when he was treating them, these things acted as an irresistible magnet to a young man brought up in the rarefied atmosphere of Rapstone Rectory.

Fred had done classics at school. He needed A-levels in science before he started his medical studies, so he lived at home, drew five pounds a week from his father and set to work on chromosomes and enzymes and the biology of the newt. Agnes got her degree but she showed no signs of leaving Hartscombe. She said she thought her father needed looking after, she didn't want to go anywhere else much, particularly not to France. Doing modern languages at Worsfield had apparently spoiled her for France. So she stayed at home, a state of affairs which suited Fred perfectly. In his happier, more optimistic moments he thought she would stay until she became the new local doctor's wife and then they would both live there forever. Dr Salter said, 'Someday someone's going to have to come and take her off my hands.'

'You used to tell me not to fall in love with her.'

'It was excellent advice. She was a child who grew up too quickly. It gave her a great deal of character. No one but a fool wants a wife with a great deal of character. I suppose you disagree?'

Fred said yes, he supposed he did.

England entered into the 1960s.

In the great world of politics sixty-nine Africans were shot at Sharpeville and Simeon Simcox wrote far more than sixty-nine letters. *Lady Chatterley's Lover* was adjudged suitable reading for the English people, an event which had no noticeable effect on the love-affair of Fred and Agnes Salter. In the Hartscombe Conservative Association there was a general feeling that Mr Macmillan was in his heaven and all was more or less right with the world. Attendance at the Y.C. evenings began to fall off in this somewhat complacent atmosphere, but Leslie Titmuss never missed a meeting. Christopher Kempenflatt, who became the Secretary, was often in London 'getting to know the ropes' of his father's firm. Leslie Titmuss offered to lend a hand by taking the minutes, which he did industriously and in great detail. When Kempenflatt became totally immersed in his father's business Leslie let it be known that he was prepared to take on the office of Secretary and, one afternoon when the Committee were anxious to get home early, he was nodded through. He was always pleasant, usually quiet and the President of the Young Conservatives began to depend on him to draw up the agenda.

The first year of the decade was also a historic one in the life of Henry Simcox. It was when he first came into contact with that brave new world where he would make his money, achieve success and finally enjoy the pleasure of disillusion. Almost two years after the publication of *The Greasy Pole* he received a letter on heavily embossed writing-paper from Atalanta Film Productions to inform him that Mr Benjamin K. Bugloss, Executive President in Charge of Artistic Enterprises, would be fulfilling a cherished ambition if he were able to meet with Mr Henry Simcox for a working breakfast in the Dorchester Hotel and would 8 for 8.30 a.m. be convenient?

Henry judged it right to present himself at the suite at 8.15 and it was some considerable time before his ring was answered. Finally the door was opened a chink and a gravelly voice said, 'Just leave it outside there, will you?'

'I'm Henry Simcox.'

'You're not room service?' The voice sounded suspicious.

'No. I'm Henry Simcox. I wrote *The Greasy Pole*. You asked me to breakfast.'

'Mr Simcox! This is a very great honour. Come in, why don't you? We were expecting room service.' The door was thrown open to reveal a large, suntanned man of indeterminate age who wore nothing except a white towelling dressing-gown on the breast of which was embroidered the simple inscription 'Hotel George V', and a pair of Gucci slippers. Looking round the suite Henry saw magazines, copies of *Variety* and a number of novels, so new that they appeared unread, including *The Greasy Pole*, which he picked up and admired, not for the first time, the photograph of the young, smiling author Henry Simcox. 'You really like it?'

'I don't like it.' Henry put his book down, disappointed. 'My dear, I love it! Tell me quite frankly. You must have become a lover at a very tender age. At what precise moment was it you first became a lover?' Mr Bugloss wandered to a bureau and discovered a cigar box. 'Don't worry, my dear. Tell me later. Do you care for a cigar?' He opened the box and discovered that it only contained one, which he took out and lit thoughtfully. 'That guy who works in a flower shop. Isn't that a hilarious conception?'

'It's a brewery.'

'What?' Mr Bugloss puffed on his cigar and frowned.

'He works in a brewery.'

'Are you sure?'

'Well, *I* wrote it!' Henry felt he had to remind him.

'So you did, my dear. And if I had my way you'd have sole writing credit. Of course, I have a partner.' Mr Bugloss went to the window and stood looking out over Park Lane. After a considerable silence he spoke, slowly and impressively. 'In our business,' he said, 'our names are written, Mr Simcox, on the sands of time. But there is one project, just one perhaps, by which someone hopes to be remembered. My dream is that your *Greasy Pole* should become a major motion picture.'

'That's marvellous.' Henry welcomed the news.

'I can give you certain things, Mr Simcox. I will fly you to the Coast. I can put a limo at your disposal. There will be a reception given in your honour. Subject to the views of my partner, my thought is that you should participate in profits. I should like to see you with a percentage, Mr Simcox.'

'Well, yes. I mean, so would I.'

'A percentage, after the deduction of my reasonable living expenses. Plus a small contribution to the cost of my boat, used for entertaining and general promotion. What's the title of your property again?' Mr Bugloss slumped into an armchair and sat smoking, thoughtful and anxious.

'*The Greasy Pole*,' Henry explained brightly, trying to cheer Mr Bugloss up. 'It's a game they used to have at regattas. A pole's covered with grease and you have to try and climb it but of course you can't. You keep sliding and falling into the river.'

'In the States they don't.'

'Don't what?'

'Have such things as regattas.' Mr Bugloss was positive. 'And a title like that might give serious offence to an ethnic minority. I have a great idea.' He got up, apparently cheerful. 'And I will present it to you as a gift with no strings attached. How do you like our title, *Indiscretions?*'

'I'm not sure.'

'And another thing, my dear' – Mr Bugloss ignored his doubts – 'how does your storyline end? Remind me.'

'Well, he could marry the girl, of course, and live in the big house.'

'The big house! I like it. Cute girl too, as I remember.'

'But he decides to stay in his job at the Brewery. Well, I suppose in a way he feels he has to be true to his class.'

'Then he's a schmuck!'

'You don't like the ending?'

Mr Bugloss went to the sofa and sat by his author, putting his arm round him. Henry tried not to look at the expanse of hairy stomach now exposed beneath the dressing-gown.

'I find it moving! I find it very artistic. I find it strikes a deep note of truthfulness, even if that makes him a bit of a schmuck. But who the hell's going to pay two dollars together with what it costs for a simple meal out and parking the car and a babysitter nowadays to see the story of a schmuck? I think my partner would have problems with your present ending. Some people think solely of finance.' Before Henry could reply Mr Bugloss went to the telephone and growled into it, 'Room service.' At which moment the bedroom door opened and a rather beautiful, nervous young woman, dressed like a Hampstead housewife, came out. 'Mr Simcox. This is an old friend of mine. Mrs Wickstead. You read Mr Simcox's great novel?'

'Never.' Mrs Wickstead sat down, sighed and pushed back her hair. She was not only beautiful but appeared to be English.

'I gave it to you. How come you didn't read it?' Henry

noticed how strangely Mr Bugloss's accent varied. Most of the time he was American; when, as at that moment, he was irritable he sounded German; when he changed again and smiled with genuine charm he might have grown up in the London suburbs. 'You two will get on, I can see that. I can sense an empathy. We shall arrange a lunch at the Green Giraffe. Are you room service?' He spoke into the telephone he was still holding and then looked up at Henry. 'You don't care for any champagne to celebrate our association?'

'Well . . .' Henry thought he might care for a little.

'No champagne,' Mr Bugloss said firmly and spoke to the telephone. 'We'll just take some of your fresh orange juice. Make it three. And a coffee. And I'll take one of your hot bread rolls, with just a little butter for the sake of energy. Do you have some nice butter?' He put down the phone, blew out smoke and said in a voice now hushed with reverence, 'Peck wants to do a picture with me.'

'Gregory Peck?'

'Who else? Mrs Wickstead knows that, don't you, my dear?'

'*Do* I?'

'She knows. Greg Peck can't wait to do a picture with me. I *see* Greg in *Indiscretions*.'

'*The Greasy Pole*.' Henry remained firm on the point.

'I think this is one Greg Peck will really go for. If we get the script right.'

Henry, suddenly determined, rose to his feet. It was about to become his finest hour. 'Mr Bugloss.'

'Oh, please. Benny.' Mr Bugloss smiled modestly.

'Benny. Have you considered that the leading character in my book is a twenty-three-year-old Englishman who works in a small country town? I don't see how he could be played by a middle-aged American actor.'

'Peck can't help that, don't hold his years against him.'

Henry started to move out of the room. He knew how Michelangelo might have felt when the Pope suggested cutting Adam out of the ceiling in the Sistine Chapel. 'And I'll never agree to change the ending.'

'Middle age will come to you, my dear, eventually.'

'I don't think I want anything to do with your trade.' Henry had reached the door. 'Nothing but visual tricks. No depth. No feeling. A few superficial snapshots of life and nothing but glamour and emptiness and using the whole wide world as a sort of stage set for inflated fantasies! I don't want any part of it, thank you very much.'

When Henry had gone Mr Bugloss turned to Mrs Wickstead and said thoughtfully, 'There goes a young man who's absolutely hooked on the movies.'

Benny Bugloss rose to power in the film world at a rare moment in history, when life in England was thought to be interesting to the American public, and when American producers found that costs and taxes were lower on the other side of the Atlantic. He was 'close to' the heads of various Hollywood studios, who liked to buy their suits in Savile Row, their pipes at Dunhill, to rent houses in Eaton Square and in general behave like their idea of an Englishman. From this position they could produce films about North Country boys whose old grandads kept racing pigeons.

'Where to now, girl?' Fred said in a Yorkshire accent, coming out of a cinema showing one such film. He and Agnes were on a rare outing to London. Agnes knew how impressionable he was – he had been speaking French when they came out of *Hiroshima, Mon Amour*. They started one of their frequent discussions about where they should go and Fred suggested her coffee bar.

'*My* coffee bar?'

'The one you say you hang about in when you come up to London. I mean, the one where you meet your friends.'

'Arturo's? Why not?' She led the way down the street from the cinema. 'I knew I'd end up by deciding.'

'*I* decided,' Fred protested.

'You decided that I should decide.'

So they sat in a dimly lit jungle of rubber plants, among a lot of people wearing duffel-coats, scarves and beards, listening to the muted music of Cliff Richard and the Shadows, with the photographs of stars on the walls, Tommy Steele, Alma Cogan and Dickie Valentine, and drank 'froffy' coffee out of see-through cups.

'Where shall we go?' Fred held Agnes's hand across the table. 'I mean, from here?'

'Back to Hartscombe on the train.'

'What about the friends in London you're always talking about, hasn't one of them got a room we could borrow?'

'No.' Agnes removed her hand. 'None that would be suitable. You'll go back to the Rectory, and drop me off at the surgery.'

'Not even go to our country place?' He smiled at her. 'Nowt Hall.' When desperate for accommodation they had been known to borrow Tom's hut in the depths of the wood where no one ever came.

'You like all that. It makes you feel grown up.'

'Enormously. I couldn't go back now.'

'Back to what?'

'Back to doing without you.'

'Please.' She sounded distressed. 'Don't say things like that.'

'I think we ought to go now,' Fred told her. 'We'll miss our train.'

'Why do you want to go suddenly?'

The reason was sitting alone, smiling and slightly drunk at the other end of Arturo's coffee bar. They had to pass Henry on their way to the door and he called out, 'The country cousins! My little brother, stumping round London with manure on his wellies. Hullo, Agnes.'

'We've got to go,' Fred told him.

'Or you'll turn back into a pumpkin. I have news for you, young Freddie. I've saved my soul. That's what I'm celebrating, and you've got time for another froffy before you go back to vegetate in rural Rapstone. You don't seem to be very interested in the state of my soul.'

'Did you say you'd saved it or something?' To his disappointment Fred saw that Agnes was sitting at Henry's table. He sat beside her and refused all refreshment.

'I'll tell you.' Henry was looking at Agnes. 'I'll tell you both. Mephistopheles appeared to me in the shape of an overweight monstrosity called Benjamin K. Bugloss. He lured me to the Dorchester. He offered me everything! A trip to Los Angeles, massage by starlets. He promised to deliver me champagne and Gregory Peck, all I had to do was to change my ending. Oh, and he wanted a new title for my book. Can you believe it? He called it a *property*. *The Greasy Pole* a *property*, like a tasteful home in Esher or something. He offered me all that, plus a dinner with a Mrs Wickstead who has beautiful frightened eyes and is clearly looking for ways of escape from Benjamin K. And what did I do?'

'Signed the contract?' Fred looked ostentatiously at the clock surrounded by brass sun-rays on the wall.

'You misjudge me, Frederick. I spurned his offer! I shook the dust of the Dorchester off my feet. I shall never see Los Angeles. I shall never meet Greg Peck. Mrs Wickstead will remain a closed book to me. I have preserved my integrity!'

In the corner of the carriage Agnes slept with her head on Fred's shoulder. The train shuddered to a halt at the small, ill-lit station, there was a sound of doors banging and an elderly guard shouted 'Hartscombe! All change, please!' Agnes opened her eyes. 'What on earth was Henry talking about?'

'His soul. I wonder where he keeps it.'

Chapter Eleven

BORROWERS AND LENDERS

After Simeon's death Henry and Lonnie were looking through the big cardboard boxes of family photographs that were kept in a cupboard under the Rectory stairs. There were pictures of the family dressed up for various entertainments, Henry as a pirate, Fred as a girl. 'Pity he never married, make a good wife to someone, old Frederick would,' Henry said. There was even a picture of Leslie Titmuss cutting down nettles. In the photographs it always seemed to be summer. Dorothy appeared rarely but Simeon was a sort of star. He was to be seen digging, greeting the Bishop, holding babies he had recently christened or upstaging the bride after various wedding ceremonies he had performed.

'Your father always looked so serene,' Lonnie said. 'So saintly.'

'It's perfectly easy to look serene if you happen to be completely off your head. Haven't you noticed that dotty people always have that wonderful saintly expression.'

Henry picked up a photograph and examined it closely. It was blurred, yellowed with age, but once in the Rectory garden a man in an old torn jacket was holding up a pair of dead rabbits which hid most of his face. Simeon Simcox was looking at the man, smiling broadly and accepting the rabbits as a gift. Dorothy was smiling in the background of the picture. Now, having taken out the coffee tray, she returned to the living-room.

'Who's that extraordinary man holding up rabbits?' Henry

gave the picture to his mother who took it over to the window and examined it closely.

'That's Tom Nowt.'

'Tom Nowt the poacher?'

'A poacher? Well, I suppose he must have been, although we didn't like to say so. He used to bring us rabbits sometimes, and I used to make pâté with them, although I expect he got them from our bit of woodland.'

'Tom Nowt, who used to have that broken-down hut in Hanging Wood?'

'Did he? I may have heard something . . .' Dorothy became vague. 'I can't exactly remember.'

'But he and our father look perfectly friendly.'

'Your father always got on with everyone.'

'Not with Tom Nowt, he didn't!' Henry remembered. 'He disapproved violently of Tom Nowt, for some reason. The only time I saw him angry was when Frederick had been hanging round Nowt's hut.'

Dorothy shook her head. 'With Fred? No, really, I'm sure you must be mistaken.' She put the photograph in her cardigan pocket and when Henry held out his hand, asking for it back, she refused, smiling. 'Whatever do you want it for? An old photograph.'

'It just might become useful evidence.'

'Of what, on earth?'

'Father's irrational prejudices.'

'You know Henry's starting a court case,' Lonnie explained.

Dorothy stopped smiling. She stood, still firmly holding the photograph in her pocket. 'I think it's disgusting.'

'It's to help you, Mother,' Lonnie went on, 'as much as anyone.'

'I can get on perfectly well without help, thank you.'

'We've got to get at the truth.' Henry did his best to control his rising irritation. At this his mother, who had decided to go out and snip off a few dead heads, turned on him instead. 'The truth! I'm not sure you'd know the truth if you found it. I mean, all those stories and films and things you're always working at. They don't have much to do with the truth, do they?'

'I suppose I could say that there's a deeper sort of truth which can only be reached by fiction.' Henry had said that often on television arts programmes.

'You wouldn't say that, Henry. You wouldn't be so silly!' Dorothy was laughing at him now.

'Henry's been to see a lawyer, Dorothy,' Lonnie was explaining, as though to a child. 'So if Leslie Titmuss goes on claiming Simeon's money . . . Well, there'll have to be a case in court.'

'You mean I'd have to stand up in public and answer questions?'

'It might have to come to that, Mother. Yes.'

'We'd hope it wouldn't,' Lonnie assured her.

'You wouldn't be frightened, would you?' Henry tried to sound reassuring.

'Frightened? I'd be humiliated!'

'I don't know why.'

'To stand and talk about our family, about Simeon, in front of a lot of total strangers, to have it all written up in the paper, for Glenys Bigwell to read, and Grace Fanner at the Manor, wouldn't that be humiliating? It's just like you, Henry, to arrange that. Just like those awful film stories you sent us to read, and your father and I were so embarrassed! We didn't know how you could bring yourself to do such things.'

Before Henry could reply his mother had gone off into the kitchen where she opened the Aga and dropped Tom Nowt and his rabbits, in the company of her smiling and departed husband, on to the burning boiler nuts, where they were quickly consumed. Then she forgot about the past, and thought of her immediate future. Now Simeon was dead she would have to leave the Rectory and move into somewhere much smaller.

Fred was lying naked under a damp blanket on the old iron

bedstead in Tom Nowt's hut. Agnes, wearing nothing but Fred's shirt, lifted the kettle she had put on the paraffin stove and stooped to light a cigarette from the flame. On the walls the antlered deer skulls and the pin-ups were expressionless. They had bicycled down to the hut an hour earlier, skidding on wet, fallen leaves, and Fred had laughed and shouted. Now he was quiet, it was time to ask the question he dreaded every month.

'No curse?'

'Nothing.'

'It's just late.'

'Nearly three weeks.' She made tea for them both and then came and sat on the bed beside him. 'What would you do, Fred?'

He looked at the shadow where the shirt divided, at her long white legs and avoided her question. 'It's awful having to start from scratch. If only I'd done science at school! Science was considered a bit common compared to Latin.'

'And now you feel a little science might come in handy?'

'If I'm going to be a doctor.'

'Oh, for that. Yes.' She drank her tea.

'You know I shan't make any money for years. I mean, I can't make any plans or anything.'

'No. I do understand. It's cold in here.' She stood up, shivering. 'I'm going to get dressed.'

He didn't say anything more then, feeling that he would never say anything right.

Ten days later Fred had persuaded himself that he had nothing to worry about. It was a Friday night when, as usual, the Stompers met for a session at Marmaduke's garage in Hartscombe. They were playing 'Ain't Misbehavin'' on an oil-stained concrete floor, under naked electric light bulbs, among gutted Ford Populars and behind a jacked-up Daimler. Glenys Bigwell, a fair-haired, strong-minded girl, daughter of Bridget and Percy, was sitting on a wooden box looking starry-eyed at Terry Fawcett with whom she had been walking out since her schooldays.

Glenys worked in a Hartscombe stationers and did part-time secretarial work for the Rector. Although her typing was enthusiastic, her spelling was weak and Simeon, too much in a hurry to correct it, sometimes signed letters to the Bishop protesting about 'apartaid' or racial 'descremination'.

Terry did his clarinet solo and then gave way to Fred, who went into a great burst of bravura drumming. When he was at the climax of his performance he saw Agnes step into one of the pools of light. His drumming quietened and finally died away, as though the sight of her, standing so quiet and unsmiling, had drained away his talents as a musician. Joe Sneeping, who was also looking at the new arrival, decided to stop the session and ask Glenys to get a brew on. Fred got up and followed Agnes into a quiet space between two cars. She said, 'I've found someone.'

'You mean . . .?'

'Yes. Someone a friend of mind knows about.'

'Where? In Worsfield?'

'You don't have to worry about where. All you have to worry about is getting hold of a hundred pounds.'

'A *hundred*?'

'Well, that's not the difficult part, is it? In pound notes, apparently, and not too new.'

Joe had lifted his trumpet and was blowing the melody of 'Snake Rag'. Agnes seemed to be crying. Fred put his arms round her and told her that of course he'd get it. Agnes sniffed, wiped her eyes on the sleeve of her duffel-coat and, suddenly saying, 'Goodbye, Fred,' released herself from him and walked away. He would have gone after her but the session was starting again. 'Get on the skins, man!' Joe called in his best New Orleans accent and Fred returned obediently to his drums and beat out the rhythm he had known so long, and which represented musical purity for the Stompers, with no taint of commercialism. A hundred pounds! He couldn't remember ever having seen a hundred pounds, all at one time. He found himself envying his father, who had nothing to worry about except the future of mankind.

Charlie and Leslie did not meet for some time after the disaster of the Young Conservatives dinner dance. She had found herself thinking of him often, as of a strange, intense creature, a foreigner in her small world, who had moved her by his unhappiness and anger. When she thought of how much she disliked the young men her mother had wanted her to go out with she found herself warming to the memory of Leslie Titmuss. One afternoon she had been to the cinema in Hartscombe on her own and sat down to a lonely tea in the Copper Kettle in the High Street, when a voice said, 'No objection to my sitting here at all?' Leslie didn't wait for a reply but made himself comfortable and ordered the set tea. He seemed in a mood of high excitement, and to have quite forgotten the humiliations he had suffered when they last met. 'I've been looking forward to telling you,' he announced at once. 'I've done it.'

'Done what?'

'Got on the Committee.'

'The Committee of what?'

'The Young Conservatives, of course.'

'You mean the people who pushed you in the river?'

'Well, that was all a bit of fun, wasn't it? I'd like to go for Secretary eventually. Do you think your father would put in a word for me?'

'I don't expect so. He's awfully vague about that sort of thing.'

'We can't really talk here, can we?' Leslie seemed prepared to accept the Chairman's vagueness for the moment and was concerned with the grey-haired tea drinkers around them.

'You seem to be managing all right.'

'Those old girls looking at us!'

'Perhaps they know about you being on the Committee. I mean, you must be famous!'

'Don't ever do that,' Leslie warned her.

'What?'

'Take the mickey.'

His rebuke startled her so that she felt in no position to refuse his suggestion that they might go out some time, and their meetings became curious oases in the desert of her life at home with her parents. Leslie seemed anxious to be discreet and suggested dates in unfrequented pubs near to the railway station or back streets behind the Brewery. During such meetings Leslie would tell Charlie about his political plans and ambitions and explain to her that the office of Secretary of the Y.C.s would, in the course of time, help him to a place on the Committee of the more senior branch of the Hartscombe Conservative Association. Whatever happened, he told her, he was determined to make something of himself. When she asked him, as she often did, what he intended to make, Leslie would smile enigmatically as though he were about to enter a new world which she would never be able to understand.

Sometimes he borrowed his father's car to take her for a 'run out into the country'. He always picked her up for these excursions at some neutral spot and explained that his parents didn't know that he was taking Charlotte Fanner out.

'Are you going to tell them?' Charlie asked.

'Of course. Eventually.'

'Why not now?'

'Oh, they're old-fashioned. My mother used to work for the Stroves. She worked in the kitchen. It made her very class-conscious. Me going out with the daughter of Rapstone Manor! She'd find that very shocking. Here, sit on this. You don't want to spoil your skirt.' He had driven her up to Picton Ridge, from where they looked down the valley and had a view of both villages and the factory chimneys around Worsfield on the distant horizon. He had taken a neatly folded tartan rug out of the back of the Prefect and was doing his best to insert it under Charlie.

'What would they do if they found out?' she asked him, raising herself for him to spread the rug beneath her.

'My father'd probably make a respectful call on yours and tell him to put a stop to it. He's quite capable of that.'

'Poor Leslie.'

'Oh no, don't feel sorry for me. In the end I'll bring them all round to my way of thinking. I say, I like your hair. In the sunshine. You're very beautiful.'

She hadn't screamed for a long time, not really since she had seen him, like a long black seal, slither out of the water in evening-dress. Now, however, she felt an awful upsurge of anger. 'Don't say that! You promised never to say that again!'

'But what would *your* father and mother say?'

The anger subsided and she felt a return of happiness. 'Mother'd be as sick as a dog but she'd have to lump it, wouldn't she?'

It was then, kneeling beside her, that Leslie Titmuss, after a slow courtship, took Charlie by the shoulders and kissed her. It was a carefully thought out, long-term move, to which she reacted with unexpected enthusiasm. To his surprise he found her kneeling in front of him, pulling at his belt as though such things were part of her everyday experience and not some long-cherished dream. Whatever fantasy it was it remained unacted. Leslie finally steered her hands to less controversial areas and, though he kissed her for a long time with concentration and zeal, it was clear that further developments still lay among his plans for the distant future.

While Leslie Titmuss and Charlie Fanner were spread out high above the Rapstone Valley, Fred sought an interview in the Rector's study. He went into the room to find his father sleeping, his long legs stretched in front of the fire, the report of a Royal Commission open and face downward on his chest. This retreat from the problems of the world, and in particular those of Frederick Simcox, irritated him. He banged the door shut and said, 'I want to talk to you.'

'Always. Always feel that you can.' Simcon opened his eyes and looked tolerant.

'About money.'

'Ah. Then I don't see that there's very much to discuss. I'm prepared to continue your modest allowance during the lengthy period it seems to take you to learn how to cut up frogs and . . .' he searched for a suitably dismissive phrase, 'pill-popping, bone-setting, and so on.' He stifled a small, remaining yawn. 'I know nothing of these mysteries.'

'They're not mysteries really.' Fred felt called upon to defend his chosen profession.

'To me, they are mysteries.'

'They're perfectly sensible, useful bits of information.'

'What a chameleon you are, my boy. You spend your days with the Salters and bring home all the Doctor's "sensible" expressions. It's like an infection.'

'I want to be sensible for a moment.' Fred sat down at the fireside also, opposite his father. 'Look, I'd be glad if you didn't tell Mother this.'

'Not tell her what?'

'You know what she is. She worries.' Fred fell silent and, when he thought it could be put off no longer, said, 'I need a hundred pounds.'

'And you shall have it!' Simeon leaned forward and put his hand on his son's knee, a gesture which Fred was too relieved to find embarrassing.

'Well, thank you very much.'

'Over the next five months, at the rate of five pounds a week.' Simeon got up, selected a pipe from the mantelpiece and began to fill it. Fred suspected that his father only smoked a pipe in order to irritate him at these interviews.

'No. No, that won't do. You see, I do need it now. In cash. You'll have it back. We've got a few gigs.'

'Gigs?' Simeon looked puzzled. 'You're talking about a kind of conveyance?'

'Jobs. With the band. Dances and . . . Well . . .'

'Oh, I wouldn't want you to neglect your medical studies and take to full-time on the kettle drum, for the sake of paying a debt to me.'

'I'll pay you back when I qualify, but I need it now. In one-pound notes.'

'You think you need it.' Simeon was exhausting his usual quota of matches. Fred knew, with a sinking of the heart, that they were about to drift away on a tide of moral philosophy.

'I know I do.'

'I'm not asking you what you think you need this money for. I shan't ever ask you that, Fred.' Tolerance was always one of Simeon's most effective weapons.

'Good.'

'It's your own life, and you must lead it as you feel it is most fitting. If you feel that it's in any way seemly to come and ask me for a hundred pounds . . .'

'*Used* notes. They don't have to be new at all.' Fred sounded as though he hoped that would make it easier.

'I'm not asking what you *think* you need it for and I don't want to know. But I will tell you one thing, Fred, it's not the answer.' He began to pace the room, as though in the early stages of composing a sermon. 'Money is never the answer! *They* think it is, don't they? Our new masters! Oh, they think money's the answer to everything. "You've never had it so good". Put a refrigerator in every cottage in Rapstone and a family runabout at every door.'

'I'm not asking for a refrigerator.' Fred felt the argument slipping away from him. 'Or even a family runabout.'

'And there'll still be a great longing, a great emptiness at the heart of the people.' Simeon was standing, looking at his son with quizzical sincerity. 'Because they do, they really do long for what money can't buy. Justice, equality, *caring* for those who aren't born with our advantages. I don't suppose you want this sum of money for any charitable purpose?'

'Not exactly charitable,' Fred had to admit. 'No.'

Simeon sat at his desk then, knocked his pipe out in the

waste-paper basket and gave some hardly welcome advice. 'Neither a borrower nor a lender be, Fred, that's a pretty good rule for life. I think you'll find a greater peace of mind, just living within your allowance. *Used* one-pound notes, did you say?'

'Yes.' Fred felt a small stirring of hope but his father was, unbelievably, chuckling. 'You'll find they're just as hard to get hold of as the nice, crisp, crackling new ones.' He ended on a serious note, 'I'm glad we had this talk, Frederick. I'm sure you'll come to agree with me when you think hard about it.'

After Fred had gone Simeon put out his hand to one of the small wooden columns that separated the little drawers and cubby-holes on the top of his writing-desk. At the touch of a spring the pillar slid forward revealing a narrow, hidden compartment from which the Rector took a long, brown envelope. He didn't open it, or read its contents, but he made a short note with his fountain pen on the back of the envelope, initialled and dated it, and after a short pause when he might have been praying, or simply doing mental arithmetic, he returned it to its hiding-place.

Fred decided against telephoning his brother; instead he took an early train to London and prepared to take him by surprise. Henry, always lucky, had been able to find three rooms at the top of his publisher's house in Islington at a minimum rent. The publisher's wife looked after him, fed him whenever he looked plaintive and put his washing into her machine. His rooms, the servants' quarters of the tall Victorian house, were small, basically furnished by his landlord, but full of Henry's books, his old Russian political posters, stills from silent movies and the general clutter of his bachelor existence. He was pleased to have the hard task of writing interrupted by a visit from his younger brother and was amused by Fred's blurted-out request.

'A hundred pounds! Dear little Freddie. Did I hear you say a *hundred* pounds?'

'It's not a terrifically complicated sum.'

'I don't know whether you were listening that night in the coffee bar, young Fred, but I've saved my soul.'

'Oh, *that*.' Fred couldn't honestly see what his brother's soul had to do with it.

'Yes. *"That"*, as you so lightly dismiss it, means that I am absolutely skint. Broke. Down to the bare bottom of my over-draft. I have rejected the appalling Bugloss and his thirty pieces of silver.'

'I don't want thirty pieces of silver,' Fred tried to explain. 'Just a hundred pounds.'

'Poor Fred, how little you understand the life of an artist.'

'I don't suppose I do.'

'Look. Let me put it to you in words of one syllable. I have given up money for Lent, or at least until I finish my next novel. I have taken money off my diet sheet. I live almost entirely on cold ham and tomatoes and Algerian cow's piss which I get in litre bottles from the off-licence.'

'It doesn't sound too bad.'

'I don't go out, Frederick. I simply never go out; have people *round*, of course.' He got up and went to inspect the view from his window. 'It's Agnes, isn't it? Agnes with what we used to call a bun in the oven. You must feel tremendously proud of yourself.'

'I'm not really.'

'I think you should have the little one. I think you owe it to the world to see what a small Frederick would be like, your one tiny hold on posterity.'

'Well, it's true I haven't written a novel.'

'No, you haven't, Fred, have you?' Henry turned away from the window and asked, quite casually, 'Do you think of what Agnes must be feeling?'

'I don't think she wants it, particularly.' Fred found the question unexpected and, coming from his brother, unfair. 'Obviously she doesn't. She asked me to find the money.'

'And you?'

'Can't you see? It's impossible now I'm going in for medicine.'

'Well, I always thought that was remarkably selfish of you.'

'I mean, our father . . .'

'Who art in Rapstone?'

'Father allows me five pounds a week, that's about all I'm going to earn for years. I mean, how could we possibly . . .'

'Dear old Fred. I always knew you were the ruthless one of the family.' Henry came and put a hand on Fred's shoulder, behaving more like an elderly uncle than a brother. 'It's impossible!' Fred was conscious that he was sounding plaintive and hated himself for it. 'I'll pay you back. I mean, you can't be short of a hundred pounds. You've only got to write a film script.'

'Write a film script?' Henry dropped his hand in mock horror, as though any contact with his brother might prove fatal. 'Are you trying to corrupt me? Get thee behind me, Frederick!'

In the days to come Fred scraped the bottom of the barrel. He found his mother rolling out pastry on the kitchen table and when he asked her if she had any money she wiped her hands on her apron, got her handbag off the dresser and said she had two pounds twelve and six. Asked if she could possibly lend him a hundred pounds, Dorothy smiled tolerantly. 'What silly things you come out with sometimes,' she told him.

As a last resort Fred walked the three miles to Picton House where he found Magnus circling a nearby wood with a gun and a spaniel. He remembered the young Strove's talent for making money at Knuckleberries and that Magnus had come into something under his grandfather's will. As they tramped through the brambles together the latest Strove told Fred of his plan to buy up Garthwaite's, the old family grocer's in Hartscombe, and start what he hoped would become a chain of Easy-Bite Dining-Parlours. 'Do an all-in evening meal, steak or scampi and French fries, cheeseboard and half a bottle of Mateus Rosé for three quid all in. Of course, my partner and I are having a bit of trouble with the Council. They keep going on about "preserving the Georgian character of the High Street" and all that type of balderdash. I expect we'll win in the end.'

'So you'll make a lot of money.'

'Bob or two, I hope.'

'So you could afford to lend me a hundred pounds. I mean, I'd pay you back.'

A rabbit came scuttling out of the bushes, death blew it into the air for a second until it fell and the dog panted off to retrieve it. Magnus smiled charmingly. 'Sorry, old boy, not with all this going on. We're fully stretched, you know what I mean, absolutely fully stretched.'

When Fred telephoned Agnes she was busy, washing her hair, or going over to Worsfield to see a girl she had known at university, or having to entertain some cousins from Canada. However, she agreed to meet him at Tom Nowt's hut the next Saturday afternoon. They could do all their talking then, she told him.

In spite of his failure to solve their problem, to come up with the money in used notes, or any sort of notes, Fred bicycled down through the woods with excitement. At least he was going to see Agnes again and he could lie down with her and share her secrets. Perhaps, after all, the situation wasn't so desperate. Perhaps it was all a false alarm, or, he imagined in some way that would still need working out, they could have a child and marry and live together without dry-mouthed telephone calls and having to borrow Tom Nowt's to go to bed together. He arrived five minutes before the appointed time, but when she was not already there he knew that she was not coming.

All the same he waited for an hour and a half and then bicycled into Hartscombe and found Dr Salter alone and having tea. The Doctor looked at Fred with pity and asked if he really didn't know that Agnes had gone to London.

'Where in London?' Fred suddenly realized how little he

knew of her friends there, or where he could telephone to find her.

'I believe she said, the usual places. It seems that she doesn't tell either of us very much.'

So Fred caught a train from Hartscombe and that evening found himself sitting alone in Arturo's coffee bar with no very clear idea of what he was going to do next. At last he tried asking the waitress who brought him his third espresso if she happened to have seen a girl with long hair who answered to the name of Agnes and smoked a lot.

'Sounds like everyone. I'll ask Arturo. Arturo! Do you know anyone called Agnes?'

The proprietor approached them and Fred looked up and saw him for the first time. His hair was slicked down, he had a small moustache and a sort of pallor as though he rarely saw the light. Arturo was wearing an Italian silk suit, a gold bracelet and pointed, patent leather shoes. He said, 'Hullo, Simcox Mi. Haven't seen you since the good old days at Knuckleberries.'

'Arthur Nubble! What on earth are you doing, posing as an Italian?'

'Nothing to it, old boy.' Arthur sat down with a sigh of relief, as though his shoes were killing him. 'It's all they want nowadays. An Italian name. A few rubber plants. Take enough black coffee to cover a postage stamp and blow a cloud of steam up its arse, add a bit of froth and charge ninepence. I'm just providing a service.'

'The last time you did that you got the sack.'

'I resigned. I'd had far too much education. Did you say you were looking for a girl? There's one working the steam pump I'm anxious to dispose of.' Fred looked at a plump girl pulling the handle of the hissing espresso machine. 'Your waitress?'

'No,' Arthur told him gloomily. 'My wife. You look as though you need a drink. Abandon that ink and candy floss. Let's go to a party!'

'You haven't seen Agnes?'

'Who's Agnes?'

'The girl I'm looking for.'

'You want one in particular?'

'Yes.'

'You were always a difficult customer to please, Simcox. Probably comes of you being Labour.' He stood up, wincing at the tightness of his shoes. 'Come to the party! There's bound to be some of Arturo's regulars around there. They may have seen your Agatha.'

'Agnes.' Fred also stood up, but without much hope. 'Her name's Agnes.'

'I'm sure you know best.'

They went out of the back entrance to where Arthur Nubble's dented, second-hand Jaguar was parked on the pavement. Fred got into the car which smelt strongly of coffee and Arthur drove very fast, coming to rest in front of a tall house in a square. The top-floor windows were open and modern jazz drifted down to them.

'This is where my brother lives.'

'Well, anyway we'll get a drink.'

'Don't be too sure,' Fred warned him as they got out of the car. 'Anyway, nothing but Algerian cow's piss.'

Fred was wrong about that. When they got up to the party a large, suntanned man wearing a silk scarf and a hugely checked tweed jacket poured him a glass of champagne. There were a lot of girls in the shadows, sitting on the sofa, whispering in corners, even dancing together to the calculated murmurs of Dave Brubeck. Some of them called out 'Arturo!' and Arthur hobbled off to join them. Fred thought that he saw some new bits and pieces, some black-shaded lamps and a new silky rug on the floor. Henry, who had clearly been buying furniture, was nowhere to be seen.

'Are you a friend of the genius?' the man who had been pouring Fred's champagne asked him.

'Which genius is that?' Fred was puzzled.

'Mr Henry Simcox.'

'Oh, *that* genius. I'm his brother.'

'Henry never told me he had a brother.'

'No? So far as Henry's concerned it's a closely guarded secret.' Fred suddenly felt a large arm round his shoulder. The man had come unacceptably close to him. 'Honoured to meet you, my dear. I'm Benny Bugloss. And I'm overjoyed to be translating your brother's great work into a major motion picture. We shall try, Mr Simcox, my dear, and we shall overcome.'

'*The Greasy Pole?*' Fred asked, extricating himself from Mr Bugloss's embrace.

'Isn't that a great title? And I'll tell you something, we're keeping it *exactly as it is*!'

'You're Mephistopheles?' Fred looked at Mr Bugloss.

'No. Bugloss. Benjamin K. Bugloss. Has someone else got an interest in the film rights?'

'Oh, I don't think so.'

'I have told your brother. I want to be absolutely true to his conception.' Mr Bugloss was deeply serious. 'You see, in the end this guy decides to give up the Ladyship and go back to his job in the Brewery. He's true to his class, you understand. Some would say he's a schmuck, but I say, "No. He's a hero."'

'What about Gregory Peck?' Fred remembered what Henry had told him.

'No.' Mr Bugloss was thinking deeply. 'Somehow I don't see Peck in this. I more likely see someone along the lines of Albert Finney, someone British. Shall I tell you something? Britain is bankable right now, Britain could be good news at the box office.'

'So you took Henry up on to a high mountain?'

'Our first meeting didn't go too well. But he called me and I met with him again. In the Dorchester, my suite, we worked something out. A *modus*.'

'A what?'

'A *modus vivendi*.'

'You showed him all the kingdoms of the world in a moment of time.'

'I told him I'd fly him to the Coast.'

'"And said unto him, all this power will I give thee."'

'Hey, what're you talking about?'

'How much did you pay him?' Fred, on his third glass of champagne, made so bold as to ask.

'Thirty thousand dollars, plus a piece of the action. It may not be all the kingdoms of the world, my dear, but it certainly ain't peanuts.'

A young woman emerged from the shadows and Mr Bugloss introduced her. 'This is a friend of mine. Mrs Wickstead. This is Mr Simcox.'

'Hullo.'

'Absolutely *loved* your book,' Mrs Wickstead told him.

'That wasn't me. It was my brother.' Fred allowed his glass to be refilled and looked towards the bedroom door which had suddenly opened. The lights were on inside and the party was beginning to spill into it. When Henry came out of the door he had a bottle of champagne in one hand and his other arm round Agnes's waist. They both looked at Fred, he thought, with a smile of faint amusement.

'Hullo, young Fred.' Henry seemed not at all surprised to see him. 'Welcome to our farewell party. I'm off to the Coast. Of course, Agnes is coming with me.'

When he thought about it, and he thought about it always, it seemed to Fred like some sickening accident, the prolonged moment when a car slithers out of control and you wait, help-lessly, for the inevitable crash, the tearing of metal, injury or death. He remembered Agnes smiling patiently as, humiliated, he held her arm, tried to drag her away from the party and back to Hartscombe. She didn't move, or try to shake him off, but waited, still smiling, until he released her and then she walked away into the kitchen where three or four girls were getting food ready for the party. He remembered Henry, also smiling, speaking as though his younger brother had left him with a heavy responsibility which he had, selflessly, agreed to discharge.

'You abandoned her, Fred.' Henry was holding a short sausage on a stick and taking small, eager bites as he spoke. 'You let her down, you didn't give her what she needed most.'

'You know what that is?' The room had become misty and Fred had an appalling suspicion that he might burst into tears.

'Of course. Money was required and I provided it. As a matter of fact I made a considerable sacrifice. Just because of you, Fred, I'm writing a film for Benjamin K. Bugloss. If you hadn't let Agnes down so badly my soul might have remained a virgin. I say. You're not going to blub, are you? I haven't seen you blub since we were at Knuckleberries.'

Fred didn't blub. Instead he drank everything he could lay his hands on until Arthur Nubble told him he looked ghastly and should be taken away. As they left, they passed Mr Bugloss in the doorway.

'Did I have a problem persuading your brother to write this screenplay? Well, artists are not easy people or they wouldn't be artists, would they?'

'I fixed it for you.' Fred assured him.

'You son of a bitch! How did you manage that?'

'Well, you see, my brother's hang-up was his soul. I can reliably inform you that he hasn't got a soul any more. There's absolutely nothing to stop him working for the movies.'

They left with several girls from the party and, organized by Nubble, went to a dark, reverberating club somewhere high over Leicester Square. In the gents, Nubble found that he had a packet of purple hearts about him and offered them to Fred.

'No thanks, really.'

'What's the matter with you, Simcox? You never want to take what anyone has to give. It was the same at school. You never really wanted the bit of pâté de foie I got hold of. People don't like it, you know, if you don't take what's offered.'

So Fred chewed purple hearts for the sake of not offending Nubble and returned to stumble round the dance area guided by a girl called Denise whom he had last seen cutting up sandwiches at Henry's flat. She appeared to him as a mildly attractive blur and he heard himself talking to her as though his was the voice of a distant stranger.

'I think you're beautiful,' the voice said.

'You're pissed.'

'You mean I think you're beautiful therefore I must be pissed? That's an a priori argument. But I'm pissed therefore I think you're beautiful. A posteriori.'

'Try not to be vulgar.'

'God's in his heaven. All's right with the world. Does that mean God's there so the world's all right, or does it mean the world's so sodding marvellous that there has to be a God?' The stranger who was talking seemed to Fred to be a pretentious and patronizing idiot.

'You're tense. That's what your trouble is.' The girl's face was almost entirely out of focus. 'You've got inner tension.'

Later he thought he was in bed with Agnes who was wearing nothing but one of his shirts, a silent, almost inert Agnes who said nothing and kept changing her shape. When he woke in the morning feeling terribly ill he looked for the deer skulls on the walls of Tom Nowt's hut and found that he was in a put-u-up bed in Arthur Nubble's Pimlico maisonette, and that his shirt was on the otherwise naked Denise, who was sitting up beside him repairing her make-up.

'Just remind me,' she said. 'Did we knock it off last night?'

In the kitchen, to which Fred had staggered for a glass of water, Arthur Nubble was wearing the sort of camelhair dressing-gown and flannel pyjamas that were uniform in the dormitory at Knuckleberries. He was grilling some lambs' kidneys he had been lucky enough to put his hands on for breakfast.

'I say, Simcox. You know that girl you were looking for at the party?'

'Yes.'

'I remember now,' Nubble told him. 'She was a bit stuck for a name and address. Well, I was able to fix her up with someone, of course, but she couldn't come up with the hundred pounds.'

When he got home, Fred went for a walk in the woods to Tom Nowt's hut. He heard his voice, hoarse, strained and despairing, calling 'Agnes!' through the trees. Overcome with exhaustion, alcohol, purple hearts and the indulgence of grief, he sank to his knees in the fallen leaves, and there he was when Dr Salter, hacking his old grey, found him. The Doctor took Fred to his house and treated all his complaints with the medicine he trusted most, the passage of time.

But when he found him, kneeling in the wood, he said, 'For God's sake, young Fred. Don't tell me you've taken to prayer!'

Part Three

Life must be lived forwards, but it can only be understood backwards.

Sören Kierkegaard

Chapter Twelve

CHEZ TITMUSS

On a Saturday morning, not long after Fred's visit to London, George Titmuss was washing and cleaning the Fort Prefect in front of 'The Spruces', according to his established practice. He hosed, shampooed, washed off and polished the car's maroon exterior, Windowlened the glass and hoovered the inside. Then he opened the glove compartment in order to give it a good dust and made an unwelcome discovery. A lipstick, a headscarf and a small crumpled handkerchief, still faintly redolent of perfume borrowed from Grace, were there found lurking. George removed these objects and took them into the house, where his son was finishing his breakfast, three rashers and two eggs on a fried slice prepared by his mother, and reading the *Financial Times*.

'You've taken to wearing lippie-stick, have you, boy?' George asked with an unwonted but not good-humoured smile. Before his son could answer, George Titmuss had gone into the kitchen, found a carrier-bag for the three exhibits, and was setting out for Rapstone Manor.

Nicholas received him in the conservatory, and there, among the begonias, George Titmuss laid out the damning relics saying, in the manner of a police sergeant giving painful evidence at a particularly repulsive murder trial, 'Traces of your daughter, Sir, have been found in my vehicle. The handkerchief displays her name-tape.' He produced Exhibit A: 'C. Fanner. No doubt she'll have had it marked for going away to boarding-school. My son, Leslie, never went away to boarding-school,' he added, as though to clinch the prosecution case.

'Of course, there's a great deal to be said for keeping the family together.' Nicholas was conciliatory.

'There's a great deal to be said for only doing what you can afford.'

'And of course, we have a magnificent state education. We must take the credit for that, you remember Rab Butler's splendid Act? It's done a great deal for the youngsters.' Nicholas avoided looking at the traces of Charlie on the table, taking refuge in wider political issues.

'We don't complain.' George was clearly speaking for the youngsters also.

'I'm sure you don't. And your young man, if I may say, is making something of himself. He chipped in at a meeting the other day. I'm not saying we'll see him on the Executive Committee for a year or two yet. But he's making his mark.'

Leslie had, Nicholas remembered, been particularly passionate at one recent gathering, when local issues had been discussed. He wanted the Hartscombe Party to get behind a plan to pull down Garthwaite's, the old grocer's shop, and allow some appalling chain restaurant to be built in its place. The Conservative majority on the Town Council, young Titmuss had told them all, must move with the times, although Nicholas didn't see the need for it himself. Now he wondered uneasily if George Titmuss had also come in pursuance of the scheme to pull down the old family grocer's shop, founded by a long-dead butler of a long-dead Nicholas Fanner. A silence fell on the two fathers in the conservatory, and Nicholas looked round at the stunted plants, too brightly coloured for their own good, which moved him to pity.

'You don't care for begonias, Titmuss?'

'Our only child will do perfectly nicely in his niche at the Brewery, just as I did before him.' George failed to answer the question. 'We don't want our Leslie disturbed by any undesirable friendships. I am referring, Sir Nicholas' – George shaped slowly up to the object of his call – 'to your daughter, Charlotte.'

'You call her undesirable? Well, I suppose that's reasonable.'

'Imagine if it went too far,' George went on gloomily. 'If it led to marriage, for instance.'

'Marriage? Is that what you have in mind?' Nicholas smiled with a tolerance which appeared to irritate Leslie's father.

'I do not have it in mind, Sir Nicholas. I certainly do not. Mrs Titmuss and I have something of a reputation around Skurfield. We are well known for keeping ourselves to ourselves.'

'Yes. I've heard that, of course.'

'Do you think we want to be invited here all the time for dinner parties, cocktails and the like? Do you think my Elsie wants to sit down to dinner with Mr Doughty Strove?'

'Well, poor old Doughty does rather bore for England, of course. But she could probably talk to whoever's on her *other* side,' Nicholas suggested helpfully.

'It's got to be put a stop to,' George said firmly, no doubt feeling that the discussion was about to drift into backwaters of irrelevance. 'Our Leslie and Miss Charlotte, they've got to be told it won't do. They mustn't see each other again, that's for the best.'

'It may be for the *best*,' Nicholas admitted, 'but we live in the world of practical politics. What can we do, even if it's not for the best?'

'It's simple, isn't it? Your daughter's not twenty-one, you've just got to put your foot down!' George looked at Nicholas who was shifting uncomfortably, as though prepared to put his foot anywhere but down. 'Or, if you can't manage that, no doubt her Ladyship can.'

Charlie had no idea whether or not she loved Leslie, but she thought about him incessantly and these thoughts puzzled her. Sometimes he looked so unnaturally pale and fragile that she felt sorry for him and afraid he wouldn't last the winter, then his almost grotesquely grown-up behaviour and serious ambition made him even more vulnerable and pathetic. At other meetings he seemed indestructible and the possessor of unnatural energy. He made Charlie, who often felt like a decent night's rest almost as soon as she had got up in the morning, tired to look at him. He was neat and precise where she was slapdash and untidy. When they were together, she would be laughing at one moment, sullen and silent the next. He was always practical and business-like, particularly when he was kissing her. Then she knew that, when his arms were round her neck, he was looking at the time through the forest of her hair. His mother was always waiting up for him.

For Charlie, Leslie's great attraction was that he was un-doubtedly one of the young men her mother would approve of least. She knew she had been a perpetual disappointment to Grace. She was never beautiful. She never wanted to spend a day in London buying hats and having tea in Fortnum's. She never discussed boyfriends with her mother, so that Grace could become, once again, a vicarious débutante. The fact that her mother disliked her had for years been a misery to Charlie, but now she revelled in it. She only wanted to feed the flames of her mother's hatred, and for that Leslie Titmuss would come in very handy. She had also, and rightly, come to the conclusion that her mother was a snob, and such a person, in Charlie's view, thor-oughly deserved all the social embarrassments that Leslie was so well-fitted to provide.

But Leslie was not only a marvellous irritant for her mother; Charlie saw him as a way of escape. Rapstone Manor, the old rambling house with its draughts, its tweed hats, gumboots and shepherds' crooks in the downstairs loo, its guns and family portraits, its domineering servants and the endless emptiness of its long afternoons, was literally, from time to time, making her scream. The dinner parties for the few inhabitants of the local big houses, or the Committee Members of the Hartscombe Con-

servative Association, or withered ladies who wore jewellery and
cardigans and who had 'come out' with Grace, were worse than
loneliness. Once settled with Leslie Titmuss, Charlie thought
she might fly to a wonderful world of sauce bottles and meat
teas, of gossip in saloon bars and holidays on the Costa Brava, of
days out in the car and of Leslie's fiercely concentrated copula-
tion on the hearth-rug in front of the electric fire, among scattered pages of the *News of the World* on Sunday afternoons. It
was a romantic dream of working-class delights which showed
how little Charlie knew of the world at that time.

Her longing to escape was frustrated by Leslie's initial determination to keep their love-affair a secret from George. But
then a change came and he invited her to meet him, not among
the dark scrub on Picton Ridge, but in the full glow of the
cocktail bar at the Swan's Nest Hotel. Whether he had gone
there to exorcize the memory of his great humiliation, or merely
to mark a change in his plans, Leslie was even more pallid and
intense when they met. His father, it seemed, had found certain
personal possessions of Charlie's in the glove compartment of
the Prefect, and their great secret was a secret no longer. Even
Nicholas had been told. They could either retreat in confusion,
or go into the attack, and Leslie had no doubt which course they
should take. One way would lead to a lifetime's separation, the
other might take them to the altar of Rapstone Church. As
Charlie burrowed into the chaos of her handbag to pay for their
gin and tonics, Leslie outlined his master-plan.

'Tell her,' he ended, 'this evening.' And he added, as though
in an attempt to temper the blow, 'After they've had their evening
meal.'

So Charlie was able to save up the revelation, as a child leaves
the largest strawberry or the cherry on top of the cake, until the
end of dinner. She sat, for the most part, in silence, hardly
answering Nicholas's well-meant inquiries or Grace's criticism
of her dress and the tedious nature of her company. She knew

that she had the power, once the long meal was over, to produce a most satisfactory explosion. She waited patiently until Bridget had brought the coffee tray into the drawing-room and then lit the blue touch-paper and announced that she planned to marry Leslie.

'Marry Leslie Titmuss!' Grace showed that her lungs, when called upon, were quite as strong as her daughter's. 'You're bloody well not going to marry Leslie Titmuss!'

'Why not? Tell me one reason why not.'

'Why not? The idea's obviously ridiculous. You're not even going out with Leslie Titmuss again and that's absolutely all I've got to say on the matter. Your father will tell you exactly the same thing.'

In fact Nicholas said nothing. He was sitting in a chair at the fireside, his knees pulled up, his long legs folded in the attitude of an aeroplane passenger anticipating a crash. He had noticed that Charlie had been looking unusually contented at dinner and had rightly interpreted the fact as a danger signal.

'Why do you have to care who I marry?' Charlie's question was triumphant. 'You can forget me! When I'm married to Leslie you can absolutely forget me. Don't even come to visit us!'

'Where do you think I'd come to visit? In some little semi-detached on a council estate in Worsfield?' Grace had picked up *Vogue* and was turning the glossy pages as though the subject was no longer worth discussing, when her husband told them that George Titmuss had paid a call on him, a fact which he had, up until then, decided not to mention in the interests of family peace.

'And I suppose he's tickled pink with the idea of his son marrying into the Fanners,' Grace sniffed. 'Probably put the boy up to it.' She pretended to make a close study of a photograph of a model wearing a fur coat and sitting in a dustbin.

'Not at all, he's violently opposed to it. I'm afraid Father Titmuss is a terrible old snob.'

'Thank God there are a few of us left!' Grace murmured piously.

'Tell her she's wrong! Tell her to mind her own bloody business. Tell her it's my own life. Go on, tell her!' Charlie had moved to sit on the arm of her father's chair.

'So far as I'm concerned, you may marry exactly whom you want.'

'Tell her then!'

Nicholas seemed to be apologizing for his beliefs as though they were begonias, a rather ridiculous sort of hobby. 'But I believe, well, I *do* believe it's up to us not to cause embarrassment, unhappiness even, to people who're not quite so lucky as ourselves.'

'Lucky? You think I've been *lucky?*'

'You're born into a certain family, Charlie. We have certain responsibilities, you might say.'

'To *her?*' Charlie looked with loathing towards the screening cover of *Vogue.*

'I was thinking more of the Titmuss family. It's going to be jolly awkward for them, Charlie, you do see that don't you? Now I'm sure young Leslie Titmuss is a perfectly decent . . .'

'Decent?' The description was too much for Charlie's mother. '*Decent!* Have you seen him? Hair oil and a row of pens in his breast-pocket. I couldn't believe it when I saw you dancing with him, Charlie, at the Y.C.s' ball. Poor child, I thought, she must be pushed for a partner.'

'You see,' Nicholas went on courageously, 'it really would rock the boat in the Titmuss household. He's an only child, just as you are, Charlie, and his mother won't want to visit here. I know that for a fact. You're going to cause a frightful lot of embarrassment, old thing.'

'Embarrassment!'

'You can't change people, Charlie. They've been going on too long.'

'All this quarrelling!' Grace slapped her magazine shut, a sure sign of bedtime. 'It's making my head ache and it's quite un-necessary. I'm going up now. You can forget all about it, Charlie, forget all about marrying Leslie Titmuss.'

'I can't forget it,' Charlie told her. 'Neither can you. I'll have to marry Leslie.'

'What *do* you mean?' her mother asked and Charlie's answer was as Leslie had planned it, although not in his exact words.

'Surely you know, don't you, mother? Isn't it the sort of thing you and your dried-up old girlfriends meet to giggle about in Fortnum's?'

After Henry had decided to contest his father's last will, he called on his daughter, Francesca, at the flat which she shared with her boyfriend, Peter. He had rarely visited that address, taking the view that anyone setting out for Tufnell Park would need a map and a compass, together with native bearers who could speak the local dialect. When he got there, after a taxi ride of no particular difficulty, he was surprised and a little shocked to find Francesca's living-room so warm and cheerful. A coal fire glowed in the grate and the place was decorated with Victorian relics, pictures and jugs depicting the Queen and Prince Albert, and Imperial battle scenes hanging on the walls. Although he sniffed cautiously, he could not detect that pungent odour of burning carpets which he always associated with the young. Henry had also come to denounce the loud and cacophonous music Francesca must surely like and he was put out to hear only a little gentle Telemann tinkling from the record-player.

'Is this *really* the sort of music you like?'

'Yes, Father. Don't you?'

Francesca was then twenty-one, only a couple of years younger than Lonnie had been when Henry had married her, a pretty, serious girl whose look of anxiety in no way reflected her firmness of purpose.

'I'm sorry Peter's not here.'

'I'm not,' Henry assured her.

'He's going into a new business.'

'Furniture removal?'

'No, of course not. Computer programming.' Francesca felt a pang of guilt, remembering the morning when she had found the Rectory empty, and only noticed the group of mourners in the churchyard after she and Peter had loaded up the van. She was prepared for an attack from her father but he was looking at the real object of his visit, Simeon's old desk which had been stripped to a naked buff colour and used as a stand for potted plants.

Henry sat down in front of it and went through the drawers methodically, telling his daughter that he was looking for anything that would spike the guns of that abominable little creep, Leslie Titmuss. At first he found nothing. The drawers had been cleared out, it seemed, and all their contents left at the Rectory. He had almost given up the search when he felt the wooden columns that supported a shelf at the back of the desk and a spring opened a secret and hidden drawer. From it he rescued a long folded paper on the back of which the words 'Last Will and Testament' were printed in archaic script.

At first Henry was enormously excited, for the newly found document in fact benefited Dorothy and the Rector's two sons. But when he took it to Jackson Cantellow it was clear that the homemade will, dated before the war, was revoked by the later, Henry thought insane, testament, made as late as 1983 in the office of a small Worsfield firm, whom, it seemed, his father had never used before.

'At least this shows what his true intentions were,' Henry said, when he called at Cantellow's office, interrupting his lawyer in a little solitary practice for a performance of Mendelssohn's *Elijah* in the Worsfield Free Trade Hall.

'What his intentions were in 1939.'

'Before he went mad,' Henry said firmly, 'and decided to benefit the appalling Titmuss.'

'I agree, it's a little strange that he should have left his money to Mr Titmuss as late as 1983, when the Minister was presumably quite comfortably off. But if that will had been made earlier, when the beneficiary was starting out in life, when he got married for instance . . . Now when was that exactly?' But Henry thought he had been away on the Coast, so the marriage of Leslie Titmuss passed without him noticing it at the time. He also refused Jackson Cantellow's offer of tickets for the oratorio *Elijah*, so their meeting was, on the whole, satisfactory to neither party.

After the initial battle between Charlie and her mother over the marriage question, there was a period of uneasy truce at Rapstone Manor. Nicholas spent as much time as he could walking round the home farm, smiling in a good-natured manner at the pigs, or he took a gun out to distant woodlands. Charlie stayed in her room a good deal and, at mealtimes, preserved a sort of triumphant silence which her mother found especially irritating. Grace's mind fluttered desperately between a number of plans which included a trip to Switzerland where Charlie might learn French and visit a discreet clinic, an accouchement in some remote nursing-home followed by immediate adoption and the wild hope that, when her immediate problems were solved, her daughter might undergo a religious conversion and become a nun. She put all these plans to her husband whenever she caught sight of him.

Grace also managed to capture the Rector after church on Sunday and, having rounded up Nicholas, imprisoned them both in the library and announced that she was seeking the help of her spiritual adviser because 'Charlie was in pod by the appalling Leslie Titmuss'. To her dismay, Simeon seemed to find the news less catastrophic than she had expected.

'I suppose people are always telling you the most ghastly things, but there can't be anything much more horrible than this! Where could we send her, somewhere quiet in the country?'

'This is somewhere quiet in the country,' Simeon told them, it seemed unhelpfully, and added, 'Young Leslie Titmuss is going to make something of himself.'

'I don't care what he makes of himself.' Grace was positive. 'I don't want him making little bastards with Charlie.'

'It might just be that Leslie Titmuss is the future.'

'If he is I'm not waiting for it. I never want to think of Leslie Titmuss again, so long as I live.'

'But there is someone you'll have think about.'

'Who?'

'Your grandchild.' And Simeon asked her seriously, 'Have you considered a really desperate remedy?'

'Of course.' She was glad to have the Church's approval.

'I mean marriage.'

'Over my dead body! I'm not having a grandchild, and Charlie's not having a wedding. I thought I'd made that perfectly clear.' And that appeared to be Grace's last word on the subject.

Simeon came away from his meeting with the Fanners curiously cast down. He became more cheerful when Leslie Titmuss called at the Rectory and requested a private audience in the study. It turned out that he wanted to book the church and, of course, the Rector's services, for a wedding. He couldn't yet name the date but it was bound to be quite shortly after the Worsfield Show. The bride's name was Charlotte Grace Fanner and, although she was under age, he had no doubt that her parents would finally give their consent.

Perhaps Leslie had hoped for a greater reaction from the Rector, a more considerable surprise or a burst of congratulations. Instead Simeon looked as though things were turning out much as he expected. He found a pencil, made a note in his diary and asked an entirely practical question.

'Where are you going to live? When you get married, I mean.'

'Sir Nicholas'll give us one of his cottages.'

'Do you think so?'

'He'll have to, won't he?'

Simeon looked up at the young man sitting opposite him and wondered, not for the first time, what it must be like to have been born without a sense of doubt. Would that be a blessing or a curse or a mere physical deprivation, like being born without a sense of smell? He failed, for the moment, to make up his mind on the question.

Chapter Thirteen

PUTTING UP A TENT

The Worsfield Show is one of the more pleasant occasions connected with that unattractive city. It takes place on Worsfield Heath, not far from the by-pass. (It can be said in favour of Worsfield that it is surrounded, and to some extent immunized, by the countryside.) It is true that the factory chimneys, now almost hiding the Cathedral tower, are visible from the site, but once a year they are fronted by sideshows, showing-rings, horse-boxes and sheep pens. The beer tents are open all day, and there farmers mix with commuters. Girls from Tesco's and the biscuit factory mingle with pigmen, stockmen, bingo-callers, fortune-tellers and dedicated showjumpers. Huge quantities of Simcox ale are drunk and great rivers of bubbling urine course down the troughs in the flapping lavatory tents and manure the common. Children in jodhpurs and hacking-jackets are mounted on midget ponies and forced over jumps by relentless parents greedy for rosettes. Worsfield Show is a place where you can still bowl for a pig, buy a horse or a pound of homemade marmalade, and watch a calm girl in a fringed cowboy suit being picked out by quivering knives hurled by her nervous and chain-smoking husband.

The show in the year of the Titmuss wedding was held in golden summer weather. The air was full of lowing, grunting, shunting, barking and the starting of reluctant horseboxes. Leslie was walking with his mother and father towards the Women's Institute bring and buy stall, when he saw his old adversaries, Magnus Strove and Christopher Kempenflatt, both dressed in precociously aged tweed suits, both with pinched trilby hats set on their foreheads, enjoying taking potshots at a number of ping-pong balls, which were dancing elusively on jets of water. Far from turning their guns on Leslie they hailed him with considerable goodwill and thanked him for the moving speech he had made at the local Party's meeting, supporting, in the name of go-ahead political thinking, their plan to tear down the old High Street grocer's and substitute a new Easy-Bite eatery.

'It was my duty,' Leslie said in answer to their thanks. 'I feel it's up to us in the Party to encourage business initiative among young people.' Both being a few years older than young Titmuss, they looked at him in some surprise, and Kempenflatt, still genial, offered to send him round a dozen bottles of the best bubbles. Leslie chose another reward, a loan of the blue and gold cardboard shield – the passport to the Steward's enclosure – which dangled from Magnus Strove's lapel.

'I'll bring it back in half an hour,' he promised, when his wish was granted. 'By the way, if you're acquiring the Garthwaite's site, have you thought about buying through a Bahamian partnership, with shares at a no-par value?'

Leslie had been reading the *Financial Times*, and taken advanced accountancy at evening classes. Kempenflatt thought he wanted to borrow the Steward's enclosure badge so that he could put on side to the other clerks in the beer tent.

In fact Leslie did as he had always planned, and went straight to the Steward's enclosure. If he hadn't been able to gain a badge he was prepared to resort to any extreme, even to forcing an entry into the back of the reserved lavatory tent and emerging, zipping up his flies and appearing nonchalant, on the hallowed ground of the 'Steward's'. As it was he walked unchallenged past the show of hunters in the ring and, crossing the grass where elderly men in bowler hats and riding macs sat perched on their shooting-sticks, he strolled into the Steward's tent. He saw the group he was looking for immediately, laughing together over champagne and sandwiches, by the banked hydrangeas at the far end of the marquee. He walked steadily towards them and, once in earshot, said like some Shakespearian messenger bringing glad tidings from the battlefield, 'I've fixed things up with the Rector.'

The faces which turned towards him at this news were variously surprised, uninterested, outraged or amused. The outrage came from Grace, who clutched her champagne glass as though for support and clenched her teeth to stop herself shouting. The group around her consisted of Nicholas, who went on looking benign, Doughty Strove, M.P., who looked his usual sullen self, and a number of tweeded friends, none of whom were as young as they liked to remember. Leslie knew exactly who they were. There stood Bridget Naboth, wife of Lord Naboth of Worsfield, one of the major local contributors to Party funds. With her was a thin, pink-faced man known to them all as the 'Contessa', who lived in a small Queen Anne house on the outskirts of Hartscombe with his aged mother and a magnificent collection of snuff-boxes (articles which a Royal aunt, on her occasional visits to Hartscombe, used to carry off as an expected tribute in her handbag after tea with the 'Contessa's' mother). There were two middle-aged sisters, enthusiastic gardeners, who were known as the Erskine girls, Uncle Cecil Fanner and Mrs Fairhazel, who, because she was the spare woman at every dinner party, carried gossip about the neighbourhood like a jungle telegraph.

'You know young Titmuss?' Nicholas smiled vaguely round the assembled company when no one seemed inclined to ask what had been fixed up with the Rector.

'Aren't you Elsie's boy?' Doughty Strove's memory went back to the days when Leslie's mother grew up in the kitchen at Picton House. 'Never get treacle tart nowadays like Elsie used to give us.'

'Titmuss is very active with the Young Conservatives now, Doughty. He speaks up at meetings.'

'Not for too long, I hope,' said Doughty, whose political philosophy had always been to avoid speaking up whenever possible. Try as he would Nicholas could think of no more small talk. He bit into a sandwich and steeled himself for his wife's inevitable question.

'What exactly have you fixed up?' She forced her teeth apart to inquire.

'Oh, the date of the wedding.' Leslie was matter of fact. 'Simeon Simcox has pencilled in the twenty-first of next month.'

'Getting married are you?' Doughty felt he should show an interest in their old cook's boy. 'Who's the lucky lady?'

'Who?' Leslie seemed amazed at the man's ignorance. 'Charlotte Fanner, of course.'

Bridget Naboth stood frozen in mid-sandwich. The Erskine girls gaped. Mrs Fairhazel's eyes shone with eager anticipation of a dozen dinner parties. Nicholas pulled a gold watch out of his waistcoat pocket and wished he had a train to catch. Grace stood motionless and closed her eyes; the thinly veined eyelids could be seen to tremble as Leslie returned to the attack.

'You know she doesn't want to be kept waiting,' he said. 'Very impatient girl, your Charlotte. Well, I can't be kept waiting either, can I, mother-in-law to be?'

Grace pulled herself together with an enormous effort. She opened her eyes cautiously and said, 'I rather think it's time we got back to the horses.' She was on the move and her group was prepared to trail obediently after her. Leslie almost had to shout after them.

'Sorry I can't join you. Got to find my people. My mother'll have all sorts of preparations to make.' And he added, for the particular benefit of Doughty Strove, M.P., 'Treacle tart and so on.'

'What do you imagine they all thought?'

'That we'd agreed to it, I suppose.'

'Of course they did. And furthermore, they must have got the strong impression that we wcrc holding a shot-gun to the repulsive head of the pimply Titmuss. I wish to God we were.'

'Well, I'm sorry. It took me completely by surprise.'

'I dare say it did, almost everything takes you completely by surprise, Nicholas. Well, it's put paid to the chances of Charlie slipping off somewhere under the cover of French lessons.'

'Couldn't we explain . . .?'

'Explain to that ghastly old Doughty Strove, and Bridget Naboth, who can't keep her mouth shut on any occasion, and your Uncle Cecil Fanner, who'll tell the entire family, and the "Contessa" and the Erskine girls, and that absolutely poisonous Fairhazel woman? Explain that Charlie's expecting by some village oik, and we have no intention of letting her marry? No. You'll have to *talk* to him.'

They were the words Nicholas dreaded. He was fully dressed, perched on the edge of his wife's bed, while she sat at the looking-glass, scrubbing at her face with fingerfuls of cottonwool and staring at herself with barely controlled despair. He had absolutely no desire to talk to Leslie Titmuss and no idea what to say to him.

'He's clearly only in it for the money.' Grace arched her eyebrows and sucked in her cheeks. Thank God, she thought, momentarily cheering herself up, I've still got my bones. Her bones, which in the past had seemed a sort of luxury, were fast becoming the sole comfort of her advancing age. 'See what he'll take to tell them it was some kind of ghastly practical joke. He can explain he was squiffy on the Steward's champagne or something. The little bugger simply has to be paid off even if it means selling woodland.' She did herself the kindness of switching off the light over her mirror and moved towards her bed. 'You'll be sleeping in your dressing-room, of course.'

'Of course.' Nicholas, getting the order for release, moved gratefully towards the door. 'I don't think you'll find he's got them, you know.'

'Got what?'

'Pimples.'

In fact the boy's skin, Nicholas thought when inevitably and at last they met, was remarkably pale but clear of all blemish. He had invited Leslie to tea on what he hoped was neutral ground, the lawn of the Hellespont Club, founded by Victorian rowing-men in a house which commands a fine view of the river. At Regatta time, white-haired ex-oarsmen, wearing the bright green socks and schoolboy caps of the Hellespont, together with yellow-ing flannels and blazers which no longer button across their stomachs, sit on the lawn drinking Pimms and lamenting the decline in rowing. Leslie, in his dark suit, burnished black shoes and remarkable pallor, seemed out of place in this setting. He was also, to Nicholas's amazement, extremely angry, and went into the attack with his eyes blazing before the waitress, who had brought them scones, was out of earshot.

'It's pretty hard on me. It really is.'

'Milk and sugar?' Nicholas was being 'mother'.

'Just two lumps. I'm just starting out, you see. I was going to make something of myself. I was going to leave the Brewery and go for my accountant's qualifications. Your daughter's put paid to all that. Now I'll have a family to see after.'

'Really, Titmuss!' Nicholas protested mildly as he handed the cup. 'What did she do? Ravish you or something?'

'Let's just say, she was very determined.'

Determination, Nicholas thought, was a characteristic of the women in his life. His Uncle Cecil had described Grace as a 'butterfly with a will of iron'. And the butterfly had made a dead set at him, a fact which he had never been able to explain. She didn't actually ravish him, of course, not as far as he could remember, but Grace's implacable persistence, when it came to the matter of marriage, made him able to understand Leslie's concern. He said, 'You pose us a bit of a problem, Titmuss. What on earth are we going to do about you?'

'What does Lady Fanner suggest?'

'I see you go straight to the heart of a matter. The family would be prepared to do something for you, of course. If we could regard the unfortunate incident as a bit of a joke.'

'What unfortunate incident?' Leslie was carefully balancing a spoonful of strawberry jam on his buttered scone.

'Your extraordinary behaviour at the Worsfield Show.'

'What would you be prepared to do?' Leslie bit into the scone and chewed steadily.

'I hardly know. What're your immediate needs?'

There was strawberry jam on Leslie's chin, bright and shiny as a drop of blood. Nicholas longed to lean forward and wipe it off with his paper napkin.

'Somewhere to live.' Leslie clearly had a list prepared. 'I can't stay with the old people for ever. And I've been taking the minutes when Kempenflatt's away, which he is the best half of the time. I'd like you to put in a word for me as Secretary of the Y.C.s with a place on the Local Executive. Oh, and I want to get a qualification and perhaps start my own business.'

Leslie wiped his own chin and Nicholas felt unreasonably relieved.

'And you'd agree to Charlie going away quietly?'

'Charlotte's never going to go away quietly.' Leslie smiled for the first time, and took a gulp of tea. 'You must know your daughter better than that. She's going to stay here and scream her head off, and she'll tell everyone what's happened. But I'm quite prepared to marry her, *if* you can see your way clear to helping us. Only thing is, one of you'll have to talk my old folks around, you know what they're like.'

'What?' Nicholas was frowning, feeling that he had lost his tenuous grasp of events.

'Oh.' Leslie's smile was wider and really quite charming. 'They're dead against me marrying Charlotte.'

Nicholas had not been looking forward to reporting the result of his interview with Leslie Titmuss to his wife. Accordingly he loitered on his way home, made a couple of calls in Hartscombe, visited the farm office, and when he reached Rapstone Manor at last, made straight for the conservatory. From there, he was surprised to see his wife and the Rector sitting out on the terrace, where Wyebrow was opening a bottle of champagne. It seemed that Simeon had been actively campaigning on behalf of the young couple. A long talk with Charlie had persuaded him that she would never abandon the idea of marrying Leslie. He had repeated his opinion of Leslie's bright future, based on legitimate ambition and tireless work, but his trump card had been the absence of other suitors for Charlie. Did Grace really want her daughter sharing their house for ever, permanently pining for Leslie Titmuss? For a while Charlie's mother sat in silence, considering this bleak prospect. Then she cautiously allowed that there might be two sides to every question. By the time her husband finally emerged to announce that he had no success in deflecting the determined Titmuss, she was persuaded to make the best of what might not be such a bad job after all. There would be no further need to explain away the extraordinary scene at Worsfield Show, and she might never have to listen to Charlie screaming again.

'Titmuss very nobly said he'd go through with it and marry Charlie,' Nicholas reported.

'Yes. That's what we've decided.'

'You've decided?' He felt like a man who has been sent out on a desperate mission to no man's land, only to return, bloodstained and exhausted, to be told that the peace was declared some time ago.

'Oh, for heaven's sake, have a glass of champagne. You can't discuss weddings without a glass of champagne. It's like having an operation without an anaesthetic. Get Wyebrow to bring out another glass.'

'I don't think you'll regret it,' Simeon smiled at them both. 'I'm sure Leslie Titmuss is going to make something of himself.'

'But what exactly?' Nicholas wondered.

'Something.' Grace was impatient. 'Does it really matter what? It's quite a relief to have it all settled.'

'Well, not quite settled.' Nicholas was still doubtful. 'It seems that someone's got to sell the idea to the Titmusses.'

*

Grace Fanner changed her mind frequently and each change was signalled by a burst of frenzied activity. Once she had decided on Charlie's wedding she wanted no delay and she certainly wanted no opposition. Accordingly she rang the musical chime on the front door of 'The Spruces' one morning, and was admitted by a somewhat flustered Elsie Titmuss who, in an overall and rubber gloves, was in the middle of washing up.

'I know exactly what it's like,' said Grace, to whom the home life of the Titmuss family was a mercifully closed book. 'Nothing but chores. All the time. Men do leave such a mess about the place, don't they? Come on, why don't we muck in together? You finish washing and I'll dry.' She was, to Elsie's considerable dismay, heading for the kitchen. 'And I do promise not to break anything.'

'Won't you take a seat, your Ladyship? I'll put the kettle on for a cup of tea.'

'Later. When we've earned it. Don't they do such amusing teacloths nowadays?' Grace had taken up one decorated with pictures of the Tower of London and was dabbing at a cup with it. 'Now do get on with the washing up, Mrs Titmuss, and we'll talk.'

'What exactly did you want to talk about?' Elsie, dazed and obedient, returned to the sink and plunged her rubber gloves into the Fairy Liquid. 'I do think the war made a tremendous difference to our lives, don't you?' Grace answered unexpectedly. Elsie, unaware of any profound change since V.E. day, felt vaguely guilty.

'It was terrible, of course. Absolutely terrible! But people did learn to muck in in the most marvellous way. Count on me, Mrs Titmuss, all hands to the pumps.'

So Elsie washed up the small number of breakfast dishes and laid them out on the draining-board, and Grace forgot to use the teatowel, releasing a flood of wartime reminiscences.

'Of course, I could've been an air-raid warden in Hartscombe, but who'd bother to bomb a few grocers' shops and the Brewery?' She remembered. 'My husband was away fighting for his country and I said, "Give me Worsfield!" Of course they were after the railways there, and they got the Cathedral. Worsfield was the place where you could get your tin hat blown off if you weren't too careful! I remember, one day in Corporation Street, it was really lovely sunshine, spring weather, and I was trudging along in my old tin hat and my boiler-suit and a truck, an American truck, passed and some doughboy leaned out and whistled at me! You know the way they did, terribly cheeky, of course, but quite appealing? And suddenly there was a terrific blast. It absolutely knocked me back into a shop doorway. Timothy Whites? I think it was Timothy Whites. And when I looked up the road, well, the truck had been hit. Smashed to pieces. Everyone in it dead. They looked so pale! He whistled at me and I was his last view of England. Well, that's where I learned to dry up. In the A.R.P. And help make sandwiches. I don't think we should ever forget what we learned in the war.' The reminiscence over, Grace stood, teatowel in hand, motionless and smiling. After a suitable and respectful pause Elsie asked almost fearfully, 'Have you come about Leslie and Miss Charlotte?'

'My husband and I have absolutely no doubt about it, Mrs Titmuss.' Grace woke from her reverie. 'We should see them married.'

'I don't know . . .' Elsie was still doubtful.

'And the Rector.'

'The Rector?' Elsie seemed startled at the mention of Simeon's name.

'Mr Simcox has gone into the whole thing most carefully and he's all for a wedding.'

'That's what Mr Simcox wants, is it?' Elsie asked, a little breathlessly.

'I told you, all for it.'

'Well, I suppose, if that's what the Rector wants . . .' It was as though, in Elsie Titmuss's opinion, God had spoken and there was no more to be said on the subject.

Charlie and Leslie went out for a picnic on the river. It was a sunny Saturday afternoon, but with a sharp smell of autumn and there were few other boats about. Charlie rowed the craft and Leslie steered expertly, past the Hellespont Club, where the tea tables were now deserted and the swans cruised malignantly, searching in vain for scraps of generously thrown scones or Dundee cake.

'Register office at Worsfield. No family. Couple of witnesses off the street. Then go for fish and chips. Afternoon in the Odeon. Don't let's do a single thing she wants.' Charlie spoke in short bursts, in time to the dipping of her oars. 'No Uncle Cecil Fanner. No Naboths. No horrible old "Contessa". No bridesmaids. No tent on the lawn.'

'We'll stop here,' Leslie told her, 'by the island.' The island was the site of a couple of bungalows, let to summer visitors, but now empty. In a few months the river would rise, flooding their gardens and loosening their kitchen linoleum. From their mooring the couple could see the Swan's Nest Hotel, the rocking punts and the landing-stage; the scene, as Leslie didn't fail to remind Charlie, of his great humiliation, a moment which he now appeared to treasure.

'You know what they thought,' he told her, when he had gone once again through the occasion which ended with him being sent home to his mother like a drowned rat. 'They thought that's the end of Elsie Titmuss's son, the boy who used to cut down nettles and hang around our kitchen.' Charlie wondered if he had ever cut Magnus Strove's nettles, but thought it better not to interrupt him. 'They're going to have to take that back, Charlie. They're going to have to take it all back.'

'Why bother about them at all? You shouldn't, you know.'

'I'm going to bother, I really am.' He looked at her and, as was rare with him, he was smiling. 'Let's make them put up a tent.'

'Perhaps marriage is the greatest test we are put to. That's what I tell my young couples. It's a case of facing up to your responsibility for the consequences of a single headstrong moment, when you may be drunk with the smell of orange blossom. How many of us think of the appalling consequences that may flow from a brief conversation in front of the altar?' Among the many wedding formalities which Leslie had insisted on was the preliminary chat with the Rector. They were gathered together in Simeon's study and Leslie listened intently as Charlie stared thoughtfully out of the window to where Dorothy was bent like an elegant and elderly croquet hoop in the border, making an early planting of winter pansies.

'That's what I say to all the young Jacks and Jills, the Harrys and the Doreens, the Leslies and the Charlottes,' Simeon assured them, although he seemed to be speaking mainly for the benefit of himself. 'The consequences may be quite unforeseen. You throw a pebble into a still pond and who knows where the ripples will end? They will end up far away, generations later, when you and your little stone will be quite forgotten. I know what you're going to ask, you're going to ask, where does God come in all this? Is God the ripples? Is God the pebble? Is God, as our Eastern friends would have us believe, simply the surface of the pond? Or are you God? Leslie and Charlotte. Are you creating a future which you have chosen not to control? Difficult, isn't it? Terribly difficult. We can only hope to do justice. Hope to . . .' Simeon's voice died away, apparently discouraged. He looked at Charlie and had to admit that no one could have called her beautiful; he turned back to Leslie Titmuss, and the task in hand. 'Of course, it's easy for you now Leslie, easy when Charlotte is in the bloom of youth. But when she's older, when she's tired of life, when she starts to be afraid of death, when her looks are vanishing it'll be difficult for you then, terribly difficult! That'll be the test.'

There was a prolonged and not particularly cheerful silence. Then Simeon knocked out his pipe with relief.

'Well now, at this stage, I usually offer my young couple a bottle of Simcox's light ale, or would you rather we strolled across to the pub for a pint of wallop?'

Nothing in the subsequent ceremony was to be as painful to Leslie and Charlotte as this act of preparation. In fact the day, when it came, appeared for both of them, and in their separate ways, to be a moment of triumph. Having made her mind up, Grace behaved as though her daughter's marriage came as the fulfilment of some long-held ambition. Nicholas greeted the guests with unfailing cheerfulness, and the 'friends of the bride', who filled most of the church, were delighted by the source of so much future speculation. Fred, who was spending long, penniless days and nights in his old room at the Rectory studying anatomy and human biology, had received a surprise visit from Leslie Titmuss, who was without a best man. 'Say you'll do it,' Leslie had begged him. 'For the sake of old times. Remember how we used to play together.' Fred couldn't recall many games with the infant Titmuss, but he had agreed to stand beside Leslie and hand him the ring. Apart from anything else, it was the only party he seemed likely to be asked to for the rest of that year.

So Leslie had everything he had stipulated, including a tent. During the course of the celebrations, Nicholas, looking across at the bride and hoping as always for the best, said he thought Charlie looked really quite handsome in his grandmother's lace.

'Do you, Nicholas?' Grace asked him with exaggerated patience. 'I'll tell you one thing she doesn't look.'

'What's that?'

'Pregnant.'

Chapter Fourteen
THE COAST

Henry took Agnes to the Coast not once but on several occasions before and after the making of *The Greasy Pole*. They travelled first class at the expense of the various production companies with which Mr Bugloss was connected, and were met at Los Angeles airport by a limousine long enough and black enough to accommodate, Agnes thought, a lengthy coffin and any number of mourners. They were put up at the Beverly Hills Hotel, where the telephone operators instantly knew their names and the staff constantly told Agnes to have a nice day, an instruction she received with an ironic smile. Henry lay in the sun, bought 'leisure-wear' in the hotel man's shop and looked to Agnes as if he were always dressed for a cruise. He telephoned his agent a good deal from the side of the pool, and, from time to time, looked anxiously at Agnes, wondering if she found the place awful enough to be enjoyable.

'It's the wonderful thing about writing,' he told her defensively, 'you can write a little novel about Simcox's Brewery, and it'll transport you to the other side of the world.'

'I know it's a miracle.' And Agnes gave him the smile which seemed to him to say, I'm awfully sorry that you can't see the joke.

On one of their visits, Mr Bugloss took them to lunch at a then fashionable restaurant on the Strip. All around them producers and agents rose from their tables like surfacing sealions to greet each other with loud honks of recognition, embraced each other with their flippers, and then sank back, gurgling towards their lunch.

'Jack Polefax, I don't believe it!' Mr Bugloss stood and grabbed a very small, grey-haired man who was about to join a similar man waving to him from another table. 'I just want you guys to meet Jack, who *is* Galaxy International.' Mr Bugloss's American accent, hardly noticeable in Shepperton Studios or the Dorchester Hotel, flowered and darkened in the sun. 'Henry Simcox wrote *The Greasy Pole*. My last picture.'

'You a writer?' Polefax spoke, with a sort of pity, a line which caused Mr Bugloss intense amusement. 'Don't let him kid you! Don't kid him, Jack. Everyone knows Henry Simcox, or they will after the next one. He's just come up with this terrific idea.'

'My God! Can you believe who's here? Julie. Julie Salario. Isn't that incredible?' Mr Polefax had spied a corpulent and balding man semaphoring desperately from a distant table, and Agnes wondered why the sight of their old friends, whom they had presumably known for years, should fill Hollywood producers with such amazement. 'I just have to go over to greet Julie. Great to meet you, Mr Simcox.' He nodded towards Agnes. 'Like to have you both come up to the house for Sunday brunch. Laurel Canyon. Get Benny to bring you.' And he was off, hallooing, 'Julie! Long time no see you at all.'

The waiter hung with chains and silver tasting-cups was hovering now, and Mr Bugloss greeted him as warmly as though he were a film producer. 'And right now, Charles,' he said, 'we could use one of your great vodka martinis.'

'I'd like some wine.' Agnes knew that if she didn't get a word in early she'd be condemned to a cocktail and iced water.

'A couple of vodka martinis, Charles.' Benny Bugloss knew that Henry had taken on the customs of the Coast. 'And bring us some nice wine.' As the waiter retreated, he went on, without drawing breath. 'You know, I've always been pretty close to Jack. When I visit the Galaxy lot, when I'm in the Commissary there, Jack will invariably come up and take me by the arm.'

'What's that a sign of?' Agnes asked.

'It's a sign that if we play our cards correctly we may get Galaxy International to distribute Henry's next movie.'

'I hadn't heard about his next movie.' Agnes looked at Henry, who wasn't giving away the fact that he hadn't heard about it either.

'Why do you think I brought you two over here again? Henry and I, my dear, are about to cook the perfect hamburger.'

'You're going in for catering?' Agnes sounded innocent, and Henry frowned.

'I speak in metaphor of the American dish that all the world loves to eat. *Pole* was fine. Good business in Britain. O.K. critical reception here. But what did it do in Tokyo? And in South America we couldn't give it away. What we need is the hamburger. We cook it right here in town and they pay to eat it in Japan and Rio and Iowa and Hong Kong – all those territories. I tell you, my dear, I have the title of the perfect hamburger. And I have had the foresight to bring it with me.'

At which Mr Bugloss put his hand in his pocket and proudly brought out a paperback edition of *The Canterbury Tales*.

'That's the perfect hamburger?' Agnes was surprised.

'I want it updated,' Mr Bugloss told Henry. 'I want you to bring out the erotic aspect. And I want these pilgrims to come from all over: Rome, Paris, New York, Tokyo. You see, each territory has its own story. That way we get the international appeal.'

'And they all end up in Canterbury?' Agnes asked.

'That is not necessary. Henry should feel free. There are people in this town who have no idea where the hell Canterbury is.'

'You mean they're all engaged in some sort of quest?' Agnes's tone of serious inquiry brought Henry no comfort.

'You've got it! A quest!' Benny Bugloss looked triumphantly at Henry. 'You see, Agnes likes the idea.'

'Well, they've always been good stories,' Henry said, and

Agnes turned on him, still asking as though for information, 'You mean, you think it's a good idea, Henry?'

'Nothing wrong with them as stories,' Henry repeated as Mr Bugloss gave the idea the final accolade.

'And it's in public domain! *Canterbury Tales* is our hamburger!'

'What's Henry have to do? Put on the ketchup? Will you excuse me a moment?' Agnes stood up and smiled down on the producer.

'Go ahead, my dear. You want to powder your nose?'

Before she went through the door marked 'Señoritas' Agnes had no fixed plan of campaign but when she was safely locked in the hispanically tiled cubicle, breathing in carbolic and air freshener, she decided that she must at all costs avoid returning to Mr Bugloss's table. She couldn't bear to see Henry mutely accepting some great storyline for Chaucer's hamburger and she was afraid of the pieces of her mind that she might be tempted to throw at Mr Bugloss. She couldn't go back and yet her only way of escape lay through the restaurant. Suddenly, in need of air, she pushed open the window of her cubicle and saw, only a few feet down, the lot used for Valet Parking. Without a moment's thought she climbed on to the seat and was out of the window and walking to freedom.

Walking was, of course, an unknown folly on the Sunset Boulevard of the early sixties. As she passed the Body Shop and the Cock and Bull, as she walked under the huge signs advertising the latest movies and the most lavish burial grounds, people stared at her from car windows, and cops regarded her with deep suspicion. Agnes walked unconcerned, as though she were in the woods round Rapstone, unconscious of the office towers and the palm trees with the rustle of rats among their high, grey leaves. A vista of hills, as beautiful as the background of an Italian painting, could be seen hovering above the smog, and Agnes's eyes were stinging and her feet aching as she set out for the pink and green palace which had become her improbable home.

While she was walking her desperation evaporated. Alone she felt safe, as she had once felt with Henry when he took over her and her problems, told her, with comforting certainty, exactly what she was going to do and arranged for her to do it. Henry had found the softly spoken German doctor in Belsize Park who had ended her pregnancy like a common cold. When she was then afflicted by an extraordinary loneliness, as if, single-handed, she had unpeopled the world, Henry had suggested journeys, aeroplane tickets and flights to the sunshine at the expense of Benjamin K. Bugloss. She had been pleased to be with him, and glad to put the greatest possible distance between herself and her old home, the surgery, the woods, Tom Nowt's hut and even Arturo's coffee bar, which seemed to her now to belong to a world of disappointment and death.

What surprised her was the amount of time that passed before Henry made love to her. She had assumed that she wasn't going to be taken abroad merely for the sake of friendship, but for a long while Henry booked separate bedrooms, kissed her goodnight at her door and talked to her about everything but themselves. It was as though her progress through so many airport lounges and hotel lobbies was a sort of process of churching and he was waiting for her to recover and be purged from the ministrations of not only the doctor in Belsize Park but his brother Frederick also.

As time and distance separated her increasingly from home Agnes became more confident, less dependent on Henry for the organization of her life and, strangely, fonder of him. He wasn't she noticed, half so self-confident as he liked to let on. He would arrive unnecessarily early at airports (Agnes had a distinct taste for catching everything by the skin of her teeth) and as he checked in she often noticed that his hands were sweating. He had an initial lack of confidence about his writing, and would only feel secure when it had been enjoyed by someone. It didn't seem to matter who praised it and Agnes, who at first enjoyed voicing her views, found that the good opinions of a secretary who re-typed the first draft were equally consoling to Henry. When she told him, as she thought, that *The Greasy Pole* was much better as a book than it ever became as a movie, he flew into a defensive rage and shouted at her in a way which she found almost touchingly helpless and quite unalarming. It seemed that Henry had pinned all his faith on Mr Bugloss as the first principle and guiding spirit of their new way of life and all his anti-Bugloss stories, of which he had many, were like jokes made by devout Catholics about the Virgin Birth. In his favour it should be said that Mr Bugloss had finally produced a sensible and well-received adaptation of *The Greasy Pole* which greatly enhanced Henry's reputation throughout the world.

Henry's second novel, which came out four or five months after their first visit to Los Angeles, was, inevitably, less well-regarded and, after a scene which left him almost speechless with despair, Mr Bugloss announced that he didn't see it as a movie property. It was then that Agnes and Henry began to make love, and if she knew she was, perhaps, only second best to a rave review, she felt pleased to repay the debt she was sure she owed him. Everything about going to bed with Henry surprised her, his gentleness, his curious lack of invention, something she hadn't expected in a writer, and his obvious need of her. It was a need she found touching but it left her, at times, remote. When she thought of Fred, which she did as little as possible, she remembered their love-making as a silent voyage of self-discovery. In bed with his elder brother she was discovering almost all there was to be known about Henry, for he was rarely silent before, during or after the act of coition. Listening to him and sensing the insecurity beneath his most extravagant boasting she fell into a trap which she thought afterwards that she of all people should have avoided. She wanted to improve Henry.

So she began to resent his trips to the Coast, his adaptations for Mr Bugloss which earned money but rarely got made into films, and Henry felt himself subject to her judgement which became the more intolerable as he came secretly to agree with it.

So their quarrels started, because she couldn't resist saying what she thought and he couldn't forgive her for it. They were tempestuous quarrels, for which Henry showed a dramatic talent, and sometimes she thought they brought them closer to each other. She couldn't remember a time when she had seriously quarrelled with Fred.

As she walked she remembered the awful evening at the Barrel of Biscuits in Worsfield which she had enjoyed in Fred's company, and wondered why the awfulness of the Hollywood restaurant gave her no pleasure. She wanted to be alone, to sleep, not to have to make conversation or pass judgement any more that day.

'Having a nice day?' the hotel doorman asked when she arrived and she told him, 'No, not particularly.'

In the restaurant, Benny Bugloss said, 'She's missing her wine.' Henry looked towards the 'Señoritas' with a kind of desperation, fearing that Agnes's failure to emerge was not due to illness or any natural cause but merely to contempt.

'I walked.'

'Don't be silly. No one walks here.'

'Somebody does.'

'You were a great help! You left me looking ridiculous.'

'You were looking ridiculous before I left. Agreeing with all that rubbish.'

Henry had found Agnes lying on a chair by the pool with her eyes closed. He thought she was pretending to be asleep. Around them on the towelling-covered day-beds, or under the yellow canopies of their private tents, lay men in bathing-trunks and women in flowered bathing-caps who were pursuing the great poolside sport of making telephone calls. One old fellow shouted greetings into the phone cupped in his shoulder, while his hands kneaded suntan oil into a woman's back. The tannoy announced names wanted for other telephone calls: 'Mr Irving Lazar, Mr Richard Zanuck, Mr Ed Pringle, Miss Gwenda Grammercy . . . to the telephone, please.'

Henry had told Agnes that some actors paid their agents substantial retainers to make these calls so that their names might be heard regularly around the pool at the Beverly Hills Hotel and Agnes thought of them going on remorselessly long after the actor had given up and left the profession, perhaps after he was dead.

'It's very easy for you, isn't it?' Henry told her. However angry he was he still kept his voice down so as not to disturb the half-naked telephoners around them. 'Oh yes. You can be so prim and superior and despise Benny Bugloss from a great height! You don't have to pay the bills.'

'You don't have to pay them like that.'

'I have to pay them.'

Agnes swung her legs off the side of the day-bed and sat up. As she spoke the twittering of telephone calls subsided, the sunbathers had begun to listen.

'Pay them by creeping and crawling to old Benny, my dear, by turning Chaucer into a hamburger, by having your arm squeezed by Jack Baby? You know what? I'd rather die than go to lunch in Laurel Canyon with a lot of old men in necklaces and women with heads covered in rubber flowers.'

'Why do you have to be so difficult?' Henry sounded genuinely puzzled.

'I don't know, I don't know why I have to be.' She stood up, snatched at her towelling dressing-gown and put it on. 'What did you honestly think when you took me on, that I was going to be easy?'

She ran away from him, past the now silent telephoners, past the puzzled Swede who was carefully folding yellow towels, past the dusty, luxuriant flowerbeds and past the great banana leaves on the wallpaper of their bedroom corridor. And Henry came after her with what dignity he could muster, moving as quickly as he could without looking as though he were chasing a woman from the pool. Once in the shadows of the hotel he made up speed and was able to put his weight against their bedroom door just as Agnes was trying to push it shut.

'You've got a short memory,' he said, when they were in the bedroom together. The calm way he spoke was calculated to drive her to distraction.

'What are you talking about?'

'The time when working for Ben Bugloss paid for what you wanted.'

'What I wanted?'

'Got you out of trouble. My little brother's trouble. You were desperate!'

'You think I'm not desperate now?'

'Agnes!' By now he was smiling at her. 'You're so self-indulgent!'

'*Me?*'

'Enjoying the luxury of feeling desperate in the Beverly Hills Hotel.'

It was a false, even a monstrous accusation; she had only wanted to save Henry from himself or at least from Mr Bugloss and his absurd pilgrimage.

She had no answer but to attack him, hitting him, scratching his neck, her fists pummelling him uselessly. He held her and they stumbled among the pink table-lamps, between the sofa and the bamboo tables, in front of pictures of fishing boats at sunset, until they fell, almost by accident, across the kingsized bed, and so their daughter Francesca was eventually conceived.

While his elder brother was away on the Coast, Fred was working towards the end of the long process of turning himself into a doctor, which seemed at times hopeless, exciting, unbearably tedious, rewarding, futile and all he had ever wanted to do. He lived in the lecture halls and dissecting rooms of his London hospital, slept, mostly alone, in a room he found in Battersea, and went back to Rapstone whenever he could to get his clothes mended, his stomach filled and to be exasperated by his mother and father. Although he felt it was perfectly normal that he should find it dull to visit Simeon and Dorothy, he expected them to be more enthusiastic about having him to stay. When he was in the country he went riding with Agnes's father, or joined the Doctor on his rounds to discover how different the theories he had learnt at St Thomas's were from the practice of medicine in the sick rooms of Hartscombe and the Rapstone Valley.

'It seems Agnes has deserted both of us,' Dr Salter said.

Fred often sat in the Doctor's living-room, a place which looked shabby by day but comfortable at night when the fire was lit, the stains on the wallpaper hidden, and the light fell softly on paintings of shot game and long-dead horses. They drank brandy and listened to gramophone records, Elgar and Brahms, and the scratchy voices of music-hall performers, Will Hay, Robb Wilton and Max Miller, at whom the Doctor would laugh until his eyes filled with tears and he had to dab at them with a huge silk handkerchief.

'Have you any idea why she should desert us?' Fred, to whom any talk of Agnes was like tearing at an open wound, didn't answer. 'You prefer not to say?' Dr Salter looked at him with his diagnostic expression. 'I'm not sure I approve of that. Our secrets have an awful sort of immortality, they return to haunt us. They went off to America did you say?'

'That's what Henry said.'

'Of course you'll miss her now, just as I missed my Annie. She didn't fall in love with my brother, not that I ever had a brother. She was unfaithful to me with a flying bomb. I thought I'd never get over it, but in time, you know, there can be compensations.'

'Compensations?'

'The silence all over the house, stretching your legs across an empty bed, an end to all the responsibility of being loved.'

'Is that a responsibility?'

'Oh yes, the greatest responsibility of all. It was really too much for you, wasn't it?'

One summer holiday Fred was with Dr Salter in a widow's house in Sunday Street, a small row of Victorian cottages that ran behind the Brewery and down to the river. Mrs Amulet was dying with quiet determination, and they had been discussing how much she should be told of her condition. Then Dr Salter had gone upstairs alone and Fred stood in the sunlit patch of garden. Among the hollyhocks and geraniums he saw, against the wall of the house, a small tombstone, of the sort that is erected for a child. Fred read the inscription on it:

IN MEMORY OF TEDDY
A TINY MARMOSET
BELOVED OF COLIN AND KATE AMULET
DEPARTED THIS LIFE THE 23RD OF MARCH 1948
WE SHALL MEET BUT WE SHALL MISS YOU

'An evilly disposed ape,' Dr Salter said when he came out of the house. 'Not house-trained, of course, and with an appalling liver condition. Spent more time and trouble trying to keep Teddy alive than Kate Amulet would want me to waste on her.'

'Does she know?'

'Oh yes.'

'You told her?'

'No. No, I didn't tell her.' They walked towards the gate. 'I shall have to tell you though.'

'Tell me. What?'

'It's difficult to know when to give out the bad news about death or marriage. It's often best to let the patient draw his own conclusions.'

'Marriage?' In the small, sunlit garden, among the hollyhocks, Fred felt as cold and helpless as the old woman upstairs.

'A lady Baptist minister married them, in a place called San Bernardino. The cable was full of unnecessary detail. Must have cost a fortune.'

'Did she want you to tell me?' Fred asked.

'She didn't say.'

The next day Simeon and Dorothy had a similar cable from Henry. His mother put a hand on Fred's arm and said, 'Poor boy. Poor old Fred.' She was smiling as she said it, but it seemed to him that her eyes were full with tears, something he didn't remember ever having seen before.

Chapter Fifteen

LIVING IN THE PAST

That year the papers were full of extraordinary news; more and more scandals were unearthed, and the serious face of the nation cracked into an incredulous smile of second-hand delight, before prim looks returned and there was much talk of the need to preserve standards in public life. The Secretary of State for War was found to be sharing a mistress with a Soviet naval attaché but this was only the aperitif before a banquet of revelations which culminated in the search for a mysterious masked figure, some person of great political distinction who, naked but for his mask, was said to act as butler and enjoy other humiliations at the dinner parties of the rich and influential figures of the time. The masked man serving the potatoes was never identified but the golden age of Conservative Government, the period when the Prime Minister had told the British people that they had never had it so good and they had believed him, seemed about to disintegrate into a widespread chorus of unseemly giggles.

Charlie Titmuss read all this news with delight each morning before she went off to pursue her social welfare course at Worsfield Polytechnic. But her husband was unsmiling and refrained from comment, as though he felt it was too early, even at their breakfast table, for him to commit himself on a great national issue, and one which, he felt, might have a considerable influence on the future of Leslie Titmuss.

In the evenings he would get home from work as soon as possible and listen to the news in the cottage Nicholas had given them, plainly furnished with Charlie's childhood books and photographs of ponies, and with few signs of Leslie's occupancy. He studied advanced accountancy while his wife drank beer in the Worsfield pubs with a group from the Poly and gossiped about problem families and their favourite delinquents.

'We can all understand your wife taking up welfare,' Elsie said when she brought a basket of her son's clean shirts round one evening. 'Even if she's never going to take up ironing. She's got to have something to look after. Ever since it turned out to be a false alarm about the baby.'

'It's not a bad thing for a politician's wife to be in the welfare service. It does no harm at all.'

'I never heard of Mrs Strove being interested in anyone's welfare when she was alive. I never heard of that at all.' Elsie had brought some homemade rock cakes for Leslie's tea and she was putting them out on a plate.

'You must have known old Doughty Strove pretty well?' Leslie asked his mother casually.

'Since I was eighteen and in service.' Leslie looked pained at the word 'service', but cheered up when his mother added, 'Quite a lad was Doughty, in his younger years.'

'What's that mean?' Leslie took a rock cake and buttered it. 'One for the girls?'

'Well, he'd come down to the kitchen for a slice of pie, something to take out shooting, and he'd try and put an arm round you, all that sort of nonsense. You wouldn't believe it, would you? Not looking at him now.' Elsie had made tea for Leslie, something she understood him not doing for himself before his wife came home, and now she poured him a cup.

'Was there anyone in particular?'

'Well, they did say Bridget Bigwell. It was all just talk.'

'Go on!' Leslie smiled, sugaring his tea.

'Bridget worked at Picton House, you know. Then she left to go to the Fanners and married Percy and had Glenys, well all on top of each other! I don't suppose there was anything in it.'

'Glenys Bigwell! She does typing for the Rector.'

'Glenys was a bright girl. Always seemed bright above her station, as you might say.'

'The Rector said she can't spell. Perhaps she inherited that from Doughty Strove!'

'No.' Elsie sat beside her son, delightedly shocked at the suggestion. 'It's talk, most likely. They were all the same, though. The young men in those days. Not enough to do and too much money to do it with.'

'*All* the young men?'

'All the same, all tarnished with the same brush. Of course, I mean the gentry.'

Leslie was munching rock cakes and looking at his mother. 'What about the Rector?'

'Mr Simcox was different.' Elsie smiled distantly. 'He was always different from all the rest.'

'In the old days. When they never got about much. Well, before the invention of the bicycle, Skurfield stayed Skurfield, and Rapstone never left its frontiers and their inhabitants simply bred with each other!' Another authority on the past of the district, Dr Salter was instructing Fred as they rode together up Picton Ridge. 'Cousins with cousins. Closer than that sometimes. Well, rabbits don't stop to ask, "Excuse me, but are you my sister by any chance?" and yet they're perfectly lively little creatures.'

Fred rode a little behind him, mounted on a small stolid hack from the riding-stable, a great deal slower than the big, black, nervous hunter, a new acquisition from the Worsfield Show, on which the Doctor was turning in the saddle, shouting back against the wind. 'Can't see all that in-breeding did much harm. They cut down their own trees, managed to turn very decent chair legs in the huts they put up in the beech woods. Look at the dates on the tombstones in your old father's churchyard, they lived far beyond any reasonable time for living. Of course

the bicycle changed all that. Then they got over to the next
village and rogered girls they weren't even related to. In the old
days there were Nowts in Skurfield and Bigwells in Rapstone,
and that was about the size of it.'

'I was thinking about Tom Nowt.'

'Oh, were you?'

'I just wondered why my father's always so against him. I
remember, when I was a child, the fuss he made when I went to
his old hut.'

'His hut?' Dr Salter sounded puzzled.

'His hut in the woods, you must know it?'

'I don't think so.'

'But I was there! When I got back from London and Agnes
had gone off with Henry to that Coast of theirs. It was where
you found me. By Tom's hut!'

'A hut in the woods?'

They had come to the top of the ridge. Their walking mounts
snorted and rolled their yellow eyes, quivering neurotically.

'I didn't notice.' Dr Salter kicked his hunter and galloped
away, a stocky figure sitting stolidly in the saddle. Fred followed
as best he could. He was never entirely at his ease with horses.

After another ride, and before another Sunday lunch, the bell
rang and Fred opened the Doctor's front door to discover Agnes
standing on the step and smiling. She had come without her key
and apologized to him, and he, looking down at her swollen
stomach, managed to congratulate her.

'I'm sorry. I so wanted you to be there,' Fred heard her say,
and was about to hug her gratefully when he realized that she
had not said it to him but to her father, who had come more
slowly down the stairs behind him.

'I was there in spirit,' Dr Salter said.

'In San Bernardino, with this female minister telling us to
take God into the bedroom with us? I don't think you were there
at all.' Then she kissed her father and they began to walk up the
stairs together. 'Henry's in London, writing very hard, so I just

came down to collect a few things. I will stay for lunch of course, if you ask me. Is it Mrs Beasley's mince? I thought of that so much in California, we used to get jumbo-sized prawns and jumbo-sized tomatoes. It all tasted of cottonwool and I used to think of Mrs Beasley's grey mince which tasted of good, honest dishwater.'

All through lunch Agnes was cheerful and unusually talkative. 'I haven't talked for so long,' she told them. 'You can't talk to American film producers, they just talk to themselves and expect you to listen.' She told them about lunch with Mr Bugloss and climbing out of the window of the 'Señoritas'. 'The last three years, we seem to have gone to the Coast so often and sucked up to Mr Bugloss. It isn't writing for Henry, really it isn't, it's more like interior decorating. But Henry's running away from Mr Bugloss too now, he's writing another novel.' Fred thought of Henry's soul, and the way it was always being saved for him. Then Agnes said, 'It's going to be extremely good. Don't say you're sorry to hear that.'

'I didn't.' Fred denied it.

'You did nearly. You'd've hated yourself if you had, wouldn't you?'

Later, in her old bedroom, Fred helped Agnes pack the clothes and books she needed. He was sorry that there were so few of them, and that their little time together would soon be over. She was silent for a long while, and then she said, 'Why have you moved in here?'

'I haven't.'

'Not yet, but why do you spend so much time with him? Why are you always helping him, why?'

'I suppose because he's teaching me.'

'Teaching you what?'

'All I want to know.'

'All?'

'Almost all.'

'It's not because of me? I couldn't bear that.'

'It's not because of you.'

'I mean that'd be like living in the past, wouldn't it?' She crammed the remaining things into her suitcase. 'Condemning yourself to stay still all the time. You wouldn't do that, would you?'

She was struggling, unusually agitated, with the suitcase and he closed it for her. As he carried it downstairs he asked her if Henry was pleased, looking again at the distended stomach which she had told him made her feel ridiculously helpless.

'Would you be pleased? I mean if you were Henry?'

'If I were Henry I have no idea what I'd feel.'

When she had gone, Fred did his best to forget Agnes and Henry and their expected child. This left him short of an obsession and he began to concern himself irrationally with the question of Tom Nowt. Why had Dr Salter pleaded ignorance when reminded of old Tom's hut and why, he wondered after so many years, had the place been forbidden to him as a child? He found Simeon, one day, sleeping in his study, or at least stretched out in his chair with his eyes closed in an attitude which he always called 'thinking up a sermon'. As the door closed, his father woke with a start.

'What do you still find to tell them in sermons?' Fred asked. 'When I was a child I can't remember you giving me any advice at all. Or only once.'

'Once?'

'When you told me not to go to Tom Nowt's hut.'

'Nowt's hut? I really can't recall.'

'I'm sure you can. Whatever was wrong with going there?'

'When did you expect to qualify?' Simeon climbed out of his chair and felt in his pocket for a pipe.

'In about three years with any luck.'

'I can't see how it can take all that time to learn Salter's trade. All he does is tell me not to cling on to life and then gives me a couple of aspirins. Oh, and he tipples my brandy.'

'But about Tom Nowt's hut . . .'

'Some people, I'm sure you'll find this out, bring bad luck.' Fred realized that any answer that might be coming his way would be lost in the mists of a sermon. 'That's the point of my sermon. God put such a lot of luck in the universe. Sometimes He seems to have thought He was creating an immense casino. I'm not suggesting that there's anything essentially evil about Tom Nowt, it's just that people like that provoke accidents.'

It wasn't until a weekend visit much later that Fred met the provoker of accidents in the public bar of the Baptist's Head. It was a crowded Saturday night with the pints of Simcox's Best slopping as the drinkers pushed their way from the bar and Fred found himself squashed into a corner inappropriately shouting the question that concerned him.

'The old hut?' Tom answered, grinning over his beer. 'Picked up a bit of something new, have you?'

'No. It's just that Dr Salter . . .'

'Keep out of the man's way. They reckon he'll see you off quicker than a shot-gun in the chest.'

'Ever been to your hut, has he? I mean, has he ever taken anyone there?'

'No questions, boy, then you won't get no lies.'

Fred considered the matter and decided on another line of inquiry. 'What've they all got against you, Tom?'

'Who?'

'My father, I remember how angry he was when I told him I'd been there. And Dr Salter says he's never heard of the place . . .'

'Don't forget her bloody Ladyshit.'

'Grace?'

'Wanted me in the nick. Well, of course, she had her reasons.'

'What reasons?'

'You want to know?'

'Yes.'

'And you're really not meeting up with a young lady?'

'I promise you. No young lady.'

'Then we'd better show you, hadn't we?' Tom held out his empty mug for a refill and said, as though it was part of his request for another drink, 'It's time you got blooded.'

Before Fred could ask for any further explanation, he saw Terry Fawcett, clarinet player of the Stompers, pushing his way towards them. It seemed they were all going on together in Terry's muddy and battered old Zephyr Zodiac. They called at a big and rather melancholy pub by Hartscombe station to collect Den Kitson, and had a surprising number of shorts for which Fred found himself paying. No one seemed prepared to tell him if the evening was to be devoted to drink or music; there was no further mention of blood, and as they came out of their final pub, the Badger at Skurfield, he had ceased to care. Den and Fred sat in the back of the Zephyr. Tom Nowt was in the front with Terry, who drove down the narrow lanes with the dark hedgerows whipping the sides of his old banger with untrimmed branches. Terry began to sing softly; Den joined in and Fred beat out a rhythm, slapping the worn plastic on the seat beside him: 'I don't stay out late. Don't want to go. I'm home about eight. Just me and my radio.' The dark shapes of trees, the straightening of a bend in the road, told Fred, who had known this landscape all his life, that they were going to Mandragola. This was a ruined farmhouse at the head of a hidden, isolated valley, a long stretch of woodland, fields and patches of grassland which had never been cultivated by the Stroves, who owned the land, so that it was rich in butterflies, shells, wild flowers and small strawberries, as well as scrub, brambles, rabbit warrens and hawthorn bushes. Soon Fred saw the shape of the farmhouse walls, and a few cottages with broken windows and fallen-in roofs which Doughty had never found the money to repair, and then the car turned and bumped down a rutted woodland track. They heard owls hoot and saw squirrels scuttle across the road.

Then, at the edge of a wood at the corner of an abandoned field, Terry stopped the car and switched off the lights. Tom put a stop to the singing. They sat for a long while in a silence which was incomprehensible to Fred, and then he heard a faraway rustling sound. Tom nodded and got out with Den. When they came back from a quiet visit to the car boot they were both carrying rifles. They sat with their barrels pointing out of the windows, so that the car looked like an old man-of-war, as Terry started the engine and it creaked slowly forward along the track. The lights were still off and the darkness of the wood seemed to press against them like fog. 'Stop,' Tom whispered, as though he had heard something else, and, after a long silence, 'Now!'

When Terry snapped on the full beam of the headlights, the woodland ride in front of them was lit up like a pantomime transformation scene and dazzled, staring motionless into the glare of the lights, was a tall deer crowned with antlers. It seemed to Fred to stand wide-eyed for a long time before the rifles cracked and it sank gently, reverently, to its knees in front of the car. He felt Den take his arm and pull him out and saw Tom take out his knife and go for the animal's throat. Then a bloody thumb was on his forehead, and he was initiated as brutally as a child who sees its first kill on the hunting-field.

After Simeon Simcox died, Kevin Bulstrode (Kev the Rev. to Henry Simcox) moved into the old Rectory from which he could direct religious operations at Rapstone, Skurfield and Picton Principal. The Bulstrode children fought and screamed and slept in the rooms Fred and Henry had once occupied, and Mrs Bulstrode held her meetings: 'Women for the Priesthood', 'Women against Discrimination' and 'Women against Rape' ('Are there any women *for* rape, I wonder?' Dorothy had murmured when she heard of the last organization) in the big drawing-room. Kevin Bulstrode took over the old Rector's study. He felt a little in awe of the place at first, calling it the Holy of Holies, and then complained, only half joking, of the fact that no journalists came to ask *his* opinion on every subject from punk hairdo's to the Resurrection. He was, he often said, only a simple parish priest, and not in the Top Ten of popular parsons.

Kevin Bulstrode was not entirely easy with what was left of Simeon's possessions; in particular the bust of Karl Marx appeared, at times, to regard him with a sort of lofty disdain and he was afraid that the Rural Dean, or even the Bishop, might call and find it inappropriate. Accordingly, he packed the bearded head and a large number of Simeon's books, pamphlets and assorted papers into tea-chests and lodged them in the attic, telling Dorothy that perhaps she would send someone to fetch them whenever it was convenient.

'Oh you can keep Karl Marx if you care for him,' she said. 'I have so little room now in my minute house in Hartscombe.'

'I'm so glad you've settled in comfortably.' Kevin did, in fact, look considerably relieved. There was a long period when he feared that Simeon's widow was going to be as much a fixture at the Rectory as the joint author of the Communist Manifesto. 'Of course we were worried about how you'd manage, particularly when we heard that Simeon has left everything to Mr Titmuss.'

'Don't worry, Mr Bulstrode. I had a little something of my own.' They were talking in the church where Dorothy still came regularly to do the flowers. The air was heavy with pollen and the dust from old hassocks.

'To leave everything to a Conservative cabinet minister!' Kevin Bulstrode pursed his lips in enjoyable speculation. 'It seems so unlike the Simeon we knew and loved.'

'I suppose he thought he should be fair, even to Conservative cabinet ministers.'

Dorothy's house was indeed small, a flint cottage in a side street. She settled in quickly, Dora Nowt came and did for her, and she thought that the house might have some advantages over the old Rectory. It was going to be impossible for her to have Henry and Lonnie to stay, for instance, and she'd hardly be able to squeeze any number of old parishioners in for tea. In fact, with any luck, she'd be left alone with her patch of front garden.

'I thought a real cottage garden,' she told Fred. 'Cabbages and roses together, and sweet peas all mixed up with the runner beans. I could never do that at the Rectory. Your father had an unusually tidy mind for a Christian Socialist.'

'It's a bit of luck you have the house.'

'And a few investments Simeon's Aunt Pauline left me.'

'Did Simeon's Aunt Pauline leave you the house? I can't remember.'

As always at the mention of financial transactions Dorothy looked vague and withdrawn, as though the conversation had suddenly taken an improper turn. She took the head of a holly-hock between her fingers and looked down on it with mild disapproval. 'Oh yes,' she said. 'I think so, don't you?'

It was only then that Fred saw something which made him remember standing with Dr Salter in the same small garden so many years before. There was the white headstone, almost covered with ivy, against the wall of the house. Half the inscription was hidden, but he could still read . . . MORY OF TEDDY . . . INY MARMOSET. Then he realized that they were in the house in Sunday Street, where Mrs Amulet and her monkey had both departed this life.

'Are you going to cut back the ivy?' he asked his mother. 'Make a feature of it?'

'Poor monkey's grave!' Dorothy shook her head. 'I think we should let it hide itself in decent obscurity.'

It was some time later, when Dr Fred was examining Jackson Cantellow as an insurance risk, taking his blood pressure and listening to the cavernous chest of the solicitor, that the question of Simeon's will was mentioned again. 'I don't believe we'll ever explain your father's will. The old Rector moved in a mysterious way, his wonders to perform. Of course it was lucky your mother had a few investments, and the house in Sunday Street.'

And Fred, who had just asked Jackson Cantellow to pull up his trousers and hop on the scales, said, 'Didn't Great Aunt Pauline leave Mother Sunday Street?'

'Oh no. Your predecessor left it to her, he got the freehold from a grateful patient. Dr Salter and your mother were old friends of course.'

'Of course.' Fred was adjusting the scales to measure Cantellow's increasing bulk. 'You need to lose a couple of stone.'

'I need the weight, for the low notes in the *Creation*. Oh yes, your mother's house came from Dr Salter.'

Chapter Sixteen

GETTING OUT THE VOTERS

In the great world, far from Mandragola and the Rapstone Valley, the revelations of scandal in high places continued to add zest and flavour to the breakfast tables of the nation. Dr Stephen Ward, who, it was suggested, had procured mistresses for the rich and powerful, was to be tried as a concession to one of the British public's periodical bouts of morality, and to commit suicide by way of a pathetically exaggerated apology. Mr Macmillan fell ill and the leadership of the Party, which numbered young Leslie Titmuss among its adherents, had been assumed by Sir Alec Douglas-Home, who had resigned his peerage and was said, for all his apparent amiability, not to show up well on television. All these doings were reported by Hartscombe's representative at Westminster, Doughty Strove, M.P., to a committee of his local Party Association meeting in Hartscombe Town Hall. After the whole sad story had been recounted and a decent silence had been allowed for those who had fallen in the great scandal, Nicholas said, with his usual fairness, 'One feels sorry for the Minister. It was the lying, of course. I don't suppose anyone cares who the fellow jumped into bed with.'

To which there was a rumbling of general assent and one small, sharp voice, 'I don't agree.'

'Titmuss?' Nicholas was displeased by the interruption.

'It's not only the lying, is it? I mean, a member's private life does have to be above suspicion. If we choose a fellow to represent us, we have to make sure he has absolutely no skeletons in his cupboard.' At which those present were surprised to see the young Titmuss fixing Doughty Strove with what looked very much like a glare of accusation.

'Well, there've been all sorts of stupid rumours, of course. Bloody tittle-tattle!' Doughty Strove was obviously nettled. 'But I've made it perfectly clear that if anyone wants to suggest that there's any connection between me and that fellow in the iron mask – they've apparently got photos of him dishing out vegetables to a party of decadents – well, I wouldn't even know where to buy an iron mask.'

An embarrassed silence met this refutation, after which Nicholas was again the conciliator. 'No Doughty. My dear fellow! Of course you wouldn't.'

'It would be quite wrong of me to suggest that there is anything in Mr Strove's past life that could cause us the slightest concern.' Leslie Titmuss went on in a voice which sounded like a prosecution and continued to give offence. 'But in my opinion our Party has attracted far too many rumours lately and they're quite likely to lose us the next election!'

'We shall weather this little difficulty and be returned next time, whenever it may be, with a handsome majority,' Doughty assured them all.

'I really don't agree.' By now his son-in-law's voice was affecting Nicholas like a rusty nail on a slate. 'We've always stood as the Party of public morality,' Leslie grated on. 'It seems to me that if we lose that reputation we might as well all go off and join the Socialists.' There was a merciful gap in Leslie's speech, into which the Chairman hurried to pour oil.

'Yes, well, I'm sure we're all extremely grateful to our member for his clear report from Westminster and for the quiet, dependable way he's represented Hartscombe. Many of you will have noticed the helpful question he asked about oil-seed rape was it, Doughty? I'm sure no one could possibly suggest that he's a man who could be connected with any sort of scandal.' Nicholas smiled vaguely around him. 'With or without an iron mask. So

I propose a vote of thanks to Doughty Strove, long may he represent Hartscombe and Worsfield South.'

'I should like to second that, Chairman.' It was Leslie Titmuss, smiling and quick off the mark. His father-in-law looked at him with the nearest he could come to real anger and, when Leslie emerged after the motion had been carried, was waiting for him by the notice-board in the cold and marmoreal Town Hall entrance.

'Father-in-law!' Leslie smiled. 'Whenever are you going to pay us a call?' Since his marriage to Charlie, Leslie had seen very little of her parents, a fact for which she was profoundly grateful but which he resented. Grace and Nicholas hadn't yet included them in their dinner parties at Rapstone Manor.

'I must say that was a bit strong!' Nicholas was clearly not in a social mood.

'Really? I thought it was a jolly good meeting.'

'People who live in glasshouses, Titmuss' – the Chairman looked round to make sure there was not a Conservative within earshot – 'should keep their mouths shut at meetings. What about your own marriage? Didn't you rather jump the gun?'

'You're not suggesting that Charlotte was pregnant when I married her?' Leslie looked pained.

'If she wasn't I don't know what all the fuss was about.'

'I really think you ought to know that the first night I slept with your daughter was on the honeymoon in Torquay you so generously paid for. I'm sure we've got too much respect for the institution of marriage. Of course we both hope to present you with a grandchild once I get settled in the new business. Best wishes to mother-in-law.'

So Leslie Titmuss went out into the Hartscombe night, and left Nicholas feeling that an act of flagrant immorality had occurred, particularly if, by some strange chance, his son-in-law were telling the truth.

There was certainly a new feeling of morality abroad: the top place on the charts was gained by a Belgian nun who sang to a guitar. The daily excitement of scandalous revelations had been forgotten. There was talk of a coming election when the New Jerusalem might again be on offer, not this time as the austere and serviceable city of Major Attlee and Sir Strafford Cripps, but as a gleaming steel and concrete Shangri-La, humming with the Mersey Sound and the mass production of mini-cars evolved by some new and mysterious technology the secret of which had, apparently, only just been discovered. The 'new business' which Leslie Titmuss had mentioned to his father-in-law was Hartscombe Enterprises, a company recently formed by Christopher Kempenflatt and Magnus Strove. They had asked Leslie to join them as an accountant, partly as a reward for his support and advice in the matter of the Easy-Bite restaurant and other property deals in and around Hartscombe, but mainly because he was prepared to work with relentless energy at all hours and leave the business lunches and 'customer relations' to them. From time to time Kempenflatt and Magnus grew fearful at the threat of another Labour Government; then Leslie, the accountant, gave them a small smile and told them that Hartscombe Enterprises had nothing very much to fear from Mr Wilson, the new technology, or government spending on buildings and public works.

'I'm coming down to Rapstone for the election.' Henry had paid an unprecedented call on his brother and been invited to lunch in his hospital canteen. 'We've both got to work, Fred. We've got to do something for this country.'

'You mean England needs you?'

'England's dying on its feet.' Henry spoke with the experience of someone who'd come back from a long time abroad. 'It hasn't even the horrible vitality of Benny K. Bugloss, or Jack Polefax of Galaxy International. My God, Frederick. What've you got? A fourteenth Earl of a prime minister who does sums with matchsticks, members of the Government chasing call-girls and waiting at table in iron masks!'

'You've become very puritanical.' Fred pushed away his cold

stew and embarked on the jam roll and custard, food which always seemed to taste faintly of antiseptic.

'About the only thing you've been able to organize decently is a train robbery.'

'I didn't organize it personally.'

'You're going to help us get rid of this lot, aren't you? I mean, I don't agree with everything our father says, as you know.'

'But you'd like to build Jerusalem in England's green and pleasant land?' Fred noticed that his brother's new taste for austerity stopped short of the jam roll.

'I don't see anything particularly wrong with that.'

They had lunch together and neither of them mentioned Agnes.

Fred was tired of the taste of hospital food, the smell of the hospital corridors and the bad jokes that were essential to keep the students' thoughts away from the hopeless reality of death. He didn't know if Henry had come to make peace between them or as some act of contrition; whatever it was he found it hard to understand why he should be beaten about the head with his father's politics during the short half hour he had before his turn to take blood in the children's ward. He wondered why Henry made everything, from an election to a love-affair, sound like some football match at Knuckleberries in which his younger brother was sure to let down the side.

'The trouble with our father's paradise is that it keeps getting put off, doesn't it?' Fred didn't mind trying to irritate Henry, who was now carefully stubbing out a cigarette by the side of his abandoned pudding. 'The promised land's always just round the corner.'

'At least let's give the people a chance and pull together.' Fred thought Henry might have added 'For the sake of the house'.

'You mean "the workers"?'

'Well, if you want to use an old-fashioned expression.'

'I went out with the workers the other night,' Fred decided to tell him. 'The workers I play all that jazz with: Terry Fawcett, who works in Marmaduke's garage in Hartscombe, Den Kitson from the Brewery and Tom Nowt. You remember Tom Nowt, don't you?'

'Vaguely.' Henry seemed to lose interest once specific workers were brought into question.

'Well, Tom Nowt. We all had a few drinks, of course, and then we went on a spree.'

'What sort of spree?'

'We drove down by the Mandragola Valley, bumped across a field, got into a wood and dazzled a deer in an old Zephyr's headlamps. Then they shot it and cut its throat. Nobody said anything about it when I met Terry and Den the week after and we did a trad night at the Badger in Skurfield. They never mentioned it at all. Tom Nowt smeared blood on me.'

'Does that mean you're against us?' Henry was frowning, trying to do his brother the credit of assuming that this anecdote, although apparently pointless, had some sort of relevance to the topic under discussion. But Fred assured him that it didn't mean that at all, in fact it meant that he was on his side.

After the encounter with his father-in-law in Hartscombe Town Hall, Leslie was daily expecting a summons from Grace. For a long time she left him and Charlie in peace. But one day, when he was walking from his old office in the Brewery, where he still helped his father at the time of the annual return, to the new office of Hartscombe Enterprises, the large black Daimler slowed up beside him, the back door opened, and his mother-in-law invited him in with all the cordiality of a hitman of the prohibition era inviting a rival mobster to take a ride. Leslie obeyed politely and looked at Grace with deep sympathy.

'I know you must have been worried, mother-in-law. Of course, Charlotte and I are enormously keen on starting a family as soon as possible.'

'You lied to us, you both lied!'

'Yes.' Leslie's answer so startled Grace that she was silent for at least ten seconds, and then he began a long, confidential explanation, carried on in a hushed tone of voice that at first angered, then embarrassed her. Before he had altogether finished she was finding the pale and by no means apologetic Titmuss strangely appealing. Did she want to know why they lied, he asked her. Because he knew it was the only way she would agree to his marriage. And because he wasn't going to spend the rest of his life working in the Brewery, coming up to the Manor once a year for tea in the garden and the tombola at the Conservative fête. It was because he wasn't going to settle for the life his father had worked out for him, nine to five in the accounts department until he was old enough to draw his pension. He was not only going to make something of himself, and of Charlotte also. He was going to become someone his parents-in-law would be proud of. In fact he was going to represent the constituency one day when Doughty Strove retired, which event might not be so long delayed as everyone might think. He, Leslie Titmuss, was embarking on a long-term programme for the development of his career and he had to start somewhere, didn't he?

'So you started with us?' Grace noticed that the window which separated them from Brooks, the chauffeur, had been left open, and slid it to, sharply, and much too late. 'Well, at least you're honest, I suppose.' She looked at him and recognized, in a surprising moment, something almost like a fellow spirit. 'What you're telling me is, you would have said anything in the world to get into our family?'

'Said or done anything. Of course there's no reason to hide the facts from you now. The point is, if I'm going to do any of the things I'm planning for me and Charlotte, I've got to begin with the people I'll meet in your dining-room. I mean, where else is there?'

It was the language that Grace understood and she invited Leslie to dinner for the following Thursday night. It was an invitation Charlie heard about with horror. If she'd wanted to eat meals with her mother, why on earth, she said, had she gone to all the trouble of leaving home? Finally she yielded to her husband's persuasion but only on the condition that he wouldn't leave her to be dragged upstairs by her mother while he stayed to drink port and tell dirty stories in the dining-room. To this condition Leslie, who could see no possible political advantage in telling a dirty story to Nicholas, readily agreed.

It was, she remembered afterwards, the first of his broken promises. When Grace threw down her dinner napkin and called on Bridget Naboth, Honor Kempenflatt, Jennifer Battley and Mrs Fairhazel to follow her upstairs, Charlie first looked pleadingly at her husband, then uttered the words 'You promised' in a resounding whisper. It was a cry from the heart which Leslie ignored, being busy telling Magnus that it would have been interesting to have had his father's views on an autumn election.

'Come along, Charlie. Let's leave the boys to their politics.' All the boys, Leslie and Magnus, Christopher Kempenflatt, Lord Naboth, the 'Contessa' and her father, had their heads turned away from her and their eyes averted, as Charlie went off as though to half an hour on the rack.

'I'm afraid Doughty had something on in London.' Nicholas apologized for his old friend.

'I expect you think he's got nothing on in London, don't you, Leslie?' Magnus was laughing. 'I mean nothing but an iron mask?'

'I'm only sorry,' Leslie replied with dignity, 'that your father has so little time for constituency matters.'

'Are you?'

'I'm sure that Doughty would tell us we're going to win the next election, whenever it is.'

'And are we all absolutely sure that would be in the best interests of the Party?'

Faces were turned to Leslie, showing more embarrassment and shock than if he'd told the dirtiest joke Charlie had ever

managed to collect from the brightest of her juvenile delinquents.

'What on earth is that supposed to mean?' Lord Naboth was
looking profoundly disturbed.

'I'm not sure we don't need a time to re-think.' Leslie smiled
in the pleasantest way. 'I don't think we can afford to go on
being amateurs.'

'You mean being gentlemen?' Nicholas's mind turned to
cricket. 'You want us to be players?'

'I'd like us to be serious. If we lost in the autumn, it might
give us time to sharpen up our image.'

'Sharpen up what, Titmuss?'

'Our image, sir.'

'Is that a phrase that has some meaning for you, Archie?'
Nicholas turned to Lord Naboth for guidance.

'I'm not sure. I'll tell you one thing though. I bet Alec
Douglas-Home isn't in the least worried about the result of the
election.'

'I bet Harold Wilson is, perhaps that's the difference between
them. Don't worry, Magnus, will you?' Leslie was now positively
affable. 'Of course we're all going to work twenty-four hours a
day to get your father re-elected.'

Upstairs, in the drawing-room, Grace knew that Mrs Fairhazel
was longing to be gently poisonous on the subject of Leslie
Titmuss and got her oar in first. 'I think Charlie's really found
something in her Mr Titmuss. He knows exactly where he's
going and, give him full marks, I honestly believe he's going to
get there. At least he pays us the compliment of wanting to join
us.' Unfortunately Charlie didn't hear this generous tribute. She
was seated in blissful solitude in the downstairs loo, a refuge
where her husband had, many years before, been found screaming. She was reading the back numbers of *Country Life* with
which the dusty table beside the seat was supplied, and when she
came across a photograph of her mother enjoying a joke at some
long-past hunt ball, she tore it out carefully, and then, even more

carefully, ripped it into even smaller pieces and flushed it down the pan.

The election was held in October. Fred drove his father's elderly Austin and Henry came down the lanes too fast, brushing the hedgerows against the sides of his second-hand Jaguar. They were both there to 'get out' Labour voters, so they found cottages on remote commons, or went down rutted tracks to unknown farms, or ransacked blocks of flats and Old People's Homes. Some of the voters came willingly, having been ready since dawn and regarding the whole occasion as a day out; many thought the election an unwarranted intrusion into their private lives and most couldn't be home until the evening. So, while the Simcox brothers were driving cars plastered with pictures of Harold Wilson, Leslie Titmuss knocked on doors, called on the residents of caravans and barges on the river and drove Conservative voters in the spruce black Rover Christopher Kempenflatt had lent him for the occasion.

Simeon and Dorothy crossed from the Rectory to the school-house, wearing red rosettes, to register their votes. Dr Salter, riding by, called from the saddle to ask them if they were about to start another revolution. 'He's only teasing us,' Dorothy explained, but Simeon waved the hand with his pipe in it and called back, 'A revolution. Of course! Guillotine all the aristocrats and their doctor.' It was a threat which was clearly heard by Grace and her chauffeur, Brooks, who had come down in the Daimler to cast their votes. By the early evening Fred had seen more village halls and schools than he knew existed, had found Hartscombe housing estates he had never visited and had helped old ladies out of bedrooms and transported babies their mothers couldn't leave. He met Ben Leverett, the Labour candidate, his grey hair blowing in the wind and his rosette flapping, as he drew up with a small catch of Labour voters outside the Town Hall.

'Hartscombe's pretty solid Tory and a lot of the villages,' Ben

Leverett said. 'But we've got South Worsfield and the housing estates. If we can get all our voters out we might just be in with a chance.'

So, in the faint hope of securing the Rapstone Valley for the People's Party, Fred drove to Worsfield with another crumpled list and inadequate information. He stopped at a traffic light on the edge of the city and looked out at sodium-lit windows on the chance of spotting Mr Wilson's photograph peering back at him. Then he heard a bleep on the horn of the black Rover parked next to him and saw the window being rolled down. In a moment he was in communication with Leslie Titmuss.

'There's a few of your voters up in Attlee Crescent. They haven't been picked up yet.'

'You're telling *me* that?'

'I thought it would be fair.' He glided off in the Rover, an unexpectedly parfit and gentil Knight of a Leslie Titmuss, and when Fred at last found Attlee Crescent he discovered that it wasn't even a hoax.

The result, when the Mayor as the Returning Officer announced it in Hartscombe Town Hall at around one o'clock in the morning, was greeted by cheers and boos and came out as follows: Leverett, Benjamin Arnold (Labour), fifteen thousand and six; Prusford, Michael Charles (Liberal), four thousand six hundred and twenty-four; Ramsden, Michael Matabele (Anti-Vivisection and Free Toilet facilities), sixteen; Strove, Doughty Picton Percival (Conservative), fourteen thousand nine hundred and sixty-seven. And so the said Benjamin Arnold Leverett was duly elected to serve as the member for the Hartscombe and South Worsfield constituency. They had, Fred calculated rapidly, a majority of thirty-nine and he wondered just how many Labour voters he had got out of Attlee Crescent, thanks to the unexpected chivalry of Leslie Titmuss.

Mr Harold Wilson went to Buckingham Palace with his wife, his two sons and his father, to become prime minister at the age of forty-eight. Doughty Strove went back to full-time farming and Leslie Titmuss worked hard for Hartscombe Enterprises. Agnes gave birth to Francesca and became mysteriously happy with the baby. Henry felt he was the only normally discontented person in the household. Fred went on learning more about the human body than he thought it safe for anyone to know, and Simeon became concerned about the military government in Bolivia.

One morning, by the woods in the Mandragola Valley, Doughty Strove's gamekeeper found Tom Nowt lying beside his shot-gun. Tom had bled copiously from a jagged wound in his chest. He was quite dead.

Chapter Seventeen

THE WRONGS OF MAN

'Let her go. Let her go. God bless her, Wherever she may be,' sang Joe Sneeping, trumpet in hand, fronting the rehearsal session in Marmaduke's garage, and Fred, on drums, heard murmurs from the other musicians. 'Accident?' ''Course, Doctor, she said it was an accident!' and 'Some it suits quite well, Tom going like that.' Those speaking were Den Kitson on banjo and Terry Fawcett on clarinet, who was resting with his instrument on his knee.

'She can look this wide world over, She'll never find a sweet man like me . . .' Joe stopped singing and looked rebukingly at Terry Fawcett who raised his clarinet to his lips, and Fred was able to overhear no more about the death of Tom Nowt. All he knew was the finding of the coroner who had heard the evidence of Dr Salter. Death was due to an accident which probably occurred when the deceased stumbled while out shooting at night. He might well have tripped over some low branch or bramble and his shot-gun, with the safety-catch off, discharged accidentally.

The cause of Tom Nowt's death brought less speculation than the future of his cottage on the Strove estate. His children had all left home and his wife, Dora, went to live with a married daughter in Hartscombe. There appeared to be available a rare commodity, an empty cottage in the Rapstone Valley, and no one, they were sure, deserved it more than Terry Fawcett and Glenys Bigwell who had been walking out for six years with nowhere to lie down together but the woods or a bed and breakfast on rare summer holidays.

Glenys could entertain Terry at her parents' and Terry could have her to tea at his mother's, but neither home afforded them permission of a bed or a space to marry. When they discussed the prospect, Bridget said Tom Nowt's place had been kept like a monkey house, and her husband was doubtful about his daughter taking over the home of a man who had crippled him by his habit of letting the sodding trees fall anywhere. Tom Nowt's cottage seemed to Percy Bigwell to be the sort of place which could bring no one any luck. However, Glenys's mind was made up. The cottage would suit them perfectly, and Terry could use the old hut in the woods for repairing his motor-bikes. She mentioned all this to the Rector one morning when she went up to type for him, and between congratulations to members of the new Government, stern warnings to the Bishop of Worsfield, drafts of letters to *The Times* on the subjects of integrated schools in the southern states of America and the situation in the Dominican Republic, Simeon composed a strong note to Doughty Strove on the justice of Terry and Glenys's claim to Tom Nowt's old cottage. He was sure that a wise and fair landlord would immediately grant them a lease. As Glenys saw the words take shape under her fingers and bite blackly into the paper, she believed that the matter had been decided by the Rector and it would only be a matter of time before she and Terry moved in together. On the same morning as she typed the letter, she booked a date for her marriage.

Both Glenys and Simeon had reckoned without a new force in the Rapstone Valley, Hartscombe Enterprises, which body, through its representatives, Magnus Strove and Leslie Titmuss, was taking a close look at Tom's old cottage in the company of Doughty Strove. Leslie had the figures Hartscombe Enterprises would pay the Strove estate – £10,000 for the property including the bit of woodland leased to the late Mr Nowt with the cottage. The cash would be immediately available and the purchasers would be responsible for all repairs and renovations.

'There's only one difficulty.' Doughty looked troubled.

'What's that, Father?'

'Had a note from the Rector, the Bigwell girl is marrying young Fawcett. As they've been walking out together for years, he seems to think they've got some sort of natural right to the place.'

'With all due respect to the Rector' – Leslie was almost apologetic – 'I wonder if he's really thought this one through. Of course Glenys Bigwell is an extremely attractive girl.'

'What's that supposed to mean?' Doughty's eyes, set like dark currants in a wide expanse of bun, became somewhat beady.

'Well, if you did that sort of favour for one particular local girl, mightn't it start old stories again?'

'Old stories?' Doughty looked round furtively, as though there might be whisperers in Tom Nowt's dilapidated cottage. 'I think all Leslie's trying to say, Father,' Magnus came in with the voice of reason, 'is that it would be much better to offer it to someone outside the neighbourhood. That's all you were trying to say, wasn't it, Leslie?'

'That's all, Magnus. That is absolutely all.'

Although she got no formal confirmation from the Strove estate Glenys assumed that the Rector's letter had done the trick. Accordingly she hung a basket full of scourers, scrubbing brushes, floor cloths, rags, Mansion polish and Gumption on to the handlebars of her bike and rode over to Skurfield one afternoon when Simeon and Dorothy had gone off to a concert in Worsfield Cathedral, and the world was let off, for the afternoon, a single letter of protest.

When Glenys arrived at the cottage she leant her bike against the hedge, found the spare key where she knew Tom and Dora had always kept it under a loose brick, went in and, after clicking her tongue a little at the state of the floors, put on an overall and rubber gloves and started to work. An hour later she was gumptioning the sink with such concentrated intensity that she didn't hear a car stop in the lane outside, nor did she hear the woman who came in at the back door.

'The door was open.' Glenys turned to see a well-preserved forty-year-old, wearing trousers and a sweater, with a bulging handbag slung across her shoulder, glasses on the end of her nose and a look of amused desperation at all the problems with which life presented her. 'You must have seen the advertisement.'

'What advertisement?' Glenys went on scrubbing.

'We put a card up in that funny little sell-everything shop. You know, paraffin lamps all mixed up with bacon and butter and old fly-papers. But,' and the woman peered at Glenys, pushing her glasses up, 'if you didn't see the advertisement how on earth did you get here?'

'Everyone knows about it now Tom's passed over.'

'Of course!' The woman sounded relieved. 'News travels fast in this little community. Well, we're delighted to see you however you got here.'

'Oh, the Rector fixed it up.' The sink was gleaming white now and Glenys looked at it, contented.

'The Red Rector of Rapstone! We haven't touched base with him yet but we hear he's perfectly charming, in spite of the funny politics. So *he* suggested you came along?'

'He wrote a letter to Mr Strove and I think that'll do the trick.'

'Well, I must say, it's extremely thoughtful of them all.'

It was then that Glenys looked out into the little patch of back garden where Tom grew a few vegetables and a good many nettles, the proliferation of which was due to the burial there of the inedible parts of much slaughtered game. A balding man had spread a rug on the unmown grass and was setting out a picnic for the benefit of two fair-haired and carsick children.

'That's my husband, by the way,' the woman explained. 'Everybody calls him Malley. I hope you will too.'

'Why?'

'His name's Mallard-Greene but everybody at the B.B.C. calls him Malley. We're having our picnic in the garden.'

'I suppose that's all right.'

'Well, thank you!' Mrs Mallard-Greene assumed that Glenys was making some kind of a joke.

'I mean, I shouldn't be here myself. It's not all signed and sealed yet but I couldn't resist coming in and making a bit of a start.' Glenys looked hungrily round at the cleaning she still had to do; she wanted to get on.

'It's most tremendously keen of you and I'm sure we'll get on like a house on fire!' Mrs Mallard-Greene encouraged her. 'We noticed that you'd brought your bicycle. How many hours are you going to be able to get up here?'

'But I'm going to be here all the time.'

'All the time? We weren't thinking of anyone living-in.'

'Living-in? Of course we'll be living-in, me and my Terry. It's going to be our cottage, isn't it?'

It was then that Mrs Mallard-Greene went to the window, pushed it open and shouted with surprising volume, 'Come here, Malley. I think there's been a tiny bit of a balls-up!'

'Tom Nowt's dead,' Fred gave his brother the news in a Harts-combe bookshop, where Henry was signing copies of his new novel *The Wrong Side of Sunset Boulevard*. ('A brilliant and savage satire on Hollywood by Britain's brightest and angriest young writer' – *Guardian*.) Fred had been walking down the High Street, wondering whether he'd end his life married to some plump nurse or eager female medical student he had met walking the wards, and then repeating the mnemonic, 'On Old Manhattan's Peaked Tops A Finn And German Picked Some Hops,' a strange, unforgettable vision which never managed to remind him of the names of the cranial nerves. Then his thoughts had turned to Stan Kenton, whose big band arrangements were polluting the purity of jazz, not that Fred thought that music should ever remain as played by a blind negro pianist in Preservation Hall. His steps were arrested by the sight of his brother's face repeated on the jackets of a pile of books. Through the shop window he was appalled to see Henry standing beside Mrs Niggs, the bookseller, drinking white wine which he didn't offer to the customers, who seemed unreasonably anxious to acquire the latest Simcox. Fred pushed open the door and joined the queue.

'Would you mind not signing this one? I plan to read it in odd moments, when Mrs Niggs isn't looking. Anyway, aren't you knocking on a bit for an angry young writer?'

'I might have known you'd be in Hartscombe, Freddie. You never seem to be anywhere else.'

'You will come over to the Rectory for dinner, won't you?'

'Why?'

'They'll expect it. Now they know you're home. Anyway, there's something I want to talk to you about.'

'What's that?'

It was then that Fred told him, 'Tom Nowt's dead.'

At dinner at the Rectory, curried lamb – the positively last appearance of the Sunday joint – washed down with a limited amount of Simcox's bottled ale, Dorothy received the presentation copy of Henry's latest work: 'To Mother and Father, without whom I shouldn't have seen Hollywood, or indeed anything at all', and looked with embarrassed amusement at the photograph on the cover.

'It's not at all like him, is it, Simeon?' She held it up for her husband to peer at from the other end of the table. 'It's not at all like Henry.'

'Not really, but then I've always found it quite difficult to remember what either of you look like,' Simeon told his sons. 'When you're not here of course.'

'Well, we're here now,' Henry pointed out reasonably.

'I do wish you'd write a "whodunit",' Dorothy sighed, as though expressing the longing of a lifetime. 'They do so awfully well in the library. Nowadays the library comes round in a van, such a strange idea, like milk.'

'Who done what?' Henry asked. 'I don't suppose anyone cares.'

'Don't you? People seem to.'

'Henry's written a satirical comedy,' Fred explained, as his brother continued to smile bravely, 'about how much he hates America.'

'Hate it, do you?' Simeon asked as though genuinely seeking information. 'Why are you always going there then?'

'Henry's not always going there,' Fred told him. 'He's always coming back.'

'Anyway, those ghastly film people.' Henry decided to shut his brother up with an anecdote. 'Agnes and I were being bored by one at lunch. You know the sort of lunches they have there – three-storey sandwiches and lethal cocktails and iced water.'

'Iced water!' Dorothy laughed. 'It'd make my teeth ache!'

'Agnes and I looked at each other in the middle of lunch and hit on this scheme, by sort of telepathy. We both went to the loo and climbed out of the window to freedom.'

'Both?' Fred raised his eyebrows.

'We walked back to the hotel,' Henry went on, ignoring his brother. 'Laughing all the way. You know, you don't walk in Hollywood, no one walks in Hollywood, it's a sort of blasphemy.'

At the end of this story Henry laughed a little on his own and Fred felt a moment of sympathy for him. Whether or not he was telling the truth he was doing his best to entertain their parents, who could be hard to please, particularly their mother. She turned big, mournful eyes on Henry, as though he had recounted a tragedy.

'Poor man!'

'Who?'

'The poor man who was buying you lunch.'

'He's not poor at all. He draws the most enormous expenses.'

'All the same, you probably hurt his feelings.'

'Impossible! I put a literal word-for-word portrait of Benjamin K. Bugloss in my book. I made him the complete comic, dotty Hollywood producer. I thought he'd sue me for libel, or at least never speak to me again. Do you know what? He thinks it's a "great piece of material" and he's bought an option on it for a movie.'

'Your Mr Bugloss,' Dorothy told him, 'sounds something of a saint.'

After dinner, when Dorothy and Simeon had retired to the double bed they still shared, Henry brought in a bottle of whisky from the car and the brothers sat in Simeon's study. 'Do you think Our Father and the Reverend Mother were getting at me slightly?' Henry swirled his drink round the tumbler and looked, with a wounded expression, at the bust of Karl Marx.

'They get at me a lot more,' Fred told him.

'Why's that?'

'Probably because I'm here a lot more.'

'Our father's an extraordinary being. Do you ever get the feeling he's not connected with us at all?'

There was silence and then Fred told him again, 'Tom Nowt shot himself by accident apparently. I can't imagine Tom shooting anything by accident.'

'Wasn't he some kind of poacher?'

'The point is, no one wants to admit knowing him very well, or his hut in the woods. You remember how angry our father was when I went there, years ago?'

'No one wants to admit knowing him?' Henry frowned.

'Dr Salter doesn't. Or Mother. I had an idea.'

'Try not to, you're not used to it.' What Henry said wasn't really an insult, only an echo of their schooldays.

'I had a strange thought that she and Dr Salter might have gone there together once, years ago perhaps.'

'God, Frederick!' Henry embarked on an outraged aria. 'They accuse me of inventing! You think *Sunset*'s an invention? I tell you. It was all exactly like that only more so. Writers are the only reliable witnesses. We know about the world, young Fred. We've got our feet firmly on the ground but people like you, the middle-class professional men like you're going to be, doctors, lawyers, bank managers, you're all lost in a world of fantasy! Or is your life so dull that you have to invent mysterious secrets about our family?'

'You're middle class too, aren't you?'

'That's hardly the point.'

'And professional.' Fred gave himself another drink out of Henry's bottle. 'Anyway, I don't suppose we'll ever know now.'

'Now?'

'Now Tom Nowt's dead.'

Disappointed of the cottage which he believed to be destined for himself and Glenys, Terry Fawcett called at the Citizens Advice Bureau. Present during his interview were a Miss Carew, in charge, and Charlie Titmuss, née Fanner, who was there as part of her training in social welfare. Miss Carew, who was caring for the row of potted plants, ferns and succulents, which stood on her window ledge, snipping off dead leaves and applying water from a long spouted can, interviewed Terry. She told him that Doughty Strove was entitled to do what he liked with his own property, that the old cottage no doubt needed more money spent on it than he and Glenys could afford, and that they could put their names down for one of the new council flats being planned for Worsfield in a couple of years' time, although priority would naturally be given to married couples with families. At which point Terry, who had been smoking with fierce concentration, deliberately applied a lighted match to the pile of case notes, pamphlets on Help for the Aged, Baby Care, Rent Tribunals and How to Register a Death, which lay on the table in front of him. Miss Carew swung round from her plants to see her small world alight and burning furiously. Unexpectedly she cried, 'What the shit, Mr Fawcett?' and doused the flames with her watering-can.

Charlie caught up with Terry as he left the counselling service and persuaded him to come for a pint or two of Simcox's. She commiserated, condoled and joined him in reviling the name of

Doughty Strove. She was late getting home to her husband, and bought fish and chips for their supper.

'Not again!' Leslie in his shirt-sleeves rose from another file of accounts and looked at the warm, damp sheets of the Hartscombe *Advertiser* unfolding to reveal the cooling, yellow fish and limp chips. 'I must set them out properly.'

'On a poncey little dish?' Charlie, without removing her mac, had sprinkled vinegar and was eating with eager, well-licked fingers.

'I can't imagine what your mother would say if she could see us.'

'Oh, I can. Mummy would think we'd got dreadfully common. Screw her!'

'It's not something I'd personally undertake.' Leslie picked up a chip, stared at it with distaste and took a determined bite.

'What's the matter with you?' Charlie looked up from her portion of rock salmon. 'You've started to make jokes.'

Leslie ignored this and gave her the news. It was time, he had decided, that they moved on. Hartscombe Enterprises needed a national centre, and London might suit Charlotte very well. It was, after all, absolutely teeming with social problems. Charlie was doubtful and reluctant.

'I don't see how I can leave Terry Fawcett and Glenys. They haven't got anywhere to live.'

'There's a plan for new flats in Worsfield.'

'They don't want Worsfield. They want Rapstone. They were both kids in the village. Why should they have to move to Worsfield?'

'Upward mobility.' As Charlie showed no signs of making coffee, Leslie plugged in the kettle.

'Up a bloody tower block you mean! In about ten years' time.'

She lit a cigarette, dropping the spent match into the paper which had contained their supper. Leslie made the coffee carefully, filtering it and setting out small after-dinner cups with a milk jug and sugar bowl on a tray. Looking at Charlie he thought that what she was was a snob. She'd been brought up deprived of fish and chips and strong tea and bottles of sauce. He remembered his daily routine at 'The Spruces'. His father always came home at exactly the same time and always said, 'Is tea ready, dear?' When he had eaten he would push his plate away with the usual words, 'very tasty, dear. That was very tasty.' If anyone in the family became ill, it was a point of honour not to bother the Doctor, and all deaths were known as 'a blessed release'. At half past nine every evening George Titmuss dropped asleep in the leatherette chair on the right side of the fireplace, his mouth fell open, his breathing became soft and regular and his wife and son would have to sew and read in silence. At ten-thirty exactly Leslie's father would wake up with a start, say 'Time for Bedfordshire!' and lock up. All hope for a different sort of life was known as 'living with your head in the clouds', all ambition had to be confined to keeping the Prefect in running order, 'The Spruces' front garden the tidiest in Skurfield and the payments to the Prudential regular. Whatever his wife might feel about the glamour of the sauce bottles on the table at tea-time, Leslie knew exactly what the world he came from was like and he was not going back there ever, not as long as he lived.

'There's not a lot I can do about Terry Fawcett's problems yet.' Leslie carried the tray to the coffee table in front of their sitting-room fireplace.

'What do you mean, *yet*?' Charlie was not following him.

'Well,' Leslie told her modestly. 'For that sort of problem, he'd have to go to his local M.P.'

So the Mallard-Greenes took possession of Tom Nowt's cottage, and the young Titmusses moved up to London, at first to a company flat in St John's Wood, and later, when Leslie was made a director, to a small company house off the Cromwell Road. Before they left, Charlie told her father to transfer the lease of their Rapstone cottage to Terry Fawcett, but he was surprised to discover that she didn't know that the cottage had already been sold to Hartscombe Enterprises, a deal he'd agreed to because Leslie had told him that having the place owned by the company would mean 'a bit of security' for Charlotte and himself. 'Really, Charlie,' Nicholas asked, 'doesn't your husband tell you anything?' Tackled by his wife on the subject, Leslie said that Magnus and Christopher Kempenflatt had insisted on the purchase, and they wanted to resell to a young chap from Hambros, who needed somewhere to pop down to for occasional weekends. He had managed to get a bit of commission on the deal which would help them in their move to London. Leslie explained all these things very reasonably and Charlie said little at the time. She felt she had failed, however, and was anxious to get away to London, where she could take a course at the L.S.E. and help such other Terry Fawcetts as she might find, without having to seek favours from her father or permission from her husband.

Some time later Mr Mallard-Greene, wearing corduroy trousers and an anorak, carrying a large tin of paraffin, walked down into the depths of the beech woods which he now owned, with his two children, Simon and Sarah. The young Mallard-Greenes followed him, somewhat reluctantly, not having been anxious to turn out on a chilly afternoon and resenting being wrapped up in gloves and mufflers by their mother. When Simon asked his father about their mission he was told, 'We're getting rid of an eyesore. It's not only because it's ugly to look at, it's because it's not what this woodland's meant for. It's meant for wild life. It's meant to be a home for the badgers and all sorts of birds and butterflies and for squirrels, of course.'

'And for worms,' Sarah suggested.

'Well, of course, for worms.'

'And for woodlice.'

'And for bluebells,' Mr Mallard-Greene summed up firmly. 'There's nothing spoils a natural bluebell wood more than having a sort of rural slum dumped down in it.' They reached Tom Nowt's hut, a scene of considerable activity. Two woodmen with a tractor and trailer, rented for the day, had loaded up all such non-inflammable objects as the cooker, lamps, pots and pans and the big, creaking, brass-knobbed iron bedstead. A couple of walls had already been knocked down and reduced to a pile of timber in the middle of the wooden floor, but the front of the hut had been left standing, with broken windows and a door which opened inwards into the silence of an ancient beech wood. Mr Mallard-Greene, known as Malley in the B.B.C. and a closet pyromaniac, told his children to stand well back and sloshed paraffin in through the front door. Then he struck a match, threw it in and retreated with the fearful delight of a child who has just lit the blue touch-paper of an enormous banger on Guy Fawkes night.

There was a wonderful whoosh, a wind of flame and then a slower crackling as what was left of the hut burned down. The damp afternoon became sultry, lit by showers of sparks and the steady burning of wooden planks and battens. So, as Malley beamed with pride, the workmen looked on without expression, and the children danced with delight and, greatly daring, darted up to throw sticks and fallen branches on to the blaze, Tom Nowt's hut, hunting-lodge and meeting-place for secret lovers vanished as his deer skulls, crowned with antlers, fell from the wall of fire and blackened on the burning floor.

Many years later, and a year after Simeon's death, Henry sat in a room in Lincoln's Inn and tried to explain his case for upsetting his father's will to a couple of barristers and his solicitor, Jackson Cantellow.

'There was an old hut in the woods,' he said. 'My brother, Frederick, once had a strange idea that our mother used to meet the local Doctor there. I really don't know what he was driving at. Perhaps that there was some sort of mystery about his birth, or mine?'

'I don't think we need be in the least concerned, Mr Henry Simcox, at what your brother, Frederick, was driving at.' Crispin

Drayton, Q.C., Henry's leading counsel, was a tall, nobbly and abstemious man, married to a lady magistrate. In court he was renowned for his high moral tone and the brutality of his cross-examination. 'Let others speculate, if they feel so inclined. You do understand, I'm sure, that if you or your brother were not the "lawful children" of the deceased Rector, we might get the one thing we *don't* want in this case.'

'What's that exactly?'

'A rational explanation for the will of Simeon Simcox.'

Chapter Eighteen

THE PARTNERSHIP

In the middle of the swinging sixties people in England were apparently under some sort of obligation to have a good time and most of them didn't. A Russian and an American walked about in space to no one's particular advantage. The Beatles received their British Empire medals and, so it was said, smoked cannabis in the lavatories at Buckingham Palace. American aeroplanes were bombing North Vietnam, but no one seemed to talk about the nuclear holocaust anymore. Even Simeon's letters to *The Times* became rarer and more benign. At such a time Fred became a doctor. He had only a nodding acquaintance with the Hippocratic oath, but was somehow aware that he was committed to Apollo the Healer to look upon his teacher in the art of medicine as one of his parents, not to give any deadly drug to anyone, even if it was asked of him, and especially not to aid any woman to procure an abortion. He knew well enough to enter a house only for the benefit of the sick and to refrain from all wrong-doing and corruption and the seduction of male or female, bond or free.

He got through his final exams without brilliance or disgrace. He was not especially proud of his results, although Dr Salter assured him that success as a healer of the sick had very little to do with being able to remember the names of the cranial nerves. He had, over the years, many of Agnes's father's definitions by heart, such as *Bedrest*: a slow and tedious introduction to death. Tell your patients to keep upright. And when they want to die, get it over quickly. In silence. Best of all is to die standing, like a horse; *Check-ups*: a process by which the customer is subjected to a minute medical examination at frequent intervals, in the faint hope of finding a fatal disease. Naturally the victim feels embarrassed unless he can produce some sort of interesting complaint to entertain the Doctor; *Dieting*: the only excuse for dieting is poverty. Voluntary self-deprivation invariably leads to a considerable increase in the original weight once the starvation period is over. By keeping this lore out of his examination papers, Fred achieved a celebration party in his room in Battersea and got moderately drunk in the company of a number of other medical novices, a few nurses, some of his guests' girlfriends and Dr Salter, who had come up from Hartscombe for the occasion, and who, after attacking Fred's more serious friends on the subject of smoking ('Why not? Saves thousands of people from going potty. Anyway, who wants to live an extra ten years in a geriatric hospital in Weston-super-Mare? There's no pleasure in the world worth giving up for that!'), issued the invitation, which Fred had half expected and half feared. 'Let us raise our glasses,' he said, having banged a beer bottle on the table for silence, 'and drink to good health, coupled with the name of Dr Frederick Simcox, soon to be best part of Salter and Simcox, witchdoctors and medicine men of Hartscombe in the County of . . .' Dr Salter looked down into his glass. 'Look here, old cock!' he said, 'the tide's gone down.'

'Did you say "partners"?' Fred filled him up and got him going again.

'For God's sake, cocky, what do you think I've been waiting for all these long years? I thought you'd never qualify.'

So Fred saw his life spread out in front of him, like the Rapstone Valley seen from the Ridge, familiar and unsurprising, a life which he might never have undertaken but for Agnes and her father, which he might have shared with her and now would have to live without her. He had no idea that only a few years later he would become solely responsible for running the Hartscombe practice.

The invitation to the partnership was not the only one that Dr Salter had issued. Fred had thought for a long time about inviting Henry and Agnes to his party, doubtful how tolerant either of them would be in the company of young medics whooping it up on bottled beer. Now there was a ring at the front door and Fred went down to find not only Mr and Mrs Henry Simcox, but also their friend Mr Bugloss, holding a magnum of champagne, and his friend Mrs Wickstead, wrapped in fur and looking as pale and perfect as a rare china object.

'Is this where you live?' Henry asked, amused. 'Wonderfully handy for the Battersea Dogs' Home.'

'Of course I asked her. Didn't you want her here in your moment of triumph?' Dr Salter said, when the party had gone upstairs. Fred offered Agnes champagne from Mr Bugloss's huge bottle but, as he expected, she preferred warm light ale taken with soggy crisps. 'Salter and Simcox,' she said. 'You're really merged into him now, aren't you? What does your father say about married people. One flesh?'

'That's absolute rubbish.'

'Oh, no it's not. You'll both do the same things, know the same things and be absolutely out of bounds, as far as I'm concerned.'

Then she turned to speak with considerable animation to the most boring young doctor at the party. Mr Bugloss approached Fred softly murmuring, 'Dr Simcox.'

'Oh yes.' Fred sounded hesitant, unused to his title.

'Do me a favour will you? Get your brother off my back.'

'He writes about you?'

'Not about me, no. He writes about some Hollywood producer, some schmuck. He blames me for the Vietnam War. It's entirely my fault, it seems, that there are now bombing targets in the North. Did I give the orders?'

'It's a bit thick.' Mrs Wickstead inserted a potato crisp between her small white teeth. She looked surprisingly young and defenceless, Fred thought, still snuggled into her coat as though likely to be on the move shortly. 'Poor Benny's not even American.' And when Fred looked surprised, she explained quietly, almost as though she didn't want Mr Bugloss to overhear, 'You know he was born in Brixton.'

'Not Brixton. Mrs Wickstead has been misinformed. White-chapel. You know the area?'

'Not intimately,' Fred had to admit.

'It has changed, it was once a deeply caring community. My father owned property there, of course.'

'But you speak fluent American!'

'Have to, dear boy, in our business. However else am I going to get close to the Vice-President in Charge of Product at Galaxy International?'

The party ebbed and flowed. Music was playing and the doctors started to dance as amorous nurses dragged them to their feet. Henry told his brother that sometimes he couldn't understand Agnes.

'Sometimes?'

'She's picked out the most tedious of your fellow medics and won't speak to anyone else.'

'Aren't you used to her doing that?'

'I suppose so. Why is it?'

'Don't you know her? She chooses the worst bar, the most horrible meal, the most tedious man in the party. Then she knows she won't be disappointed. Do you think you can manage it?'

'Manage what?'

'Living up to her expectations.'

In a corner, Dr Salter had started to sing, an ancient and obscene ballad remembered from his distant past as a medical student. Someone put on a Charlie Parker record and Fred was called to do his act of accompaniment. He sat at his drums in a corner of the room and joined the rhythm section behind the Great Birds soaring alto saxophone. He saw that Agnes was dancing and that her father and Henry had discovered one of the few bottles of whisky left under the table.

'You do that rather well.' Fred looked round. Mrs Wickstead was sitting beside him, judging his performance.

'Yes.' Well, he'd practised long enough.

'I've never tried a doctor.' This was what he thought she said but she spoke very quietly. He reduced his playing to the swish of wire-brushes and a diminished thud. Mrs Wickstead seemed to be telling him about the people she *had* tried.

'Film people, producers and all that, you're something they want to have sitting next to them to impress the Executive Vice President. You're meant to smile and say, "Great idea, Jack," and that's all you're meant to say. Of course you get trips. But it's having to smile all the time, the muscles of your face begin to ache.'

'You think I could treat that, medically?'

'Ring me some time, if you want to. I'm not in the directory.' Then Mr Bugloss called from across the room. Fred stopped drumming and tried to hear the whispered figures.

'Two four six, eight oh two six. Did you get that?'

'No.' He couldn't be sure. But all she said was, 'It seems we're going now,' and wandered away, leaving Fred lonely at the drums.

> 'Drain the Worthington out of my kidneys
> Get the whisky fumes out of my brain,
> Get the night nurses out of my bed boys
> And start up the motor again . . .'

So sang Dr Salter as Fred took him down the stairs to his car. He made his senior partner move over and announced that he was going to drive him back to Hartscombe.

'Why?'

'Because you are pissed out of your mind.'

'So early in your career, Doctor,' the patient murmured obediently. 'And you have come to a completely accurate diagnosis.'

As he drove home, the numbers were arranging and rearranging their series in Fred's mind: eight oh two, two four two six.

No. Two four oh, eight six two? Or was it two oh six? The more he thought about it the more endless the possible combinations became. But the next morning he began to dial hopefully.

'Eight oh six two,' said the voice on the telephone. 'Excelsior Meat Importers.' After six or seven calls like that he decided to file his conversation with Mrs Wickstead away in his archive of missed opportunities.

So the partnership began and Fred, whose own life was in some disarray, became clothed with the magic of his profession and, calling on his patients with his black bag, made them feel alarmed or instantly better and turn to him for guidance although most of them were wiser and a great deal more experienced than he was. Giving coherent advice, trying to fathom the complexities of other people's lives, saved him the trouble of understanding his own or laying down any particular treatment for himself. When he started he was excited by being a doctor. On the whole, his customers liked him, and although he had by no means discovered how to live, he became, in time, able to reconcile those he treated and their families to death.

The partnership prospered and in time took on another young doctor, Geoffrey Hardison, who was extremely serious and satisfyingly shocked by everything that Dr Salter had to say on the subject of bedrest, check-ups, diets and smoking.

While Fred lived unnoticed by the world in Hartscombe and Simeon spent more time in the garden and less dictating manifestos to Glenys Bigwell, Henry took on the task of public pronouncement. He signed letters to *The Times*, he sat on the platforms, he read poems and went to rallies, protesting about the Greek Colonels and the continued war in Vietnam, mourning the blacks killed in Detroit riots and the death of Che Guevara. Simeon, listening to his portable wireless while Dorothy weeded, frequently heard his elder son sounding off on *Any Questions?* and wondered why people who once took the advice of statesmen and priests now seemed so anxious to be guided by writers of fiction.

Henry, Agnes and their child, Francesca, moved to a flat just off the King's Road, an area where Arthur Nubble had opened a boutique called Sam and Samantha, which did well for a time. Henry was often to be found having lunch in nearby Italian restaurants, meeting-places for models and agents and film directors, where he would sit among the gleaming white lavatory tiles, the low-slung lights and tall dark wooden chairs, wearing a white polo-neck sweater, drinking Verdicchio and holding forth on the injustices of the world.

Charlie was taking a new course in Social Administration at the London School of Economics, an institution made the more exciting for her by the large number of strikes, sit-ins and student protests. In the evenings, when Leslie was dining with clients in the Caprice or the Mirabelle, his wife would meet student activists, for whom she bought many drinks, and would sit on the edge of the group, listening and saying little. On some nights she would go out with young men whose hard cases formed part of her practical training. She found herself in big, noisy pubs, round King's Cross or in the East End. She went drinking in Soho clubs which were open all the afternoon, and, on certain occasions, she was made love to in the students' rooms or in the backs of borrowed cars.

At such times she believed herself to be happy in a world far away from Rapstone and the small, neat London house, forever humming with the carefully controlled chatter of property developers, which was Leslie's home in London. When she came in, her husband didn't ask her where she'd been, nor was he interested in her explanations about late seminars or committee meetings. He went to sleep quickly, tired out by his business dealings. He didn't seem to care that their worlds had divided and, to her great relief, never expected her to join him and Christopher Kempenflatt in their working dinners in Mayfair.

In time Mrs Mallard-Greene became discontented in Tom Nowt's old cottage. Her children were away at boarding school and Malley left at six o'clock each morning for his job in the

B.B.C. She never quite knew what he was doing there although she suspected that he was taking his secretary out to long lunches where they gloated over the sweet trolley together and then what? He always came home exhausted and never hungry, and obliged her by going to sleep in front of the telly at half past nine. Left in the country Mrs Mallard-Greene attacked the earth over the buried deer bones, bought a lot of plants from the Hartscombe Garden Centre but finally surrendered to the weeds. She made the acquaintance of a few similarly abandoned wives and had coffee and nips of brandy with them in the mornings, quarrelled with them and had difficulty keeping a cleaning lady. In the afternoon she often sat watching the rain on the hedge-rows, the mounting willow herb and the blossoming cow parsley. She felt a tightness in her chest and sent for Dr Simcox.

'What's the trouble?'

'Look out there, that's the trouble! It's so green and quiet and it's always bloody raining.'

'That's England, Mrs Mallard-Greene. I'm afraid there's no known cure for it.'

In the last months of her pregnancy, Glenys and Terry Faw-cett were at last moved into a two-roomed flat at the top of a Worsfield tower block. Glenys thought they could make it quite cosy once they got the curtains up, and they would be able to put the pram out on the narrow walk-way overhanging the precipice on which they were perched. Far below was a small patch of green where dogs were not allowed and, on a section specially railed off, their children might be allowed to play. As Glenys outlined her plans for the future, Terry assembled his clarinet and began to play 'Ain't Misbehavin'', even before he had laid the carpet.

About six months after he qualified Fred stopped for a beer in a pub on Picton Ridge and made a final attempt at dialling Mrs Wickstead's number. Up, like a row of cherries on a fruit machine, came her voice apparently not in the least surprised. If he ever came to London she would certainly have lunch with him, dinner wasn't so simple, nor was it sensible to ring her in the evenings, she was usually out. Fred named his next day off and a restaurant in Jermyn Street that Henry had often talked to him about.

He arrived almost twenty minutes early for their first lunch together and Mrs Wickstead was exactly a quarter of an hour late. He was in a state of near despair when he finally saw a waiter, a man who had been studiously avoiding his eye, escort her proudly over to him. He had bought a new shirt and tie, and taken what had seemed an immense sum out of the bank and realized in a panic that fifteen pounds was only just going to cover their lunch.

When she was sitting beside him, Fred forgot about the money; he staked everything on Mediterranean prawns, grilled sole and a bottle of Chablis. Mrs Wickstead ate exactly what he had ordered and she listened to him talking about his patients, and the extraordinary views of Dr Salter, wide-eyed and enthralled. When it was over she said, 'You know, you shouldn't have spent out on all those Mediterranean prawns. Quite honestly, I'd rather have had the money.' She was smiling and he was sure it was a joke. 'The trouble with lunch is thinking where to go afterwards.'

'Where do you live exactly?' He had put his hand on hers as they sat side by side on the plush bench, under the red satin walls and shaded electric candles which imparted a pink glow to Mrs Wickstead. 'Couldn't we go there?'

'Oh I don't think you'd like that. I don't think you'd find that at all suitable.' Then she was laughing at his look of disappointment. 'I do have a girlfriend though, with a sort of a flat. It's in Notting Hill Gate. For God's sake, next time, don't spend so much on lunch. We could bring sandwiches.'

'Are we going to have a next time?' Fred continued to hold on to Mrs Wickstead, conscious that his hand was hotter and probably damper than it should be for the accomplished luncher-out and boulevardier.

'Oh, I think so, don't you?'

'I was wondering.'

'What?'

'About Mr Wickstead.'

Only then did she remove her hand. 'Mr Wickstead,' she said, 'is entirely my business!'

Fred took the train back to Hartscombe, feeling that fate, which hadn't been very generous to him since he parted from Agnes, had handed him a huge slice of luck on a plate. He began to 'see' or 'go out' (which really means staying in) with Mrs Wickstead. Three weeks later they met in a small Italian restaurant in Notting Hill Gate, lunched hurriedly and walked to the flat for which she had a key. Making love to Mrs Wickstead was a far simpler, even more innocent experience than Fred had expected. She was laughing as they undressed, then enthusiastic, and finally sleepy. As she closed her eyes, Fred who had become domesticated during his bachelor life, put on one of the two towelling dressing-gowns that hung on the bathroom door and made tea. He wondered a little about Mrs Wickstead's girlfriend who seemed to have left few traces of her personality on her home. He could see no pictures or books, no photographs, and only half a bottle of milk and a bottle of champagne in the fridge. He wondered if the fitted cupboards in the bedroom were full of her clothes but before he had a chance to investigate, Mrs Wickstead opened her eyes, sat up and put out her hand for a cup of tea.

'This girlfriend of yours seems extremely tidy.'

'She works. She's frightfully well organized.'

Mrs Wickstead, sitting up naked in bed, put down her tea and stretched her arms towards him. Fred asked no more questions about the girlfriend.

Sometimes he didn't see his new-found friend for weeks, even months at a time. After their long partings she would turn up suntanned and murmuring about Nassau or Gstaad or the Greek Islands, but she never showed him snaps or recounted her adventures on these holidays, apparently preferring to hear him talk. Sometimes, when he had tried to telephone her for weeks without reply, she would call the surgery and leave a message. On his next day off he would wait for her in a big, gloomy pub by Notting Hill Gate tube station and she would arrive smiling, always in a rush to get there a quarter of an hour late. They had given up restaurants now, bought rolls, pâté and cheese in a delicatessen, together with bottles of champagne, which Mrs Wickstead insisted on paying for. When they got to the flat they would make love at once, she apparently as eager as he was after weeks of separation. Then they had a high tea, always washing up and leaving the flat as tidy as they found it. She had, of course, he discovered, other names but he always thought of her as Mrs Wickstead, because that was how she had been introduced to him, and because his use of her Christian name, Virginia, didn't make him feel that he knew any more about her.

So on and off, punctuated by long intervals and enthusiastic revivals, secret, simple and satisfying, Fred's friendship with Mrs Wickstead continued. The surgery receptionist got used to leaving notes with her name on them and Dr Salter asked no questions. One Christmas in the flat they opened their presents to each other. Her gifts to him had been lavish: cufflinks, a shirt from Harrods, a pair of shoes which fitted, because he never bought shoes for himself, and LPs, old recordings of Louis Armstrong and the Hot Five with the original crackle.

'There you go. Have you got everything you want?'

'Except for one thing.'

'What's that?' It was the most anxious he had ever seen her look.

'I'd like to show you where I live. I mean I want you to see Rapstone and all my country.'

'Well.' She looked relieved, as though she had been expecting an impossible claim. 'I don't see why not.'

'Mrs Shelley's in the clear.' The lab tests had arrived and were on Dr Salter's desk in the surgery. Fred had come in to his senior partner's room to learn the secret constituents of his patients' blood, and was considerably relieved about a young mother in a sudden panic about the cause of her exhaustion.

'That's very good.' Dr Salter was slitting open an envelope. He glanced at the report it contained and, as his partner was searching for the names of his other patients, slid it under the blotter on his desk.

'This weekend . . .' Dr Salter began, but Fred, who had been waiting for a chance to mention it, interrupted him. 'Oh, I was going to ask you about this weekend.'

'Were you?'

'I've got . . . Well, a friend of mine's coming down from London.'

It was a weekend when Fred would normally be on duty, and the only one when Mrs Wickstead could make an expedition to the English countryside.

'I think, I rather think I shall have to go hunting.' Dr Salter lit a cheroot and blew out smoke. Fred felt a great wave of disappointment, like a child who had been suddenly deprived of a long-promised treat.

'Oh, well. In that case . . .'

'Yes. I feel the time has come for a brisk ride to hounds. Don't worry though, old cock. Young Hardison can look after the shop.'

After Fred had gone, Dr Salter took the report out from under his blotter. He read it again carefully, although he knew quite well that there had been no mistake. Then he tore it into strips and set fire to them in his ashtray.

The hunt met at Rapstone Manor on a Saturday morning when the trees were still black lines across a grey sky and spring was a faint hope for the future. Nicholas came out to chat, Dr Salter took a stirrup cup from Wyebrow, and Grace shivered as she viewed the proceedings from her bedroom window. Fred, standing on Hartscombe station, telling himself not to expect too much, was amazed when a train arrived, a door opened and the single passenger not going on to Worsfield was Mrs Wickstead. She stepped out, looking puzzled, as though she had arrived in a strange country and didn't expect to hear English spoken.

'I'm glad you came.'

'I do think it was quite brave of me.'

He put his arm round her, trying to keep her as warm as possible on their way to the car park.

The hunt was moving off down the lanes and across the fields away from Rapstone as Fred drove up to the ridge and showed Mrs Wickstead the view down the valley. He felt he was letting her into his childhood. 'It hasn't changed,' he told her. 'Not really very much, ever since I can remember it. Some of the cottages have been converted, of course. And the summers don't seem so hot now. That's Skurfield over there. We think of it as full of rather glum, short people who keep chickens in clapped-out Austin Sevens. You know the sort of thing?'

'Not really.'

'What do you think of it?'

'Cold.'

The hunt was fanning out now, across a stretch of open country. Dr Salter was up with the leaders riding the big hunter he had first seen at Worsfield Show on the day that Leslie Titmuss announced his engagement. He was smiling, taking jumps easily, as though enjoying the best day out in his life.

Fred had no intention of taking Mrs Wickstead to visit his parents at the Rectory. He wanted to spare her Simeon's Olympian curiosity and Dorothy's amused unconcern. However he risked a visit to the church. 'It's Norman basically,' he told her. 'Of course it's been added to a lot. There's some Victorian bits.' He opened the door of the vestry, breathing in the familiar smell of mice and hassocks. 'When I was a child, I used to sit in here with my father. Cutting up bread for Communion. What's so funny?'

'Englishmen.'

'Why?'

'Once they start going to bed with you, they always want to take you into churches.'

The hunt had walked round a square of ploughed field and was now moving again, the hounds following a straight line towards a copse on a hillside, the riders spreading out, the leaders galloping with mud flying, others struggling to keep up. By a hedge the protesters shouted, blew whistles and waved their banners, angered by the bright coats, the beauty of the horses and the concentrated and elaborate pursuit of death. Fred and Mrs Wickstead lay together, warm at last, in his bedroom above the butcher's shop in the Worsfield Road. Later they planned to eat the food he had bought and drink a celebration bottle of champagne.

Those in the lead at the hunt remembered Dr Salter moving away from them. He left the line and galloped diagonally across a stretch of pasture, pounding the thin grass so that black earth was thrown up by his horse's hooves. He was riding at a high, an impossibly high hedge with a gate leading to a road. But he swerved from the gate and went straight for the huge hedge, faster and faster for a jump which his horse took bravely, hopelessly, into a tangle of dark wood, and below the dim light of the sky.

'Don't answer it, please!' Mrs Wickstead said when the telephone rang, but Fred got out of bed and stood naked in his living-room while Hardison told him the news. And then he was dressed and walking down a rubber-smelling corridor in the Worsfield General with a white-coated houseman. The walk seemed endless, but at last they swung open a pair of doors and were in a room where Dr Salter lay flat on his back with his eyes open.

'Sorry,' he muttered when Fred looked down at him. 'I seem to have made the most almighty cock-up!'

*

Some months later Simeon called on Dr Salter, whom he found in a room above the surgery, somehow diminished in size, and seated in a wheel-chair in which, from then on, he would spend his waking hours. Simeon entered the room with an expression of serious concern and was a little taken aback to be greeted by a burst of laughter, nothing like the sound made by the old Dr Salter, but all the same, the patient seemed to be enjoying a joke.

'You can laugh?'

'About all I can do. I'm still alive but unfortunately not kicking. He's got quite a sense of humour, your old practical joker.'

'Mine?' Simeon declined to be identified with whatever power had prescribed the Doctor a broken back.

'The old gentleman you claim as such a close acquaintance. The one with the beard and the irritable expression. A great prankster, apparently. No doubt time hangs heavy on His hands, waiting for you to lecture Him on the joys of the Welfare State every Sunday from Rapstone pulpit. Probably longs to get hold of a bit of fire and brimstone and smite a few backsliders for idolatry.'

Simeon waited for the Doctor's speech, which he clearly relished and had, possibly, rehearsed, to be over. It took a little longer.

'When you're next on your knees tell Him it was very funny but hardly worth His while. I mean, hasn't He got enough on His hands with wars and earthquakes and famines without spotting one ageing G.P. on the hunting-field, a fellow out with the sole purpose of getting his neck broken, and turning him into a useless sort of lump that can't even *walk* to hounds?'

Silence fell between the two men, and then Dr Salter thought to ask, 'I say. Do you think the Almighty's a member of it?'

'Of what?'

'The League Against Cruel Sports?'

'Of course not. Why should He be?'

'Well, according to you, He's a paid-up member of the Labour Party.'

Simeon smiled patiently, and asked the Doctor a question. 'Did you say you went out with the sole purpose of getting your neck broken?'

'Of course. I always told you they did you a decent death on the hunting-field.' But then the joke was over and he said seriously, 'Tom Nowt did it far more efficiently.'

'What did Tom Nowt do?'

'We get these little verdicts you know.' Dr Salter gave what he seemed to feel was the obvious explanation. 'Decisions. Lab tests. Quite simple. They either condemn you to death or let you off provided you promise to be of good behaviour and not get ill. Tom Nowt and I were found guilty of the serious crime of carcinoma for which there can only be one penalty. He mitigated the sentence with a shot-gun; on the hunting-field I simply added a few minor disabilities to the final judgement.'

'Tom Nowt shot himself?'

'I was never a shooting man.'

'You told the Coroner that Nowt's death was an accident.'

'Didn't want any rubbish talked about unsound mind. Box of cheroots on that table by the gramophone, mind passing them? Might as well assault the lungs as well as everything else.'

Simeon stood up and moved across the room. He felt guilty, a tall, walking man in his sixties, looking down at the helpless Doctor who had been forced to surrender to illness, his life-long enemy.

'Would you like me to come and sit with you? I've plenty of time now.'

'No.' Dr Salter selected a cheroot from the box Simeon held for him. 'I don't think I should like that at all.'

So Fred took over the running of the Hartscombe practice, with the help of young Hardison and occasional advice from the wheel-chair in the room upstairs. When Agnes called to see her father, Dr Salter said he didn't want visits to the sick, then he told her to go back to London and look after her child. It was as though he were ashamed of his condition and didn't want his daughter exposed to such an obscenity. Mrs Beasley cooked for him and did the housekeeping, otherwise Dr Salter was looked after by the District Nurse. Smoking, drinking brandy, listening to his records and disliking the District Nurse were now his occupations.

Part Four

'Who breaks his birth's invidious bar,
And grasps the skirts of happy chance,
And breasts the blows of circumstance,
And grapples with his evil star;'

from *In Memoriam*
Alfred, Lord Tennyson

Chapter Nineteen

LESLIE'S LONG WEEKEND

Leslie Titmuss came down for breakfast at Rapstone Manor and almost fell headlong over Bridget Bigwell, who was frantically polishing the brass stair-rods.

'Oh, do mind yourself, Leslie!' Then she remembered that he was a guest. 'I'm sorry, Mr Titmuss. Once a week we have to get all our stair-rods up.'

'You were always thorough, Bridget, I always heard that, when you were at Picton House.'

'Twelve bedroom fireplaces to be done when the visitors were down for their breakfast and coal scuttles to be polished so you could see your face in them.'

'My mother told me a lot about when you were in service with Doughty Strove.'

'Mr Doughty! He was more or less a young lad then.'

'Well, yes. Exactly.'

And Leslie was off to join his host and hostess at breakfast. Nicholas was hidden behind *The Times* and Grace was opening envelopes, reading the scrawled handwriting of friends she had 'come out' with, bringing her news of death, disease and divorce. Leslie, having helped himself to a full plate of eggs, sausages and bacon, was determined to chat.

'Mother-in-law . . .'

'Do try not to call me that.' Grace didn't look up from her correspondence.

'What would you like me to call you?'

'Call me Grace. Call me Lady Fanner. For heaven's sake call me Mother Teresa if you want to.'

'But not mother-in-law?' Leslie was anxious to get it right.

'It's the sort of expression that might be used by Mr Harold Wilson.'

There was a pause while Grace opened more letters and Leslie got stuck into his breakfast. Then he said, apparently seriously, 'If I say anything like that again, Grace, anything that irritates you in any way, I'd be very glad if you'd let me know.'

'Don't you worry.'

'We're sorry Charlie couldn't come with you.' Nicholas peered round the edge of his newspaper.

'Charlie's studying.' Grace knew.

'Yes. They're keeping her pretty busy at the L.S.E.' Leslie was now at work on the toast and marmalade. 'So I thought someone should come down to give the parents all the latest news from the big city.'

'To give your parents?'

'Well, no. I meant the Fanner family. You, Grace and Nicholas, of course.'

'In my day a young wife wouldn't think of studying.' Grace harked back to an earlier deception. 'She'd think of babies. And real ones, this time, *if* you please.'

'Well, not yet, Grace, not until the business really gets established. Magnus Strove and I are hoping to pull off the big one. The Tasker Street development.'

'What on earth's Tasker Street?'

'It's a row of little shops at the moment, not far from Liverpool Street station. We're hoping to develop it.'

'You make it sound like a photograph.' Grace went back to her post.

'Offices for people to sit in while they plan to build more offices.' Nicholas was not convinced. Nor, when Leslie suggested it, did he want to come in with them. He remembered Magnus Strove as a small boy: 'Every time I saw him he seemed to be able to make me part with ten bob! Some story about collecting for disabled seamen, or poor children in the East End. He could be very convincing.'

'Well, he's managed to persuade the bank. It's our first, our only, real gamble. If we can pull this one off we can have everything, babies, anything you like.'

'I didn't say I liked them exactly.' Grace was gathering up her letters, resigning from the task of keeping her son-in-law entertained until Monday morning. 'I suppose you can amuse yourself this weekend?'

'I was wondering, Nicholas,' Leslie asked as though for the realization of a childhood dream, 'if there would be any chance of having a look round the farmyard this morning?'

'My dear boy, of course. We'll go now. Finish up your coffee.' The world was surprisingly short of people who actually asked to see Nicholas's pigs.

'How absolutely super!'

It was in the farmyard, picking his way through the cowshed in a pair of borrowed wellies and admiring the new milking-machine, that Leslie delicately approached a subject which lay considerably nearer to his heart than a conducted tour of the home farm. He didn't, of course, come at it head on, but in a circuitous fashion, by way of the lack of support the politicians of the day were giving to the Great British Breakfast. Speaking for himself, Leslie didn't remember Doughty Strove asking a single question in the House about bacon.

'You may be right. More of an oil-seed rape man is Doughty.'

'Of course the old fellow's done yeoman service for the Harts-combe constituency.'

'I seem to remember some suggestions you made about the purple past of Doughty Strove.' Nicholas saw no reason why one of his contemporaries should be called 'old'.

'Rumours! I was only reporting on some rather damaging tittle-tattle. Personally I don't believe there was a word of truth in it. I'm sure we all want to see Doughty reap his just reward.'

'Glad to hear you say so.' They had arrived at the sties and Nicholas was mollified, not only by Leslie's retraction, but by the sight of the well-fattened animals with small intelligent eyes snorting with contentment. Those with red crosses on their rumps were destined for an early visit to the abattoir. 'But what sort of reward are you talking about exactly?'

'His elevation.'

'The elevation of Doughty.' Nicholas laughed, having a sudden vision of his stout neighbour levitating mysteriously, and in a bad temper.

'To another place,' Leslie explained patiently. 'The Upper House. Well, they're bound to offer Doughty the Lords, aren't they? He's been the member here for so many years, off and on.'

'You mean they'd give Doughty a peerage?' Nicholas raised his eyes reluctantly from his pigs. 'I never heard any talk of that.'

'But it's possible, isn't it?' Leslie was pushing gently. 'Quite likely in fact.'

'I suppose' – Nicholas felt it would be disloyal to dismiss the suggestion out of hand – 'it is reasonably likely.'

'Well, we'll have to start looking round, won't we?'

'Looking round? Whatever for?'

'A new Conservative candidate. For the Hartscombe and Worsfield South constituency.'

Grace didn't have to entertain Leslie much that weekend. Magnus Strove had invited him to dinner at Picton House, partly to discuss Tasker Street and partly to persuade his father to try and make some money out of his gloomy and underpopulated house and the large park that surrounded it. For instance, a pop festival in the grounds might be profitable and Hartscombe Enterprises would undertake the organization. 'Popular music?' Doughty had a momentarily comforting vision of a band playing selections from Gilbert and Sullivan, but he knew that was not what the young men had in mind. 'Look at it this way,' Leslie suggested. 'At the moment Picton represents locked-up capital with a minus income factor. Let it pay its way occasionally.'

'I wouldn't have to have lions, would I?'

'No, Father. Not lions. Just a lot of frightfully nice people wearing beads.'

'Of course.' Leslie refused port, keeping a clear head for this delicate stage of the conversation. 'Picton'll become even more famous after you've gone up.'

'Gone up where?' For an appalled moment Doughty thought that young Leslie was planning his death.

'Oh, haven't you heard anything?'

'Anything about what?'

'It's just that Nicholas was saying this morning that it's more than likely, in fact it's pretty well certain. Of course they don't tell people, do they?'

'What don't they tell people?' Pale old Doughty had an edge of panic in his voice.

'It's all meant to be a tremendous secret, I suppose that's why Nicholas won't talk to you about it. Well, I promise you I won't say a word.'

'Won't say all word about what? For heaven's sake, Titmuss. I've absolutely no idea what you're talking about.'

'Such a pity it's only life peerages with the Socialists in power. Still, I suppose he'll be the Honourable Magnus.'

'Honourable Magnus?' Doughty savoured the future which he understood at last. 'I've always wanted the House of Lords. I think it would be right for the family.'

'No one deserves it more, according to my father-in-law.'

'Vague sort of chap in many ways, but Nicholas is pretty near the heart of the Conservative Party.'

'I'd rather you didn't mention it to him. It was told me in confidence and one simply doesn't gossip about these things.'

'What would the style be, I wonder?' Doughty sounded dreamy. 'Lord Strove of Picton Principal? Lord Picton?'

'Not Lord Skurfield, Daddy.' Magnus laughed at the inelegant title and Leslie paused, like a snooker champion planning a long pot into a distant pocket. Then he played the shot. 'Of course, you'd have to give up the idea of fighting Hartscombe in the next election.'

'Give up the parliamentary candidacy?'

'They'd want you to make that clear before any final decision. I mean if you get in they wouldn't want to move you to the Lords, couldn't risk a by-election.'

'I see.' Doughty thought that he did.

'It'll be a bit of a relief to you, won't it?' Leslie was understanding. 'To be out of the dust of the arena? Leave the hard slog to a younger man, won't that be a relief?' Doughty Strove seemed to think that perhaps it would.

On Sunday morning, Leslie went to church. In the evening he sat by the fire in Rapstone Manor watching Grace playing patience while Nicholas read dutifully through the proceedings of the Begonia Society.

'So Charlie's studying to love the poor?'

'Something like that, yes. You could put up your Red Queen.' Grace's refusal to wear glasses when they had visitors, even such visitors as Leslie Titmuss, made her miss many tricks in her solitary card games. 'I suppose she's got to love someone. She can't love me.'

'And the Black Jack.' Leslie moved it for her.

'I don't think it's at all necessary to love a person, just because they happen to be your mother or your daughter. There's no need for anyone to feel guilty about such things.'

'The Ace can go up.'

'I may not be the most practical person in the world, but I *can* manage my own patience.'

'I'm sorry, moth . . . I mean, I'm frightfully sorry, Grace.'

'And don't feel sorry about things! There's far too much of that about, if you want my opinion. Anyway, stop watching me like a hawk. I fully intend to cheat a little.'

So Leslie moved away obediently and told Nicholas that old Doughty Strove seemed to be slowing down a bit. 'He complained to me that he gets tired very easily. Politics are beginning to take it out of the old chap.'

'Lifting a heavy brandy glass in the Members Bar must be absolutely exhausting!' Grace dug into the pack and extricated the Red Seven she had been hoping for.

'In fact he's extremely doubtful whether he's going to stand at the next election,' Leslie was able to tell them. 'No sort of final decision on that as yet of course.'

Although he left early on Monday morning, Leslie didn't go directly back to London. He spent the day doing some business with local estate agents and had a drink at lunchtime with the editor of the Hartscombe *Advertiser*. George had just got home from the Brewery when Leslie called at 'The Spruces'. The table was set with lettuce and tinned salmon, slices of bread and butter, cake and biscuits. 'There's more than enough for three,' Elsie said, and started to lay another place.

'Thank you, Mother, but I'm having dinner in London. Magnus and I are meeting a couple of fellows from the bank.'

'Feed up, boy.' George was thumping the bottom of the salad cream bottle, which then emitted a hefty white dollop. 'You've got a journey to go.'

'He'll be having his later, Father, in the form of dinner.'

'And I can't go out with the fellows from the bank and not be hungry. It wouldn't be polite.'

'So it's more polite to come here and not be hungry, is it? I mean it's all right not to be hungry in your own home.' George took a large mouthful and chewed steadily, as though it were now his duty to eat for his son as well.

Then Leslie told them that he might, he might just possibly be offered something rather important. Elsie guessed that it was a position, but he said he couldn't tell them any more about it because it wouldn't be fair to 'someone who isn't in the very best of health'. However, he wanted them to know that he'd always be proud of them, proud of having been brought up in Skurfield and proud of having been taught not to be above going out to cut nettles to earn a bob or two when it was needed. After this speech Elsie sat looking at her son in silent admiration, and George, pushing away his emptied plate, said, 'Very tasty dear. That was very tasty.' At which moment there was an unexpected chime at the door and Leslie hurried to admit a Mr Narroway, a photographer from the *Advertiser*, who had, it seemed, called to take a family group of the Titmusses. At last a somewhat bemused George was persuaded to stand on the left of his son in front of the fireplace, while Elsie was on Leslie's right. Prominent in the background was the statuette of the bather from Clee-thorpes which, as a boy, Leslie had once rashly given to the Rector. 'Will all this be something to do with your new position?' his mother asked, and Leslie murmured, 'Let's hope so,' as Mr Narroway caught them all three, startled and wide-eyed in the flash.

Although Elsie searched the *Advertiser* with excitement during the next months the photograph was delayed until the Tasker Street development was securely launched and Leslie started to acquire the fortune which would allow him to devote his life to the work to which he had apparently become dedicated. '*Politics*: the thankless task of bossing around a lot of people who don't want to be bossed and don't care who's trying to do it. The work is extremely dull and its only reward is a temporary illusion of power' (Dr Salter's definition). Such was the mysterious 'position' which he had hinted at, and which his mother had hoped to be something moderately high up in a bank.

On the day the demolition gangs moved into Tasker Street, Elsie was rewarded by the sight of her family, her own front room and the bather from Cleethorpes featured in the *Advertiser*. 'City Developer at Home in Skurfield', was the headline, and the readers were told that it was Mr Leslie Titmuss, a partner in Hartscombe Enterprises, now involved in an important development scheme in the City of London, pictured at home with his parents. 'Mr Titmuss Senior has just completed forty years' service in the accounts department at Simcox's Brewery.'

Elsie posted a copy of the paper to her son but he was more interested in the scarcely prominent paragraph in the *Daily Telegraph* which appeared later. He read it aloud over breakfast, while his wife was standing, gulping coffee and chewing toast, on her way to what was to be a rare working-day at the London School of Economics: 'Doughty Strove, the former Conservative Member for Hartscombe and Worsfield South, has announced that he will not be contesting the seat at the next election. "I hope I shall be able to be of service to my country," Mr Strove said, "in another capacity." Hartscombe is a Labour marginal where Ben Leverett, M.P., had a majority at the last election of only thirty-nine.'

'Is that the big news in the paper?' Charlie asked on her way out. 'Of course,' Leslie told her. 'It's the big news for me.'

Chapter Twenty

THE LOST LEADER

'Henry Simcox. May I ask you what you're writing now?'

'Something we started on a few years ago, but couldn't get off the ground. You know about movies? They die and get resurrected time and again before they appear in public. This is an idea I had about characters who come from all over the world to go on this – well, this pilgrimage.'

'But it's not religious?'

'No. I promise you. I'm more interested in live sinners than dead saints.'

'Are you a contemplater?'

'Am I what?'

'Have you got a god-sized hole in you? I mean one takes the point about Christianity, but the religions of the East . . .'

'Eastern complacency's even more repulsive than English complacency. I've got no time for blokes who sit in Kathmandu contemplating their navels and putting up with poverty and starvation, and the worst class system outside Bournemouth. I'd like to see all those gurus get off their backsides and start demonstrating . . .'

'Camera reloading,' a voice called from the shadows stopping him in mid-flow. The interview was being filmed in his flat. He sat in a pool of white light and chatted until the camera was ready to receive the image of Henry Simcox once more.

'You know we've got a cottage in your neck of the woods.'

The interviewer was Mr Mallard-Greene of the B.B.C. Arts Programme. 'My wife absolutely adores it.'

'That was terrific stuff! Going very well,' the director called from the darkness. 'Pick it up from "get off their backsides and start demonstrating".'

'Bit of a dry mouth,' Henry discovered.

'Lonnie! You've got Mr Simcox's coffee?'

'Yes. Yes of course.' An enthusiastic girl appeared in the pool of light carrying a mug of Instant. Although not especially pretty she was remarkable for her soft voice and expression of deep concern. 'I can easily heat it up again if that's what you'd like.'

'It's fine thank you. I only wanted a swig.'

'When you're finished I'm going to pluck up courage and ask you to sign one of your books for me.'

'Of course.'

'Please. Don't forget.'

They were ready for another take and Henry gave his mug back to the girl, who retreated with it reverently, as though she had just been handed the Holy Grail.

'So you are in favour of demonstrating?'

'Certainly. What are we supposed to do about Vietnam? Well, at least we still have the right to shout!'

As though taking her cue from this, the four-year-old Francesca, who had just fallen over in the bedroom, let out a series of piercing shrieks. 'All right, cut.' The director sounded weary. 'Lonnie, see if you can do something about that child.' So Agnes, comforting her daughter, was surprised by a plumpish girl whose eyes seemed to be rather too close together and who looked at her with a kind of tolerant despair. 'Please. Could you try and keep the child quiet. After all we *are* shooting.'

Agnes went to Grosvenor Square because she believed in the protest and thought that Henry believed in it too. Although there were many women there with toddlers, and even babies, she left her child at home with a babysitter, thinking that

Francesca was not yet able to make decisions in matters of world politics. She and Henry were together at first, marching in the detachment from Oxford Street. In front of them she could see the helmets of policemen trying to stop the column but the helmets retreated. Agnes was marching solemnly, like a new recruit, still anxious to do her best. Henry walked excited beside her. He was shouting and seemed to be protesting for everyone he could think of: Czech students, as well as children in Asian villages, American blacks and even the inhabitants of Rapstone who found themselves short of cottages. His anger came out in great whoops of delight and he smiled frequently at the marchers around them. Although he was a well-known writer he seemed to pass unrecognized and, like his wife, he was merely a private in this army. Round them the placards waved like banners and there was a great deal of shouting of 'Hey, hey, L.B.J., how many kids have you killed today?' It was when Henry joined in this cry that Agnes noticed that he did so with an American accent.

It was far removed from the gentle walk across the English countryside which Fred had escaped from to meet Agnes when the threat of war had seemed less important than love in a churchyard. The reality of fighting on the other side of the world, the burning villages and the laid-out bodies of dead children, received the tribute of a pale, imitation war in the West End of London. When Agnes got into the square she saw that the garden in the centre was already occupied and a column was wheeling round to advance on the front of the American Embassy. She saw people running, throwing stones, clods of earth from the garden, and over the crowd she saw the mounted police and the heads of the horses. Smoke bombs and fire crackers went off in front of her and she began to run with the rest of the demonstrators.

Even as she ran, Agnes thought of the absurdity of the situation. What would a stone thrown, a policeman's helmet knocked off in Grosvenor Square, do to stop mass killing on the other side of the world? The shouting, the waving placards, seemed as ridiculous as the solemn cavalry, brought out as if to fight some ancient battle, forgotten in the history books. Yet as she realized the day's pointlessness, she became excited. She began to get nearer the horses, she wanted to see the charge. It was then that she looked round and saw that Henry was no longer with her.

It wasn't until she was on the pavement opposite the Embassy that she saw him again. She was standing against some railings looking towards South Audley Street, as a crowd of reinforcements tried to force a police barrier. She saw a large, silver-coloured motor car parked, and beside it stood Henry talking to, of all people in the world, Mr Bugloss. Had Benjamin K. suddenly become a peace demonstrator, was he about to risk his valuable connection with Jack Polefax and Galaxy International for the sake of one glorious shout in front of the Embassy? Agnes tried to wave at him and to call out words of encouragement. Then she saw both men get into the car and Henry was driven away from the battlefield. Agnes left the railings as the police horses began to trot in the face of the crowd. She stood still, amazed by the sudden beauty of the sight.

'Judging me! You're always sitting there judging me!'

Agnes didn't say anything. She was giving Francesca her tea, egg and toast soldiers, after she had arrived home from the engagement in Grosvenor Square. 'I suppose' – Henry was walking up and down the room in increasing anger – 'you think I haven't lived up to your extraordinary standards.'

'Just one more bite, Francesca.' Agnes offered a yellow-dipped soldier.

'One more bite! To end the Vietnam War.'

'You were the one who was keen on the demonstration.'

'Look! Ben Bugloss heard about my interview on television. He's just on the point of doing a deal for *Pilgrims* with Galaxy. Naturally he didn't want his writer arrested for storming the American Embassy!'

'Very reasonable, I'd say.' Agnes was eating the soldiers for Francesca.

'Well, I was there, wasn't I?'

'Oh, yes. You were there, Henry. You stood up and were counted.'

'Why do you have to say it like that?'

'Say it like what?'

'Looking down from a great height! Passing judgement.' He turned away from her and opened the stripped pine cupboard where the bottles were kept. 'I'm having a drink. Do you want a drink?'

'No, thanks. I've just had Francesca's tea.'

'My little brother Fred ran out on a demonstration.' Henry returned to the attack. 'He sneaked off to see you, as I remember. You snogged in a churchyard. You didn't blame little Fred for that!'

'No. That wasn't what I blamed him for.'

'So it's just *me*, is it? You only want to condemn *me*! That's what really makes you feel good.' He was into one of his speeches now, Agnes knew, spreading the ointment of words on the pain he felt. 'That's what gives you your great, warm, comforting assurance of feminine superiority. "I married Henry Simcox, but he turned out to have feet of clay. Just like everybody else. Did you hear how he ran out of the Battle of Grosvenor Square? Of course, I stayed on. So I wouldn't be ashamed when Francesca asked me, 'What did you do in the Great Demo, Mummy?'"'

'That's quite funny.'

'Well, not for me, it isn't! For me it's like going to bed with an amateur Joan of Arc.'

'I'm sorry.'

'Where's the whisky?' Henry returned to the cupboard.

'I'm sorry it's like that for you.' Agnes was serious.

'Somebody's drunk all the bloody whisky!' He held up the empty bottle as though it were part of the conspiracy against him.

'I think you gave it to that film crew. You were being very generous.'

'All right. I'm going to the pub.' He moved away from her. 'I'll be back later, for a night of penance. Why don't you start ironing the hair-shirt?'

Henry went to a number of pubs that evening. He rang Lonnie, whose telephone number he had secured when he signed his book for her, from the Cross Keys. He bought a bottle of whisky and took it round to her bedsit near the World's End and there they went to bed together for the first time. It was an act which Lonnie took as a compliment and Henry felt no sort of judgement was being passed on him. She was particularly understanding when he told her he had to get home and helped find one of his socks under her bed. 'Of course,' she said. 'Of course, you must get back.'

'To all that disapproval.'

'I don't know what Agnes wants.' Lonnie gave him a puzzled smile. 'She must have everything anyone could wish for, you and Francesca.'

'Even the child looks as though it's condemning me for something. I think she teaches it.' Henry was sitting on the edge of the narrow bed, putting on his sock. 'Agnes thinks I should do more demonstrating.'

'That's silly. Your work's your demonstration, isn't it?'

'I suppose it is.' He stood up and kissed her, it was so much what he wanted to hear. 'I'm glad you were in when I called.'

'Oh, don't worry. I'll always be in.'

That was the great thing to be said for Lonnie, she always was.

Chapter Twenty-one

THE CANDIDATE

One evening that summer, Leslie Titmuss, neat in his dark blue suit, sat with Doughty Strove in the study at Picton House, discussing some business of mutual interest to Hartscombe Enterprises and the Strove estate. Lifting his eyes from the drink his host had poured him, Leslie saw a girl with pale hair loom out of the dusk and, waving her arms and legs rhythmically, appear to swim past the window. From where he sat he couldn't be sure if she were dressed in some light-fitting garment or if the colours in whirls and scrolls, flower and heart shapes, were painted on her body. He looked down into his glass and when he looked up again she was gone. Outside the still uncurtained windows, from the lakeside and the park, there was a sound like a distant storm and the flashing of lights. The other guests had gone out to join in the festivities and the two men, young and old, sat huddled together in the study as though for safety, discussing business. Doughty rose and drew the curtains, feeling that what they couldn't see wouldn't harm them.

'Magnus tells me I'm going to make money out of this.'

'I'm sure he's right.'

'Is he? I wish to God it were all over.'

So did Terry Fawcett. He stood under the trees with Glenys, far away by the side of the lake, where the group of the moment pranced and strutted like marionettes on the small, lit stage. The music came to them doubled and redoubled, crackling and echoing from amplifiers in the trees. Terry looked at the crowd, strangers from London, perhaps some from Worsfield. Like the music they were alien to him, and seemed to come from another age.

If the crowd in Grosvenor Square had been a pale imitation of an army at war, the mass of young people at the Picton House Pop Festival seemed to parody the idea of peace. The badges they wore like campaign medals not only said 'Make Love Not War' but 'If It Moves, Fondle It', 'Down with Pants' and 'Position Wanted'. The boys' hair was not yet shoulder-length – many of them looked like chunky young van drivers, storemen or roadworkers wearing cowbells, beads and an occasional flower behind the ear. The girls had long, straight hair and short dresses. They sat or lay in the grass, speechless beneath the blare of the music. Most of them stared or frowned at more ornate figures, wealthier students in embroidered Nehru jackets, who strutted among them like officers walking aloof through a dispirited encampment. The strong smell of pot which came to Terry on the summer breeze produced isolated giggles but little laughter. Now and again, a girl stood up to dance and some, closer to the lake, threw off their shirts or peeled off their jeans and attracted little attention. Now and again fights broke out under the trees.

'It's not music,' Terry told his wife. 'Not in any understood sense of the term.'

'You mean it's not the Riverside Stompers.'

'We shouldn't have put your mother to the trouble of babysitting, not to have our eardrums blasted off.'

'Terry!' He looked round and at first didn't recognize Charlie. She had added to the short, cotton, Indian-patterned dress she had worn at dinner with Doughty Strove, and had put on more beads, bells and a button which said 'I'm a Hippie'. A flower was painted on her forehead, her legs and feet were bare, and she looked lonely and pleased to see him. 'Look, Terry,' she said, in an accent which she had carefully flattened and sent down-market since her husband had begun to imitate the clenched-teeth delivery of Magnus Strove. 'Bloody awful about Tom's old cottage. And ours.' She apologized. 'I did try, really.'

'We're quite comfortable, thank you.' Glenys sounded brisk. 'The Council fixed us up with one of the new flats in Worsfield. There wasn't no need for all them drinks you took Terry for, round the Citizens Advice.'

'It's a great evening.' Charlie looked towards the crowd. 'Don't you think it's great? Everyone's so relaxed.'

'Terry isn't relaxed, he's going to request, "Ain't Misbehavin'"'. Come along, Terry, we might as well go and look at them dancing.' As Glenys removed her husband, Charlie said, 'Enjoy!' and raised her hand in a gesture of peace which looked dispirited. She stood alone for some while before taking a deep breath and walking down to the crowd by the lake, like a nervous bather steeling herself to plunge into a cold and possibly dangerous sea.

Leslie looked at his watch and decided that it was time to take his wife home. He left Doughty and set out for the terrace, where he saw three hippies passing round a joint which hovered between their fingers like a glow-worm. They were Magnus Strove, wearing a long, silk, high-necked jacket and a headband with a feather in it, Jennifer Battley with carnations and tinsel in her hair, and Christopher Kempenflatt complete with an embroidered Afghan waistcoat and ornate boots.

'Charlie's gone to the ball,' Magnus told him. 'She's already lost both of her slippers.'

'At midnight she'll probably turn into a hash cookie,' Jennifer thought.

'Or Mrs Leslie Titmuss.' Kempenflatt made it sound a grimmer fate. 'Come and sit down, old boy. Join the party. Now we really have got something to celebrate.' Buyers had been found for the Tasker Street offices, and both the bank and Kempenflatt's family construction firm had breathed huge sighs of relief. Leslie accepted the invitation, and sat for a while on the terrace wall beside them. When Jennifer held the rather sodden joint towards him he shook his head.

'You're a puritan!' Kempenflatt took it instead.

'I suppose I am.'

'Not a bad thing having a puritan in charge of the accounts.'

'Not so much of a puritan, our Leslie,' Magnus told Jennifer. 'He's not above a bit of mini-skirt accounting.'

'What's that?'

'Shows off all the figures except the vital parts!' They laughed loudly above the sound of distant music. Then Kempenflatt announced that, as their trickiest bit of business was settled, and now Doughty was no longer in the contest, he was going to do what he had always wanted and become the parliamentary candidate for Hartscombe and Worsfield South. 'I can count on your support, Leslie,' he supposed, 'in the constituency Party?'

'I'm sorry.' Leslie spoke quietly out of the darkness. 'Can't be done.'

'Why?'

'I mean to be adopted for Hartscombe.'

'A *Titmuss*, representing Hartscombe?' Kempenflatt was incredulous.

'You find that more outlandish than a Kempenflatt?'

'Well, there is a slight difference, isn't there?' There was light from the windows in the house and Kempenflatt could be seen smiling.

'Oh, I agree.'

'It really comes down to a background, doesn't it?' Christopher Kempenflatt was at his most kindly. 'No one can say it's the least little bit your fault. No doubt it's due to circumstances entirely beyond your control. And I must say the way you've pulled yourself up by your boot-straps does you enormous credit.'

'Pulled himself up by what?' Jennifer was puzzled.

'His boot-straps, apparently,' Magnus told her.

'But able as you may be, Leslie, confoundedly able, as a matter of fact, where's your background, eh?' Kempenflatt demanded. 'Tell me that now.'

Leslie got off the wall then and moved into the light. 'No. I think I'll save that to tell the Selection Committee.' And then he started down to the lake to fetch his wife.

*

Charlie had been dancing around a young man with bare feet and no shirt. The flowers, leaves, lips and crosses painted on his chest and arms, scrawled across his cheeks and nose, looked like wounds. He had large hands with a cigarette between his stubby fingers, short hair crowned with a plaited hairband and he danced on flat feet with heavy, unsmiling concentration. For a long while he seemed not to notice her but then he changed direction, plodded towards Charlie in time to the music and they were dancing nearer to each other, she smiling and clapping, he stamping as he stared at her. Then Leslie grabbed his wife's arm and pulled her out of the crowd. She resisted only a little, but laughed at him. 'Look at you,' she said. 'Can't you relax ever? Just for once couldn't you climb out of that tired old business suit?'

'We're going home now. When we get to the car I'll have something to say to you and you'd better listen!'

'Something to say? That'll be a turn up for the book.'

When he got her into the car, he didn't speak immediately. He drove out of the Picton gates, through Skurfield and stopped on a quiet stretch of the road to Rapstone. Then the words poured out of him. 'I've put up with you,' he started. 'I've put up with you without complaint. That's because I promised someone I respect that I'd look after you, no matter how difficult it was. No matter how you resented it. Well, I've done it!'

She sat silent, whether or not she was listening to him. He had twisted himself towards her and she thought how pale he looked in the reflected light of the dipped headlamps.

'I've put up with you taking courses in social services, where you learn nothing because you're always on strike. I've put up with your "caring" activities which are designed to make you feel good and help no one else at all. I've accepted the fact that you find any gormless slob in a T-shirt morally superior to me in my tired old business suit, as you call it. You owe me for all that, Charlotte. And now I'm calling in the debt.'

'I don't know what you mean.' She was listening to him now.

'I'm sorry. I should have remembered, the subject of money is something far beneath you, isn't it?' He moved closer to her; she could smell his breath faintly tinged with Doughty Strove's whisky. 'Let me put it in terms even you can understand. I can win the Hartscombe seat. That's not the problem. The problem is, I've got to be selected and nowadays they look at wives. God knows why but they do. And if they took one look at you at the moment I'd be out on my ear. Scrubbed! Ruled out! Not chosen! Understand what I mean? Do you?' He grabbed her wrist, pulling her up sharply when she tried to lean back and away from him. 'So listen to me, Charlotte. Scrub that bloody chrysanthemum off your forehead. Get yourself a dress you can't see through. Get your hair done at Chez Giorgio in Hartscombe. Get yourself a hat. And stop fawning on all those drug-headed, overpaid, screaming teenagers who think you're a joke anyway. Just till I'm elected you'll bloody well practise your caring skills on your husband. You get behind me, you see – what do they teach you to say – in a supportive situation?'

He let her go. She looked down at the red mark on her wrist and gave a small smile. She remembered then why she had liked him in the first place. He was rough trade.

Nicholas was in the garden, seated on a low stool and cutting dead heads off the begonias, when Christopher Kempenflatt, uninvited, approached him across the lawn. 'I'm down here with my people for the weekend. I thought I might drop in for a word.'

'What word is that?' Although what he was doing wasn't in the least interesting, Nicholas didn't like being interrupted.

'Of course you'll be chairing the Selection Committee for the new candidate, when the time comes. There *is* something. I couldn't really say it on the day, as it were, more of a word of warning in your shell-like, about Titmuss.'

'About my son-in-law? You don't think he'd make a suitable member?'

'So far as I can see he's hard-working, clever and extremely ambitious.'

'Not the sort of fellow we're used to in the Conservative Party?' Nicholas smiled faintly in the direction of the flowerbed.

'Not that. Actually, the word of warning is about his wife, your daughter.'

'About Charlie?'

'I don't suppose you know this, but she's been getting into some rather unusual company.' Nicholas didn't react so Kempen-flatt tried to explain tactfully. 'You know what comes of helping lame dogs over stiles . . .'

'Can't say I do, Kempenflatt. It just doesn't seem to have arisen. I mean, I've never seen a lame dog that *wanted* to get over a stile.'

'No doubt she gets friendly with that sort of person from the best of motives.' If there had been a joke, Kempenflatt ignored it. 'But you can get a little too close to them, if you know what I mean. People are bound to talk. Not the sort of talk that's particularly healthy, when it's about a candidate's lady.'

There was a silence then, and Nicholas looked to the begonias for help. 'Such a lot of them to water. Hideous plants, aren't they? And they get uncommonly thirsty.'

'Just thought it was worth mentioning.'

'And they have a tremendous appetite for bone meal. Your people will be expecting you, won't they? Do get Wyebrow to show you out.' Nicholas was suddenly very angry so he spoke with unusual gentleness.

The Selection Committee was due to meet in November. In October, Dorothy, arranging flowers in Rapstone Church, saw Leslie kneeling in solitary and silent prayer, a proceeding which Simeon of course permitted, but never did much to encourage. She knew enough of the local gossip to be quite sure what he was praying for. It must be the first time, she thought to herself, that God had been asked to select the Conservative candidate for Hartscombe and South Worsfield.

'I think they want to see you now.' Christopher Kempenflatt emerged from the Committee Meeting and called in on the little room where Leslie Titmuss was still waiting. His rival's pallor had that day, he noticed with some pleasure, taken on a positively greenish tinge. He thought he had done pretty well. He had assured the selectors that his wife, Honor, was behind him every inch of the way. He had gently reminded them of the Kempenflatt background and the Kempenflatt family money, ever a productive source of Party funds. He had assured them of his soundness on the question of the death penalty and his intention to live permanently in the constituency. There had been perhaps a slight coolness in the Chairman's manner but he put this down to Nicholas's determination not to show his preference too openly.

'Off you go then, Leslie. May the best man win.'

'Oh yes.' Leslie got slowly, almost reluctantly, to his feet. 'I think he probably will.'

Once faced with the Selectors, sitting on an upright chair in front of a long table, stared at by men and women, most of whom were as old as his parents, and none of whom were his age, Leslie embarked on his carefully prepared speech in answer to the inevitable question 'Why do you think you're particularly suitable to represent this constituency?' which Nicholas was deputed to ask him.

'Background!' he started. 'I expect you've been hearing something about background. Let me tell you mine. My father was a clerk all his life in the Brewery. My mother worked in the kitchen for Doughty Strove. What you call your "living-room", they call the "lounge". What you call "dinner", they call "tea". Perhaps you think they talk a different language from you?'

Leslie had begun by speaking very quietly, so that his hearers had to strain their ears and pay attention. He also looked ill and so gained some puzzled and embarrassed sympathy. As he got into his stride, his voice became louder and a hint of colour returned to his cheeks.

'I went to the village school,' he told them. 'Then I got a

scholarship to Hartscombe Grammar. Weekends I used to go out on my bike and help people with their gardens. I grew up to understand the value of money because it took my father five years to save up for our first second-hand Ford Prefect. Every night he finishes his tea and says to my mother, "Very tasty, dear. That was very tasty." He always says the same thing. He falls asleep in front of the fire at exactly half past nine and at ten-thirty he wakes up with a start and says, "I'll lock up, dear. Time for Bedfordshire!" Always the same. Every night. Just as he got to work at exactly the same time every morning for forty years. He's loyal to his job and my mother was loyal to the Stroves. You know what my parents are? They're the true Conservatives! And I can tell you this. They're tired of being represented by people from the City or folks from up at the Manor. They want one of themselves! You can forget the county families and the city gents and the riverside commuters. They'll vote for you anyway. What you need to win is my people. The people who know the value of money because they've never had it. The people who say the same thing every night because it makes them feel safe. The people who've worked hard and don't want to see scroungers rewarded or laziness paying off. Put it this way, ladies and gentlemen. You need the voters I can bring you! They are the backbone of our country. They aren't Conservative because of privilege or money, but because of their simple faith in the way we've always managed things in England!'

A small man in a tweed suit and rimless glasses seemed disposed to clap but he restrained himself and there was a silence. Leslie sat back in his chair smiling. Some of the Committee smiled back. Lord Naboth seemed interested, and leant forward to speak. Leslie prepared himself to give his views on a balanced budget. Instead he heard, 'Mr Titmuss, we haven't had the pleasure of meeting your wife.'

'Really? She's your chairman's daughter.' Lord Naboth smiled and papered over what might have been seen as an appeal to nepotism.

'I mean, we haven't all had the opportunity of asking her how she feels about taking on the rather onerous constituency duties.'

The Association Secretary, who had been called out of the room during Leslie's speech, came back quietly and whispered a message to Nicholas.

'Well, Charlotte is a hundred per cent behind me, naturally.' Leslie was showing as much conviction as possible.

'It seems she's here,' Nicholas announced, as surprised as anyone. 'Charlie is here apparently.'

'Very well' – to Lord Naboth it appeared perfectly simple – 'why don't we have her in?'

Nicholas whispered to the Secretary who went out. The Committee Members doodled, coughed or whispered together. Nicholas stared up at the ceiling as Leslie looked anxiously at the door. He saw the Secretary usher in his wife, set a chair for her and leave. He saw Charlie, but a Charlie transformed. She had had her hair done in Hartscombe. She was wearing a tweed jacket and skirt, sensible shoes and a hat. Had she been out of doors, she gave the impression she would have been wearing a headscarf.

Nicholas nodded to Lord Naboth who asked the question, 'Mrs Titmuss, would you be prepared to appear on your husband's platforms and undertake social engagements, fêtes, coffee mornings and so on? We do depend a good deal on our coffee mornings.'

'Of course,' Charlie started to say, 'I'm a hundred per cent behind Leslie and . . .'

'Oh, I don't suppose Charlotte'll be able to do too much of that,' her husband interrupted her.

'Why ever not?' Lord Naboth frowned.

'Well, you see, we're doing what every other young couple with faith in Britain longs to do. We're starting a family.'

There was a murmur of approval. Leslie looked pleased, proud and relaxed. There were certain people in the world, he thought to himself, whose prayers deserved to be answered.

Chapter Twenty-two

THAT CHRISTMAS

'I thought we might have a word about the case.' Henry had called on his mother at her house in Sunday Street, about a year after his father's death, and not long before the Probate Action about the validity of Simeon's will was to come to court. 'Our barrister wants the answers to certain questions. You see the other side, that is the toad Titmuss and his gang, will try and find some logical reason for father turning against his family. It's most important that we shouldn't give them the slightest encouragement.'

'What an extraordinary device!' It was just before Christmas again – Dorothy thought that Christmases seemed to come round far more often these days, and Henry had brought her a present wrapped in bright paper. 'I'll open it now,' Dorothy had said. 'I can't have it standing about here for days with me wondering if I'm going to like it.' To her surprise it seemed to be some sort of a machine. 'What can it be, a bomb?'

'It's a Teasmade, Mother. Lonnie thought of it. It'll wake you up and give you a cup of tea.'

'But I can give myself a cup of tea when I wake up.'

'This will wake you up at a certain time, Mother.'

'But nowadays I don't have to wake up at a certain time. What can Lonnie have been thinking of?'

'What I was trying to say' – Henry returned to the real object of his visit – 'is that we don't want to hand evidence to

272

Titmuss on a plate. Obviously every family has misunderstandings, but there are certain incidents it would be better not to mention. Speaking of Christmas . . .'

'It's not yet you know, not for another week. Lonnie's got her dates mixed up.'

'There's really no need,' he told her firmly, 'to mention that Christmas when we all came to stay, Mr Bugloss and everybody.'

'Oh.' Dorothy appeared to be re-wrapping her Christmas present. 'You mean *that* Christmas.'

That Christmas, the Christmas of 1969, the year after Leslie Titmuss was selected as Hartscombe's Conservative candidate, was certainly the most disastrous that Fred ever spent at the Rectory. It was one of those occasions in which a malign fate seemed to take a special interest. It began for Fred, shortly before the festivities, on the day he visited old Mrs Fawcett in her cottage in Rapstone. 'I always took the work easy. Slow and steady, not like Bridget at the Manor. Bridget goes at her stairrods like a hurricane, always has done. Yet it's me that gets the heart, isn't it?' Maggie Fawcett complained.

'We're going to move you somewhere where you'll be more comfortable.'

'The Worsfield General?'

'Well, yes.'

Maggie Fawcett lay, beached in bed, a huge and alarmed woman, who, ever since Fred could remember, had helped out at the Rectory. 'We'll get you a bit of treatment, and hope to have you back here.'

'Before Christmas?'

'Let's say, before the spring.'

'I don't like to leave the old cottage. My Tina's got her plans. She and her Gary. They've got their arrangements.'

Tina Fawcett was an overweight, broody and determined

young woman. Fred found her and her boyfriend Gary Kitson, the younger brother of Den, the banjo and double bass of the Stompers, sitting at the table in the downstairs room drinking tea and smoking. Fred told them that he was going over to the pub to call an ambulance and they said they'd reckoned he'd be taking her away.

'Gary's going to do this old place up,' Tina told him, 'when we get married.'

'Well. That'll be something for your mother to look forward to, won't it? When she gets back from hospital.' It was not a thought that seemed to please either of them particularly, so Fred left to make his telephone call.

Ted Lawless was sticking holly up over the photographs of old aeroplanes in the Baptist's Head. As he stood at the pay phone on the wall, Fred looked at the cold and dripping church-yard and was surprised to see his brother and Mr Bugloss appear from the west door and walk briskly towards the lychgate. By the time he had finished his call they were in the bar.

'Quite typical!' Henry greeted him. 'While Ben and I are in church, you're sozzling in the pub.'

'I'm waiting for an ambulance.'

'Feeling seedy? Three pints, Ted. Simcox Best Bitter.'

'Your village church is going to make a great location for *Pilgrims*.' To the film producer, Fred thought, it seemed as though Rapstone Church had found its destiny at last.

'This is our country, Benny,' Henry told him. 'We were born here, among these hills. You need to get back to your roots occasionally.'

'I guess so. I never felt all that longing to get back to White-chapel, I must say,' Mr Bugloss told Fred. 'Your father has been very gracious. We have a Midnight Mass scene in *Pilgrims*, so the Rector has generously invited us to stay over on Christmas Eve to get the feel of the occasion.'

'Invited us?' Fred looked at him doubtfully. 'You mean you and Henry?'

'I mean me and a friend of mine.' Mr Bugloss sounded modest. 'Hey. Didn't you once meet Mrs Wickstead?'

'I'm putting her in the parrot room, and Mr Bugloss in Henry's old room.' Dorothy was trying to work the sleeping arrangements out on the back of an old envelope while Fred and Simeon decorated the Christmas tree. 'There's nothing of any sort *between* them is there?'

'Oh I don't think so,' Fred told his mother. 'Mrs Wickstead's extremely respectable, she lives in Hampstead.'

'Hampstead, eh?' Simeon was threading coloured bells on to the branches. 'Do the sins of the flesh stop short at Hampstead?'

'I just don't want to dread going to the lavatory for fear of meeting them creeping about the corridor. However, she is called *Mrs* Wickstead, that sounds reassuring. Henry and Agnes can have the pink room. I'd put Mrs Wickstead there but she's not used to the boiler.' Dorothy consulted her envelope. 'Francesca can go in the pink room too, on the camp bed.'

'On the camp bed!' Simeon approved. 'She'll be excited about that.'

There were four bedrooms on the first floor of the Rectory, two on each side of the corridor. At the front, looking out on the cemetery, were Simeon and Dorothy's matrimonial bedroom and a room with wallpaper covered with parrots (known as the parrot room), in which Dorothy had planned that Mrs Wickstead should sleep. At the back there was a double bedroom with pink wallpaper (known as the pink room), in which Francesca's camp bed had been set up and in which Henry and Agnes were to have the large bed. Also at the back was a small room where Henry used to sleep. This was to be awarded to Mr Bugloss. Fred's old room, in which he was to stay over Christmas, was up a narrow staircase and once formed part of the servants' quarters. He had been put there as a child so that Simeon could be removed as far as possible from the sound of his drums.

These carefully worked-out arrangements were challenged,

when the guests arrived on Christmas Eve, by Francesca who immediately announced that she wanted to sleep with the parrots, that she loved the parrots on the wall, and that anyway she always had the parrot room at her granny's house. Agnes was left upstairs trying to persuade her child of the many superior advantages of the pink room, while the other members of the party, except for Simeon who was writing his sermon, assembled in the sitting-room.

'Mrs Wickstead' – Dorothy came up to her smiling – 'may I hang up your coat?'

'Oh, please can't I keep it on?' Fred had been prepared for her coming, but not entirely for his suddenly urgent need of her as she stood clutching her coat about her, standing as near to the sullen fire as possible. It had been a bad year for their meetings. Mrs Wickstead had been away a lot, the practice had been extra busy and now the only present he wanted was to be with her in the anonymous flat in Notting Hill Gate. What he didn't want was to be tormented by the sight of her unattainable across a stretch of cold carpet, surrounded by Henry, his mother and Mr Bugloss.

'You find the Rectory a little fresh?' Dorothy looked at the gently shivering object of Fred's desire. 'Simeon used to say that the only talent you need for a career in the Church is an ability to survive draughts. You've never dined with the Bishop of Worsfield?'

'Can't say I have.'

'The water has been known to freeze in the fingerbowls. I've put you in the parrot room, it looks over the churchyard. I do hope you'll be comfortable.'

In the end, Francesca was reconciled to the pink room and was looking at a book and waiting to be settled down for the night, her stocking on the end of her bed and a glass of sherry and a mince pie ready in the fireplace, when the door swung slowly open, and, not to her surprise, for she had seen such manifestations before, Simeon entered on his knees, one arm swinging like a trunk in front and the other like a tail behind him, trumpeting like an elephant. She laughed politely, and when he came to sit on her camp bed, he told her she should go straight to sleep, and, when she woke, she might find that a miracle had taken place.

After dinner the party were to walk through the churchyard to Midnight Mass. Tina Fawcett was bringing her boyfriend Gary Kitson in to babysit, although Dorothy said that if she were a child and had to choose between waking up alone next door to a churchyard or having Tina Fawcett looming over her she knew which she'd choose.

They were all assembled in the hall, wrapped up against the cold night and the colder church, except for Simeon who had already gone over. Dorothy pulled open the front door. Fred saw Mrs Wickstead shiver and Mr Bugloss take her arm. Then Henry said, 'I'll catch you up.'

'Why?' Agnes wanted to know.

'Last chance of a pee before the sermon.' When Henry was left alone he went to the telephone on the hall table, dialled a number and said, 'Lonnie. Thank God you're there!' Although really it came as no surprise. 'What are you doing? Tell me everything you're doing!' She sounded breathless, as though she had been waiting for the call for a long time, and then when he told her, she asked incredulously, 'Not going to *church*?'

Halfway across the churchyard, Dorothy noticed that she had left her handbag containing her spectacles and money for the collection in the sitting-room. Agnes volunteered to go for it and turned, scrunching back along the gravel path. She opened the Rectory front door and saw her husband standing with the telephone to his ear.

'It's just that I probably won't get a chance to ring you on Christmas Day, my darling. Well, family. Yes. Can't get a moment to myself. I'll be thinking of you at midnight. Thank you for being there.'

'I'm always here,' Agnes said, as Henry put the phone down and saw her. He said nothing. She went into the sitting-room, got Dorothy's handbag and they walked in silence across to the church together. They prayed together and stood together to join in the final carol, 'O Come All Ye Faithful'.

At about half past twelve they got back from church. Gary and Tina were interrupted in the middle of a snog, paid and departed. Dorothy went into the kitchen and returned with a tea-trolley on which she had set out coffee and sandwiches. Fred opened the bottle of whisky he had brought with him. He poured drinks and they wished each other a Happy Christmas. Agnes was silent. Mrs Wickstead took her whisky neat, and kept her coat on. The telephone rang and Agnes went to answer it.

'Who can it be at this time of night?' Dorothy asked, handing round sandwiches. 'It can't be good news.' Agnes came back from the hall to announce that Mr Bugloss was wanted. At the same time, Simeon came in in his belted cassock, having said Happy Christmas to the last of his congregation, and asked Mrs Wickstead if she'd enjoyed the service.

'I've been a lot more bored in movies.'

'I'll take that as a compliment.' The Rector accepted a whisky and soda from Fred.

'At Midnight Mass' – Henry was frowning – 'to celebrate the mysterious birth of Christ, do we really want a lecture about low-rent accommodation in the Rapstone Valley?'

'I thought Christmas was a story about low-rent accommodation,' Simeon smiled.

'Oh, Henry's very keen on mysteries nowadays.' Agnes bit into a sandwich. 'Mysterious trips, mysterious phone calls, he finds it terribly inconvenient to explain anything.'

Simeon sat beside Mrs Wickstead on the sofa. 'I suppose it might have saved an awful lot of trouble if it had never happened,' he suggested to her.

'If what had never happened?' Henry felt that he was being attacked from all sides.

'Christmas!' Simeon was still speaking confidentially to Mrs Wickstead. 'I mean, before that, absolutely no one had to feel sorry for slaves. You could watch gladiators being killed as part of an afternoon's entertainment. Wars were glorious and probably rather enjoyable. Nobody minded a bit about infant mortality or starving tribes in Asia Minor or the housing shortage south of the Tiber and all that sort of thing. If Christmas had never happened, it would have saved all those petitions, and appeals and letters to the Bishop and marches. Well, it would have saved a fortune in stamps, wouldn't it?'

Fred was put out to see that Mrs Wickstead listened to his father with the same flattering attention she gave him. In the silence that followed Simeon's views on Christmas, Mr Bugloss returned to them and announced that Jack Polefax had just flown in from the Coast and checked in to Claridges. He wanted a breakfast meeting on *Pilgrims*. Much as he regretted it, Benny would have to drive back to London, so that he could set out some figures to 'lay on Jack' in the morning.

'Surely your Mr Polecat can have breakfast on his own?' Dorothy was puzzled.

'I'm afraid he's not used to that. Anyway it's all to the good of Henry's project. Shall I drive you back, Mrs Wickstead?'

'Oh, but surely you'll stay?' Dorothy turned to Mrs Wickstead who had greeted Mr Bugloss's suggestion with a prodigious yawn.

'It's very kind of you. So sleepy.'

So Mr Bugloss wished them all a Happy Christmas and left. In a short while Simeon and Dorothy went up to bed and Mrs Wickstead, after a last drink, braved it up to the parrot room. Fred, who could feel that Agnes's stormy silence was about to explode in thunder, pushed the trolley helpfully out into the kitchen, where he gave himself a final drink. He shut the door carefully behind him, cutting himself off from the scene which then took place.

'It's that girl, isn't it?' As she said it, Agnes was sickeningly conscious of all the wives, at all times, who had started a quarrel with the same form of words.

'It's what girl?'

'I could tell when you poured the last of the whisky out for her. I could tell by the awful way she came oiling up to you and asked you to sign your book. "Oh, thanks ever so, Mr Simcox, I shall treasure that. Always."'

'She didn't say that!'

'She didn't say what?'

'"Thanks ever so". Lonnie doesn't say things like "thanks ever so".'

'"Lonnie",' Agnes said with deep contempt, 'that's who she is. "Lonnie!"'

The door opened to admit Mr Bugloss in his overcoat, carrying his case. 'I'm sorry about this. It's been a most moving occasion. A great experience . . .' And when no one answered him he ended with a heartfelt 'Happy Yuletide!' and left. There was a short, unhappy silence before Agnes burst out again.

'You know what Lonnie is? She's your easy option. You won't have anything difficult in your life now, will you? No demonstrations. No fights. No *me*! You can sit forever in a warm bath, soaping yourself with mysticism and little Lonnie's adoration, until you get old and pink and your skin begins to pucker. How comfortable for you. How horribly comfortable!'

Henry went to the door, opened it and stood looking at her. 'Bugloss has gone.'

'What on earth's that got to do with it?'

'I can sleep in my own bed.'

'How wonderful! Henry can go to sleep in his own little bed again. Henry Simcox who was going to change the world and ended up with Lonnie!'

He was gone and the door banged after him. She lit a cigarette and blew out smoke, then she heard Francesca crying.

Woken by the banging door, Francesca had discovered that she was not in her favourite parrot room and staggered out on to the landing to protest loudly. Mrs Wickstead, who had not undressed, came out of the bathroom to see a child seated at the top of the stairs with Agnes trying to comfort her. At the same time Fred was coming up from the kitchen.

'What's the tragedy? I know so little about children.'

'It's nothing really. Just that she wants to sleep in the room with parrots on the wall.'

'The one I'm in?'

'That's what I told her.'

'Then we'll swop. Not a problem. I've been far too cold to unpack.'

'It's incredibly kind of you.' Agnes looked up, genuinely grateful, and when Fred reached them, and asked if they were all going to spend the night on the stairs, the situation was explained to him. So Agnes and Francesca climbed together into the big bed in the parrot room and, to some extent, comforted each other. Mrs Wickstead went into the pink room and Fred retired up the stairs to the old servants' quarters. Henry lay on his back in his small bedroom, staring at the photograph in which he appeared as head boy at Knuckleberries.

When he tapped on Mrs Wickstead's door and pushed it open, after what he judged to be a discreet interval, Fred found her with the fur coat still fastened on like a life-jacket, sitting by a small and ineffectual electric heater, looking nervously at the white bed which stood like a glacier in the middle of the pink room. She looked up regretfully. 'I daren't go to bed with you.'

'Because of my parents?'

'Because it's freezing.'

He held her, warmed her. At last they dived between the sheets like crazy swimmers who break the ice on Christmas Day. They were stung by the first frosty moments into frenzied activity, zealous, enthusiastic and hungry after a long separation. Then, as their movements became slower, as they searched for, and finally found, a corner of warmth in the draughty house, Fred saw Mrs Wickstead looking over his shoulder, her eyes wide, her expression startled, as though she had just seen a ghost enter the room. He turned his head and saw, by the dim light of the pink-shaded bedside lamp, not a ghost but his father, the Reverend Simeon Simcox, Rector of Rapstone Fanner, white-bearded and fully tricked out as Father Christmas, advancing stealthily towards them with a stocking full of Francesca's presents.

Early on Christmas morning, Fred went into the kitchen to make tea before driving Mrs Wickstead to Worsfield Junction so she could catch one of the few trains back to London. He found Simeon seated at the table, warming his hands on a mug of coffee, all ready, in his cassock, for the day's business. It was the first chance they had had to speak since his father backed hastily out of the pink room. Fred thought it best to dive in at the deep end.

'Did you manage to deliver Francesca's stocking?'

'Oh yes. I guessed she must have got her way about the parrot room. It's the one she always wanted.' There was a silence, then he said, 'Mrs Wickstead seems to be a very pleasant person.'

'Yes.'

'Do you know *Mr* Wickstead at all?'

'Not at all. No.'

'Not know Mr Wickstead at all!'

Fred sat at the table with his father, who was carefully consider-ing the matter. 'It's a case of acting up to your responsibilities,' he said at last. 'You throw a pebble into a still pond, and who knows where the ripples will end?'

'They will end up far away, generations later. When you and your little stone will be quite forgotten.' Fred supplied the words for him.

'You knew what I was going to say?'

'It's what you said to all those married couples.'

'I never told you.'

'We used to listen at the door.'

'You wanted to find out what we used to call "the facts of life"?' Simeon was almost laughing.

'We wanted to find out if you knew them,' Fred told him. 'I

was just thinking about the beard and the Father Christmas uniform. Francesca would have been asleep. She'd never see it. Was it honestly worth it?'

'I don't see that it matters in the least whether she saw it or not.' Simeon finished his coffee and spoke with some pride, 'Even if she saw absolutely nothing, I have played my part.'

'Patients and nurses. That's how you can divide the world,' Dr Salter said when Fred called on him on the afternoon of Christmas Day. 'I was a nurse who got conscripted into the Patients' Brigade. Your father's definitely one of the patients. We always had to look after him.'

'We?'

'Your mother and I. Can't say I noticed you or your brother putting in much time at the bedside.'

'*You* looked after my father?' Fred was puzzled.

'I helped your mother, it was a bit too much for one nurse however devoted. What's that you've brought me?'

'I know you've got it.' Fred handed over the wrapped gramophone record, the *Enigma Variations*.

'I'm glad I've got it. I don't want to embark on new music.' He was in his wheel-chair, a small grey shadow of himself, exhausted by the effort of tearing at the wrapping paper.

'Yours had got a bit scratchy.'

'I rather enjoy playing the scratches.'

Then the door opened and Agnes joined them. Her father looked at her, unsmiling. 'You've come over from Rapstone?'

'Yes.'

'Alone?'

'Yes. Alone.'

Dr Salter looked from one to the other of his visitors, judging them.

'And you two are both nurses. That's true.'

'What about my husband?'

'Yes. What about Henry?'

'Oh, I'd say one of the world's natural patients, wouldn't you?' Then he smiled and asked Fred to put on his new, unscratched record.

'Are you going to throw me out again?' Agnes asked.

'Don't be ridiculous.'

Then she knelt beside him, putting her arms round her father, as the musical variations, whose basic theme is never stated, played and Fred stood watching.

Chapter Twenty-three

AND A HAPPY NEW YEAR
TO YOU, TOO

Grace had invited the in-laws, George, Elsie and Leslie Titmuss, to lunch that Christmas Day at the Manor. It was a small party – the cook had gone off to her family and Bridget managed the turkey and plum pudding. They sat now, with the food eaten and the crackers pulled, round the table. Grace, Elsie and Leslie were crowned with paper hats, Nicholas, Charlie and George were bareheaded. The talk didn't flow freely and, after George had told them that he planned to spend his retirement digging a small lily pond in the garden of 'The Spruces', silence fell. Then Grace asked what on earth there was to do on the afternoon of Christmas Day.

'The Queen,' George told her. 'We usually watch the Queen.'

But Grace was away, on a flood of reminiscence about Christmas afternoons in various country houses in the golden days pre-war. 'Of course we used to do all sorts of things. Charades. Treasure hunts. Or we'd roll up the rugs and have dancing. Private, private dancing from tea-time to breakfast. Come on!' She looked at their somnolent faces. 'Why don't we have a bit of fun, why don't we roll up the carpet in the sitting-room? I've still got my records.'

Only Leslie smiled politely. Charlie sighed and said, 'Oh, please, Mother. For heaven's sake!'

'What's wrong, Charlie? You're always the same, when you were a child you were a most terrific spoilsport!'

They moved into the sitting-room and Grace put Leslie to

work on the carpet, while she opened a cupboard and took out her old pile of 78s. She found what she was looking for at last, and smiled round the room with delight, not noticing that Nicholas had slipped off unobtrusively to the conservatory.

'I've found Pinky's record! The one he gave me. "You're the Top!"'

'Pinky?' Leslie was on his knees, rolling up a long strip of Turkey carpet revealing the naked floor. 'That'll have to be polished again when you've done standing on it,' Bridget warned when she came in with the coffee tray. And Elsie, enthroned by the fireplace, said, 'First-class meal you put on, Bridget. You did really well.' 'Very tasty,' George added, from the edge of sleep.

'Pinky Pinkerton,' Grace explained. 'A simply enormous spade in full evening-dress, killingly funny! Sang at the old Café de Paris, before the bomb got it. Voice like black treacle poured out terribly slowly. Surely *you* remember Pinky, George?'

'Don't think we ever visited the old Café de Paris, did we, Mother?' George Titmuss was enjoying a joke.

'Leslie' – Grace handed him the record – 'we simply have to dance to this.'

'Please don't!' Charlie was on the edge of despair but Leslie told her that it was Christmas and surely if her mother wanted it . . .

'"You're the Top!", and Pinky put in some words for me.' Grace sang them in a surprisingly high, girlish voice:

> 'You're the top!
> You can trump the A-ace.
> You're the top!
> You're the Lady Gra-ace . . .'

'I remember dances too.' Elsie was still wearing her paper hat. 'When Mr Doughty was a young man there was always a dance at Picton House, New Year's Eve. Of course they've stopped all that since the war.' Grace wasn't listening, she was looking ecstatically at the strip of dance floor. 'Oh, well done, Leslie, awfully well done! All that shining parquet for us to glide about on, just like the old Café de Paris before the Jerries got it.'

'I'm not going to be able to stand this.' Charlie was convinced.

'Of course you will, Charlotte,' Elsie reassured her. 'Your mother's only having her bit of fun.'

And then the music started. The dark velvety voice of Pinky Pinkerton emerged above the scratch and hiss of the old record to pay its tribute and Charlie was faced with the awful spectacle of her husband dancing with her mother. She heard Grace carrying on a long, staccato monologue directed at Leslie's right ear. 'Nicholas was away at the beginning of the war. Where was it? Bognor? Some such nowhere. Doing something tremendously heroic in Army Intelligence. And I used to go up to London by train. In the black-out, to the Café de Paris! The bombs didn't worry me at all. Not at all. There was something so exciting about the sound of broken glass. And in the mornings, after the all-clear, the streets were so wonderfully quiet. Such times! Now it hardly seems worth the trouble of going up to London.'

It was then that Charlie clenched her fists, stood up and screamed, filling Rapstone Manor with a sound not heard since her marriage. Eventually she let her husband take her upstairs and she lay on her bed sobbing, while he read her the chapter of 'Biggles' with which Simeon used to calm her nerves before Leslie Titmuss came into her life.

In the dead days between Christmas and New Year's Eve events happened to Nicholas which he didn't entirely understand. He received a visit from Tina and Gary, who told him that they had been to see Maggie Fawcett in hospital, where she was likely to remain for some time. It seemed she was very worried about losing her cottage during her long absence, and it would take a great weight off the old girl's mind if the rent book could be put in Tina's name. Of course Nicholas agreed to this reasonable request, and sent them off to his estate office for the change to be made. Later he was able to tell Simeon that he had put his Midnight Mass sermon into practice and secured low-rent accommodation for the villagers of Rapstone.

During that week also Nicholas went on a shoot, and had a conversation with Doughty Strove, during which he wasn't sure that he quite followed the old boy's drift. They had stopped for lunch, which was laid out on trestle tables in the farmhouse at Mandragola. As they munched cold steak and kidney pie and drank cherry brandy, Doughty admitted that he was looking forward to New Year's Eve.

'Paper hats? Singing "Auld Lang Syne"? I've never cared for it personally. You having a party, Doughty?'

'Not *a* party. Service to *the* Party, you might say. I mean it should be published by then, shouldn't it? Our little secret.'

'*Ours?*'

'When it's announced, perhaps you'll join me for a dinner. In another place.'

'What other place?'

'Do I really have to spell it out for you, old fellow?' Doughty's voice sank to a confidential whisper and he looked round nervously in case the beaters should overhear. 'The House of Lords.'

'Oh, I'm not expecting anything like that,' Nicholas said modestly. 'Not for a local chairman of the Party. We don't get a leg up to the Lords. Besides, it's a terribly dangerous place, Bob Naboth was telling me.'

'Dangerous?'

'You can't get into your seat without tripping over fellows' crutches. Bob Naboth tells me that in the corridors you're likely as not to be run over by a peeress in her own right, driving a self-propelled invalid chair. The House of Lords! Believe me, it's a place to be avoided.'

'But it's not *you* that's going there, is it?'

'I suppose it's not.' Nicholas looked at Doughty and chewed thoughtfully. 'What are we talking about?'

'My dear old Nicholas.' Doughty Strove was laughing as he cut himself another slice of pie. 'You do play your cards remarkably close to your chest.'

Fred was also looking forward to New Year's Eve. The Riverside Stompers had been asked to provide the entertainment at the Badger which had become bigger and brassier under new management. They rehearsed their favourite standards in Marmaduke's garage and decided to give the inhabitants of Skurfield a whiff, as genuine as they could make it, of the brothers of New Orleans in the great days. 'What do we do if they request "White Christmas"?' Den asked.

'Ignore it!' said Joe Sneeping. The Christmas rush had made him sick to the teeth of paper streamers, Santa Claus wrapping-paper and 'Jingle Bells' or 'Once upon a Winter Time' which his employers wanted to emerge from a record-player in the off-licence to stimulate the sale of cut-price spirits. 'The only concession we make is "Auld Lang Syne" at midnight. Otherwise we stick to the stuff we've always wanted to play. Who knows? They may even like it.'

Both Joe Sneeping and Doughty Strove were due for a disappointment. Unable to contain himself any longer, Doughty rang the *Daily Telegraph* on the night before the Honours List was due to be published. He sat in his study and asked for the news desk. He told a reporter who had just come back from the pub that he was the ex-Conservative member for Hartscombe and, although apparently unimpressed, the young man was full enough of the spirit of goodwill to read out the list of peerages announced in the next day's paper. 'Is that all? You're sure that's all? No mention of Strove? That is s, t, r, o . . . No? Well, it's extremely decent of you to let me know. Yes. And a happy New Year to you too, of course.' When he had put down the receiver, Doughty sat for quite a long while, staring at nothing very much.

*

On New Year's Eve, Gary Kitson, Tina and a group of their friends called at the Mallard-Greenes' cottage and collected young Simon, who, though under age, was tall enough to be accepted in pubs and had enough money to pay for a good many rounds of drinks. Malley was up in London, doing a B.B.C. *Arts Review of the Year*, and his mother was prepared to let Simon go on the promise, which she knew wouldn't be kept, that he be home before midnight.

The big, gloomy Badger had been redecorated in the age of affluence, but not improved. It now had fake beams, plaster bas-reliefs of porridge-coloured horses and pictures of tearful clowns and pool-eyed children. The bar was full. There were still a few jazz fans, now growing middle-aged, and wearing duffel-coats, who had travelled to hear the Stompers, but most of the clientele were buying drinks, chattering or trying to dance to unfamiliar rhythms. Simon, free with his Christmas present money, was buying a good many rum and Cokes, snowballs or vodka and blacks. His party agreed that the music was depressing, got you down, made the place sound like a bleeding funeral parlour and needed livening up.

'Ssh!' Glenys had come to hear Terry play and wasn't going to have his evening spoiled by Gary and Tina, even though she sometimes felt her husband should move with the times.

'Council flat all right, is it, Glenys?' Tina challenged her.

'Course it is. We were lucky to get it,' Glenys whispered back against the din of the bar.

'My Gary wouldn't consider no council flat in Worsfield.'

'Well, your Gary may have to.'

'I don't reckon he will. He's going in for window-cleaning. Setting up his own business. If he wants something he gets it. Not like your Terry. My big brother don't think about nothing but tootling his little clarinet.'

Terry was tootling, apparently happily. Fred was behind the drums, contented with the music if not the venue. Joe Sneeping lowered his trumpet to sing a verse of 'St James Infirmary':

'When I die I want you to dress me in straight lace shoes,
Box back coat and a stetson hat,
Put a twenty dollar gold piece on my watch chain,
So the boys'll know that I died standing pat.'

And then, young Simon Mallard-Greene shouted from the bar, 'Cheer up, sounds like you're going to a funeral!' Joe stopped singing and looked pained as the barracking came at them like rifle fire from Simon, Gary, Tina and their friends. 'Don't you know no groovy sounds?' 'Nothing we can dance to!' 'How about "Honky Tonk Woman"?' '"A Boy Named Sue".' 'Listen, Grandad, we've got a request here. "Honky Tonk Woman".' 'He can't hear you, Simon!' 'Get your hearing aid in!' 'Wash your ears out!' And then an empty Coke tin came tumbling through the air and thudded against the front of the drum. The band was silent and Joe stooped to pick it up.

'Who chucked that?'

'My sodding little brother,' Den Kitson, with his banjo on his knee, called out. 'Isn't it past your bedtime, Gary?'

'We came here for a bit of entertainment,' Gary shouted. 'Not to hear you moaning away up there.'

'What are we going to do?' Joe asked the Stompers in a kind of desperation.

Fred looked at his watch. It was ten minutes to midnight but he had no doubt of the solution. 'Play "Auld Lang Syne". Bloody loudly!' They did, and, in an instant, the crowd in the Badger was linking arms, singing, kissing, hugging and making breakable resolutions. So the year 1969 slid into history, was forgotten or only occasionally brought to mind.

Chapter Twenty-four

THE MYTH OF HAPPINESS

A few days before he died, Dr Salter, lying in his own bed, with a full-time nurse now in attendance, spoke to Fred, who sat by him whenever he could get away from the practice.

'Never jump your fences too soon. I jumped mine years too soon. Bloody silly thing to do. Look after her, won't you?'

'Agnes?'

'Your mother.' Dr Salter's voice was fading with his life. 'She may suffer from his sense of justice. Nothing more unfair, you know, than a sense of justice.' After a silence he said, 'What's happening in the world outside?'

'Nothing very much. There's a new Conservative Government. Leslie Titmuss won Hartscombe.'

'Leslie Titmuss? Sounds a good time to go. Look after her won't you?' He put an almost weightless hand on Fred's arm. 'I should've liked to have stayed on till Friday. Mrs Beasley does fish pie on Friday.'

Fred, Henry and Agnes had Mrs Beasley's fish pie on Friday after the funeral. Henry wanted to know if it was really what Dr Salter wanted – Worsfield Crematorium, in all its ugliness, no music, no flowers, no prayers, nothing. Agnes asked, 'Why? Do you think that your father feels done out of a funeral?' and Fred told him, 'Nothing. That's what he wanted.'

There was little left to arrange. Everything belonged to Agnes, but Fred was going to buy the house from her. He and the remaining partners would take out a mortgage, so that the practice could continue there. She wanted him to have the gramophone records and some of her father's pictures. Henry thought that final details should be left to the lawyers. So Dr Salter was divided up, passed on and his ashes scattered. When Agnes and Henry had gone Fred went back to work. He could think of nothing else to do.

Later Henry felt excluded by his wife's grief as he had felt obscurely jealous of Francesca when she claimed so much of Agnes's attention. Some weeks had gone by when he said with a hint of impatience in his seriously sympathetic voice, 'It was bound to happen some time.'

'Some time. Yes.'

'He was an extraordinary man.'

'He told the truth.'

Henry, wrongly, took that as a reference to himself. He didn't answer it, however, but went to his desk and picked one off a pile of newspaper-cuttings. 'We've got away with it. My new book, remember? Bloody great piece in *The New York Review of Books*. Socking great caricature of the author.'

'I'm glad.'

'Do you want to read it?' He held the cutting out to her. She shook her head. 'I said I was very glad.'

Henry had changed since the retreat from Grosvenor Square. His new enthusiasms were for tweed suits, the Church of England, English watercolours and Victorian animal paintings. His latest book, *The Myth of Happiness*, was a collection of essays in praise of these articles and denouncing the modern fallacy that the human race is born with some sort of divine right to work, financial security and personal satisfaction. Its publication coincided with the defeat of Harold Wilson's Government, but Henry claimed no credit for this. Indeed he found Mr Heath's Conservatives just as crassly materialistic and blind to the virtues of human suffering as their Labour alternative. He restored the press-cutting to its pile. 'I'm glad that the new book's got away with it. Just as well. I don't think Benny's having much joy raising the money for *Pilgrims*.' He poured them both a drink; Agnes took hers without speaking. 'You're still thinking about your father?'

'His illness came between us like another woman. He was ashamed of it so he didn't want to see me. When I was young,' she remembered, 'when I was living with him over the surgery, I felt so safe. I could really enjoy anything awful.' She gave him a small, regretful smile. 'Nowadays I'm so grateful for anything a bit pleasant. It's pathetic!'

'For God's sake! I've tried to make you happy. I have.'

'I know.'

'I've given up . . .' He claimed the credit. 'Given up having anything to do with anyone else.'

'I never thought I'd develop into a person someone had to give things up for.' She took a gulp of her drink and looked at him with regret.

Fred and Mrs Wickstead never talked much about the eruption of Father Christmas into the pink bedroom. When his father had withdrawn Fred had gone back to his own room, and when he drove her to the station she seemed to have forgotten the incident. Afterwards they continued to meet, only a little less often than before, and such meetings were rare oases of pleasure in the dry months of his practice. He talked to her about all sorts of things but never about Christmas. Strangely enough the absurd incident made him feel fonder of Simeon; the old man hadn't preached him a sermon, nor did he seem anxious that his son should feel ashamed. So Fred began to see more of his father and, on his afternoons off, they would go for walks together, exploring the countryside in a way which took the place of his rides with Dr Salter.

Maggie Fawcett came out of Worsfield General after a long spell and discovered that her daughter had become the tenant of her cottage. She spent most of her time upstairs in her room, avoiding the company of Tina and Gary. 'I can't sit down there,

Doctor,' she said when Fred called to see her. 'Not with them fish goggling at me. "However much does it cost," I said, "to keep them awful little animals in tropical waters?" "Don't you worry your head," he says. "We can afford it." So they can afford the electric organ and all the other stuff they got. He's given up the building, you know, and gone into cleaning windows. Perhaps he *has* got a good business.'

'You say you signed something in hospital?'

'Letter they brought round from Sir Nicholas. Said it made sure the family kept the cottage. If I was away a long time, like. It meant *they* kept it.' The sound of Pink Floyd percolated up through the floorboards. 'It's the record-player too, all hours of the day and night. It was always so peaceful in the General.'

'I'll have a word with them.'

'Don't upset them, Dr Fred. My Tina can be ever so spiteful when she's upset.'

Downstairs, Fred found that Gary had come home for lunch and was sharing a cardboard box of chicken and chips with Tina. They were sitting on the plastic leather sofa, their feet on the mock leopardskin rug, backed by the knotty pine wallpaper. Round the room the huge telly, the record-player and the small electric organ gleamed metallically. In a large bubbling tank mournful but brightly coloured fish threaded their way through imitation mother-of-pearl obstacles such as underwater pagodas. 'Your mother's not been well.'

' 'Course not. Been in hospital, ain't she? Better now though.'

'I want you to keep her comfortable.'

'She's comfortable all right.' Gary was sure. 'In her bedroom all the time. Can't trouble herself to come down here and be a bit sociable.'

'I don't think she likes the fish.' Fred looked at the tank and decided he didn't like them either.

'What's she got against Gary's Oriental Hot Lips?'

'And she says the music keeps her awake.'

'Did you put her up to that? I could tell you had no love for music, Doctor' – Gary smiled at him over a grey and hairy chicken drumstick – 'that night down the Badger.'

On Christmas Day, after having been surprised at the telephone, Henry promised that he would never see Lonnie again. After the death of Agnes's father he seemed almost anxious that she should discover evidence of his broken undertaking. He left stubs of air tickets to Manchester on his desk on which Lonnie's name was still legible. He often put the phone down when Agnes came into the room, or got up early to collect the post, sometimes leaving an envelope with what she suspected was Lonnie's hand-writing, postmarked SW10, crumpled in the kitchen tidy-bin. In a way, Agnes started to feel sorry for Lonnie. Other girls got trips to the South of France or Venice from their married lovers, poor old Lonnie got a literary lunch in a room full of ladies in hats in Manchester. All that would be on offer, Agnes knew, would be grapefruit segments, chicken and frozen peas, and Henry making a speech about himself. And then Lonnie had to man her phone twenty-four hours a day. It was no doubt a tough assignment, being the other woman in Henry's life.

Jack Polefax of Galaxy International had, so Mr Bugloss ex-plained, 'gone cold' on *Pilgrims*, so the movie was once more postponed. Henry was working on a new novel and taking part in a series of television documentaries called *Writers' England*, in which various authors could reveal the parts of the country which had most inspired them. For his number Henry was 'going back to his roots' in the Rapstone Valley. One day he said to Agnes, 'Look, I want you to be very sensible about this.'

'What've I got to be sensible about?' she asked nervously.

'Lonnie Hope'll be working on the project.'

'Lonnie Hope's been working on the project for some time, hasn't she?'

'I honestly don't know what you mean. She'll just be doing her job. You won't object to that, will you?' He was clearly not prepared to believe that any woman could be so unreasonable.

Agnes thought about it and finally said, 'No, I suppose I wouldn't object to that.'

'I'm glad' – Henry looked relieved – 'we understand each other.'

When Henry had first told her that he was making a film about his roots, Agnes said that it sounded like *Gardeners' Question Time* and he hadn't laughed. Lonnie at least took him seriously as he stood in front of the camera with the Rectory behind him and said things like: 'I could see the whole of village life from that window. The children brought for christening and the old people brought for burial. Perhaps that's why I was never entirely convinced by facile optimism and all the claptrap about the right to health and wealth in the pursuit of happiness. The only undisputed right anyone had was to six foot of earth under the cedar trees in *that* churchyard.'

One night he arrived back at the flat with Lonnie who was carrying a briefcase and a long-legged doll dressed as a clown. 'I brought Lonnie back for a drink,' Henry explained. 'She's just going to type out a bit of script for tomorrow.'

'I hope you don't mind me turning your front room into an office? We met the last time we filmed with Henry. I'm Lonnie Hope.'

'Yes. I know.'

'Campari and soda, Lonnie?' Henry was pouring drinks.

'Henry knows what I like.'

'Apparently.'

'And how's little Francesca?' Lonnie asked as she sipped her drink. 'I brought her a present.'

'Lonnie brought that marvellous clown for Francesca.'

'Really? How amusing. Perhaps I'll give it to her in the morning.'

'Oh, I say. I do like the way you've done your front room.' Lonnie walked round it admiringly. 'What gorgeous cushion covers! Are they antiques?'

'Henry's mother gave them to us. They come from the Rectory.'

'Oh, we're filming there. Henry's promised to introduce me to his father. The old Rector sounds an absolute sweetie! Your father was a doctor, wasn't he? Henry told me that your two fathers were always arguing – in the nicest possible way, of course.'

'I don't know if I'd describe my father as "nice".'

'Oh I'm sure he was if you're anything to go by.'

'You think I'm nice, do you?' Agnes spoke in a voice of doom, apparently unnoticed by Lonnie. Henry thought they had better get on with typing the scene.

'Your husband's so marvellous on screen, you know,' Lonnie said, as she settled down to work. 'He does it so naturally.'

'Well, it's something he's used to, isn't it?' Agnes was leaving for the kitchen. 'Talking about himself.'

Shortly after that evening, Agnes looked for a flat in Fulham. When she had found one she left, taking Francesca and all their possessions except the clown doll. As she told Henry, she couldn't really enjoy anything awful any more.

Chapter Twenty-five

THE PARTY

After only two years on the back benches, Leslie Titmuss got a job in the Government and became a parliamentary private secretary at Advanced Technology. This news was welcomed particularly by Christopher Kempenflatt and Magnus Strove, who saw that Leslie would have to resign his directorship and leave them in control of the now extremely profitable Hartscombe Enterprises. 'Do you think we could bear life without Titmuss?' Magnus asked, and Kempenflatt thought that they might be very brave about it. When Leslie was approached he surprised them by saying that he wouldn't only resign his directorship, but sell all his shares. He expected to get a pretty good price for them.

'Don't worry, old man,' Kempenflatt said. 'We're prepared to buy you out at a substantial profit. More than you ever dreamed of getting your hot little hands on when you were working at the Brewery.'

'Of course it would have to be deferred.' Magnus took it for granted. 'Well, you wouldn't expect readics, would you?'

'Haven't you got a future interest you could raise a bit on, if you're short of cash, Magnus? I mean the Strove estate? By the way how *is* old Doughty?'

'Daddy doesn't get out much nowadays. Fred Simcox says it's depression. He's given him a handful of pills for it.'

'I'm terribly sorry to hear that.' Leslie looked concerned. 'You will give him my best wishes, won't you? After all he kept the seat warm for me, all those years.'

In fact Doughty Strove had fallen into strange habits. The staff at Picton House were dismayed to find him wandering, tieless and unshaven, about the upstairs corridors, muttering, 'Strove, Doughty Picton Percival, Lord Strove of Skurfield in the County of . . . First Baron. Doughty Picton Percival Strove, first Baron of Skurfield in the Peerage of England . . .' So Doughty was in no condition to join the drinks party that Nicholas and Grace felt they should give to celebrate their son-in-law's promotion.

Grace said that, in the old days, they didn't have to wait for someone to become Secretary to the Water Works or whatever it was before they had an excuse for a party. However she climbed into a cocktail dress, took a few pieces of jewellery out of the bank and the hall at Rapstone Manor was filled with familiar faces and some unfamiliar ones, eager, youngish men with dark suits and businesslike expressions who were Leslie's new colleagues. Fred, who had called in after a day's work, found himself talking to someone who was quite unknown to him, a man who had smooth, dark hair like a seal, a suit, shirt, tie and breast-pocket handkerchief in various shades of blue, a heavy gold wristwatch and Gucci shoes. He spoke in a controlled and persuasive voice, as though he were forever selling some product.

'Never seen Leslie in the ancestral surroundings before.' The man was looking across at the Fanner family. 'Doesn't go with his image, really.'

'What's his image?' Fred wondered.

'My firm does P.R. for Hartscombe Enterprises,' the man explained. 'We've taken on Leslie's political profile as well. You know, gritty man of the people, all that sort of rubbish. Good thing there's no press about. He ought to be at the Young Business Man of the Year do at the new Worsfield Motorway Inn, not swigging champagne up at the Manor. Known Leslie a long time, have you?'

'Oh, since we were children.'

'I imagine he's changed a lot since then.'

'Oh no,' Fred told him. 'Hardly at all.'

On the other side of the party, Mrs Mallard-Greene had introduced herself to Simeon. 'Sorry we haven't got round to coming to church yet.' 'That's all right,' Simeon assured her. 'As a matter of fact, I hadn't noticed.'

'Of course, *we'd* like to go. But our *young* aren't in the least interested. Such a difficult time for young people, isn't it?'

'It usually is.'

'We always hoped our Simon would follow Malley into the B.B.C., but now it's come to the crunch they've got nothing to offer him. All the same, I've got to hand it to Simon. Rather than hang about round the house he's going into window-cleaning with Gary Kitson. I think they're doing rather well but it wasn't what we had in mind when we sent him to Bedales.'

Simeon smiled and wandered away from her then. He wanted to speak to Bridget whom he had seen taking out a tray of empty glasses. He followed her into the kitchen corridor and called after her, 'Bridget! It's been so long since we've seen anything of Glenys. I do miss her typing so.' She stopped with her back towards him. 'Is she well? And the baby, not a baby now, I suppose.'

Bridget turned slowly to face him and stared silently over her tray. 'I've got my fires to do,' she said.

'You're not working too hard, Bridget, I hope?'

'Fireplaces need blacking. You've got to get up early for that. I can't stand here gossiping.' She turned away from him, leaving him for a moment alone and staring after her. Then he went back to the party where he was immediately engaged in conversation by the 'Contessa', who wanted to know why Grace kept telling everyone that Leslie had joined the Water Board.

'Wonderful types you get in country houses, like a lot of antiques. That cleric talking to the old queen in the corner, for instance. Terrific face!'

'You think so?'

'Get a face like that to endorse a product and you could sell cannabis to nuns. Good old Church of England parson, is he? The Tory Party at prayer.'

'As a matter of fact,' Fred told him, 'my father's a Socialist.'

'Your father?' The man looked at him, apparently amazed. 'What did you say your name was?'

'I didn't. But it's Simcox, Fred Simcox.'

'Not *Doctor* Simcox.' Fred nodded and it was then that the man started to laugh. 'Good God, that perfectly wonderful story! So it was you who got the Christmas stocking. What a life you must lead, down at the Rectory. I say, we never got properly introduced. I'm Wickstead. Kenneth Wickstead. I believe you know my wife.'

Fred looked at him and could think of nothing whatever to say. Luckily there was a diversion – Leslie appeared on the staircase carrying the baby he had just insisted that Charlie should allow downstairs. 'Great bit of P.R.,' said Mr Wickstead and wandered off towards his client.

'My Lord, Lady Naboth, Sir Nicholas and Lady Fanner, ladies and gentlemen,' Leslie called out to them all. 'Will you please welcome a future prime minister, Nicholas George Titmuss!'

'Well!' Grace murmured. 'I must say we had to wait long enough for him.'

But Dorothy moved to the bottom of the stairs, put out her hand and touched the baby's head. 'He really *is* rather handsome, isn't he?' she said.

'He knew! Your husband knew all about Christmas. And everything.'

Fred had met Mrs Wickstead, not in their usual pub in Notting Hill Gate but in the bar of the Great Western Hotel at Paddington station. 'Yes.'

'But how did he know? That's the point.'

'I told him, of course.'

'You what?'

'We're very honest with each other. We don't have secrets.'
Fred had come up from Hartscombe in the afternoon, deliberately missing lunchtime. Now it was six o'clock: the bar was full
of businessmen with briefcases and large ladies with Harrods
bags all having a stiffener before facing the long train journey
back to the country. Mrs Wickstead looked into her vodka and
tonic. 'You rather like secrets, don't you, Fred?'

'Some secrets. I mean, some things *are* private.'

'Priests have secrets, doctors and lawyers, all those sort of
people. Well, Kenneth's just an ad-man. We find it works to tell
each other the truth.'

'What about Mr Bugloss?'

'What?'

'What about Mr Benjamin K. Bugloss? Did you tell Kenneth
about him too?'

'Of course, not that there was much to tell. Benny's so in love
with the movie business that he hasn't got much energy for
anything else. He really kept me on for the sake of appearances.'

'And does Mr Wickstead keep you on for the sake of appearances?'

'Not entirely. But he doesn't mind. Can't you get that into
your thick head? He really doesn't mind at all.' She looked at
Fred and smiled. 'That shocks you, doesn't it?'

'Yes.'

She finished her drink and spoke quietly. 'I've been stupid.'

'I didn't say that.'

'I should have pretended that it was all a great mystery and
we were deceiving Mr Wickstead. You'd've liked that better,
wouldn't you?'

Instead of answering her, he asked, 'The flat in Notting Hill
Gate, was it for both of you?'

'I suppose so. From time to time.'

There were shouts and chuckles from the other end of the
bar. One of the businessmen was telling his friends and the
barman a joke.

'Did Mr Wickstead laugh a lot when you told him about Christmas?' What Fred couldn't put up with was the thought of them both laughing at his father.

'I knew he'd think it was funny. That's why I told him. Oh, come on, Fred. It *was* funny, wasn't it?' When he didn't answer, she said, 'I've blown it, haven't I?'

'It's probably my fault.'

'Why miss something enjoyable, just because Mr Wickstead knows about it?'

'I know it sounds unreasonable.' He took out his wallet and left a note on the table to pay for the drinks.

'But you've got a train to catch?'

'Yes.'

'And I'm not coming with you?'

'Not tonight.'

'Or any night. I'm sorry you had to find out about Mr Wickstead.'

Fred's anger soon died. It gave way to a dull ache and a long period of emptiness during which he only just resisted the temptation to telephone Mrs Wickstead. He thought about her perpetually at first, then less often, and finally only with a stab of regret when anyone mentioned Notting Hill Gate, or he saw a young woman immerse herself in a fur coat.

Leslie had less than two years in the government job before the miners went on strike. There were power cuts and fuel shortages and the great British public, reduced to working a three-day week, was expected to make an important decision. The young P.P.S. at Advanced Technology took his family down to Rapstone for the weekend so that he could put the Chairman of his local Party in the picture. 'Ted Heath's going to call an election.'

'Your Mr Heath's making a mistake,' Nicholas thought.

'Why? Do people really want the country run by the miners?'

'I don't think people want to be asked. They put Ted Heath

there to get on and deal with things like miners' strikes. They want to get on with watching their telly boxes, and filling in their pools and . . .'

'Watering their begonias?' They were in the sitting-room after lunch, and Charlie spoke from behind the shelter of *New Society*.

'Well, exactly! They don't want Ted Heath asking them questions all the time. I think they may teach him a lesson.'

'I expect to double my majority in Hartscombe.' Leslie was confident. 'Meanwhile, it's up to all of us to save the country.'

'Are we having a war again?' Grace was cheered by this call to arms. 'I must confess I did rather enjoy the last one.'

'We've got to take the situation seriously,' Leslie told her. 'I mean, we've got bricks in all the toilet cisterns. Speaking for myself, I do clean my teeth in the dark.'

'Well, I hope your Mr Heath doesn't expect Nicholas and me to "take a shower" together! That's all I hope. I'm going up to my room. It's not exactly entertaining down here. Discussing bricks in the lavatory.'

'I had a good letter today, from Nicholas George's headmaster,' Leslie told Charlie when her mother had gone.

'Nick's only three. He hasn't got a headmaster.'

'The Headmaster of Knuckleberries,' he explained to Nicholas. 'Your grandson's been down since birth, of course. I've been writing regularly, keeping the Headmaster in the picture. Simeon put in a word for me.'

'He did that, did he?'

'Oh yes. The Rector's taken a considerable interest in him. So in due course we'll be packing young Nicholas George off to Knuckleberries.'

'Don't you be too sure,' Charlie warned him.

'Of course I'm sure. You know who really governs the country? Not Ted Heath *or* the miners. It's the fellows who went to Knuckleberries, so that's why Nick is going to be one of them.'

Up in her bedroom Grace wasn't resting. She was playing

Pinky Pinkerton's old record of 'You're the Top!' and dancing to herself. She thought no one saw her, and, in her elaborate turns, didn't notice the window-cleaners. Gary Kitson, up his ladder, could see her and he called down to his partner, Simon Mallard-Greene, to join him. Watching the old woman pirouette on her own they laughed so much that Simon nearly fell off the ladder.

Chapter Twenty-six

COLLECTING THE EVIDENCE

SIMEON HENRY SIMCOX
BORN 1ST JANUARY 1903
DIED 21ST MAY 1985
FOR FIFTY YEARS RECTOR OF THIS PARISH
BELOVED HUSBAND AND FATHER
'"I KEPT MY WORD," HE SAID.'

Such was the inscription on Simeon's tombstone. Dorothy was busy with her trowel and secateurs, cutting the dead heads off the standard rose she had planted at the head of the grave, and then clearing the weeds that had grown up around it. As she knelt she saw that a pair of uncleaned black shoes and unpressed grey flannel trousers had come to join her. The Rev. Kevin Bulstrode told her that he did like to see a family caring for the grave.

'I suppose most families have got better things to do.'

'Your son was here the other day. I saw him from the Rectory window.'

'You saw Fred?'

'No. Your eldest son.'

Dorothy stood up and thought that it was rather disgusting how well roses did on graves – she could never get a Mrs Sam Macready to flower like that at home.

'Henry? What on earth was he doing here? Never weeding!'

'So far as I could see he was taking photographs.'

'Whatever of?'

307

'Of the headstone so far as I could tell, and of the inscription.'

When Dorothy got home, unloaded her small car and struggled up to the front door with her handbag, shopping bag and tray full of gardening tools she found Jackson Cantellow, the solicitor, smiling and anxious to help.

'Are you very busy?'

'Extremely, the Bishop's coming to tea.' Dorothy didn't want to be bothered with Mr Cantellow.

'Is that true?' Cantellow was carrying her possessions into the sitting-room. 'No,' Dorothy told him. 'It's a thundering lie. What on earth can you want with me?'

'Don't you know, Mrs Simcox? Didn't you get my letters?' She had seen the envelopes neatly typed and marked Cantellow and Machin. She told him that she burnt them unopened. 'You couldn't have anything of the slightest interest to say to me.'

Cantellow smiled, prepared to take his time. 'Aren't we going to have a cup of tea?'

'I am.'

'That's very thoughtful.' But when he followed her into the kitchen she used only one cup, one tea-bag and a little milk. She drank on her own.

'Mrs Simcox' – Cantellow ignored the lack of hospitality and perched himself on a high stool . . . 'if you had read my letters you'd've been aware that your son, Henry, is attacking his father's last will on the grounds that the late Rector was of unsound mind, memory and understanding. We shall need your views on that.'

'Well, of course Simeon was mad.'

'Really?' The solicitor was gratified.

'Aren't we all? Aren't you, Mr Jackson Cantellow?'

'Me?'

'I would say, mad as a hatter.' Dorothy was sitting at the kitchen table, sipping her tea. 'Writing me letters which I have no desire to read. Asking a lot of questions I have no desire to answer. Singing in those awful concerts.'

'I really don't see what the Worsfield Choral has to do with it.' For the first time Cantellow looked hurt.

'Ha! Ha! Ha! Ha! Ha! Ha . . . le . . . lu . . . Hallelujah! Taking forever just to sing one word! On and on and on until everyone dies of boredom. Why couldn't you just say "Hallelujah" and get it over with, like a normal person?'

'The evidence we already have shows signs of unfortunate mental instability growing in the late Rector since the end of the last war.' Cantellow decided to ignore Dorothy's attack. He opened his briefcase in a businesslike manner and took out a typewritten statement. 'We give instances,' he went on. 'An occasion when he appeared on the doorstep of Rapstone Manor on his hands and knees, apparently trumpeting like an elephant. A time when he opened the front door to a couple seeking guidance on the Christian approach to marriage and was seen to be clad in female attire. An incident during an election when he wished that the guillotine might be reintroduced, for aristocrats and their doctors.'

'This is total madness! What's that you're reading from?'

Cantellow handed her the document. 'A draft, Mrs Simcox, of your proof of evidence. I thought we might go through it together and I can include any further little nuggets that you might wish to add.'

As soon as she had it Dorothy tore the 'proof' into small strips and dropped them into the tidy-bin. Cantellow seemed not at all perturbed as he told her he had a copy, of course, back at the office. 'Some time you'll have to tell us about these matters, Mrs Simcox, painful as they may be. Steps can always be taken to compel a reluctant witness to come to court, in the interests of justice.'

'In the interests of justice I have to be visited by the awful little slimy hymn-singer! I have to be besieged in my own living-room! I have to be asked the most ridiculous questions about your father! Naturally Simeon went down on his hands and knees and trumpeted like an elephant. It was something he thought amusing.' Dorothy had burst furiously into Fred's consulting room, surprising the local bank manager who had come to chat about his piles.

'Please, Mr Grimsdale. Could I ask you to wait outside? Just for a moment.' When his patient had gone, Fred protested mildly, 'This is a doctor's consulting room, Mother. I don't know if you remember?'

'Well I wish you'd prescribe something for Mr Singing Cantellow, preferably rat poison. And you must stop Henry bringing this wretched case. You must know how to do that,' she ended somewhat illogically. 'You're a doctor.'

Fred told her that it would take more than a doctor to stop Henry, a feat which could hardly be performed by a battleship armed with Exocet missiles. So far as he could tell the only thing which would prevent Henry going on to contest the will in court was something he could see no sign of, a logical explanation.

'A what?'

'A sane reason for our father leaving his money to Leslie Titmuss.'

'It was his money, wasn't it? I suppose he could do exactly as he liked with it.' Dorothy was still trembling with rage after the solicitor's visit. 'That Mr Jackson Cantellow thought I was going to make him a cup of tea. But I didn't, you know!'

When Dorothy had left him, Fred telephoned his brother. He said he was coming up to London that evening and might he call in for half an hour? As he drove out of Hartscombe, across the bridge, up the hill and towards the motorway, Fred began to feel that he had a new purpose in life, that of protecting Simeon's memory. He saw no reason why any court should find his father guilty but insane because of his will, or his jokes, or his political beliefs, and the fact that the Rector was no longer in a position to explain himself made Fred even more determined to discover the truth. If he had been entirely honest he would have had to admit that not allowing Henry to get his own way had its place somewhere in his list of aims and ambitions.

When he arrived at the flat off the King's Road he found Lonnie laying the table for a dinner party in the big room. While Henry poured drinks, Fred looked idly down at his brother's desk and saw, to his considerable surprise, a photograph of their father's tombstone.

'Rather an important part of the evidence, don't you think?' Henry handed him a glass. Lonnie was muttering to herself as she laid out forks, 'Is Fred staying for dinner? If he is it's going to play silly buggers with my placement.'

'You remember the inscription?' Henry said it as though putting his brother through some kind of basic intelligence test.

'Do you think I'm likely to forget? "'I kept my word,' he said." From the Bible, I always thought.'

'You always thought! The trouble with you, young Frederick, is that you hardly ever think at all. As for the money wasted on your so-called education at Knuckleberries . . .'

'It would mean sitting Fred next to another man – I could put him beside Ronnie Archpole.' Lonnie was worrying round her dinner table.

'"'Is anyone there?" said the Traveller, Knocking on the moonlit door."' Henry took a drink to his second wife and handed it to her as he spoke to Fred. 'Does that ring a faint bell?'

'"'Tell them I came, and no one answered, That I kept my word," he said.' Lonnie recited it as she moved the place-mats around. 'Walter de la Mare.'

'The brilliance of a well-stocked mind!' Henry applauded her.

'Of course Ronnie Archpole is tremendously gay. Fred won't mind that, will he?' Lonnie wanted to know but her husband was asking his brother the next difficult question.

'Have you considered the significance of our father choosing that quotation for his final resting-place?'

'Have you?'

'The climax of megalomania! Simeon clearly regarded his

passage through the world as a sort of Second Coming. He called on the great, inert masses to answer his call and accept the Kingdom of Equality, Christian Socialism and the Welfare State! Poor old Father. Nobody answered. That's how he saw himself. The Great Prophet rejected. The misunderstood Messiah! Our psychiatrist says his hospital's full of them.'

'Our psychiatrist?'

'The one we're calling to give evidence.'

'Anyway.' Fred was thinking about the inscription. 'Our father didn't quote the lines about no one answering. He quoted the bit about keeping his word.' He had picked up a dish of nuts and was eating thoughtfully. Lonnie removed them from him.

'I was just going to set those out on the coffee table.'

'Perhaps he gave his word to someone,' Fred suggested.

'You mean to Leslie Titmuss?' Henry was contemptuous. 'If he tries to say *that* . . .'

'It might be true.'

'It can't be! Simeon had no possible reason to promise Titmuss anything.'

'But if he *had* a reason your case would collapse, wouldn't it?'

'What reason can you suggest?'

'Perhaps I can find one.'

'Why would you want to try?'

'Your solicitor . . .'

'*Our* solicitor.'

'Cantellow's been pestering Mother. She'll never give evidence.'

'She may have to.'

'Would you force her?'

'It isn't because you're so concerned about Mother, is it?' Henry, much pinker than he used to be, flushed to a deeper shade. 'She stands to gain as much as any of us. It's because you can't bear a fight. One thing you can say for the terrible Titmuss, he's a fighter! You've always been the same, Frederick. You couldn't even fight me all those years ago. You had to cave in, over Agnes.'

Lonnie, reacting to the mention of the Numero Uno, dropped a spoon, picked it up, flustered, and wiped it with a table napkin. 'Well, is Fred staying to dinner or isn't he?'

'He isn't,' Fred told her. 'I'm leaving now.'

'Going to sample my ex-wife's experiments with herbs, down the wrong end of the Fulham Road?' Henry asked him.

'You know about that?'

'You'd better take it I know most things about you.'

After this visit to his brother Fred was more anxious than ever to discover the true reason for their father's will. He thought how little he really knew about Leslie. What secret did this politician, whom Fred had always found faintly ridiculous, have which made him deserve Simeon's sudden and secret generosity at the Simcox family's expense? Intent on discovering some clue to the Titmuss mystery, Fred thought of Leslie's long-time friend and business associate. He invited Magnus Strove and his wife, Jennifer (née Battley), to lunch at the Swan's Nest Hotel. They accepted eagerly and arrived dead on time.

Their table was in the new Old Father Thames Carvery, where they were attended by a malign-looking Portuguese waiter wearing a soup-stained purple dinner-jacket. Piped music tinkled and gurgled incessantly and Fred noticed that the platform, where he had once played for a dinner dance with the Riverside Stompers, had been abolished. Magnus's boyish good looks had faded, he was now a balding, disappointed, middle-aged man, wearing a blazer and an old Knuckleberries tie. His wife, Fred thought, had worn rather better. She had become a determined and rather tough woman, the organizer of a family which had fallen on harder times than they ever expected to encounter. Both the Stroves looked down at their plates with approval. 'It's a while since we had smoked salmon, isn't it, Magnus?' 'Rather a while. Of course, you quacks must be making a fortune out of the National Health. And when you and Henry win the battle for the Simcox shares . . .'

'That's what I wanted to ask you about. I want your help.'

'Well, absolutely anything we can do to scupper the toad, Titmuss. Isn't that right, Jennifer?'

'Absolutely anything to scupper the toad.'

'You know my father left his whole estate to Leslie?'

'Then he must have been off his chump, quite definitely. What do you say, Jennifer?'

'I'm awfully afraid to say that the late Rector must have been entirely off his chump. Not hereditary, of course,' Jennifer added hastily.

'Tell me a bit more about him, Magnus. After all you were in business together for a long time.'

'Hartscombe Enterprises. Its name's engraved on my heart.' Magnus looked pained.

'Was he ever in need of money?'

'Leslie in need of money?' He gave a small and mirthless laugh. 'That's pretty rich, isn't it, Jennifer?'

'Yes, it is. Pretty rich.' These Stroves, Fred thought, clearly supported each other.

'Look. You remember when Leslie first got into the Government? Under-Secretary for Public Urinals. Some damn thing or other . . .'

'Advanced Technology.'

'Jennifer knows all about it. Anyway, he had to get out of Hartscombe Enterprises just at the top of the property boom. We couldn't go wrong at the time. Offices, hotels, blocks of flats were going up like mushrooms. And we were coining the stuff. So Christopher Kempenflatt and I were delighted to buy the toad out, even though we had to pay through the nose for it, in readies.'

'Cash down!' Jennifer told Fred.

'That was it. We didn't want to deplete the company so I borrowed a load on my expectation of the Picton estate.'

'The house?'

'Of course, and the cottages and woodlands, couple of farms

in hand – the whole bloody boiling. Well, Daddy was going into a state of depression about the peerage he never got and I knew it'd all be mine in pretty short order. I thought I'd pay off the mortgage out of the company profits. That's what I thought!'

'That was when Hartscombe Enterprises went broke?'

'Worse than that. When he was our accountant, do you know what the toad made Christopher and me do? Only give our personal guarantee to the bank. Of course we needed a loan to expand in those days.'

'And Leslie didn't give a guarantee?'

'Toad Titmuss? He wouldn't guarantee his own child the price of a Mars bar.'

'So when Doughty died Magnus had to let the whole estate go back to the mortgage company.' Jennifer carried on with the story as Magnus seemed to momentarily weaken with disgust. 'And you know who was the principal shareholder of *that* little enterprise?'

'He can guess, Jennifer. Fred can guess.'

'Yes, I suppose I can.'

'The Honourable Member for Hartscombe and Worsfield South, otherwise known as the Toad. Now we're left with nothing. Of course, Jennifer's got her physiotherapy and I fill in as part-time secretary at the Golf Club. That's the poor, starving little brewery clerk your father decided to leave his money to.' Magnus looked out of the restaurant window at the river and the line of punts which still bumped gently against the landing-stage. 'We made a big mistake that night at the dinner dance,' he said. 'We ought to have drowned the little bugger.'

The events which Magnus Strove had described took place in the years after 1974, when Mr Heath fell prey to the miners and Leslie in opposition was able to devote his time to his new business interests. The quick upward climb of 'fringe' banks and property companies, such as Hartscombe Enterprises, was over and they began to slide towards disaster. Leslie had jumped for safety just in time. So, in due course, the changes in the market and the death of Doughty delivered him Picton House and the Strove estate. When he first took possession of Magnus's old house Leslie stood for a while on the terrace, surveying his domain. Then he walked through the rooms, huge, empty and dusty with marks on the walls where the Strove ancestors had once hung. Standing in the hall he heard a strange sound in that house, the sound of laughter. He went down a number of draughty corridors to the kitchen and there found his mother in rubber gloves and an overall preparing for a good clean-up. She was laughing her head off.

After he had entertained Magnus and Jennifer at the Swan's Nest, Fred had a further opportunity to research into the character of Leslie Titmuss. He came back from a call and Miss Thorne, the receptionist, told him, with a certain amount of pride, that the Minister had been on the phone asking for Dr Hardison to visit; the great man had lost his voice.

'I might go over to Picton myself.'

'He did especially ask for Dr Hardison.'

'But Hardison's not back yet, is he? I mean we can't leave a politician without a voice.'

Leslie was not delighted to see Dr Simcox. Owing to the pending case, he whispered, he felt it was quite improper for Fred to treat him. 'You mean it might be contempt of court to look at your larynx? Don't be ridiculous!' Fred got out his torch and spatula. 'Now if you'd just sit down and open your mouth.' Such are the magical properties of the doctor's black bag that the Minister obeyed him.

The Picton living-room was now furnished according to Leslie Titmuss's specification and looked as though everything had been ordered in one lot from Harrods. On the gold striped wallpaper there were oil paintings of watermills and cardinals drinking wine. On the copy antique console table stood signed photographs of the Queen visiting Leslie's department, President Reagan, Mrs Thatcher, Lee Kwan Yew and the Pope. For all the money spent on it the room gave no more sign of individual taste than the Residents' Lounge of a chain hotel; it was warmer but not less grim than it had been in Doughty's day. In the midst of this splendour the Cabinet Minister sat with his chest bared, his mouth open and his tongue depressed by Fred's spatula.

'Really you and I don't have to quarrel about anything.'

'Oo–shoo–arr . . . ber . . . hat.'

'What did you say?'

'You should ask your brother that,' Leslie croaked when Fred removed the spatula.

'Henry thinks my father was mad to leave his money to you.'

'Do you agree with him?'

'My difficulty is finding any sort of logical explanation.'

'It's obvious, isn't it? Your father was . . .'

'Open again, will you? I'll just take another look at those remarkably overworked tonsils.'

'En . . . essly . . . sappointed . . .'

'What?'

'Endlessly disappointed.' The spatula was removed and the croak returned. 'Your brother left his wife for some sort of typist, didn't he? I don't imagine that went down very well at the Rectory. Besides which he used to be a Socialist, now he's criticizing Margaret for being soft on the unions. Did you read his article on Sunday?'

'I thought you might approve of that.'

'The Rector wouldn't have.'

'He might have been disappointed in Henry but that doesn't begin to explain why he should have left everything to you.' Fred took out his stethoscope in as authoritative a way as possible. 'I mean, you're somebody who's led a totally wasted life.'

'Wasted! My life wasted?' Outrage and laryngitis silenced Leslie.

'You *have* got a nasty cold.' Fred was listening attentively to the Titmuss chest.

'What do you mean wasted?' A still, small voice returned. 'Ever since I was a kid, ever since I cut your nettles, I've been determined to make something of myself.'

'What went wrong? Just cough again for me, will you?'

Leslie coughed and was about to protest when Fred went on. 'I mean you were set for life, you might have done a very decent job as head of the accounts department at the Brewery, getting the beer circulating efficiently. You might have done a lot of good in the world.'

'Look.' Titmuss spoke in a furious whisper. 'I told you I'd asked for Hardison.'

'But you couldn't stick to it. You had to go into property, turning corner shops into offices and doing no possible good to anyone. And getting into the Cabinet! Where's that got us all? Back to where we were before the war: wasted lives, no jobs, back to the years before Simeon made his well-meaning offer of Paradise. Why on earth would our father have left everything to a person like you? You can do your shirt up now.'

Leslie stood and did so. Anger gave him back some of his voice.

'God! You're arrogant,' he rasped. 'I always thought Henry was the bloody superior one. Always on television, always writing about himself, knowing everything, laying down the law. Henry's got nothing at all on you! You're the one for arrogance, aren't you? You don't do anything, don't commit yourself to anything. It's all far beneath you, isn't it? Politics! Business! Property! Writing books! Even getting married and giving birth to another human being. All that's far beneath your dignity!'

'I wouldn't say that.' Fred was writing out a prescription.

'You're so pure, aren't you, Doctor Frederick? So uncorrupted. Doing your rounds in your tweed jacket and old flannel trousers. The decent, quiet country doctor and we all know why Simeon cut *you* out of his will!'

Fred packed up his medical bag, the consultation almost over. 'Do we? I'll leave this here.' He crossed to put the prescription on the mantelpiece. 'You'll probably get better just as quickly without it.'

'*That* Christmas in the Rectory,' Leslie muttered.

'*That* Christmas?'

'The respectable country doctor was found tucked up in bed with someone else's wife when the simple-minded Rector was delivering a Christmas stocking.'

'Who told you that?'

'Someone I can call to give evidence in court.' Leslie, triumphant, suddenly spoke clearly.

'Mr Wickstead, I suppose. Isn't he in charge of your image? At least I've done one thing for which you ought to be extremely grateful: you seem to have completely recovered the power of speech.'

As Fred left the room he heard the front door bell ring, and in the hall, Janet Nowt, one of old Tom's daughters and now part of the Titmuss household, was letting in a portly figure who announced himself in an ingratiating manner.

'The name's Nubble. I was told that the Minister was working at home this morning.' And then, with a grin, 'Hullo there, Simcox Mi.'

'What on earth are *you* doing here?' Fred asked.

'The "Creevy" column.' Nubble sounded inexplicably proud of himself.

'The what?'

'You know what the name of the game is nowadays?'

'Coffee bars? Boutiques? Flower power accessories?'

'Gossip! People love it. All the truth about everyone you'll never meet. I'm interviewing Titmuss. What've you been doing?'

'Much the same thing.'

The living-room door opened and Leslie came out to find Nubble and Fred renewing their acquaintance.

'Minister!' Nubble was obsequious. 'So awfully decent of you to see me.'

'Do you two know each other?' Leslie was whispering again now and puzzled.

'Of course,' Arthur Nubble told him. 'We were at Knuckleberries together.' The old school fellows stood silent and Leslie looked at them both with deep suspicion, as though he suspected them of forming some sort of alliance against him.

Part Five

As it will be in the future, it was at the birth of man –
There are only four things certain since Social Progress
began:
That the Dog returns to his Vomit and the Sow returns
to her Mire
And the burnt Fool's bandaged finger goes wobbling
back to the Fire;

And that after this is accomplished, and the brave new
world begins
When all men are paid for existing and no man must
pay for his sins,
As surely as Water will wet us, as surely as Fire will
burn,
The Gods of the Copybook Headings with fever and
slaughter return!

from 'The Gods of the Copybook Headings'
Rudyard Kipling

Chapter Twenty-seven

THE BEST FOR NICKY

'Rough shooting's better since Tom Nowt left us. Fellow had a talent for luring away my pheasants. Never saw a hare either, not when Nowt was alive.'

'He had his ways, Sir, did old Tom Nowt.'

'Of course my wife could never stand him, wanted me to prosecute if I remember rightly.'

'Tom was a red rag to her Ladyship.'

'For goodness sake, we've got enough rabbits to go round. I mean if you own a decent bit of rough shooting, you're under an obligation to have your game pinched occasionally. My wife can't see that. Do you remember when she summoned in the Constabulary?'

Since the death of his friend Doughty, Nicholas went round with a gun, a dog and Wyebrow who had become, after years of secret practice, an excellent shot. They walked along the edge of the woodlands, and through the sifting rain, two old men, master and servant, indistinguishable in their tweed caps and jackets. A lurcher and a spaniel sniffed and dived under bushes, causing an occasional drum roll of wings or the streak of a rabbit.

'Of course the officers of the law never found Tom's old hut and I didn't give them directions.' Nicholas sneezed. He was coming up for a cold on a bleak day in the 'winter of discontent', a time when hospital porters and gravediggers went on strike, and those hostile to Mr Callaghan's Labour Government could ask what sort of a Britain was this in which the luxuries of falling ill and being buried in the ground were apparently denied to the citizens. Nicholas, being in a privileged position, fell ill privately and at home. His cold developed into pneumonia. Fred called, dosed him with penicillin, and Simeon, smiling and ruffled like a cheerful bird of ill omen, came to sit by the patient. 'Haven't come to administer the last rites, have you?' Nicholas asked. 'If you want to hear my confession, I must say you're in for a damn dull evening.'

Simeon felt for his pipe, changed his mind about smoking in the sick room, and settled down to listen. 'It's a terrible thing, you know, to look back over a long life and have no sins worth confessing. Not that I've had many opportunities to sin. Married Grace when I was a young man and before that I was living with Mother.' Nicholas looked back, dismayed by a blameless life. 'Of course, I might have had a sin or two when I was parted from Grace during the war. But I never took advantage of that. More fool I! I suppose some people would say.'

'No. I'm sure they wouldn't say that.'

'I might have done a bit of sinning when I was stationed at Bognor,' Nicholas calculated. 'Grace was always dashing up to London for evenings out. She enjoyed the air raids, you know. All I did was go for walks along the sea-front or over the Downs. I stayed away from home – not that I stayed away *with* anyone, you understand.'

'I understand.'

From along the bedroom corridor they heard the strains of another Pinky Pinkerton special, 'Smoke Gets in Your Eyes'. Grace, determined that her husband should not be the only one to spend a comfortable day in bed, was listening to her gramophone, propped up on her pillows and sorting through the contents of a mother-of-pearl box which she usually kept on her dressing-table. She reminded herself of old bits of jewellery buried in it and in its depths she found a brooch in the shape of a Maltese Cross, set with garnets which flashed in the glow of her bedside light. It was nothing very grand or expensive, of course,

nothing like his mother's pieces which Nicholas had given her
and which were always kept in the bank, but she was glad to see
it because it reminded her of something that happened during
the war. Under the jumble of rings and necklaces, ear-rings and
bracelets, was a letter on pale blue notepaper together with a few
other scraps of correspondence that she kept for the same reason.

'You never liked Grace, did you?' Nicholas asked Simeon over
the distant sound of music.

'You want me to tell you the truth?'

'Isn't that what we're here for? A truth-telling occasion.'

'No. I never liked her.' Simeon smiled. 'In fact, I think I
disapprove of everything about her!'

'Spoilt, overprivileged, selfish and intolerant?' Nicholas suggested.

'Yes.'

'I thought that's what you'd say. But there's always something
I shall remember about Grace. She was so beautiful and I was
rather dull, but she married me, you know. Do you do much of
this nowadays?'

'Much of what?'

'Hearing confessions.'

'Hardly any at all.'

'People don't believe in it, eh? I'm not sure I do. Good
heavens! What's the point of remembering things that never
happened so long ago?'

From Rapstone, Simeon drove to Picton House. He was
admitted by Janet Nowt, and found the curtains drawn in the
hall and the standard lamps at the foot of the stairs illuminating a
theatrical scene. The Rector was delighted to see a small figure,
wearing a beret of Janet's with a pheasant's tail feather stuck in
it, a black, curly moustache painted on his face, clad mainly in a
tartan car rug, climbing the stairs with a bread knife at the ready,
undoubtedly intent on murder. Half-way up, the nine-year-old
Nicholas George Titmuss struck the old dinner gong, a relic of
the Stroves, and recited the only lines he could remember:

'. . . the bell invites me.
Hear it not, Duncan; for it is a knell
That summons thee to heaven or to hell.'

So, with a bloodcurdling laugh, Nick vanished into the shadows, and Simeon, standing at the back of an audience consisting of Charlie, Elsie Titmuss and Janet Nowt, clapped loudly.

'We did it when I was at school,' he said. 'I had the other part. And my boys did it with me, one Christmas at the Rectory.'

'They were taken to see it at Stratford, and they've been doing scenes,' Charlie explained. 'Such a good school! I can't imagine why Leslie wants to move him.'

Elsie shivered. 'I don't think it's right to teach children things like that.' At which moment Nicky ran delightedly back down the stairs. 'I've done it now. I've stabbed the old King! Ring the bell and pretend it was the servants.'

'Oh that's not fair!' Elsie protested but Nicholas, his face, hands and the bread knife liberally smeared with crimson water colour, hit the gong again.

'Ssh,' said Charlie to the mother-in-law. 'It's the sort of thing Thanes do.' But the show was suddenly over; Nicky bowed to prolonged applause, then Elsie took him away to clean him up and Janet Nowt went off to get tea. 'I've been summoned by your father,' Simeon told Charlie when they were alone. 'He wanted to make a confession.'

'He's not seriously ill?'

'Fred hasn't said so.'

'Poor Father.' Charlie smiled. 'He finds it hard to do anything seriously.'

'Yes. Well, what I wanted to say to you, is' – Simeon was positive – 'he has absolutely nothing to tell you.'

'To tell me?'

'Has he tried to say anything to you?'

'No. Nothing serious.'

'Well, that's the point, isn't it? So, well, if he summons you to tell you something, it'll really be nothing very much. Nothing for you to be concerned about in any case.'

'I'll try to remember that.' Charlie was laughing, then she went back to the question that concerned her most. 'Why does Leslie want to send Nicky away from me? Would you send a child of yours away?'

'It's something we've all done,' Simeon admitted.

'Doesn't he understand?' He saw Charlie's fists clench, her back stiffen and he remembered how she used to be just before she started to scream. 'For God's sake! Who else is there for me to talk to?' Simeon wondered if he'd have to resort, as he had before, to a reading of *Biggles of the Royal Flying Corps*. Then the door opened to admit Nicky, still in his costume, Elsie Titmuss and Janet with a tray. 'We've washed the blood off our hands,' Elsie told them. 'But we've decided to keep our nice moustache.'

When Charlie said that Nicky was the only person she had to talk to, she was scarcely exaggerating. Her longing to have someone helpless to look after, which had disposed her towards Leslie when he was thrown into the river, and had been distributed among a random selection of hard cases and students she thought badly done by, had concentrated itself powerfully on her child. She forgave Nicky everything, including not being homeless or underprivileged or living below the poverty line or in constant trouble with the police. Deprived of these disadvantages, she thought her son had compensating problems. He had a father who had managed to become extremely rich and too busy to see much of him. Nicky was an only child, as she had been, and therefore must be lonely. In fact he grew up to be a pale, contained but self-reliant small boy, who wore glasses, read a lot of books and never minded being left alone. He found little to say to his father and thought of his mother as someone who needed a great deal of looking after.

When her son was growing, Charlie decided he should be

brought up in the country. Leslie agreed. It was no bad thing that his family should live in the constituency although he spent most of the week in London. He thought it politic for Nicky to start his education at the village school, although he was later sent to a small fee-paying day school in Hartscombe. So Charlie gave up her social studies, her case work and her clientele of lame dogs. She spent no more time in afternoon drinking clubs in Soho, students' bedrooms or the backs of vans. She enjoyed her days in the country and looked forward to Nicky coming home at tea-time far more keenly than she did to her husband's return at weekends. A shadow hung, however, over the peaceful landscape of Nicky's childhood. As doom-laden as the pronouncements of the witches in *Macbeth* came Leslie's constant references to the day when their son would have to go away to Knuckleberries.

When Charlie tried to argue about Nicky's education, Leslie merely smiled tolerantly and changed the subject. The date was fixed, it seemed to Charlie, like that of an execution. Pleas for clemency were met only with a polite smile and a quick glance at the calendar. It's fair to say that Nicky, reading on his stomach in the long grass all the summer, seemed unaware of the condemned cell in which he was waiting.

'Leslie never went away to school. You kept him at home. Did you want to get rid of him?' Charlie did her best to get her mother-in-law to sign the petition for a reprieve.

'Get rid of him?' Elsie smiled at the absurdity of the idea. 'Of course not. He was always his mother's boy. I never thought George really understood his ways. Besides which Leslie was always one for my cooking.'

'Then will you tell him not to send Nicky away?'

'He wants him to have all the advantages.'

'The advantages of being buggered and beaten and brought up by a lot of bloody snobs?' Charlie sometimes reverted, at moments of emotion, to the language of the London School of Economics.

'There now.' Elsie was making rock cakes for tea. 'I'm sure
Leslie only wants the best for Nicky.'

It was still two years before the date of his son's banishment,
when Leslie Titmuss found himself fighting his third election. It
was the end of the sad seventies, a decade whose contributions to
history, the Watergate scandal, President Carter, hot pants and
the skate-board, vanished from the memory more quickly than a
Chinese dinner. The country, it seemed, was prepared to atone
for the greatly exaggerated sins of its past. The dreams which
Simeon had were dying at last, and a new age was coming to
birth. Young people in black leather, loaded with chains, with
white faces and pink, green and purple hedgehog hairdo's hung
round the market square in Hartscombe, some wearing swastikas
and iron crosses, nostalgic for an old horror. Leslie stood on an
empty beer crate at the Brewery entrance and addressed his
former workmates through a loudhailer. Stuck on his campaign
van were posters, showing Mrs Thatcher looking prepared to
face a grim future for a lot of other people with considerable
fortitude. 'You're worried about your jobs?' Leslie's magnified
voice bounced round the vats, the barrels and piles of hops to be
disregarded by a group of drivers enjoying their mid-morning
pints; although someone in the accounts department stuck his
head out of a window to listen. 'Of course you're worried with a
Labour Government giving you one and a quarter million unemployed! Thank your lucky stars Simcox Ales hasn't been
nationalized. It hasn't been taken over by the Socialist bureaucracy. This is just the sort of small business we want to see
prosper. Your jobs are going to be safe after the election.'

And after the election Leslie found himself a job as a Minister.
His rise, as always, was rapid, and, in an early reshuffle, he
entered the Cabinet.

Hartscombe is in the more fortunate half of England and was
not as desolated by the abandonment of old industries, or the
complete hopelessness of unemployment, as the remote and
foreign North. All that happened in the riverside towns was a

little 'slimming down', a bit of 'rationalization' and 'cutting down on overmanning'. There were also a large number of bankruptcies. Fred went away on a holiday and came back to find a change had come over Marmaduke's garage. The pumps were now self-service, and the only attendant was a lumpy girl sitting in a burglar-proof booth who handed out, through a tiny grille and with the change, green plastic men. Collecting about five hundred 'greenies' could mean the infliction of garden tools, Pyrex dishes or a cuddly toy. Marmaduke's had given up repairs, and had also given up Terry Fawcett, who sat in his tower block, thinking of his dwindling two thousand pounds redundancy money, and wondering why it was proving so unexpectedly difficult to find another job.

'Glenys is back typing for your father,' he told Fred when he visited. 'I do the shopping and fetch the kid from school. I'd make a lovely wife.'

'I tell him he ought to go into window-cleaning. Look at all Tina's got round her, it's through Gary's window-cleaning. That's what she's always telling us.' Glenys had just got home from work.

'Gary doesn't want me in his business. Well, who needs to live with a lot of tropical fish, anyway?'

'Do you ever get the feeling the whole world's going backwards? It's as if we got tired of chugging on slowly and put the whole engine into reverse. Back to the dole queues and poverty being thought of as a shameful little secret, something respectable people don't get involved in. Nicholas wouldn't have approved however much he called himself a Conservative.' Simeon and Fred were on one of their walks together, threading their way down a long, overgrown bridle-path, walking in single file so that the Rector's random thoughts were shouted back over his shoulder. 'Poor old Nicholas! At the end he seemed to let go of life. Not that he ever had hold of it very firmly.'

'Not like you!' Fred smiled at his father, who was striding

along as though on a Fabian Society walking tour of the Lake District. 'You're remarkably tenacious.'

'Your predecessor, Dr Salter, used to tease me about that. He said Christians ought to give death a warmer welcome. Well, Salter was an unbeliever but he went first.'

'So he did.'

'And he was always so strong.' Simeon was hitting at brambles with his walking-stick, clearing the path for both of them, with as much relish as if he were using a machete in a jungle. 'Of course, I've always known you were the tough one of our family.'

'Am I?' Fred was surprised.

'Henry's not as strong as you. But he can look after himself, don't you think?'

'Does he have to? Now he's got Lonnie to look after him.'

'Lorna! Your mother doesn't hit it off with Lorna at all.' They were slithering down the steep end of the path. The wood stretched out around them, coloured by pools of bluebells. 'There *is* something rather unsettling about her, though. About Lorna, I don't mean about your mother.'

'What's that?'

'Lorna would appear to be deeply religious,' Simeon said as though it were much to be regretted.

'Oh dear!' Fred laughed.

'Of course, Henry goes to church whenever they come down for the weekend. He's become such an old English country gent, it makes me feel quite young sometimes. You don't go to church, do you?'

'Not at all.'

'Can't say I blame you. But I look across at Lorna during prayers. Most people – well, there aren't many of them now – adopt the usual sort of Church of England crouch: bottoms on the edge of the pew, head stuck forward, you know the sort of procedure? Not Lorna! She's down on her knees, hands together, eyes tightly shut, lips moving. Sometimes I want to leave the altar and go over to her and say, "For heaven's sake, my dear girl, give it a rest! Don't try so hard." I don't think God likes to be pestered, do you?'

'I suppose not.'

'So you admit the existence of a God who doesn't like to be pestered?' Simeon asked quickly.

'I didn't say that.'

'No.' There was a gate at the end of the path. The Rector climbed it and sat for a moment, perched on the top bar. 'But you're all right, Fred. You'll always be all right. Are you happy?'

'Not particularly.'

'Of course not, foolish question.' Simeon dropped from the gate. Fred followed him and they came out on the edge of a cornfield. They walked for a little and Fred saw a track going back into the wood behind them. He suddenly realized where they were, in that part of the Mandragola Valley in which, one long past night, he had seen Tom Nowt shoot a deer.

'You know we all think, I certainly thought,' Simeon told him, 'that our lives are so different from our parents'. We think differently, feel differently, all that sort of thing. But it's not true, is it? We all find out the same things, and when we've found them out, well, then it's time to go.'

'Not for a long while yet.' They were walking side by side along the muddy edge of the field and Fred took his father's arm.

'Why? Do you think I'm about to make some great new discovery?'

As the date crept slowly towards Nicky's first term at his big school (Leslie's description) or his imprisonment, his execution, his being sent off to the front (as Charlie called it), the process seemed to his mother to have a sickening inevitability. Leslie was quite set on it. Elsie was not going to help. Grace, Charlie knew without asking her, would be worse than useless. Faced with what she regarded as a huge disaster, Charlie could only exercise the right that Henry had once claimed in the face of the Vietnam War. She did not, it's true, organize a march with banners or attract the attention of the mounted police; she demonstrated in the sitting-room at Picton House after dinner and shouted at her husband.

'You hated them once, didn't you? You really hated them when they threw you in the river! That was when I thought I could love you. You were some sort of a person, I thought, a real, live, fighting, kicking, human person.' She turned away from him and started a journey up the carpet. 'Now you've stopped hating. Now you feel so safe and smug and sure of yourself. What are you now? Nothing.'

'Nothing?' Leslie sat in front of the coffee tray. He was nibbling at an after-dinner mint, always having had a sweet tooth. 'Only a member of Her Majesty's Government. Only in the Cabinet.'

'Exactly what I said. Nothing!' The last word rose in volume to just under a scream. Leslie put the rest of the mint into his mouth, wiped his fingers delicately on his handkerchief and urged his wife not to shout. '*They'll* hear.'

'Who'll hear?' Charlie pounced on his fear. 'The servants? My God, let them hear, if it interests them in the least.' She went to the door, wrenched it open and yelled down the kitchen corridor. 'Listen to this, Janet Nowt. Listen, Cook. The Right Honourable Leslie Titmuss is *nothing*!' There was no reply from the brightly lit kitchen where the radio and the washing-up machine were both playing loudly. Charlie banged the door shut. 'Pity the gardener's gone home. He might have been interested.'

'For God's sake, Charlotte. I've tried to make you happy.'

'Happy? Does that include separating me from my child?'

'You're being ridiculous. It happens to everybody.'

'Everybody? Who's everybody? Magnus Strove and that horrible Christopher Kempenflatt and all those braying imbeciles who threw bread rolls and laughed at your dinner-jacket. Have you forgotten? Have you quite honestly forgotten?'

'It's a long time ago.' Leslie finished another mint and this time he licked his fingers quite delicately.

'And now you want Nicky to join them?'

'Your father went away to school.'

'My father! Poor man.'

'His main problem in life was being married to your mother. I must say' – Leslie couldn't help smiling – 'you get more like her every day.'

'Don't say that! Don't ever say that!'

'Now I suppose you're going to scream?'

'No.' Although Charlie was controlling herself with difficulty. 'I'm not going to have to scream any more. I'm going to leave you, Leslie. I'm going to live in London. We'll find a flat somewhere.'

'We?'

'Nicky and I. He can go to school on the state. Just like you did. He'll be like you, a mother's boy. But I'll tell you one thing. I'm not staying here, living with a nothing who can't hate any more.'

'Breakfast meeting with the Americans.' Leslie stood up and stretched. There was a little chocolate stain on his top lip; his tongue emerged and licked it away. He had behaved, he knew, with perfect manners and considerable restraint. 'Isn't it time we both went to bed?'

When Charlie went into Nicky's room, she found his light on and that he was fast asleep wearing his glasses and holding *Vanity Fair*. She took his glasses off gently and put his book away, being careful not to lose his place. She switched off his light and closed the door, full of hope for the future.

During those long summer holidays, both Grace and her daughter came in contact with the law. A detective sergeant and constable were summoned to the Manor. 'No one in Rapstone ever locked their doors. Ever!' Grace stood in the hall in her dressing-gown and lectured the two bewildered young officers on the decline of civilization as she knew it. 'And all we had was one bobby, Harry Jimpson. He had an old push-bike, of course, not some luxurious motor with flashing lights like you've parked out there. But nothing ever got stolen when Harry Jimpson was our bobby!'

'You say it was a box with some pieces of jewellery?' The sergeant looked at such notes as he had been able to take, and wondered why the old bag wanted to get him back on a bicycle. 'And there's no signs of a break-in?'

'Well, there wouldn't be, would there? They must have been far too clever for you. Yes, a mother-of-pearl inlaid box. Locked. With some jewellery and other personal things.'

'No very costly pieces you say? Sentimental value only.'

'And that's exactly why I want them back.'

'We'll do our best, your Ladyship.'

'Your best may not be good enough!' Grace squared her small jaw. 'My son-in-law's in the Cabinet you know. He sees the Prime Minister every day. Law and order's very much her thing, isn't it? I don't suppose she'd like to discover she's being let down badly by the police in the Rapstone Valley.'

Charlie met the law in the shape of a Mr Rattling, a tall, grey-haired and dignified man, the sort of solicitor who acts for Cabinet Ministers. Rattling had walked through the garden at Picton and she first saw him as he stood, a dark and alien figure, beside the croquet lawn, where she was being ruthlessly defeated by her son.

'Mrs Titmuss? I'm Ted Rattling, by way of being your husband's solicitor.'

'I don't need a lawyer,' she told him, squinting in the sun.

'If we could just have a word in private? Before anyone takes a step they're going to regret.'

'You play, Nicky.' Charlie crossed the lawn and stood looking up at the strange man who seemed to have grown in height as she approached him.

'You'll take independent advice, I'm sure. This is just to get the position quite clear.'

'Mr Rattle . . .'

'Rattling. Ted Rattling.'

'Mr Rattling.' She paid no attention to the 'Ted'. 'I've no idea what you're talking about.'

'Have you not? It seems that in conversation with your husband, you suggested a parting of the ways. Look, shouldn't we discuss this indoors?'

'Where are you going, Mum?' Nicky called after her as she allowed the man to lead her across the terrace and in by the french windows. 'Won't be long,' she told him. Indeed, it was not to be a lengthy interview, just a preliminary sniff round the problem as Ted Rattling described it, just so Mrs Titmuss could know what her husband's present 'thinking' was, just so she could 'take on board' his probable reaction.

'I don't really care *what* he thinks. I'm going to London and taking my son with me. Has my husband got any objection to that?' From the living-room window, Charlie could see Nicky working out several devastating shots with mathematical precision. 'If you embark on that course,' she heard Rattling tell her, 'your husband's instructed me to take divorce proceedings, based on your intolerable conduct.'

'That'll suit me down to the ground.'

'And immediate proceedings for the custody of the child of the marriage. Nicholas George, is it?'

'That's ridiculous.' Charlie turned towards him, full of contempt.

'In the normal case, of course, one would expect an order of custody to the mother. However, it seems that you, Mrs Titmuss, were a student and later active in the social services.'

'Is that some sort of crime?'

'Not in itself. No.' Rattling could sound very judicial, indeed many judges behaved more like common or garden solicitors than he did. He prided himself on being able to see at least two sides to every question. 'But what your husband has instructed me to allege, in any proceedings, would be "intimacy" on quite a sizeable scale, as I understand it, with the young males who happened to be in need of the social welfare services. Your husband used the words 'rough trade', Mrs Titmuss. Of course, all custody cases are distressing, but when it comes to an incident, which the child himself might be asked to recollect . . .'

'What incident is that?'

'I'm sure you remember, Mrs Titmuss. When your husband was up in London and a young person "on probation" came to spend the night here. When the child was in the house?'

It was then that Charlie remembered Percy Denham from Wandsworth. He had been one of her special cases and he still telephoned her occasionally. Percy had been after a job in Worsfield and seeing friends, he explained, 'in the area'. She asked him to visit Picton and gave him a meal, and, to Janet's silent disapproval, a bed for the night. Some time during that night, Charlie, long ignored by her husband, had visited Percy in one of the spare bedrooms. She had felt healthy for about two weeks afterwards, and yet it seemed to her that one night had lost her the battle. Now, she thought, it was all inevitable, the endless sewing on of name-tapes, the sorting-out of clothes' lists, shirts blue, shirts white and shorts running, the bleak farewell at the railway station, the tea out at Half-Term, when they would neither of them know what to say. She had come to the centre of a maze of loneliness and there was no escape except by the way she had come in.

'I'm sorry to disappoint you, Mr Rattling,' she said, 'but there isn't going to be a case.'

Leslie was able to get away from his Ministry in time to join Charlie and Nicholas at Liverpool Street station. Father and son said goodbye to each other with distant politeness, although Nicky treated his mother with unusual consideration. When the train had gone, the Minister said he hoped Charlie would be responsible for writing the letters. He had, after all, so little time. They parted then, and she went back to Picton.

She couldn't stay in the house that night, and, after a lonely dinner, she took the car and drove down to the Baptist's Head, planning to buy cigarettes. She was sitting alone at the bar, when someone spoke to her.

'Hear you had a friend of mine down to visit you. Percy, wasn't it? He said you were very hospitable.' She looked round at Gary Kitson.

'Yes.' Charlie saw a well-nourished young man with black ringlets and brown eyes, dressed in jeans, cowboy boots and a leather jacket. 'I expect you'd like a drink.'

'Large rum and black, please, Ted.' Gary held up his empty glass. 'And the lady's paying.'

Chapter Twenty-eight

JUST LIKE OLD TIMES

'Sovereignty is not negotiable. We've made that perfectly clear. What we have is ours, and nobody else's.'

'There may only be a few of them, but they're our sort of people, aren't they?'

'Are you a sheep farmer, Contessa?'

'No, my dear. But I am Scottish, somewhere in the dim and distant past.'

'Are *they* Scottish then?'

'Bound to be. Nobody but the Scots would think of going to live in a place like that.'

'I wish someone would make it clear to me exactly where the Falkland Islands are.'

'It's going to be quite a problem with combined ops. It's going to be quite a party.'

'Not a *garden* party?' Charlie had been drinking a good deal and the dinner-table conversation stopped for a moment around her.

'I mean more like a D-Day party, Mrs Titmuss. On a far smaller scale of course. But it'll be quite like old times.'

Leslie was entertaining the neighbours, regulars like the Naboths and the 'Contessa', Mrs Fairhazel and the Kempenflatts, the Erskine girls and a few members of the Committee of the local Conservative Association and their good ladies. As they ate their Black Forest gâteau, the British Navy was steaming off to the South Atlantic, to take part in a war which brought back irresistible memories of the Empire, maps on classroom walls, largely coloured pink, and newspapers full of distant campaigns which didn't put them in the slightest danger. A dozen miles away Worsfield Heath had become an American Air Force base in preparation for a different sort of war entirely. It was left to Lady Naboth to draw the parallel. 'When I think of our fellows steaming out there. To the Arctic? It *is* the Arctic, really. And those ghastly women in bobble hats and smelly anoraks camped round the Heath. Deserting their husbands and talking about peace as though they'd only just invented it. Peace! I'd like to see them doing it in Russia.'

'Doing what?' Charlie wanted to know.

'Camping in their horrible bobble hats. I really don't know what they're thinking about.'

'Perhaps they're thinking about Nicky.'

'I say. Your lady isn't one of the disarmers is she, Leslie?' Mrs Fairhazel was alarmed.

'I am.' Leslie spoke with the sort of quiet conviction that Charlie had discovered he adopted when he didn't altogether mean what he said. 'I've got a certain amount of respect for the women of Worsfield Heath, but I'd go a lot further! I want the whole world to disarm at the same time. That's all. Not just us. Not just the Americans. Not just the Russians. All of us. Until then, of course, we must keep up our defence capability. I'm sure that's what Charlie has in mind.'

'Oh well.' Mrs Fairhazel looked relieved. 'I suppose that's all right then.'

His wife might have said more but Leslie looked at the clock above the large painting of dead game on the dining-room wall. 'Perhaps it's about time, Charlotte.'

'About time for what?'

'Wouldn't you like to take the ladies upstairs?'

'Take them upstairs?' Charlie pretended ignorance of a ceremony she detested.

'People usually do it,' Leslie explained patiently, 'after dinner.'

'Do they?' Charlie didn't move. 'I thought people usually had a nice cup of tea and went to sleep in front of the telly after dinner.'

'Well, shall *I* lead the way?' Mrs Fairhazel took command of the situation.

'Lead the way? Where?'

'Upstairs, of course. The ladies want to go upstairs.'

'Well, of course. Up you go.' Charlie gave her permission. 'If you're absolutely bursting for a pee.'

In the weeks that followed Leslie had no chance of coming home to Picton. He sat, with his Cabinet colleagues, in remote control of a distant war which came flickering on to the television screen in the saloon bar of the Baptist's Head. There was news of Marine casualties at a beachhead and of Argentine Sea Hawks shot down. Ted Lawless stood behind the beer handles, backed by photographs of Spitfires, of himself with a silk scarf, sheepskin jacket and Brylcreemed hair, and of Ivy, his wife, as a W.A.A.F., and felt young again.

'A drink for the lady, Ted. They can get on and capture Goose Green without you.' Gary Kitson shouted for the landlord's attention; Charlie had just come into the Head to join him for the evening.

'An estimated forty aircraft took part in the attack, and some got through the missile defences to drop their bombs on the ships below. The Argentine planes were finally driven off by the Navy's Sea Harriers, flying almost continuous combat patrols.' The television set in the Rectory described the victory at Goose Green. 'Shall I turn the machine off?' Dorothy wondered.

'If you like.' Simeon was looking depressed.

'If I'd known it was going to have that sort of thing on it I'd never have let it in. Now what exactly do we do to quieten it?' She could never remember so Simeon got up and found the switch. 'I told Fred we were going backwards. That's not exactly right. What we're doing is going round in circles. I mean, is this where we came in?'

'What do you mean?'

'We used to go to the pictures at the Hartscombe Odeon.'

'Did we do that?' Dorothy went back to her mending.

'Of course, even before we had the children. And we were always late.'

'*You* were always late.' She remembered that.

'Yes. So we'd sit on and watch until we said, "This is where we came in." Films used to go round and round in those days. First attraction. Second attraction. Then start all over again.'

'In the last war at least we only had wireless.' To Dorothy that seemed to have been a mercy.

'And we sat glued to it for the latest news of people killing each other,' Simeon reminded her. 'So much enthusiasm. So much hope. Where do you think it all went to?'

'I was never all that concerned about the New Jerusalem.' Dorothy attacked another sock. 'I suppose I've always had far too much to do in the garden.'

'It's going to go round and round, like at the old Hartscombe Odeon.' His pipe had gone out and he started to strike matches to little effect. 'Is that all that's ever going to happen?'

'Probably.' Dorothy sounded reasonably cheerful about it.

'What can we do?'

'Only what we have to.' She looked at her husband and repeated more positively, 'Do what we have to, that's all. And hope for the best.'

On the night when Goose Green was captured Charlie and Gary Kitson entered the Rapstone Cricket Pavilion by forcing a window. After a long evening's drinking at the Baptist's Head they made love on a bed of towels in the middle of the floor. When it was over, Gary zipped up his jeans, buckled his belt, did up a few shirt buttons and combed his hair carefully before putting on his leather jacket.

'You don't really like me, do you?' he asked Charlie, who was sitting naked in a patch of moonlight, ransacking her handbag for a cigarette. 'I don't suppose I like you,' she told him. 'No.'

'What is it then?' Her nakedness irritated him. 'You lonely?'

'That must be it.'

'Where's your husband?'

'Up in London. Winning the war.'

'He's done pretty good for himself then, hasn't he?'

'I suppose so.'

Charlie was sitting under a plaque on the wall which announced that the Pavilion had been donated to the village by the Rt Hon. Leslie Titmuss, M.P., in memory of Sir Nicholas Fanner.

'What about your kid?'

'He's away too.'

'So you've just got your mum?'

'Oh, no. I haven't got her.'

Gary finished work with the comb, cleaned it with his fingers and stowed it in his back pocket.

'I know a bit about your mum. It might surprise you.'

'What?'

'Oh, just things. Things I heard about her, I mean.'

'I can't believe you heard anything interesting.'

'I'd say it was pretty interesting, yes. I mean, perhaps it's something you really ought to know.'

'Tell me.'

'All right. But for God's sake, get your clothes on.'

She looked at him for a moment, then she obeyed him. Later, he told her something which she kept as a secret, entirely to herself.

To understand his father's will, Fred told himself, he had to understand Leslie Titmuss, but nothing that he had learnt from Magnus Strove, nor while examining the larynx of the Minister himself, seemed to throw much light on the problem. Simeon was beyond questioning. To whom should he turn next? He had been to visit a patient on the ridge, and was driving back along a narrow road through a wood near Rapstone, when he saw a familiar grey-haired figure, wearing an old mac, stooping to fill a plastic sack with kindling wood. He stopped his car and went to help his mother, although she said, 'Really, shouldn't you be caring for the sick or something? I'm perfectly capable of getting my own kindling.' All the same, he picked up dead and fallen sticks for her, snapped them and loaded up her bag in silence until he felt able to raise her least favourite subject.

'All this business, about father's will.'

'For heaven's sake, doesn't anyone remember anything about Simeon except his wretched will?' She whacked a branch against a tree to break it. 'Firelighters are so expensive nowadays.'

'I know what you want is to stop the case coming to court.'

'It takes no time to get a bag of kindling.'

'I can stop it. I think I can stop it if I can tell Henry the truth.'

'Anyway, it's a treat coming out to Rapstone Woods, much better than a trip round Tesco's.'

'Tell me what you know about Leslie Titmuss.' Fred tried to make it clear that he hadn't stopped to discuss firewood. 'I mean, who *is* Leslie Titmuss?'

'Isn't he the Minister of something or other? I thought everyone knew that.' Dorothy moved further into the wood but her son followed her.

'Is he . . . I mean, it would make father's will understandable at least.' Fred tried to put the suggestion as tactfully as possible. 'Is he related to us?'

'Related?' She had turned away from him, filling her sack. All he saw was the stooped back and the old, flapping mackintosh. 'Perhaps.'

For a moment Fred thought his mother was going to explain everything in a way that even Henry would have to accept but, when she straightened up and turned towards him, she was laughing. 'Perhaps in the Middle Ages, there was some romance between an old Lady Simcox and a medieval Titmuss! What a perfectly killing idea. I can't really imagine a medieval Titmuss, can you? A Titmuss in shining armour!'

'You know, if we can't explain it, they're going to say father was a lunatic.' Fred tried to persuade his mother of the seriousness of the situation but she was unimpressed. 'It won't be the first time,' she told him.

'No?'

'When he was a young curate in Worsfield I'm sure the Bishop called him a lunatic. Simeon got his revenge, of course. He never stopped writing the poor fellow letters.'

'But about Leslie Titmuss?'

'There.' Dorothy tugged her sack to his feet and left it there. 'I think that's about filled up now. As you don't seem to have anything better to do, Fred, could you put it into my motor? Try and be careful not to drop any out.' And after that she was answering no more questions.

The sitting-room at 'The Spruces' had seen a few changes since Leslie made his fortune: wall-to-wall carpeting, a giant colour telly, a velvet-covered three-piece suite and central heating were some of the new amenities. 'He wanted us to move into the big house, you know,' Elsie explained to Fred when he came to call. 'But George didn't think it right, me going back to live where I used to be in service. George gets funny ideas sometimes. He sits out there all weathers now, by that old bit of pond he put in when he retired.' Mr Titmuss the elder was visible, through the sitting-room window, with a rug over his knee like a traveller on a transatlantic liner. He seemed to be asleep. 'Of course, his memory's not what it was. He forgets they've retired him sometimes and worries about getting along to the Brewery. As though the accounts department couldn't do without him! What've you called in for, Doctor? We're not ill, surely?'

'No of course you're not.'

'Anyway, we usually have Dr Hardison.' Elsie looked at him with suspicion. 'Are you collecting for something?'

'I suppose you might say so. I'm trying to get hold of a few facts.'

'Oh yes.' Elsie had suddenly lost interest in the Doctor's visit.

'You know about my father's will?'

'The Rector was always so kind to our boy.' Elsie smiled. 'Isn't there going to be a court case? Between you and Leslie?'

'Between my brother and Leslie,' he corrected her. 'I don't want any court case. I just want to explain the will. Look, you knew my father when you were young.'

'Of course, everyone knew the Rector.' Elsie was noncommittal.

'You probably got on well with him?'

'George had a quarrel with him once. It was about a statuette. Leslie gave the Rector one of our ornaments, and his father was quite angry about it. He thought the Rector shouldn't have held on to it, you see.'

'Was that the only time?' Fred asked the question gently as though he were trying to diagnose a disease. 'That George was angry about my father?'

Elsie moved to the mantelpiece and touched the plaster figure of the lady from Cleethorpes. From this contact she seemed to derive the strength to conclude the interview.

'I shouldn't be answering your questions.'

'Shouldn't you?'

'Not with the court case coming on. You shouldn't be asking them either. Anyway, if Leslie's had a bit of good luck over the will, he deserves it, doesn't he?'

'Does he?'

'After all he's gone through. After all *she* put him through, more likely. I must ask you to go now, Doctor. I've got George to see to.' She went out then to straighten the old man's rug. Fred left 'The Spruces' with none of his questions answered.

Chapter Twenty-nine

WORSFIELD HEATH

One autumn evening, after the glory of Goose Green had been almost forgotten, and as the women of Worsfield Heath bedded down in their sleeping-bags, Charlie went to meet Gary Kitson in the Badger at Skurfield. She waited a long time in the almost empty bar, sitting on a stool, drinking whisky and refusing to notice the stares of the two boys in the corner. They had Youth Opportunity Programme jobs, short-term employment, sweeping floors in a Worsfield biscuit factory and had come to Skurfield where the only entertainment they found was in watching Charlie and whispering about her. At last, at very long last, the door was pushed open to admit Gary Kitson, his wife, Tina, and their friend Simon Mallard-Greene. This trio advanced to the bar, apparently for the sole purpose of buying cigarettes and announcing that the place was dead, had no one in it, and that they would try the bar of the Station Hotel, Hartscombe, in search of a bit of life. As Simon paid for the Rothmans King Size, and Tina just popped into the toilet, Gary apologized to Charlie. 'Sorry about tonight. Tina insisted on coming with. Know what I mean?' Yes, Charlie knew what he meant. Gary left with Tina and Simon in a bad mood. He was angry with his wife for coming out with them and angrier at her for having foolishly set out wearing a garnet brooch in the shape of a Maltese Cross, a glowing piece of sentimental value only. Gary had made Tina take it off before they got into the Badger.

When she was left alone again, Charlie went over to the

YOPs and, in order to wipe the silly grins off their faces, bought them both a drink.

She was late getting back to Picton. She and the YOPs had gone to a pub up on the ridge without a bar, where Simcox bitter was poured out of barrels in a front room with a stained carpet, and a sofa leaking stuffing, a place where the licensing laws, if ever known, had been long forgotten. It was past midnight when she arrived home, her lipstick smeared and her step unsteady. She had some difficulty unlocking the front door. When she did so she was surprised to see a light on in Leslie's study and its door open. She couldn't get to the staircase without being seen by him as he sat at his desk, a red dispatch box open in front of him. He called out to her, and, as she couldn't escape him, she went into the room.

'I thought you were in London.'

'I'm sure you did.'

'What happened, no war this week?'

Leslie kept some decanters on a side table for visitors who came on constituency business, and she poured herself a drink. 'I had dinner alone,' he told her. 'Where've you been?'

'Out.'

'That's obvious.'

'I needed some air. I was driving. I walked a little.'

'Where did you have dinner?'

'Nowhere. I had dinner nowhere.'

'You do lie awfully badly, Charlotte.' He smiled at her in a way calculated, she thought, to unhinge her. She gripped her glass tightly. 'Of course, you're speaking as an expert,' she told him. 'Have you heard yourself on telly?'

'Your dinner consisted of too many whiskies and a packet of onion-flavoured crisps in some pub or other.' He was still smiling. 'With a lot of undesirables.'

'Who's undesirable?' She was angry and the words came flooding out of her. 'You mean with one or two *desirables*? Anyway, what's wrong with onion-flavoured crisps? I thought you got where you are on onion-flavoured crisps. And bottles of sauce. And meat teas. And money in the Prudential. Aren't you the good old working-class lad with his pint of Simcox Best and his heartfelt ambition to buy his own council house? That's who you taught me to admire. What did you call yourself? The backbone of England!'

'I wasn't talking about a handful of spivs.'

'Spivs? What a charming old-fashioned word! They wouldn't know what it meant.'

'They'd know what it is, though. Scrounging on the welfare. Everything on the never-never. Or dropped off the back of a lorry, more likely. Taking advantage of the rest of us. Taking advantage of you.'

'You've never been taken advantage of, have you, Leslie? You should try it some time. It's really quite enjoyable.'

'You're letting me down, Charlotte.' He got to his feet and stood over her. 'You're letting yourself down and Nicky.'

'Don't talk to me about Nicky!' She stared up at him. It was a look of contempt such as her mother might manage.

'I don't expect you to stay here, all by yourself. I know it's lonely.' He had put on the reasonable and disarming voice he employed at Question Time in the House of Commons.

'Do you?'

'Of course it is. But couldn't you get some sort of decent interests?'

'What a good idea! You mean the Women's Institute? Fruit-bottling? Flower-arranging? Evening classes in basket-weaving?'

'Something more serious,' he suggested. 'History, perhaps. Or politics.'

'Politics?' She looked at him, took a gulp from her glass and managed a slow smile. 'Is that what you'd really like me to do?'

On Worsfield Heath, once the site of the Annual Show, where stockmen paraded heifers and children in jodhpurs gritted their teeth and kicked their ponies towards the jumps, it was rumoured that the cruise missiles would come out at night to take exercise. The women hung their washing, their scarves and brightly coloured anoraks, even their plastic buckets and frying-pans, on the tall, wire fence, guarded the gates and waited in the hope of seeing and deriding these expeditions. They slept in tents until such shelters were removed by the police. Then they hung plastic sheets across the branches of trees and slept under their flapping cover.

They moved seriously, importantly, about their tasks, although occasionally cheerfulness or anger would break out and they would shout at the police on the other side of the wire; young men who would react with embarrassed silence or occasional obscene suggestions. Some of the younger guards said they would come out from behind the wire and ravish the women, converting them, by the joy of sex with an energetic military policeman, to a true appreciation of the value of nuclear missiles. It was a plan they had no intention whatsoever of putting into practice. The women asked the military police if they were on the side of death or life, a question the young men seemed to find difficult to answer.

Debates about the missiles, arguments destined to have no influence whatever on the course of events, continued. Leslie gamely agreed to attend one such discussion at Worsfield University. His ministerial Rover forced a slow passage through a crowd of angry students outside the Convocation Hall, and policemen reclined backwards on struggling bodies. He was met with a hailstorm of eggs, ink bombs and abuse through which he smiled as though with real enjoyment, perhaps feeling that being thrown into the river by Young Conservatives marked an important stage in his political development.

After he had been hustled into the hall, where his speech was to be made inaudible by boos and cat-calls, the demonstrating crowd drifted away, leaving one older than the rest, Charlie, who had come to join in the chorus of abuse. She stood quietly for a moment, pleased to have taken part in the event. Then she went back to Rapstone to call on her mother, whom she found in the conservatory, watering pots of begonias.

'You're keeping them on?'

'Well, they're here so I might as well water them. Is Leslie with you?'

'Leslie's never with me nowadays. That's the difference.'

'What do you mean, the "difference"?'

'Father was always here, always in Rapstone. You saw him all the time.'

'He was away in the war.'

'Yes. In the war. Of course he was.'

'Doing what he felt to be his duty. I expect Leslie's doing the same, isn't he?'

'Oh yes. Leslie and his friends who arranged to put a lot of wonderful new things for blowing up the world on Worsfield Heath. They're meant to make us feel safer.'

'Leslie understands, Charlie.' Grace watered on like a woman who had never felt any particular hostility to bombs. 'He's got all the information.'

'Oh yes. Leslie understands. It seems these things have to be exercised like dogs. They have to go out walkies.'

'Are you quite well?' Her mother put down her watering-can and looked closely at Charlie, as though she suspected her of being about to get some tedious childhood complaint like measles. 'What've you come here for? You never come here.'

'I just thought I ought to warn you, Mother, if you ever meet one on your way home from Bridge at the Hellespont Club. Don't try and pat it, that's all.'

'Do stop talking nonsense, Charlie! Leslie knows these things are necessary. For our protection.'

'Yes of course. Leslie always knows best.' And, after a silence, she said, 'I'm sorry for you, Mother.'

'Sorry for me! Whatever for?' Charlie, quite unexpectedly, put out a hand and touched her mother's arm. 'Having to have a child you couldn't love.' She moved to the door, on her way out.

'Oh. By the way. That burglary you had, did you ever hear any more about it?'

'Nothing.' Grace was outraged. 'I asked your husband to mention it to the Prime Minister.'

'Terrible, isn't it?' – Charlie was going – 'how many old crimes go undetected.'

On Worsfield Heath, a small boy, about three years old, wandered away from his mother, who was washing up plates in a plastic bucket, and ran across a patch of ground, a small, bright figure in scarlet gumboots and a mac. Charlie, standing alone and lost, saw him trip and fall. She picked him up to comfort him. The child stiffened and cried in her arms and wouldn't be consoled. In a little while the mother came to claim him, looking at Charlie with what she felt was hostility.

Although she knew no one there and felt lonely and ridiculous, Charlie stood about near the fence, shouted when the others shouted, and later simply sat on the grass until daylight ended. Then the fires were lit, kettles started to boil, and Charlie finally found a group who appeared not to resent her. She offered round her cigarettes, and sat warming her hands on a mug of tea they gave her. Later on, a fat, grey-haired grandmother, bundled into layers of clothing, began to sing, and the others joined her.

> 'Early one morning before the bombs were falling
> I heard a woman singing in the valley below
> Politicians hate us
> They'd obliterate us
> Don't let them treat a poor world so.
>
> I will be gone and gone will be my true love
> Gone will be the trees in the valley below
> If we don't stop them
> Now let them drop them
> Don't let them treat a poor world so.'

The small children joined in enthusiastically, as though it

were a nursery rhyme, and Charlie sang, also, with gratitude. She clapped in time to the music, and when a tall, thin-haired woman sat beside her and began to talk about her social security, Charlie was able to give her a few tips she remembered from her days in the Welfare. Then others began to talk to her, about the things they had shouted over the wire, and about the way they had run round the Heath keeping their tents out of the way of the police. They seemed excited and cheerful, as though they had got away from unwanted husbands to go on some illicit holiday. Only occasionally did they sit silent and brooding, staring into the ashes of the fire until someone threw on another branch and then they started to sing again. None of them seemed to have the slightest doubt of the usefulness of their mission.

It was almost midnight before they saw the police cars coming. The blue lights revolved and flashed and delivered reinforcements to line the road that led from the gates of the encampment. The women started to run away from the fires and out of the shadows. Some clung to the wire and tried to climb it, until they were pulled down. Others formed up on a length of road the police had left unoccupied. Charlie ran with them, not sure of what was going on, unaware of the rain which had begun as a few heavy drops sizzled in the camp fire and now ran down her cheeks and flattened her hair. The women she was with burst through a clump of bushes and came out on a tree-lined stretch of road. There they linked arms and formed a close, warm, wet barricade. They waited a long time, but remained in possession of the road. The police guard was still between them and the gates of the Air Force station.

At last they saw a high and distant light moving through the tops of the trees, illuminating the driving rain. It came on to shouts of derision from the unseen women and the hum of an engine. Her arms held on each side of her, Charlie peered into the darkness. Then there were two other points of light far down the road.

'And if one cruise missile
Should accidentally fall . . .
There'd be you and I my darling
Left hanging on the wall . . .'

The women were still singing and she heard shouts of 'Walking the dog, darling?' and 'Daddy wouldn't buy me a bow-wow-wow!' Then the lights got bigger and seemed to rush towards them, becoming clear as the headlamps of police outriders. Charlie felt released by the women on either side of her as they scampered to the side of the road. She was alone on the wet, black surface, under the dripping trees, and, as the lights came towards her, she started to scream. It wasn't desperate or unconsolable, nor the sort of cry that needed a chapter of *Biggles* to calm it. It was louder, stronger, more like a battle call or a yell of triumph.

The policeman on the first bike, helmeted and oil-skinned, saw Charlie and swerved to avoid her. His heavy machine skidded on the wet surface, slithered helplessly out of control and crashed into her sideways, silencing her and blacking out her world which had become strangely and unaccountably happy.

'My wife was always interested in social work and the caring professions. One of her projects was to visit the women of Worsfield Heath. Many of them were experiencing marriage problems, and the strains and stresses of bringing up children in one-parent families. My wife's death occurred during one of such visits and was purely accidental.'

Leslie stood on the terrace of Picton House and read out a prepared statement to the news cameras, microphones and notebooks of a group of reporters. The wind fluttered the sheet of paper in his hand and slightly dislodged his hair, exposing his bald patch. 'No blame of any sort can be attached to the officer whose motor bicycle skidded, and I wish him a speedy recovery. He was doing his duty and playing a vital part in the defence of our democratic way of life. My wife died carrying out duties which she also believed to be important.' He folded the paper and put it into his jacket pocket. 'Thank you. That's all.' Of course, it wasn't. Questions were hurled at him, and Leslie, an old hand by now, fielded them expertly.

'Minister. Did you approve of your wife going to Worsfield Heath?'

'Of course, I had the greatest admiration for her social work.'

'Are you saying she took no part in the demonstrations against cruise missiles?'

'My wife wasn't interested in politics. She was simply dealing with the women's social problems.'

'Minister. Was your wife a member of C.N.D.?'

'I can categorically assure you that she was never a member of that organization.'

'Minister.' Someone was holding a microphone up to Leslie's face. 'Can you explain why your wife was doing social work after midnight?'

'I'm afraid there isn't any "knocking off time" for the caring professions,' he explained with charm. 'Both of us were accustomed to work all the hours that God gave us.'

'So far as we can discover, your wife wasn't attached to any of the regular social services.'

'Charlotte wasn't a great joiner, she was impatient of bureaucracy. Aren't we all? She was very much her own person.'

'The women at Worsfield Heath don't seem to have known her.'

'I don't suppose those women like to talk to you about their personal problems.' Leslie smiled at them all. 'I can't say I enjoy it much myself.'

'Minister. You don't *approve* of the Worsfield women?'

'I respect their sincerity,' he answered carefully. 'I think they're terribly misguided. But we're all after the same thing, aren't we? Peace in our time. Now, ladies and gentlemen. If that's all . . .' He was about to move back into the house when he was asked: 'What are your future plans?'

'To go on doing my job as long as the Prime Minister wants me.' A modest smile. 'And she hasn't said she doesn't.'

'Apart from that?'

'My life' – he was serious now and it was the last thing he said before he vanished into the house – 'will be devoted to the care and upbringing of our son.'

Some time after Charlie died, Simeon did what he didn't recommend to his parishioners. He went into Rapstone Church alone and knelt for a considerable time in prayer. Meanwhile, Leslie and his son Nicky faced each other from opposite ends of the dining-table at Picton House. Their meal seemed endless and they found little to say to each other. Nicky didn't want to talk about his school, and his mother's death was a subject both of them avoided.

Chapter Thirty

VISITING

'I was expecting you to call,' Jackson Cantellow said. 'I've left countless messages at your surgery. Where on earth have you been?'

'Trying to find out the truth.' Fred had called as part of his own investigations. 'Not the sort of thing you would encourage, I suppose, as a lawyer.'

'We put our case. The truth remains a matter for the trial judge to decide.'

'You must know it though.' Fred looked at the large, complacent face opposite him and wondered if he did.

'*I* must?'

'You must know why he made that will.'

'How should I know that, Dr Simcox?'

'You were my father's solicitor for years.'

Cantellow got up and went to a filing-cabinet from which he took a tin of throat pastilles. He selected one with care and popped it into his mouth.

'Alas, we know so little of our clients. In any event, the Rector chose a Worsfield firm for his last, his extraordinary last, will.'

'There must have been a reason! You don't want to find it though, because you're arguing my brother's case.' There was something about the singing solicitor that made Fred understand Dorothy's rage. 'That's what he's paid you to do.'

'We have to live, don't we, Dr Simcox? I suppose some might

say we both thrive on the sickness of mankind. That, I feel, would be an uncharitable view.'

'My father must have told you *something*.'

'Very little. I don't think he had a great deal of respect for lawyers.' Cantellow was starting to shuffle the papers on his desk. 'Wyebrow's statement,' he muttered and put it away. 'Ah, yes.' He found his place in the notes he'd been making. 'Perhaps you could throw some light on the Tom Nowt incident. We have these rather over-simplified headings.' He apologized. 'Your brother has seen photographs of Nowt and the Rector looking entirely friendly, but didn't your father suddenly forbid you to visit the man's cottage?'

'Not his cottage, his hut in the woods.' Fred thought about it.

'Wasn't *that* rather extraordinary?' Cantellow looked up. 'Your father was supposed to be so liberal, such a democrat, the friend of all the world. Did he object to you visiting any of the other cottages?'

'No. No, I don't think so.'

'A sudden irrational phobia, you see. That's the view of the psychiatrist we shall be calling. He turned against people for no reason.' Cantellow was delighted. 'I really would like to take a witness statement from you, Frederick. Couldn't you just help me by remembering all about the Tom Nowt incident?'

'Why should I want to help you?' Fred, having decided that he was only going to be asked questions and given no answers, got up and started to leave. 'Who do you want to help? Not Leslie Titmuss, surely?' Cantellow asked, pained, but Fred was gone.

After visiting the solicitor Fred had to call at Tom's old cottage. Mrs Mallard-Greene, in a state of high anxiety and rattling with tranquillizers prescribed by a London doctor, had rung up for a visit, although her trouble, as it turned out, was hardly of a medical nature. The problem was her son, Simon. His car had been stopped after midnight and in the boot the police had found a certain amount of hi-fi equipment, reported missing by a Hartscombe dentist. 'Thank God you've come.' There was a brandy bottle on the kitchen table, and an ashtray overflowing with stubs. 'I just couldn't sit in the queue of National Health patients with everyone looking at me, hearing them whispering about Simon. You know he's due up before the Magistrates?'

'Mrs Mallard-Greene, I'm a doctor. If you need a lawyer . . .'

'Receiving stolen property! He was just selling a few bits and pieces he'd bought off some fellow in the Badger.'

'If that's true, no doubt he'll be triumphantly acquitted.'

'But if it isn't true?' Mrs Mallard-Greene had obviously considered the possibility.

'Well then . . .'

'You've known Simon since he was a schoolboy. He was highly strung as a child and he's always been extremely nervous.'

'A nervous window-cleaner?' Fred was doubtful.

'I don't think Malley ever understood Simon. And there was the sibling rivalry with Sarah, of course. Simon was always trying to *prove* himself against a powerful father with a job in the B.B.C. All that achievement! I'm sure you could tell the Magistrates that it's a well-known psychiatric condition.'

'Receiving stolen property?' It wasn't a disease that Fred had learned about at St Thomas's.

'He needs help, Dr Simcox.'

'Don't we all?' Fred went to the window and looked out. 'I've told you, I think, that I remember this when it was old Tom Nowt's cottage.'

'I wish to God it was still Tom Nowt's cottage!' The words came from the bottom of Mrs Mallard-Greene's heart. 'It's supposed to be so restful in the country, so secure, so peaceful. You know what it's really like? Extremely dangerous! Simon's arrested, not for drugs, not for something like everyone seems to do when they're young, but for being mixed up in stealing! We'd all have been so much better off in Highgate.'

'Would you mind if I took a look at your woods? There used to be an old hut . . .'

'Oh, that's gone. I think it went years ago. Malley was clearing up there when he was terribly rustic. You will tell them, won't you?'

'Tell them?'

'Tell the Magistrates about Simey. It's no use them trying to blame him really.'

'He'd better come and see me.'

'I knew you'd help us!' Mrs Mallard-Greene was enormously relieved. 'Underneath that cold professional manner, I knew you'd understand.'

At the place where Tom Nowt's hut once stood Fred picked up part of a deer's antler, blackened by fire. He looked across to a patch of sunlight at the edge of the wood and heard children's voices. Still holding the antler, he walked towards them and found Dora Nowt, Tom's widow, Janet, his daughter, and three of his grandchildren, Janet's nephew and nieces. The children seemed to be searching in a patch of rough, chalky grass, a meadow isolated between two patches of woodland that had never been ploughed. Dora Nowt, an old woman now, saw Fred first.

'Dr Simcox. You don't remember me, do you?'

'Of course.' In fact he had hardly recognized her, and said, 'Dora Nowt,' hoping for the best.

'No one used to take much notice of me, not of the wife. Tom was the one who had all the posh friends, wasn't he? Now, did you ever call on *me* when you was a little boy, did you? No, you come straight down to see Tom in his old hut.'

'It's gone.' Fred dropped the burnt and broken antler into a patch of brambles.

'Oh yes. They had it burnt down, them townees got our cottage now. Your mother must've been upset about that.'

'My mother?' Fred was surprised, but before he could pursue the matter, a small boy brought the spike of a picked wild flower and gave it to Dora. 'Is this it?'

'Yes, Tom. But you mustn't pick it. You mustn't ever pick

those. I bring the children down here for the flowers,' she told Fred, and took the flower from her grandson to give it to him. 'There's the spider orchid. Hope it brings you luck. You don't see many of the late ones. You know where to find them, of course.'

'No, I never knew.' Fred had to admit it.

'The late one's rarer, very rare, Mrs Simcox told us.' Fred had no idea that Dorothy had played such a large part in the life of the Nowts. 'She used to visit Tom and me, and the children. She showed us the orchid places. Always very good to Tom and the family, was your mother.'

Janet had moved away with the children, who were finding snail shells and butterflies. Dora seemed talkative and anxious to make up for having been so much ignored by Tom's friends in the past. 'When Tom couldn't get work anywhere, just after the war when Lady Grace put the police on to him, no one would give him anything, not beating, not wooding, nothing! Well, your mother helped us out when Tom wanted to build his hut in the woods. We've always been grateful to her for it.'

'What about my father?' Fred looked at her and waited for an answer which might have been important to him.

'Tom used to see a lot of the Rector in the old days. He used to take up rabbits to him. After it all happened, well, he never used to see so much of your father, then.'

'After *what* all happened?'

'After Tom fell foul of her Ladyship. Well, Tom was never a churchgoer, was he? And your father was that busy putting the world to rights.'

Then the old woman was called by the children about the find of a bird's skull. Fred remembered that it was Thursday, his mother's afternoon for doing the flowers in Rapstone Church. He found her in the vestry, surrounded by vases, attacking long grasses and delphiniums and sprays of leaves with her secateurs. He held out his hand on which lay the warm and wilting spider orchid found by young Tom Nowt.

'You know what this is, Mother?'

'You don't surely?' Dorothy looked amused by him.

'A late spider orchid. Rather rare. You know where they grow?'

'I think so,' she admitted.

'By Tom Nowt's old hut. Why did you never tell us?'

'Tell you what?' She bashed the end of the long stem of a rose.

'When we were young. Why didn't you tell us where the wild orchids grew? Isn't that the sort of knowledge parents usually pass on to their children?'

'I didn't tell you' – Dorothy sounded reasonable enough – 'because you weren't in the least interested in that sort of thing. Henry was always writing the most unsuitable stories, from all I ever heard of them! And you were stuck up in your room drumming. I didn't think either of you cared tuppence for wild flowers.'

'I suppose the Nowts did?' Fred asked her. 'Brian and Annie and young Janet Nowt and the grandchildren as they came along. You helped them find the orchids in their own wood?'

'We used to go for walks and find flowers. Before Simeon, well, before . . .'

'Before *what*, exactly?'

'Before he got so occupied.'

'You helped Tom Nowt' – Fred tried not to make it sound like an accusation – 'when he was down on his luck!'

'That was the sort of thing Simeon approved of.'

'But he didn't approve of Tom.' Fred was far from understanding. 'He was angry when I talked about the old hut. What sane reason did he have for that?'

'What *sane* reason?' His mother looked at him with mistrust.

'You'll have to tell me some time. And when I've found out I'll tell Henry he hasn't got a case.'

'Will you enjoy doing that?' She looked towards the open vestry door and seemed to welcome the sound of someone moving about in the church.

'For heaven's sake, Mother, help me to do what you want.'

'What I want? What I want is for everyone to stop asking me questions.' She went to the door and called, 'Mr Bulstrode!' Kev the Rev. trotted in, obediently, having been pinning up children's drawings in the Sunday School area.

'So good of your mother to go on helping with the flowers,' he told Fred. 'Of course, my wife should take it over if it ever got too much.'

'It's not too much, thank you.' Dorothy suddenly lowered her voice as though repeating a scandal. 'Do you know Dr Simcox was never confirmed?'

Fred was surprised that his mother should raise such a subject. The Rev. Kevin Bulstrode looked at him with sympathy.

'Simeon said the boys could wait to be done until they'd made up their minds. Freddie, it seems, never has.'

'Mother!'

'Couldn't you oblige him with some sort of ceremony for those of riper years? Why don't you have a nice long talk with Mr Bulstrode, Freddie?'

'I say, I'd love to have a go.' The new Rector was enthusiastic. 'I'm not your father, of course, so I haven't got all the answers. What's troubling you exactly?'

'A few unanswered questions.' Fred was looking at his mother.

'Oh, I do know.' Bulstrode was beginning to enjoy himself. 'Why the good, the omnipotent God allows wars and concentration camps, and children with leukaemia . . .'

'And that awful music in the Hartscombe supermarket!' Dorothy nodded, refilling her vases.

'I'm as much in the dark as you are,' Bulstrode admitted to Fred, 'I rather suspect. But if you could spare half an hour in my den, well, your dear old father's den, in the Rectory, we might sort of feel our way into the darkness together.'

'I'm afraid . . .' Fred started to retreat.

'Aren't we all? But talking does help sometimes. It really does.'

'I'm afraid I've got a lot more calls. Illness you know. There's a lot of it about.' When Fred walked past her out of the vestry, his mother whispered, 'Coward!'

So he left the church, passing the marble tablet which commemorated certain dead Fanners whose names were written under the scrolled bas-relief of a lady in Regency costume, weeping over an urn. The lastest words to be carved were:

CHARLOTTE GRACE
23 MARCH 1940 TO 19 APRIL 1984
BELOVED WIFE OF THE RT HON. LESLIE TITMUSS, M.P.

and under the inscription stood a small, newly arranged vase of flowers.

Rapstone Manor was next on the list of visits, there was a problem, Miss Thorne had said with awe, 'about her Ladyship's leg'. Wyebrow led him upstairs and Fred let him know that he had heard that the butler was to be a witness in the coming Probate Action.

'I think that's a matter we probably shouldn't discuss, isn't it, Doctor?' Wyebrow smirked proudly, knowing that he had it in him to give a devastating account from the witness box of the late Rector on all fours, trumpeting like an elephant. 'But I'll be doing my best to help Mr Henry Simcox.'

'I'm not sure that's what my mother wants.'

'I shall be sworn to tell the truth, shan't I? On my Bible oath.' Wyebrow gave a pious sniff. 'I shall tell it all, exactly as I saw it happen.'

Grace had fallen while dancing. She lay on her bed in her lace nightdress and padded dressing-gown, showing more of her white, matchstick legs than was essential for the examination of a sprained ankle. 'Not bad, are they?' She squinted critically downwards. 'And they used to be absolute stunners!'

'Does that hurt?'

'Absolute agony! But better a little pain than no one ever

coming to visit. You won't believe this, my dear, but during the war years, all through the Blitz, the Allied Forces would have queued up to touch that ankle.'

Fred started to bandage. 'I'm afraid you'll have to stop dancing for a while.'

'Dancing alone, ridiculous isn't it? I do everything alone now. I can't even have my grandchild to tea. Have you ever heard of such a thing? Nicky,' she told him, 'used to come bicycling over from Picton.' It seemed he enjoyed having tea up in Grace's bedroom, looking at the old photograph albums, the holiday snaps of St Moritz and Cannes and the Bahamas, and of the fancy dress parties at Rapstone when Simeon came dressed as Rudolph Valentino and Doughty Strove, not a pretty spectacle this, as Mae West. Nicky also showed an interest in Grace's old dresses, her Teddie Molyneux evening-jacket which was like a shower of gold coins and her Chanel sewn with pearls. Nicky said that in the Molyneux she looked like Danaë, a legendary figure who, it seemed, was someone he learned about at school. And then, just when they were enjoying themselves, Leslie had driven over, pushed his way past Wyebrow in the most loutish manner and sent his son home, with orders never to return again. He had also said things to her that could never be forgotten, told her, for instance, that Nicky had better things to do than spend his afternoons stuck in a bedroom going through Grace's moth-eaten wardrobe. According to Leslie the Fanner family had brought him nothing but ill luck – even Charlie would never have gone off on her dotty causes and died if she'd really cared for Nicky. He said other things which Grace didn't repeat to Fred, among them that she was a lonely old drunk with no one but a child to bore with her stupid stories about useless people and the scratchy records she had once danced to. But she did tell him that she and Nicholas had made his career by putting up with his spotty presence when a young man at their dinner parties and trying to ignore the appalling noise he made when eating soup.

'I also remember him as a ghastly child screaming when the

lights went out in our downstairs loo. He was scared out of his senses, perhaps that's what he's got against us. Anyway he told me that I was unsuitable company for young Nicky. Perhaps I was unsuitable company for old Nicholas too.'

Fred had finished strapping the old and fragile ankle: 'Rest and keep it up as much as possible.'

'You look extraordinarily like your father sometimes,' Grace told him.

'I'll give you some pain killers.' He scribbled a prescription. 'You mean I look mad?'

'Why should I mean that?'

'My brother wants to prove my father was insane. Your Mr Wyebrow's going to provide evidence in support of the proposition.'

'I shall give him the day off to go to court.'

'Because you believe it's true?'

'Because we all want to do in Titmuss, don't we?'

'Do we?'

'Of course. He wanted to join the family circle, we let him in and he kicked us in the teeth. He's got my grandson, in fact he's got it all. And your father's money!'

'How did he manage that, do you suppose, without any legitimate claim?'

'I'll tell you one thing, *Doctor* Simcox. That four letter Titmuss hasn't got a legitimate claim to more than a charge of shot up the backside of his awful little city gent's off-the-peg suiting!'

'I don't think he gets them off-the-peg any more.'

'Get that into your head, absolutely no legitimate claim of any sort. Is the operation over?'

'Quite over.' Fred was packing up his bag.

'Then it's time for the anaesthetic. You'll find it in the bathroom. We'll use toothmugs – Wyebrow looks disapproving when I ask him to bring up a drink. It's what I hate most about growing old, you're so at the mercy of the servants.'

'Most of my patients don't have that problem.'

'I shock you, don't I, Dr Simcox?' Grace was looking more cheerful. Fred went into the bathroom and came back with the bottle of champagne he found nestling in the washbasin. As he filled their toothmugs he happened to mention, 'What did you have against Tom Nowt?'

'Nowt?' Grace took a swig of tepid Moët. 'He was a poacher.'

'Is *that* what you had against him?' Fred was unconvinced.

'He got above himself. He tried to interfere with other people. He was the first symptom of the national disease that spread alarmingly and became Leslie Titmuss.'

'My mother got on well with him.'

'Your mother got on well with the most extraordinary people. Before you go, would you mind putting on a record?'

Coming downstairs, Fred saw Wyebrow waiting for him in the hall. The muted music reminded him of a children's party, years ago, with nervous Charlie, the birthday girl, being pushed down the stairs, and musical chairs, two children anxiously circling an empty seat and the manservant switching off 'You're the Top!' to decide the contest. When Wyebrow opened the front door, Fred paused to ask him a question, with no particular hope of an answer. 'You don't know why Lady Fanner quarrelled with Tom Nowt, do you? I mean, it can't have just been the poaching?'

'That's all, as far as I know. Bridget was in the house when he came up and they had their disagreement. She never talked much about it.'

'And Bridget's in "The Meadows",' Fred remembered.

'Oh yes. It's my opinion Bridget always took her work far too serious.'

'The Meadows' was Hartscombe's one small hospital, a modern glass and concrete square built in the expansive seventies, along the Worsfield Road, as an alternative to a theatre or an arts centre. It housed a few geriatrics and a labour ward. The Out Patients department came in useful for those who got kicked by their horses or maimed by chain-saws. Bridget, whose journey back to the hard days when she was first in service was now complete, had been there for almost a year. She was quite sure that the bleak and modern building was Picton House, where she worked as a young girl.

'You come for the weekend, Dr Simcox?' She smiled at Fred as they sat in the Day Room, among the potted plants, the reproduction Van Goghs and the old people inert in front of *Play School* or tottering round on their Zimmers. 'I got up early to see to a nice bright fire in your bedroom.'

'You like it here, do you, Bridget?'

'Lovely old house, of course, but so inconvenient. The job I have finding the fireplaces! They've got to be done, you know. Mrs Smurthwaite's that keen on her fireplaces and her stair-rods. Well, I've always been particular about my stair-rods. But it's not too bad, I help with the silver in the butler's pantry. We get a few laughs sometimes, when Smurthwaite's up in her sitting-room.' Bridget giggled like a young girl. 'Having her little nap or is it her "nip", we wonders. There's rules though, and regulations. Everyone in by ten o'clock and no followers.' A nurse came with cups of tea for both of them. Bridget whispered, 'Old Smurthwaite doesn't half keep her running.' She sat smiling around her, her cup held closely under her chin.

'I was going to ask you. You remember Tom Nowt, I'm sure. Old chap who had a hut in the woods.'

'He doesn't come here no more.' Bridget sipped tea with great delicacy. 'Ladyship sent him away. Well, he had no right to do that.'

'Do what, Bridget?'

'No right to come round asking her for money.'

'You heard that?'

'I was on the stairs polishing up. I couldn't help hearing.'

'Of course not. Of course you couldn't help it. What did he want money for, do you remember?'

'Something he'd noticed in the park.' Bridget nodded.

'The park?'

'Tom Nowt'd seen something there and he wanted money for it. 'Course, Ladyship sent him about his business! Said she'd ruin him in the district. But it's my belief he was ruined already. He never came to any good, did he?'

'He died,' Fred admitted.

'There now! I knew he came to no good.' She drank her tea with satisfaction. 'Whatever made you think of Tom Nowt?'

'You've got everything you want, Bridget?' Fred didn't answer her question.

'It's just not easy to find the fireplaces.' Bridget shook her head. 'And that Percy Bigwell! I just don't want him to come here at all odd hours. Smurthwaite won't tolerate followers.'

Fred was shown out by the Matron. 'She seems to have trouble finding the fireplaces,' he told her. He breathed the air in the car park, free from the smell of old people.

'Well, of course she does.' The Matron was young, and kept resolutely cheerful. 'Seeing we're all central heating. Sometimes I think we ought to send her home but when I suggest it to her she cries and thinks I'm giving her the sack. How did you find her, Doctor?'

'Nothing wrong with Bridget's memory.'

'So far as it goes.'

'Yes.' Fred was thoughtful. 'I just wonder how far that is, exactly.'

A few days later, just as he thought he had finished his surgery, Miss Thorne told Fred of one last patient, and Simon Mallard-Greene came in, flopped into the patient's chair and spoke as though he were in a position to put a bit of welcome work in the Doctor's way. 'You're going to be my expert witness, aren't you? You'll be able to tell them about my childhood and all that.'

Fred had been given the Mallard-Greene notes. 'You come from a comfortably off, middle-class family and you got a good education. Isn't that your background?'

'I never got on with my father, know what I mean?'

'It's not a particularly obscure remark.' It was what Fred's father used to say.

'He was totally orientated to his career at the B.B.C. He was unsupportive to my mother and to us as a nuclear family.' Fred looked at the pale, unsmiling Simon, whose fair lashes and eyebrows gave his face a curious look of nakedness; he seemed perfectly qualified to act as his own social worker. 'I suppose, looking back on it, I was doing it all as a challenge to my father.'

'Buying bits and pieces of stolen hi-fi equipment in a pub in Worsfield?' Fred was trying to understand. 'To rival his telly programme on *The Arts in Our Time?*'

'Basically, I did it that way because I wanted to get into trouble.'

'Well, at least you've had one resounding success.'

'It wasn't really a crime at all, you see. It was more of a . . .' He looked suspiciously at Fred, who didn't seem to be paying him serious attention. 'What's the matter?'

'I thought for a moment you were going to say a "cry for help".'

'We're not having you on the National Health, you know.' Simon frowned. 'We're doing this private. I don't think my father cares what you charge within reason.'

'I'm sorry. I'm not a psychiatrist.' Fred stood up to terminate the interview.

'All the same, I do reckon you'd better help me, Doctor.' Simon smiled in a chilly and unattractive manner. 'I don't think it'd do your family any good if you didn't.'

'My family?'

'Gary knows all about your family.'

Fred went back to his seat, and looked at the young receiver of stolen property. 'Gary Kitson? What does he know?'

But Simon wasn't giving anything away. 'Things I don't suppose you might like to have said around, that's all. He didn't tell me the whole story. He would though. He's a good friend is

Gary.' The young Mallard-Greene was no longer giving instructions to his medical man – what he said came out as a threat. 'I think you ought to take Gary Kitson seriously, Dr Simcox. And you'd better be there to help me, on my day in court.'

Fred finished the interview by promising to think about it and then he drove over to Rapstone. He stopped at Gary Kitson's cottage and saw the For Sale notice in the front garden. Then he went over to the Baptist's Head, where Ted Lawless told him that the Kitsons had cleared out suddenly and no one knew their address. 'Did he owe you money too, Doctor?'

'No.' Fred took a gulp of Simcox bitter. 'Information.'

Chapter Thirty-one

NEVEREST

The Probate Action 'In the Estate of Simeon Simcox deceased, Simcox *v.* Titmuss' was fixed for a date in the spring and estimated to last two weeks. Leslie told his lawyers that there could be no question of a compromise – winning outright and getting possession of the Brewery shares was something he felt he owed his son. Henry was also prepared for a fight to the finish. Whatever the Brewery shares might be worth, and they had not yet had a final valuation, he was determined to see they remained in the Simcox family. Their attitude was extremely welcome to the lawyers on both sides, who saw a profitable piece of litigation ahead. Roderick Rose, Henry's junior counsel, was so sure of the number of refresher or daily fees that the case would provide that he organized a little dinner party in his Kensington house to which he invited his leader, Crispin Drayton, Q.C., their instructing solicitor, Jackson Cantellow, and, almost as an afterthought, their client, Henry Simcox. 'An informal get-together for your legal team,' Rose told Henry. 'Just so we can have the picture quite clear and get our "act together" as no doubt you show-folk would say.' The only ladies present were Roderick Rose's wife, Pamela, and Lonnie, who became enthusiastic about the food provided.

'Super sort of herby taste! Provençal?' she suggested. 'Well, I don't know. I can't help you about that actually.' Mrs Rose was vague on the subject, and offered no further information when

Lonnie guessed, 'Oregano! You must have relied heavily on oregano.'

'And not a bad drop of Beaujolais either.' Henry sniffed at it. He had lately taken up the study of wine and could be quite boring on the subject.

'I thought something light' – Rose refilled his glass – 'if we're going to go over our plan of attack.'

'We have to face up to the fact' – Crispin Drayton as the Q.C. in charge of the case put an end to the gourmet chatter – 'that the burden will be on us to prove your father's insanity.'

'Did he *honestly* dress up in drag to give marriage guidance?' Pamela Rose was giggling with delight. 'Of course, I suppose that might be considered quite trendy nowadays.'

'I'm sure we all understand' – Drayton looked at his junior's wife with disapproval – 'that the late Rector's extraordinary behaviour must have been deeply distressing to his family.'

'Or is it a touch of tarragon I'm detecting?' Lonnie stared thoughtfully upwards as she masticated her *coq au vin*.

'Of course it was extremely embarrassing for all of us. My mother always tried to cover up for him,' Henry told his leading counsel. 'I think that's why she's refusing to get involved.'

There was a short, almost reverent pause of understanding, and then Rose struck a cheerful note. 'I think our medical evidence is pretty clear. Monomania, or an insane aversion to members of his family.'

'Or an insane affection for Leslie Titmuss?' Lonnie suggested.

'It went deeper than that,' Henry told them. 'What he suffered from was an insane optimism about the future of mankind.'

'With respect, we want to avoid generalizations.' Drayton struck a note of caution, but Henry launched yet another attack on the myth of happiness. 'He suffered from the great insanity of our times. The pathetic fallacy that we'll all get better and better, nicer, kinder, more concerned about each other, more disinterested, more enthusiastically against fox hunting, capital punishment and nuclear war. These idiotic beliefs took hold of him like a disease. They haunted him like strange hallucinations. In the end they corrupted his judgement and addled his brain. He became terrified of his own wealth and decided to unload it on the most undeserving object he could find.'

'You mean, he wished to leave you the gift of poverty?' Drayton was afraid they might be finding a motive.

'It sounds appropriately idiotic.'

'I'm not sure that I like that.' Drayton shook his head. 'It might have some sort of sound religious basis.'

'You're thinking of the eye of the needle?' Rose suggested.

'We're safer with psychotic monomania, and the specific acts of insanity we've pleaded in our defence,' Cantellow said firmly, and Drayton, who had formed the view that Henry would have to be kept on a tight rein in the witness box, found himself in complete agreement with his instructing solicitor.

'Can anyone manage a tiny bit more?' Pamela Rose invited them all, and Lonnie asked whether it would be frightfully piggy of her. Piggy or not, Mrs Rose took Mrs Simcox's plate to the service hatch, slid it open and said to whoever was on the other side, 'Just seconds for one, could we? If that's at all possible.'

Agnes knew that it would have to happen some time. She had been cooking for years in houses which Henry and Lonnie might have visited, doing dinner parties for publishers and actors, television producers and literary agents. She hadn't expected any such accident to occur when she was rung up and asked to cook by a barrister's wife, who insisted, much against Agnes's better judgement, on avocado with prawns and *coq au vin*, the whole to be topped up with chocolate mousse. She stood by herself in the kitchen full of knotty pine and blunt knives, a place which seemed to have been used merely for providing scrambled eggs to be eaten in front of the television, and tried not to listen to her ex-husband's voice which came booming through the open hatch as she spooned out another plateful for Lonnie.

'My brother Fred is either a natural traitor, or he's inherited our father's insanity. I can't really figure out his game. Apparently he's going round asking questions, behaving like some ridiculous kind of amateur sleuth.'

'Thank you so much.' Pamela Rose took the plate, the hatch door was shut, and Agnes could hear no more. In the dining-room, Lonnie tucked in gratefully. 'I really must ask you for the recipe.'

'To be brutally honest,' Pamela confessed, 'the recipe is the Flying Kitchen.'

'Oh really.' Lonnie seemed to have gone off her food.

'The person out there does rather look as though she despised our fitted cupboards, but she leaves it all surprisingly tidy. I can give you the telephone number, if you want it.'

'That's very kind, but I don't think we need it, do we, darling?' Her husband, in a voice of doom, agreed, 'We don't need it.'

When they were saying their goodbyes Henry asked to be pointed in the direction of the loo, went down a passage and, hearing the whirl of a washing-up machine, pushed open the kitchen door. Agnes was sitting at the wiped-over table, smoking a cigarette and finishing the Beaujolais.

'Did Fred send you here to spy on me?'

'You didn't *like* the wine, did you?' Agnes didn't seem to think his question worth answering. 'I mean talk about thin . . .'

'Fred's taken to playing detectives. How else did you get here?'

'I was rung up by Mrs Rose. She found me in the Yellow Pages. I didn't know they were part of your legal Mafia.'

'How much did you hear?'

'Not a lot. I was busy doshing out Lonnie's seconds.' Henry came and sat on the edge of the table then, swinging his legs, took a swig from her glass and tried to sound friendly. 'You ought to be on our side.'

'Ought I?'

'For Francesca. She'll benefit eventually if we end up with the Simcox shares.'

'You mean if you end up with them.'

'Money never did much harm to anyone, even Francesca.'

'How much should she take for having her grandfather found insane?'

Henry got up from the table. Before he left her he looked round the kitchen and sniffed. 'All those herbs!' he said. 'They smell of our old quarrels.'

The next day, Fred decided what to do about young Mallard-Greene. He drove to Tom Nowt's old cottage, outside which a window-cleaning van, with a ladder fastened to the top, was parked. Simon was at home resting between windows, drinking a cup of coffee and listening to Radio One. He switched off Wham! and looked reassured when Fred told him that he was prepared to give evidence before the Magistrates at Simon's trial.

'You'll tell them I'm sick?'

'Oh yes, of course. You're suffering from a fairly well-known condition.'

'What's that, Doctor?'

'Greed. You were injected by a strong desire to make a quick wadge of folding money for some bits and pieces of hi-fi equipment you and your precious friend, Gary, nicked when you went cleaning windows. It's a condition which may lead to a term of close confinement, in serious cases.' For a moment Simon thought he was getting helpful medical advice. When he understood that he wasn't his colourless face set in a look of hatred.

'You want me to go in there and say what Gary knows about you Simcoxes?'

'What does he know?'

'I'll have to ask him, won't I?'

'You may find that hard. Mr Kitson seems to have deprived Rapstone of his company. Perhaps he didn't want to share the limelight with you in the Magistrates' Court.'

'His friends know where to find him.' Simon smiled in a way that wasn't in the least engaging. 'So why don't you go and get your act together? Court's in two weeks' time, Dr Simcox.'

About fifteen minutes after Fred had left the cottage, Simon Mallard-Greene went out to his van and looked up and down the road. He saw no one so he got in the driver's seat and started towards Hartscombe. Waiting in a side road, Fred saw the ladders moving above a hedge and set off to follow at a discreet distance. When he got to the town he took a route away from the main street and emerged to see the window-cleaner's van crossing the bridge to the London road. He waited for a couple of cars and a lorry to get between him and Simon and then went after him.

Up the long hill through the wood, past soggy autumn fields and in and out of villages, Fred followed the van to the motorway entrance. Simon, bucketing along in the fast lane, looked in his mirror and saw only the lorry behind which Fred was concealed. So they travelled towards London and at last Fred saw the van dive away down the Paddington exit. He followed, and, for a long minute, was stuck at a traffic light, which Simon had driven through. He was lost in Bayswater, and then he looked down a side road and saw the van turning into a mews. He went after it, parked in the main road, and saw Simon walking into the office of O'Leary's Mini Cabs, '24-hour service'. Fred waited and after ten minutes, Simon came out and drove out of the other end of the mews.

A pair of legs was sticking out from under a wounded Consul. A face peered out as Fred asked the man if Gary Kitson worked there.

'There isn't no Kitson, my friend.'

'Who owns this place?'

'O'Leary. Desmond O'Leary.'

'Where's he?'

'Ask her in the office.'

The office was small and dark, littered with spare parts; a plump girl sat clattering on an upright typewriter with her back towards the door. Above her a brown and naked calendar beauty stood on some faraway beach, sand on her buttocks, advertising brake-linings.

'Mr O'Leary's not here today. I'm sick of telling everybody.' Then Tina Kitson turned round. 'Dr Simcox!'

'Everybody? You mean Simon Mallard-Greene or the police?'

'I mean everybody.' Her eyes were red and puffy. 'He doesn't tell me anything.'

'I'm sure he doesn't.'

'I'll let him know you want him. *If* he happens to call.'

'I think he's got something I might be interested in.'

'They all say that. I'm sick and tired of it. Honestly I am.'

Fred moved to a cluttered mantelpiece over a broken gas fire. He saw a business card, clean and white, among the crumpled bills and notes for drivers. He picked it up and read the name of the Neverest Detective Agency and an address in Fetter Lane.

'You're trying to have him traced?' He showed Tina the card.

''Course not! I'm not as worried as all that. That's a guy who called. Gary was here then.'

'What happened?'

'I don't know, do I? How could I know?'

'Try and remember.'

Tina looked at him, and decided to do her best. 'I think Gary sold the man something. Did some sort of a deal anyway. He seemed pleased. Anyway I haven't seen much of Gary since then.'

'Sold him what?'

'I don't know do I?' Tina was becoming angry and near to tears again. 'Could have been an old banger for all I know. Could have been anything.'

'Yes.' Fred put the card carefully back on the dusty mantelpiece. 'Yes, I suppose it could.'

As he left, Tina went back to pounding the old typewriter, writing letters for a business her husband had apparently deserted.

Fred couldn't find a parking meter, so he squeezed his car into a space between two vans in Fetter Lane. He pushed his way into a dim hallway, went up three floors in a groaning lift, and found himself in the outer office of the Neverest Detective Agency: 'All Inquiries Undertaken. Complete Confidentiality Guaranteed'. 'I'm after a detective,' Fred explained to the depressed secretary who was knitting at her desk, clearly short of work. 'I think a client's gone in.' 'Yes,' Fred told her, 'me.' He opened the door into the inner office. 'Of course,' he said when he got inside. 'I should have guessed.'

It was a small room. On the wall a group photograph of the boys at Knuckleberries, taken in the Summer Term of 1948, hung beside a certificate of affiliation to the Private Inquiry Agents Association. Arthur Nubble was sitting behind the desk, eating a sandwich, drinking a packet of milk through a straw and reading the *Tatler*.

'Oh, hullo Simcox Minor. I thought you might be turning up.'

'The last time I saw you, you were a journalist.'

'Bit of a cover that, actually.' Nubble smiled modestly. 'Of course, I do manage to pick up a little gossip from time to time. Some of it finds its way into the papers.'

'And some of it you keep for your clients?'

'Well, that's the name of the game nowadays, isn't it?'

'What is?'

'Information.'

Fred sat on a rickety office chair and wondered how many games Arthur Nubble had known the name of since he ran a delicatessen in an old double bass case at school. Now, he supposed, it was divorce cases, the following of errant husbands, industrial secrets and, perhaps, wills.

'Who's your client in the estate of the late Simeon Simcox?'

'Titmuss *v.* Simcox and Others?' Nubble seemed to enjoy the formality of the title.

'Words to that effect. I suppose you're acting for Leslie Titmuss. Didn't we meet at his home?'

'I say, steady on.' Nubble looked hurt. 'You're doing me an injustice. Anyway, I understand Titmuss is a bit of a shit.'

379

'They speak of him as a future prime minister.'

'That's probably why. No, I wouldn't act for Titmuss. One has a certain loyalty. After all, we were all at Knuckleberries together.'

'All three of us.'

'You and I. And your brother, of course.'

'Henry!' Fred stood up. 'He hired you to check up on Leslie Titmuss?'

'And to collect evidence for his case. Yes.'

'And to stop me collecting evidence which might make his case impossible. Is that what Henry asked you to do?'

'I really don't know what you're suggesting, Simcox Mi.'

'There is a bit of evidence. I'm not at all sure what it is, except that it throws a good deal of light on our family circumstances. An appalling youth called Gary Kitson got hold of it by some means or other, probably theft, and you've just bought it from Gary. I don't imagine it's anything that my big brother thinks I ought to know about.'

'Your brother hasn't said anything about it.' The Neverest detective appeared to be enjoying a joke.

'Hasn't he?'

'In fact, we haven't had time to discuss it.'

'Have you not? So it's a piece of virgin evidence untouched by the interested parties.'

'If it exists.'

'And if it exists I'd like to see it.' He held out his hand. 'Please.'

Nubble didn't answer at once. Then he said, 'You never got on with Simcox Major, did you?'

'Not especially.'

'I took to you at school, you know. I wanted you to be my friend. None of the others had much time for me.'

'I remember.'

'You told me you were treacherous. Was that true?'

'Possibly,' Fred admitted. 'Treacherous to Henry.'

'Why?'

'My father may have had his failings, plenty of them. But he wasn't insane. I'm never going to let that be said. Never!'

Nubble looked at him and then stood up. Panting slightly he went to a battered safe in a dark corner. After searching for his keys he unlocked it and modestly produced a couple of sheets of blue notepaper, a letter that Grace kept at the bottom of her box of cheaper jewellery among other objects of sentimental value only.

'What are you offering me for this?' He held it to show the address printed on the first sheet.

'Money?' Fred supposed. 'Isn't that the name of the game nowadays?'

Chapter Thirty-two
FAITH UNFAITHFUL

The Miners' Strike, the prolonged war over dying pits and dying towns and villages, struck only a small echo in Hartscombe. There was a little posse of pickets outside Simcox's Brewery and placards which read 'Hands Off Our Beer', 'Save 300 Jobs', 'We Demand the Right to Work', and even 'Drink to the Workers!' From time to time a number of police and pickets enjoyed a brief push as some anxious secretary tried to get in or out. It had been Christopher Kempenflatt's scheme: unlike Magnus Strove he had recovered his fortunes since Leslie dropped a dying Hartscombe Enterprises on them and his eye finally lighted on the large Brewery site by the river in Hartscombe. What a waste of space it was, and how much more profitable might the area be if it were turned into a shopping precinct. Kempenflatt saw a pedestrian walk-way, a fine selection of shoe shops, music centres, and boutiques, all paying high rents and employing far fewer people than were needed to brew a beer which, in any event, was losing ground to cans of imported lager in the self-service winery.

Trafford Simcox, a thin, anxious and good-natured cousin to Fred and Henry, had been brought up to be Chairman of the Brewery. He sat in the office which had seen generations of Simcoxes, men who no doubt thought that their ales would last as long as the river which flowed past the windows, and worried a great deal. He worried about the loss of jobs, the destruction of the old buildings and the departure from the world of Simcox

Best Bitter. Yet the offer was one his shareholders could hardly refuse, and, in the absence of Best Bitter, it might keep him and his family in champagne for the rest of their natural lives.

'There's only one slight complication,' he finally had to admit to Christopher Kempenflatt. 'The law-suit going on about the old Rector's shares.'

'Who do we have to buy them from?'

'I suppose that will depend on the result of the case.'

'I may have to deal with Leslie Titmuss,' Kempenflatt supposed gloomily. He was looking down into the yard, where a disturbance of a minor sort was going on. Leslie's father had arrived at the gate, apparently suffering from the delusion he still worked there. 'You've got to let me in,' he told the pickets. 'There's things I've got to do in Accounts.' Some of the younger men told him to get lost, and one, who had no idea who George was, called him a scab. Den Kitson, bored on the picket line, was relieved to see Elsie arrive in her car and take the retired pillar of Accounts home to tea. 'He's been rctircd,' Den explained to the others. 'For donkeys' years.' 'Yes,' Elsie said, as she shepherded her husband away, 'and sometimes he forgets all about it.' 'All right, Dad,' they shouted as he left, 'call again, when the dispute's over.'

When they had finished tea and George had called it tasty, he went to the mantelpiece in 'The Spruces' and picked up that lady from Cleethorpes his boy had once given to the Rector. 'It's a while since we went on that holiday.' Elsie was clearing away.

'Leslie shouldn't have done it. He was all take was the old Rector.'

'The boy meant no harm. Leslie was always made welcome up at the Rectory.'

'I had to go and speak to the Rector about it.'

'You did, George. We all remember it clearly. It was the only time in his life Leslie took anything to which he wasn't strictly entitled. We all remember when you went up to speak your mind to Mr Simcox.' Elsie took the ornament from George and put it carefully back on the mantelpiece. 'You came home with our ornament in your pocket and there it's been, safe and sound, ever since.'

'The Rector always got that much more than what he was entitled to.' The old man yawned, thinking that it was time for Bedfordshire. 'It's been a worry to me.'

'If you win this wretched case, I'm going to have to buy the old Rector's shares from you.'

'And if I lose, you'll do a better deal with Henry Simcox?'

'At least he's a human being. He doesn't live entirely for money.'

'If I win, I shall charge you top price. It's the least I can do for Nicky.' Leslie looked at his watch. He saw no point in continuing the interview with Kempenflatt, who had called, without warning, one weekend at Picton House.

'Which leads me to wonder . . .' Kempenflatt showed no sign of leaving.

'To wonder what?'

'If you should be fighting this case at all, a sordid sort of legal scrap about the will of a well-known constituent. There are those in the local Party who think . . .'

'That it doesn't look good?' Leslie smiled at the simplicity of the Kempenflatt approach.

'Exactly!'

'Like rented dinner-jackets' – Leslie's smile turned to anger – 'and made up bow-ties and meat teas and string vests on summer holidays. I don't give a damn how it looks.'

'Perhaps I ought to warn you, you're a little more vulnerable these days.'

'You mean since I became a Minister?'

'I mean since you married one of the Worsfield peace women.'

'Charlotte was never one of them,' Leslie answered quickly. 'You read my statement to the Press.'

'Oh, everyone read that.' Kempenflatt got up to leave. 'The

trouble is not everyone believed it. Underneath their sensible hats and blue rinses, some of our dear Conservative ladies have got remarkably suspicious minds.'

When Fred left the Neverest Agency, he experienced a feeling of great elation. It was the end of a quest, a task he had set himself. Something had been achieved, finished with, done. The past was no longer a mystery and its solution was far from the warring contentions of Henry and Leslie Titmuss. When he walked out into Fetter Lane, his face was hit by rain. Peeling the wet parking ticket off his windscreen, he was prey to a sudden temptation. He might crumple it and the letter he had bought, throw them into the gutter and keep the secret he had discovered to be shared only by himself and the other two who must surely know it. Henry and Leslie could keep on battering each other in blind ignorance, and he would go quietly about his practice, knowing what they would never learn, and might, in any event, never clearly understand.

He drove into Fleet Street, crawled with the traffic down the Strand, peering out between his windscreen wipers, and, when he reached the park, found, almost to his surprise, that instead of turning north towards Paddington, the motorway and Harts-combe, he went on towards the Fulham Road. When he got to Agnes's flat, he sat for a long while in the car before he decided to ring the bell. Even then he decided she wasn't in, and was turning away when the buzzer went and her disembodied voice invited him up.

'I knew I couldn't escape cooking Lonnie's dinner for ever.' He had come to tell her of a revelation, but she had immediately started on her own story, half in outrage, half in amusement. It seemed she owed him an explanation for waiting on Henry. 'Do you think it's funny?'

'I suppose it is.'

'Your brother wasn't at all amused. He came into the kitchen to accuse me of spying on him.'

'Spying? Whatever for?'

'For you.' He felt unexpectedly flattered by Henry's accusation, and by the fact that Agnes accepted his visit as part of her day, with no particular motive behind it. She was making a steak and kidney pie to drive off to that night's dinner party, cutting out a pastry flower to decorate the top. 'What've you been doing anyway?' she asked him.

'More or less what your father did. Oh, and I've started to play again with the Stompers.'

'Aren't they getting a bit old by now?'

'All jazz players are getting a bit old. We've got another gig at the Badger in Skurfield. We might be a bit less pure this time. Perhaps they'll only throw tins cans during "St James Infirmary".' She had finished decorating and was wrapping the pie in silver foil, ready for the journey. 'Why don't you come?'

'To hear you play the drums?'

'You haven't for a long time.'

'Aren't you any better at it?'

'Come and see.'

'Would you like coffee?' She put the pie into a cardboard box with other silver-wrapped courses. 'Or a drink or something?'

'A drink or something.'

There was a bottle of white Rioja open in the refrigerator. She splashed some into tumblers and they drank. 'Why did Henry think I might want you to spy for me?' asked Fred.

'He said you were playing at being a detective. Is that true?'

'It was. I've finished now.'

'Good.'

'I've got the truth.' He tried not to sound triumphant.

'What are you going to do with it?' She was sitting at the kitchen table, in front of her drink, her lighter and packet of cigarettes, prepared for a chat. He sat opposite her and thought clearly for the first time in his life about his father and felt a surge of affection for the man who had often seemed remote and too involved in the simple solution of world problems to notice his immediate family. And, as he understood Simeon, he knew he couldn't let his brother go on publishing his misunderstandings to the world. 'I'm going to stop Henry making out our father was an idiot,' he told Agnes. 'At last I can shut him up.'

'Is that what you really care about?'

'What?'

'Shutting up your brother.'

'No. Of course it isn't. But he needs to be given a little truth, after all these years.'

'What sort of truth exactly?'

Fred took out his wallet, extracted the folded blue letter and handed it to her. Agnes took it reluctantly and, for a while, didn't care to look.

'Please. I want you to see.'

She started to read and he was glad that she was the first person to whom he had shown the letter. After a while she looked up at him. 'Careful,' she warned him, 'how you go about it.'

When Dorothy had moved out of the Rectory she had left a lot of bits and pieces from the study, books and papers, articles of no particular value, and promised to pick them up sometime. She had never done so and Kev the Rev. had often telephoned Fred to say he had a tea-chest full of Simcox memorabilia in his attic, and what would be a convenient time to call for it. Fred, wondering if he really had room for dozens of Left Book Club volumes and Fabian tracts, had put off this transfer of property but now he decided that it was a convenient moment.

The Reverend Kevin was on his way out when Fred arrived at the Rectory. 'Twenty-four-hour vigil in Worsfield Cathedral for better industrial relations.' He impishly displayed a paperback of *The Dogs of War*. 'Jolly naughty of me, I know, but these occasions can get deadly boring. Have you come for a good old bash at the problem of evil?'

'No, I told you, for my father's bits and pieces.'

'Oh, right. I'm sure Monica'll show you. It's Dr Simcox, darling!' Kevin Bulstrode shouted back through the front door. 'Can you let him have the stuff in the attic?'

Fred went past his old bedroom. Through an open door he saw a pile of clothes on the floor and a child's unmade bed. He went up a ladder to push open a trap-door, and climb into the dark, flyblown cavern above the rafters. He switched on a naked, dangling light bulb and recognized some of his and Henry's old toys, a tailless rocking-horse, toy guns, an old cricket bat and a box of dusty Christmas decorations. And there was his first, childhood drum set. He worked the pedal and produced a sagging, hollow thud. Then he saw the tea-chest with the bust of Karl Marx in a nest of pamphlets. When he got it home he found even more treasures, pipes, tobacco jars, faded posters, petitions for forgotten causes together with African carvings and Indian gods which had been presents from politicians, peace groups and bishops in distant lands. At the bottom he found an old 78 record; he looked at the label and was not particularly surprised. He took it out of its envelope and blew off the dust, then he adjusted his record-player and put the old disc almost reverently on the turntable. Karl Marx's bust was lying on its back, staring at the ceiling with sightless eyes, as Pinky Pinkerton's piano tinkled and his soft voice began to caress the old Cole Porter number 'You're the Top!'

Once more Mr Bugloss had bought champagne. After so many years, after so many hopes and disappointments, a city consortium had put together a deal with a Canadian, an Italian and several Germans, and the first day of principal photography, the day when everyone hoped to get paid for *Pilgrims*, was fixed. 'I shall be there,' Henry told him, 'provided it doesn't clash with my giving evidence in court.' 'My dears' – Mr Bugloss raised his glass in Henry's flat – 'good luck to our dear movie, and all who sail in her! She has a great script. May she receive twenty Oscar nominations, and make us all rich and famous. Jack Polefax must be kicking himself he never took up his option. Remember when we first had the idea? In that restaurant on the Coast, and you' – he looked at Lonnie more in sorrow than in anger – 'you disappeared into the john, and never came out again.'

'That was his other wife.' Lonnie was displeased.

'Of course.' Mr Bugloss smiled, not at all put out. 'And she walked home. I mean, his other wife walked.'

'Agnes wasn't dull, was she? You couldn't say that about her.' The phone began to ring on Henry's desk at the other end of the room, and he went to answer it. 'Not dull!' Lonnie muttered when he had gone. 'He says that to me!'

'She *walked*!' Mr Bugloss was still amazed, after so many years. 'About thirty blocks along Sunset. I can bear witness to that . . . er, Mrs Simcox.' Mr Bugloss played for safety. 'You've been right behind your husband through eight re-writes of *Pilgrims*. It's paid off, you see? We've got the end money guaranteed.'

'And what do *I* get for always supporting Henry?' Lonnie asked him. 'For always being on his side against everyone? He tells you, "There was one thing to be said for Agnes, she was never dull"!'

'That was Fred. He wants us to come down to Hartscombe and see our mother.' Henry returned from the telephone with other things to talk about.

'See Dorothy?'

'He thinks she might be ready to make a statement.'

'Is Fred on our side now?' Lonnie wondered.

'I honestly don't know what he's up to now. I've got to find out. Do you want to come?'

'Oh, yes, I'll come.' Lonnie included Mr Bugloss in her sigh. 'I'll be there supporting you, naturally I will.'

On the day that Henry and Lonnie were to come down to Hartscombe, George Titmuss, temporarily eluding his wife, presented himself once more at the Brewery gates and talked to

Den Kitson, who was again on picket duty. He still wanted access to the accounts department. 'Mistake to retire,' he said, 'Mother doesn't want me at home, get under her feet all the time, nothing to do but sit out in the garden. 'Course, we always paid the old Rector his wages.' He went on talking at random. 'Not that he did a stroke of work for it, other than marches and pinching other people's ornaments. It's the pre-war balance sheets, that's what needs to be looked at.'

'You mean you want a look round your office for old times' sake?' On that basis, and although it was an official dispute, the pickets were persuaded to let George in as a tourist for a trip down Memory Lane. Later that afternoon, Trafford Simcox, working on the final details of the Brewery sale, was disturbed by sounds from the deserted accounts department. He went along the corridor to find old Titmuss surrounded by dusty ledgers, annual statements and balance sheets which hadn't been looked at for years. 'I'm not blaming you, Mr Trafford.' George spoke calmly, as though he had been expecting the interruption. 'It was done in your father's time. It was done in Mr Pym's day. I think it was kindly meant at first, and then it got written up wrong. I shouldn't have passed it, not when it was written up like that. It's got to be put right some time.'

'What's got to be put right, George?' Trafford Simcox, forever anxious, sat down beside George Titmuss and had it explained to him, at considerable length.

'Young Dr Fred's still out on his rounds,' Mrs Beasley, Dr Salter's old housekeeper, and now Fred's, told Henry and Lonnie when they arrived at the surgery. 'He wants you to go on up.' In the living-room Henry wondered what you had to do to be called 'young' in middle-age. 'Never move on,' he suggested to Lonnie. 'Stay where you're planted, and like Fred, you can be called "young" till the day you die.'

'He hasn't put much of himself in here, has he?' Lonnie looked round at Dr Salter's old furniture. 'Except the drums.'

'It's the room of a man totally unaware of his surroundings,' Henry agreed. 'Or of a man pretending to be totally unaware of his surroundings,' he added. 'That's the impression Fred wants to give; he's very devious.' He helped himself and Lonnie to drinks from the sideboard. 'There's absolutely no limit to the deviousness of little Freddie. For instance, he'd like us to believe that he's quite uninfluenced by the thought of money. It's dishonest. People who say they don't care about cash are usually lying, or they're after something far more unpleasant.'

'Such as?'

'Moral superiority,' Henry decided. 'The principal vice of our father.'

'I thought your father was meant to be mad.' Lonnie had learned to answer back a little, over the years.

'That too, of course.' Henry defended his position. 'Madness was his other vice.'

Fred came in then and apologized for being late. One of the Hunt boys, up near Mandragola, had got his hand caught in a tractor belt; it had given the Doctor a chance to do a bit of stitching.

'Jolly considerate of the Hunt boy to get his hand caught then. Is Mother coming here?'

'No. But I thought we should meet here first. At Sunday Street the drink flows like cement.'

Lonnie wondered where in the evening's events dinner would be fitted in. Her heart sank when they arrived at Dorothy's house and her mother-in-law greeted them with 'I really don't know why you should want to come all this way. I'm not putting on a dinner party you know.' As they went in and disposed themselves round the living-room, a place which in its own small way preserved the Rectory's reputation for howling draughts, Dorothy expanded on the subject of her not providing food. 'Simeon and I always avoided dinner parties. I started to notice the way people eat. I never listened to what they were saying then, I just watched them chewing or trying to slip food into their mouths when they thought you weren't looking, or, worse still, picking their teeth furtively with a little finger-nail. Once you notice people eating it's an end to dinner parties.' She looked round at her visitors with amusement. 'All the family!'

'I suppose I'm a bit of an outsider.' Lonnie was hungry.

'Yes.' Dorothy looked at her thoughtfully. 'Still, you go with Henry, don't you? You always go with Henry.'

'Perhaps a cup of coffee?' Henry suggested. He looked at Dorothy who didn't move, so Lonnie got up and went out to the kitchen.

'Mrs Nowt . . . You know old Dora Nowt lives in Hartscombe now? Anyway, she brought me some elderflower wine. I do wish she wouldn't,' Dorothy whispered confidentially. 'It's particularly revolting.'

'Fred told us' – Henry called the meeting to order – 'that you felt ready to make a statement.'

'A statement? Good heavens, what about?'

'About our father.'

'I think what Henry's looking for,' Fred told her, 'is some sort of explanation.'

'Oh, dear. I do hope an explanation won't be necessary.'

'It wouldn't be if Henry decided to give up the case.'

It was, Fred knew, an impossible request. The truth would have to be shared and he supposed it was better done in the sitting-room in Sunday Street than in a law court, with a judge writing it all down and barristers to ask questions and throw doubt and newspapers to report it and old men in macs, wandering in off the street for the sake of the central heating and the free entertainment, to hear all about it. All the same he avoided looking at his mother, and came to the matter obliquely, by way of the tea-chest in the attic.

'Perhaps I should tell you what I did this afternoon,' he said. 'I got a box of our father's bits and pieces out of the attic in the Rectory. You know what I found?'

'Not another will?' Henry had little hope of it, all Simeon's papers had been searched by the solicitors before they were stored away.

'More important than that. I found a gramophone record.' Fred looked at Henry, still turning away from his mother. 'Down at the bottom of the box was Pinky Pinkerton's rendering of "You're the Top!" If you remember, it contains the immortal line "You're the Top! You're the Lady Gra – ace!" It's something Grace Fanner plays to everyone. It even got played at children's parties. She gave a copy of it to our father.'

'What on earth's the point of bringing us here to tell us someone gave Simeon a gramophone record?' Henry acted superhuman patience.

'There would be no point at all if only you hadn't said our father was insane.'

'Go on then, what do you want to have said about him?'

'He wasn't in the least mad. He wasn't a saint either, not a saint at all. He was a man, like anyone else, who falls in love and can't possibly explain it.'

'Of course, his behaviour was completely irrational.' Henry was triumphant, and then he said, more quietly, 'Who are you suggesting he fell in love with?'

'Do you want to tell them?' Fred looked at Dorothy, but she offered him no help, only murmuring, 'I don't see why any of these things have to be said.'

'Some things have to be.' Fred stood up. Now the time had come he felt tired, as at the end of a long day's work with the most difficult patients still to treat. 'I suppose it was about the beginning of the war, before the bomb hit the old Café de Paris, when the late lamented Sir Nicholas was doing his bit in Bognor. I suppose it was the time Charlie was conceived.'

'Charlotte!' Henry was genuinely puzzled.

'Oh yes,' Fred told him, 'she's one of us. She *was*. She was really the problem, wasn't she, Mother? She wasn't beautiful. She wasn't interested in clothes. She wasn't even a snob. So Grace hated our father's child.'

'It can't possibly be true!' Henry looked at Dorothy, angrily, accusingly, as if whatever had happened must have been her fault. She started to speak then, as though released by his disbelief, and the words, held in so long, came flowing out of her. 'That's why he always felt so guilty. Poor Simeon. He was guilty about practically everything, living off shares in Simcox's Brewery.' She smiled. 'Just like any other capitalist, not having sufficient faith in Socialism. Not believing enough in God, and then, of course, having a child he couldn't acknowledge, who got no love from her mother.'

Lonnie chose that moment to come back from the kitchen with a tray of coffee and biscuits, cheerfully announcing, 'It's only Instant.' The others seemed not to notice her, and Dorothy didn't stop talking. 'And having a secret from me, I suppose. Of course, it couldn't stay a secret forever, because of Tom Nowt. I'm afraid Tom saw Simeon and Grace, oh, I don't know exactly where. He wasn't bad you know, Tom was never bad. He probably wouldn't have said anything if that stupid woman hadn't gone after him about his poaching. She complained to Nicholas so that any stories Tom spread about her could be called malicious slander. In the end, Tom never told Nicholas. The only person he told was me. Perhaps he thought I should know about it. Anyway, we were friends. We both knew about the woods. I used to show his children where to find the spider orchid. He told me about Simeon, and I persuaded Tom not to tell anyone else. I gave him a bit of help for his hut for instance, things like that. I really don't think I could have managed it on my own but I did have a friend.' Lonnie bit audibly into a biscuit. Dorothy noticed her but went on telling them. 'A friend to advise me. He was a sensible man. Much more sensible than Simeon, of course. And he was kind to me. He knew that Simeon might want to pay for his . . . his adventures in the end. So Dr Salter left me this little house.' She looked round the room, smiling. 'I must say, it's a good deal easier to dust than the Rectory.'

There was a long silence. Henry was not prepared to give up without a struggle. 'None of that explains why Simeon could possibly have wanted to benefit Leslie Titmuss.'

'Poor Leslie!' Dorothy was still smiling. 'He was never a really happy child. Of course your father must have been delighted when Leslie married Charlotte, and there was someone to look after her. It was a load of guilt off his mind. But then Charlie became unhappy, and of course she died. Simeon thought perhaps she'd killed herself and it was all his fault again. He had to pay a debt to her and to her child. So he left his money to Leslie Titmuss.' She looked round at them all, at Henry silent and Lonnie, apparently frozen, holding up her half-eaten biscuit. 'It wasn't entirely his idea,' Dorothy explained. 'I thought that if he left the money to Leslie, Nicky would benefit. I'm sure he will.'

'*You* thought . . .' Henry couldn't believe it.

'It made Simeon feel better, about all the wrong he imagined he'd done to Charlie. It was such a little thing, after all. He knew you'd be all right. "Henry'll be all right," he said. Only that character you put on, I suppose it's some sort of reaction against your father, pretending to be a crusty old English blimp; Simeon was afraid that'd grow on you and you'd be trapped in it forever – if the wind changed or something. But he always said, "Henry's got the gift of the gab. He'll be all right." And you . . .' She looked at Fred. ' "Fred's indestructible," he said. He thought Leslie was the one who needed help. Poor Leslie. He loves money and power and all that sort of thing so much, he's bound to lose them in the end. These things only stay with those who have a certain contempt for them. Simeon was afraid for Leslie's future. He was afraid for the future of poor dead Charlie's child.' Suddenly she had had enough of talking, the explanations were over and she hoped they'd all go away. 'It's such a long story,' she said, 'and it was all so long ago.'

'I really don't see what it's got to do with our case.' Henry was still determined to look on the bright side. 'After all there's absolutely no proof that any of it ever happened.'

'Only the letter our father sent Grace when Charlie was born. It was something she kept with old gramophone records, bits and pieces of jewellery, scraps of her past. I don't suppose she really cared if Nicholas found it or not.' Fred took the blue sheets out of his wallet, looked at them, but didn't unfold the letter.

'Where did you get that?' Henry stood up and crossed the room in a purposeful way.

'It was being offered for sale, more or less on the open market.'

Henry put his hand out for the letter, but Fred returned it to his wallet. 'The case is over. Leslie Titmuss knows just why our father left him the money. At least, he can prove it wasn't in-sanity.'

'Prove it?' Henry was contemptuous. 'What can he possibly prove?'

'Oh, most of it.' And then Fred told him. 'You see, I sent him a copy of the letter too.'

There was a cry of agony from Lonnie. 'You've lost our case!'

Henry, of course, told them that it wasn't over at all, not by a long chalk. He was going to see the lawyers, he wasn't going to let Fred's treachery do any of them out of their legal rights and he doubted whether the precious letter was evidence of anything. And yet, as he and Lonnie left, Fred knew that it was over, and that Henry knew it also. After a while they would meet again, in a world where their father was not demonstrably insane, and they were the two half-brothers of Charlie Titmuss.

When Henry had gone Fred tried to explain himself to Dorothy. 'It was the only way, Mother. I had to stop him somehow.'

'Oh, yes.' She withdrew her interest from him. 'I suppose you did.' She stood up then and went to lock the back door, ready for bed. 'Just don't expect anyone to love you for it.'

Chapter Thirty-three

THE SIMCOX INHERITANCE

When they had all gone, and the story had been told, Dorothy took the cold, untouched Instant coffee Lonnie had made and poured it away down the sink. As she washed the cups she thought of the big Rectory kitchen on a day at the end of the summer, early in the war. She had evacuees, she remembered, three small boys who had come to escape the bombs on Stepney. They were copious bedwetters who looked at a field of cows with more terror than they had ever felt for the Luftwaffe. Simeon had put himself out for them, taking them on long country walks which they disliked, or playing 'Beggar My Neighbour', at which they cheated, with them in the evenings. Dorothy found little to say to them but they followed her about the house with extraordinary devotion. She remembered the events which came on them as suddenly as the black-out curtains, the sound of bombers droning through the sky towards Worsfield, or the three prematurely aged children with their luggage labels pinned to their jackets. 'I don't think anyone else knows,' she told Simeon as they stood in the Rectory kitchen. 'Only Tom Nowt.'

'I can't explain it.' He seemed genuinely puzzled.

'No.'

'I can't explain it at all. I've always, really always, tried to believe in fairness and equality, all the things she finds completely ridiculous!'

'I don't think it's about politics this time.' Dorothy was looking for something in the larder.

'And she's selfish and spiteful and trivial as well,' he admitted. 'Quite funny, I suppose. A woman who paints her finger-nails purple and wears pyjamas in the day-time and enjoys the Blitz, God help her. She's everything I most despise and I found her irresistible.' He seemed to be faced with a mystery darker than any he'd met in his profession. 'How can that happen?'

'It's over now.' She found the big basket in a dark, cluttered corner of the larder floor and pulled it out of its hiding-place.

'I suppose I'm back to some sort of sanity.'

'I hope you don't regret it.'

'The affair with Grace?'

'No. Getting back to sanity. Come on, let's pick the crab apples.' It was something they always did at this time of the year, so they went down to the trees together.

'He let me marry his little by-blow, his wrong side of the blanket. He let me have one of the Simcoxes, and I didn't know a damn thing about it!'

A copy of Simeon's letter had arrived on Leslie's breakfast table at Picton House. Before embarking on the long day ahead (opening a Worsfield Job Opportunities Centre, a flight to a speech at the Euro-Computer Exhibition in Birmingham, a five o'clock meeting at the Ministry and dinner at the Worshipful Company of Breeches Makers) he stopped his ministerial Rover outside Rapstone Manor, and found Grace in her dressing-gown, submitting her face to the filtered sun in the conservatory.

'I can't imagine how Charlie ever came to marry you,' was her answer to his opening volley.

'I must seem very disagreeable to you. I don't know anything about lying and cheating and saving up traces of old adulteries as though they were something to be proud of! That's not the way people carried on where I was brought up.'

'Your family had extraordinarily dull lives, I've always thought so.'

'Just let me tell you this. I've got my lawyer coming out to meet me and if Henry Simcox goes on fighting this case I'll drag you to court on a subpoena and make you spit out the truth, the whole truth and nothing but the truth.'

'The truth? We had nothing in common, Simeon and I. Absolutely nothing. I suppose, when all's said and done, it was some sort of challenge.' She gave a small and satisfied smile. 'I made him fall for me, you know.'

'God help him.' Leslie looked at his watch because he was working to a tight schedule. 'Who else knew about this? Did his wife know?'

'The long-suffering Dorothy? Of course she knew everything.'

When Leslie had gone Grace felt nothing but hatred for him, and yet his visit had been an event at a time when life produced few surprises. It brought back memories of a past which had once excited her. Perhaps she would call on Dorothy. They would have something to talk about now, even if it were only Simeon's guilt about Charlie, and its expiation in showering favours on the appalling Titmuss. She told Brooks to get the car ready.

'I'm going out, Dora.' Dorothy in a mac and headscarf found Mrs Nowt washing the kitchen floor in Sunday Street. 'I'm going up to the Manor.'

'To her Ladyship?' Dorothy had told Grace's story. She had spoken of something she had thought never to have to speak of again, although it hadn't been her intention to give away Grace's secret. Surely she should explain that to the woman? Well, perhaps, after all, not. She sat down on a kitchen chair. 'I don't think' – she undid her scarf – 'that there's any more to be said.'

'You're not going out?'

'No, Dora. I'm not going out at all.'

Grace, walking a little unsteadily, reached the car door which Brooks held open. She also had second thoughts. She looked up at a sky which threatened rain and gave further instructions. 'Put the motor away, Brooks. Really, I have nothing at all to say to Dorothy Simcox.'

As soon as he got Fred's letter, and even before his visit to Grace, Leslie Titmuss, puzzled but triumphant, had telephoned his lawyer with the good news and ordered an immediate meeting. The problem was finding a free half hour of the Minister's valuable time, so he suggested a car to bring Rattling to Worsfield's minute airfield where they could discuss the new evidence before the helicopter took off for the Birmingham Exhibition Centre. So, in the airport building, which was little more than a collection of huts, with his secretary and a man from his Ministry hovering in the background, Leslie gave his solicitor the copy of an old love letter. 'That wraps it up surely? A perfectly clear, rational explanation for wanting to benefit my family. They won't go on with it now, will they?'

'No, I don't suppose they will,' Rattling agreed.

'So we've won!' Leslie was a little irritated by the lawyer's look of embarrassed gloom. He hadn't expected the man to cheer loudly but there was surely cause for a good deal of quiet satisfaction.

'The question is' – Rattling wore the expression he kept for the funerals of important clients – '*what* have you won exactly?'

'The Simcox estate. We know what that is don't we?'

'Let's say,' Rattling sounded a note of caution, 'we thought we knew.' And then he took a deep breath and explained. 'When the Simcox family business was reconstituted, back in the early twenties, in a certain Pym Simcox's time, the Reverend Simeon was given a large number of B shares. They carried no voting rights whatsoever. They should have produced no income.'

The windows rattled at the sound of the helicopter landing. Leslie looked confused by the noise and the information.

'But he was always paid, every year.'

'Indeed.' Rattling looked as grave as if he were describing some hitherto undetected murder. 'It seems at the time the family realized the Rector had no means of support other than a pretty miserable stipend. So they doled him out a comfortable voluntary income. As he was paid regularly, it came to be assumed in the accounts department that he had A shares, producing regular lolly. So' – Rattling coughed nervously – 'a bit of a mistake crept into the annual returns.'

Outside on the landing strip, the helicopter fell silent. The building was quiet and airless, the only sound that of a distant telephone ringing unanswered. Leslie looked at his feet and seemed to find them, for some time, objects of interest. When he raised his head his habitual air of jaunty self-confidence had left him. He looked his age.

'Worthless? The shares worthless?'

'An old fellow who used to work in the Brewery Accounts spotted it. It'd been on his mind. The Brewery rang Jackson Cantellow this morning, and Cantellow got on to me before I left London.'

'I think I know who the old fellow is.' And then Leslie asked again, 'Worth absolutely nothing?'

The telephone had stopped ringing. There was the squawk of an announcement on the tannoy, and the two men with briefcases told the Minister that the chopper was at his disposal. They were puzzled when he looked at them and repeated, 'Nothing!' Then he walked out of the building, the wind ruffling what remained of his hair, to go about his business with no benefit whatever from the Simcox estate.

In Cantellow's office the same news was given to Fred. 'Shares with no voting rights. Paying no dividends. Producing no income.' Jackson Cantellow rolled the words round his tongue like a lament from an oratorio. 'Of course they'd been wrongly entered for years. A gross piece of negligence.'

'All you lawyers and Q.C.s from London have only just discovered that?'

Cantellow asked, 'What on earth's the matter, are you quite

well?' for Fred, sitting back in the client's chair, seemed to be overcome with laughter.

There was no laughter, however, in 'The Spruces' when Leslie called on his parents. George sat in his armchair after tea, feeling, for the first time in his life, frightened of his son although, to be fair, Leslie hadn't blamed him for anything and agreed that the truth would have had to come out in the end. Elsie also looked nervously at the silent figure who stood in front of the fire, suppressing his anger. She didn't know why he had come except to blame them and she wished he'd do that and go back to Picton House where she felt he belonged. 'Your father's right,' she said. 'The truth had to come out.'

'He had nothing to give us.' Leslie picked up the lady in the red bathing-dress, who had been for years in the act of diving off a rock. 'I wanted to give him that,' he said. 'It was all I could think of. And he gave us nothing.'

'Our ornament!' Elsie cried out as her son sent the object crashing against the opposite wall. And then she was down on her hands and knees, carefully picking up the pieces.

None of these events were completed. All had life left in them and continued to stir and trouble their participants, although, with time, strength was spent. Like the pebble in Simeon's well-used pond, they produced diminishing effects. Simon Mallard-Greene, defended by an expensive barrister, was fined by the Magistrates, and his mother told Fred that they had decided to sell up and move to London. 'We're getting rid of what you call Tom Nowt's old cottage,' she told him. 'I've always known that there was something evil about the place.'

Christopher Kempenflatt, without any particular difficulty, got hold of a list of members of the Worsfield branch of the C.N.D. and sprung a surprise under Any Other Business at a Conservative Association committee meeting to which Leslie was invited. He startled the members by charging the Minister with lying to the Press, having categorically denied that his wife was ever a member of the organization when her name was clearly listed in a document which had conveniently fallen into Kempenflatt's hands. Of course there was nothing illegal about C.N.D., but a Member for Hartscombe must have an unimpaired reputa-. tion for veracity. Did they not all remember, in the distant days, a certain Minister for War . . .?

'Of course I lied,' Leslie interrupted sharply, cutting off what seemed to him Kempenflatt's pathetic attempt to be revenged after the collapse of Hartscombe Enterprises.

'You admit it?' The accuser was disappointed. He had wanted to see his old partner wriggling on the hook.

'Did you want me to give a boost to the pacifists? Think of the publicity they'd've got out of that: "Minister's Wife One of the Worsfield Women". Did you honestly want that sort of head-line?'

'The point seems to be . . .' Lord Naboth looked at the photo-stats of the old press-cuttings Kempenflatt had unexpectedly tabled. 'There does seem to have been a lack of frankness . . .'

'You've told us you lied.' Kempenflatt would allow no eu-phemism. But Leslie, with his look of patient sincerity, smiled round at their worried faces. 'And wouldn't you lie, Mr Kempen-flatt, wouldn't every man in this room lie to protect the honour of the dead wife he had loved above all things?' It was not much of a tight spot, but Leslie had got out of it, as he would get out of many in the years to come. 'Never apologize for winning,' he told Nicky, when his son came home for the holidays. 'Never apologize and never explain. And when you win, you're entitled to feel triumphant.' But the boy seemed uninterested in this advice. He left the dinner table because, he said, he wanted to get on with his book.

'Our father was deceiving us all those years,' Henry told Francesca. 'He let us think he was well off.' Peter, Francesca's boyfriend, had been converted to high-tech and the flat in Tufnell Park was now filled with black metal shelves, chromium lights, canvas deckchairs and banks of stereo equipment. She was wearing a white boiler-suit, and Simeon's old desk, empty of all wills, had been painted black and, with its top drawers removed, was fitted with chrome handles. 'It's you I'm thinking about, Francesca,' her father told her. 'I was planning to do something for you.'

'Do what? Give me money?'

'Don't you undervalue it. I've had to work for every penny.'

'Down the film studio, every morning. Hacking scripts out of the coalface.'

'Sometimes you look exactly like your mother,' Henry noticed. 'Sometimes you sound exactly like Agnes.'

'You never got to know much about me, did you?' Henry didn't answer. 'You might have quite got to like me. I ought to have told you that I hate loud music, I've never taken drugs and, here's another thing, I absolutely don't give a damn about whales.'

Pilgrims was being filmed at last, and vans were parked outside Rapstone Church, together with camera cars, a catering wagon for the incessant procession of sausage butties, cakes and tea, and a generator from which a complicated system of cables snaked across the churchyard and in at the west door. None of this activity was visible to Dorothy as she walked across the fields to do her flowers. She had been cutting willow and beech sprays to go with the flowers she had brought. Inside the vestry, she put her basket on the table, unconscious of the activity in the church, where silence had just been called for. She filled a bucket from a tap outside, plunged her flowers in the water, and then opened the door which led into the church to collect the vases.

Light, white and almost blinding, struck at her. Perhaps, in the shadows, there were a good many people. All she could see was the back of a stooping figure in an old tweed jacket, who turned towards her. He was smoking a pipe, wearing a dog-collar and had the look of a rather bothered eagle. In a moment of extraordinary, unreasonable hope, she called out, 'Simeon. Oh, my dear!'

From the darkness, the director shouted, 'Cut.' The actor sighed, knowing that he would have to start the scene all over again.

Whether it was because the audience at the Badger had grown more tolerant, or because the Stompers were less relentlessly traditional and gave their own jazz versions of such popular numbers as 'Hello Dolly' and 'As Time Goes By', the gig was an unexpected success. Joe smiled in a superior manner during the rendering of these tunes, as though he had chosen them as a sort of private joke against himself. Den, who had been delighted to discover no sign of his young brother in the bar, slapped the double bass he had available for the night with the enthusiasm of a man enjoying an evening of dubious delight. Terry Fawcett played his clarinet with new invention, having had long and empty days to think about it. Only Fred, with a nervousness which he despised in himself, was drumming with moist hands and a dry mouth, waiting for something to happen as though he were a young doctor again setting out for his first lunch with Mrs Wickstead. They played 'St James Infirmary' for the sake of auld lang syne, and no one threw a Coca-Cola tin. So, as a reward to the audience, Joe Sneeping nodded to signal that he was going to permit the piece of commercialism which Fred had played since childhood. 'One, two, three, four. We know what we're waiting for,' Joe murmured in his deep South Hartscombe accent, in order to give it some sort of style, and then he went into the first bars of 'Slow Boat to China'. The Stompers played a chorus together, and Joe sang.

> 'Get you and keep you
> In my arms evermore,

Leave all your lovers
Weeping on the faraway shore . . .'

Terry Fawcett was allowed a perfect eight bars on the clarinet, and then Joe, raising the bell of his trumpet to the sky, went into the solo Fred had heard so often that it was as familiar to him as the common cold, Mrs Beasley's arthritis, or the road to the surgery. When Joe had exhausted his repertoire of clichés, during which Den Kitson leant on his double bass and softly chatted up a youngish girl, while Terry drank most of a pint, Joe grudgingly waved his trumpet at Den for his solo. Then they all took up the tune.

'Out on the briny,
With a moon big and shiny,
Melting your heart of stone,
I'd love to get you
On a slow . . . slow boat to China,
All to myself alone.'

It was Fred's moment for the final outburst. He started quietly, being careful not to become too busy to lose the beat, and it was when he was doing a little complex work on the side drum that he saw her. She was moving out of the shadows beside the bar, as she had once stepped into the light in Marmaduke's garage at the moment he had failed her. That was over too now, even, perhaps, forgiven. She had come a long way to meet him, and he started on a triumphant drum roll to welcome her.

Some time later they were walking through the beech woods together over a spot which no longer showed signs of fire and there were no charred antlers.

'So that's it,' Agnes said. 'No one got anything from your father.'

'We got what we are, Henry and I, in our different ways.'

'Leslie got nothing.'

'I think he created Leslie more than any of us. Poor old Dad, God help him!'

They were walking side by side, but with a yard separating them, between the grey-green trunks of trees. He thought how old it would be now, the child they had never had. And he thought of his father's child, of Charlie, whom the old man had loved.

'That's a bit sad!' Agnes gave him a look of mock despair. 'You think we're just what our fathers and mothers made us. Haven't we got any choice?'

'We had a choice once. You and I, I mean. I made the wrong one.'

'It's a bit late to think of that now.'

He walked in silence and then kicked up a small cloud of dead leaves as he had when he was a child. 'I don't think it's late.'

He looked at her trudging beside him, her fists pushed down into her pockets, smiling as though at a joke so awful that no one else could see it, as he had always known her.

'It's never really too late,' he said. 'To begin.'

Titmuss Regained

For John and Myfanwy Piper

Today

What would the world be, once bereft
Of wet and of wildness? Let them be left,
O let them be left, wildness and wet;
Long live the weeds and the wilderness yet.

'Inversnaid'
Gerard Manley Hopkins

CHAPTER ONE

About a mile to the north of the village of Rapstone there was an area of mixed woodland and uncultivated chalk downs. The woods included some beech, birch, field maple and yew. The grassland, owing to the centuries of peace it had enjoyed from the depredations of farmers and builders, was rich in plant and insect life. The violet hellebore and the bird's-nest orchid did well there and gentians and wild thyme proliferated. The Duke of Burgundy's fritillary and the chalkhill blue butterflies were to be seen, as were the trapdoor spider, fallow and muntjac deer, badgers, foxes, adders and slow-worms. At the foot of the hill there was a stream said to be haunted by two kingfishers, although their nesting-place had never been found.

One afternoon in April a Volvo stopped on the road by the stream. An observer standing on the crest of the grassland might have seen, indeed did see, a young couple, hand in hand, climb the hill towards him. They were a good-looking pair. The man had heavy, regular features, fair hair which covered the tops of his ears and a moustache. At serious moments his face could assume a look of sullen brutality, but now he seemed cheerful enough. The girl with him was sturdily attractive, with white, slightly protruding teeth. Such clouds as there were hung high in the sky. The early sunshine gave promise of a hot summer, never to be fulfilled.

Half-way up the hill the observer saw the couple stop and stand still, facing each other. They had chosen a patch of clear scrub where the turf was soft and springy, much undermined by rabbits. They did not kiss or touch each other, but the girl laughed, causing a colony of fat pigeons to tumble out of the trees in alarm. Then they prepared to make love.

They did this in a businesslike way, with an efficiency born of experience. They moved deliberately but seemed to be under pressure of time, like soldiers at a military tattoo racing against the clock to assemble a gun. Buttons and belt buckles were undone and shoes kicked off and they then fell to the ground in one movement, as though they were under fire. Only then did they embrace, but as soon as their mouths joined they were interrupted.

'Can't you lot read? There's notices where you came in. This place is reserved for nature!' The man standing over them was short, square and bristling with anger. Hair covered the lower half of his face so profusely that his eyes seemed in a perpetual panic at the danger of being overgrown. With his green sweater and leather patches, his beret, knapsack and stick, he had the appearance of a soldier beating the countryside for terrorists. His name was Hector Bolitho Jones. 'I,' he told them, 'am keeper and warden of the Rapstone Nature Area.'

'Tell him,' the girl muttered, avoiding the eyes of the infuriated warden as she stood up, straightening her skirt. 'Tell him who you are.' But her companion remained motionless, staring up, unamused.

'You know what we get on this natural downland which has never known pollution by any form of artificial manure or pesticide of any nature whatsoever? You know what you may be laying on there? Do you have any idea what you may be crushing?'

'We're going,' the girl said. 'We wouldn't want to stay here, anyway.' And once again she advised her lover, 'Tell him who you are.'

'Just on a stone curlew's nest. I don't suppose you realized that, did you? In your ignorance. The stone curlew habitually makes its nest on the ground. On the natural chalk. You could have got that from our fact-sheet at the area entrance. If you lot can read.'

'We're moving, anyway.' The girl, glancing down, found another button and did it up.

'That'd be a bit late if you've laid on a stone curlew's nest. If you've smashed the eggs or frightened away the mother. You might have had a death on your hands then, mightn't you? As if you lot cared!'

The man didn't move but spoke for the first time. 'Why don't you shut up and mind your own bloody business.'

'It's not *my* business!' Hector Bolitho Jones raised his voice as though talking to the deaf or to a foreigner. 'It's S.C.R.A.P.'s business. S.C.R.A.P. owns this ground, the Society for Conservation, Rural and Arboreal Protection. S.C.R.A.P.!' he shouted, so that his voice echoed across the woods and set the pigeons off again. 'I suppose that means nothing to you?'

'Of course it does.' The man got slowly to his feet, on which he towered over the small, infuriated Jones. 'It means I'm your boss. I just happen to be at H.E.A.P., the Department of Housing, Ecological Affairs and Planning. It may come as news to you out here in the sticks, but we have just taken over the S.C.R.A.P. Nature Areas with a view to privatization!'

'After all the government money you've had poured into you!' The girl, who seemed to understand such matters, looked at Hector Bolitho Jones accusingly.

'So you'd better keep a civil tongue in your head. If you value your job, that is.' Her friend was even more threatening.

Hector Bolitho Jones drew a breath. His chest swelled and his beard bristled. He was about to start on a lengthy speech about stone curlews being the business of all of us, together with rain forests, the black rhino, badgers, otters, the greenhouse effect, lead in petrol, seal slaughter, mink coats, fox-hunting, hedge destruction and non-organic farming. He looked at his audience and decided, like a Victorian missionary facing a hostile couple in war-paint with rings through their noses, that a sermon would be a waste of breath. 'I don't care who you are,' he said. 'I give you five minutes to get off this Nature Area.'

'And if we don't?'

'You'll find yourselves mentioned in S.C.R.A.P.'s annual report.'

'Oh, Christ.' The man smiled coldly. 'You're scaring us to death.' He was strong, with muscles that stretched his neat grey suit, clothes which looked too formal for courting in the countryside. For a moment he seemed about to strike the warden but, surprisingly, he took his girlfriend's arm and they walked away down the hill towards the road where their car was waiting. Hector Bolitho Jones watched them leave with undiminished hostility and only when the lovers had driven away was he satisfied that he was once again in command of a small kingdom where nature might pursue its uninterrupted course.

'What're you going to do?' In the car the girl, whose name was Joyce Timberlake, twisted the driving-mirror and leant sideways to repair her lipstick. 'You going to get him the sack?'

'Probably not worth it.' Her companion drove with one hand, the other was lying coldly on her thigh. 'But it's not something I'm going to forget either. You can be sure of that.'

Hector Bolitho Jones, true to his word, did mention the sacrilegious behaviour of the lovers in the Nature Area in a report to his masters at S.C.R.A.P. Months later, watching television, he saw an interview with Ken Cracken, M.P., on the subject of planning permission for a theme park in the Lake District. He at once recognized the fair moustache, the wary and hostile expression of the youngish man who had become, with a rapidity which alarmed many older politicians, Minister at the Department of Housing, Ecological Affairs and Planning, a position only junior to that of the Secretary of State himself, the Right Honourable Leslie Titmuss.

CHAPTER TWO

'What a swine God was!'

While the forces of nature were in collision on the chalk down-land, and Ken Cracken and his girlfriend, who was also his personal assistant and political adviser, were being expelled from the paradise of the Rapstone Nature Area, a woman of eighty, her legs and arms shrunk as though from enforced starvation, lay waiting, with growing impatience, for death. Grace Fanner was unaccustomed to being kept waiting for anything. Her bedroom in Rapstone Manor was dark and gloomy, its windows curtained by the spreading yew tree in front of the house; patches of damp stained the wallpaper which was decorated with lighter squares from which pictures had been removed and auctioned off as Lady Fanner's overdraft climbed to dizzier heights. She lay now, an unpaid-for and half-drunk bottle of champagne beside her, her diminutive body scarcely swelling the coverlet on the bed in which her husband Nicholas, over a decade before, had met death with the polite but puzzled smile with which he had greeted all his visitors.

'I've been reading the Bible.'

The Rector of Rapstone, Kevin Bulstrode, known to many of his parishioners as Kev the Rev., looked at her as though this activity were a sign of mental weakness, like astrology or studying the measurements of the Great Pyramid.

'Not the Old Testament?' he asked nervously.

'*Particularly* the Old Testament. What a swine God was, most of the time.' Lady Fanner said this with a tight smile of admiration. 'Smiting people in a way I've hardly ever done. Right, left and centre.'

'I don't think we see God as so much of a smiter nowadays,' Kev the Rev. explained. 'We see Him more as the depth of our being.'

'Certainly the depth of *my* being,' Lady Fanner agreed. 'Smiting away like that. Bully for Him!'

'The God that's within us all' – Bulstrode was still patient – 'is above all things a God of love.'

'God is within *you*?'

'I'd certainly like to think so.'

'It seems' – Lady Fanner looked at the clergyman with ill-disguised contempt – 'a most peculiar place to put Him. The tide's gone down.' She put out a matchstick arm and her hand trembled as it felt for the glass on her bedside table. 'Pour!'

'Are you sure that's absolutely wise?'

'Pour!' she repeated in a voice which rose towards an enraged squawk. Her eyes widened with anger and the Reverend Kevin obeyed her immediately, although he could have sat still and left her impotent and thirsty. Being unused to pouring champagne he sent the liquid bubbling up over the top of the glass. Life, Lady Fanner thought, had deteriorated in Rapstone. The previous Rector, the Reverend Simeon Simcox, although a life-long Socialist, could at least pour a glass of champagne without letting it overflow and ruin the furniture.

'I read the Book of Job.' She lifted the great weight of a half-filled glass to her lips and pecked at it in the manner of a blue tit at a bird-bath. 'God certainly gave that poor bugger a hard time. Boils!'

'I think you'll find that He has grown a little more civilized down the centuries. As, perhaps, we all have.' Kevin Bulstrode did his best to sound reassuring. 'I don't think the Old Testament God should be taken as a model of behaviour.'

'Oh, I do. I quite definitely do. I'd love to see my son-in-law afflicted with boils. That is if the Right Honourable Leslie

Titmuss hasn't got plenty of them already. As a young man, I hate to remember, he appeared to suffer from terminal acne. What my poor Charlotte saw in him, I really can't imagine. But then Charlie was such a beggar in the looks department, she couldn't be much of a chooser, could she?'

'I always heard your daughter Charlotte was a bit of a saint, Lady Fanner. Didn't she die in a C.N.D. demonstration at Worsfield Heath?' Kevin sounded like an old-time army padre, remembering those who fell on the Somme and at El Alamein. His head was bowed and his hands locked between his knees.

'She was run over there. In some foolish demonstration.' Once again Grace Fanner pecked at the liquid in her glass and then waved it wildly in the air, trying to restore it to the bedside table, an operation which her visitor just saved from disaster. 'At least she caused the terrible Titmuss extreme embarrassment. He was something rather pompous in the Government at the time. Having a wife who went to bomb protests was worse than tucking up with a tart in Mount Street.'

'Did he do that?' His nose was twitching and Grace Fanner thought how eager the little cleric was for gossip. No doubt that was why he came to visit her; though her gossip was mainly about a vanished society and persons long dead.

'Did he do what?' She was tired and testy.

'"Tuck up" . . . with whoever you said?'

'Oh, no. So far as I can tell he didn't tuck up with anyone. Leslie Titmuss wouldn't have the gumption. On his way up from being the spottiest and commonest little boy in the village to Minister of Something Incredibly Boring he thought it might help his career to marry my daughter. Well, Charlie put him right about that. We've got to give her the credit. Bloody near scuppered his miserable career, my Charlie did.'

She smiled proudly and then fell silent for so long that the Reverend Kevin thought she had gone to sleep or died. Her eyes were closed but her brain was whirling. She was thinking, not of Leslie Titmuss, her son-in-law, or of Charlotte, her dead daughter, but of their son, Nicholas, who once used to visit her, riding over on his bike and listening, while she fed him cocktail biscuits and let him take sips of her champagne, to her long, involved stories about the South of France and the old days at the Café de Paris. She would ask Nick, 'Do you know who I mean by Nancy Cunard?', at which the schoolboy would smile tolerantly and nibble at a Twiglet. Sometimes, in the long winter afternoons, she would show him her photograph albums or the old Molyneux dresses she kept hanging like tattered banners in her wardrobe. All that had ended when the toad Titmuss, dressed for Westminster, with his hair slicked down like a counter-jumper, had burst in and accused her of being drunk and of corrupting his boy with stories of useless people whom she had probably never known anyway. Titmuss's driver had packed Nick's bike into the boot of the government Rover and the boy, silent and tolerant of all adult outbursts, had been driven away, never to visit his grandmother again at Rapstone Manor.

'If he thinks I'm going to leave this house to young Nick so *he* can plonk himself in it,' she suddenly called out, 'the toad Titmuss has got another think coming.' She opened her eyes to see Kevin Bulstrode creeping, as though from the bedroom of a fractious child he hoped was now safely asleep, towards the door. 'And where do you think you're going?'

'You will excuse me.' The Rector was stopped in mid-flight. 'One has certain duties.'

'Oh no, one hasn't. Not until Sunday and they're not exactly full-time then, are they? One sits down and one tries to think of something nice to say about me at my funeral.'

He obeyed her. In fact he had spent many unprofitable hours thinking of any kindly words that could be used at Lady Fanner's obsequies without inducing cynical and incredulous smiles on the faces of the attendant mourners. 'Positive', 'always knew her mind', 'a genuine character', 'one of the Old Brigade': these were about as far as he had got. 'Never one to suffer fools gladly'. He reflected that on his duty-visits he always seemed to be cast as the fool who wasn't suffered gladly.

'The Titmuss family shan't have a brick of Rapstone Manor. Not a stick of furniture. Not a lavatory-paper holder, if I have anything to do with it.'

'Lady Fanner. Isn't that a matter for your lawyer?'

'Jackson Cantellow! That idiot who spends his time bawling out the Hallelujah Chorus with the Worsfield Choral Society. Of course not. It's a matter entirely for me. You know what I'll do?' Her smile was suddenly girlish, set in a pale, skull-like face that had once been beautiful. 'I'll leave the whole shooting-match to the anti-bomb brigade. That should teach Titmuss!'

CHAPTER THREE

The town of Hartscombe lay about five miles to the south of the
Rapstone Valley. In the days when Grace Fanner was about to
dispose finally of her property it had changed from the town it
was when she was carried over the threshold of Rapstone
Manor by her stumbling husband. This ceremonial was insisted
upon by Grace, mainly for the purpose of impressing those of
her former lovers who were present. It had also changed since
the days when the Right Honourable Leslie Titmuss had been a
silent and deeply mistrusted boy at Hartscombe Grammar. It
was then a small and sleepy riverside town. Streets of brick and
flint houses, some half-timbered, a few square and Georgian
with surprisingly large gardens, led down to the river where
swans hissed at the children who threw bread to them, and punts
and skiffs for hire were moored under the bridge. There were
grocers' shops where hams hung from the ceiling, a draper's
where the change travelled on an elaborate system of overhead
railway, the Copper Kettle Tea-Room – a popular place of resort
after visiting Boots Lending Library – and a cinema, built in the
thirties, where the patrons were entertained by a magnificent
organ which rose from the floor in a haze of purple light and
played a selection of golden oldies. Double seats were available
in the back rows for couples who wished to show extra friendli-
ness. Hartscombe's pride and main source of employment, however, was the building where Simcox ales had been brewed for
generations. Its brick had worn to a dusty pink and dray horses

used to stamp and jangle their brass on frosty mornings outside the yard gates. The cinema had now been torn down to make way for a pedestrian precinct through which the wind howled, blowing the cardboard remains of Chinese take-aways against the concrete plant-tubs. In it the shops sold life insurance, shoes, electrical appliances and such essential objects as scented and upholstered coat-hangers or His and Her embroidered knicker-bags. A thriving business undertook to supply jacuzzis and gold-tapped bidets to converted barns and former labourers' cottages. There was a health-food bar and a herbal cosmetic boutique. There was not a butcher, an ironmonger or a fish shop. Behind this disappointing market-place, an almost exact replica of those implanted into the hearts of hundreds of once-healthy towns in Southern England, towered a huge supermarket and a concrete multi-storey car park, to enter and leave which required an advanced knowledge of computer technology. The brewery building had been sold and converted into flats for upwardly mobile executives and money managers who commuted on the motorways to London, a city which, when Leslie Titmuss was a boy, many Hartscombe inhabitants had never visited. Simcox ales were now brewed in a new factory in the industrial zone and their Fortissimo lager was held to be responsible for the youthful violence that brought some sort of life to the shopping precinct on Saturday nights.

It was into this new Hartscombe, which had been dragged, without too many screams of protest, into the age of prosperity, that the Right Honourable Leslie Titmuss was driven a week or two after his former mother-in-law had told Kev the Rev. what she thought of her former son-in-law. He felt, he could never help feeling, like a king returning to his own small kingdom. Had he not, a despised and laughed-at boy, who earned his scant pocket-money cutting down nettles and doing odd jobs in the Rapstone Rectory garden, fought his way up and over the Hooray Henrys, bank managers and country gents in his local party to become the M.P. for Hartscombe and Worsfield South, which seat he had held by an impregnable majority for twenty-five years? Was he not the candidate who had first preached the gospel, learnt he used to say from his father, a clerk in the Brewery, of respect for thrift, a constant appreciation of the mystical power of money and a deep suspicion of those who wished to hand it out to the undeserving poor? Armed with this simple creed, which had since become the accepted doctrine of his party, Leslie Titmuss had helped to change the face of England. After years of toil he had cut the ribbon that threw open the shopping precinct and had given planning permission for the new trading estate. And if the old-fashioned landlords in his local party complained that the new motorway cut across their fields, or that lorries on the way to the trading estate blocked the lanes and frightened the laying birds, so much the worse for them. They had been, some of them, those whooping little snobs who had pushed him into the river for wearing a hired dinner-jacket, redolent of mothballs, at his first Young Conservative dinner dance in the Swan's Nest Hotel.

He walked by the river, having sent his driver to cope with the mysteries of the car park. Hartscombe Bridge was as yet unaltered, although another four-lane span would soon have to be built to accommodate the increase in traffic. The big pink and white, gabled Edwardian riverside villas still looked raffish – places where long-forgotten actresses and retired army officers had once lived in decorous sin; their windows still stared out at the island, flooded each year, with its bungalows and tangled gardens. The footpath, after the boat-houses, still led past flat meadows where cows stumbled down to the water. It was part of the scene of Leslie Titmuss's youth but as he walked he didn't think of standing barefoot in the squelching mud among the rushes or trying to catch tiddlers in a jam-jar. His childhood was a prison from which he had long escaped. Once over the wall he had wanted to put as much distance as possible between himself and that place of confinement. Although he made much of his father's values for political purposes, the memory of the old man's life filled him with horror. The complacent acceptance of a job with no prospects, the self-satisfied assurance that the good things in life were not for the likes of him or of young Leslie, the nightly routine of polishing off his tea, telling his wife that it was 'very tasty' and falling asleep in the armchair – this was the expected fate the young Titmuss had escaped by courtesy of a head for accountancy and the voters of Hartscombe and Worsfield South.

So he walked, a man now in his fifties, with a long, dark overcoat flapping round his knees in spite of the spring sunshine. He strode energetically, with no particular pleasure, as though always late for a vital meeting. His hair had receded, leaving an expanse of bony forehead; he was pale with a pallor inflicted by overwork. He rarely smiled, although he was known to make unexpected, often wounding remarks which were thought to be jokes. Although he walked rapidly, his pale eyes missed nothing of the riverside scene. The area, he saw, was ripe for development. There would have to be some pretty radical changes made if Hartscombe were to meet the challenge of Europe. In Leslie Titmuss's world nothing was allowed to stand still for very long. Having made that decision without difficulty, he rang at the door of one of the older riverside houses which bore the brass plate of Cantellow & Bagley, Solicitors and Commissioners for Oaths.

'I am afraid Lady Fanner is not well, not at all well. You will be dropping in to see her, I suppose?'

'You suppose wrong,' Leslie answered.

Jackson Cantellow was a man who had conducted a long love-affair with his own voice. So delighted was he with its rich and rumbling tones that his account of his client's ill-health came out as a recitative. 'Skin and bone,' he intoned with apparent enjoyment. 'Skin and bone, I'm afraid. And that's the best that can be said of her condition. I'm told she eats nothing.'

'But makes up for it by drinking?'

'Her bills for champagne at the Simcox off-licence. Pheenominal!' Cantellow hit a low note and then pursed his lips and put a finger to them. 'Tales out of school.' He seemed tempted to slap his own wrist.

'I expect you will tell me what I need to know.' The politician did not stoop to remind Jackson Cantellow how many of his clients were gambling on getting planning permission for various expensive projects, still less to hint at how many of such applications might be looked on favourably by his department.

'Lady Fanner, I'm told, eats nothing.' Jackson Cantellow's conversation proceeded by constant repetition, like an oratorio.

'What's that mean?'

'It means that I wouldn't expect her to last until . . .' He rolled his eyes to the ceiling. 'Until September.'

'September's a long time ahead.'

'Well' – the solicitor had chosen the month more for the resonance of its syllables than for any medical reason – 'she may go, of course, at any moment, but she always had this extraordinary energy.'

'For destruction?'

'As one of the family you knew her, of course, as well as anyone.'

'I'm not one of the family. I never felt one of the family. I suppose my son is, though. What's going to happen to the house?'

'The house?' Cantellow did his best to look innocent, as though he had never heard of Rapstone Manor.

'It's about all she has left. I suppose she's made a will of some sort?'

'I'm sure you wouldn't expect me' – Cantellow looked down modestly, as though he had been propositioned – 'to divulge the contents of any testamentary document of a client who, in spite of being a shadow, a shadow is how I would describe it, of what she was, after all a great beauty, rather before your time, of course, is still, to all intents and purposes, alive, so they tell me. The Rector visits regularly, although I believe he finds the task painful and sometimes humiliating. You wouldn't expect me to divulge anything further, would you?'

Leslie Titmuss didn't answer but kept his eyes fixed on Cantellow in the pale stare which he used to send his permanent staff out of the room in terror.

'Of course you would assume she had made wills. Various wills. In fact in her later years will-making has come upon her as a sort of disease.' Cantellow looked at his visitor. Surely he had now said enough, more than he should have, to satisfy his curiosity? But Leslie still stared at him and said nothing.

'Some of the wills were notably eccentric. Perverse, I might say. Particularly the last. Let us devoutly hope it will be the last.' Jackson Cantellow felt he had to fill in the silence and immediately regretted it.

'Now you've told me she hasn't left the house to my son, Nick.'

'I didn't say that!' Cantellow retreated in a panic. 'You mustn't put words into my mouth. I didn't say *what* she had done. The question, at any rate, is purely academic. It's really quite pointless to speculate. It's always a pleasure to see such a distinguished member of the Cabinet in the constituency, Mr Titmuss. But now if you'll excuse me . . .' He looked, in vain, for some important papers on his desk.

'Did you say *academic*?' Leslie pounced on the word and worried it as a terrier might worry a rat. 'Why did you say academic?'

'Well, shall we say not of enormous *practical* importance, in the circumstances.' Cantellow now knew he had said too much.

'The circumstances being, I suppose, that the whole caboodle is in hock to the bank. She's drunk away the equity and they'll foreclose as soon as her Ladyship is boxed up.'

'I didn't say that.' Cantellow looked pained at the idea that he could possibly have used words so brutal.

'You never could hold your tongue.' Leslie stood up now that the meeting was over. 'You've told me exactly what I needed to know. I'll find my own way out, Cantellow. All I can say is, thank God you're not my lawyer. I might as well conduct my private business on the "News at Ten".'

After his visit to the lawyer's office Leslie Titmuss was driven out of the reconstituted Hartscombe and deeper into his past. The car turned towards the Rapstone Valley. It passed the gates of the Manor but didn't stop. The next village was Skurfield, an untidy collection of houses strung out along the road, a grey place of corrugated-iron sheds, chickens roosting in the wreckage of old motor cars, pebble-dash walls and bungalows built with concrete blocks. Isolated from its neighbours stood 'The Spruces', a small, detached house with a scrubbed appearance, its privet hedge neatly trimmed and white paint shining against its red brick walls. Although there was no plaque to record the event, this was the house where, bellowing his lungs out in the upstairs bedroom, the Right Honourable Leslie Titmuss had first seen the light of day. It was the home of his mother Elsie, now over eighty, who spent her days dusting and polishing the labour-saving devices her son sent her and which she never used. She had resisted all his attempts to move her into larger and more luxurious accommodation.

'This place was good enough for your father,' Elsie said as she poured tea for her son, 'and it's good enough for me to end up in. Shouldn't I take a cup to the poor man outside?' She looked out pityingly towards the driver of the waiting Rover.

'He's used to waiting. I wanted to talk about something.'

'If you'd told me you were coming, I could've done you a steak and kidney. I know how you love your steak and kidney.' Elsie Titmuss had been in service as a cook with the Stroves of Picton Principal. Her pies had been the delight of the neighbourhood shoots.

'Old mother Fanner, it seems, is on her way out at last.'

'You never had no time for her, did you, Leslie? May God forgive her.'

'God can do what he likes. I see absolutely no reason to forgive her. Ever. But if we manage to get hold of her house for Nicky . . .'

'Rapstone Manor? Whatever would young Nick do with that?'

'I don't know. Live in it, I suppose. Eventually. Anyway, that family owes my son something. I suppose you'd agree with that?'

'His mother should never have gone out with those bomb women. Not when she had a child to think of.' Elsie lifted the teapot, snug in its knitted cosy, and refilled her son's cup. They sat in silence for a moment, in comfortable agreement on the subject of the wickedness of Mrs Charlotte Titmuss, now long dead.

'Anyway, when Nicky gets it . . .'

'You seem quite sure of that.'

'Oh, yes. Absolutely sure. Well, there's rooms there. Floors of them. We could make a nice little conversion for you, Mother. There'd be a place for someone living-in, to look after you.'

'Living-in!' She spoke with contempt. 'I've done enough living-in not to want anyone else doing it for me. Livers-in take advantage. I know that. I've taken advantage in my time.' The memory clearly caused Elsie Titmuss satisfaction.

'We could make it very comfortable for you. Living in the Manor. Isn't that what you'd like?'

'Leslie Titmuss!' In her days as a cook, Elsie had been greatly desired by all the male inside- and outside-workers and, it was said, by members of the Strove family also. When she looked at her son she was a still pretty and flirtatious octogenarian. 'I'm not going to have it. Not from her Ladyship or from you or anyone. And I'm not leaving this house, not till I join your father in Rapstone churchyard. Don't move me out of here. Will you promise me?'

Leslie wasn't smiling but he thought, at the time, that he meant it when he said, 'I promise you, Mother.'

So the immediate future of the big house at Rapstone remained unsettled, which was what gave Leslie Titmuss his great opportunity, and also what brought him more trouble than he had had since the days when he first entered politics and was pushed unceremoniously into the river during his first Young Conservative dinner dance.

'Fallowfield Country Town. A proposed development of ten thousand houses. It will entail a new commuter high-speed rail-link and the construction of a spur to the motorway. Architect-designed town centre, with civic buildings, sports and leisure complex. Multi-storey shopping facilities with extensive car parking. Pedestrian walkways and traffic-free zones. Site: between the towns of Worsfield and Hartscombe, making use of hitherto undeveloped areas such as the village of Skurfield and the Rapstone Valley' – Ken Cracken was laughing as he read out these specifications in his room at H.E.A.P.

At a desk in the corner Joyce Timberlake, his political adviser, wearing a neat black suit and glasses, was evolving a scheme, to be discussed with her opposite number at the Home Office, for the sale of specified National Trust houses for use as privatized youth custody centres.

'What's so funny about that?'

'The Rapstone Valley. It's the Secretary of State's back garden. That's what's so funny.'

'His back garden? Leslie sold his place in the country, didn't he? Doesn't he have a flat in Waterside Mansions?' Joyce made it her business to know most things. Leslie Titmuss had disposed of the big house he had bought at Picton Principal, where his mother had once cooked, shortly after Charlotte's death. To have had a wife suspected of being an anti-bomb Worsfield Heath woman, coupled with farming interests, would have been, he felt sure, too much for his political career. So he had managed, with some skill and much expedition, to disown them both.

'He's still involved in Rapstone. His mother's house is in the next village. And his old mother-in-law lives there. I wonder how they'd like to wake up next to Tesco's in Fallowfield Country Town. It might be interesting to hand our Leslie a political hot potato. See where he drops it.'

'You want to be a bit careful of Leslie,' Joyce warned him. 'He's used to winning.'

'Oh, he won't know who handed it to him. It'll come as a planning decision. Through all the normal channels. Anyway, there's another excellent reason for laying down a bit of concrete on the Rapstone Valley.'

'What?'

'It's where that bearded lunatic made us get up off the grass.'

'You mean,' Joyce asked, although this was the sort of matter they hardly ever discussed at work, 'when you were hot to trot?'

'Yes.' Ken Cracken wasn't smiling. 'That's what I mean exactly.'

CHAPTER FOUR

'So you're a widow?'

'Well, not really.'

It was a word Jenny Sidonia never used, not under any
circumstances. The fact that Tony Sidonia with his sad, dark
eyes – the eyes, his ex-girlfriend Sue Bramble had once said, of a
lemur after a passionate weekend – his untidy greying hair and
his untidier tweed suits and unbuttoned collars, his exhaustive
knowledge of the Renaissance Popes, his long, anxious face and
his rare smile, eagerly awaited, had left her never to return was
something which, like most unpleasant facts, she chose to ignore.
She didn't forget it; she hid it away in some remote cupboard of
her mind, like an unwelcome Christmas present, and couldn't
always remember exactly where she'd put it. Tony was with her
because she thought about him constantly and she never thought
about him as dead. Above all she'd never seen herself as a
widow. A widow was a ridiculous figure, dumpy, dressed in
black, sexually frustrated and on the look-out for another man.
'The Merry Widow' – that was something she would have hated
to be.

'Not really what?'

'Not really a widow.'

Her neighbour was pale and stared at her with colourless eyes.
He had been asking her questions with great intensity but he
didn't seem to be interested in her as a woman. She was used to
men looking at her hopefully as they went through their old

routines or pretended to be fascinated by her in order to excite some sort of interest in themselves. The strange man on her left asked, 'What sort of an answer is that?'

'I'm sorry.' It was something that Jenny said a lot, smiling, although she didn't feel any need to apologize.

'I mean about your husband. Is he dead or isn't he?'

It was, she supposed, a fair question. Tony had given her so much and most of all a sense of fairness. He had brought her standards of truthfulness and decency. Now that the question was put to her so bluntly she had, in all honesty, to answer it.

'He's dead,' she admitted and was struck again, as she was whenever she allowed herself to be, by the bleakness of her situation. 'I suppose you could say that.'

'Well' – the man beside her attacked his food, satisfied – 'now we know.'

On the other side of the table the Master of St Joseph's, in whose lodgings the carefully calculated lunch-party was taking place, looked at the couple with glee. It had been a brilliant idea to sit the Secretary of State next to Jenny Sidonia. She had, above all things, a talent for making men feel that they had her entire attention, even though her thoughts were far away in some private and distant country of her own. Although fragile, she always managed to look healthy, her eyes shining, and she appeared to be continually amused, even when her thoughts were sad. Sir Willoughby Blane wasn't above squeezing the knees of many of the ladies he sat beside at lunch and he sometimes received unexpected encouragement; but he had never dared lay a straying hand on Jenny. Her good looks were awe-inspiring, even to a marine biologist who had made a lifetime's study of the prawn and who regarded human beings as only a little more developed than the minor crustacea. Jenny had been invited to that sunny Sunday lunch-table not to be flirted with by the Master but to charm the Secretary of State and later, when they were strolling round the great mulberry tree, the Master might do a little trade with the Right Honourable Leslie

Titmuss on the matter of government support for an addition to the college, to be christened – whatever else? – the Willoughby Blane Biology Library. Politicians like Leslie were, so Sir Willoughby felt, alien beings, creatures from outer space, far from the crumbling walls and the soggy lawns of Oxford. Some heads of colleges would flinch at the name of Titmuss; they would mutter despairing imprecations and hastily change the subject as though the topic were somehow obscene. Not so the Master of St Joseph's. He prided himself that he could do business with a potentate so foreign, rather as the Government boasted it could do business with the Soviet President. Whatever our differences, he was prepared to say, we're both practical sorts of chaps, aren't we? No doubt the transaction would be easier after Mr Titmuss had spent luncheon in close proximity to Jenny Sidonia.

'Why do you get asked here?' Leslie was interrogating her as though she were under suspicion; but, away from the subject of her personal tragedy, Jenny seemed to find the experience comic. 'Are you anything to do with this lot?' The people round the table – Hector and Gudrun Lessore, an ex-ambassador and his wife, a Liberal peer, someone in publishing, her Honour Judge Phyllis Durst and her silent husband, a smattering of dons and their wives – were all older than Jenny and yet, when she came to look at them, she supposed they were her friends.

'They're my friends,' she said.

'They don't look your sort.'

'What do you think my sort is, exactly?'

'A bit better than this, I should have said.'

Their fellow guests deliberately avoided looking at the Cabinet Minister, rather as people avoid staring at those disfigured or in some way maimed. Before Leslie arrived they had been denouncing his government, but now he was among them they talked about books, or the theatre, or the heads of colleges who weren't present.

'It must be terrific to be the wife of a head of college,' Judge Durst said. She was a highly perfumed lady whose flat, pink face emerged like a cutlet from an elaborate, white ruffled collar. 'You get put next to all the male heads at dinners.'

'And what if you're a male head of college?' Willoughby Blane asked her in his old aunty's posh Edinburgh accent, his bald head on one side, his hands clasped across his stomach.

'That must be terrible. You get put next to their wives!'

'Willoughby often asks me to his lunches. And Tony ... That's my husband. Of course, Tony taught here,' Jenny explained patiently to Leslie Titmuss.

'*Was* your husband.'

'What?'

'You mean Tony *was* your husband.'

'Oh, yes. Of course.' For once it seemed simpler to say it. 'When he was alive.'

Leslie nodded and for a moment they sat silent. Jenny wondered whether to turn to the ex-ambassador on her left, but he was involved with the Lady Judge and it didn't seem altogether right to abandon her pale neighbour, who looked lost. To leave him now, she suddenly felt, would be like ditching a blind man you have helped half-way across the street.

'Why're *you* here?' she asked him. 'Apart from the obvious reason.'

'What's the obvious reason?'

'Well. Willoughby's always on the look-out for someone who'll help the college.' Jenny was in no way a party to the Master's ploy; he had used her as an attractive antelope tied up to lure the tiger within range of the rifle. 'And I'm sure you have terrific influence and all that sort of thing.'

'I'm here because of my son,' Leslie Titmuss said. 'Young Nick is up. About to do his finals, in fact. And I didn't have to offer to build another wing on the place to get him in here, either.'

'I'm sure you didn't. About to do his finals? That must be exciting.'

'Finals in English? I don't think that excites me much.'

'Perhaps it excites your son.'

'He knew English before he got here. Even I know English. I don't know why he can't learn something that'll help him get on.'

'Get on where, exactly?'

'Well, to where I've got. Somewhere near it. Nothing wrong with that for an ambition, is there?'

'No. No, I'm sure not. Nothing wrong at all.' Jenny was used to men who begged her for reassurance and, if possible, praise. She gave it generously, knowing what was expected of her, so that at the end of such a lunch as this, she felt physically tired and her arms seemed to be exhausted from massaging so many egos. The man beside her clearly needed no such therapy. He was convinced that where he had got was everybody's distant, usually unattainable, goal in life.

'I told him, I can't see how reading English is going to be the slightest help to the economy. It's not going to produce jobs. It's going to do damn all for the prosperity of the country. Isn't that what these places should be for?'

'Is it?' She looked at him, smiling, feeling that she owed it to Tony Sidonia's memory to take some sort of a stand. 'I'm not *absolutely* sure about that. My husband spent his life with Renaissance Popes. I don't suppose that did much for the economy.'

'Renaissance *Popes*?' Leslie looked at her, incredulous.

'Of course, they behaved appallingly, but for some reason he felt able to forgive them. He was awfully good at forgiving people. He said you had to do a lot of that, when you took on ecclesiastical history.'

'Ecclesiastical history,' Leslie said with disgust. 'What luxury!'

'Luxury!' Jenny was suddenly angry, as she had it in her to be. The accusation was absurd and entirely unfair to Tony. The extraordinary man beside her spoke as though her husband had devoted his life to fast cars, drugs and exotic women and hadn't

spent his holidays in the Vatican Library in order to produce
Humanism or Indulgence? The Papacy 1492–1534. 'What's *not* a
luxury? Learning how to operate some sort of giant computer so
we can all have our bank balances flashed on the screen every
moment of the day and get pre-cooked Thai dinners sent round
without even having to go down to the shops? Is that how Tony
ought to have spent his life? Well, I'm sorry but I really can't
agree with that.'

'I don't expect anyone round this table would. Not until they
wake up to the world we're living in.'

'Jenny!' Sir Willoughby called to her like some disapproving
nanny who has spotted two children, invited to make friends,
about to pull each other's hair in a corner. 'Will you be at
Covent Garden on Monday?'

'I don't think so. What is it?'

'Placido. In a brand new *Ballo*. This Greek producer woman,'
the Master remembered, 'has set it all in Stalin's Kremlin.
Should be rather fun.'

'The love duet!' The Lady Judge sighed unexpectedly on the
Cabinet Minister's left. 'Don't you simply adore *Un ballo in
maschera*?'

'Never seen it,' Leslie told her. 'I'm not a great one for
dancing.'

'Dancing?' Gudrun Lessore, the ex-ambassador's wife – a
large, glacial woman Sir Hector had met when posted to Iceland
and had brought home rather to everyone's regret – was the only
one daring enough to ask.

'Yes. I know nothing about your ballet, *In Maskera*.'

'The garden!' The Master stood, as though announcing the
treat for which they'd all been longing. 'What about a small,
digestive turn around the mulberry tree? It really is looking
rather fine.'

Then, as they trooped down the narrow, dark staircase of the
lodgings and out into the sunshine, Jenny, walking beside Leslie,
took his arm. What did it matter if he couldn't tell a Verdi opera

from a ballet, even if he confused *Traviata* with *Les Sylphides*? She had seen him surrounded by faces which just, only just, concealed their owners' mockery and contempt. They had a story to tell, which would be laughed at in all the country houses and at all the high tables they visited, about the incredible Philistines in control of their government; but then government was, perhaps, always a matter for Philistines. She put her arm into his as a sign that she disapproved of their cruelty and because she imagined, wrongly as it so happened, that Leslie had been made to feel awkward and miserable by it. Her sense of fairness was outraged and she lavished the sympathy on him which her late husband had even been able to feel for the Borgia Pope. It was a moment, as they went down the dark staircase together, which was the start of all their troubles.

'You and I —' The Master now had his hand on Leslie's arm, a contact which he found, unlike the gentle touch of Jenny Sidonia, irritating and which he wished to shake off as rapidly as possible. 'We both look at education in the same way, from an entirely practical point of view.'

'Practical? I thought you specialized in shrimps?' Leslie Titmuss was nothing if not well informed.

'Crustacea. The whole range from the lobster to the woodlouse. Not forgetting the minute pelagic copepods, useful little blighters, who swim in mile-wide shoals and guide whalers to the most profitable fishing-grounds.'

'Didn't you read my Birmingham speech? We've come out in favour of the whale.'

And your concern for the larger cetaceous mammals, Sir Willoughby thought, may, I suppose, distract attention from your plans to concrete over the South of England. It is the smallest possible concession you can make to the growing, and irritating, army of greens. What he actually said was, 'There's scope for a study of labour-intensive prawn cultivation. On a strictly commercial basis, of course. Now *there*'s a valuable food source for you!' He was one of those who believed that Leslie's political supporters never entered a restaurant without ordering prawn cocktail, followed by steak 'and all the trimmings', to be topped off with a liberal helping of Black Forest gâteau. Delighted by his private gastronomic joke, he giggled in his most aunty-like way. 'Labour-intensive food production. Isn't that the name of your game? Now, all that know-how needs proper technological back-up, which is why we at St Joseph's feel that the Blane Library is going to be so enormously cost-effective. Most of the information would be computer-stored so it won't have to be an *enormous* building.'

'I saw my son this morning. We had a drink together. In the Randolph.'

'Did you? Oh, good. Now *we* know, *you* know, *I* know, that enough food can be produced to feed the ten thousand by a couple of men and a computer. Particularly in coastal waters. Farming land is just a luxury nowadays. And I'm sure you chaps have plenty of other uses for it.'

'Getting on all right, is he? Nick doesn't tell me much.' Across the low wall which bounded the Master's gardens was the wider territory open to the undergraduates. They lay together, kissing, rolling over like baby seals, pretending to read their notes, pretending it was summer, listening to their ghetto blasters. Leslie couldn't see Nick among them. Where was he? Shut up in his room doing – what exactly? He had boasted, around the corridors of power, when Nick had got into Oxford. No doubt his boy would join the Union and the Conservative Association; the political and business contacts which Leslie had made with such difficulty would come easily to his son. He expected to hear in the mutter of conversation before Cabinet meetings, 'Your Nick's invited me to come down and speak at Oxford. Suppose I'd better keep in with a new generation of Titmusses.' He had prepared speeches, apparently half angry and envious, in reality proud and even adoring, which he would make to Nicholas: 'I never had a head start like I'm giving you,

Nick. I had to fight my way up, every inch of the way. I'd've saved years of hard work if I'd've had your chances. You've got it with jam on, son, and don't you ever forget it.' But because Nick showed no sign whatever of taking advantage of his position, as he seemed to have joined nothing, made no speeches, invited no Cabinet Ministers, these carefully prepared sentences seemed inappropriate. So they had sat that morning in the hotel bar with Leslie, determined to be one of the boys, nursing a pint of bitter, and Nicholas staring, secretly smiling into a Coke, and they had shared long periods of silence.

'I may have some good news for you soon, Nicky.'

'What sort of good news?'

'Something you may be coming in for. A house.'

'A house?' Nick looked at his father, amazed, as though he were offering him something totally impractical, like an ocean-going yacht or a château on the Loire.

'It's somewhere you always liked. Somewhere you were always taking off to. On your bike.'

'I don't think I need a house.'

'Not yet awhile. But in time, of course. Well, there're not many better investments.'

'What would I do with a house? I don't know where I'm going to be. I don't know that at all.' Nick still smiled.

'You never know what you're going to need. I wanted you to know. Something's going to come your way. That's all I can say about it.'

'I don't know what this place is doing for Nick,' Leslie told the Master of St Joseph's later as they walked across the garden. 'Hardly what I expected.'

'I've made inquiries about him, of course.'

'I hope you've found out more than I have.'

'He's a hard worker. I do hear that about him. And well liked. Everyone seems to agree about that. Young Fanner is very well liked.'

'Fanner?' The Minister stood still beside the great mulberry tree. The laughter and the thumpings from the ghetto blasters and the subdued gossip of the other guests walking behind him died away. He seemed to be listening to other voices, coming at him from the past. 'Why the hell do you call him Fanner?'

'Stupid of me.' Sir Willoughby smiled. 'I'm sure some of his friends call him that. I must have heard it somewhere. Is that not part of his name? Not double-barrelled, is it?'

'It certainly isn't.' The Minister's tone was icy, and help for the Blane Biology Library faded into the distance. 'There's absolutely nothing double-barrelled about my Nick.'

CHAPTER FIVE

'I'm bored with dying. Let's have a cocktail party,' Lady Fanner said. 'For God's sake, let's organize a cocker!'

The Reverend Kevin Bulstrode had flirted, during his first curacy, with the idea of joining a mission to Central Africa. He had felt a calling to care for the sick, educate the children, comfort the persecuted in some distant land, but fear of being hacked to pieces by machetes on a hot, African night had deterred him. He had set his eyes on a less adventurous path and become the Rector of Rapstone. Now, as he sat by Grace Fanner's bed trying to decipher the spidery numbers in her ancient address book and dial them for her, his thoughts turned with longing to any dangerous spot on the Zimbabwe border. The fragile but alarming old woman demanded his full attention. She telephoned the Rectory day and night to call him to her bedside. He had a terrible fear that, unless he obeyed her, she might contrive to leave her bed in a final burst of manic energy and appear, her nightdress fluttering against her skeletal body, in church to interrupt the service. Visiting the dying was no doubt a pastoral duty, but he hadn't taken orders to become the unpaid secretary, champagne pourer and telephone operator to an old woman whose accounts of high life in the thirties, at one time entertaining, had been so often repeated that he now knew them all by heart.

'Betsy von Trump. Isn't she there? It's Kensington some-where.'

'It's ringing. There's no answer.'

'Probably tucking up with some lover-boy. Who's next?'

'Jack Annersley-Vachell.'

'Well, he can't be dead. Not Jack. That wouldn't be his line at all. Telephone up, why don't you?'

Kevin's finger got to work again. The instrument whined. Jack Annersley-Vachell, whoever he might have been, was no longer obtainable.

'What do I say to these people, if I get hold of them?'

'Tell them to come down for a cocker, of course. If they don't get their skates on I'll be gone, and most likely the house'll be gone with me. Tell them that. If I know Jack, he'll go anywhere for a glass of Bollinger and a couple of cheese straws.'

Grace Fanner was right about one thing. Rapstone Manor was going with her. Centuries ago, at the time of the Civil War, when the Cavalier Fanners fought the Roundhead Stroves of Picton Principal, their lands stretched far from the valley and down to the riverside near Hartscombe. A Fanner cousin, a man with a head for politics, had joined the Parliament army as a wise insurance against the King's defeat, which had therefore brought no loss of family acres. At the Restoration a number of Strove farms were added by a grateful monarch and the eighteenth-century Fanners could ride for almost a day without leaving their boundaries. Gambling during the Regency, and a vague lack of interest in money in later years, had considerably reduced the family's estate and by the time Grace's husband had died it was owned by farmers who had once been Fanner tenants. Only that sacred area of wood and chalk downs, bought by S.C.R.A.P. as a place of safety for the stone curlew and the Duke of Burgundy's fritillary butterfly, remained unavailable for commercial exploitation.

But still, as Grace planned her final party, the cultivated land and pastures around her looked much as they had done in her husband's, and his father's and grandfather's day. Only the garish yellow fields of oil-seed rape were different and the old farm-labourers' cottages, converted with open-plan kitchens and extensions containing granny flats and saunas, had been sold off to bankers and men in satellite television. And they, appearing at weekends in their waxed jackets, driving their Range Rovers, were loudly eager to maintain the rustic appearance of their neighbourhood.

Market forces, however, were sweeping up the Rapstone Valley and secret plans were being made to change it as it had not been changed since the Fanners, with a commercial sense not much apparent in their subsequent history, had fought on both sides in the Civil War. The scattered farms had, without anyone paying too much attention, amalgamated and formed a consortium. They had approached Kempenflatts, the builders, a firm which had done well erecting multi-storey car parks, communications systems factories and office blocks. Kempenflatts had long wished to attract new business, change their image and 'go into the countryside'. Accordingly they formed a wholly owned subsidiary, Fallowfield Enterprises Ltd. Fallowfield was prominent on the list of subscribers to all societies out to protect the environment and contributed largely to Friends of the Planet, Friends of the Maypole (The Folk Art Preservation Society), Friends of the Rain Forests and Friends of the Leopard. It extended the hand of friendship to the farmers of the Rapstone Valley and paid them a handsome sum for an option to buy their land in the event of planning permission being granted for the building of Fallowfield Country Town. If all went well and the scheme were finally to be approved by the Secretary of State, the farmers would make half a million pounds an acre, a sum unattainable by slaving over oil-seed rape or battery hens.

These seismic movements in the countryside had not yet touched Rapstone Manor, and its small area of surrounding parkland, as Lady Fanner planned her cocktail party and Kev the Rev. made telephone calls to people, most of whom seemed to be either dead or in hiding. When he had, at long last, managed to escape from her bedside and the nurse, whose services added so considerably to Lady Fanner's overdraft, was downstairs making tea, the invalid, stimulated by champagne and telephone calls, suddenly jerked herself out of bed. The sitting-room! It was a long time since she had seen it but was it, could she be sure it was, in a fit state for a cocker? Was it warm, was it comfortable, were the cushions plumped on the sofa and was the chandelier sparkling? It must be as it was when they had their first parties, before the war ended and everything got so dull. She had to make sure. Her small, white feet, dangling from the bedside, searched in panic for her slippers. Then, with her lips pursed and her hands held out in front of her as though the room were dark, she made the long journey to the door, which seemed enormously heavy as she tugged it open.

Heaven alone knew how she got down the stairs. She was like a marionette operated by a drunken puppeteer. She floated, she stumbled, she almost fell in a pile of dislocated limbs. By an extraordinary effort she crossed the marble hallway and pushed open the sitting-room door. She switched on a light and what she saw caused her to cry out and bite her knuckles.

There was no chandelier, dim or sparkling; a dusty bulb dangled from a wire in the middle of the ceiling. Everything of value had gone, including the Georgian bookcases, the console tables, the Chesterfield, the claw-footed wing-chair in which Sir Nicholas had sat after dinner and infuriated her by falling asleep. What remained, mostly wickerwork covered in chipped white paint, she seemed to remember from the conservatory or the garden. What she didn't remember were the bedside conversations with Jackson Cantellow during which he had given her the news, which she had done her best not to hear, that a great deal of furniture had to be sent to auction to satisfy the ever more anxious demands of the caring West Country Bank.

She stood, swaying, wide-eyed and dismayed, until she saw, on a table which had lived somewhere quite different (the scullery, the potting-shed?), her old wind-up gramophone. It was among a clutter of unsaleable objects, broken lamps, cracked decanters and family photographs. She had used it often, particularly to play her favourite record made by Pinky Pinkerton, her immaculate spade from the Café de Paris, who had sat at a white piano and added, in his black treacly voice, a special verse for her in 'You're the Top!'. She made for this beloved object and clung to it. In her head she sang, in a high, girlish voice, her own particular words:

> You're the top!
> You can trump the A–ace.
> You're the top!
> You're the Lady Gra–ace . . .

but no sound came from her. She managed half a turn of the handle and then fell, as though the wires which held her up had been dropped at last.

When Grace Fanner died, her few friends and numerous relatives felt that some invaluable subject of gossip and entertainment had been removed from their lives. Her funeral was well attended and the Reverend Kevin Bulstrode conducted the service with considerable relief. He made use of all his long-prepared phrases and said that she was 'a genuine character', 'one of the Old Brigade' and 'never one to suffer fools gladly'.

She was buried in Rapstone churchyard and whether her grave would look over damp fields and dripping woodlands, or at the bleak prospect of a multi-storey car park and another pedestrian shopping precinct, was a matter which the Right Honourable Leslie Titmuss, as the Secretary of State for Housing, Ecological Affairs and Planning, would eventually have to decide. Lady Fanner's future was in the hands of H.E.A.P.

CHAPTER SIX

'Some people. People with plenty of money who can enjoy the privileges of living in the "green field areas" will talk a lot about not disturbing the peace and tranquillity of the English countryside. Strangely enough these are often the same whingers and belly-achers who criticize the Government for not providing enough houses, who accuse us of lack of compassion, or of not being "fair". Well, if they're so keen on fairness, why don't they want to share their little corner of England with ordinary folk who have worked and saved enough to buy a decent, newly built house of their own in these privileged areas? [Applause.] "Oh, no," say the green welly brigade of the Countryside Clubs and the Rural Preservation Societies, "we want the government to be fair, but please, not in our back garden!" [Laughter and applause.] My old father had a word for their sort. Dogs, he would have called them, in the manger. [Prolonged applause.]

'I would say to them, I would say this. Don't come to me in your tweed hats . . . [Laughter.] . . . and lecture me. I know all about England's green and pleasant land. I was born there! [Applause.] In a little two-up and two-down where my father died and my old mother, bless her, still lives. We didn't take in *Country Life*. [Laughter.] We didn't have a herb garden or breed up pheasants for the pleasure of their ritual execution. We didn't have a woman from the village in to do the washing. My mother did that herself in the old copper.

[Applause.] I got to know about country life by cutting down nettles in the Rectory garden for sixpence a day and a glass of ginger-beer, if the Rector's wife was feeling generous. [Laughter.] My mother got to know about country life by cooking steak and kidney pie for the local big-wigs. And it's no reflection at all on this five-star eatery, ladies and gentlemen, to say that my mother could have taught them a thing or two when it comes to steak and kidney! I knew what the English countryside meant to me. It meant damned hard work and a decent home for anyone with the determination to save up for it. [Loud applause.] That's more than the rich Socialists who live in their converted farmhouses will ever understand. Here's what I would say to the Rural Preservation Society which means the Keep the Other Folk Away Society. Oh, we shall have whiners, ladies and gentlemen. We shall have whingers. We shall have petitions and we shall have protests and we may get a vote against us in the House of Lords. But a wind of change is blowing through the English countryside. And let me say this to you. While I'm at H.E.A.P. there shall be very few No Go areas for the operation of the free market economy. Thank you.' [Prolonged applause mixed with 'Hear, hear!', 'Sock it to them!' from the partially intoxicated lady wife of one of the guests, and a solitary attempt to start the singing of 'For he's a jolly good fellow', quickly silenced by the Chairman, who rose to thank the Secretary of State for his wise and genuine understanding of the problems of the construction industry.]

Leslie Titmuss sat at the top table, with a winged collar sawing at his neck like a blunt execution, and, his speech over, he thought about the past. He thought about it particularly because the Chairman of the United Construction and Developers Association (U.C.D.A.), who was making such a gracious speech of thanks, was that same Christopher Kempenflatt who had led the baying band of ex-public schoolboys who had pushed the young Leslie into the river. It was Kempenflatt also who had, many years ago, invited the young Titmuss to go into a property business with him, a venture which had left Leslie with enough money to devote the rest of his life to politics and Kempenflatt temporarily in debt. It goes without saying that neither man mentioned these past events, although no doubt they had not forgotten them.

'It was a tremendous speech,' Kempenflatt said as he sat down to renewed applause beside his guest. 'They loved every word of it. I hope you've enjoyed the evening.'

'I always enjoy a speech.' Leslie never tired of the way he could affect an audience.

'Because you're so good at it.'

'I have an uncanny knack of bringing out the baser instincts in any gathering. That's what the Leader of the so-called Opposition said about me.'

'That's not true.'

'Isn't it? I rather hoped it was,' Leslie Titmuss said seriously, and Kempenflatt paused, a lighted match in his cupped hand on the way to his cigar. Then he laughed at what he could only assume was a joke. 'Well, you certainly gave them what they wanted to hear.'

'I like it better, though, when I give them what they *don't* want to hear. And they have to take it. That's when politics begins to get interesting.'

Kempenflatt, a big, square-shouldered man, an old rowing Blue fast going to seed, tried to establish a little more common ground with the Secretary of State that he would need when Fallowfield Country Town came up for planning permission. 'I'm sorry to hear about poor old Grace.'

'Are you? Can't say I am.'

'Well, I suppose it was a merciful release.'

'About the only merciful thing she ever did.'

'I forgot. Your wife never got on with her mother.'

'Lady Fanner thought her daughter ugly and me common. I needn't tell you what we thought of her.'

'What's going to become of the house?' As soon as he had asked it, Kempenflatt regretted the question. His guest of honour looked at him, stony-faced and silent. Ken Cracken, Leslie's second-in-command, whom Kempenflatt called a 'personal friend', had advised him to say nothing about the proposals to 'develop' the Rapstone Valley until he gave the word that the time was ripe. Ripeness was clearly not yet.

'She's only just cold in the ground,' Leslie said reproachfully. 'Isn't it a little early to be talking about that?'

'Smashing speech that Leslie made at the U.C.D.A. dinner,' said Joyce Timberlake.

'Yes. The old boy was terrific. From our point of view.' Ken Cracken put his hands behind his head, leant back in his desk chair and looked at his political adviser with every sign of satisfaction.

'What's that meant to mean?'

'Just that now he's said all that, he'll find it very difficult to backtrack. Even in a difficult case.'

'What sort of difficult case?'

'I mean difficult. For him personally.'

'He doesn't know yet? About that new country town at Rapstone?'

'He hasn't said anything. And I'm not telling him. Yet. I'm worried about Leslie, though. He seems to have got culture.'

'You mean he's read a book?' Joyce, who had a degree in the History of Art from Exeter, was often contemptuous of the Secretary of State's reputation for reading nothing but Green Papers and Cabinet minutes.

'Worse than that. He asked me about the ballet.'

'Oh, Christmas!' Joyce, even as a political adviser, sometimes went too far. 'I don't fancy seeing him in tights!'

'The funny thing' – Ken Cracken didn't laugh, but then he rarely did – 'is that he asked what was so amusing about the ballet, *In Maskera*. I was able to tell him it wasn't a ballet at all.

It's an opera.' Ken's friend Christopher Kempenflatt often invited him to his firm's box at Covent Garden and so he was not altogether uninformed about such matters. 'You know, he has been behaving rather strangely.'

'Why? What did he say when you told him that? About the opera, I mean?'

'He said, "Bastards!" And that's all he said.'

'What on earth is it?'

'Well, I suppose it's a flower.'

'It looks dead.'

'It looks laid out. Embalmed.'

'In that awful little plastic coffin.'

The women speaking were Jenny Sidonia and her friend Sue Bramble. Sue had been, was perfectly well known to have been, the girlfriend of Tony before Jenny married him. They had, however, liked and trusted each other for a long time. Sue had told Jenny she was absolutely right for Tony, and Jenny had felt that the other woman, five or six years older than herself, had understood her husband whereas she could only love him. Now, in the London flat Jenny had bought when she sold the spiky, Victorian Gothic house in North Oxford in which she had been happy, they had their heads together. Sue was blonde, freckled, slightly sun-tanned – even in the most unlikely weather – went hunting and smoked like a chimney. Jenny was dark, delicately boned, ivory-skinned, amused and slightly aghast as she looked at the object which they were examining, nothing more or less than a single orchid lying on a bed of velvet in a see-through box, tied up with gold ribbon.

'It's got some sort of pin up its bum,' Sue discovered.

'Perhaps it's a corsage.' Jenny made the appalling suggestion.

'A what?'

'Well. Something you pin on. For going out to dinner. Don't some men send them to some women? Before they take them out, I mean.'

'Some men? I don't think,' Jenny's friend said with certainty, 'that Mr Sidonia would ever have sent a girl anything like that.'

'Tony wouldn't,' Jenny agreed.

'Well, who would?'

Jenny said nothing.

'Have you any idea?'

'Some idea. Yes.'

'Not that ghastly little politician?' Sue, who was not easily shocked, sounded as though she would rather have heard that her friend was considering an evening out with a bisexual Californian drug addict with sado-masochistic tendencies.

'Well, he's not so little. Quite tall, as it so happens.'

'I don't believe it.'

'Why don't you? I told you he telephoned. He said, would I like a bite of dinner?'

'Typical.'

'What?'

'"A bite of dinner". How typical of him to say that.'

'You can't say it's typical. You don't know him.'

'Aren't I lucky!'

'Probably.' Jenny looked gloomily at the orchid lying in state.

'You didn't say you'd go?'

Jenny nodded guiltily and Sue asked, '*Why*, in the name of God?'

'It was that lunch at Oxford. They were laughing at him because he didn't know about opera.'

'There must be millions of people who don't know about opera. But you don't have to go out to dinner with all of them.'

'I suppose I was sorry for him.'

'But that's the worst possible reason.'

'Yes,' Jenny admitted it, contrite.

'What on earth would Tony have said?'

'I suppose he'd've said it was a bit of a joke.'

'He'd certainly have laughed. Tony would.'

'But not to his face. Tony wouldn't have done a thing like that. It was awful really. Poor Mr Titmuss was looking round the table and he had no idea he'd said anything wrong.' Jenny was carefully removing the orchid from its box. Sue looked at her with growing incredulity. 'You're not going to pin that thing on you?'

'Well. I suppose I'd better.'

'Why on earth?'

'I don't want to seem rude.'

'You take my advice. There are times when seeming rude's the best possible thing to do.'

Later, when Jenny Sidonia was changed and ready, Sue, looking out of the window of the flat, saw a large black car draw up.

'Something's arrived.'

'He said he'd send a car for me.'

'It looks like a hearse.'

'I think it belongs to the Government.'

'That's so much worse! Oh, Jenny, what *have* you got yourself into?'

So, feeling apologetic, Jenny went off on her first and, her friend sincerely hoped, her last date with Leslie Titmuss.

CHAPTER SEVEN

Hector Bolitho Jones, warden of the Rapstone Nature Area and servant of the Society for Conservation, Rural and Arboreal Protection (S.C.R.A.P.), had not always been green. It would be true to say that he came of a shooting family. Hector's father had been a gamekeeper on the Rapstone Manor estate; he was a large, gentle Scot who occupied a cottage which had been expanded after his death. Part of it now housed the Area's audio-visual instruction material; the other half was used as living accommodation for the warden. When Hector was a boy, in the long-gone days of rabbit pie and outside lavatories, when many of the cottages were still inhabited by woodmen, gardeners and farm workers, he had followed his father about his work and at an early age he could name the wild flowers, identify the butterflies and predict the weather with astonishing accuracy. He had also assisted in the more bloodstained part of his father's profession. He took strangled rabbits from snares, he baited rat traps, he hung up on a branch, like a gallows, those magpies which the gamekeeper had shot for poaching pheasants' eggs and wanted displayed as a dire warning to other criminally minded birds. He would go out with old Jones on moonlit nights and stalk deer in the depths of the woods and, at that time, he had no objection to venison steaks or even a dish of deer's liver for his tea. He helped beat the woods when the pheasants were old enough for execution and piled up the corpses of birds shot by the Fanner family and their guests. He was a stocky and unusually silent child who shared his father's devotion to animals. The difference between them was that, while old Jones's concern was to provide the wild creatures he cared for with a dramatic and splendid death, the young Hector wished above all to preserve their lives. It was this devotion to animals which had caused him to rage at Ken Cracken and Joyce Timberlake who had, when returning from a lunch in the country with Christopher Kempenflatt, felt the urgent need to be alone on a hillside.

Hector had worked hard at school and, to his father's considerable pride, taken a degree in forestry at Worsfield University. When the Rapstone Nature Area was set up he seemed, as a local boy who had been born in these woods, an ideal candidate for warden. The public career of Hector Bolitho Jones was upwardly mobile.

His private life was not so successful. Whilst a student he had met a girl named Daphne Bridgewater at the folk club. She had come from a large family, was naturally gregarious and studied sociology. She thought that Hector, with his large, perpetually anxious eyes, was deeply concerned about a number of causes. She was also, as she would have been the first to admit, the sort that went for beards and Hector's had sprouted profusely since his first year at college. They went on several hunt sabotage expeditions together and for long walks in the country. When she suggested that they visited Rapstone Wood at bluebell time and lay down together on the misty blue carpet, however, he wouldn't hear of it. 'There's wildlife there,' he said, 'and who are we to disturb it?' At the time she liked him all the better for his caring nature.

When they were married and living in the extension to old Jones's converted cottage, and especially after their daughter, Joan (named after Joan Baez, a heroine of the folk club), had turned four and was old enough to play in the woodlands, Daphne became disenchanted with her lot as a warden's wife. The trees seemed to grow rapidly and crowded round their home, shutting out light from the kitchen windows. Hector was away from early morning until long after nightfall, in the woods or clearing scrub on the grassland. In the shadowy kitchen there was always some animal recovering: a tiny fox cub, perhaps, that had to be fed milk from a baby's bottle, or a young caged barn owl with a broken wing. Hector seemed more and more reluctant to leave the Nature Area and his passion for rain forests (everywhere felled to make way for beef cattle) ruled out a Whopperburger after the pictures at the multi-screen in Worsfield. Above all she grew weary of his conversation, which came to consist almost entirely of grim warnings of environmental doom.

'That hair-spray of yours,' he said. 'Do you want to kill off *all* our oak trees, Daphne? Can't you be made aware, dear, of the death and destruction you're causing, penetrating the ozone layer like that?'

'I don't think your oak trees are going to drop dead because of one little hair-spray.'

'That's not the point. The point is, we've got to set an example.'

'Oh, have we? We don't hardly see anybody to set an example to.'

'It's the attitude. That's what I object to. There's forests the size of Europe disappearing all the time. And what are you doing about it? Spraying your hair, that's all. Adding to the terrible toll of destruction. Sometimes I wonder, Daphne. Don't you care at all?'

'Not when I can't do much about it.' Daphne took a gulp of the homemade wine which they drank to avoid chemical additives and longed for a long, cool gulp of Fortissimo lager in the bar of the Olde Maypole in Hartscombe.

'That is exactly the type of attitude' – Hector sighed and looked up at the ceiling – 'which is going to lose us the black rhino.'

'Oh, bugger the black rhino!' Daphne's patience with her marriage was running out.

'What's that, Daphne?' Hector spoke very slowly and softly; he sounded enormously calm, a sure sign that he was nothing of the sort. 'What did I hear you say?'

'I said, bugger the black rhino. And I shan't be all that sorry to see the last of the whales, either.'

'I took you, Daphne,' Hector said, after a long and disapproving silence, 'for a genuinely caring sort of person. It seems I took you wrong.'

'Listen, Hector. There's men sleeping in cardboard boxes by the canal in Worsfield. There's old ladies with all their worldly goods in plastic bags, kipping down in the bus shelters in Parkinson Avenue. There's a couple turned out of their home for being behind with the rent as are sleeping rough in the pedestrian walkways. What use is the black rhino to them? That's what I'd like to know!'

'It doesn't have to be any *use*, Daphne. It's a form of wildlife and has rights which we have to respect. I think I'm off out now. I might get a sight of the badgers. At least they're creatures you don't catch polluting the atmosphere with hair-sprays!'

'Sod badgers!' Daphne Jones said after her husband had gone out. And then she did something which she had promised to confine to Christmas and her birthday. She lit a cigarette.

People, Hector Bolitho Jones reflected as he walked through the woods in which fallen branches were left undisturbed as a home for a variety of insects, people, no doubt about it, were what caused all the pollution in the world. People drove cars with lead-filled petrol and felled rain forests. People, unless watched incessantly, dug up orchids and primroses, they frightened the foxes, lit fires in the bracken and threw plastic bottles into the undergrowth. He emerged from under the tall beeches to the top of the downland and, looking down towards the stream, he saw two more of them, no doubt also intent on intruding on to the gentle privacy of the animals. His boots thudded through the brambles and scrub as he strode to the attack. The man wore a city suit and looked older than the small, fragile woman, elegant in black and white. They were townees, he felt sure, who once again would have no respect for the nesting birds. And as he tramped forward he began to call, hoarsely, so that his voice sounded, from a distance, like the calling of rooks.

Hector Bolitho Jones saw them turn away and stood still, triumphant, his feet planted firmly and apart on his patch of uncultivated downland. He had been too far away to recognize a local boy made good and thought that whatever polluting activity they wanted to get up to they now had to do it somewhere else.

Jenny Sidonia's first dinner with Leslie Titmuss had been an occasion of some embarrassment. They had gone to an expensive restaurant where minute quantities of monkfish and prawns, accompanied by a wisp of dill and a small puddle of pink sauce, decorated the octagonal plates. (The Secretary of State had asked his Junior Minister to recommend somewhere to eat; he now decided that it was the last time he was going to take Ken Cracken's advice on anything.) Jenny felt that the orchid, pinned to her dress, hung there like a dead weight. The conversation was equally heavy and when they had talked about the lunch in Oxford, and failed to mention the confusion about the *Ballo in maschera*, it was apparently exhausted. In the long silences Jenny wondered how soon she could ask for a taxi home, but whenever she glanced furtively at her watch the hands scarcely seemed to have moved.

'Your job,' she tried desperately, 'must be very interesting.' She hoped this trite remark would switch on an endless speech during which she could retire into her own world and close the door.

'So far to go,' he said, 'before they grow up.'

'Who grow up?'

'People.' Leslie looked morosely down at his plate. She wondered if she were to be numbered among the un-grown-ups and thought such a description of herself might well be justified.

'They expect the Government to wipe their noses, see they wear their vests in the winter. Do everything for them.'

'I don't think I expect that.'

'Of course you don't. Oh, and make sure they have a nice view of empty fields from their bedroom windows. So they can pretend there's no one else in the world except them. They're very keen on the rights of Patagonian Indians but they won't allow the right of an English builder to put up a few houses within ten miles of their view. That's what's got to change. Am I boring you?' He asked the question perfectly seriously, without a smile.

'No,' she said. 'No, of course not.' If only, she thought, I had some talent for being impolite. If only I could say, Naturally you're boring the pants off me, Mr Titmuss. For God's sake, pay the bill and let's get out of this dimly lit place where the waiters pad reverently up and serve out these plates of nothing very much as though it were some religious ritual. Please, Mr Titmuss, let me go home and make myself toast and marmalade and go to bed. Aloud she said, 'It's very interesting.'

'I don't think it interests you at all.' He managed to make her feel guilty. She resented this, even though she tried to look fascinated as she said, 'Planning and all that sort of thing. I know so little about it.'

'Don't bother. It's something we want to get rid of.'

'But perhaps' – she felt she owed him a little discussion, for politeness' sake – 'you can see their point.'

'Whose point?'

'People who live in the country. After all, that's what they went there for. Peace and solitude. You can understand that.'

He looked at her in silence and she nerved herself for the impact of another public address. Instead he said, 'Is that what you'd really like, Jenny?'

In the short time she had known him she couldn't remember his having used her name before. It was as though he had moved one step nearer her and it made her nervous.

'What?'

'Peace and solitude. Living in the country all the time.'

'Oh, yes,' she said truthfully. 'Sometime, perhaps. That's what I'd like. Tony and I were always planning to do it. When he lived by writing and didn't have to teach any more.'

Leslie Titmuss seemed to be thinking this over carefully and the silence grew to a disconcerting length until relief flooded over her as he said, 'What do you think we have to do to get a bill here? Drop dead?'

When it came she saw that he was adding it up, checking the items, even making an inquiry about a minute plate of scarcely cooked vegetables, the price of which was finally deleted by the head waiter with a pencil stroke of unutterable contempt. Tony Sidonia had never read a restaurant bill in his life; he used to go on talking, teasing her gently, making her laugh as he dropped money on to the plate with the bill on it. 'Waiters have got to live,' Tony used to say. 'Anyway, it's the duty of people who can afford restaurants to be cheated a little.'

When the argument about the bill was over and Leslie had left a tip of punitive size, he smiled at her and said, 'You look hungry.'

'Well, yes. As a matter of fact, starving.' She was angry about the fuss over the bill, irritated by the restaurant, annoyed with herself for having been weak-minded enough to accept this bizarre invitation. She thought that by being uncharacteristically rude she might nip what looked like becoming a most unsuitable acquaintance in the bud.

'Good. Then we ought to go on somewhere.' He seemed delighted by what she had said. 'It won't take long.'

'I really need an early night.' It was true. The strain of dinner with Leslie Titmuss had exhausted her.

'I told you. It won't take long at all. The car's outside.'

Sitting behind his driver, she cursed her own fatal tendency to agree. What did 'going somewhere' mean? A terrible club, perhaps, with hostesses and a cigarette girl in fishnet tights where he'd buy sweet champagne and go on talking about town and country planning until her eyes closed and her limbs ached with tiredness. He couldn't think for a moment that she'd go back to his flat with him, somewhere, he'd told her, extremely convenient on the Embankment, with a porter who'd smile knowingly as they got into the lift. It was true that he had made no move towards her, leaving as much space as possible between them in the back of the car, but could that be because he was sure his opportunity would come later? Was he arrogant enough to think that? Was he not arrogant enough to think anything? Well, if he imagined she'd put one foot into the entrance hall of Waterside Mansions, or whatever it was called, he was suffering the strangest of illusions. However much ruder would she have to be, she wondered with some dread, before she was shot of him forever? Then she saw that they were not at the entrance of any mansion flats, but surrounded by the bright lights of a street running into Leicester Square. She hadn't heard his muttered instructions to the driver and now the car stopped.

'Wherever . . .?'

'At least we'll be sure of a decent helping!'

It wasn't dark, like the unmentionable club she had imagined, but brilliantly lit, decorated with bright pink plaster pillars and murals of scenes on the Costa Brava, which made her eyeballs ache. Piped music and the fairground smell of frying oil pervaded the place. They sat at a table with a fully loaded ashtray and Leslie asked her, 'What would you say to a couple of eggs and a large go of chips? We might as well live dangerously.'

'I think it'd be wonderful,' she said.

'It was the worst thing he could do.' Sue Bramble looked horrified when Jenny described the evening to her. 'It made you like him.'

'Well, it did almost. It was so sensible.'

'Jenny! How could you have done it?'

'Easily. You know it doesn't matter what I eat. I mean, I don't get fat or anything.' This fact, Jenny knew, was one that Sue, who often dined on white wine and cigarettes, found intensely irritating, but then she was beginning to get tired of her friend's grim warnings about the disaster of Mr Titmuss.

'What on earth did you talk about?'

'Well, nothing very much. We didn't stay that long.'

In fact they had talked about his dead wife.

'Charlotte used to like this sort of thing,' he said. 'Fish and chips, eggs and sausage; all with plenty of sauce. She'd've eaten sauce sandwiches if I'd let her. She thought that was "terribly working class". She was very keen on anything working class, was Charlotte. Coming from where I did, I couldn't see the attraction.'

'Where did *she* come from?'

'Oh, the decaying gentry. She was the girl from the local manor house. The sort that's desperately in love with their ponies until they discover some lad who works round the stable and likes sauce sandwiches.'

'So that was you?'

'Not me. I suppose I was the next best thing. By the way, you can take that flower off if it's worrying you.'

Jenny unpinned the orchid and put it down between the sauce and the mustard where it stayed after they had left, forgotten. 'You're not married to her now?' Asking about himself, she knew, only involved her further; but she was curious and wanted to know.

'Oh, no.' He looked solemn. 'Charlotte passed away.'

In his family, she thought, everyone 'passed away', the most terrible illness was 'feeling poorly' and death itself was 'a merciful release'. She watched as he dipped a long, golden chip into the yoke of his egg and thought how near we all are to childhood.

'I'm sorry.'

'I thought you'd understand. That's why I told you.'

'Because I'd go for people who like lots of tomato ketchup? I have to say, Tony couldn't stand it.'

'No. Because he's dead too.'

She stared at the wall, at a garish señorita with a carnation between her teeth, dancing some sort of clumsy fandango against an electric blue sea. They were the words, it seemed, that her new acquaintance always wanted to make her say.

'Yes.'

'We're alike, aren't we? Both married to people who're dead.'

Was death what they had in common? Not much, surely. The world was full of widows and widowers with absolutely no links between them. 'Does that make us alike?' she asked, giving him another opportunity to approach her.

'We're both alone.'

'Well, not quite alone. Friends count for a good deal. Don't you think?' What she said sounded to her as trite as 'he passed away', or 'it was a merciful release'.

'Friends?' he asked. 'I suppose I've never really tried them. That's why I asked you to dinner. Hope you enjoyed it?'

'I enjoyed the second dinner very much.'

He paid the bill then, without any argument, and she was driven home.

'What about in the car?' Sue asked. 'Did he leap on you?'

'Nothing,' Jenny told her truthfully. 'Not even a kiss on the cheek.'

'Well, thank God for that, at least.'

'Yes,' Jenny said. 'Thank God for that.'

There was then a long silence from Leslie Titmuss. Jenny spent her days in the art gallery, having been lucky, she told herself, to find a job among beautiful things, although many of the works on the stark white walls of the room in Bruton Street were not, she had to admit, particularly beautiful. She sat behind a desk smiling at the visitors, cataloguing paintings at prices which would have bought her the longed-for house in the country, something which, as the empty days and late nights of her London life dragged on, she wanted more than ever. In the evenings she went to dinner parties and was put next to men thought to be likely partners for her, men unhappily married, divorced, or, and here her hosts always assured her that such was not the case, gay. She was usually relieved when this turned out to be the fact, and then she could talk easily, laugh at their jokes and suffer no fear of attack. The heterosexuals were more difficult. They either hinted at past successful seductions and assumed, without any encouragement, that because they had been placed next to Jenny they would spend the night with her, or they poured out their souls to her, described the way their children were being brought up to hate them, or the greed of their ex-wives and the inferiority of their ex-wives' present husbands. In neither case did they ask her anything about herself, and never mentioned the fact that her husband was dead.

'Tracked you down!' She was yawning one morning in the gallery over the proof of a new catalogue, and looked up to see Leslie, his dark suit and pale face striking an unusual note of realism among the art works. 'I rang your flat and there was a girl there. She didn't want to tell me where you worked.'

'Your Mr Titmuss,' Sue said, 'is so horribly persistent. He just wouldn't get off the phone until I spilled the beans. Can you ever forgive me?'

'Oh, yes,' Jenny said later. 'I forgive you.'

'What've we got here?' Leslie Titmuss asked, looking about him. 'Portraits of bath-towels?'

'I'm afraid it's the New Abstraction.'

'Dull, isn't it?'

'Yes,' she had to admit. 'Very dull.'

'Well. I've come to take you away from it all.' He spoke as though he were a rich Victorian squire offering to save a girl from long hours in the sweatshop. 'What would you say to a breath of country air?'

'It would be wonderful. But I can't possibly.'

'Who says you can't?'

As though summoned by the Secretary of State's peremptory questions, the proprietor entered the gallery. He looked, as always, nervously exhausted, his grey hair ruffled, his bow-tie askew and a scratch on his cheek, which was, perhaps, a war wound from the battles of his love life, which involved the constant unhappiness of at least five people. He lived in fear of women, in fear of his landlord and in the faint but constant hope that he would discover, in some villa owned by an insane old lady who had once been the artist's mistress, an unknown Modigliani which she would give him for love and make his fortune.

'Mark. This is Mr Titmuss. Mark Vanberry.'

'Not *the* Mr Titmuss?' Mark's perpetual guilt was such that his heart missed a beat whenever he saw a policeman. The sight of a Cabinet Minister caused him instant terror, which he did his best to suppress.

'*A* Mr Titmuss, anyway,' Leslie told him.

A member of the Government, Mark began to calculate, who might have some say in the funding of the arts and in the buying of pictures for countless offices. He said, 'I'm so glad you dropped in. This is a very patriotic show. We're entirely given over to the British Abstract stuff. We got an absolutely *super* notice in the *Guardian*. Does it interest you at all, Mr Titmuss?' Mark looked proudly at the monotonous canvases.

'Not in the least. We were just saying how dull they all were.'

'Dull?' Mark was pained.

'Nothing abstract about life, is there? I suppose my job might be a deal easier if people were no more complicated than bath-towels. I want to take your assistant away from you.'

'You want to take Jenny?' Mark sounded deprived.

'Only for a day in the country. Don't you think she could do with a breath of fresh air?'

'Well, yes.' Anxious to appease this overbearing and un-doubtedly influential man, Mark said, with an air of great concern, 'You do look a little peaky, Jenny.'

'She doesn't look peaky at all. She looks glorious. All the same, she'd appreciate a day in the country.'

'Perhaps we can spare her.'

'Of course you can spare her. You're not going to get much trade with these things, are you?'

'I really do have work to do.' Jenny resented having plans made for her as though she wasn't there.

'I suppose they might make room for one of the small tea-towels in the Oslo Embassy,' Leslie speculated. 'Very abstract sort of people, the Scandinavians.'

'Oh, do please go, Jenny. We can manage here easily, just for today. And it would do you good,' Mark pleaded and she fell, once more, a victim to her reckless longing to help the underdog.

When they were in the car she asked what country they were going to.

'My country,' Leslie Titmuss said.

CHAPTER EIGHT

It hadn't been a good summer, but as they turned off the motorway and took the road to Hartscombe the rain stopped, heavy gun-metal clouds were dragged away and a shaft of sunlight lit the church tower and the swollen river. When they reached the Rapstone Valley the whole sky lightened and, switching down her window, Jenny smelt the wet countryside. She saw a stream at the foot of a chalky hillside which led up to a beech wood, and asked Leslie to stop the car. They got out and walked down a path where the bracken and the white lace on the cow parsley were steaming like drying laundry.

'It's beautiful!' Jenny was looking up the hill. The wind from behind her blew a dark veil of hair across her face.

'It's where I was a kid,' Leslie Titmuss told her. 'I didn't think it was beautiful then.'

'But now?'

'I suppose so. Anyway, it's been designated under the Nature Areas Act.'

'Then it must be beautiful.' She pulled the hair away from her face and laughed at him.

'They always said there were kingfishers by that stream.'

'Truly?'

'I don't know.' The rook call grew nearer and sounded distinctly human. 'I never did have the time for bird-watching.'

'There's a man up there.' Jenny was worried. 'He seems to be shouting at us.'

'Well, for God's sake. Who does he think he is?'

'Who is he?'

'Jones! Looks after this place. Obviously they don't give him enough work to do.' And Leslie added, lacking his Junior Minister's taste for anonymity, 'Doesn't he know who he's talking to?'

'No.' Jenny put a hand on his arm. 'Don't let's have an argument. Not here.'

'We can't let him shout at us.'

'Please. Let's go.'

'All right. Anyway, I wanted to show you something.'

They drove on up the valley, between a fold in the hills and then high over fields and little woods. They turned down an avenue of decrepit lime trees, planted, it was always said, to celebrate a young Fanner's return from the Peninsular War, and through an open gateway into a long drive across a park, in which the deer were lit dramatically as the clouds blew away from above them. They came to the empty Manor with its jumble of architectural styles, its pillared portico and its stone green with age, as though it had at some point in its history emerged from under the sea.

'What's this?' Jenny asked.

'Well, a house.'

'I think I can see that.' She laughed at him.

'I just thought you might like to look it over.'

He's like an estate agent, she thought, as he took a key from his pocket and opened the heavy front door, trying to sell me something. 'Well,' she humoured him, 'I suppose it might suit me. How many bedrooms, did you say?'

'I think about ten. A lot for the servants, of course. When they had servants. Most of the rooms haven't been used for years.'

'Ten?' She was still laughing. 'It might just do me. There's a gun-room, I hope. And billiards. And a place for the butler to clean the silver.'

'Oh, yes. There's all that.' Standing in the black-and-white marble paved entrance hall, looking up the wide staircase that twisted away into the shadows, towards a domed ceiling on which falling angels had been badly painted, she felt an extraordinary peace come over her. It was all a huge, a ridiculous, joke; but for some absurd reason she would have liked to live there, quietly perhaps, in one of the rooms, causing no harm to anyone.

'This is the sitting-room, madam.' He pushed open some high double doors, playing the part in which he seemed to know she had cast him. 'Madam might be quite cosy in here.'

She went through, on the echoing boards, into what seemed to be a sort of stateroom containing nothing but a table and some old garden furniture. Through the tall windows she saw the deer again, moving in and out of the shadows.

'Will you be taking it?' he asked.

'On my wages from the gallery and the nothing much Mr Sidonia left me? Well now, why ever not?'

'Didn't your husband leave you anything very much?' Leslie Titmuss was concerning himself with an old wind-up gramophone he had discovered on the table and blowing the dust off a record.

'Tony didn't have anything to leave, except the house in Oxford. I bought my flat with that. Money bored him.'

'What a luxury, to be bored by money!' Quite unexpectedly a deep voice and a tinkling piano came to them through a fusillade of scratches.

> You're the top!
> You can trump the A—ace.
> You're the top!
> You're the Lady Gra—ace . . .

'What on earth's that?'

'My ex-mother-in-law's favourite song. She liked it because it was about her.'

'It's *her* house!' How could she have been so stupid, so intoxicated by a rare day out in the country, not to have understood at once what he was up to?

'Yes.'

'Your wife lived here.'

'Not for very long. Or very happily.'

'You used to come here with her?'

'As little as I could manage. I told you, the old lady hated me.' He switched off the gramophone, causing Pinky Pinkerton, Lady Fanner's beloved singer, to skid into silence.

'What about her father? Did he hate you too?'

'Sir Nicholas? He was a country gent. He wore an old tweed suit and gave his tenants blankets and pounds of tea at Christmas.'

'He sounds rather nice.'

'He was the sort that went out with the dinosaurs.'

'The sort of country gent?'

'The sort of Conservative. We've got rid of them all now. Swept them into the dustbin of history. Thank God.'

Jenny was surprised at herself. He had brought her here and involved her in his past life without warning and without her permission. She should have been angry. What did she have to do with his dead wife, his dead mother-in-law who hated him, the dead old man who went out well-meaningly with presents for the village? She should insist on leaving and after, well, perhaps after, lunch in Hartscombe (why was she always so inconveniently hungry?), she should make him drive her home and avoid seeing him again. Was he trying to stage a repeat of his past life with her, Jenny Sidonia, of all unlikely people? She ought to have been angry but the situation was so curious that she thought of hanging on to see what happened next.

'We're going to have a picnic in the kitchen.'

'Why?'

'You'd like that, wouldn't you?'

Unfortunately she supposed she would.

The driver brought in a cardboard box with sandwiches in plastic wrappers and tins of beer, the sort of lunch Leslie would have sent out for while he stayed working at his desk. They sat in the kitchen by a rusty cooker the size of a steam engine, installed to feed dinner parties which hadn't taken place for years, and families who had long stopped visiting. They sat under iron hooks from which hams had once been suspended, and well-populated fly-papers, beside tarnished saucepans and shelves which supported no more than a few pieces of broken china, beside the electric kettle and the two-ringed cooker which had been enough to provide Lady Fanner's light meals. Jenny ate gratefully, having decided to stop worrying for the moment – the sort of decision she came to easily.

'What I want to know is' – she chose something harmless to ask – 'are you going to get some embassy to buy one of Mark's dreadful pictures?'

'Of course.' He looked at her seriously. 'Did you think I'd deceive him?'

'I wouldn't put it past you.'

'Well, madam.' He changed the subject. 'Would you like the house?'

There was a long silence and then she said, 'Yes, I would. Very much. It's madness, of course.'

'Why is it madness?'

'How could I possibly buy it, or live here? It's quite im-practical.'

'Nothing you want's impractical. It's people who don't know what the hell they want that are the impractical ones.' So that, she thought, was the Titmuss philosophy of life and no doubt simple enough.

'All right,' she laughed at him, 'I'll buy it.'

'You can't.'

'Why not?'

'It's already sold.'

'Who to?'

'Me.'

She unwrapped another sandwich, wondering where on earth they had got to now.

'I happen to be a good friend of my ex-mother-in-law's solicitor. He told me the whole damn thing had been pawned to the bank, oh, for years before she died. So I got the bank to sell it to me. Quite quietly, of course. They tried to get some fancy price on the ground that there might be a new development round here, a bloody great new town.'

'You mean they'd build over this valley?' Jenny was dismayed. 'That'd be sacrilege.'

'It won't happen,' Leslie assured her. 'Not if I have anything to do with it.'

'So you're going to live here?'

'That depends.'

'What on?'

He stood up, brushing crumbs off his dark suit. 'Would you like to see upstairs?' he asked her.

They inspected servants' bedrooms, with crumbling ceilings and peeling wallpaper. They saw guest bedrooms and the room where Charlotte Titmuss, when a young girl, had pinned up the rosettes she won at gymkhanas and her many photographs of horses. They went into her mother's bedroom, where the furniture had not yet been sold and the big bed was stripped to the mattress, and smelt the sour smell of old age and spilt wine and the sweet smell of death. It was there that, suddenly and with great authority, Leslie Titmuss kissed Jenny Sidonia for the first time. She was not, she supposed, surprised that it happened, but she was astonished by the result. Like a skier who had been standing nervously and then, without taking a breath, pushes off down the steepest part of the mountain, she felt elated, irresponsible and in extraordinary danger. Whatever the Titmuss kiss was like it was far from the comforting warmth and reassurance provided by Mr Sidonia.

The incident of the kiss was curiously isolated. When it was done they left the bedroom and continued their tour of inspection. They walked for a while in the overgrown and neglected garden and then drove into Rapstone village. Leslie, now acting as a tour guide of his past life, showed Jenny the church, starting with his father's grave, and then took her inside, where they found the Reverend Kevin Bulstrode pinning up notices about a vigil for Aids Week.

'Mr Titmuss! This is an honour.' Although he preached weekly sermons about the lack of compassion and true Christian principle of the Government, Kev the Rev. became effusively respectful to the Cabinet Minister. His eyes sparkled and he blushed like a young girl in the unnerving presence of a pop star. 'I see your mother, of course, and she tells me all about your doings. We're very proud of you in Rapstone.'

'This is Mrs Sidonia. She's thinking of taking a place in the country.'

'Am I?' Jenny smiled, but the Rev. Kev ignored her, having eyes for Leslie alone. 'Terribly expensive here now, of course. For the smallest two-up, two-down. That is, unless you're like me and work for the C. of E. Then you get a tied cottage.'

'You mean that draughty great Rectory, falling to pieces?'

'I'm afraid so. In the church we have to accept draughts like the Thirty-nine Articles.'

'Your organization needs to slim down. Sell the Rectory to the highest bidder and put you in a decent bungalow. With double-glazing. I used to cut nettles for the old Rector,' Leslie told Jenny. 'Sixpence a day and a glass of ginger-beer. The Reverend Simcox was a Socialist. You're not a Socialist, are you, Rector?'

'Only' – Kev the Rev. blushed more deeply, horribly torn between good manners and his obligation to the truth – 'in so far as Our Lord was a Socialist.'

'How far was that? Paid-up member of the Nazareth Labour Party, was He?'

Now Jenny was torn. She thought what Leslie had said quite funny, but she hoped the Reverend Kevin wasn't being bullied.

She gave him one of her most glittering smiles and said, 'It's so lovely round here. Quite extraordinary.'

'Well, we think so. And we hope it'll stay that way. There have been rumours –'

'Never believe rumours,' Leslie advised him, 'until you hear them officially denied. By the way, Bulstrode. I wanted to thank you for what you did for my ex-mother-in-law. At the end. Apparently it was well beyond the call of duty.'

'I did what I took to be my pastoral job. She wasn't an entirely easy woman to visit.'

'She was impossible.' Leslie spoke with feeling. 'She must have been hell when she was doing anything as common as dying. You did very well. And I'm not going to forget it.'

What did he mean? As a member of the Cabinet, Leslie Titmuss obviously had considerable influence. Might it be Rural Dean? For a heady moment the vision of a mitre swam before Kevin's eyes. He accompanied his visitors down to the lychgate and saw them into their car, bowing like an old-fashioned Hartscombe shopkeeper who has been patronized by royalty.

They drove out of Rapstone into the next village. Jenny saw that it was in every way uglier and looked more down at heel than the cluster of old brick and flint cottages and half-timbered houses they had left. 'This is Skurfield,' Leslie told her. 'My village. That's ours – "The Spruces".'

'The birthplace?' she asked, and he didn't laugh. The small house, as neatly kept as his father's grave, was where his mother lived.

'Don't you want to call on her?' she asked politely.

'Another time, perhaps.'

'She'll be upset, won't she, if she finds you've been down here without calling?'

'If you don't mind, then.' He looked grateful.

They rang a bell which chimed and went into a strong smell of furniture polish and an array of gleaming china ornaments. Jenny was surprised at how pretty the old woman was, and how pleased she seemed to be to see her. They stayed only long enough for a cup of tea to be made and drunk. Jenny admired the house and Leslie's mother said, 'I told my son, I don't want him to move me from here. Not ever.'

'Don't worry,' Leslie laughed. 'I've given up that idea.'

When they left, Elsie Titmuss said to Jenny, 'I hope you're not the sort to go on demonstrations?'

'Not really,' Jenny smiled.

'And I hope to see you back in my house, dear. I really hope so.'

After that they drove back to London. When he dropped her at her flat Leslie said, 'See you next week,' and she said, 'Yes.' They met regularly but they didn't sleep together, nor did he kiss her seriously again for a long time. This puzzled her. She knew that there was about to be a great change in her life and she was eager to begin it.

'What on earth,' Sue Bramble said, 'can you possibly see in him?'

'He's like no one else.'

'Thank goodness.'

'And he knows exactly what he wants. That's quite an unusual thing to know.'

'What he wants is you, undoubtedly.'

'He comes from the country.' Jenny ignored Sue's remark. 'A most beautiful place. I think he really loves it there.'

'You mean, he's just a local yokel at heart?'

'Something like that.'

'Jenny. The man's a Cabinet Minister. In the Government. He's always on the television. You don't get there with a straw in your mouth and a few rustic sayings, do you?'

'I don't know. I don't know anything at all about Cabinet Ministers.'

'Just watch him on the box. Especially when he's trying to be terribly sincere. Then you can tell how devious he is. And his suits! He looks like a man with his foot in the door who's trying to sell you encyclopaedias.'

'I don't think that's in the least bit fair.'

'Jenny Sidonia,' her friend told her, 'it was a bad day when you decided to be fair to Leslie Titmuss.'

Whether or not Leslie was as devious as Sue Bramble said, he hadn't told Jenny the whole truth about his purchase of Rapstone Manor. Certainly he had had several conversations with the manager of the caring West Country Bank in Hartscombe and it was true that they had discussed a deal. He had waited, however, until he had shown Jenny the house before he decided to buy. The day after their journey into the country he made his final offer. Then he strolled, in his shirt sleeves, into the office of his Minister of State.

'Ken,' he said. 'I could do with a word with you in private.'

Joyce gathered up some papers and left the room, confident that she would soon share in any secret the Secretary of State had to offer.

'Are you trying to be funny?' Leslie asked when the two men were alone.

Ken, also wearing a striped shirt, braces and no jacket, as was the working custom at H.E.A.P., looked up innocently from his desk. In his heart was the great hope that he had got his superior rattled.

'Funny about what exactly?'

'About the proposed Rapstone Valley development.'

So he knew. Ken thought that Leslie would find out sooner rather than later. 'Oh, that. Well. I didn't want to trouble you at this stage.'

'Trouble me, Ken. That's what I was put here for. And if you don't trouble me, my lad, I'm quite likely to trouble you.'

'It's very early days. I just happened to hear something in confidence.'

'From Kempenflatt and his construction company? When you were at the opera together?'

'Something like that. Yes.'

'In future, when you hear something in confidence, Ken, you share it with me. Otherwise I might lose confidence in you. There's a bit of a minor reshuffle in the wind, you know.'

He's threatening me, Ken thought. He really is rattled. 'I didn't think you'd be interested in every little development scheme that just might be applied for.'

'Or did you think I'd be particularly interested in this one? Did you decide not to tell me until it was all nicely sewn up?'

'I couldn't do that, could I? The final decision will be entirely up to you, of course.'

'Of course. I think, Ken, that's something you should bear in mind. That's my advice to you, my lad.'

'But Fallowfield Country Town, if it ever happens, is something I thought would be absolutely in line with your present thinking.'

'Is that your view of the matter?'

'It's yours, isn't it? You put it so well in that smashing speech you made at the U.C.D.A. dinner. The one about the whingers and belly-achers who don't want to share England's green and pleasant land with any upwardly mobile young couple who can save up enough to buy a house. You remember, when you talked about "not in our back gardens"?'

'I didn't realize' – Leslie sat down, half-despairing, half-amused, in the armchair from which Ken Cracken habitually held forth to particularly privileged journalists – 'that I'd got a Minister of State who was entirely wet behind the ears. Politically speaking.'

Politically speaking, Ken thought to himself, I think I'm doing rather well.

'What I say to one pressure group or another, Ken' – Leslie spoke quietly, patiently, as though instructing a child – 'doesn't pre-judge any decision I may have to make. At the end of the day. The whingers and belly-achers, as you called them –'

'As *you* called them.' Ken was confident enough of his own position to interrupt.

'I may call a good many people, including you, all sorts of names from time to time. But at least have the sense to remember that the whingers and belly-achers have votes. The green welly brigade is going to support us at the next election, unless we push them too bloody far.'

'The construction industry's likely to vote for us too.'

'Exactly. Maybe they've got enough to be grateful for already. They don't need any more favours. And it's not just the green wellies, Ken. It's not just the lot with converted barns you mix with at Glyndebourne Opera House or wherever you choose to spend your leisure hours. There are millions of little people, perfectly decent people in small businesses, up and down the country, who are deeply concerned about the environment.'

'You mean the Save the Whale nutters?' Cracken did his best to sound sceptical.

'Have you got something against whales, Ken?'

'Well, not personally.'

'Well, you'd better not knock them. They may not be very much use to anyone, swimming about the ocean and suckling their young, or whatever it is they do. They may not add much to our gross national product. But don't knock them, lad! There are plenty of votes in whales. People find them sympathetic. Just like they worry about rain forests and the ozone layer. I hope you're not going to call good folk who're concerned about the ozone layer belly-achers, are you, Ken?'

'Well, no, of course not,' said the Minister of State, who had been tempted to do so.

'In the same way there are plenty of people, decent, small people, who are concerned about our beautiful English country-side. They're not snobs, Ken. They're not down-at-heel country gents with stately homes. They're folk who were born there. Take my mother, for instance.'

I don't believe this, Ken thought, amazed at the effect he was having on the head of his department. He's going to go on television and start talking about his mother.

'What about your mother?'

'Well, her vote is just as good as Christopher Kempenflatt's, I should think.'

'Just as good,' Ken conceded.

'Concern for the environment' – the Secretary of State stood up, as he reached his peroration; he was no longer rebuking a Junior Minister but making a public pronouncement – 'is vitally important. What we are doing to this world of ours. Can we keep the place free of litter and pollution? That's the great political question of our time. And remember this, Ken. It's a *safe* political question. It's got damn all to do with socialism or public ownership, or the so-called welfare state or the politics of envy, as we knew them in the Winter of Discontent and the bad, sad old days of Harold Wilson, who didn't give a fart about whales, from all that I can remember. It's everyone's concern, from the chairman of the building society to the girl in the local hairdresser's who's prepared to give up aerosol sprays for the sake of her convictions. It's the way we can appeal to the whole country, including –'

'Including your mother?'

'I think you've got the message.' Leslie gave his subordinate an extra-long stare and then moved slowly to the door. 'Keep me informed on the Rapstone development, will you? Every inch of the way.'

When Joyce returned to the room she found Ken alone and barely able to contain his mirth. 'It's Leslie Titmuss,' he told her. 'He's gone green!'

Tomorrow

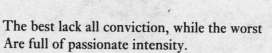

The best lack all conviction, while the worst
Are full of passionate intensity.

'The Second Coming'
W. B. Yeats

CHAPTER NINE

Kempenflatts, the builders, opened their attack on the Rapstone Valley, not with a salvo of bulldozers and a bombardment by concrete-mixer, but with a delicately understated exhibition which the public was graciously begged to attend in Hartscombe Town Hall. To the piped music of Purcell and Edward Elgar the citizens could see an artist's impressions of Fallowfield Country Town which made it look, not a blot, but a thing of beauty on the landscape. Fallowfield, it seemed, would be a tastefully conceived Camelot with pedestrian precincts and parking facilities, an up-to-date version of the lost Atlantis which had that mythical city's talent for disappearing tactfully from view. Just as Atlantis dived beneath the waves, Fallowfield Country Town was, it seemed, quite capable of vanishing between folds in the hills and behind newly planted municipal coppices, so that it would not, God forbid it ever should, give the slightest offence to the critical eye of the most dedicated rural conservationist.

So the water-colour paintings in the Town Hall showed ponies trotting, badgers building, birds nesting and fox cubs sporting in the foreground and, somewhere in the leafy distance, a vague impression of rose-red desirable homes, an occasional elegant church spire or a slimmed-down municipal clock-tower peeped shyly over the brow of some well-positioned hill. Nothing, it was stressed in the captions to the surrounding photographs, would be lost by the proposed development. Rapstone Nature Area, and here Hector Bolitho Jones was shown

bottle-feeding a baby lamb on his patch of ancient chalk downland, would be kept intact and carefully preserved as a public
park for the delight of the fortunate citizens of Fallowfield. The
public-spirited Kempenflatt was, out of the kindness of his heart,
prepared to add many facilities to the Nature Area, including a
children's play area, hand-rails for senior citizens who wished to
climb the steep path to the woodlands, and the free supply of
Walkmans to visitors so that they might stroll through an area of
unspoiled countryside with rustic information plugged into their
ears.

More photographs showed the enhanced quality of life in
other Kempenflatt developments. There were carefully selected
views of children laughing in school playgrounds, old people
feeding ducks by municipal ponds and string quartets performing
in shopping piazzas. Over this part of the exhibition ran the
modest legend HOW KEMPENFLATTS BUILT JERUSALEM IN
ENGLAND'S GREEN AND PLEASANT LAND.

The local inhabitants didn't, at first, react strongly to this
exercise in gentle persuasion. The exhibition was mainly attended
by old people who were not allowed to return to their bed and
breakfast accommodation until nightfall, and children seeking
free gifts of Genuine Old Rapstone Country Mint Humbugs
and I LOVE FALLOWFIELD T-shirts to add to their collections.
They showed little interest in the photographs and drawings on
display and were unimpressed by the news that an application
was in hand to twin the as yet non-existent Fallowfield with
Siena.

An underground movement opposed to the Kempenflatt
occupation was soon to find its voice, however, and freedom
fighters were to hear a somewhat muted call to arms. The centre
of the resistance was, at first and appropriately enough, centred
on an isolated spot above the Rapstone Valley. There was a field,
so high that it was sometimes obscured in low clouds, which on
bright days commanded a view of no less than three counties. It
should have been in itself an area of great natural beauty. To be

honest, it wasn't. To be brutally honest, it bore a close resemblance to those make-believe shantytowns which privileged American students erect on their campuses as a protest against the intolerable conditions in Soweto.

There was a rickety fence round the field and two posts on each side of the gateway which supported, except on the frequent occasions when it blew down in the high winds sweeping the area, the ranch-style notice CURDLES RABBIT HACIENDA: ANGORAS OUR SPECIALITY — ALSO BRED FOR YOUR TABLE DELIGHT. Beneath it, in smaller letters, was the invitation *Come in and Take Your Pick of Rapstone Free-Range Lapin Dinners — Prepared for Your Freezer in Handy Packs*. Behind the fence, in a number of home-made buildings of various shapes and sizes, assembled from scraps of available corrugated-iron, hardboard, tea-chests, sheets of asbestos and the bodies of defunct pick-up trucks, the rabbits, destined to become Tasty Segments or Cuddly Sweaters, bred with enormous rapidity and little assistance. These buildings were also liable to collapse like card houses in the wind, sending the liberated occupants bounding off to ravage the carefully tended gardens of the neighbourhood. Further into the field, and under the shelter of the trees, three huge mobile homes, sunk up to their axles in foul weather, housed the members of the Curdle family who had been as fecund as their charges. These homes, which also served as the hacienda's offices, were connected by an elaborate system of outdoor wiring to a huge generator, for the Curdles went without no modern aid to living and were lavishly supplied with coffin-sized freezers, calculators, video machines, cordless telephones, microwave cookers and even a small but powerful electric organ which none of them could play. A large dish, also sunk perilously into the mud, picked up a flickering supply of soft porn and children's cartoons from satellites wandering above them in the heavens. Around these dwellings another shantytown provided sheds, workshops and an outside lavatory. Cropping the remains of the grass was a shaggy and under-exercised pony on which the Curdles offered to give riding lessons to anyone foolish enough to pay them for such a service. The rabbit hacienda was a matriarchy. Dot Curdle, a huge, astute woman who had in her youth, and indeed in middle age, called on the amorous services of most of the personable young men, and many not so personable, in Hartscombe and the surrounding countryside, regulated the affairs of her family and her business down to the minutest detail. She was up before dawn, cobbling together hutches, skinning, dividing and freezing small corpses, cutting angora, sending out bills and concealing her excess profits in a number of biscuit tins under the flooring of the mobile homes. She supervised the lives of her children and grandchildren with a benevolent despotism and if any task didn't fit into her extended timetable (she rose at dawn and liked to wait up until Billy, at sixteen the youngest and least law-abiding Curdle, was safely home from the lager battles in Hartscombe) she would say, with an air of total confidence, 'Wilf will see to it,' and her diminutive husband Wilfred, a withered apple of a man who was always smiling, invariably did so.

Dot was the child of the long-deceased Tom Nowt, a well-known Rapstone poacher who had fallen foul of Lady Fanner long before the war and had found himself before the magistrates for the offence of snaring rabbits in the Fanner woods. He had been imprisoned for a noisy week in Worsfield gaol, which institution he left to the enormous relief of the staff; his habit of using his cell as though it were some dark corner of the Rapstone woods had not made him a popular prisoner. Neither he nor his family had ever forgiven the Fanners for this humiliation and it was perhaps in tribute to her father's memory that Dot had devoted her life to the proliferation of rabbits.

One day, taking a quick meal on a copy of the *Hartscombe Sentinel*, Dot saw, for the first time, the full details of the Fallowfield proposals. She discovered that the hacienda was due to become a suburban supermarket area, architecturally adjusted to a hilltop position, with abundant parking facilities. She guessed that the farmer from whom they had, for many years, rented their field was proposing, if the plans received official blessing, to sell their home and business from under them. The whole life of the Curdles would vanish under an area of parked cars, piled groceries and supermarket trolleys.

'Hang about, Wilf,' she said. 'This is not on!'

'What's not on?'

'Dumping a bloody great town on our rabbit farm.'

'Oh, that.' Wilfred, ever philosophic, seemed to regard the changes as inevitable and not worth discussing, like death or the weather. 'After we've gone, perhaps. This place'll see us out.'

'We're not going anywhere. We're going to stay here and stop their tricks.' Dot was reading voraciously every inch of print on the subject of Fallowfield Country Town: '"The scheme presented by Kempenflatts the builders,"' she announced to Wilfred, '"is likely to run into considerable opposition from rural pressure groups and other protesters."'

'What's that mean?'

'It means,' Dot explained patiently but with considerable force, 'that's what we're going to be. Our family. A rural pressure group and other protesters.'

'What do we do then?'

'We protests.'

'How does it say we do that?'

'It doesn't say. Most likely because it doesn't want us to know. It's crafty.'

'So what do you reckon?'

'The old Rector would have known,' Dot remembered. 'The Reverend Simcox was one for protesting about most things.'

Simeon Simcox, Kevin Bulstrode's predecessor at the Rectory, had been a life-long Socialist to whom shares in the Simcox Brewery had given a secure vantage point from which to set right the evils of the world. Wearing his dog-collar, an old tweed jacket with leather patches and an expression of benign joy he had headed innumerable protests against the Bomb, against apartheid, against the war in Vietnam and in favour of low-rent accommodation in Worsfield. His younger son, Fred, had long worked as a doctor in Hartscombe, having taken over the practice of old Dr Salter who, diagnosing his own cancer, had sought death by attempting an impossible jump in the hunting field, had failed to find it and had lived on, paralysed, for several painful years. This was a practical joke of fate which he had been able, incredibly, to laugh at. Fred had been more attracted by the old Doctor's acceptance of the immutable facts of life and death than by his father's optimistic march towards a paradise which became ever more distant and unattainable. Unlike his elder brother, Henry, who had started out as an angry young novelist and had now become a crusty old blimp, writing articles for the newspapers denouncing as dangerous illusions their father's most dearly held beliefs, Fred had opted out of all political activity, being content with the quiet life of a general practitioner in the countryside where he had spent his childhood. Sometimes, but not often, he wondered how he had come to pass over half a century on earth and travelled so little distance from his home.

Fred had once, many years before, joined a march for nuclear disarmament, which he had deserted in order to meet a girl with whom he was in love. He didn't expect to be involved in any similar demonstration for the rest of his life. However his consulting room was invaded during one morning surgery by the huge and urgent presence of Dot Curdle. He was pleased to see her, for although he despaired, like most people, of the mess the hacienda made of the field above Rapstone, Dot's great bulk had long been a familiar feature of his landscape. As a small boy he had greatly admired her father, Tom Nowt, and he had watched the old poacher bait fish-hooks with raisins soaked in brandy to catch pheasants, and ridden with him at night when he shot deer dazzled in the headlamps of a car. Until his father suddenly forbade this friendship he had spent much of his school holidays in Tom Nowt's hut in the woods, listening to tall stories of

drunken nights and unlikely seductions. He had heard the amorous cries of Tom's caged calling-bird, which lured the game
from the Strove and Fanner woods into his traps. His predecessor
in the practice, Dr Salter, had brought Dot Nowt into the world
and had given her, as he always said, 'a slap on the bottom and
told her to get on with it, which is the most you can do for anyone
embarking on life'. On the whole, Dot had made the most of this
encouraging start and Fred had seen her children and grandchildren
born, treated them when they were ill, which was seldom, and
tried, without any success, to worry her about her huge weight
which seemed to have no adverse effect on her health whatsoever.

'I want to talk to you, Dr Fred. Urgent.'

'You're not ill?'

'Not me. No.'

'Or any of the family?'

Dot seemed, suddenly, shy of embarking on the non-medical
subject of her visit.

'Well,' she said. 'There is my Evie.' She mentioned a pale,
sullen thirty-year-old who was always known as the brightest of
the family and who had supplied the foreign words used in the
hacienda advertising. 'I think the girl's sick,' she added with
undisguised contempt.

'What's the matter with her?'

'She says she can't fancy her sex.'

'Her own sex?' Fred Simcox speculated wildly.

'She says she can't abide doing it, Doctor.'

'And that's a worry to you?' Fred heard his doctor's voice and
wanted to burst out laughing at its concerned pomposity.

'It's a worry to Len Bigwell, seeing as he's her intended.
We've got a big wedding planned for the autumn time. What's
the matter with young things today, Doctor?' Dot settled back in
his creaky patient's chair and seemed prepared to enjoy a trip
down memory lane. 'We never had any trouble not fancying it,
from what I remember. Looked forward to it, more or less, as I
still manages to this day.'

Fred tried to picture the diminutive Wilf climbing aboard this great old steamer and said, again in the doctor's voice with which he was becoming bored, 'You want me to speak to her?'

'Wouldn't do any good. She can't bear talking about it either. She reckons it's the rabbits what put her off.'

'A marriage guidance counsellor from Worsfield comes to the Town Hall once a week.' Fred said this with little conviction. Old Dr Salter had always taken the view that the only possible marriage guidance was contained in the sentence, 'If you like it, enjoy it; if you don't like it, piss off out of it.'

'Marriage guidance.' Dot appeared to think this over. 'That might bring her to her senses. To be honest, Dr Fred, and I've got to be honest, that's not the reason I dropped into the surgery.'

'I didn't think it was.'

'Your dad. He used to protest. Organized a few demos and that, didn't he?'

'Oh, all the time.'

'He knew how to stop things happening that didn't ought to happen.'

'He thought he did.'

'And he put a stop to them?'

'Well, not very often.'

'But he had a go?'

'Oh, yes. He had a go.'

'And he might have won the day, like. If he'd gone on persistent.'

'I suppose he might. About some things.'

'So you'll remember how he used to do it.'

'Oh, yes. I remember quite well.'

'You're the one that's got to undertake it then.'

'Undertake what, exactly?'

'Stop them dumping a bloody great town on my hacienda.'

Even Dot Curdle's call to arms might not have immediately

moved Fred into activity had it not been repeated by a number of his patients and fellow citizens after the full account of the Fallowfield plans appeared on the front page of the *Hartscombe Sentinel*. Crossing the road on his way to a lunchtime sandwich in the entirely rebuilt Olde Maypole Inn (it now had all the advantages of muzak, one-armed bandits and the Seafood Platter which had ousted Dr Salter's favourite beef and pickle sandwiches), he was hailed by a Mrs Virginia Beazley, the wife of Mr Vernon Beazley who took the long journey to London each day to work for a prosperous firm of charity organizers. Mrs Beazley called them the Two Vees and often said they worked as a team for the humane concerns which, in less enlightened times, an idle populace had left to its government. Virginia had taken on the Worsfield Drug Therapy Unit, the Safe Sex Advisory Service and a growing organization called Help the Homeless to Help Themselves. 'All I want to do,' she often said, 'is to get people off their backsides and into the tough old business of "love thy neighbour".' She often added that she and the other Vee 'got their kicks' from such work. She was a tall, handsome woman of great energy and a commanding presence, and Fred sometimes had the unnerving suspicion that she was in love with him.

'Hi there, Dr Fred!' she called to him from the pavement as he was trapped on a traffic island. 'Who's going to get Hartscombe up off its bottom now?'

'I don't know.' He did his best to make his answer inaudible.

'Well, you are, of course!' she shouted, and when a lull in the traffic forced him to her side she explained, 'Vee and I are forming the Save Rapstone Valley Society and I can't think who the hell else we should ask to be chairman.'

'Chairman? I've got my practice –'

'But you're here all the time! Not like poor old Vee, who has to travel a hundred and fifty miles backwards and forwards to work every day. Anyway, Vee says you're just the chap we ought to scrounge for the job. He thinks you'd look quite reassuring on local television if only you'd invest in a few new shirts and not cut your hair as though you'd just come home from National Service. Also he'd like to give you a bit of advice about your specs.' And she invited the Doctor to buy her a large Kir in the Olde Maypole Inn.

While there they met Daphne Jones, who had escaped from her husband, Hector Bolitho Jones, and the Nature Area on the pretext of her monthly visit to the Hartscombe Cash & Carry. She was drinking Fortissimo lager with Barry Harvester, the young proprietor of the herbal boutique in the pedestrian precinct, who had a witch's knowledge of country remedies for all ailments and smiled in a particularly embittered manner whenever he saw a registered medical practitioner.

'Hullo, Doctor,' he said. '*Still* poisoning people with penicillin?' Fred resisted the temptation to answer, 'Whenever I get them out of your clutches.' Instead he offered to buy them all a drink, thinking that the female Vee was safest when lost in a crowd.

'It's not as though it's going to provide any low-rent council houses,' Daphne Jones said, with justice. 'It'll just be more homes for well-heeled business people like your old man, Virginia, commuting up to London.'

'It's another battle in the class war' – the herbalist was a one-man cell in the Hartscombe Workers' Revolutionary Party – 'and this one we've got to win.'

'It's a matter of preserving our national heritage,' Mrs Vee said. 'I don't see why we have to drag politics into it.'

'You try dragging politics out of it.' Barry Harvester fixed her with his most unfriendly smile and bit noisily into a radish. 'I don't think you'll find we get very far.'

'It's Titmuss we're up against in the end.' Daphne Jones was a great deal better informed than her friend Barry on matters of political reality. 'He's the one who wants to concrete over the South of England. For yuppies to live in it.'

Fred said nothing, thinking of yet another stage in what felt like a lifetime's battle against Leslie Titmuss, the boy who had once come in on Saturdays to cut his father's nettles. Mrs Vee said, 'The important thing is we all have to pull together. Us and our little group of founding fathers. Now, who are we going to be? Apart from us four – and Vee, of course, to deal with the charitable aspect.'

'We ought to ask the Curdles,' Fred told her.

'Really?' Mrs Vee was unenthusiastic.

'They stand to lose their rabbit farm.'

'Best reason I heard yet for the new town.' The She Vee giggled and punched Fred lightly on the upper arm. 'No, pax! Don't slap me down. I suppose it'd be democratic to ask the Curdles, or a representative selection of them.'

'Yes! Try being democratic,' Daphne advised her quite sharply. 'It doesn't hurt much.'

'Oh, and I think we should invite the Mayor, as a matter of courtesy. And the Head of the Hartscombe Grammar.' Mrs Vee ignored Daphne's advice. 'And Colonel and Mrs Wilcox for the footpaths. And the Church ought to have a place.'

'The Church has got no place. Not in the world today,' the herbalist told her, but in the end they decided that Kev the Rev. would be invited to serve on the committee. 'For our first meeting' – Mrs Vee was in a generous mood – 'I don't see why Vee and I shouldn't lay on a buffet. That is, providing everyone is willing to chip in, of course.'

'And I hope you'll be serving out the Armalite rifles and the ammo with the quiche, Mrs Beazley.' The herbalist, who had nothing whatever to do with firearms and who was prominent in animal welfare, downed his Fortissimo. 'I reckon we're going to need them to stop this lot in the end.'

'I'm prepared to take that remark entirely as a joke,' Mrs Vee said. 'I think fifteen quid each would cover a reasonable selection of salads and, let's say, one glass per head of carafino rosé. After that I'll put Vee in charge of a small cash bar.'

So, at this historical moment, an organization was formed to deliver a small part of England from subjugation by the Kempen-flatts and the dangerous domination of Leslie Titmuss.

CHAPTER TEN

Driving through the Rapstone Valley, along hedged lanes which he could have negotiated in his sleep, past the patches of bracken where he had hidden and built shelters when he was a child, the diminishing ponds in which he had squelched and hunted frogs, the common where, at night, he had found glow-worms and occasionally made love, and through the tall beech trees, thin and grey as elephants' trunks, where he had ridden shot-gun with Tom Nowt, Fred Simcox was filled with anger. What had his patients done, what offence had they committed that their small world should suddenly be taken from them? Death, he knew, would deprive him of the hills and woodlands which had been for so long a part of his existence; death was the great, the accepted, robber but he saw no reason in the world why he should be so deprived by Kempenflatts the builders or, and here his rage, an emotion to which he was usually a stranger, rose to a level which was almost as intoxicating as Fortissimo lager and perhaps as likely to lead to violence, by the shadowy but apparently infinite power of Leslie Titmuss.

Fred had read reports of the now famous Titmuss speech at the Construction and Developers Association dinner. The *Fortress* had welcomed it, as it welcomed all his utterances, as a refreshing blast of common sense and plain speaking. Henry Simcox, writing what he called one of his 'Why, oh why?' pieces, had said it was time country dwellers stopped regarding it as their inalienable right not to have to look at their fellow citizens and were dragged, green wellies and all, into the glories of Britain's new industrial revolution. People who lived in the country, together with farmers, school teachers, hospital nurses and social workers, formed that group of mendacious malcontents of which Fred's brother, Henry, especially disapproved; and the fact that he spent his life in the gentle confines of South Kensington and found his rustic pleasures in a villa in Tuscany meant that he didn't have to bump into many of them. 'Why, oh why,' he wrote in a much-quoted article, 'if these pampered people want to live so close to nature don't they move to the Outer Hebrides and leave us to our prosperity?'

And the Titmuss war, Fred reflected as he entered the stuffy bedrooms of the few remaining villagers, or tried to convince weekending television executives that there was no magic potion for avoiding death, could even be thought of as funny. It was comic, no doubt, that opposition to the best-laid schemes of Titmuss should have to come from a country doctor who wanted to be left alone, and from a Trotskyite shopping-precinct huckster who sold nettle tea as a cure for arthritis. No doubt it was entertaining for Titmuss to know that their forces were to be assembled at a buffet in the Hartscombe home of Mr and Mrs Vee, to which Colonel and Mrs Wilcox, representing the footpaths, and Kev the Rev. were also invited. What else, after all, could they possibly do? The more hopeless the battle against Titmuss seemed, the more intensely it had to be waged and the more completely did Fred feel he had to dedicate himself to it.

Much of his feeling about Titmuss went back, as did his devotion to the Rapstone landscape, to the days of his childhood. It was Leslie Titmuss who had seen the young Fred skiving away from the C.N.D. march and who had informed the old Rector of his son's lack of dedication to that, or probably any, cause. It was Leslie again who had figured so improbably as a beneficiary in the Reverend Simeon Simcox's will, a matter which had only been explained, as a result of the Doctor's painstaking investigation, by the discovery that Charlotte, Grace

Fanner's daughter and Leslie's wife, had been a child of the old Rector's passionate and unsuspected past. It was true that Simeon Simcox's legacy had turned out to be financially worthless; the affair had split the family and caused the Doctor's mother, a woman slow to show any feelings except dry amusement at the vulgarities of the world, a good deal of carefully concealed pain.

Fred always thought of Leslie Titmuss as he first knew him, an irrepressibly cocky small boy with an unnatural pallor, short trousers and socks which concertinaed round his ankles, who used his nettle-cutting to ask endless questions of the Rector's two sons and to worm his way into their father's favour. At the end of every corridor which led into Fred's past, on every pathway of that half-remembered landscape, that figure seemed to stand, causing unnecessary trouble. So, when the Doctor saw the Cabinet Minister's picture now, in newspapers or on television, he remembered him as an intolerable small boy and hoped against all reasonable hope that Titmuss's undoubted power would thereby be diminished.

'We need an acronym,' said Mr Vernon Beazley, who knew about such things, 'and a logo.'

'What's he talking about?' Wilf Curdle whispered to his wife, and was immediately told to keep his mouth shut.

'I thought we'd agreed to call ourselves the Save Rapstone Valley Society.' Fred was already beginning to find his duties as chairman (Chair, as Daphne Jones insisted on calling him) unacceptably absurd.

'S.R.V.S.? That doesn't do anything for us. What we need are initials that make up a word you can say,' the He Vee explained patiently to those unacquainted with the needs of charity organizations. 'Like U.N.E.S.C.O. and S.C.R.A.P.'

'Hands Off Our Valley?' Daphne Jones was anxious to help. 'H.O.O.V.'

'Sounds like a vacuum, doesn't it?' Mrs Wilcox of the footpaths piped up unexpectedly.

'What about Piss Off Out Of Our Valley?' said Dot, who was surprisingly quick at crossword puzzles. 'You could say that. P.O.O.V.'

'Please, Mum, don't be disgusting.' Evie Curdle, tight-lipped and disapproving, thought her mother had a one-track mind.

'P.O.O.V.?' the She Vee said. 'I'm not sure that's what we're looking for, is it?'

'It doesn't *absolutely* ring a bell,' the He Vee agreed. 'Hang about a bit. What about, Say No Over Fallowfield?'

'That makes S.N.O.F.,' Dot told them with quiet satisfaction, while Evie explained that the one thing she couldn't eat was salad, probably, Fred thought, because she'd seen so many rabbits at it.

'Save Our Valley,' Mrs Vee said suddenly, and added with the authority Fred appeared to lack, 'I think that has a quiet dignity. Don't you, Chair?'

'S.O.V.?' Mr Vee tried the word out. 'I rather like that. Well done, Vee!'

'S.O.V.? Sovereign. What's that meant to sound like?' Barry Harvester was suspicious. 'On Her Majesty's bloody Service?'

'When Dad shot hisself,' Dot told the world in general, 'we found five gold sovereigns sewed up in the lining of his best breeches. Worth a fortune today, they'd be. We got rid of them to some bloody Scotsman who kept a stall in Worsfield Market. Wet behind the ears, we was, in those days.'

'Save Our Valley. Save Our Souls. That has, to me, the right note of urgency about it.' Kev the Rev. spoke excitedly, a plate balanced on his knees, eating as though his life depended upon it.

'I propose S.O.V.,' Mrs Vee said, 'and the Reverend Kevin Bulstrode seconds me. Will you be kind enough to put the motion, Chair?'

Chair was kind enough, and after a short and heated debate, and despite Dot's insistence that their logo should be an artist's impression of 'our hacienda bunnies', it was decided that a drawing of one of the valley orchids should adorn all their communications.

Fred listened to this with half his attention, thinking that the suggestions for protests and fund-raising and publicity, the printing of leaflets and the approaches to the Great and the Good and, it was to be hoped, the Generous, would end in the inevitable contest with Leslie Titmuss. It was Titmuss they must be prepared to fight, Fred decided, and Titmuss who would have to be defeated before the valley was out of danger and he could resume his normal life without the necessity of further buffet do's with the Beazleys. Meanwhile the voices around him rose and fell, coming to no definite conclusion.

'They can't just do away with the footpaths,' Colonel Rudolph Wilcox said. 'They've been there since the Middle Ages.' He and his wife, fearless devotees of rights of way and wearing similar types of tweed trilby in winter and white cotton billycock hats – of the sort well-off children used to play in at the seaside – between May and September, would tramp uncompromisingly across lawns, even through french windows and across carpets, to keep open what they knew to be ancient rights of passage. They don't know Leslie Titmuss, Fred thought, if they believe he's going to pay the slightest attention to anything that happened in the Middle Ages.

'When Doughty Strove tried to put a grass court across the bridlepath at Picton,' Mrs Wilcox said, 'Rudolph and I threatened to get a couple of hacks and ride across it every tea-time. That put a stop to his tennis.'

Ten thousand houses, Fred thought, wouldn't be so easily moved by an elderly couple on horseback. In the respectful silence that followed, he saw Hector Bolitho Jones, still wearing his anorak as though he didn't mean to stay long, staring at him over his encroaching beard. 'Perhaps we should hear from Mr Jones,' he suggested, 'as the expert on the wildlife in the district.'

'I don't see all that harm,' Hector surprised them by saying. 'I read as how the Nature Area's going to be preserved. They've given their word about that.'

'But as a park! In the middle of a town?' Fred argued.

'If they keep people that come into the area in order, I'm not so concerned what they put around it. Perhaps it'll be all the better for a strict enforcement of the bye-laws. As it is, there are those who think they can take all sorts of liberties.' Hector turned his bright, hostile eyes on his wife and the herbalist, of whom he entertained well-justified suspicions.

'You mean, you don't want human beings to have the same rights as your badgers?' Daphne Jones challenged him, and the group felt uneasily that they were in the presence of private grief. Fred knew that they had all formed only an impermanent and uncertain alliance to defeat the stolid determination of his old enemy.

In spite of everything, S.O.V. acquired a good deal of support in the locality, although it was not universally welcomed. Some of the doctors looked forward to the influx of patients a new town would bring; many lawyers had, like Jackson Cantellow, clients anxious to invest in the development; many shopkeepers said they would profit, and the Mayor felt that his high office required him to remain neutral in the matter (he had managed to acquire a small patch of woodland in the Rapstone Valley and hoped, when Fallowfield was triumphant, to sell it and build himself a lavish retirement home on the Costa del Sol, to which he would retreat with his long-time mistress, the manageress of a local chemist's, and finally ditch the Mayoress). Some teachers in Hartscombe dreamed of promotion to a huge Fallowfield comprehensive and the local undertaker welcomed the idea of a steep increase in deaths.

On the whole, S.O.V. could count on the support of the remaining villagers, who knew that Fallowfield houses would be more than they could afford, and the recent immigrants who had paid up to half a million pounds for cottages they had assumed would be in the countryside. A Mr Peregrine Lanfranc, who had opened a ruinously expensive hotel in the old Strove country house at Picton Principal, became hysterical at the thought of his clientele compelled to consume their marinaded duck and Château Latour between Safeways and the Doner Kebab House in Fallowfield High Street. He offered to raffle a free weekend for two in aid of S.O.V., but when the prize was won by Evie Curdle's fiancé, Len, she rejected the opportunity with disgust. Many other well-wishers organized coffee mornings, Bring and Buy sales and recitals in local churches and from these small contributions Mr Vernon Beazley's charity organization company took 25 per cent. 'It's the name of the game in giving nowadays,' the He Vee explained. 'You can't just sit outside the Cash & Carry with a begging-bowl, you know. Appealing to people's better natures is part of the new technology.' Fred Simcox, becoming aware of the Beazley commission, created a row he found enjoyable until the She Vee, taking his part against her husband, kissed him clandestinely and moistly in the ear after a stormy meeting. The Beazley take was reduced to 10 per cent, only to be paid on the basis of work done, and Fred tried to avoid lonely moments with the She Vee.

And he became aware of a momentous event which seemed likely to alter the whole future of the Rapstone Valley. One of the numerous small Bulstrodes ran a soaring temperature and the Doctor was called out to the old Rectory that had once been his home. He passed through the familiar rooms full of unfamiliar clutter and sat on the bed of a little, feverish girl who seemed to be facing, with admirable courage, the difficulties of being a child of the clergy, an experience which Fred remembered as like a lifetime of uneventful but emotional Sunday evenings. When he had diagnosed the measles and prescribed for her, and as he was moving into the damp air of the churchyard, he asked Kev the Rev. about the builder's lorries he had noticed at the gates of Rapstone Manor.

'Haven't you heard?' Kevin Bulstrode, swollen with inside

information, shared it proudly. 'Leslie Titmuss has taken it over. He's coming to live. Isn't that marvellous news?'

'Is it?' Fred was doubtful.

'Well, he's hardly going to allow a new town to be built in his own back garden now, is he?'

'I don't know.' Fred thought this over. 'There's one thing I have learned, over the years. You can never trust Titmuss.'

'Oh, I do hope and pray that that's all over now. I don't know how I could face Mr Titmuss in church while I'm campaigning against him as an active member of S.O.V. That' – Kevin looked proud of his interesting dilemma – 'would be so very embarrassing.'

'I can't see why you'll have to face him in church. Titmuss hasn't taken to God, has he?'

'I can't think Mr Titmuss is an unbeliever. You see, and of course I tell you this in the strictest confidence, he's asked me to marry him.'

For an absurd and entertaining moment Fred supposed that the Right Honourable Leslie Titmuss had proposed to Kev the Rev. Then he said, 'He's marrying who?'

'Ah, that' – the Rector had run out of information – 'remains to be seen. But Rapstone Manor, no doubt about it, is going to see a bit of life again. Perhaps the old place will see children . . .'

A long line of Titmusses, stretching out into the future? It was a thought Fred found hard to tolerate.

CHAPTER ELEVEN

Jenny Sidonia had been going out with Leslie Titmuss for a long time before anything in particular happened. 'Going out' was the expression she and her friend Sue Bramble used for staying in, in particular for staying in bed with someone; but when it came to Mr Titmuss 'going out' meant exactly what it said. They met for dinner almost once a week in one or other of the small restaurants near her flat, places she supposed he liked because they never saw any of those he insisted on calling his 'colleagues' there. These colleagues, presumably other members of the government, were shadowy figures whom Leslie spoke of, if at all, with undisguised contempt. Jenny, who had little interest in politics and to whom the names of the colleagues meant little, listened to his revelations of life in government, which seemed to consist mainly of internecine strife, without any particular attention. Then she asked him, because she supposed it would be polite to do so, what had made him wish to enter so strange and unrewarding a world in which people never seemed to wish each other well.

'I got pushed into the river,' he said – something which he hadn't spoken about for decades.

She felt an irresistible urge to burst out laughing and then she looked at him and realized that he was about to make a painful and intimate revelation.

'At a Young Conservative dinner dance, in the old Swan's Nest at Hartscombe. It was a formal occasion!'

'Oh, yes,' she could hardly trust herself to say, 'I bet it was.'

'And this snotty little gang of old Etonians pushed me in. Because I was wearing a hired dinner-jacket. They said I smelt of mothballs. Oh, and I had a ready-made bow-tie. You ought to tie it yourself, but I didn't know that. Bastards!'

His look of hatred was so intense that she could no longer stop the laughter bubbling out of her. 'I'm sorry,' she made a breathless apology. 'I really am most terribly sorry.'

He looked for a moment as though he were going to strike her, as she felt she probably deserved, or at least rise up in fury and slam out of the restaurant. Instead he stared at her in bewilderment and then, very slowly, smiled. At last a low, rasping sound emerged from him, which she found difficult to identify as a laugh.

'I suppose,' he said, 'it is funny.'

'Not really,' she gasped. 'Not really, at all.'

'I never laughed at it before. Not ever.'

'You can now?' She was able then to become serious.

'Well, yes. I suppose I can.'

'So that's what made you take up politics?'

'Oh, I wanted to before that. But then, well, I knew just what I had to do.'

'What?'

'Take it away from those old school twits. That's what I set about then. If you want to know the truth.'

'You mean, make the world safe for people with rented dinner-jackets?' Now he seemed not to mind being mocked.

'Anyway, I wanted to prove it wasn't enough to be able to tie your own dicky-bow. That didn't entitle you to a seat in Cabinet.'

'But you got one.'

'Oh, yes. I knew I'd manage it. In the end.'

What an extraordinary thing to know, she thought, for anyone sinking into the mud and clinging rushes, with the water ruining his first rented tuxedo. And she became aware of Leslie Titmuss's determination as though it were a pungent smell.

'There's one thing I've been meaning to ask you.'

She was sure she knew what was coming, but she was wrong.

'Take me to the opera.'

'What?'

'You go there, don't you? I don't want them to enjoy any more little sniggers at my expense. Like that day at Oxford.'

These were the things that drove him on, she thought, being thrown into the river and being laughed at by a collection of elderly academics. They forced him to seek things that might have been thought unattainable to the young Titmuss – a Ministry and perhaps, well this was such an enormous perhaps that she hardly admitted the possibility to herself, the lonely widow of Tony Sidonia. 'All right,' she said, 'I'll take you, if you promise me one thing.'

'What's that?' He looked wary as he always did when asked for promises.

'That you'll wear a rented dinner-jacket.'

'What's on next week?' Jenny telephoned Sir Willoughby Blane, who was on the Board of the Opera House, as he was on many boards dealing with subjects as diverse as prawns and Puccini.

'Give me a minute, Jenny darling.' Sir Willoughby felt for his folder. '*Simon Boccanegra*. Rather a heavy evening. Do you fancy that?'

'I might do. Wasn't he a politician?'

'A pleb politician in Genoa. Of a rather ruthless variety.'

'That'll do fine, then.'

'Wonderful. You'll be my guest, of course? I'll see if I can scrounge the Royal Box. Anyone you'd like to sit next to, apart from me?'

'Sorry. But I'd love you to get me a couple of seats. Somewhere in the back of the Grand Circle'd do fine.'

'Don't tell me you're being taken by a young man?'

'He's not all that younger than you are. I'll pay for the tickets.'

'Won't he?'

'I won't let him. This is entirely my treat.'

A politician, Sir Willoughby thought to himself as he put down the telephone. The word led him to a wild speculation, which he dismissed as impossible after he had laughed out loud and for a considerable time.

'Go out and get me,' Leslie said to his secretary, 'a tape of Verdi's *Simon Boccanegra*. And the words in English. Oh, and for God's sake, make sure the bloody thing's not a ballet.'

Jenny Sidonia enjoyed taking Leslie Titmuss to Covent Garden. The marble staircase up which she could see them climbing in a welcoming mirror, the buzz in the Crush Bar where she ordered a bottle of champagne to be put ready for them, in the interval, under the bust of Sir Thomas Beecham, as Tony had always done when they could least afford it – these things excited her as they had before. What added to her entertainment was the fact that she was standing Leslie a treat; he clearly found this confusing. By now long accustomed to command, being under her orders as to where they were to go, where they should sit and when they should have their first drink didn't come easily to him, and he was confused by not being the one who paid.

'How the hell much did these tickets cost?'

'I'm not telling you.'

'Why not?'

'You're such a puritan. You wouldn't approve.'

'And our government's handing out tax-payers' money to help this lot go to the opera.' He looked round at the well-nourished faces in the Grand Tier.

'Well, at least that's one good thing about your government.'

'Jenny. Why don't you let me pay?'

'Because you asked me to take you and I'm very obedient. At least I hope you've kept your side of the bargain.'

'What was that?'

'You mean you've forgotten? Just another of your politician's promises.'

He looked at her, puzzled, and she had to remind him. 'Didn't you go to Moss Bros and hire that suit?'

'Well, no. I have to wear it rather often. At functions.' He looked, she was glad to see, guilty. So she pressed home her advantage.

'And the bow-tie? You're not going to tell me you tied it yourself?'

'I've got used to doing it,' he admitted. 'Over the years.'

The lights dimmed and she was able to rebuke him with 'Leslie Titmuss, you've let me down completely' before the conductor bobbed up like a distant jack-in-the-box, received his applause and the overture began.

'The champagne's there. Under Sir Thomas Beecham.'

'Follow me.' Leslie Titmuss felt he was of some use at last. 'I can elbow my way through this lot.' He went through the Crush Bar crowd like a knife through butter. Some opera-goers fell back and smiled nervously, recognizing a well-known face; others gazed in amazement, having always thought the Minister's idea of an evening out would have been all-in wrestling, or dinner overlooking the Wembley dog races.

'Are you enjoying it at all?'

'Good God, yes. A people's politician! Elected by public acclaim. No wonder all the toffee-nosed Italian aristocrats hated him.'

'He came to a bad end.'

'I know,' Titmuss conceded. 'Poisoned by an underling.'

Jenny was surprised at his grasp of the plot. 'What about the music?'

'Oh, that's all right. In fact it hardly gets in the way at all.'

'You're joking!' She was suspicious; surely that was a bit of Titmuss self-parody?

'Yes,' he agreed. 'Do you mind?'

'I never thought that the Opera House was your particular stamping-ground.' Ken Cracken was suddenly upon them, leading

Joyce Timberlake, Christopher Kempenflatt, a Mrs Armitage who was Kempenflatt's lady, and a large man called 'Jumbo' Plumstead, with his wife – he being the merchant banker who was placing large stakes on the proposed Fallowfield Country Town development.

'I don't think you know everything about my interests, do you?' Leslie was unwelcoming.

'I'm Ken Cracken,' the youngish man with a fair moustache told Jenny. 'Joyce Timberlake, Christopher Kempenflatt, Mrs Armitage, Sir Hugh Plumstead, Lady Plumstead.'

'"Jumbo" Plumstead.' The banker was proud of his nickname. 'This is one of the long ones, isn't it?' He seemed to be talking about the opera.

'Jenny Sidonia,' she had to say, as Mr Titmuss clearly had no intention of introducing her to these people, whom he was looking at with smouldering distaste. They had spotted the Secretary of State's unlikely presence from their box, whose privacy they had left, together with a large plate of smoked salmon sandwiches, to satisfy the greater hunger of their curiosity about his beautiful and mysterious companion.

'Such a wonderful place to unwind!' Mrs Armitage, a woman whose hair, skin and jewellery were all the same shade of burnished gold and from whose crustaceous dress her powdered breasts were in danger of being ejected, told Titmuss as though in confidence. 'Christopher always says he forgets all his business worries after the first two bars of the overture.'

'We usually bring the Japanese customers here.' Jumbo Plumstead still had his mind on commerce even at the end of the first act. 'Such a relief not to have the little fellows bowing at you all over the Crush Bar and downing whisky. At least this is a night out with the Brits!'

'We're all still talking about that absolutely super speech you made at the U.C.D.A. dinner, Leslie.' Christopher Kempenflatt's mind also seemed to have returned to business with the cessation of the music. 'It's given us a great deal of encouragement on the Fallowfield project.'

'Hear, hear!' Jumbo rumbled. 'A hundred and fifty years ago those Save Our Valley blighters would have objected to Manchester.'

'Live in Manchester, do you?' Leslie asked Jumbo in what Jenny realized was a tone of considerable menace.

'As a matter of fact we've got a place near Lewes. On the South Downs.'

'The South Downs, eh?' The Titmuss eyes were particularly cold. 'We ought to remember them next time we want to dump a new town somewhere.'

'Of course you're joking!'

But Leslie didn't smile. He turned on his one-time tormentor. 'You ought to take the lady's advice, Kempenflatt. Put business right out of your mind when you go to the opera. This is neither the time nor the place to discuss important matters of planning policy. But you'd be much mistaken if you thought that anything I happened to say at your little dinner party meant that I've even begun to make up my mind about the Rapstone development. One way or the other. Come along now.' And he took Jenny's arm as she had once, so long ago, taken his. 'I reckon this show's costing you about two quid a minute. We can't afford to miss any of it.'

'That Christopher Kempenflatt,' he told Jenny as they found their way back to their seats, 'is one of the bastards who pushed me into the river.'

'I wish you'd told me,' she said. 'I'd've spat in his champagne.'

Later Leslie and his car delivered Jenny to her flat, as he always did after their evenings out. She had never seen the inside of his mansion apartment, nor had she any wish to do so. Sue Bramble, who was her lodger, was away for the night and Jenny felt suddenly miserable at the thought of turning on lights in empty rooms and of going to sleep, once again, with no one to say goodnight to. As usual Leslie kissed her cheek while his driver stared politely at a lamp-post.

'Thank you,' he said. 'That was a treat. I enjoyed it.'

'Shall we go again?'

'I'll start saving up.' He smiled at her.

The strange thing was, she thought, looking back on it, that what happened then was entirely her responsibility. 'Why don't you come in?' she asked as quietly as she could.

'What shall I tell my driver?'

'You can tell him to go home.' And so it was decided.

Very early the next morning, just as it was starting to get light, Jenny Sidonia woke up next to a naked Leslie Titmuss. He was quite motionless and breathing regularly, but his eyes were open. She had heard somewhere that this was how horses slept.

When they had reached the flat they had gone, almost without a word, into the bedroom. There Leslie took off his custom-made dinner-jacket and hung it carefully over the back of a chair. Jenny said, 'I won't be a minute,' and went into the sitting-room where she looked, for a little, at her outstretched hand. Then she took off her wedding-ring and put it in the drawer of a writing-desk which had once been the property of Tony Sidonia. She went into the bathroom and spent a short while taking off her make-up and cleaning her teeth. When she came back to her bedroom Leslie Titmuss was already undressed and between the sheets. The room was in darkness which was apparently how he preferred it.

His eyes always seemed cold but she was surprised by the heat of his body and, although he was so much older than she, he behaved as though he were enjoying a youth long postponed. At the same time she was made to feel as though she, Jenny Sidonia, was the height of his ambition, long awaited, like his position in the Cabinet, the Right Honourable in front of his name and the black official motor car always in attendance.

When he lay motionless, asleep, she thought, with his eyes open, he spoke.

'You like Rapstone, then?'

'I told you. It's beautiful.'

'You like the house?'

'I told you I did.'

'They want to build a town there.'

'The man who pushed you in?'

'Yes. That's his idea.'

'He can, can't he?'

'I don't think you should worry.'

He had said planning policy shouldn't be discussed in the Crush Bar of the Opera House. To talk about it when they were in bed for the first time, just after five o'clock in the morning, seemed equally inappropriate. She closed her eyes and fell into a deep sleep and when she woke again he was still looking at her.

'My son, Nick,' he said, 'is a librarian.'

'Is he?'

'He's got himself a job. Somewhere in the North-East.' Leslie had travelled to the sprawling town in an area untouched by the prosperity his government had brought to the South of England. He had walked through the rooms which smelt of disinfectant and floor polish, where pensioners slumbered over the news-papers and schoolchildren giggled and searched vainly for rude bits in the *Encyclopaedia Britannica*. He was enraged because the fear that he had had in the college garden was realized. His son was calling himself Nicholas Fanner. 'Mr Fanner,' they had told him, 'is in cataloguing.'

'He doesn't want me to help him,' he told Jenny. 'I don't want your name because I want to do something on my own,' Nick had said. 'I don't want to be given jobs just because you're in the Cabinet.'

'Are you ashamed of me, then?' Leslie had covered his hurt with anger. 'Not ashamed. Of course not. But we're different, aren't we?' Nick had tried to explain. 'We're two entirely different people.'

'Surely it's understandable,' Jenny said. 'He wants to be independent.' She felt sorry for Leslie and liked him better because of this unhappiness.

'I don't know. I don't really know about Nick. Just as I didn't know about his mother.'

'The one who liked men who ate sauce sandwiches?'

'Yes. That's the one.'

'Well. How do you get on at understanding me?' Jenny wanted to cheer him up; he seemed a prey to such sad thoughts.

'I think we've got something in common.'

'What, for instance?'

Loneliness, that's what she thought he might be going to say. Instead he laughed at her, 'Opera!' Then they started to make love all over again.

Sue Bramble, who shared Jenny's flat, had been to visit her lover, a trainer of horses who lived near Newbury. They had argued for a great part of the night about his apparent inability to so arrange matters with the wife from whom he said he was separated, so that he might marry Sue. Finally he confessed what she had half suspected, that this wife of his was only staying with relations in America and he had not, in fact, plucked up courage to break the news of Sue's existence to her. Filled with rage and swearing never to bestride one of his horses or travel to the races with him again, she had got into her Triumph motor car at dawn and driven back to London, disillusioned with life, love and the reliability of husbands. She arrived at the flat early and there found a tall, pale man in a dinner-jacket making tea in the kitchen. Although unshaven he had taken the trouble to tie his black bow.

'Hullo,' she said. 'I'm Sue Bramble. I suppose you're Mr Titmuss.'

He looked at her as though he was considering the possibility of denying it, and then said, 'Yes.'

'If you're making that for Jenny, she likes Lapsang. I'd better show you where it is.' And she added, quite unnecessarily, 'It was Tony's favourite.'

After she had made the tea he thanked her and took it away in silence. She heard voices and then the front door open and shut.

Later she sat on the end of Jenny's bed. To her disappointment, her friend looked unreasonably contented.

'The things you get up to the moment my back's turned!'

'I thought you were away till tomorrow.'

'I don't think I'll ever be away again. Men are such *liars!*'

'I'm sorry.'

'And I'm sorry I scared your Mr Titmuss. I thought he was going to jump out of his skin.'

'I don't think he was scared, particularly.'

'Nonsense. He bolted out of here like a rabbit.'

'He had to get home and change.'

'Well, I imagine he didn't want to turn up at the Ministry in his tuxedo.' Sue Bramble lit a cigarette in some gloom. 'Is he terrified I'll talk and it'll be all over the *News of the World*?'

'He did mention that possibility.'

'What did you say?'

'I told him you were totally reliable.'

'Too bloody reliable. That's my trouble.'

'Oh, Sue.' Jenny looked at her friend with great concern. 'Teddy has let you down, hasn't he?'

'Don't worry about me. You're the one we've got to worry about. Promise me, Jenny. You will be careful, won't you?'

'I'm sorry.' Jenny Sidonia gave the matter some thought. 'I don't think I can promise that.'

Later that morning, when Jenny was sitting contemplating the unsold and quite probably unsaleable New British Abstracts, the telephone rang and a female secretarial voice said, 'Mrs Sidonia? I have the Secretary of State here for you.'

'Jenny.' Mr Titmuss came on the line immediately, sounding brisk. 'I meant to tell you. I have to go to Rome next month. Something to do with my opposite number in the Community.'

It was a one-night stand, she thought with unexpected despondency, and this is his way of saying goodbye. 'I hope you enjoy it,' she said.

'And I've been thinking . . .'

'About me?'

'Yes.'

'What exactly?' She was not, whatever happened to her, about to weep.

'Well. Wouldn't Rome be rather a good place for a honeymoon?'

'What on earth can you be talking about?' It was ridiculous, the great swing on which her spirits were rising.

'I've rung the Rector of Rapstone and suggested a date for him to pencil in. They're both dead, I told him, so there's no reason why we shouldn't be married in church, is there?'

After they had spoken, she sat still for a long time, then she telephoned Sue Bramble and offered to buy her lunch in Soho. She wanted to cool off, as soon as possible, in the icy waters of her best friend's disapproval.

CHAPTER TWELVE

'What on earth would Tony think?' Jenny found the question particularly irritating, partly because it assumed that Tony was still around somewhere and watching everything she did with puzzled disapproval, but mainly because it was what she had avoided asking herself. Now Sue Bramble had, with a true friend's lack of mercy, faced her with it.

'How on earth should I know?'

'Well, what do you *think*?' Sue wasn't going to let her off lightly.

'I think Tony always wanted me to be happy.' Jenny played for safety.

'Oh, yes. I'm sure he did. But would he have wanted you to be happy with *Leslie Titmuss*?'

'I think he'd've left it to me.'

'Chalk and cheese?'

'What?'

'Your extraordinary Leslie and Mr Sidonia. By the way, was he wearing a made-up tie?'

'What do you mean?'

'When I caught him in full evening-dress at seven o'clock in the morning. Was that a ready made-up bow he was wearing?'

'I can tell you without a doubt' – in this new and confusing world there was one thing Jenny was sure of – 'he tied it entirely himself.'

'A real bow-tie which managed to look phoney! Only your Mr Titmuss could do that.'

'If he were exactly like Tony. If he wore all the right clothes, only he looked as though he slept in them and didn't give a damn anyway. If he knew all the poetry and history I'd never heard of, and read all the books I've never even opened and could be quite serious, particularly when he was making jokes – Well, then, I suppose Tony might be upset because I'd found someone who could do all he could do and perhaps better. But my Mr Titmuss, as you insist on calling him, can't do any of those things. He's chalk and cheese, as you said. So why on earth should Tony be jealous of him?'

She was, she realized, being absurd. Where on earth was Tony, to be jealous or not? If not on earth, was he floating through space, dodging secret weapons and television satellites, deeply distressed by her new friendship? She could only think of him in his fraying basket-chair in the untidy garden of their house in North Oxford, holding a book too close to his eyes and laughing tolerantly at the nefarious connivings of some long-dead Pope. No doubt he would be laughing at her and Leslie's strange behaviour, and when she thought about it she decided he might be right and laughter was the only possible reaction.

'I'm not saying he'd be jealous. I'm just saying he might not be very happy about your prospects.'

'You think Mr Titmuss is going to ditch me?'

'I think he'd ditch his own mother, if it'd get him higher up in that awful Cabinet or whatever it is he belongs to.'

'I tell you, you're wrong.'

'Am I?'

'Oh, yes. Mr Titmuss and Mr Sidonia aren't as entirely different as you think. There's a sort of honesty about both of them.'

'You really believe that?'

'Oh, yes. I do.'

'All right, Jenny.' Sue Bramble smiled in her most irritating and grown-up way. 'I just hope you go on believing it. That's all.'

*

This question of honesty was an important one to Jenny. Her mother, from whom she had inherited her looks but not her character, moved naturally in a world of lies, where the climate suited her. When she was a child Jenny thought that lying was a sort of game her mother played in the car, like Animal, Vegetable, Mineral or I Spy. She gave, Jenny soon realized, totally inaccurate information about where she'd been, what she'd bought, where she'd left her handbag and who had telephoned. She lied, it seemed, out of pure high spirits or for the pleasure of exercising her undoubted talent for invention. She would tell her husband, who was something in engineering and travelled a lot, that she had been shopping in Tesco's where there was this extraordinary crowd of Japanese tourists holding them up at the check-out, when they had gone to Sainsbury's and hardly been kept waiting at all. Jenny had heard her mother say to her father, when she was meant to be asleep but could hear them talking in the next bedroom, that she had taken their daughter for lunch at the zoo when she had, in fact, been left to play with her friend Sheena Dalrymple. She even heard some of the comical things she was alleged to have said about the animals she never saw. For a moment she wondered if she had gone mad and had never been in Sheena's house playing tedious games of Mothers and Fathers but had actually been staring at a camel and saying brightly, 'A horse with a house on its back!' Then she supposed it was one of her mother's peculiar games. Not until she was older did Jenny deduce that these games had some connection with the constant sounds of her parents quarrelling, the slamming of doors, cars driving away and then returning to further shouted accusations, denials and footsteps on the stairs. Then her father's travels seemed to last longer and her mother often met her from school in a strange car, driven by a man in a fawn overcoat who smelt like the hairdresser's and offered Jenny, to her intense embarrassment, curiously strong mints which he kept in his waistcoat pocket.

This was also a time when her mother began to go on travels

and Jenny was sent to stay with her grandmother in St
Leonards-on-Sea. Granny Paget was a small, bright-eyed woman
who swam in the coldest weather, picking her way barefoot
across the frosty beach to flop into the grey water, wearing a
one-piece woollen bathing-suit and a pink plastic shower-cap,
large as a tam o'shanter, propelling herself afloat by thrashing
her arms in a sort of windmill motion which she called 'the
crawl'. Then she and Jenny would walk home across the shingle,
the wind blowing so strongly at them that they were hardly able
to move and stood for a long time poised for the next step, with
Jenny's hair and her school mac billowing out behind her. When
they got home they always had what Granny Paget called a 'slap-
up tea' to recover from the swim and Jenny was allowed as many
scones and as much anchovy toast as the old lady, although she
never entered the water because of her intense fear of the cold.
At these teas they would sit together and Jenny would go
through the events of the day to be sure that all she remembered
had actually occurred.

Granny Paget would also give Jenny Sidonia details of life in
Hong Kong, where her grandfather had been stationed when in
the army. Jenny was glad to have it confirmed that her mother's
general account of life in that city was accurate, although when
she got down to details the evidence became more shaky. 'Mummy
says her nurse took her out for a walk and then pulled her into
this terrible low den where Chinamen were sitting round smoking
opium and playing cards. She said you had to pay a lot of dollars
to get her back.'

'Fairy tales!' Granny Paget said with impatient scorn as she
brushed crumbs off her lap and smeared another scone with
raspberry jam. 'The nurse took her to Sunday School and I didn't
want her to go because she was far too gullible already. So far as
I remember, your mother believed in Father Christmas until
puberty! And I never paid a penny to get her back.'

Once they received a faint telephone call and Jenny's mother,
sounding as though she were under water, announced that she

had travelled to Tenerife but would be back on Thursday morning and come straight down to St Leonards. She said, 'I can't wait to see you, darling.' Although they laid on extra supplies of scones and Jenny had a new dress, her mother never came. A week later a postcard from Malaga told them, 'Stuck here longer than I expected, darling. Just can't wait to see you.' 'Fairy tales!' Granny Paget said, as though she had never expected anything different. From that time truth-telling seemed to be more important than ever to Jenny.

When her parents were divorced, Granny Paget said, 'Your mother never found out the importance of sticking to things.' Jenny's father travelled to Oakwood, California, where he sired a large new family. Photographs of new half-brothers and sisters dandled by a strapping blonde at some distant poolside were posted to Jenny almost annually, accompanied by the briefest of notes from her father: 'Peter (or Barbara Joy or Hepworth) begs to be introduced and can't wait to meet his/her big sister.' Like her mother, these siblings seemed able to contain their impatience and she spent more and more of her holidays in St Leonards watching the pale, blue-veined body of her grandmother sink into the water and walking home along the wind-torn promenade. As she had little else to do she worked very hard and got into Oxford.

There, as a student, she was at first lonely and then, when word of her beauty was put about, much sought after. She embarked on a few love affairs with young men she expected to prove unreliable and in this, at least, they didn't disappoint her. It wasn't until her last year at the university that she was taught by Tony Sidonia. 'History,' he told his students in his first lecture on the Roman Church during the Renaissance, 'is an account of the way our ancestors lied to each other because they were too evil, or ambitious, or manipulative, or simple-minded, or cowardly to face the facts. Our great advantage over them is that we are able to tell the truth and that's the justification of our existence.' These words appealed greatly to Jenny and she copied them carefully into the front of her notebook. She was surprised, as Tony continued his lecture, to discover that the Borgia Pope was even less truthful than her mother.

Tony Sidonia rented, at that time, a cottage about ten miles to the north of Oxford and, in the summer, he used to invite his friends for Sunday lunch. Jenny came out in a car with some other students and felt privileged. She lay in the sun on the long matted grass of a 'lawn' which apparently had never seen a mower. She helped wash up and peel vegetables and she thought she had been invited to make herself useful. Tony was clearly attached to Sue Bramble, who was always there, and Jenny thought they trusted each other far too much to get married in the sense in which she understood the word.

Towards the end of her last year she was seeing Tony Sidonia more often – at dinner parties or visits to the movies, or when opera companies came on tour – but they were always with other people, for Tony had a wide circle of friends, ranging from white-haired Euro-Communist scientists to old Etonians from Christ Church and their girlfriends. For one thing Jenny was grateful; she was always invited on her own and no attempts were made to pair her off, as happened after Mr Sidonia's death. One Sunday, just after she'd done her finals, Tony arranged to pick her up and drove her to his cottage where she found that they were alone together and that the table, with bread, cheese, wine and pâté, was laid with two places only.

'Where's Sue?' she asked as she went, as usual, to wash the lettuce.

'She's not coming here this weekend. I told her it had to be over.'

'You quarrelled?' Jenny couldn't believe it. 'You never quarrel.'

'We didn't quarrel. I just told her I had something to do, and I couldn't do it with any honesty while we were living together.'

Jenny was silent. She had no idea of what was to come.

'Anyway, she agreed it was much better we told each other

the truth. Saves an awful lot of mess. She said she hoped that you and she would stay friends. I said I hoped so too.'

'Friends? Why shouldn't we be friends?'

'That's exactly what Sue thinks.'

She was washing the lettuce now, keeping her hands in the cold water with the tap running. She discovered a slug sleeping in a pale-green bed and dislodged it with a fingernail. Then she imprisoned the lettuce in a wire censer and went to the door where she swung it briskly through the air, producing a fine rain which glittered in the last of the year's sunshine.

'So now you've done your finals,' he said. 'Now we're free.'

'Free of exams.'

'Well, free of having to behave ourselves, like a teacher and a pupil. It's no good getting that relationship tangled up with emotions. No good at all. It always leads to a complete mess. I've always made that a golden rule.'

'Have you?' It was true. He hadn't given her a hint of what she now knew he must be talking about.

'So now,' he said, 'I can do what I've wanted to do for such a long time.'

'What's that?'

'Proposition you. I suppose you'd call it that.' He laughed then, as she had discovered he always did at the things he took most seriously.

All that happened almost exactly fourteen years before she was propositioned again, this time by Leslie Titmuss.

As he had suggested they went to Rome for their honeymoon.

She felt, not as though she had embarked on a perilous future, but as though she were flying back to a familiar past when she had always been looked after. In fact the looking-after was even more efficient than it had been in the days of Tony Sidonia, who often missed buses, was late for meals or forgot about aeroplanes in his constant preoccupation with trying to point out the truth to long-dead and self-deceiving pontiffs. With Leslie Titmuss the small details of life were reliably looked after, the car was waiting at the airport and a man from the embassy was there to dispense with any tedious formalities at the hotel reception. As she opened the windows and looked down on to the Spanish Steps where she and Tony used to sit among the sleeping students and guitar-players and sellers of cheap belts and costume jewellery, and eat their lunch-time *paninis*, Leslie Titmuss said, 'There's only a day and a half of meetings and one lunch and a boring dinner we'll have to go to. For the rest of the time you can educate me. I've never been to Rome before. Have you ever been to Rome?'

'Oh, yes,' she told him. 'Rather often.' The last time had been when Tony came nearest to popular success. The B.B.C. had asked him to make a historical documentary called 'In the Shadow of the Triple Crown'. They had been here with a film unit and stayed in the unusual splendour of the Eden Hotel.

Now Leslie was eager to learn the Italian phrases Tony had taught her, which she still wasn't entirely sure how to spell when he insisted on writing them down in his Filofax. They stood with their faces upturned among the crowds that filled the Sistine Chapel as though it were an airport in high season, and Jenny took her husband down the familiar corridors to the Vatican Library. They walked among the plane trees and statues in the Borghese Gardens and he found the white naked figure of Napoleon's sister, Pauline, carved in marble to be alluring. 'It's you,' Leslie Titmuss told her. 'Absolutely. It makes me think of you.' And Jenny remembered that, although they were as different as chalk and cheese, Tony Sidonia had said almost the same thing.

Nor were the one formal lunch and the official dinner a particularly high price to pay for Rome. She sat beneath painted ceilings smiling enchantingly as German and Dutch representatives, delighted to be free for an hour from the appalling tediousness of their jobs, flirted with her ponderously. On their last night Leslie asked Jenny to suggest somewhere for dinner and she took him across the river to a place she remembered.

The streets leading to the square of Santa Maria in Trastevere were darker and dirtier than when she had last seen
them. The young people lurking in doorways, astride parked
Lambrettas or sitting on the bonnets of other people's cars
were no doubt up to no good, dealing in noxious substances or
worse. Leslie strode through them bravely and held on to her
as tightly as if she had been his wallet. But the square, the
fountain and the golden mosaic front of Santa Maria were
unchanged. 'We'll go in here before we eat,' she said, and led
him into the church built on the spot where a stream of pure
olive oil flowed during the whole day of Christ's Nativity.
'Give me some lire,' she said. 'I'll buy us a couple of candles.'
'Why? Are you religious?' He looked at her suspiciously. 'Not
at all, but you can't be too careful. Not when it comes to
luck.' They lit their candles together and speared them on
spikes next to the guttering flames lit by those in fear of
death, or the police, or pregnancy, or failure in examinations,
or the general nerve-racking anxiety of getting through the
day.

They sat in front of Sabatini's, protected by dusty shrubs
through which children peered and thrust hands clutching for lire
or cigarettes. And when she tasted the pale white wine and the
metallic flavour of the spaghetti vongole Jenny was overcome
with a terrible longing for the husband she had lost and in whose
honour she had just lit a candle.

'You're crying!'

'No, really.'

Leslie Titmuss touched her cheek with his knuckles, and then
withdrew his hand as though her tears had scalded him.

'It's him, isn't it? You used to come here with *him*. You're
crying for Tony Sidonia.'

'Of course I'm not. Honestly. It's just that I'm tired. That's
all. Tired, after all the excitement. You do like this place, don't
you?'

She dried her cheeks carefully with her table napkin and, for the first time since their marriage, she felt miserable. The question of honesty meant a great deal to her and she had just lied and, in lying, betrayed Tony.

CHAPTER THIRTEEN

When Leslie Titmuss met Jenny Sidonia at lunch in St Joseph's, Oxford, he had achieved all but two of his ambitions. He had reached high office in a government which had ruled the country for so long that most young people could not remember another. And he had survived some temporary embarrassments, such as the death of his wife in the anti-nuclear protest at Worsfield Heath, to become a national figure. He was respected, enjoyed, if not liked, as a sardonic wit, a card, a man who gave honest utterance to the feelings of all ordinary citizens and who didn't give a damn for what the liberal intellectuals thought of him. Liberal intellectuals were responsible, after all, for most of the ills of the modern world, from drug abuse to the B.B.C. Some of his phrases had become part of the language, as when he called the welfare state 'The Scroungers' Charter', or the opposition 'The Ageing Hippies' because their principal concern seemed to be free hip-replacements in a population annually growing older. 'One chap's plastic hip,' Leslie Titmuss had been fond of saying when he was at Health, 'is another chap's crippling taxation.' The man who promised the Archbishop that he'd guarantee not to preach in Canterbury Cathedral provided that cleric kept his nose out of politics, who referred to barristers as 'wallies in wigs, wrapped in the tattered gowns of class privilege' and who had called the unemployed 'ladies and gentlemen of leisure' was always sure of a headline or a place on any chat show. He was then at the height of his power and his popularity

– and the England that had grown up in the last decade had been born in the image of Leslie Titmuss.

At the time of the lunch at St Joseph's all this had been achieved. Leslie was like a climber who scrambles up, with bleeding hands and boots lodged in precarious toe-holds, to the top of the apparently unassailable mountain and then has nothing to do but sit down, eat his sandwiches and admire the view. Although the first flush of triumph may have gone and the excitement of the ascent is over, it is still far too early to think about the way down.

Looking about him he saw only two more peaks to conquer. He would, what politician wouldn't, have liked to be Prime Minister, but only death, it seemed, would part the present incumbent from that office. He also wanted, he positively longed, to obliterate the memory of a failed marriage; and the only way he could think of doing this was by a marriage which would be a resounding success. He was tired of the sympathy hostesses bestowed on him for his widowerhood, as though it were some sort of physical deformity. His loneliness, he felt, put him back among the underprivileged, the no-hopers he had devoted considerable energy and talent to leaving far behind him. He wanted to marry but none of the ambitious personal assistants or party workers who were granted, for an occasional night, the freedom of his mansion flat came near to the idea of the sort of wife he thought his position demanded. He wanted a wife who would make him the envy of his few friends and, more satisfactorily, his many enemies. He wanted to hear the likes of his Minister of State Ken Cracken whisper, 'My God, how did old Leslie manage it?' Even, 'What the hell can she see in him?' would have been music to his ears. In the pursuit of matrimony he wanted to bring off something as seemingly impossible as the young nettle-feller from Rapstone Rectory earning a place in the Cabinet. When he found himself next to Jenny Sidonia for the first time he was presented, he thought, with the ideal challenge. He could hear the voice of his long-dead father, George Titmuss, who had no ambitions beyond being an accounts clerk at Simcox Brewery, saying, 'She's got class, boy. Undoubtedly class. Girls like that are not for the likes of you.' To which Leslie, calling over the gulf of the years, would have answered, 'Get stuffed, Dad, and just watch me.'

No doubt he overestimated the difficulties of capturing Jenny; he never understood her loneliness and consequent vulnerability. She was never that glacial and unscaleable peak he imagined her to be when he first took up the challenge. He thought, and this was perhaps Leslie Titmuss's most serious weakness, that people would never do what he wished unless they were bribed or threatened. There could, of course, be no question of threatening Jenny Sidonia, so some sort of inducement had to be offered to her. He guessed, quite rightly, that his political success meant nothing to her for as soon as politics were mentioned her gaze would wander round the room as though seeking means of escape. She would never have dreamt of allying herself with a man simply because he was in charge of the Department of Housing, Ecological Affairs and Planning; indeed such a position might well have an offputting and anaphrodisiac effect upon her. But he must have something she wanted because Leslie Titmuss, for all his apparent confidence, couldn't bring himself to believe that such a girl as Jenny Sidonia would love him for himself alone. And the perfect bribe, he came to convince himself, was Rapstone Manor.

Leslie had persuaded himself of the justice of his claim to the Fanner house many years before. He felt it was his because the family owed it to him. He had married their only daughter, who had not only been consistently unfaithful but indulged in political activities which were anathema to his party. The fact that he had married Charlotte Fanner because her father was chairman of the local Conservatives represented a debt which he had long since paid off. So he planned to acquire the house, when Grace Fanner died insolvent, from the deeply caring West Country Bank. But if he bought it the question was, what should he do with it?

His mother didn't want it and his son, at any rate for the moment, seemed to regard the prospect of owning a large country house in an appalling state of disrepair, as akin to a sentence of death. Then Leslie met Jenny Sidonia and thought that, although she might find the idea of life with him a doubtful prospect, life with him in a house which had impressed her, in a place she found beautiful, would prove a temptation she could not resist. So he decided to go ahead and buy the place. It was while the sale was going through that he picked up the information that Ken Cracken, his Minister of State, had been careful to keep from him, that there were plans afoot to submerge the Rapstone Valley in Fallowfield Country Town. He thought of the pointlessness of offering the girl he hoped to make his bride a charming and historic country house situated within hailing distance of the municipal Leisure Complex and the bus centre, bang in the middle of the pedestrian precinct. From that moment Leslie Titmuss became a secret underground member of S.O.V.

Nipping in the bud such an expensively fertilized plant as Fallowfield presented him with a problem which even he felt was a challenge to his political skills. His speech to the construction industry had been a great success and he didn't intend to retract a single word of it. However, as he had said to Ken Cracken, in the encounter that led Ken to the astonishing conclusion that his boss had gone green, free scope for market forces and healthy commercial development must be balanced against the claims of the environment, and there was, surely, more environment round the Rapstone Valley than almost anywhere else in the British Isles. Moreover, there was another powerful reason against the erection of Fallowfield Country Town. Christopher Kempenflatt stood to make an extraordinarily large sum of money out of it and Kempenflatt, as the Secretary of State would remember until the day he died, had publicly humiliated Leslie Titmuss at the Young Conservative dinner dance.

The question was how to prevent Fallowfield without the

charge that he was doing it to provide a quiet and privileged home for his new family. The answer was, Leslie thought, perfectly simple. There would be a free and independent public inquiry, and the function of a free and independent public inquiry was, the Secretary of State had no doubt, to reflect his preferably unstated wishes. When the inquiry had reported that, after careful deliberation and having heard all sides, the Rapstone Valley was not, after all, a suitable site for urban development, he would have no alternative but to accept its recommendations. There might be a few snide comments in some discontented newspapers, jokes about his back garden, but his reputation would merely grow greener and thereby more attractive. Jenny and he, together with the deer and badgers and the Duke of Burgundy's fritillary butterfly, could enjoy the valley unmolested, and the best-laid schemes of Kempenflatts the builders would come to nothing.

It was a time for weddings in Rapstone. Dot Curdle, using her full authority as head and undisputed ruler of the Curdle family, ordered her daughter, Evie, to take Dr Simcox's unpalatable medicine, somewhat hastily prescribed, and 'have a go' at marriage guidance. It was a command that Evie felt she had to obey, so she presented herself, wearing an extremely sullen expression, at the office under the Town Hall in which the marriage guidance lady appeared once a week to give counsel. With Evie was her fiancé, Len Bigwell, a ginger-haired, plump and perpetually smiling young man who loved her tenderly and was deeply moved by her heroic efforts to adjust herself to the unpalatable business of loving him.

'Sit down, both of you, and do just relax.' Mrs Tippett, the marriage counsellor, was a substantial, dark-haired woman with tragic eyes who wore a knitted suit, boots and numerous bangles. Evie and Len sat, perched nervously on the edge of their chairs. 'Sex,' Mrs Tippett opened briskly, 'is really nothing to be afraid of, is it?'

'Isn't it?' Evie looked profoundly unconvinced. 'I don't know so much.'

'Now then, Miss Curdle.' Mrs Tippett's voice became softer, more cajoling. 'I'm sure you're very much in love with your Les.'

'No.' Evie's small mouth shut tight as a mousetrap.

'You mean, you *don't* love Les?'

'No.' Evie's mouth was only opened wide enough to admit the smallest morsel of cheese and then snapped shut again.

'And yet' – the counsellor's eyes moved imploringly towards heaven – 'you're going to become his wife.'

'No.' Evie felt she was winning.

'Oh, dear. Has something gone rather wrong? A lovers' tiff sort of thing? This is *marriage* guidance, you know. That's what we're here to help you with. Now tell me, dear. Why aren't you going to marry Les?'

'Because I don't know no Les.' Evie feared that she had let herself down and said too much.

There was a moment of real panic in the counsellor's large eyes. Seldom or never had she given marriage guidance to a couple who were not only not married but didn't even know each other. And then the smiling man broke his silence to say, 'I'm *Len*. Len Bigwell.' 'Oh, dear. Silly me!' Mrs Tippett laughed musically and her bangles rattled an accompaniment. 'Of course you are. Sorry, Miss Curdle. I'm sure you're very much in love with your chap, Len.'

Evie sat with her mouth shut, giving no more away.

'Len loves *you*. I'm sure about that. Don't you, Len?'

'No problem,' Len assured her. 'Never has been.' He looked at his fiancée and blinked away tears, apparently of happiness.

'And you love Len, I'm sure. Don't you love Len, Miss Curdle? And may I call you Evie?'

'I don't care.'

'You don't care for Len. Really?'

'I don't care if you calls me Evie.'

The bangles jingled again as the counsellor looked at her watch; so far the interview seemed to be getting nowhere. 'You do want Len to be happy, Evie, don't you?'

'I'm not worried.' Evie Curdle looked longingly at the door.

'What?' The counsellor looked deeply concerned.

'She's honestly not worried,' Len explained, still smiling proudly, 'if I'm happy or not. That's what she's trying to tell you.'

'That's Len's business, isn't it? If he's happy.' Evie agreed so far with her fiancé.

'Your business too, Evie. When you're married to him. And if you make Len happy, then perhaps you'll make yourself happy too.'

'Not by doing it I won't.'

'Evie. Can I ask you this? Have you ever tried?'

'I haven't.'

'I have,' Len admitted proudly. 'On numerous occasions.'

'Well . . . how did Evie react?' Mrs Tippett clearly felt as though she were getting somewhere at last.

'Told me to get lost.' Len still looked admiringly at his future bride.

'But Evie. Don't you think Len loves you?' Mrs Tippett seemed increasingly pained.

'He says he does.'

'And you believe him?'

'I suppose so.'

'Well, then . . .'

'If he loves me he can do without it. Loving me ought to be quite enough for him. Anyway, that's what I reckon.'

'Evie.' The counsellor got up and paced the room, her arms crossed on her bosom, her military-style boots clicking on the linoleum. 'Evie, my dear . . .' She was about to embark on an inquiry which she knew might prove long and painful and she feared it might be difficult to obtain a stream of recollection from a client who was addicted to monosyllables. 'I wonder if we could go on a little journey together. Into your past. Now, I want you to be a hundred per cent honest about this. Is there anything in your childhood, anything at all, which might account for your distaste for . . . the physical side of married life?'

'Yes.' Evie answered immediately and the counsellor felt she had been pushing at a door which opened far too quickly and overbalanced her.

'Reeaally? How . . . how interesting! Do you feel you might be able to tell me?'

'I was brought up with a lot of bloody rabbits.'

'Rabbits?' The counsellor was slow to take in the relevance of the answer.

'Angoras and eaters. And I works on her family's rabbit hacienda *with* Evie. We are fellow workers,' Len explained.

'The angoras is the worst,' Evie told her counsellor with disgust. 'Always at it.'

'I see. Yes, of course. I do see.' Mrs Tippett sat down and consulted her watch, causing another jangle of jewellery. 'I think we must have a long chat about this. A real heart-to-hearter. Do you think you'd be able to come regularly on Thursdays? And it would be a terrific help if Les, I mean Len, would come with you.'

'You mean for marriage guidance?'

'Well, yes.'

'How long'd we have to keep coming?' Len was prepared for anything.

'Until we've helped you sort out your little problem.'

'You mean, until I give him sex?'

'Well, I suppose you could put it like that. Yes.'

Evie thought it over. 'If I do it once a week, I won't have to come?'

'Well, no. I'm sure Len thinks that reasonable. In view of your rather unusual upbringing. Wouldn't you, Len?'

'I'd settle for that.' Len was his usual cheerful self. 'Thank you.'

'Then it's either sex or marriage guidance?' Evie looked at the door again.

'Well, I wouldn't put it exactly like that.'

'I'll do the sex,' Evie said with the grim air of a youthful offender opting for a short, sharp shock rather than a long period on probation. 'I'd rather do that than come here again.' And then she made for the door with Len hurrying eagerly after her.

Not long afterwards and influenced by her intense dislike of marriage guidance, Evie and Len made love in a darkened caravan on the rabbit farm. The effect on her was not noticeable, but Len became a changed man. He smiled less but his self-confidence increased hugely. He worked out new ideas for packaging the freezer joints and toured the countryside looking for more retail outlets. 'Health food is the name of the game nowadays,' he told Dot Curdle with his new-found enthusiasm. 'We've got to sell rabbit as nature's greatest health food. Country-fed rabbit. A genuine green dinner.'

'Green?' Dot was doubtful. 'Only if it's gone off.'

'And I bet rabbit cures a lot of illness.'

'Does wonders for your love life, anyway.' Dot laughed. 'You found that, didn't you, Evie?'

'Please, Mum. Don't be disgusting!'

All the same, Evie admired the new, entrepreneurial Len Bigwell and, by the time they walked down the aisle of Rapstone Church together, she felt able to tolerate his love-making, which was already having such a beneficial effect on the family business. As for Len, he was so overcome with emotion brought on by the day, the organ music, the smell of orange blossom and Evie's new compliance that he looked at his bride through another blur of devoted tears. Fred, who had been invited to attend the ceremony, wondered at the success of Mrs Tippett's marriage guidance as an aphrodisiac in which he had not, up to then, had a great deal of faith.

A few weeks later he was back in the same church for another wedding, that of the Right Honourable Leslie Titmuss, M.P. and Jenny, only daughter of Edward and Joanna Banks. Leslie, who had had the invitations printed, had not included the name Sidonia on them.

As he sat in the church crowded with the notable inhabitants of Rapstone and the surrounding countryside, Fred wondered why he had been invited and why he had accepted the invitation. More years ago than he cared to remember Leslie had asked him to be his best man when he married Charlotte Fanner, and Fred, a young medical student with a love affair in tatters, had welcomed an afternoon away from the study of the central nervous system. Over the years they had grown so apart that they now seemed like strangers from distant countries, brought up in alien cultures: the country doctor who despised politicians, and particularly politicians of the Titmuss variety, and the Secretary of State who found Dr Simcox's retreat from the world of great issues and tough decisions into the safety of a country practice merely pathetic. So why had Fred come? Curiosity, he supposed, and – he thought how little, on the whole, he had changed since his student days – on an impulse to break up the monotonous routine of his life. As for why Leslie had asked him, the reason was obvious as soon as Jenny, crowned with flowers and smiling as though still amazed at what she was getting up to, entered the church on the arm of a conveniently tall cousin she hardly knew. He was standing in for her father who couldn't get away from his considerable family in Oakwood, California. Leslie Titmuss clearly wanted to show her off and fill his few friends and many enemies with wonder and envy. Leslie had no doubt that Fred had patronized him from his childhood and had despised his ruthless pursuit of fame and fortune. And now, Leslie had wanted to say, what have you got for keeping your hands out of grubby politics? Nothing but the prospect of a lonely old age, whereas I am now standing in front of the altar, where your father once prayed in vain for the coming of a new Socialist Jerusalem, waiting for a slim and beautiful young woman to deliver herself to me, forsaking all others. This may not have been exactly how Leslie Titmuss would have put it, but Fred Simcox thought it was, and Fred was never able to attribute high motives to the man he looked on as a threat to England in general and to the Rapstone Valley in particular.

It was all done with considerable dispatch. Kev the Rev. gave a short address in which he managed to mention 'compassion' four times, 'values beyond the marketplace' three times and 'England's green and pleasant land' at least twice. He had nerved himself to give this homily, which he thought of as a daring attack on government policies, but Leslie sat smiling imperturbably and Jenny seemed lost in thoughts of her own. Then the organ played and the happy couple, together with Elsie Titmuss and Jenny's mother, a flustered and larger edition of her daughter, who had arrived late and spent most of the service whispering loudly about the present she had bought and forgotten to bring, or forgotten to buy and therefore hadn't brought, or meant to buy as soon as she got a moment, set off down the aisle. So Jennifer Sidonia, feeling that she had said goodbye to her name and so to much of her past, became Jennifer Titmuss.

When they came out of the church and into the rain they were met by a political demonstration. It seemed, at first sight, to consist mainly of members of the Curdle family, with Evie prominent and showing all the joy and vitality she had lacked at her own wedding ceremony and waving a S.O.V. poster tacked on to part of a disused rabbit hutch. HANDS OFF OUR VALLEY, TITMUSS, other placards read, and IT'S YOUR BACK GARDEN TOO, LESLIE. Dot Curdle grasped in one fist a threatening placard reading DON'T LET THE BASTARDS CONCRETE OVER OUR FURRY FRIENDS, whilst the other opened to hurl a cloud of confetti at the newly wed Titmuss. She shouted, 'God bless you, sir, and your lovely lady!' Colonel Wilcox and his wife, who had refused an invitation to the church on grounds of conscience, stood to attention in their cotton hats, it now being officially summer, holding up the only insignia of the Ramblers' Society they had been able to find readily, a cheerful drying-up cloth showing a well-marked footpath snaking across a green landscape. Mr and Mrs Vee were among the assorted demonstrators, having organized the occasion without reference to their Chairman, who now came out of the church and looked at them with considerable surprise. Dr Simcox, the Vees felt, was far too old-fashioned to take advantage of the magnificent photo-opportunities the Titmuss wedding would provide.

'Not much of a demo, Fred. I was disappointed. Couldn't your Friends of the Earth have done any better than that?' Leslie Titmuss spoke with smiling belligerence. 'I thought at least you'd have had a bit of manure thrown, or organized an attack with reaping hooks by outraged yokels in smocks. Bit of a damp squib, wasn't it?'

'I'm sorry.' Fred felt, as his champagne glass was refilled by an elderly waitress hired from the Hartscombe Rowing Club, that the least he could do was apologize. 'I really didn't know it was going to happen.'

'But aren't you Chairman of the Save Our Valley Society? That was certainly my information.'

'Well, yes. I suppose I am.' It was Fred's way to smile at the pomposity of the title.

'You mean you're the Commander-in-Chief and the troops don't tell you when they're going to attack?'

'Not on this occasion, no,' Fred admitted.

'I'd call that mutiny.' Leslie Titmuss laughed. 'I suppose you'd say it was democracy at work?'

'I think they should have stayed away from your wedding.'

'Oh, I didn't mind in the least. I don't mind anything now I've got Jenny.' Leslie looked across to where his wife was talking to the Lord Lieutenant of the county with wonderfully simulated animation. 'I'm going to make it work, you know. This time I'm honestly going to make it work.' And he said it with such intensity that Fred was even more uncomfortable than

537

he had been when he spotted Colonel and Mrs Wilcox holding up a tea-towel in the rain.

'You ought to try marriage,' Leslie advised him. 'Give up politics. You've clearly got absolutely no talent for it.' Fred didn't answer. He was looking round at the newly decorated walls, the fresh plaster and restored chandelier of the Rapstone drawing-room. There was every sign that Titmuss in his new-found happiness was planning on a long stay and he thought that, even without the ill-timed S.O.V. demonstration, the threat of Fallowfield was receding.

'The trouble with you and your father before you –' Fred was now looking across the room at Jenny, the house's newest and most beautiful acquisition. He heard, as though from a great distance, yet another attack by Leslie on the late Rector of Rapstone, whose memory still seemed to haunt him. 'You think your consciences are so much more important than other people's. You think you've only got to parade your precious consciences in some sort of bedraggled procession, take them out for a walk as though they were relics of the One True Cross, and all sorts of miracles will occur. Isn't that what your old dad thought? He imagined the Bomb would go away if he went out marching with a few mums pushing prams and a handful of weirdos playing guitars.'

Is *that* what this beautiful woman had done it for? Fred asked himself in bewilderment. Had she dressed herself up in lace and decorated her hair with orange blossom to listen to this sort of thing from Titmuss over and over again for the rest of her life?

'Wankers of the world unite, you've got nothing to lose but your self-advertising liberal causes!' Leslie laughed and Fred became increasingly uncomfortable in the presence of such an obviously cheerful Titmuss. Then he felt the politician's hand on his arm and Leslie's voice sank to a conspiratorial murmur. 'If you really want to fight the Fallowfield development there're a lot of better ways of going about it. Oh, there's the folk from satellite T.V. I'd better go and give them a welcome.'

There were several groups in anoraks piling their plates at the buffet, representatives of the news programmes who had covered the Titmuss wedding. As Leslie went to talk to them Fred, whose view of his host's conduct was never generous, thought he was probably going to lean on the broadcasters to exclude the S.O.V. demonstration. On the contrary, and to the delight of the Curdle family, whose shouts of self-recognition echoed from their mobile homes that night, the demonstration was prominently featured. Dot Curdle, waving her poster and flinging her confetti, was bounced into space and back into millions of homes, and the protests seemed electronically multiplied to sound like a substantial popular uprising.

The Secretary of State for Housing, Ecological Affairs and Planning gave a brief interview to camera before he left with his bride for Rome. The following is an extract.

INTERVIEWER: Minister. Does your acquisition of this lovely home, Rampton Manor House –

TITMUSS: Rapstone. Get it right, young man.

INTERVIEWER: *Rapstone*. I'm sorry. Does it mean, sir, that plans for a new town here are unlikely to go ahead?

TITMUSS: It means nothing of the sort! If the inquiry decides that Fallowfield Country Town can be built, it will be a great experience for my wife and myself to live as part of such an exciting new development.

INTERVIEWER: And the value of your property will no doubt increase?

TITMUSS: We hope the value of everybody's property will increase. We're not in the business of seeing decent, hard-working householders lose money as they did in the days of the last Labour Government.

INTERVIEWER: So it all depends on the public inquiry?

TITMUSS: Of course. That's the way we do things in a democracy.

INTERVIEWER: And if it happens you'd happily live next door to a new town?

TITMUSS: Of course we would. Just like any other young couple, starting out in life. Is that it? I've got a plane to catch . . .
INTERVIEWER: Thank you, Minister. And many congratulations on your marriage.
TITMUSS: Oh, yes. Marriage is a wonderful thing. You should try it some time.

Although the interviewer may have had a somewhat ambiguous appearance he was, in fact, the happy father of two and the Secretary of State's last remark was uncalled for. Most of his audience found it appealing, however, and a sure sign that their much appreciated Leslie Titmuss had lost none of his zip.

Leslie had been happy in Rome. He couldn't help noticing and enjoying the looks of envy and increased respect caused by having Jenny at his side. She spoke a little Italian and he encouraged this performance with pride, although so far as he was concerned an inability to speak any foreign language was an essential feature of the no-nonsense politics he embodied. Foreign languages, in Leslie's book, were for wets and international socialists, although from Jenny's lips the words sounded entrancing and musical to his ears. He assumed she would be interested in clothes and she agreed, after some argument, to let him buy her a dress and a pair of shoes, but a tiny part of the expensive wardrobe he offered her. Clothes shops, she said, bored her and she took him on short visits to picture galleries, insisting that no one could really take in more than a few paintings on any one visit. He was grateful for this wisdom and failed to wonder who had taught it to her. He found the religious subjects, the pale saints bristling with arrows and the agonized crucifixions, embarrassing. He was more interested in the portraits of Popes and Emperors, persons of authority at whom he looked with fascination and some understanding.

During these days he felt that he had his new wife's full attention. When they were together she looked at him in a way he found flattering and he was engrossed in watching her, so that her smallest movement, the doubtful way she frowned at herself in a mirror, her habit of running a long finger round the rim of a wine glass as she talked, delighted him. He assumed she had picked up her knowledge of the language and the pictures on other visits, but he didn't worry about that until their last evening when she said she knew somewhere for dinner. It was when they had come out of the narrow streets of the drug-dealers into the square with its fountain and its gold mosaic church, that he felt, for the first time, the presence of an intruder. As they crossed the square of Santa Maria in Trastevere he knew that she was concerned, not with him, but with whoever her last companion there had been. When she lit a candle in the church he knew that it was not in tribute to her future but to her past. And when they sat together outside the restaurant her sudden, unexpected tears seemed an act of infidelity to him. They were married and alone, she was wearing the dress and the shoes he had bought her, they were going back to the house she had wanted, in the countryside she found beautiful. He had been consistently kind and considerate and had taken the greatest care of her at all times. If she were weeping it wasn't because of him; her tears, like her candle, were a tribute to another man.

Leslie Titmuss's jealousy of Tony Sidonia began that evening.

CHAPTER FOURTEEN

In the place on the Rapstone Nature Area, once known, although the fact is forgotten except by Hector Bolitho Jones and a very few former villagers now lodged in the Hartscombe Old People's Home, as Hanging Wood, there were, when Hector was a boy, at least fifty badgers. Their numbers had considerably diminished over the years. Some had died, like operatic heroines, of tuberculosis. Some had been frightened by poachers' lights and killed by poachers' lurchers, long-legged, sharp-toothed dogs who could run faster than they. A few had even, so it was suspected, been flushed out by terriers and kidnapped by the likes of sixteen-year-old Billy Curdle, who organized furtive and illicit dog and badger fights in a remote corner of the rabbit hacienda to make money. In these prize fights the badgers, heavily built and with tight-locking jaws, were sometimes able to defeat and kill the smaller dogs. At the top of Hanging Wood, where the old and close beech trees abruptly gave way to a corn field, there was a sett which was no less than four hundred years old. Now it contained one family of four. The sow had the scar of a deep and inadequately healed dog-bite in her stomach, but she had given birth to two cubs, born blind and now, at two months, just about able to find their way into the open air. At nightfall this family left the sett and the complicated system of tunnels which surrounded it and ventured out to feast on roots, fruit, eggs, insects, young birds and small mammals.

When out foraging, the badgers, short-sighted but with a keen sense of smell, recognized their family by the musk which they sprayed from their bodies. They had sprayed some of this pungent odour on Hector Jones's boots, so he was always a welcome and recognized member of the group. As his relations with Daphne deteriorated he would spend more of his nights with the badgers.

One moonlit night towards the end of that summer Hector had gone out after a supper with Daphne noted for its prolonged silences and deliberate, resentful chewing. He had climbed to the top of the wood, carrying no light which might alarm nocturnal creatures. The moonlit hills were not silent. Dogs barked distantly, owls shrieked and whirled down on mice stirring among the fallen leaves. There was a sound of running in the ground cover of brambles, which Hector took to be a deer on the rampage. So he climbed steadily to the top of the wood and was there rewarded by the sight of the old sow badger tirelessly collecting bedding of dried grass, twigs and leaves to make her family comfortable.

Then, from a clump of bushes far down the wood, Hector saw a little light. It was a distant pin-point but its presence, and the addition it gave to a feeling of danger provided by the sharp calls of birds of prey and the sudden flutter of death, sent the sow scuttling into the safety of her sett, her carefully gathered bedding forgotten. Hector looked after her with regret and then up to stare at what was happening in the clearing half-way down the hill.

Three men had emerged from the shadows, running, crouching, bent almost double, carrying objects that had the undoubted appearance of guns. They were dressed in flak jackets and berets, their parti-coloured trousers tucked into huge boots and their faces daubed with camouflage paint. 'Christ!' said Hector Bolitho Jones, seeing that they were undoubtedly soldiers.

Soldiers, but whose? He tried to remember what little he'd read in the papers, or seen on the television when Daphne insisted on having it on. The Russians, surely, had become friendly. But could the Russians be trusted? He strained his ears to listen for commands in a foreign language as the men vanished into the shadows beside a great holly bush. If not Russian, were they Chinese or Arabs – the spearhead perhaps of an Islamic invasion, a terrifying crusade in reverse, set off to burn the church and rape the women? Hector's mind raced. His father had told him about the war, about the nights they had watched in Hanging Wood for Germans landing by parachute; how some of the Home Guard had laid hands on a man from the Electricity Board with a small toothbrush moustache and thought, for a single intoxicating moment, that they had 'got Hitler'. Well, the foreigners were obviously back, looking leaner, healthier, more determined and better armed. Alone in the wood he thought how he might raise the alarm and if he would be heard above the owls' shrieks and the distant barking, and the rattle of wind in the treetops. In his pocket he kept a whistle which he used to command the dogs who corralled sheep in the Nature Area. He raised it to his lips and blew a deafening blast.

Then he heard a charge and a thunder of boots. He turned and saw another platoon in uniform rushing towards him. They ran, grinning with triumph and excitement. He raised his whistle again, but as he did so the leader of the second platoon aimed his gun at Hector's face. Their eyes met and, in spite of the camouflage paint, Hector Jones had no difficulty in recognizing the fair moustache and heavily lidded eyes of Ken Cracken, the Minister at H.E.A.P. Whether Ken had been recognized seemed not to trouble him. He had seen an old enemy unexpectedly delivered into his hands. He pressed the spray-gun he held and the warden of the Rapstone Nature Area was struck dumb by the great spurt of yellow paint filling his mouth and dripping down his clothes towards the boots on which the badger sow had so sympathetically sprayed her musk.

'All in all, I think, one of our better exercises. Would you say that, Jumbo? As O.C. of the Yellows, old fellow. And, by the way, bad luck.'

Christopher Kempenflatt, still in his flak jacket but with his camouflage paint washed off, stuck his legs out towards the log fire in his country house, a listed mill which was in no danger at all of redevelopment. He held up his glass and the devoted Mrs Armitage refilled it. In the room a number of other men, still in bits and pieces of army uniform, were gathered. They included Ken Cracken and 'Jumbo' Plumstead, who looked as game as an old colonel. Joyce Timberlake was also of the party; there was still a spot of camouflage paint on her face, for she had been a fully combative W.R.A.C. girl for the Reds.

'I was commanding from our base,' Jumbo admitted, 'but from what came over my radio it sounded like a damn close-run thing.'

'Doesn't matter about being close run,' Kempenflatt told him. 'When it comes to war, you either win or lose. There's no half measures.'

'Much the same in politics,' Ken Cracken said. 'By the way, I think our battlefield got a bit extended. Weren't we meant to keep to your chum's woods, Christopher?'

Kempenflatt had got cooperation for his latest war game from the farmers who had sold him options to build Fallowfield on their land.

'We moved our operations to another wood. We'd organized a really great pincer movement but some old fart with a whistle tried to hold up our advance,' Ken Cracken told him.

'Oh, really? What did you do with him?' Christopher Kempenflatt was only moderately interested.

'Let him have it with my paint-gun. Full in the kisser! As a matter of fact, it's something I've been waiting to do for a long time.'

When he got home Hector Bolitho Jones cleaned the paint off his face and out of his hair and put his clothes aside for Daphne to take to the dry cleaners. He told her that he had been attacked by lager louts with a paint-gun, but he didn't think they'd dare to do it again. However, he wrote another report to his superiors at S.C.R.A.P. to say that the hooligan who had been about to make love on a possible site of stone curlews' nests had returned to Rapstone Nature Area with a party in military attire. He had been sprayed with paint by a man he was now in a position to identify positively as Kenneth Cracken, M.P., Minister of State at H.E.A.P.

A few days later Hector visited the attic of the converted cottage in which he still kept, neatly packed away, certain of old Jones the gamekeeper's possessions. There was a tea-chest which contained his father's boots, carefully cleaned and wrapped in newspaper, his much worn and leather-patched jacket and an assortment of caps, his clasp knife, his silver watch and some homemade snares. There was also the gamekeeper's shot-gun, oiled and packed away in its case, and a khaki shoulder-bag still full of cartridges. Hector had never used this weapon. Now he often took it out of its case, raised it to his shoulder and aimed it, unloaded, at an imaginary target. He had no intention of using the gun against any of the wild creatures under his care, but ever afterwards, on his night-time patrols, he went armed.

The war in Rapstone woods had one other result. Leslie Titmuss was invited to lunch at the Sheridan Club by Lord Skirmett, President of the Society for Conservation, Rural and Arboreal Protection (S.C.R.A.P.). It was not an invitation he welcomed. Skirmett was exactly the sort of silver-haired, well-meaning and tweedy old Tory who was inclined to give trouble in the House of Lords on such subjects as the closing of rural schools. Leslie distrusted clubs like the Sheridan where the food was adjusted to the tastes of those who had been brought up in nurseries. However, as soon as his apologetic Lordship had explained the reason for the invitation, Leslie was glad he'd come.

'Of course the fellows at S.C.R.A.P. don't want to embarrass the Ministry in any way. But we can't have members of the Government running around spraying our wardens with paint! I mean, one can understand a bit of high spirits . . .'

'High spirits?' Leslie shook his head sadly. 'I'm afraid I take a far more serious view of Cracken's conduct.'

'I'm glad to hear it. I must say . . .'

'And I mean –' Leslie held up his hand to stop Lord Skirmett, who shuddered to a halt in mid sentence like an elderly motor car conking out on the road. 'I mean –' his voice sank to a low and menacing tone – 'to take this on board at once. I'm grateful to you for coming to me on this one, Lord Skirmett. I suppose I can rely on your organization to see that the whole matter remains absolutely confidential. I know you won't wish to embarrass the Government, at the moment when we're considering leaving some of our best reserves in your control.'

'No privatization?' Lord Skirmett asked hopefully.

'Wait for the statement. That's the trouble with the House of Lords. You all panic so easily. I think I can say that the proper preservation of nature is something which comes very high on our list of priorities. And I'm sure you'll understand how green our thinking is.'

'Green thinking?' Skirmett looked vaguely up to the ceiling as though trying to imagine what thinking of such a colour might look like. 'I'm so glad we've had this chance to exchange views, Secretary of State. It's been extremely helpful.'

'Oh, I agree.' But Leslie Titmuss did nothing with the knowledge he had gained for some time. He had no doubt that it would, in his future dealings with Ken Cracken, prove very useful indeed.

The Next Day

As I was going up the stair
I met a man who wasn't there.
He wasn't there again today.
I wish, I wish he'd stay away.

'The Psychoed'
Hughes Mearns

CHAPTER FIFTEEN

At last the orchids and the foxes, the ancient beech woods and chalk downlands, the rare butterflies and the unusual snails were to be submitted to the processes of democracy, which would decide whether they should survive or be obliterated for ever. This was the judgement which Leslie Titmuss wanted to be pronounced by others in accordance with his secret and never-to-be expressed wishes.

The heart of Worsfield, the town hall built to resemble a gothic château, the railway station built to look like a cathedral, the old biscuit factory which was, in its way, more imposing than either, had been demolished. Now its centre was filled with toy-town architecture. Immensely tall office buildings, the colour of raw liver embellished with blue-painted iron-work and plate-glass windows, looked as though some giant child had been let loose in the ruins with an infinite number of huge building bricks. Around these buildings the traffic swirled. Beneath the four-lane highways, in a warren of shopping malls, among boutiques and record stores and hamburger havens where the light of day never penetrated, the citizens of Worsfield went about their business like the rabbits which scuttled through the complex system of tunnels under the Rapstone Nature Area.

High up in one of the Worsfield towers the twenty or so members of the planning committee of the District Council assembled under the energetic chairmanship of a Mrs Babcock-Syme. She was a tireless local politician with flashing eyes and a husky voice which could rise to sudden rage or sink to a tone of naked sensuality, even during the discussion of planning matters, which would startle and fascinate the male members of the committee to such an extent that many of them became clay in her hands. It was not, in fact, a hard committee to manage. The majority of those who had the time to stand for election and go to meetings were either local builders or farmers. The farmers, quietly spoken men in business suits, were longing to sell their land at a handsome profit to developers. The builders, dressed in old tweeds and corduroys and keen on rustic pursuits, were always on the look-out for somewhere new to build. Neither of these groups had any fundamental disagreements with the alluring 'Chair', who was inclined to give out permission for most things to be built in most places because, as she was fond of telling the admiring men by whom she was surrounded, 'The name of the game is consumer choice.'

'When I was a girl at Worsfield Grammar' – Mrs Babcock-Syme was a local – 'we could only get three sorts of yoghurt at the corner shop. At the last count Luxifoods in the Mall had twenty-three. I call that a smashing victory for consumer choice. Yes, Mr Parsloe?'

Ted Parsloe, a retired headmaster whom Mrs Babcock-Syme suspected of not taking her entirely seriously, had raised his pencil and now said, 'Thank you, Madam Chair. I must say, I've never cared for yoghurt.'

'It's the same principle, Mr Parsloe. Applied across the board. We're giving the consumer the choice of living in an old town like Worsfield or a new town like Fallowfield.'

'With respect, Madam Chair. What if I, as a consumer, don't want to live in a town at all?'

'Then I would suggest, Mr Parsloe' – the Babcock-Syme voice sank almost to a whisper of flagrant sexuality – 'you move to the North of England where I understand there are still lots of empty spaces.'

'With respect, Madam Chair –' Mr Parsloe was grateful for

the fact that his advanced age made him safe from the allure of Hermione Babcock-Syme. He plodded gamely on like the only surviving explorer in a group otherwise gone down with an exotic tropical disease. 'There are plenty of empty spaces in the old Worsfield station area and all the empty warehouses by the canal. Why not build there if we need new houses?'

'May I, Madam Chair?' A red-faced builder smiled at Hermione Babcock-Syme in a roguish sort of way.

'Oh, yes, Mr Entwhistle. Please do.'

'It's far cheaper and easier to build houses on green field sites. Cost a fortune to clear the old station and the warehouses.'

'I'm sure we're grateful,' Mrs Babcock-Syme purred to Mr Entwhistle, 'for that very practical contribution. Yes, Mrs Tippett?' Mrs Tippett, the marriage guidance counsellor who had done her best to make sense of the love life of Evie Curdle, rattled her bangles, sighed heavily and said they still needed more houses in the middle of Worsfield for one-parent families on Income Support. When Mrs Babcock-Syme said that Fallowfield Country Town would provide rows of houses for such unfortunates no one thought to remind her that low-income one-parent families would never be able to afford the delights of the new town.

The Chair was now ready to sum up the discussion: 'The Secretary of State has given us the lead in his super speech to the builders. We can't have No Go areas for the operation of market forces. A new town would make Rapstone England's Silicone Valley of prosperity.' The Chair grew more eloquent as she saw a wide thoroughfare, bejewelled with the neon signs of fast-food outlets, leading between Parkinson Close and Titmuss Gardens to an imposing civic centre. Its name, she had reason to hope, would be Babcock-Syme Boulevard and her immortality would be assured. 'What I think most of us see here, with a very few exceptions' – she flashed a lethal smile at the headmaster – 'is a tremendous opportunity to make – yes, what is it, Mr Plant?' This was the planning officer whose secretary had just come in with a message. Certain plans, it seemed, concerning road access and a new sewage system had still not been supplied. Certain questions still had to be answered. With considerable irritation the Chair announced that, although she had little doubt of what the majority would decide, the matter would be adjourned until the next meeting.

That night Eric Babcock-Syme, who owned a garage on the Hartscombe Road, a business he saw growing to supply the Fallowfield motorway-exit service area, told Vernon Beazley that S.O.V. might as well pack it in because, without a doubt, Hermione's committee would give the green light to the new town. On the same evening the Right Honourable Leslie Titmuss made a speech to the Nottingham Chamber of Commerce. He made, of course, no reference to Fallowfield, which was, he was anxious to give the impression, no concern of his, at any rate for the time being. However, dedicated Titmuss-watchers were surprised to see that he spoke with considerable respect for the tiger, the black rhino and the world's diminishing supply of elephants. He showed a new interest in the ozone layer and announced that all H.E.A.P.'s vehicles were now running on unleaded petrol. He made a number of jokes at the expense of the Greens, townees most of them he said, who probably thought a badger sett was something trendy you ordered at the hair-dresser's. 'I wonder how many of them,' he told his delighted audience, 'earned sixpence a day cutting nettles, weeded a potato bed, scared off birds in an orchard or picked a big bunch of bluebells in the local woods on the two-mile walk home from school on Mothers' Day?' Unlike most of those who only noticed nature when they got bored with preaching socialism, Leslie Titmuss reminded his audience that he was 'a countryman born and bred. I was brought up sniffing country air, that potent mixture of new-cut grass, cherry blossom and farmyard muck. My message to all of you is have no fear. So long as I'm at H.E.A.P. our environment is safe for future generations.' It appeared that the greenish tinge, noticed by Ken Cracken with such amusement, had deepened and somewhere, although not necessarily in the Rapstone Valley, there would always be a wood where the small Titmusses of the future might disport themselves and gather bluebells. On the distant African plains the few remaining rhinos might also snort their relief that Titmuss, at least, was on their side.

Although the new town seemed set for an early victory, the opposition to it was growing in strength. From its small and unpromising beginnings S.O.V. advanced rapidly and, greatly to his surprise, Fred found himself at the head of a substantial and fairly well-financed army of protesters. The converted barn, extended cottage, jacuzzi and carport owners were entirely with him. Although Fred disliked their habit of decorating the commons with gothic-lettered signs announcing the close proximity of their houses, 'Badgers End', 'The Coppice', 'Nut Trees' or, in the case of an old chapel converted to house two youngish men in designer knitwear, 'Shrivings', he was glad of their support and their subscriptions. Going on his rounds he would come across old ladies in gaunt grey houses in the back streets of Hartscombe, or in the middle of villages, who had played in the Rapstone woods when they were children and gone there for long walks with husbands, now long dead, who knew the names of the orchids and the gentians. They opened attics and descended cellar stairs to return with three-pronged Georgian forks, wine coolers, tarnished candlesticks, old lamps, spotted mirrors, dusty glass candelabras, dim oil paintings of the river and Hartscombe Bridge, sabres once used in the Crimea and silver teapots carefully wrapped in newspaper and hardly used at all. They gave these treasures to Fred to sell so that the valley might be saved, although for years past it had been a place they only visited in memory. In addition to these small donations, S.O.V. received, from a firm of solicitors who said their client wished to remain anonymous, a cheque for five thousand pounds to 'help in the propaganda war against Fallowfield Country

Town'. Fred banked it gratefully and with no idea who their unknown benefactor might be.

So, with a growing membership and bank account, Fred felt saddled with something he had never been used to – power. Could he and his strange assortment of allies hold their ground against what he still thought of as the Titmuss invasion and defeat the advancing tide of concrete, commercialism and pedestrian precincts? In moments of depression it seemed absurd even to try. But one day Mrs Vee told him that she had spent the morning walking in the Rapstone Valley. 'You think it's all yours, don't you, Fred?' she accused him. 'Just because it's where you lived all your life. You think we only got here lately and we're nothing but trippers, the sort you see with their little folding-chairs and Tupperware spread out all over Rapstone Common any Bank Holiday.' 'Of course, I don't,' Fred protested, although if the truth were told this was very much what he had, uncharitably, thought of the Vees from the time he had first met them. Now he felt, guiltily, that he must devote himself more whole-heartedly to the cause. After all, Mrs Vee spent her days sitting on strange sofas, chattering with incessant brightness and achieving, either by charming or by boring her victims, cheques of a size he would never have dared ask for.

'It's all the fault of that ghastly woman.' Mrs Vee rang him during his morning surgery.

'What ghastly woman?'

'The appalling Babcock-Syme. She's about to bully the District Council into giving planning permission. For Fallowfield. Only one person that can do anything now.'

'Really? Who's that?'

'You know Titmuss, don't you? He asked you to his wedding. You know him well.'

'Extremely well. In a manner of speaking.'

'He's the only one who can stop Babcock-Syme killing our valley. You can do it, Fred. You don't know your own strength. You can charm Titmuss.'

Fred had been expected to pull off many medical miracles, most of which were quite beyond his power; but he had never before been called upon to perform such a Herculean task as charming Leslie Titmuss. In view of Mrs Vee's clear devotion to the cause and the trust of the old ladies who had ransacked their attics for him, he felt bound to try. He phoned the Ministry, penetrated to the Secretary of State's office and left a message in which he felt no confidence. Then, driving on his morning rounds, he turned into the driveway of Rapstone Manor. It was not that he thought his diminishing fund of charm could be better spent on the new Mrs rather than the old Mr Titmuss. He told himself he would do better to call as an old family acquaintance and so arrange to talk to the Secretary of State. He could remember his short meeting with Jenny at her wedding and how her beauty had astonished him for many reasons, not least because it had so unexpectedly surrendered to Leslie Titmuss.

Jenny came round the corner of the house when she heard a car scrunch the gravel of the drive and then a ring at the front doorbell. There was earth on her hands and under her fingernails and a mark on her forehead where she had brushed back her hair with dirty fingers. The knees of her jeans were damp and muddy.

She stood still for a moment, looking at the back of the tall man by the front door. She noticed that his elderly tweed jacket hung from his shoulders as though from a coat-hanger. Something about the way he was standing, his hands in his pockets, at ease but in no way assertive, reminded her painfully of the lost husband she had been made to think of more often than she would have wished.

CHAPTER SIXTEEN

It was not that Jenny was unhappy living at Rapstone with Leslie Titmuss. Her life contained almost all she hoped for and very little of what she feared. The house itself had more than fulfilled her expectations. She spent a lot of time alone in it, but was never in the least lonely. The soft greenish light that filled the rooms, the constantly changing views of the park and the garden that greeted her as she moved from room to room, her new obsession with growing things which, instead of taking years, as she had supposed, to come to fruition, seemed to shoot up and proliferate with magical rapidity, all these acted on her like a drug, so that during any prolonged time she had to spend away from Rapstone she suffered acute withdrawal symptoms. Old Bigwell, father of Len Bigwell who was now happily married to Evie Curdle, continued to do the garden, coming full-time instead of the few hours a week that Lady Fanner had been able to afford. Spurred on by Jenny's constant praise and encouragement he resurrected the fruit cage, discovering in the jungle which filled it loganberries and white raspberries, as well as giant gooseberries which Jenny liked to explode in her mouth as she helped with the weeding. Slowly, like archaeologists excavating for traces of a lost civilization, they uncovered rose beds, bits of herbaceous border, patches where the strawberry plants were hidden under brambles and, under a rubbish tip, what must have been a forgotten rockery. Mr Bigwell, although secretly pleased by Jenny's flattery, made it a rule, like most professional gardeners, never to do what she suggested. She was only occasionally able to outmanoeuvre him by telling him that one of her favourite plans was impossible and never to be attempted. She would then retire to the house and keep watch from an upstairs window in the hope, sometimes fulfilled, of seeing him start to demonstrate his independence by digging the bed, applying the manure or sowing the seeds she had suggested.

Now she had taken to cooking and was proudest when she prepared the vegetables, or flavoured the meat with the herbs she and Mr Bigwell had grown together. Tony Sidonia had been a dashing cook who often improvised and she had thought herself a dull performer. But now she gained confidence and was happy in the kitchen, opening a bottle of white wine, chopping vegetables, listening to music and waiting, often for a long time, until Leslie got home. When he came he was always appreciative and rewardingly hungry. He praised her as fulsomely as she praised the gardener, and she was both pleased and unconvinced by his praises.

One night Leslie, who had cleared his plate, pushed it away and said, 'That was very tasty.'

'What?' she laughed at him.

'That was what my father always said. Every bloody night of his life. After tea he said, "That was very tasty, Mother. Very tasty indeed." I promise I won't do it again.' He looked at her, almost beseechingly. 'Don't let me, will you?'

What was unexpected about him were the jokes. She and Tony Sidonia had ritually voted for the Labour Party and, between elections, just as ritually denounced and derided the government of which the Right Honourable Leslie Titmuss was a member. Tony Sidonia's derision, however, was gentle compared to the savagery with which Leslie, at home with his wife, spoke of those of his colleagues who filled the other great offices of state. One might just as well have sent his suit to Cabinet meetings as it was 'the only smart thing about him'. Another was thought to have been extremely intelligent 'when he was alive'. A third had less idea of how to present a Bill than 'a waitress in a teashop'. And so it went on, to such an extent that Jenny often felt, quite mistakenly, that her new husband shared at least some of the views she and Tony Sidonia had taken for granted. Leslie was careful never to discuss politics in general at home, nor did he ask Jenny to read his speeches. When they watched him on television and she raised her eyebrows at some of his more outrageous utterances, he assured her that he was only having 'a bit of fun' or 'tweaking a few tails' and she was inclined to share the general view that political life in England would have been a great deal duller without the tail-tweaking propensities of Leslie Titmuss.

What she got from him was constant protection. From the start of their marriage he seemed determined to submit her to nothing she might find objectionable or even boring. He didn't ask her to go to meetings or cocktail parties in London. If they were invited to dinner with the 'colleagues', he would get his secretary to ring up with a convincing excuse if she showed the slightest reluctance to go. She was convinced that he only wanted her to be happy. She was right about this, but his feelings had changed since their wedding. He had once thought he wanted Jenny as a new possession to show to the world. Now he was like a millionaire who buys a painting of rare beauty, perhaps from a dubious source, and wants it kept in his home, never to be lent out for an exhibition, for his eyes only. He treasured her in his private not his public world, but he wanted her to be happy. He was perceptive enough to understand that this would not be the case if she had to go on trips with him to Chambers of Commerce or to many dinner parties with other government wives. He suspected that the 'colleagues' laughed at him for keeping his much younger wife under wraps, but he didn't mind, and when it came to laughing at people he could always win on points.

So, contrary to all reasonable forecasts and to the amazement of her friend Sue Bramble to whom Jenny spoke on the telephone almost daily, the Titmuss marriage had every appearance of success. They got on well in bed, a fact Sue found impossible to accept. Leslie would return home with as sharp an appetite for making love as he had for his dinner and Jenny, intoxicated by the fresh air, the silence, the small dramas of the garden and the white wine she got through whilst cooking, received him gladly and as though in a continuing dream. Perhaps one of his attractions for her was that danger which Sue Bramble had assured her lurked somewhere in Leslie Titmuss but which she had seen no sign of so far.

It was Leslie who said they should have Sue to stay. Jenny was grateful to him for the suggestion, although nervous about the outcome. In the end she couldn't resist showing off the house and the garden to her friend. Sue Bramble drove herself from London on a bright, spring day when the daffodils and the cherry trees were out and the azaleas in bud.

'Well?'

Sue had walked round the house as silent and non-committal as a police officer inspecting the scene of the crime. Now, when she had opened a bottle of wine in the kitchen and started to get the lunch, Jenny could stand the suspense no longer and asked again, 'Well? What do you think of it?'

'Terrible.'

'This house, and the garden? Terrible?' Jenny was standing in front of a chopping-board holding a half-moon shaped blade, frozen into puzzled immobility.

'Terrible that it's all so beautiful. Mr Titmuss used it to seduce you.'

'You don't think I married him for the house, do you?'

'One day I suppose I shall understand what you did marry him for.'

Jenny didn't answer that but started to chop parsley energetically, producing a clean, grassy smell and getting rid of the irritation she felt at Sue's obstinate disapproval. Then she chopped more slowly, smiled and said, 'You won't be too hard on my Mr Titmuss, will you?'

'Is he so delicate?'

'I'm not sure. He got rather badly laughed at once. He's remembered it all his life.'

'Don't worry. I'll treat him like a rare china ornament. I mean, I'll try to take him seriously.'

'I ought to tell you this.' Jenny pushed the chopped parsley into a neat pile with her blade. 'Something quite extraordinary's happened.'

'You're not . . .?'

'What?'

'Well. Not up the spout, are you?' Sue knew that her friend had been told that she couldn't, that she never would, have children. Had this extraordinary marriage, she wondered, produced some sort of medical miracle?

'No. Nothing like that. It's just that, well, we seem to be sort of entirely happy together.'

'I'm glad.' Sue seemed to accept the fact. 'Of course I want you to be extremely happy. Always.' Sitting at the kitchen table Jenny's friend raised her glass and drank to that.

'What were the games we used to play?'

The first evening of Sue's stay was going well. Leslie got home early and was perfectly polite, listening to her with studied concentration, as though it were important for him to understand everything she said. He was proud rather than embarrassed that they had met under strange and compromising circumstances and reminded her, 'You remember me? I was the one in the dicky-bow making early morning tea.' During dinner he enjoyed the company of two women, the blonde and the dark, laughing together in the candlelight. He opened more wine, spared them news of his day at the Ministry and listened sympathetically to Sue's accounts of the deceptive nature of men in general and racing trainers in particular. After dinner she lay back in a chair by the big log fire and reminded Jenny of the games they used to play.

'Charades. Wink Murder. "In the Manner of . . ." Oh, and The Truth Game, of course.'

'The Truth Game?'

'Oh, yes.' Sue explained it to Leslie. 'If you did something wrong – I mean, failed to drink a glass of wine in one gulp, or let the ash fall off your cigarette – then you got asked a question and you had to answer truthfully.'

'How did anyone know if you were telling the truth?' Leslie was interested.

'Oh, we could tell. We all knew so much about each other. Of course' – Sue looked at Jenny – 'Tony never had any problems with that game.'

It was the first time Tony Sidonia's name had been mentioned since their honeymoon. Jenny was quiet, hoping it would not be said again. But Leslie, raising his eyebrows, asked, 'Why didn't Tony have any problems?'

'Oh, because he always told the truth. Quite naturally. All the time. Didn't he, Jenny?'

'Well, yes, as a matter of fact. Who's for more wine?' Jenny got the bottle off the table and refilled their glasses, wishing for a change of subject.

'Such a truthful person, Tony. It really wasn't any fun playing the game with him.'

'But how can you be sure it was always the truth?' Leslie seemed eager for information.

'Oh, because he just couldn't lie. He wouldn't have been the slightest good at it. Would he, Jenny?'

'What would you like to do tomorrow?' It was Jenny and not Leslie who wanted to stop the Tony reminiscences. 'Would you like to go out to lunch somewhere?'

'Sunday lunch in the country. You remember those ridiculous great parties in Tony's garden?'

'In the summer?' Leslie's interest was apparently undiminished.

'The summers seemed so much better then, and longer. There

were always such an extraordinary number of guests. All sorts of people, writers, painters. Tony's mother, who was once a ballet dancer.'

'Myra was wonderful,' Jenny explained. 'Huge dark eyes and this amazingly straight back. She was really quite old then, but she'd play the piano for us and even dance occasionally. She danced so beautifully. No wonder so many men fell in love with her.'

'All sorts of writers, and wasn't there a general or something?'

'Oh, yes. Definitely a general. She said she took his mind off the war.'

'Do you remember,' Sue started to laugh, 'Willoughby Blane's shorts?'

'You were *outrageous*!' Jenny couldn't help laughing at the memory.

'Sir Willoughby Blane.' Leslie was smiling. 'The old bore who can tell you all you never wanted to know about prawns?'

'The man who brought us together.' Jenny did her best to bring the story up to date, but Sue remained firmly in the past with Tony Sidonia. 'It was so hot that year,' she said. 'We were all wearing, well, not very much really. And Willoughby Blane turned up in these vast, voluminous shorts. Tony had a long table with oh, about twenty people round it, out in the garden. I was sitting opposite Willoughby and he was next to that dreadful ex-ambassador's wife. What was her name?'

'I always forget.' Jenny was trying to put the past behind her.

'Mrs Lessore?' Leslie, who never forgot a name, had met her at the Oxford lunch.

'Gudrun Lessore was next to Willoughby Blane. On his right, I think.' Sue was apparently blessed with total recall. 'And, as I say, I was sitting opposite. Now you've got to understand that Tony's garden was always in a hell of a mess. This was before he married Jenny. The grass was never cut and was full of old bones and bits and pieces the dogs couldn't eat. Well, I looked under the table and I saw, what do you think? A chicken's foot! I suppose we'd had chicken for lunch and this old claw had got out into the garden. I hadn't got any shoes on so I somehow got this awful old yellow chicken's foot between my toes. And I managed . . . Jenny saw me do this, didn't you, Jenny?'

'Yes,' Jenny had to admit, 'I saw you.'

'Well, I managed to lift up my leg under the table and insert this terrible dead claw up Willoughby's baggy shorts. And he thought Gudrun Lessore was making a most intimate pass at him. He became all giggly and flirtatious.'

When she finished there was silence. Jenny looked anxious. Sue, not in the least contrite, smiled down into her glass. Leslie sat forward in his chair, frowning as though seriously trying to assess the full significance of this story, and then he burst into loud laughter. Much relieved, Jenny then laughed with him, as though the incident were much funnier than it had seemed at the time.

That night in bed Leslie lay quiet again, apparently asleep with his eyes open. Jenny watched him for a long time and then he said, 'Was he really like that?'

'Who?'

'Tony Sidonia.'

'I'm sorry,' Jenny apologized for her friend. 'I don't know why Sue kept on about him. It was stupid of her.'

'How did you *know*?'

'What?'

'How did you know he was always telling the truth?'

'I'm not sure.' She tried to think of a reason which would convince him and failed. 'I just did know. That was all.'

'And that was important to you?'

'Oh, yes. The most important thing in the world.'

He seemed to think about that for a while, then he closed his eyes and was really asleep. The subject wasn't mentioned again that weekend and Jenny wasn't troubled by thoughts of Tony Sidonia until much later when she saw the back of Fred Simcox as she walked round the house.

*

'Of course, I remember you at the wedding.'

Now that she was facing Fred in the sitting-room she could see that he didn't really look in the least like her late husband. All the same Tony Sidonia felt nearer to her at that moment than he had been since he died. Jenny thought again of Tony when Fred said, with a kind of self-confident modesty, 'I've become the sort of pest who dumps leaflets on people.' Indeed, he had a glossy folder in his hand, decorated very much like the developers' propaganda, with a picture of sheep grazing. This document had been prepared for S.O.V. by an advertising agency well known to Mr Vee.

'Why?' she asked. 'What's it all about?'

'The new town we're threatened with.'

Jenny took the folder politely, feeling he was glad to be rid of it. 'I mean,' he said, 'I'm sure you're attached to the valley.'

'I've come to love it. Of course, you know it much better than I do.'

'Since I was a child. Your husband and I were boys together. My father was the Rector.'

'And Leslie used to cut his nettles.'

'He's told you that?'

'Oh, yes. Quite often.' He smiled when she said that and she felt she had been disloyal to her husband. 'I don't think you need worry too much,' she said. 'Leslie doesn't want this valley spoiled, either.' So she established Leslie's credentials as a responsible and caring politician.

'I just hope' – Fred looked at her, smiling – 'he's going to tell the District Council that.'

'What've they got to do with it?'

'Quite a lot. If they say "yes" no one can appeal. And it seems they're all ready to give the green light to Fallowfield.'

'Does Leslie know that?'

'I'm sure he knows most things. But it wouldn't do any harm to remind him. I'll give him a ring, if I can, over the weekend.'

'I'm sure he'll be glad to hear from you.'

Fred wasn't so sure. All the same he felt he'd gone as far as he could with the beautiful and apparently receptive Mrs Titmuss. 'Well,' he said, 'I won't bore you any longer.'

'Your patients'll be waiting.'

'Not many round here. They're terribly healthy in this valley and seem to live forever.'

'Like Lady Fanner?'

'She was well over eighty when she died,' he told her. 'A pretty good advertisement for a diet of gossip, champagne and cigarettes.' He was looking out of the tall windows. 'You've tidied up the garden.'

'If you've got time I could show you what we've done.'

'I'd like to see.' And when they were walking down the long border she'd planted and he was admiring the white cloud of narcissi in the rough grass of the orchard, she wondered what old Lady Fanner had been like. 'Extremely malicious. She had a bad word to say of everyone. I must admit, I miss her dreadfully. The Rapstone Valley's a much duller place without her.'

As she walked him to his car she said, 'I'm glad you're fighting for the valley.'

'I don't know about fighting. I seem to spend my time asking people for money. Oh, and organizing strange sorts of events. I want to get some jazz evening going in aid of S.O.V., but the people I used to play with are knocking on a bit.'

'*You* play?' Tony Sidonia didn't perform on any instrument but she remembered the piles of old records he listened to, Bix Beiderbecke, Coleman Hawkins, Dizzy Gillespie, Django Reinhardt and Le Hot Club de France.

'On drums with the Riverside Stompers. That's what we used to call ourselves. We might try the pub at Skurfield again. If we manage it I'll send you a ticket. And your husband, of course.'

Jenny tried to imagine Leslie at a jazz evening in a pub and failed. As Fred opened the car door she said, 'I'm sure they'll come in droves to hear you drumming for the valley. Everyone'll want to help.'

'Including you?'

'Of course. I told you.'

'You mean you'll join S.O.V.? You get all sorts of treats.' He laughed, inviting her to laugh at his organization also. 'Not only me on drums. Car-boot sales. Sponsored footpath walks with Colonel Wilcox. Wine, cheese and poetry reading in the Hartscombe Town Hall. How can you possibly resist it?'

'I don't suppose I can.'

'Good. I'll send your membership card.'

And he drove away, leaving her alone and wondering, only for a moment, whether she had done the wrong thing. What she had done, in fact, was to kick away the small stone which would start an avalanche.

CHAPTER SEVENTEEN

Fred drove back to Hartscombe in a distinct glow of triumph. He told himself that by enlisting the support of the Secretary of State's wife he had struck a powerful blow for the salvation of his native countryside. He also allowed himself to feel that he had scored a victory over Leslie Titmuss, undermining that hitherto undented self-confidence which assumed that everyone connected with him would always do exactly what he wanted.

So, when he walked into the bar of the Olde Maypole Inn at lunch-time and found Mrs Vee running through the agenda of the next S.O.V. meeting with Daphne Jones, Fred couldn't resist taking his beer over to them and raising his voice above the muzak and the squeals of computer games to say, 'What do you think? Jenny Titmuss has joined the group.'

'You invited her?'

'Well, yes. I was up in the valley, so I called.'

'Mr Chairman!' Mrs Vee spoke in a tone of vibrant admiration which filled Fred with immediate foreboding. 'You're a political genius!'

'It wasn't at all hard. She's very sympathetic.'

'God!' Hector Bolitho Jones's wife was also awestruck. 'Think of the publicity we're going to get.'

'Front-page stuff. No doubt about it,' Mrs Vee agreed. 'PLANNING MINISTER'S WIFE JOINS ANTI-PLANNERS. S.O.V.'s really going to be put on the map. Thanks to our Chairman. We ought to give an exclusive to the *Fortress*,' she suggested, 'and then they'll be sure to make a big thing of it. I'll ring Vee and get him to take it on board.'

'No.'

'What?'

'No announcement in the papers.' Fred had decided.

'Why ever not?'

'Because that's just what they'd do.'

'What who'd do?'

'The opposition. If something like that happened to us they'd get the newspapers full of it. We've got to show them we're different. So let's keep quiet and treat Jenny Titmuss just like any other member.' To his surprise his words came out with authority. But he was thinking, Why am I tangling with a world I was never cut out for? All I shall succeed in doing is making trouble for a woman I found myself liking very much.

Mrs Vee looked at him in a penetrating and deeply understanding way. 'Is that your decision, Mr Chairman?' she said in the solemn tones she might have used if he had just announced that he was terminally ill.

'Yes,' he said. 'That's what I've decided.'

'For God's sake.' Daphne Jones had no doubts on the matter. 'I don't agree with that. If I catch my enemy with his balls hanging out and I happen to have an axe in my hand, I strike!' This was a political precept which she had heard enunciated by the President of the Worsfield Students' Union and she had been much impressed by it.

'No, Daphne!' Mrs Vee was prepared to behave with nobility. 'Fred has his principles. We've got to respect them. That's why we chose him to be our Chairman. All right, Mr Chairman. Sir.' She put a proprietorial hand on his knee where it remained visiting. 'No publicity from us, although God knows what the gentlemen of the press are going to find out for themselves.' So Fred finished his lunch and went about his business visiting the sick, feeling that he had, in some way, betrayed both Jenny and Mrs Vee and he hoped, so far as Jenny was concerned at least, that he had done his best to repair the damage.

It goes without saying that as soon as she was left alone, Mrs Vee telephoned her husband with the news and he then put through a call to the *Fortress* into whose Mr Chatterbox column he often dropped hints about clients who employed him in their charitable concerns. The name Mr Chatterbox did not, as might be expected, mask the identity of an elderly, grey-haired gossip but a languid, comparatively young, untidy and dissolute old Etonian called Tim Warboys who, although he found anyone who hadn't been to Eton, and many who had, totally absurd, had a strong sense of self-preservation. He was about to be promoted to the Whispers from the Gallery parliamentary column and he knew that writing stories hostile to Leslie Titmuss in the columns of the *Fortress* was the journalistic equivalent of searching for a gas leak with a lighted match.

So, after getting the news from Mr Vee, Tim Warboys rang the press officer at H.E.A.P. and was told that any suggestion that Mrs Titmuss had joined a group at war with her husband was totally untrue, that any hint of such news would be met with a writ and that the Secretary of State would no doubt be speaking to the *Fortress*'s proprietor Lord Dowdswell, who, as Tim well knew, was a close personal friend. As all this was relayed after a pause for consultation with the Secretary of State himself, Mr Chatterbox said that he had never believed the story anyway and had thought it only right to alert the press officer to so scurrilous a rumour. He then went to the first of four cocktail parties persuaded that it was true but that his column had much better concentrate on the ludicrous attempts of an allegedly socialist M.P. to get himself elected to White's Club. So, in the course of one day, Jenny's membership of S.O.V. was pushed towards centre stage and then back into the wings to become a matter of concern for no more than three people.

'What did you think you were doing to me? Or did you just not think at all?'

'I told him what I felt. That's all.'

'What a luxury! That's perfectly all right for you, of course. You can go round the world saying exactly what you feel. That's the privilege enjoyed by people who have no responsibility for anything.'

'Of course I'm responsible. I have to be responsible for what I say.'

'And what about me? Did you think about me for one single moment, during the Doctor's visit?'

Elsie Titmuss had come to dinner that night and had helped Jenny in the kitchen, talking a lot about her distant past, taking little swallows of gin and tonic and revealing old scandals about people in big houses of whom Jenny had never heard. As always they got on well and were ready to receive Leslie with interest and excitement. When he came home he was in a black mood which Jenny did her best to ignore. He waited until Elsie had gone and the dinner cleared away before launching his attack and Jenny, who thought it must have been one of the 'colleagues' that had infuriated him, was surprised to find the cannonade directed at her. At first she wasn't alarmed by his fury; she was busy trying to follow an argument which seemed to involve people she hadn't met, in a world she hardly understood.

'Did you?' he repeated, staring at her like some cold lawyer cross-examining a hostile witness. 'Did you think about me at all?'

'Of course I thought about you, Leslie. I knew exactly how you felt.'

'Oh. How did you know that?'

'Because you told me.'

'What did I tell you?'

'You told me they'd never build a new town in the valley. Not if you knew anything about it. You told me that the first day we came here.'

'I don't mean . . .' Leslie sighed and looked at his wife with exaggerated patience. 'I don't mean how I felt about the new town. I meant how I felt about people *knowing* how I felt.'

'I'm sorry.' She looked back at him in genuine confusion. 'I don't know what you're talking about.'

'Of course you don't. I'm talking about politics. That's a dirty word to you, isn't it?'

'Not necessarily.'

'It's another world to you, beneath your notice. A world where you have to say what you don't mean in order to get what you want. It's a world where you may have to tell lies. That wouldn't have suited your precious Tony Sidonia, would it? He could sit in some old library somewhere and feel cosy and contemptuous of squalid politicians who have to practise a few deceptions to get anything decent done in the world. Well, I have news for you. The time has come to forget Mr Sidonia!'

There was a silence and then Jenny seemed to crumple at Tony's name, which had never been thrown at her with such violence before. Now Leslie looked down at her as she sat crouched in a corner of the sofa, her hands hugging her elbows and her knees bent sharply. He seemed surprised at the result of what he had said because he lowered his voice and made an effort to sound reasonable.

'All right . . .' And he repeated 'All right' as if trying to get the attention of the House of Commons at Question Time, although what he had to say would never be heard in Parliament. 'I don't want the town. You don't want the town. The bloody interfering doctor doesn't want the town. You know I don't want it. But Jo Public mustn't know that!'

She looked up at him. He assumed an unspoken question and was encouraged to answer it.

'Why mustn't they? Because I'm the man of the free market. The patron saint of the builder and the upwardly mobile property investor. That's why they elected me and why I got my job. If I come out against the new town they'll say it's for one reason and one reason only. Because I live here. Because I want new houses everywhere except in my own bloody back garden. You understand that, don't you?'

He waited for an answer but she didn't give it to him. On the other hand she looked at him constantly and didn't turn her face away. He took that for encouragement and went on being reasonable.

'So let's spell it out, my darling. I have to keep absolutely quiet. Not take sides in any sort of way, you understand? There's going to be a full public inquiry, a judicial proceeding with arguments from all sides. Evidence taken. All the trimmings. Plenty of money for the lawyers. And at the end of that, you want to know my own, personal, entirely private prediction? This is not for publication, just between you and me, strictly off the record. I promise you that Fallowfield Country Town will be dead as mutton! So we'll be able to go on living here in peace. That's what you want to know, isn't it?'

'Yes,' she said. 'Yes, I suppose so.'

'But none of that can happen if I'm seen to be personally involved. That's why I had to wake up old Dickie Dowdswell in Palm Springs and get him to kill the story in the *Fortress*.' Confident now that he had won the debate and that the final vote would be in his favour, Leslie went to a table between the two tall windows and poured himself a drink.

'What story?' Jenny frowned, no longer understanding.

'The story about your joining Dr Fred's tin-pot resistance movement. The Doctor's no doubt a specialist in hopeless protests. He learnt the art from his father who was a pacifist vicar.'

'My joining?' Jenny was puzzled. 'They were going to put *that* in the paper?'

'Of course they were. It's news because you're my wife.' And why on earth, Leslie wondered as he drank whisky, did he find himself involved with women who insisted on joining inconvenient organizations? He remembered the trouble he'd had convincing the world that the undoubted fact that his first wife had signed on with the Campaign for Nuclear Disarmament was a pure invention. 'Don't worry your pretty head,' he told Jenny. 'The story's killed. And now all you have to do is tell the Doctor you never meant to join in the first place.'

She was looking at him, without understanding. He brought his glass and sat down beside her, and then he remembered to ask her if she wanted a drink. She shook her head.

'Tell him he must have misunderstood. You talk quietly, so he probably didn't hear what you were saying. He wanted you to join, so he seems to have assumed you agreed when all you were doing was being politely interested.' He drank. 'You'll know how to get out of it, I'm sure.'

'You mean,' she had found a voice now and spoke quite loudly, 'you want me to lie about it?'

'We all have to from time to time. I bet even Tony wasn't busy being George Washington every day, was he? It wouldn't surprise me at all to discover that he found a use for a good thumping lie occasionally.'

Then she said that she was going to bed and left him.

Leslie finished his drink slowly, determined not to hurry after her. He felt he had nothing to reproach himself with. His argument, he thought, had been moderate, sensibly put and unanswerable. He had, he hoped, done something to shake Jenny out of an unreasonable obsession with her departed husband. He climbed the staircase slowly and when he reached the bedroom he saw a small shape under the covers. Her face was turned to the wall and her dark hair spread over the pillow. He smiled at her and made a final concession.

'I'll do the dirty work for you, if you like. I'll explain to Dr Fred that it was all a misunderstanding. Would *that* make you feel better?'

But, it seemed, it wouldn't. That night Jenny moved away from him in bed, a rejection he had never suffered before. He lay in the darkness and his feeling of having been unfairly treated hardened into a deep hatred, not of Jenny or even of Fred Simcox, but of the late Tony Sidonia.

The next morning the storm between them seemed to have passed. Leslie got up when Jenny was still asleep and went to bath and dress. When he came back to the bedroom to say goodbye, he was as friendly as before their quarrel and seemed to bear her no ill will. The last thing he said was, 'I'll look after everything. No need for you to worry.' When he had gone she reviewed their quarrel with the fairness which, she sometimes worried, might have been her way of avoiding trouble. Perhaps, after all, his embarrassment was understandable. If she'd known there was a danger of it getting into the papers would she have joined S.O.V.? As she wandered into her natural home, the kitchen, in her dressing-gown, put the kettle on the Aga and listened to the comforting sound of Mrs Bigwell's Hoover, she was about to give Leslie Titmuss the benefit of the doubt. Then she remembered what he had said about Tony, the unexpected attack on a dead man which had unbalanced her like a blow. Was that forgivable? And could it be forgotten? As she had been used to doing for so many years she consulted her friend Sue Bramble.

'Well, I've never been absolutely crazy about your Mr Titmuss, as you well know, although he was perfectly civil to me that weekend. Much to my surprise, I must say. But what's he done that's so terrible? He just didn't want you to join this Save the Badger Club, or whatever it is.'

'He wanted me to tell a lie.'

'Well, he might have wanted you to do much nastier things. Like climb into a rubber suit and squirt soda-water at him. Men have such unfortunate wants sometimes.'

'He did want me to lie,' Jenny repeated.

'And then he told you you needn't. And he'd do it for you.'

'That's right. Yes.'

'Well, it's so rare to get a chap to do anything for you nowadays. My bloody trainer wouldn't even change the wheel on my car, let alone put himself to the trouble of getting a divorce. If you've found a man who'll do things for you, I say be grateful. Even if he does have a row of pens in the breast pocket of his business suiting.'

'He doesn't.'

'Not do things for you?'

'No. Have a row of pens.'

'Oh, well. He looks the sort who would.'

'It's the way he attacked Tony.'

'What did he say again?'

'He more or less called Tony a liar.'

'Well, he didn't know Tony, did he?'

'Of course not.'

'Then he's talking nonsense. He's just jealous.'

'Of Tony?' Jenny couldn't believe it. 'I mean, Tony's not here to be jealous of.'

'I bet your Mr Titmuss wants to think he's got you all to himself. No memories. Nothing. He probably longs for you to have been a virgin when he married you.'

'Do you think so, honestly?'

'Don't worry, darling. Absolutely nothing you can do about that.'

So Jenny was surprised by her friend's lenient attitude towards Leslie Titmuss and she felt she had been unnecessarily upset. This suited her very well because she wanted, above all things, to avoid another quarrel.

Fred Simcox sat in his consulting room faced, once again, with the immense bulk of Dot Curdle. When he asked her why she had come to see him, she muttered a word which sounded to him like 'perdition', so that he was inclined to say that she needed the services of Kev the Rev. rather than his. 'Perdition?' he asked, and she nodded her head in a meaningful manner and withdrew a bundle of papers from a Tesco's bag. 'It's a perdition which I wants everyone to sign, but you should sign it particular as a doctor who knows about things.' Then she read out a preamble which she had composed and Evie had typed out in rough.

'"Science has taught us,"' Dot thundered, as though

announcing the end of civilization, '"that eating of chicken pro-
duces salmonella and the gastric. It's dicing with death to eat beef,
lamb and pork meat, or tinned tongue, as these fatty substances
gives you heart attacks. For a healthy diet keep to regular meals
of pure, local raised, free-range rabbit meat, low in fat or starch
which raises the blood pressure. Rabbit will cure heart disease.
It can be cooked in a variety of ways ranging from haute cuisine
to peasant. We the undersigned being consumers, producers and
experts in the field are gravely concerned" – Len Bigwell told us
to put that "gravely concerned". He says as how everyone's
gravely concerned on the news nowadays – "are gravely blah,
blah . . . at the prospect of our locality losing a huge natural
source of this vital food by the closure of the Rapstone Valley
Rabbit Hacienda."' Here Mrs Curdle paused and looked at Fred
triumphantly. 'So will you put your name on the dotted?'

Fred was tempted to sign any document, however misleading,
which was designed to protect the valley. Then common sense
prevailed and he said, 'Perhaps I could have that and tidy up the
scientific side a bit.'

'You do that, Doctor. I'll trust you to get it right, after all you
done for Evie.'

'Marriage guidance worked, did it?'

'Puts me in mind of old Dr Salter as was here before you. If
ever us children got ill he'd come round with a big black bottle of
medicine and say, "This tastes like liquid cow-pat and if you
don't get better at once you'll have to drink it all up." Well, we
was well again before he left the house. You got the same idea,
didn't you? 'Course she'd rather have the sex than that nasty old
marriage guidance.' Then the telephone rang and Fred's panic-
stricken receptionist announced a person of great importance who
insisted on coming in to see him. Before he could ask for further
details his door was pushed open to admit Leslie Titmuss.

'Mr Titmuss.' Dot Curdle heaved herself to her feet. 'We'd
like your signature to my perdition too, sir. Save the Rabbit
Farm. I'll leave it with you.'

When she had gone Leslie looked at the document, dropped it on to Fred's desk and said, 'Are you going to sign this rubbish?'

'I'll have to edit the medical bits. But, yes. I want to help her keep her rabbit farm.'

'Poor old Fred!' Leslie looked at him with pity. 'Why don't you give up politics?'

'It is my morning surgery. Could we make a time to talk?'

'You're even more ridiculous than your old father was when he went on marches all over the place. Neither of you had the faintest hope of achieving anything. Why don't you just give up?'

'I suppose I could ask you the same question.'

Leslie looked at Fred with particular coldness and didn't bother to ask him to explain.

'If you hadn't taken up politics, if you didn't go around making speeches about market forces and consumer choice, we might have had a bit of peace in the Rapstone Valley.'

'So you and your well-heeled friends can enjoy the rural life?' Leslie was, in fact, far better heeled than Fred would ever be but the Simcox family had, since childhood, represented his idea of wealth plagued by guilt and a half-hearted hankering for socialism in order to ease their consciences.

'So long as there's any countryside left for everyone to enjoy.'

'It's not going to be saved by you having a few jumble sales and coffee mornings. You know that. It'll be decided by people who've got power, and that hasn't been your lot for a long time and it may never be again.'

'You mean it's going to be decided by you?'

'It'll be judged in due course by a proper, fair, public inquiry.' Leslie repeated the words which he was going to use again and again to distance himself from the future of his new home.

'In the end you'll have to decide whether to accept the inquiry's decision. If there is an inquiry. As of now the District Council seems about to condemn the valley to death without an inquiry.'

'Please, Fred.' Leslie smiled at him tolerantly, as though he were a child. 'You may be the world's greatest expert on prescribing the pills my government has to pay for when you can't think of how else to treat your patients, but please, don't try to teach me my job.'

'Doesn't everyone have a right to teach politicians their jobs?'

'Oh, Fred.' Leslie now managed a look of genuine pity. 'You used to have a bit of life in you once. You used to chase girls, although as far as I can remember most of them got away. You used to play mournful jazz numbers rather badly on the drums. Now you're growing old with nothing better to do than chatter about democracy.'

'I notice you chatter about it quite a lot.'

'I know what it means.'

'Look, I've got a whole line of patients waiting.'

'It means handing over power to whoever's got a majority in Parliament and then forgetting about it for the next four years. And it doesn't mean calling on people when they're out and trapping their wives into joining their funny little pressure groups.'

'Did you say, trapping?' Fred was genuinely puzzled.

'Jenny was reasonably polite, as she always is. And then you ran away and claimed she'd joined your Save Our Back Gardens Group, or whatever you call yourselves. Very pleased with yourself, weren't you? You even had to ring up and tell the bloody newspapers.'

'I didn't do that.'

'Oh, no? And you didn't make my wife a member, without her consent?'

What was going on? Fred thought that Jenny must have lied in the face of her husband's anger. Clearly she needed help.

'Did she tell you that?'

'Of course she told me that. Why do you think I'm here? I'd be a great deal too busy to waste my time in National Health surgeries if you hadn't involved Jenny.'

'Then I must have been mistaken.'

'Or shall we say pushing your luck?' Fred noticed that Leslie Titmuss had come very close to him, so that their faces were almost touching. It was an unnerving way he had, Fred remembered, when he was a perpetually obtrusive small boy.

'Say what you like.'

'Then will you kindly remove my wife's name from your list of members?'

'Of course,' Fred told him. 'If that's what she wants.'

Leslie left then, feeling, with some contempt, that his victory had been far too easy. Fred spent the next two hours listening to long stories of vague complaints, wishing he could threaten his patients with Dr Salter's horrible black bottle, and being sorry for Jenny Titmuss.

CHAPTER EIGHTEEN

It was now early autumn, the sunniest time of the year, with the leaves only just on the point of changing, a smell of damp earth in the woods and heavy dew on the bracken fronds or sparkling in spiders' webs among the ripe blackberries. There were mushrooms and toadstools scattered like lost golf balls on the Rapstone downland as the District Council postponed its decision. Leslie Titmuss got into his car to drive to his Ministry each morning before the day warmed up and he would shiver a little at the hint of frost soon to come. It was in those days, when Kev the Rev. filled his church with giant marrows, ripe apples and bunches of corn, which were duly prayed over by a congregation of stockbrokers and P.R. men kneeling in rustic ritual, that the marriage of Hector and Daphne Jones suffered an irretrievable breakdown.

Their daughter Joan Baez Jones had grown into a large, awkward thirteen-year-old whose passage through the Nature Area was noisy and destructive. She often disturbed nesting birds, broke hospital cages and, on one never-to-be-forgotten occasion, rode her bicycle over a nest of curlew's eggs. When Hector lost his temper with her daughter, Daphne accused him of preferring the young of animals, who proliferated thoughtlessly and with no idea of schooling or career prospects, to that of their own child. Thinking over what she said, in the quietness of the woods, Hector had to admit that his wife had a point. The fury which he had directed at the thoughtless Joan Baez would have turned into gentle and loving concern if she had only been born a badger cub. It was when he was out watching badgers that it happened. He came home a little before dawn, put his gun in the shed where he always hid it, and was surprised to find the house lit up and unlocked. He went upstairs to find the beds unslept in and the suitcases gone from the top of the wardrobe.

In the sitting-room he found a note written on a page torn from one of his daughter's school exercise books.

Dear Hector [he read with mounting excitement] I have rung Barry and he's coming up at once to fetch us in his car. It's obvious you prefer anything that has four legs on it to your wife and daughter. Often I think you haven't noticed how many legs I've got for a long time and I've had about enough of it. I don't think you give a damn about Joannie and her school problems. She complains that all you've told her about nature study her teacher disagrees with, particularly when it comes to the intelligence of such things as foxes which everyone knows fully deserve to be treated as vermin. Anyway, Barry has a couple of rooms over his shop which he says we can use till the Council finds us something. I'm going to try and get back into the Social Services. I'll put nothing in the way of your seeing Joannie, not that I suppose you'll bother. But if you have her out I'm not letting you take her into the woods. She's a young woman now, though I don't suppose you've noticed that either.

Hector read the note over again, and a third time, savouring its news to the full. In such a way do punters read telegrams telling them they've won the pools, applicants enjoy the good news of their selection for important jobs or actors relish favourable notices. The silence, the luxury of his new-found, hard-won solitude lapped around him like the water in a warm and comforting bath. He climbed the stairs, undressed as far as his shirt, vest and underpants, a comfortable form of night attire of which his wife disapproved, and fell asleep breathing gratitude on Barry Harvester, the Hartscombe herbalist, who had brought him the peace he had longed for.

The next morning he rose early and enjoyed his silent breakfast and his walk into the Nature Area. Now all he had to fear was the time when the schoolchildren came filing along the nature trails. They had to be watched for flower picking and wandering from the marked footpaths, just as the senior citizens on their organized rambles had to be prevented from picnicking or sitting on the grass. He wondered, as he often did, what the flowers and the animals had to do with these forked radishes, dressed in bobble hats and anoraks, who did nothing but destroy their peace.

With his wife and daughter gone, Hector Bolitho Jones hoped that, in time, other human intruders would go also. In his new-found happiness he had forgotten the prospect of a great sea of human faces surrounding the Nature Area with the coming of Fallowfield Country Town. This was the concern of politicians in distant offices, whose days were spent far from the cry of curlews or the late fluttering of fritillary butterflies.

'We have got him,' Ken Cracken said, 'on toast.' He spoke with his mouth half full of the sausage sandwich Joyce had got him from the Ministry canteen. It was their habit to arrive at work with the cleaners and, although their nights had been devoted to love, at dawn their talk was all of politics.

'You're very sure of yourself.' Joyce Timberlake spoke in admiration.

'I'm sure of the Worsfield District Council. They're about to put a new town in Leslie's back garden. He won't just have to go green. He'll have to become a wet. Can't you see the headlines: TITMUSS TO ACT AGAINST FREE MARKET ECONOMY. And at that moment' – Ken Cracken refreshed himself from a plastic mug full of strong, sweet, instant coffee – 'he's going to lose the Prime Minister's love. It'll really be quite heartbreaking.'

At which moment the telephone rang. Leslie Titmuss had got in earlier than the earliest cleaner and wanted to see his second-in-command without delay. 'On toast,' Ken said as he moved triumphantly towards the door, 'with a nice dollop of sauce on the side.' The image seemed to fuel his hunger and he returned to his desk and took a final mouthful of sausage sandwich to sustain him on the journey upstairs.

'I wanted to talk to you about the Rapstone development.' Leslie sat very still and spoke quietly. The room was as impersonal as the top of his desk, where a framed photograph of Jenny stood alone and out of place on the bleak stretch of mahogany. Ken Cracken smiled, invited himself to a chair and sat with his legs stretched out, still thoughtfully chewing. 'I thought you might,' he said.

'I'm told the District Council's inclined to say yes.'

'Well, no wonder. After your smashing speech to the builders.'

'As I tried to explain to you, Kenneth. A new town's going to upset a lot of ordinary voters.'

'Ordinary voters, eh?' Ken Cracken was relishing the moment. 'Well, we mustn't upset *them*. As I always say, we ought to have abolished local government long ago. It's always been a pain in the bum. Still, if that's their thinking . . .'

'I'm assured it is.'

'And you don't want the damn thing built . . .'

'I never said that.'

'I mean, if their decision is likely to be contrary to the present high priority the Government's giving to the preservation of wild life, wilderness areas and broad-leafed woodlands . . .' Ken spoke with a kind of brutal cynicism which was almost a parody of the way in which his Secretary of State used to mock the ideas of the green welly brigade.

'Advise me, Kenneth. I'd be very grateful.' Leslie's voice had become gentle, almost caressing, a dangerous signal which Ken Cracken was unwise to ignore.

'Well, if you really don't want it to happen, just say the

building of a new town is too important a matter to be decided at local level and you're calling in the papers and ordering a full public inquiry. You could say that, couldn't you?'

'No.'

'Of course' – Ken Cracken smiled with delighted understanding – 'now you've gone and bought yourself a house in the place, I do see the difficulty.'

'I couldn't say it. You'll have to say it.'

'Me? But you're the boss . . .'

'Exactly. That's why I'm telling you what to do.'

Ken felt a moment of uncertainty as he watched Leslie get up and go to the window.

'You can say that as I've bought a house in Rapstone it would be inappropriate for me to make the decision. Go on to say that you have advised me to order a public inquiry as the matter is too important to be settled at local level. Not a brilliant phrase, Ken. Not headline stuff. You'll never make a first-class speech. But it'll do. You'll say that you recommended putting the question to a full public inquiry so all the objectors could have their say. You'll make it clear that was your advice. You can ring Tim Warboys on the *Fortress* and start leaking the story now.' Leslie looked down into the street below. The workers at H.E.A.P., self-important and anxious men in mackintoshes, bright chattering girls, older women loitering to exchange gossip, postponing for as long as possible the start of another day in the typing-pool, were arriving, stepping off buses or emerging from the Underground. They would initial files, stamp orders, copy letters, photostat plans and slowly but surely England would change. Old buildings, streets filled with memories, would tumble to make way for office blocks, desirable apartments or shopping centres. Fields once sensitive to the seasons would freeze into commuter towns, drive-in supermarkets or eight-lane motorways. Often such changes occurred after the flicker of a word processor and initials scrawled by someone who would never see the results of their decision. Leslie looked down as his staff hurried up the big stone steps into the Ministry and, in the silence, Ken Cracken so far forgot himself as to say, 'You can't expect me to do that.'

'What's the matter, Ken, my lad? Are you hoping to embarrass me?' Leslie looked from the window to his Junior Minister.

'No. Why should I?'

'I don't know. Perhaps you want to take over my job. You like living dangerously, don't you?'

'I don't know what you mean.'

'Trouble with you, Ken, is that you missed the war. Oh dear, oh dear, what a pity we can't organize a nice little bit of fighting so you could work off some of your high spirits. I might persuade the Prime Minister to invade the Scilly Isles. You'd appreciate that, wouldn't you?' Leslie sat behind his desk now and looked like an indulgent headmaster half-amused by an inadequate pupil's tiresome habit of letting off stinkbombs in the lavatory. 'I can imagine you jumping off the landing craft, shrieking with excitement. Until they started chucking live bullets at you, of course.'

'Well, if that's all for the moment . . .' Ken sat forward but didn't get up as there was more to come.

'You were even too young for National Service, weren't you?' Leslie, who had done his time in the Pay Corps, spoke like a veteran of World War Two. 'What a shame. You might've enjoyed the square-bashing. The spit and polish would've turned you on. It might, I say it just might, have saved you from making a rare idiot of yourself in other people's woods at night.'

'Leslie' – Ken tried a friendly smile which came out a little crooked, hoisting his moustache up on one side only – 'I honestly have no idea what you're talking about.'

'Have you not? War games. That's what I'm talking about.'

'War . . .?'

'Don't look so bloody innocent. I gather it's the latest craze among hooray bankers, building tycoons and upwardly mobile politicians. Provided they're young enough to have missed the real war, of course. It's taken over from pushing people into rivers.'

There was another silence. Leslie looked down at the naked wood on top of his desk and seemed to sink into deep thought. Ken, wondering if it were all over now, got up as quietly as possible, but stood still when his superior looked at him again. 'You leak what I told you to leak, my lad,' he said. 'And stand by it, or I might leak the news of the daring commando raid with paint-guns in the Rapstone Nature Area. What are the ordinary voters going to think of that, eh? A so-called responsible Minister playing silly games of soldiers.'

'I'll give Warboys the story.' Ken now needed no more time to make up his mind. 'From a government source. That do?'

'Perfectly. Oh, and you can say I'll stick by the finding of the public inquiry. Whichever way it goes.'

'Of course.' Ken was on his way to the door. 'Is there anything else?'

'Only one thing. Don't eat the canteen sausages for breakfast. They spurt grease all over your tie.' And here Leslie Titmuss did a parody of Christopher Kempenflatt's old Etonian accent. 'Rather lets the Ministry down, that sort of thing. Wouldn't you agree, old chap?'

Joyce looked at her scowling Minister of State when he got back to his room and decided that, in one way or another, Titmuss must have slid off the toast.

'There's going to be an inquiry,' Ken told her. 'Leslie must have a lot of faith in it. He's going to accept the result, whatever it is.'

'So he'll get away with it.'

'What?'

'No town in his back garden, and no political fall-out. I always told you. It doesn't do to underestimate Leslie.'

'We'll have to wait and see about that, won't we? Just for now, I've been given a job.'

'In Northern Ireland?' Joyce looked at him with pity.

'Oh, very funny! No. I've got to ring Tim Warboys at the *Fortress*.' Beneath his moustache, Ken's lips pursed as though he were about to take some peculiarly nasty medicine. 'I'm going to square the press for Titmuss.'

IN MY BACK GARDEN IF YOU LIKE. That was the headline of Tim Warboys' Whispers from the Gallery column and it went on:

> Leslie Titmuss might have been put in an embarrassing position by the proposal to build a new town next to his lately acquired home, Rapstone Manor. Opposition hopes that Titmuss would block the development for selfish reasons were dashed by the Secretary of State's decision to leave the question to the high-flying Ken Cracken, Titmuss's Number Two. Cracken has decided that there should be a full public inquiry and Titmuss has told friends and Cabinet colleagues that he'll accept its findings. Once again the man who the Prime Minister calls 'our Leslie' has shown he is a Minister who accepts democratic decisions and the changing face of England. What a contrast to such out-dated snobs as the Labour Member for Smoketown South who's burnt his cloth cap and is trying to oil his way into White's Club in the faint hope of being bought a small dry sherry by a Duke.

One evening not long after he'd read this paragraph, designed to preserve its author's position as the Government's favourite journalist, Fred got a telephone call which astonished him and led him to turn down the volume of his Charlie 'Bird' Parker record. His caller was Mr Chatterbox of the *Fortress*.

'We've got a story about you, Dr Simcox. Rather an odd one.' Tim Warboys, calling from his bed which contained an insatiable married lady from the Home Maker section of his paper, sounded exhausted. 'Do you really think that eating rabbits is the way to avoid heart disease?'

'Absolutely not. I've never said that.'

'Apparently it was in some sort of manifesto you signed.'

'Whoever told you that?'

'Come on, Dr Simcox. You know we don't reveal our sources. But this one couldn't be more reliable. Was it in this document of yours?'

'Well, yes. But I didn't sign it –'

'Do *you* eat a lot of rabbit, Dr Simcox?'

'Not since I was a small boy and my mother made rabbit pie.'

'Delicious, was it?'

'Not very. My mother wasn't much of a cook.'

Tim eluded another sticky embrace from his partner to make a note on his bedside pad. Then he said, 'Well, thank you, Dr Simcox. I think we can get a paragraph out of that. Oh, by the way, wasn't your father a pinko vicar? Always marching for peace and stuff like that?'

'Well, yes. But look. I want to make it absolutely clear that I don't think there's the slightest connection between heart disease and eating rabbits.' But the telephone was buzzing nonchalantly and Tim Warboys had turned, in a desultory way, to satisfy his partner once again.

This strange conversation produced the following paragraph written by Tim Warboys under the headline COUNTRY G.P. BASHES BUNNIES:

It's a case of 'run rabbit run' in the Rapstone Valley. Hartscombe doctor Fred Simcox says other varieties of meat are responsible for all sorts of ills, including heart attacks. The bunny-bashing doctor lives, it seems, on rabbit pie as his mother made it. 'Delicious,' he says, 'and twice as tasty as chicken.' Older readers may recall the name Simcox. Fred's father, the Rev. Simeon Simcox, was always popping up in the Swinging Sixties when he led marches for the C.N.D., the A.N.C. and any other set of letters that took his fancy. Has Fred inherited his father's quirky love of lost causes? He has admitted he is desperate to help the owners of the local 'rabbit hacienda' which is in danger of being swallowed up by a new town. And the Rapstone rabbits are in danger of being swallowed up by the Doctor's health-conscious patients!

As a result of this story Fred wrote a number of letters to the *Fortress* and left messages for Tim Warboys, who never returned his calls. Finally he was rewarded by a short piece in the Healthy Living section of the paper headed IS BUNNY DOCTOR RIGHT? EXPERT SPEAKS OUT. It continued:

Bernard Wheatkins, Professor of Dietetics and Longevity at the University of Worsfield, has backed rabbit-eating G.P., Fred Simcox. Professor Wheatkins, who first established the connection between arthritis and fried fish, told our medical correspondent, 'Rabbit meat may help keep many people free of heart failure. Research has shown that poachers in the early years of this century, who fed mainly on rabbit, lived to an extraordinary age.' The Professor, who has made a close study of the psychology of illness, says, 'Rabbits are life-loving and active little blighters. Think of how they breed. Who knows if this positive attitude may not derive from the chemical make-up of the food product?' He foresees a day when bunny may take the place of beef at the British Sunday lunch table.

The result of these events was a further extraordinary increase in business at the Curdles' hacienda and, as a sign of their new prosperity, Len Bigwell was seen driving a second-hand Porsche. He asked a Worsfield advertising agency to plan a new 'promotion' for the hacienda's products and appointed Jackson Cantellow his solicitor with a view to forming a company which might, at some date, be floated on the Stock Exchange. Fred wondered how on earth this nonsense had started, and remembered that the only person who had seen Dot Curdle's 'perdition' in his consulting room was Leslie Titmuss.

CHAPTER NINETEEN

Fred Simcox had only been in love twice in his life before he met Jenny and both times it was with the same woman.

He had known his old partner's daughter, Agnes Salter, since they were children. When he was a young man they had made love, passionately and often, in an old hut Dot Curdle's father, Tom Nowt, the poacher, had built in the woods and which he made available to them in exchange for a few pints of beer in the Baptist's Head in Rapstone. There, under the skulls of poached deer, among the shot-guns and snares and the skins of foxes and squirrels, under an army blanket on an iron bedstead which squeaked and rattled its complaints, warmed by a wood-burning stove which belched acrid smoke when the wind was in the wrong direction, Fred had made love with a white-skinned, red-headed girl in ways which he had the privilege of remembering all his life.

When Agnes, in those days before the pill, became pregnant, Fred, then a medical student, had failed either to marry her or find the money for the abortion she subsequently had. She had married his brother Henry who finally went off with a young lady in television. Fred, of course, forgave Agnes but never himself. At last, when Henry was safely married to Lonnie, the television researcher, Agnes and Fred came together and he fell in love with her once again.

Their second love was entirely different from their first. Although they didn't live together it was much more of a marriage. Agnes had a flat in London and made her living cooking other people's dinners. Fred had the house which went with his practice in Hartscombe. They stayed often in each other's homes and, because they had inflicted such wounds on each other, they now behaved with almost too much consideration. Lacking any element of danger, their relationship finally lost its passion. It was as though they were so determined to be friends that friends, in the course of time, was all that they became. They still visited each other, confided in each other and, very occasionally, went to bed together to try and rediscover that ridiculous excitement they had known in a hut on a blanket that smelled of wet dog. Although it was never found again, Fred had loved Agnes for the second time. Because she was undoubtedly an original spirit, a woman who enjoyed the awfulness of life, laughed at loneliness and detested things like summer holidays and Christmas, he had found it hard to love anyone else better.

Of course he had tried. He had taken girls driving across Europe; girls had stayed in the room over the surgery and listened to his old jazz records or even more devotedly sat at the bar while he played the drums with his old friends in the Riverside Stompers. He had liked many of them and thought there was no reason why they shouldn't have become excellent wives for a local G.P., but the memory of Agnes as she had been somehow made them seem tame and colourless, and the duty he felt he owed to Agnes as she was made him reluctant to take on another life-long commitment. In his forties the turnover had been quite rapid; something, a toss of the head, a way of lighting a cigarette, a smile of derision at some pomposity, would prick his desire and set him off, believing he felt all the wild and breathless excitement he had known when he bicycled off to meet Agnes at Tom Nowt's hut in the woods. But finally, when it became clear to him that he wasn't going to meet Agnes or anyone like her, and when whichever partner it was felt her attention wandering because the Doctor's was wandering also, they would part, usually without rancour. So Fred went to the weddings and looked after the children of old lovers who rarely thought about him now and he, with his mind still full of Agnes, found it hard to remember exactly when, or in one case even if, he had made love to them.

Then he fell in love for the third time in his life, with Jenny Titmuss.

Although he felt no older, and certainly no wiser, than he had been when he was first sent away to school, or when he disappointed his father by defecting from a C.N.D. march to meet Agnes, Fred had reached that time in his life when he knew where he had got to and was prepared to settle for it. He still went to London and had dinner with Agnes, enjoying her hilarious denunciation of all the things women of her age were meant to value most; but now he rarely sought out new companions. Most of the time he felt he would have liked to have been left in peace, without the demands of the Rapstone Valley protest or the lure of a slim back, a narrow waist, a cascade of red hair pushed back, swaying in front of him in the street. Now, if such a vision turned towards him he felt a sense of relief if the face didn't touch him. He would be spared, at least, the long process of getting to know someone new, the dinners in country house hotels, the repetition of his old stories which had come to sound to him like the words of an actor whose play has run too long. But just as S.O.V. came to involve him in the affairs of the district and in the making of protests, however absurd, his sudden love for Jenny Titmuss shook him out of his contentment, bringing him an excitement which he had hoped never to feel again.

He didn't fall in love when he saw her at her wedding, although he knew there was nothing in her face to save him from that predicament. He didn't even fall in love with her when he called on her at Rapstone Manor and she had, he was sure she had, promised to join his organization. He only fell in love, suddenly and hopelessly, on the morning that Leslie Titmuss called on him in his surgery. This event occurred after Leslie had left and he felt sorry for Jenny. He thought she must be in distress and had been forced to change her mind about her membership by the domineering Titmuss. He found it hard to imagine anyone married to Leslie not being in distress and that, as well as her beauty, moved him almost unbearably. So his love for Jenny was, although he didn't admit as much to himself, brought about by his lifelong dislike of Leslie Titmuss.

As soon as Leslie had gone about his business, Fred had explained to Mrs Vee that there had been some confusion and Jenny Titmuss wasn't a member and had never agreed to become one. When he had arranged this matter Fred telephoned Jenny to set, as he told himself, her mind at rest. He chose to ring in the morning, when she was likely to be alone, but the voice that answered him was that of Leslie Titmuss in a hurry.

'Oh, it's you.'

'Of course it's me. You sound disappointed.'

'Not at all. I just wanted to tell your wife I've made it clear to everyone here that she never agreed to be a member.'

'You mean you told the truth? I hope it wasn't too great an effort. I'll let her know.' The telephone clicked and then buzzed angrily. Fred put it down and set off on his rounds. He thought that ringing Jenny again might make life difficult for her and he didn't want to encounter Titmuss. For their next meeting he would have to rely on chance. Until that happened he thought more often about Jenny and less about many years ago when he went to meet Agnes Salter in a hut in the woods.

A few weeks later in the Badger in Skurfield, Fred sat behind the old drum set, got down from the attic, and in remembrance of things past underlined the deep, mournful and persistent beat of 'St James Infirmary'. The Riverside Stompers had got together again. The group consisted of Joe Sneeping from the off-licence in Hartscombe on trumpet (he also supplied the vocals and tried to confine the band strictly to music played in New Orleans during the prohibition era), Terry Fawcett from Marmaduke's garage on clarinet, and Den Kitson from the Brewery who performed no better on the banjo than he did on the guitar or bass. They hadn't played together for a number of years and now they had blown the dust off their instruments in the hope of blasting the developers out of the Rapstone Valley. Once, in the heyday of rock 'n' roll, they had been shouted down by teenage tearaways in this same pub and had Coca-Cola cans thrown at them for singing that very blues number. Now the belligerent teenagers, filled to the brim with Fortissimo lager, were busy fighting more dangerous battles in the pedestrian walkways of Hartscombe and Worsfield. The audience for the Stompers' jazz were elderly and respectable, the sort that, when Fred was young, had sat respectfully through Gilbert and Sullivan operas. They wore anoraks and Fair Isle sweaters and the girlfriends they had once taken to hear Humphrey Lyttelton or Chris Barber were now grandmothers who in some cases brought their grandchildren. This newer generation sat wide-eyed at music as remote from their times as Byrd or Monteverdi, amazed that its sadness should give such obvious pleasure to those who played it.

And then, finishing a complex riff on the drums, Fred looked up and saw Jenny standing by the bar, ferreting in the depths of her handbag to pay for the half pint of bitter she had ordered. Looking dizzily down a precipice of years he saw himself sitting behind the drums in the garage where the Stompers used to rehearse, on the night when Agnes Salter walked in and stood, listening quietly until she announced her need for money because she was pregnant, a situation which he then proceeded to mismanage. Now, when Joe Sneeping, in the New Orleans accent he had learnt off countless records, told them they could take ten, Fred stepped off the platform and made his way towards Jenny. In her way, it seemed to him, she was in trouble and he didn't mean to fail again.

'It was good of you to come.'

Jenny and Elsie Titmuss, in their new-found friendship, sometimes shared pub lunches. Jenny had seen a notice pinned up advertising the Stompers concert on a night when Leslie was the guest of the Euro M.P.s in the Midlands, an event which he had considerately spared her.

'You like jazz?'

'I'm not exactly an expert. My husband used to listen to it all the time.'

'That's odd' – Fred turned from her for a moment to order himself a pint of the family bitter – 'I can't remember Leslie being so ecstatic about the brothel music of the Deep South. I mean, we were never offered Titmuss on tenor sax. Not so far as I can remember.'

'Not Leslie!' Jenny smiled. 'My first husband. Who died.' She was surprised by how easy it had become to say it.

'I'm sorry.'

'It was a long time ago.' She lifted the mug of beer which her wrist looked too thin to keep steady. 'I ought to say I'm sorry. That silly muddle about me joining your group of protesters.'

'I hope that didn't get you into trouble?'

'Not really.' She was looking at him across the surface of her beer. Then she drank, put her mug down on the bar and said, 'Of course, Leslie's got his politics to look after.'

'That's what he told me.'

'Did he? When?'

'When he came to see me. To tell me you didn't mean that about joining us.'

'Is that what he said?'

'I'm sorry. I must have misunderstood . . .'

'No.' Although she was looking away from him now and down at the bar, and though her face was hidden from him by a veil of dark hair, her voice was clear and determined. 'You didn't misunderstand. I told you I wanted to join.'

'And now you can't?' It was as far as he could safely go in trying to form an alliance against the deviousness of Titmuss.

'I suppose not. What a ridiculous position to be in. I just didn't want you to think I'd, well, lied about anything.'

'Of course I didn't think that.' But he had thought that she had, or had been forced to do so by her husband. That moment, when she looked up at him and seemed to be on his side, was the most splendid that the Save Our Valley Society had yet produced. Then he heard Joe Sneeping call him from the platform and he had to go back to open the second half with 'St Louis Blues'. He played with a new vigour and, it seemed to him, a return of youth. In the middle of 'Slow Boat to China', introduced into the Stompers' repertoire despite the purist protests of Joe Sneeping, Jenny left quietly to go back to her house and wait for her husband. She lifted her hand to Fred on her way out and he felt that, in returning her salute, he was waving goodbye to a small soldier off to the front line of battle.

CHAPTER TWENTY

Leslie Titmuss couldn't find a photograph of Tony Sidonia.

What he now felt about Jenny's first husband was something different from the vague and jealous unease which had come over him in a Roman square during their honeymoon. Now it was as though Sidonia had entered their marriage, deliberately challenged him and made him look mean and dishonest. When he had dealt with the matter of Jenny's sudden adherence to S.O.V., and had arranged it in the way he was accustomed to settle countless small difficulties in the course of his working life, Leslie felt that Sidonia was observing him, looking down with amused contempt at the way he rearranged the facts to suit his own purposes. And in this conflict between two men, one of whom was dead, he was afraid that he knew which side his wife was on.

Thinking about it, as he found himself doing a lot of the time, Leslie came to the conclusion that he couldn't believe in Tony Sidonia and the thought brought him much comfort. On the whole, and in spite of the comfort and reassurance of power, Leslie still held a simple view of human nature. Mankind, it was his considered opinion, was motivated by greed. The carrot was money, the stick failure, bankruptcy, 'jobloss' (as he liked to call unemployment) or, in the most obstinate cases, a cardboard box to sleep in by the Worsfield canal. This was the simple mechanism by which people moved forward, obtained a larger share of the market, built tunnels and motorways, erected new cities and gutted and rebuilt old ones. Money was to be found, not in building ships, tilling the land or mining for coal but in countless 'service industries', selling computers to revolve money, peddling insurance policies, advertising more and more different varieties of indistinguishable washing powder, lager or cigarettes. By and large, it might be said, and even was said by Leslie when in a more than usually caustic mood, England had become a nation of hairdressers. But if they were happy hairdressers, well supplied with cars and videos and a large variety of undemanding television channels, if, above all, they were hairdressers who were content to go on voting for Leslie and the 'colleagues', he had no particular objection to them. What he couldn't stand, what enraged him and made him mutter 'Humbug!' and 'Hypocrite!', although not at present in the hearing of his wife, were people who suggested that human behaviour could be attributed to motives other than a laudable desire to 'do well' and provide a decent home for the children. Such a one, he saw quite clearly, was Sidonia.

And yet, in spite of his high moral attitudes, his unreasoning addiction to telling the truth, his bloody air of uncalled-for superiority, what had Sidonia done in the world? He had died leaving nothing but a still mortgaged house in Oxford. He had devoted his life to digging up unsavoury details about the lives of long-dead Princes of the Church, work which created no jobs and trained no one to survive in the harsh world of the marketplace. Sidonia, for all his pretensions, had achieved nothing. And then he remembered that his rival had achieved something which was very precious to Leslie, he had achieved Jenny.

'I have absolutely no idea what he looked like.'
  'Who?'
  'Sidonia.'
  'Why should you want to know?'
  'Curiosity.'
  'I see.'

But Sue Bramble didn't see. Neither did she have any idea why Leslie had asked her to lunch. Having seen him with Jenny, and been startled by his obvious pride in her, and the intensity with which he seemed to look only at her, it never occurred to Sue that there was anything even mildly flirtatious about the invitation. And yet she believed that Leslie, like God, did nothing without a purpose, however obscure his aims might be to ordinary mortals. So they sat together in the restaurant where he had once dined with Jenny, near the flat which Sue now had to herself, and she was nervous, not knowing what precisely was going on, and afraid for her friend. She said, 'You will look after Jenny, won't you?'

'Of course. Don't you know that's all I want to do?'

'Yes. I do know that.' Although she couldn't bring herself to trust him entirely, she was prepared to take his word about looking after her friend. She also, in spite of herself, felt flattered to have been chosen to receive the politician's confidence.

'The odd thing is that Jenny hasn't got a picture of him at home. Absolutely nothing.'

'You've asked her?'

'No. I've looked.'

'I see.' Sue felt a chill at the idea of him choosing some moment when Jenny was out shopping, or in the garden, to quietly open drawers and peer into possible hiding-places, putting things back so that his search shouldn't be discovered. And then the head waiter interrupted them to ask Leslie to sign a menu for some admirers at the next table. Men in suits and grey-haired women were smiling at them and Sue couldn't help feeling important in the politician's company.

'I've looked and I can't find any trace of him at all,' he said when he had signed with a flourish.

'She left behind all the traces when she moved in with you. You should be flattered.'

'Should I?'

'Of course. So you don't have to think about it really, do you? Just go on as if Tony Sidonia never existed.'

'But he did, didn't he?'

'Oh, yes. And I don't suppose anyone who knew him will forget him.'

'Why?' Leslie looked hard at her and spoke with sudden bitterness. 'Was he a perfect person?'

'Of course not.' She laughed at him, but was not unfriendly. 'No one is. But somehow he seemed to know what was right. And if you had Tony on your side you knew you couldn't be so bad after all. Now, why don't you forget about him?'

'Because he's dead.' He frowned when he said that and looked, Sue thought, tormented. She began to get the vaguest idea, a mere glimmer of his troubles. 'And you're afraid he isn't?' she suggested. 'Not in Jenny's mind, anyway.'

'I do want to understand her. Completely. That's the way I feel I can do most for her. Of course I only want Jenny to be happy with me.' Leslie spoke with the sudden unexpected sincerity which had won him, many years ago, his party's nomination for the Hartscombe seat and had convinced the House of Commons at a few dangerous moments since then. It wasn't wasted on Sue Bramble. 'I just feel I could make her happier if I really knew about her life. I mean, I haven't kept any secrets from her.'

'I don't think she's kept any secrets from you, either. She probably just didn't want to trouble you with a lot of old photographs.'

'So she burnt them?'

'Well, not exactly.'

'What exactly?'

'She left them in the flat.'

'You've still got them?'

Sue was silent for a little and then she told him, 'Yes.'

'If I could only see him. See them together.'

'You think you'd know what you're up against?'

'I do want to feel close to Jenny. As close as you are.' He gave Sue Bramble the sincere look again.

'Because you're really not up against anything,' she tried to reassure him. 'Quite honestly you're not. Tony Sidonia's lost and gone forever.'

But, in the end, she was persuaded to let him come back to the flat with her and there, in a bottom drawer where sheets and blankets had been put away, were two photograph albums and Jenny's old wedding ring. It was the ring she had taken off on the first night she spent with Leslie, wrapped in cotton wool and put into an envelope. Sue handed the books to Leslie, telling herself that it was somehow touching that he should want to know as much as possible about Jenny and also feeling some pride at having information to impart.

He stood impassively, turning the pages without any particular expression of interest. At first she tried to give him a bright running commentary. 'That was Tony's cottage. Oh, there's Willoughby Blane in his famous shorts. Their house in Oxford. Jenny's birthday party. That was the Christmas when we did charades. Tony as Marlene Dietrich. That was them in Rome. Tony standing in front of St Peter's and Jenny kissing his ring. Shocking, really. Tony with a crowd of students. Of course they all adored him.' The picture showed him in a big basket-chair in a garden with girls and young men sitting on the grass, listening to him talking. 'Tony's old mum. Myra Sidonia.' And then, as he said nothing, she stopped guiding him round the photographs and went out to make the tea he had asked for.

When she came back with it he said, 'I put them back. I think I remember them well enough.'

'I hope it's made you feel better.'

'You've been an enormous help.' He stirred the tea into which he'd asked her to put two spoonfuls of sugar.

'It was another world. But like I told you, it's gone forever. I'm not even sure she still thinks about it.'

'Just one thing.' He looked at her solemnly. 'It would be better if you didn't tell Jenny you'd shown me these things. Could you promise me that?'

'I suppose so . . .' She felt involved in a conspiracy, a sensation she didn't particularly like.

The day after his lunch with Sue Bramble, Leslie Titmuss directed his ministerial Rover towards a turning off Fetter Lane, a jammed little thoroughfare handy for the Law Courts, barristers' chambers and similar resorts for persons in trouble. He got out in front of a narrow and gloomy building, went up in a lift which sighed with the hoarse complaints of worn-out machinery and entered the offices of the Neverest Detective Agency: 'All Inquiries Undertaken. Complete Confidentiality Guaranteed'. He was ushered without delay into the office of the head of the agency, a man called Arthur Nubble, of whom he had some previous knowledge.

It was not the first time that Mr Nubble had been concerned in the affairs of the Cabinet Minister. He had been a small, fat boy at a boarding-school with Fred Simcox and his brother, and a faded school photograph now hung above his desk beside his certificate of affiliation to the Private Inquiry Agents Association. Since his school days Arthur Nubble had gone into various service industries fashionable from time to time: coffee bars, boutiques, gossip columns and, finally, detection. With a recent increase in divorce and industrial espionage he had prospered, although it suited his romantic view of his trade to keep his premises as squalid and down-at-heel as they would have been in fiction. He had been engaged by Leslie Titmuss on a previous occasion in proceedings concerning the Reverend Simeon Simcox's will and, although he had done his best to serve both sides in that case, Leslie had not learned the full extent of Nubble's duplicity and was prepared to engage him again in a matter which was unlikely ever to surface in a court of law.

'Leslie' – Arthur Nubble liked to call all his clients, especially criminals and Cabinet Ministers, by their Christian names – 'I was delighted when I heard you'd called. Thank you for having faith in us.' His soft brown eyes pleaded for a compliment as urgently as a spaniel begs for a tin of dog food.

'I was brought up to trust nobody,' Leslie told him. 'Especially a professional peeper into other people's bedroom windows. All the same, this is something pretty simple. You can't really mess it up.'

'It's good of you to say so.' Arthur Nubble smiled with delight, as though he had got the praise he was asking for. He also mopped his forehead with his handkerchief, as he always seemed to be suffering from over-heating, however chilly the weather.

'It's this man.' Leslie felt in an inside pocket and brought out a photograph. 'I want you to find out everything you can about him.'

'Is it a divorce matter?' Nubble picked up the photograph and saw a tall man in a garden talking to some admiring young people who sat before him on the grass.

'No. It's a private matter. There's no question of divorce. The chap's name is Anthony Sidonia. He's the one in the chair, holding forth.'

'And where do I find him, Leslie?'

'In some North Oxford cemetery, I imagine. He's dead.'

'Then what do you want me to find out about him?' Nubble always tried not to seem surprised by any instruction. On this occasion he didn't succeed.

'Everything you can. Especially . . .' Leslie was silent for a long time, as though he found the next words hard to say. 'Especially if he always told the truth.'

CHAPTER TWENTY-ONE

It's no sort of comment, favourable or otherwise, on the general integrity of planning inspectors, to say that Gregory Boland was a peculiarly honest man. His honesty wasn't anything he could help. It had been with him all his life, like a birthmark or a stammer. Some of those who knew him found it faintly ridiculous, some inconvenient. His wife felt sure this unfortunate defect was what had caused Greg's failure as an architect in private practice. That, she told him, and his resolute refusal to join the Freemasons. Building developers, it was well known, always gave jobs to the architects they met whilst swearing strange oaths in the banqueting rooms of provincial hotels. Greg had smiled and announced in his soft Scottish accent that if he couldn't get the contract for the new bacon factory without putting on an apron and pressing the point of a pair of compasses to his naked bosom he'd rather stay at home and build kitchen cupboards. His home was well furnished with fitted cupboards, but Sir Joseph Buddle, F.R.I.B.A., whose membership of the ancient order of Masons in no way improved his brutal style of architecture, got the bacon factory with the geriatric ward of a local hospital thrown in.

Gregory Boland was also rare among architects as he lived in a house he had built himself. Jo Buddle, who had dumped the pile of vast building-bricks on the centre of Worsfield, who wrote regularly in the *Architectural Review* saying that we must forget the past and stamp the culture of the 1990s on our towns and villages, lived in a Georgian rectory with a walled garden, a place he furnished with Chippendale and English water-colours. Gregory, who also built in the modern manner, was prevented by the handicap of honesty from living in a house any more or less beautiful than those he was able to design for his customers. Accordingly he and his family inhabited a smallish concrete block in an area to the south-east of London where planning permission was not too hard to come by. This home which looked, in a poor light, like a small bunker built to withstand the onslaught of World War Three, was a source of derision and complaint from the neighbours and of regret to Mrs Boland and the children, who pined for a thatched cottage beside an old mill stream. Living with cheerful determination in this unsympathetic residence, Gregory Boland found his practice fading away and so, looking for a regular source of income, became an inspector with the Ministry of Housing, Ecological Affairs and Planning.

As such he presided over inquiries where his height and his flaming red hair made him an imposing figure. Having been brought up by a father who had been a postman, lay preacher and an elder of his church, and having fought his way up without losing his faith in a punitive God, Gregory Boland was quick to smell a whiff of corruption in any planning application or council proceeding. His clear blue eyes behind gold-rimmed spectacles were always on the look-out for builders who gave councillors peculiar and talismanic handshakes before the proceedings began. Such was the upright judge who was to hear the application for permission to build Fallowfield Country Town. In due course his recommendations would be laid on the desk of Leslie Titmuss, who had, in the particular case of Fallowfield and the Rapstone Valley, agreed to accept them, however inconvenient they might be to his own life and happiness.

'The Inspector's Greg Boland.'

'What's he like?'

'Scottish Wee Free. Straight as a die. Slightest touch of

pressure being put on him and he'll be off like a shot in the opposite direction. I've made the fullest inquiries.'

Ken Cracken and Christopher Kempenflatt were in a corner of Bettina's, an upper-crust disco tucked away in a Mayfair mews. The music overlaid their voices, as the shadows in the corner where they sat drinking a late-night bottle of champagne almost concealed their presence. Their companions for the evening, Joyce Timberlake and the gold-burnished Mrs Armitage, had gone off to exchange confidences in the Ladies, leaving the two men to discuss business.

'He doesn't sound quite the right chap for us.' Kempenflatt was doubtful.

'He's absolutely the right chap for us. Anyway, if he hadn't been straight Leslie Titmuss wouldn't have let them appoint him.'

'I thought you said that Titmuss was leaving the whole Fallowfield business to you.'

'That's what he *said*.' And Ken Cracken laid his finger along the side of his nose in a gesture used by generations of the Cracken family to mean 'pull the other one, it's got bells on'. 'Leslie's got to make sure this business is done strictly on the level. If anyone thought he was swinging it in favour of his country house he'd be finished.'

'I thought that was rather what you wanted.'

'There are more ways than one of skinning a dead cat.' Ken Cracken again used a phrase which had been a great favourite with his grandfather when the old man was in the fur trade. 'But you're right. I wouldn't mind Leslie retiring gracefully to the back benches, after years of valuable service to the country and the Party. All that sort of rubbish. Perhaps the time has come for the old boy to take things easy.'

'And let you pinch his job?' Christopher Kempenflatt had never, since the day when he pushed the great servant of his country into the river, favoured the subtle approach.

'Of course, although that'll be entirely up to the Prime

Minister. And you need to build Fallowfield. With a bit of luck we may both get what we want.'

'How're we going to manage that?'

'Politics, Christopher. Some of us were born with a bit of a talent for it. We might as well finish the bottle, before the girls get back.'

Dancing with minimal movement in the company of the wildly gyrating editor of the Home Maker pages, Tim Warboys noticed the Minister at H.E.A.P. drinking in a corner with the Chairman of Kempenflatts building consortium. Any story about Leslie's Ministry, he felt instinctively, might result in his own immediate transfer to the obituary column, so he averted his eyes. In another corner he saw the much-pilloried Labour M.P. who had tried to get into White's, doing his best to present a swinging image to his research assistant. The absurd hypocrisy of such a fellow behaving like a conservative started an avalanche of column inches in Warboys' mind. His dancing became minimally more animated as he shaped his first sentence: 'A Bettina's Bolshevik takes the floor, but not in the House of Commons. Who is the unknown blonde with whom Labour leftie Dudley Dumpton seems anxious to form a liberal alliance?' Exhausting though it undoubtedly was, and however absurd he felt swaying slightly and clicking his fingers in time to the music, Tim Warboys thought there was nowhere like Bettina's for getting an insight into politics.

Ken Cracken was right. Leslie Titmuss had discovered the name and character of the Inspector who would hear the Fallowfield inquiry. Leslie had no rooted objection to honesty, provided it was not used, as in the case of Jenny's previous husband, to make wounding comparisons with himself. The honesty of Gregory Boland could only underline his own incorruptibility. He had agreed to abide by the result of the inquiry, and the inquiry was to be conducted by an inspector who was above suspicion. How could he conceivably be criticized for that?

It might be thought that Leslie was taking a risk, but having examined the case with the iciest impartiality he came to the conclusion that he was betting on a certainty. Apart from Christopher Kempenflatt and two or three farmers who hoped to make millions, there seemed to be few people who could see any good reason for building over the Rapstone Valley. The number of new houses could easily be fitted into many villages and on the outskirts of Worsfield. A new town would block the roads, pollute the rivers, lay waste the countryside and provide a permanent blot on a much-loved landscape. Given the fact that Gregory Boland was clearly closed to any dubious approach by the Kempenflatt consortium, Leslie Titmuss didn't see how he could possibly decide in favour of Fallowfield Country Town.

He had only one worry. Could the opposition to Fallowfield get its act together? His plan depended on a well-organized outcry by the public, to whose demands, after judgement had been pronounced in its favour, he would bow graciously. He would have every opportunity of showing the human heart beneath the rugged Titmuss exterior. Could Fred Simcox, never to be classed among nature's politicians, get the outcry going effectively? Leslie thought back to the ease with which he had won the skirmish over Jenny's membership of S.O.V. and didn't feel encouraged. At least he could see that the protesters had a decent Q.C. to argue their case. He arranged for his solicitors to send another cheque from an anonymous benefactor to help with the legal expenses of the protest group. 'Send it to Dr Simcox,' he told them. 'It'll be a rare treat for him to get a glimpse of so much money.'

Leslie and his wife also discussed Gregory Boland's character.

'He'll say exactly what he thinks and the hell with the consequences.'

'Well, that's good, isn't it?' Jenny, stretched in front of the fire that autumn evening, flicking through a catalogue full of hopelessly optimistic pictures of a herbaceous border, had almost forgotten they had ever quarrelled.

'He won't try to guess what I want and do it. He'll come to a perfectly honest decision.'

'Isn't that what we want?'

'Just the sort of chap your ex would have approved of.'

'My ex?' She was genuinely confused. 'Exes' to her were living husbands of the sort constantly complained about because of their failure to provide for the children's school fees or the awful hairdo's of their new wives. Death was not, surely, a similar act of infidelity, a ground for divorce, and it was only slowly, and with a distinct feeling of unease, that she realized who he was talking about. 'I don't know what you mean, exactly.'

'Only that Sidonia put such a high value on honesty. Never told a lie, all that sort of thing.'

Jenny stopped turning the pages, apparently engrossed in a portrait of lupins. She didn't know what to say.

'Isn't that what he said?'

'No. He didn't say it much. It was the way he behaved.'

'Admirable, of course. What did he talk about?'

Not to answer him seemed likely to prolong an inquisition of which she felt no good would come. 'He made jokes a lot of the time. About the things he did. The people we met. You can't expect me to remember everything.'

'No. No, of course not.' He sounded understanding and fell silent for a while. Then he said, 'I wish I could've met him.'

'Why?' She could imagine no two men less likely to understand each other than those she had married. Their meeting would, no doubt, have been a disaster, but it was also an impossibility. So why did she feel in such a panic?

'He must have been enormously entertaining.'

'Yes,' she said. 'He was that.'

'Judging by what Sue said about him.'

'You mean, when she was staying here?'

'Yes, of course. She talked about him then. And his wonderful old mother. What was her name . . .?'

'Myra.' Jenny smiled, feeling they'd moved to safer ground. 'She was tremendous value.'

'You said she'd been a ballet dancer.'

'With Sadler's Wells, I think it was. Oh, before the war. And she was with the Russians too. The Monte Carlo company. I can't remember who else.'

'I was never a great one for ballet.'

'I wouldn't think you were.' Jenny smiled at the thought of Leslie watching grimly as young men pranced about in revealing tights. 'Have you ever seen one?'

'Well, not so far as I can remember.'

'I didn't think so.'

'And she danced under her own name?'

'No. She called herself something else. What was it? Myra Zirkin. She said that was the name Fokine gave her because it sounded vaguely Russian. It seemed a bit pointless when her own name was so . . . impressive.'

'Is she alive?'

'Oh, no. She died before Tony. That was a good thing in a way. It would have been a terrible blow to her.'

'Pity. It might have been fun to ask her down.' Leslie opened his red dispatch-box and sat with it on his knees. He began reading documents with great rapidity, scribbling comments which were mostly dismissive and sarcastic. It was late, the fire was dying and Jenny got up to put on another log.

'What would you like? Tea, a drink or something?'

Leslie didn't answer but looked at the flaring wood and said, 'What about Tony's father?'

'Oh, he was killed in the war. When Tony was very young. Why do you want to know that?'

'I thought the dancer might have married an exiled prince or something romantic. She must have had a hard time getting Tony educated. I mean getting him so very educated.'

'I think his father left some money. A pension perhaps. He went away to boarding-school. Nothing else you want to know?'

She felt that Tony should be allowed to rest in peace and not be summoned to answer some sort of interrogation. She was prepared to say as much in answer to Leslie's next question.

But now he smiled at her and said, 'Did you say tea? That would be very nice.'

It was Arthur Nubble's practice to travel by bus and charge for a taxi, and it was only a short bus ride from his office to the narrow passage leading into the Charing Cross Road where he walked into the Entrechat bookshop. He pushed open a door, the bell pinged and a young man in a bow-tie uncurled himself from behind a pile of books, programmes, posters and other souvenirs of the dance to look at him with an expression of considerable hauteur. 'Yes,' he said. 'And what can we do for *you*?'

Arthur Nubble explained he was a solicitor wishing to trace the whereabouts or family of a certain Myra Zirkin in order that she might hear something to her advantage. The young man registered increasing distaste until he heard that Nubble's clients would pay generously for information. Then he burrowed into pre-war programmes, searched indexes and finally unearthed a Zirkin who danced minor roles at Sadler's Wells, in the Ballet Russe de Monte Carlo and, above all, in Dame Felicity Capet's Empire Ballet which, before the war, occupied a now defunct theatre in High Holborn.

'Zirkin? Of course I remember Zirkin. I knew all the secrets of all my girls. They used to confide in me. I insisted on that.'

This time Nubble had gone on a long bus ride to the furthest reaches of Putney and there, in a small flat at the top of a dull grey block, he had found Dame Felicity, a very old lady with huge, saucer eyes who had known Pavlova and who now sat among photographs of fauns, firebirds and sylphides in a cluttered room which smelt overpoweringly of cats. There was a black tom on Nubble's lap, marching round in search of the most comfortable position to sleep, its open claws pricking him through his trousers. 'Do push Dr Coppélius off if he's being a bore. You did say you loved cats, though?' Her long, white fingers were wrapped round the handle of the walking-stick she used to rap on the rehearsal room floor to stop the music so that she might abuse the dancers. 'And you say you're writing about the Empire Ballet?'

'With special reference, Dame Felicity, to your own career.' Nubble liked to vary his cover stories to add interest to his work.

'I don't know why you bother with Zirkin. She had very little discipline and, as I remember, particularly unfortunate knees. Only one good point,' Dame Felicity allowed grudgingly. 'She had a face like a magnolia.'

'She also had a son?' Nubble asked.

'Not as far as I was concerned she hadn't.' The old woman seemed to have no doubts. 'And I'd certainly've known about it if she had.'

'Really?' The cat had gone to sleep now, a hot, dead weight on his groin. 'I think I met her at Oxford after the war. She used to come and stay with her son who was a friend of mine.'

'I don't know what you're talking about!' In the old Empire Ballet she had never suffered fools gladly. 'After the war Zirkin wasn't in Oxford, or anywhere else in this world, for that matter.'

'I'm sorry, Dame Felicity. I don't quite understand what you're telling me.'

'I'm simply telling you, my dear man, that she went out to Germany with a concert party to entertain the troops during the war. She danced the Dying Swan as one of the turns, something she was quite unqualified to do. Anyway, the concert party's train was bombed, apparently by mistake. I suppose you could say' – the old lady was smiling gently – 'she died in action. Of course' – she forced the smile off her face – 'it was extremely sad. An amusing girl but hardly a genius.'

So Zirkin, the dancer, died during the war, a time as he knew from his briefing before the second Mrs Titmuss had been born. Nubble felt relieved that the interview was over and he could get out into the fresh air, away from this old woman who treated him as though he were some sort of idiot. Before he went he tried a final question.

'Dame Felicity. Does the name Myra Sidonia mean anything to you?'

'Myra Sidonia?' The huge, disapproving eyes were turned on him; the voice rose as though he'd tripped over the prima ballerina in the finale. 'Why ever should you bother me with questions about her?'

CHAPTER TWENTY-TWO

Pale sunshine continued until December and then withdrew, discouraged, as north winds and heavy skies promised snow. At midnight mass Kev the Rev. prayed, 'Oh Lord, guide the hands of Thy ministers and officials at Housing and Ecological Affairs to spare, if it be Thy will, this valley from falling victim to a materialistic society.' As his congregation shook his hand and came out into the cold, the doors of their Range Rovers were glued with ice and their children woke to a snowy morning which seemed intent on preserving the traditions of rural England. How God the Great Planning Officer would conduct Himself when the inquiry opened the following month remained a subject of endless speculation. In the Baptist's Head Len Bigwell was offering two to one against Fallowfield Country Town ever being built now the protesters had suddenly found themselves able to engage a Q.C. reputed to be the best planning lawyer in England.

After Christmas the snow lay fresh on the Rapstone Nature Area, marked with the hierographics of many pads and claws. In Worsfield it turned as grey as dirty washing, clogged the gutters and made the steps of the District Council offices a peril. Inside, in an atmosphere made soporific by central heating and legal argument, Gregory Boland, the Inspector, sat high over a sea of plans and towers of documents. The lawyers whispered, made jokes and passed each other notes. Young men and girls from Kempenflatt's office dozed, then woke with a start and tried to look interested. In the public benches sat the members of S.O.V., who did their best during long hours of anaesthetizing boredom to preserve their high mood of concerned outrage. The Curdles had arrived in force, dressed as for a wedding, and passed round tubes of wine gums and Polos. They then sat with their jaws working in a threatening manner. The Vees took copious notes of the proceedings which would later be fed into the computer in Mr Vee's office and circulated to many people who would never read them. At the press table the elderly man from the *Worsfield Echo*, who lived in an area so entirely bereft of natural beauty that the issue didn't concern him one way or the other, filled in his football pools and waited for something dramatic to happen. Such was the scene in the council chamber when Dr Frederick Simcox was called into the witness-box.

Every group throws up its own leader but Fred wondered, as he swore to tell the truth and tried to look as though he were taking the whole thing seriously, if S.O.V. hadn't thrown up the wrong one. Dot Curdle would have overflowed the witness-box, dominated the room and given everyone a piece of her mind. Mrs Vee would have had the facts at her fingers' ends and Mr Vee would have been able to lower his voice to that tone of quiet urgency which was so effective in gathering money which would go, after the payment of his considerable percentage, to feed children in remote parts of Africa.

The expensive barrister hired with Leslie Titmuss's secret contribution was a Mr Alistair Fernhill, who was about to become a judge. So he would go, after a lifetime in town planning, to a new world of murder, mayhem and indecent assault, of which he had no experience whatever. In that moment in a barrister's life, before being enveloped in scarlet and ermine and whisked into a position above the battle, Mr Fernhill had come to do his cases in a detached and world-weary manner, as though already remote from the struggles of lesser men. This aloof Alistair Fernhill, Q.C., revealed that Fred was a doctor who had been in practice locally for over a quarter of a century, and who, as Chairman of the Save Our Valley society, was one of the principal objectors. What would the new town do to the amenities of the countryside, the beauty of the landscape, the safety of the roads and the health of the population? Fred was taken through his evidence rather as an unwelcome visitor is led through the corridors of some grand house by a superior butler. His answers, he felt, lacked conviction.

It was as though all the talent for belief in his family had been taken up by his dead father. The old Rector of Rapstone had believed passionately in everything: Socialism, pacifism, Ban the Bomb and some essential good in human nature. After such an immense outpouring of faith the Simcox stock, it seemed, had been exhausted. If Fred believed in anything it was the countryside he had grown up in, the dark woods and secret hiding-places in the bracken, the memories of afternoons of love in Tom Nowt's old hut and moonlit swims in the muddy water of the river. And yet, as he tried to find words for these feelings which would be acceptable in a court of law, he thought of other arguments, different points of view. Might not childhood be as vivid in a Worsfield housing estate? Might not love be equally memorable if it were crammed into the back seat of a Ford Cortina behind the multi-storey car park? It was Fred's curse to see two sides to every question; it was freedom from this unfortunate character defect which had brought Leslie Titmuss his considerable success.

'You're a medical doctor, aren't you?'

The superior butler and embryo judge had sat down, to be replaced by another learned friend. This one had a voice like a hacksaw blade, gold half-glasses three quarters of the way down his nose and an expression of puzzled incredulity. This was Carus-Atkins, Q.C., Counsel for Kempenflatts, the builders.

'Not a doctor of botany, or forestry, or other rural mysteries?'

'Not at all.'

'So you are not an expert on the countryside?'

'No. I have just known it all my life. Perhaps I have a special feeling for the Rapstone Valley –'

'As a doctor you will be paid by the number of patients you attend.' The barrister interrupted the answer.

'I understand that's the intention of the present government, yes.'

'Then won't a new town suit you very well? You'll have a great many more people to provide pills for. You might make a great deal more money, might you not, Doctor?' There was some obedient laughter from the staff of Kempenflatt's office.

'I'd rather have less money, fewer patients and no new town.'

'Some people might think that rather an eccentric view.' Carus-Atkins peered over his spectacles at his supporters in the Kempenflatt camp. 'But then you are a somewhat eccentric doctor, aren't you?'

'I don't think so.'

'Given to acting as a drummer in a local public house?'

'I'm a member of a jazz group. Yes.'

'Enlighten me, Doctor.' The builders' Q.C. dug his hands deeply into his pockets and leant forward, his head on one side, his ear cocked as though he were eager to receive knowledge. 'Do you think eating rabbits an excellent cure for heart failure?'

Gregory Boland, the Inspector, pursed his lips and looked as though someone had just burst into song or started to undress in the course of the proceedings. The Curdle family nodded wisely, in total agreement with the proposition, and Mrs Vee hid her face in her hands and whispered, 'Oh Christ, here it comes!'

'No,' Fred answered without hesitation.

'How very strange.' Carus-Atkins received a newspaper cutting from an attentive junior and took it with the delicacy of a great surgeon about to employ a scalpel. 'Did you not say as much to a journalist working on the *Fortress*?'

'No, I didn't. That report was totally inaccurate.'

'Where do you suggest the journalist got the idea from?'

'From someone who came into my surgery and might have seen a document containing that piece of information.'

Looking round the council chamber Fred noticed Jenny for

the first time. Had she been there long or had she wandered in late, as she had done when he played with the Riverside Stompers? Seeing her brought the whole room into sharper focus. He felt suddenly younger, more energetic and, for a moment, mercifully unable to tolerate the opposition. At least there was no possible doubt about his dislike of Mr Carus-Atkins.

'Are you prepared to tell us who that person was?'

Fred looked at Jenny and was not prepared to supply the information.

'Dr Simcox. Are you really here to *help* this inquiry?' the Inspector intervened.

'So far as I can.'

'Then perhaps we could ask you to deal with the matter in hand.' Gregory Boland looked at him with a severity which Fred felt should have been reserved for his inquisitor. 'That matter is about building houses. It's got nothing to do with the medical properties of rabbit meat. May I ask you to remember that, Doctor?'

'Exactly my view, sir.' The Carus-Atkins effrontery astounded Fred. 'Now, Doctor. Please direct your mind to the issues in this case. You have told me you have a special feeling for this countryside, around Rapstone.'

'That's perfectly true. Yes.' Fred was looking at Jenny and the sound of the hacksaw voice seemed to grow faint as she gave him a small smile of approval.

'Are you a selfish man, Doctor?'

'Not particularly.'

'Isn't it rather selfish of you, if you love it so much, not to want to share it with other people?'

'If it's all built over, there won't be anything to share with anyone.'

'He's improving,' Mrs Vee whispered.

'Slightly,' Mr Vee whispered back.

'Dr Simcox. I understand your father, the Reverend Simeon Simcox, was a clergyman who indulged himself in a large number of anti-government protests.'

'He had strong beliefs, yes.'

'And he used to march all over the place. Organize demonstrations.' Carus-Atkins waved his spectacles aimlessly to suggest mental confusion in the old Rector. 'And the like.'

'Certainly.'

'Is that a characteristic you have inherited?'

'I hope I have inherited some of his concern for social justice. Yes.' In the ordinary course of events these were words which would have made Fred squirm with embarrassment. With Jenny looking at him from her seat among the protesters, he felt a certain pride in his answer.

'You have also inherited his dislike of Conservative governments.'

'My complaint against this Conservative government is that it's failing to conserve anything.'

Fred was rewarded now, not only by Jenny's interest but also by some laughter and a clearly audible 'Doctor got you there, then, didn't he?' from Dot Curdle.

'And I'm bound to suggest' – Carus-Atkins was leaning back on his heels now, looking at the witness with an indulgent expression such as might be used to a tiresome child – 'that your Save Our Valley society simply exists to satisfy your family craving to protest against the Government. However much employment and wealth and prosperity it brings, you'll never be satisfied, will you, Doctor? You'll just . . . carry on marching.'

'I don't think it's necessary to involve this inquiry in a political argument.' Again the soft Scottish rebuke from the red-haired Inspector seemed directed at Fred rather than at his assailant.

'I think it's entirely necessary for me to answer the question.' Fred raised his voice and felt he was speaking directly to Jenny. 'As a matter of fact I've got no particular interest in politics. I don't want to spend my time organizing protests or going on marches. Protests and marches make me feel ridiculous. I'd like to be left alone to look after my patients and go drumming in public houses, as you put it so charmingly. But you won't leave us alone, will you? Your clients want to buy up the farmland and make money out of us. The Government wants to change our lives and wreck our valley forever. Nobody who lives around Rapstone wants that to happen. Nobody! But it seems we're all at the mercy of strangers –'

'Dr Simcox!' The Scottish protest rose suddenly to a bleat, but Fred carried on.

'Do you think I enjoy spending an afternoon standing here answering your ridiculous questions about rabbits? I'd rather be treating carbuncles and changing dressings. But you don't give us any choice. When you come down here, hired by people trying to make money out of us, what else can you expect us to do?'

Fred had listened to himself in some surprise. He was further surprised to see Mr Carus-Atkins sit down and look triumphantly about the court, his cross-examination over. Perhaps he thinks he's proved I'm a total nut-case, Fred thought, and then the red-haired Inspector said, 'Thank you, Dr Simcox,' and he left the witness-box.

'You were splendid!' Jenny told him.

'I sounded like a diehard old Tory, didn't I? Keep the world safe for peasants and game birds. That sort of thing. That's the trouble with these people. We used to feel like young revolutionaries, now they seem to have turned us into the last defenders of the old regime.'

'Which people?'

'What?'

'Which people is it the trouble with?'

'Oh. I mean the new radical, tear it all down and start again, Conservative party . . .'

'You mean people like Leslie?'

'Well . . .' Fred hadn't wanted to say that, not knowing how Jenny might take an attack on her husband.

'That's who you mean.' They were in a pub, cosy as an aircraft hangar and only a little smaller, opposite the council offices. Jenny took a gulp of the white wine she had asked for and pulled a face.

'Is it all right?' Fred was concerned.

'Fine. Except that it tastes of slightly chilled, watered-down paraffin with a touch of vanilla essence.'

He laughed at the accuracy of her description. 'I'll get you a beer. It's probably safer.'

'I don't know what Leslie wants, quite honestly,' she said when he came back from the bar. He looked at her with excitement, feeling that she was about to confide in him. Indeed, she was. She felt at home with Fred, as she had with Tony, and that she could tell him anything and he wouldn't laugh at her, or make her feel an idiot, and probably, in nine cases out of ten at least, tell her something which would be a help. She was on the point of saying, I don't know what Leslie wants. He's started to ask me all sorts of questions about my first husband, a man who has been dead for six years now, who was as different from Leslie as chalk from cheese, who I couldn't explain to Leslie if I sat down and talked from now to September but who, in some ways, which I feel is slightly unnerving, was a little like you, Dr Simcox. She might have said all that but she knew she would have regretted it. It would, after all, have been disloyal to Leslie. So she said, 'I'm still sure he doesn't want the new town.'

'That's encouraging. Let's drink to that.' So they raised two glasses of Simcox's lager and clinked them together.

CHAPTER TWENTY-THREE

'Mr Sidonia? He's been dead a long time.'

'Of course I know that. But he was one of your most famous dons, after all, at St Joseph's. I just wondered if you remember him?'

'Remember him? Of course we remember him. Everyone except my colleague, that is, who was no doubt still in his rompers when Mr Sidonia passed on.' The square-faced porter peered out of his cubby-hole at the college entrance; somewhere in the background his colleague, who wore a single discreet ear-ring, was fitting letters into pigeon-holes. Girls and young men surrounded Nubble, reading notices and holding hands or embracing so flagrantly, despite the freezing weather, that he felt soured by jealousy. He was also tired and out of breath, having walked from Oxford station so that he could make a small profit on the cab fare. 'Mr Sidonia,' the porter said, as though to close the conversation, 'was a very nice gentleman. Very nice indeed.'

'Popular with the students?'

'I expect so.'

'You had girl students when he was here, didn't you?'

'If you've got an appointment with Sir Willoughby, he doesn't like to be kept waiting. Through the arch and in the far left-hand corner. That's the door to the lodgings.' So Arthur Nubble was sent about his business and he crossed the quad, whipped by the icy wind from the cloisters which had frozen generations of undergraduates on their way to the bathroom. When the secretary showed him into the Master's presence, Nubble reminded Sir Willoughby that he was writing a series on famous heads of colleges for the *Fortress* colour magazine, which was the cover story it had amused him to adopt. The Master, who knew the value of publicity in these tough, fund-raising times, received him with an effusive handshake and a small glass of the sherry he kept aside for students. He then talked persuasively about his own career, his remarkable insight into the life-cycle of the prawn and the essential part the Blane Biology Library would play in Britain's future. The Government had been amazingly short-sighted about it and he wondered if some great philanthropist, such as the proprietor of the *Fortress*, might perhaps be interested.

'He might well be.' Arthur Nubble considered the matter seriously. 'Particularly in view of the distinguished scholars you've had at St Joseph's. I was thinking of Anthony Sidonia, on history.' This journalist said it, Sir Willoughby thought, rather as though history were a musical instrument in a jazz band. 'He was very popular, wasn't he, among the students?'

'Tony?' Sir Willoughby looked suitably distressed. 'Tragic early death, of course. So many of our older dons wouldn't have been missed *half* as much. Yes. Of course he was popular with the students. Not quite so popular with other history teachers.'

'Oh, really?' Nubble opened his notebook for the first time during the interview. 'Why was that?'

'Well, he spoke about his subject on television. He did it rather well and *looked* quite attractive. A lot of less photogenic historians felt rather sour about it. Touch of the showman, they said, about Tony Sidonia.'

'Jealous?'

'Oh, yes, I think so.' The Master liked nothing better than to relay old gossip. 'They suggested he only got the job because his then girlfriend worked in television. But she was only a researcher, I believe, and I don't think that had anything to do with it. Anyway, the programmes were very popular. Academics hate that.'

'Of course they were extremely interesting,' said Nubble, who hadn't seen them.

'Indeed, yes.' Sir Willoughby hadn't seen them either. 'I'm sure the criticism wasn't justified. Although I believe Tony never really got to grips with Savonarola. Not that I'd know. I'm only a poor biologist.'

'I think I might have met the girl who worked on those programmes. What was her name again?'

'Briar, was it? Something decidedly prickly. No. Bramble. Sarah, or perhaps Susan, Bramble. She turned up at a secretarial college here and then she found her way into the B.B.C. Most girls seem to, in the end.'

'I suppose he met her before he married.'

'Oh, yes. He knew La Bramble long before he met Jenny. Moved her out, I believe, before he proposed anything so outrageous as matrimony. Not that Jenny isn't an absolutely *super* girl. You've spoken to her, I suppose?'

'No. Not yet.'

'I've never known what mental aberration led her to take up with that appallingly common Cabinet Minister. We had a sweet, gentle fellow here who taught Anglo-Saxon, and he fell passionately in love with a most disagreeable Detective Inspector who used to treat the poor old dear just like a criminal, interrogate him and so on . . . By the way, that's not for publication.'

Nubble, scribbling energetically, looked up sharply at the Master's description of his employer. Sir Willoughby wondered if he had gone too far; the *Fortress*, after all, was not a paper to look sympathetically on critics of the Government.

'Who was the chap you say Tony never got to grips with?' Nubble was frowning at his notebook. 'Savannah something?'

'Savonarola.'

'I wouldn't mind meeting him, if he's still around.' History had never been Nubble's strongest suit and he had soon left the public school he attended with the Simcox brothers to open an espresso coffee bar.

'I'm afraid not. They burnt him in Florence quite early in the sixteenth century.' The Master tried to be fair and tell himself that no doubt persons with no particular claim to education now wrote on academic matters for the quality papers. He decided to give the dubious candidate one more chance.

'Tony wasn't the only distinguished St Joseph's man. You know, we did have Isaac Newton.'

'Of course.' Nubble, who had heard of Isaac Newton, nodded wisely. 'I'll remind my readers of that, Sir Willoughby.' But the Master, feeling that every schoolboy should know that Newton went to Trinity, Cambridge, fled to his secretary's room where he telephoned Tim Warboys, another St Joseph's man who had achieved stardom, and discovered that nothing was known of Arthur Nubble in the *Fortress* features department or, indeed, of any article on famous heads of colleges. He didn't reappear but the secretary told Nubble that a crisis in the marine biology lab had brought the interview to a premature end.

Despite this sudden conclusion the sleuth felt reasonably satisfied with his morning's work. He was getting closer to Tony Sidonia and although he had as yet learned little to his subject's disadvantage he felt that his employer would admire his persistence and the ingenuity of his various disguises. When he got back to London he started to make inquiries of the B.B.C., becoming an independent film and television producer interested in a reissue of Tony Sidonia's brilliant programme 'In the Shadow of the Triple Crown', and perhaps speaking to some of the people who had worked on it.

Sue Bramble was in low spirits. She felt something she had not experienced before. She was lonely. Naturally high-spirited and gregarious she thrived on variety, changing her jobs as frequently as she changed her lovers, and greeting each new arrival with the enthusiastic certainty that she had hit upon the perfect answer to her problems. She had not found work or love difficult to come by. When she was doing her secretarial course at Oxford she had been a constant figure at undergraduate and indeed graduate parties. She'd worked in bookshops, as a waitress in a succession of restaurants and in a shop full of exotic second-hand dresses in the covered market. When she parted from Tony and he married, she moved to London and got her job at the B.B.C. She progressed rapidly from secretary to researcher to the director's assistant during Tony's programme on the Renaissance Popes. Later, working on a documentary about the turf, she met her trainer, helped out in his office for a while and made many new friends. When her situation with him grew complicated she came back to Oxford and wrote stories for various racing papers. When Tony Sidonia died she and Jenny seemed to be drawn more closely together by the disappearance of the man they had both loved. So they had decided to share a flat in London.

Now she was alone in the flat. Teddy Blaze, the Newbury trainer, whom she had urged for so long to leave his wife and marry her, and who had so often promised and failed to do so, rang to say that he was to be divorced. He was now free and available. He drove up to London at great speed and knocked at the door of the flat, loaded with champagne and roses. As Sue saw him standing there, flushed with his belated achievement, she felt the excitement drain away from their relationship like cooling bath-water. Not only could she no longer marry him, she could hardly bear to be taken out by him. In the restaurant they went to she sat mostly in silence, only criticizing him occasionally. At last she had to beg him, for his own protection, not to ring her or try to take her out again. When he wrote to tell her that he was engaged to marry a girl groom some twenty years younger, who lived in Didcot, she felt nothing but relief.

Since her friend had got married, Sue had taken over Jenny's job. She sat all day, dazed by the white walls and bored by the abstract paintings, trying her best not to become involved in the disastrous private life of Mark Vanberry, the gallery owner. In this she succeeded but, far too often for her own self-esteem, she came home to an empty flat to wash her hair and watch the television. On many such evenings she wanted to ring Jenny and laugh and gossip as they once did. What stopped her was not just Jenny's marriage – her amazed disapproval of Leslie had never come between them – but she had felt, curiously enough, more remote from her friend as she had come to find Leslie Titmuss more bearable. And now there was another reason: she had shown him Tony's photographs, she had had what amounted to a secret lunch with him. She had been manoeuvred, against her better judgement, into a conspiracy and she had promised to say nothing to Jenny about it. It was that small act of treachery that made Sue uncomfortable at the idea of telephoning. And Jenny didn't ring her. She was reluctant to tell Sue about Leslie's curious questions about Tony, and yet she didn't want to keep this latest development a secret from her friend with whom she had always discussed everything. So the shadow of Leslie Titmuss fell between them, and Sue was left wondering why on earth she had done what he asked her.

So, when the telephone rang one lonely evening, she half hoped it was Jenny and dreaded that it might be Mark Vanberry. In fact it was a somewhat husky male voice who made sure she was Miss Bramble and then announced that Atmos Films Limited was going into the production of historical and artistic documentary films. Would she be interested in joining the team? 'I was much impressed by the work you did on that beautiful programme "In the Shadow of the Triple Crown". Might I have the pleasure of taking you to lunch? Shall we say tomorrow, if you're free, at the Groucho Club? The name's Nubble. Arthur Nubble . . . Oh, and by the way, can you put me in touch with anyone else who worked on that magnificent production?'

The snow turned to slush which was washed away by incessant rain. Hector Bolitho Jones slid and skidded round his woods, shrouded in a yellow waterproof cape. He shook the drops from his beard as a dog shakes itself dry. The badgers emerged at night into a cold monsoon and scuttered back into their setts.

Although there were signs of buds on the branches and specks of green pushing through the black earth, Rapstone Nature Area was then no place for lovers. Through that month and the next Gregory Boland sat in the spare bedroom of his concrete-block house, surrounded by piles of maps documents and transcripts of evidence, and wrote his report on the future of that particular countryside. During the bad weather Arthur Nubble completed his inquiries.

When the sun returned, making the soaked grass steam, two men in overcoats were to be seen walking past the great mulberry tree in the garden of St Joseph's College.

'It isn't so much a moral question,' Sir Willoughby was explaining. 'It's more a problem of educational technology.'

'You mean, dons shouldn't go to bed with their students?'

'It's not the bed part so much. It's what it leads to. A warping of the pupil–teacher relationship, favouritism in tutorials, sexually induced marking, and then, when it all busts up, tears in lectures and feelings of rejection that may seriously impair the performance at Finals. That's why we don't find bed-hopping with pupils acceptable conduct at St Joseph's. Of course, there have been exceptions.'

'What exceptions?'

'Well. I can't remember exactly.' The Master became vague and avoided Leslie Titmuss's pale and persistent stare. 'But there must have been exceptions.'

'I wanted to ask you a few questions about one of your dons. Sidonia.'

'Well, he does seem to have become the flavour of the month. The last few months, anyway.'

'Has he?'

'I had a most extraordinary fellow here asking about Tony. This man said he was working for the *Fortress*. I suspected that was a lie.'

'It was.'

'You know about him?'

'He was working for me.'

The Master thought it best to conceal his astonishment and to say nothing.

'He was making certain inquiries for me about Sidonia.'

'This Mr Nobble?'

'Nubble. I suppose he made a prize idiot of himself, didn't he?'

'He knew absolutely nothing about Savonarola, and very little about Sir Isaac Newton.'

'He had his uses, filling in the background. I'm relying on you to complete the picture.'

In a moment of wild speculation Sir Willoughby guessed that Tony had been a crypto-Communist, a spy, a traitor, the fifth man, or sixth, and now, after his death, the subject of government inquiries. He was not to know that his crime was to have been the first man in Jenny Sidonia's affections.

'I don't see how I can help. I really didn't know a great deal about Tony's private life.'

'Nonsense! You know all about the private lives of everyone in your college.' Leslie stopped on the spongy lawn, apparently not feeling the east wind which was making the Master long for tea and anchovy toast by the fire in his lodgings. 'Is that where it's going to stand?'

'What exactly?'

'The Blane Biology Library.' Leslie was looking at a great expanse on which, he had reason to suppose, planning permission might be given. 'I've made some inquiries, the D.E.S. has a certain fund for educational developments of special value to industry and commerce.'

As in a dream the Master saw the tasteful building in Cotswold stone. In the hallway there would be a statue, wouldn't there, or at least a bust, of his good self? It would be, as he had no child, his single, magnificent claim to immortality.

'Secretary of State. Is there really any hope –?'

'I shall have, of course, to talk to colleagues.' Now Leslie gripped Sir Willoughby's forearm and turned to more immediate matters. 'For the moment I have just a few more questions about Sidonia. Number one. I expect you remember a girl who was a friend of his called Susan Bramble?'

CHAPTER TWENTY-FOUR

Gregory Boland worked long and tirelessly on his report. He tabulated the evidence and classified and reclassified it under various headings, 'Sewage', 'Traffic Volume', 'Rail Access', 'Population Density' and 'Commercial Opportunities'. He looked again and again at the beguiling drawings of children playing in the pedestrian precincts and he remembered the walks he had taken on the site, the cathedral hush in the middle of beech woods soon, perhaps, to be broken forever and to be broken by him. And yet, he told himself, being a reasonable man as well as honest, neither life nor architecture could stand still. The English, sooner or later, must face up to the fact that it was a myth that they lived in a series of delightful villages, strung like jewels across some rustic landscape. They would have to wake up and realize that they lived along motorway routes and by service stations in some vast and anonymous suburb which stretched from Land's End to John o' Groat's, punctuated by theme parks and shopping malls. If that was the future, was it after all so terrible? It meant jobs for many people, including architects and town planners as well as policemen, sewage workers and girls at supermarket check-outs. The country needed houses which, like motor cars, were a sign of healthy prosperity. Those who wished to spend their days in uninterrupted contemplation of the great crested grebe could, as Counsel for Kempenflatts had ventured to suggest in a peculiarly acid final speech, move to the Highlands of Scotland. Gregory Boland, who had come from the

Highlands, had no intention of going back there, however the English landscape developed.

And yet, and yet ... As Gregory fed more and more facts into his computer, hoping that the ingenious machine would come out with the answer he found it so hard to arrive at, as he remembered the stream of experts, planners, botanists, porers over archaeological remains, politicians and sociologists who had passed before him during that long hearing, he couldn't help remembering Dr Simcox. He hadn't at first taken to the Doctor, who seemed lacking in respect for the tribunal and to regard all the evidence, including his own, with the same amused detachment. But then something Fred had said returned to him: 'We're all at the mercy of strangers.' Gregory had protested at that, he remembered. It had seemed irrelevant to the proceedings. But now, thinking about it, he saw Fred's point; although it was one which would never be understood by a computer.

He, after all, had been born in a small country which had fallen into the hands of the alien English. The Scots, in Gregory's view, had done nothing to deserve such a fate and what crime had the inhabitants of Rapstone and Hartscombe and the countryside in between committed that they should be punished by Fallowfield Country Town? It was not their fault that three of the farmers who lived in their midst were prepared to sell the past to a hungry developer who, like some vulture wheeling in the sky, was only on the look-out for a defenceless body to pick to the bones. Their homes were not to be razed to the ground and their woods destroyed because they occupied the perfect site for a new town, but simply because it was there that Kempenflatts had found an opportunity to make money. Slowly, painfully and with minute attention to detail, Gregory Boland was coming to the view that he would decide against Fallowfield.

Such were the Inspector's thoughts when his wife knocked at the door, something she rarely did when the computer was wrestling for his soul, and announced a telephone call from the Ministry of Housing, Ecological Affairs and Planning. He went downstairs to have his ear filled with the voice of Ken Cracken, calling him as though on a loud-hailer.

'Boland. I suppose you've broken the back of the Fallowfield business?'

'Ay.' Gregory was, as always, cautious. 'I think I see light at the end of the tunnel.'

'And you've done a splendid job, by all accounts. How about a celebration lunch? Give yourself a day off and come up to town.'

'I don't think that would be quite appropriate.'

'Not to discuss Fallowfield, of course. That's entirely off limits. But we're up to the bloody neck in these applications now. We're looking for someone of real experience to become chief adviser in a brand-new planning department. Salary not yet fixed but appropriate to the responsibilities. And naturally your name came up in preliminary discussions. Think about it and give me a bell, why don't you?'

Once Gregory had mentioned this to Mrs Boland the result was inevitable. Was he to lose a last chance to gain some of the prosperity he had missed by not joining the Masons? So, a couple of days later, Gregory Boland entered the Savoy Grill to be lavishly entertained by Ken Cracken and his political adviser.

'What we're looking for is a bloke with a real knowledge of planning law and a reputation for being clean as a whistle. Naturally you were first on our list.'

'I am suitably gratified.' Although he had protested that he never drank at lunch-time Gregory had been persuaded to share the bottle Ken chose, the second most expensive on the list. 'The Ministry doesn't often get a chance to show its gratitude.' As he raised the glass of Pichon-Longueville and was filled with its costly benevolence, Gregory felt himself at the beginning of a new career. 'This is a treat,' he said. 'A rare treat.'

'What attracts us to you' – Joyce Timberlake was looking at the Inspector over the rim of her glass with wide-eyed admiration – 'is that you understand politics.'

'I'm an architect by trade.' Gregory was flattered but modest. 'I don't quite know where politics comes into it.'

'Comes into everything, doesn't it?' Ken was carefully weighing up the rival claims of profiteroles and bread and butter pudding on the sweet trolley. 'The trick, in your present inquiry, is to come up with the right decision at the right moment.'

'I thought we weren't going to discuss Fallowfield.' There was a slight rise of the Boland hackles.

'Of course not. That would be quite inappropriate,' Joyce reassured him.

'Improper,' Ken agreed.

'Entirely wrong.'

'Until you've announced your decision.'

'Which, of course, we're looking forward to with enormous interest.' Somewhat mollified, Gregory returned his nose to his wine glass. 'But it would be pretty short-sighted,' Ken went on, 'not to recognize the political climate in which all these decisions are taken nowadays.'

'You mean a general free-for-all?' Gregory put down his glass and resumed his severe expression.

'That's one way of putting it.' Joyce laughed as though he had made a joke. 'In government we like to call it the operation of market forces.'

'I'm well aware' – Gregory looked like one of his Wee Free ancestors winding himself up to denounce the Pope – 'that there are those in government who think it a sign of our national well-being that the whole of Southern England should be concreted over to accommodate banks, shoe shops, hairdressers, building societies and other light industries. It's surely my job to see that the outcome of this particular case is my free and independent decision!'

There was a silence while the product of so many elders of the kirk fixed his listeners with a glare of defiance, and then Ken Cracken sat back and clapped his hands in a loud gesture of applause which disconcerted the waiters.

'Damn good!' Ken raised his glass. 'Let's drink to your free and independent decision.'

'So long as that's perfectly understood.' Gregory Boland then drank to his independence.

'Of course,' Ken began again after a suitable pause for reflection, 'if you'd said all that about concreting over England a year or two ago I'd've entirely agreed with you.'

'A year or two ago the only song we sang was about the free market economy,' Joyce bore him out. 'It was all on one note. Fallowfield might have seemed the answer to all our problems.'

'But there's been a bit of a difference in the political climate, quite honestly, Greg.'

The Inspector looked warily from the Minister to his political adviser. What were they getting at now?

'The truth is' – Ken Cracken now leaned forward confidentially – 'Leslie Titmuss has become ozone-friendly.'

'He's come out for the rhino and broad-leafed trees, hedgerows, butterflies, chemical-free farming, unpolluted streams. The rumour is' – Joyce laid a strong hand on Gregory's cuff and smiled to indicate that she wasn't to be taken entirely seriously – 'that he's given up using a hair-spray!'

'Oh, he never used a hair-spray,' Ken corrected her. 'I don't believe he's got beyond brilliantine.'

'We're off the H in H.E.A.P. and on to the E.'

'It's not housing. Ecology's the buzz word nowadays.'

'Well,' Gregory told them. 'I'm very glad to hear it.' Indeed he was. As his mind was turning towards saving the Rapstone Valley for the badgers he was delighted that he would have his Secretary of State's approval.

'But the major political development in the last two years' – Ken now looked at Gregory in a way the Inspector found uncomfortably conspiratorial – 'is something entirely different. Not really anything to do with the environment.'

'No,' Joyce agreed. 'More something to do with housing.'

'I'm afraid I don't understand.' Gregory was again afraid that he might understand them too well. Ken Cracken waited ostentatiously until the waiter had cleared away the pudding plates – he had gone for the profiteroles with a touch of bread and butter pudding on the side – and then he leant forward to make it quite clear to anyone of the meanest intelligence that Gregory Boland was being invited to take part in a plot.

'The outstanding event of our time,' he said in a stage whisper, 'is that Leslie Titmuss decided to buy Rapstone Manor.'

'Mr Titmuss's house.' Joyce made it painfully obvious. 'So naturally he's a bit concerned about what goes on in his back garden.'

'I'm sure you're not suggesting, either of you' – Gregory thought he knew quite well what they were suggesting – 'that I should allow the position of the Secretary of State's house to have the slightest effect on my decision?'

'Of course not,' said Joyce, apparently horrified.

'God forbid!' Ken echoed her.

'No effect at all,' said Joyce.

'Your decision will be based, I'm sure, on sound environmental principles.'

'Fulfilling our duty,' Joyce intoned, as though it were part of a new and recently learned litany, 'to our planet earth.'

'Of which we've but got a lease for a short number of years.' Ken Cracken took up the response and then added, in a more businesslike manner, 'I'm sure the Secretary of State would be delighted if you made that the basis for your decision to stop the development.'

'The basis for my decision?' Gregory Boland, his eyes alight with the strength of his principles, looked at his hosts with scorn; in such a way the early Protestant martyrs no doubt faced the threats of the Inquisition. 'What's Mr Titmuss got to do with the basis of my decision?'

'Absolutely nothing,' Ken Cracken agreed with a smile. 'Provided it doesn't mean a new town being planted on top of him. If that can be avoided, I know he'll be extremely grateful. And we'll look forward to your joining us, as our new overall planning adviser.'

'I'm sorry. I'll have to go now.' So Gregory the martyr thrust aside temptation and stood up proudly in the Savoy Grill. 'I have a great deal of work to do. Redrafting my conclusions. You may tell the Secretary of State that he will have my full report before the month is over.'

'Worked like a charm,' Ken said when the Inspector had gone home to disappoint Mrs Boland and he had ordered a couple of Remy Martins to go with the coffee. 'We've certainly got the right character. He'll go to the stake for Fallowfield Country Town after that.'

'You handled him beautifully,' Joyce told her lover with admiration.

'Well, you've got a great deal of political talent yourself. As well as being an absolutely delightful screw.' Ken didn't bother to lower his voice for the benefit of the waiter who was warming two huge balloon glasses. 'Hardly worth going back to the Ministry this afternoon, is it?'

'Hardly worth it at all.'

So, on a bright and windy April morning Gregory Boland's report thudded on to his Secretary of State's desk, to coincide with a well-timed paragraph leaked to Tim Warboys by Ken Cracken, which had appeared in the *Fortress*. LESLIE TITMUSS TO JOIN THE HOMELESS? it was headed at Ken's suggestion, after Warboys had been assured that Leslie would welcome so dramatic a statement of his promised sacrifice.

Now, as I am informed, the Planning Inspector's report is to give the go-ahead for a new country town in the Rapstone Valley, will Mr and Mrs Titmuss of Rapstone Manor be out on the streets? Hardly likely. Titmuss made a sizeable fortune before he devoted himself to becoming one of the country's most outspoken and abrasive politicians. He won't be driven to sleep in a cardboard box. What is certain is that Leslie Titmuss, with the unshakeable integrity which has been a characteristic of his political career, will keep his promise to follow the public inquiry's recommendations. He is not likely to allow his own personal comfort to get in the way of what he considers best for England. Whatever his critics may say, that has never been the Titmuss style.

'Did *you* write this? It seems to have the Cracken ring to it.'

Ken and Joyce were entertaining committee members of his constituency party and had brought them out to admire the view down the river from the House of Commons terrace. The silver-haired women and red-faced men who helped Ken Cracken to his huge majority in the London suburbs smiled with adoration as their favourite Cabinet Minister came up to them. But Leslie was tight-lipped and furious as he held the folded paper under the nose of his Minister of State.

'I'm not a journalist, Secretary of State. And I'm here with my constituency party.'

'You may not be a journalist but you've got as many leaks in you as a rusty sieve. It's about time you and I had a word together.'

'Why don't I take you all to find a cup of tea? And a drink, of course. Perhaps you'll join us later, Ken.'

'I do realize it's very embarrassing for you,' Ken Cracken said as Joyce rounded up the party and they left, disappointed to be missing what looked like being an enormously enjoyable row.

'Not half as embarrassing as it's going to be for you, my lad.' I've got him, Ken Cracken thought. Now he's starting to threaten me. He looked away, down the water towards the dome of St Paul's and smiled serenely. Then he said, 'I don't know why you're so worried about that piece in the paper. I mean, it's perfectly true, isn't it?'

'True he's given the go-ahead to the town. Yes.'

'And true you promised to abide by his decision.'

'I know what you want, Ken Cracken.'

'I'm not sure I want anything in particular. After all, I don't live in Rapstone.'

'You may not. But you're thick as a couple of thieves with Christopher Kempenflatt. How much did he contribute to party funds last year?'

'That's ridiculous. All sorts of businessmen contribute to our party funds.'

'Oh, I'm not suggesting you're out for money. Although I'd like to bet you and that toothy little researcher of yours have got a summer fixed up on Kempenflatt's boat round the Greek islands. Just watch he doesn't push you in, that's all. If he doesn't, I might. I know exactly what you're after.'

'I wish you'd let me into the secret.'

'You want me to go back on my word, don't you? You want me to reject the Inspector's finding. You want me to make a decision to save my own back garden. Titmuss, you'll be able to tell them all in the bloody tea-room, is using his job to protect his own interests. How very unlike Ken Cracken, who is as pure as the driven slush.'

'I've no doubt you'll find a very convincing way of putting it. If you want to stop the new town, that is.' Ken was smiling imperturbably at his master's insults.

'Oh, yes? How would you suggest I do it?'

'Start "In view of all we now know about the environment, and having regard to this government's very real commitment to preserve the British countryside . . ." How about something along those lines?'

'Do you want to write the speech for me? Then you'd be quite sure it sounded like a load of lies!'

'I really can't understand why you're taking this attitude.' Ken now assumed an expression of pained innocence, which didn't suit him. 'It seems to be a matter between you and Gregory Boland, the Inspector. If you want him to think again about his report . . .'

'I think I'll leave that sort of monkey business to you.'

'I was going to say, you know as well as I do that the Inspector's as straight as a die. If you or I asked him to do anything he'd fly off in the opposite direction.'

As soon as he had said that, Ken Cracken regretted it, because his Secretary of State looked at him and asked, almost with admiration, 'Is *that* how you managed it?'

CHAPTER TWENTY-FIVE

On the day when the warrant for the execution of Rapstone Valley was leaked in the *Fortress* and while Leslie confronted Ken Cracken on the terrace of the House of Commons, Jenny was at work, as usual, in the garden. It was her best time of the year, full of promise but before the weeds took over, when the first blossom was starting to appear and she hoped it would be dealt with gently and not shaken down by the wind. She took out the sweet peas she had started in the greenhouse and planted them in the earth which had been prepared for them. Then she straightened up with the trowel in her hand and looked about her, noticing the changes, the opening of buds, the length of the shoots, since yesterday. She had a premonition of disaster, as though the whole landscape were about to be blotted out, as must happen at the moment of death. She blinked, told herself not to be ridiculous, and went in to start on the dinner.

When he had finished eating, Leslie pushed his plate away, and, instead of saying, 'Very tasty!' as his father always did, he smiled bitterly and said, 'Well. It's happened.'

She didn't ask him what had happened because she didn't want to know.

'The Inspector's report's come out in favour of Fallowfield Country Town. So far as he's concerned the bulldozers can move in tomorrow.'

Jenny felt her afternoon's vision return. She said, 'And what about as far as you're concerned?'

'I undertook to accept the result of the public inquiry. You'd want me to keep my promise, wouldn't you?' And when he said that, he turned on her with such a look of fury that she wondered what on earth she had done wrong, although she was soon to discover.

'I've got to keep my word, haven't I? Otherwise I'd be just a shifty politician. Not someone you could mention in the same breath as the wonderfully honest Mr Anthony Sidonia.'

'I don't know what you mean,' Jenny said, after a long silence.

'No. You probably don't.'

She didn't answer him, but collected the plates and took them out to the kitchen. Mrs Bigwell was coming the next morning but she washed up slowly and with enormous care, taking as long to do it as she could and trying not to think about what Leslie had said to her. When the glasses were polished and the saucepans scoured and put away, she went into the sitting-room where she found her husband watching himself being interviewed about the result of a by-election. The man smiling and making jokes on the screen and the other Leslie, slumped in an armchair, pale and angry, appeared as different people. She collected a book and went upstairs to bed. If she couldn't avoid an argument she could, at least, put it off for as long as possible.

She was sitting in front of the dressing-table brushing her hair when she heard his footsteps on the stairs. As soon as he had opened the door he said, 'He's got to be got rid of.'

She didn't ask him who or what he was talking about, but she sat still with the brush in her hand, wearing a nightdress and with her face clean of make-up.

'You've got to get rid of him,' he repeated.

'If you mean Tony' – she tried to smile – 'I think he's gone already.'

'He's not gone yet. He's been here. All the time since we've been married. I knew that in Rome. In that restaurant of his you took me to. Sitting between us. So you could compare me with him!'

'Why are you saying all this now? Please don't.' She looked at him, pleading. She was ready, even though he had gone so far, to forget what he had said.

It was her calmness that infuriated him. The way she sat there quietly, with her dark hair shining, dressed in white as though for some sort of sacrifice, forced him to attack her. He had so much information, such a huge weight of evidence which he had carried around for so long that he had to be relieved of it. He had to prove at long last that he was, in every sort of way, a better man than Sidonia, whose shadow had kept him in the cold.

'You're wrong about him. You've got it all wrong.'

He had meant to wait. When a time came, as he knew it would, when she would say, 'Tony wouldn't have done that', he could have presented his unanswerable case and banished this superior, smiling ghost forever. But Jenny never did speak the words he was waiting for, although he imagined that she always thought them.

So it had gone on, during the long period of investigation. Each night he had come home and been friendly, funny in his way, had praised her, appreciated her, even made love to her, and said nothing. But that evening was different. He had been beaten, cheated and forced into a position where he would have to keep his word. Sidonia, he knew she was thinking, wouldn't have found that difficult at all.

'Please,' she begged him again. 'I'm tired.'

He wanted to say, I'm tired also. Tired of your late husband. What he did say was, 'This won't take very long.' And then, as though he were dealing with a matter of politics, he said, 'I'll just run over the main points. His mother, for instance.'

Now she knew it was a nightmare. What on earth had Myra to do with Leslie Titmuss? She said, 'She was a dancer.'

'Don't you believe it. She worked in the wardrobe. Even then she was always pretending to be someone important. All her stories about dancing, the parties she went to, probably her lovers, they all came from another girl. A dancer who died. Do you think your Tony didn't know?'

'You mean Myra made things up?' Her smile was more infuriating to him than any look of shock would have been.

'Most things. Including the husband killed in the war. So far as I can discover she never married anyone.'

'So far' – she was looking at him, amazed – 'as you can discover? What've you been doing?'

'Finding things out,' he told her. 'I made it my business. Don't you think I had a right to?'

'Things about Myra. What on earth does it matter?'

'Not much. Except that I had to tell you. Sidonia comes from a family of liars.'

He had to tell her. Jenny wondered why he should have to tell her anything.

'When it comes to *his* lies, of course, it's difficult to know where to start.'

'I don't want to hear.' She wanted to cover her ears now, shut out his cold, deliberate voice.

'I expect you don't. You've *got* to listen, though. Now. It's only fair.'

'Fair?'

'Fair to me. You've never been that, have you? You're not going!'

She stood and tried to get out of the bedroom. He positioned himself between her and the door.

'How should I start? The affairs with students. He told you he didn't have them, didn't he? That was his way of making you feel special, specially wanted, until you'd passed the exams and got your reward. All lies. Blane told me. At least twice the college nearly got rid of him. Because of the girls who passed through his bed on the way to their exams.'

'Even if that were true' – she didn't believe him – 'what does it matter now?'

'Doesn't it matter? About him and Susan Bramble?'

Relief flooded over her. He was going to tell her nothing she didn't know already. 'Of course I know,' she said. 'Sue was Tony's girlfriend for years.'

'For years.' He looked at her and smiled. 'Years after you were married.'

'I know that's not true.'

'When he went to London to lecture, to go to dinners of the Historical Association and was supposed to be staying in his club. Such a gentlemanly, old-fashioned excuse, wasn't it? And when Sidonia went to do his film in Rome, the one your friend Bramble worked on. He didn't want you to drive down through France with the unit, did he?'

'I flew out to Rome. I was with him.' She hated herself for arguing, for admitting that Tony needed defending.

'You joined them. After he'd slept with your friend in all the hotels during a scenic trip through Europe. And then he lied to you about it. Come to that, they both lied to you.'

'You don't know!' Now she was trying to defend Tony. 'Anyway, how do you know?'

'I had a man' – for the first time he seemed defensive – 'a man to find out.'

'A man to find out things about Tony?' She found it impossible to believe.

'Yes.'

'You mean a detective?'

'Yes.' And then he said, as though this made it better, 'I couldn't rely on him. He's a bit of a fool, quite honestly. In the end you always have to do these things for yourself.'

'You did it for yourself!' She felt herself choking with anger, a feeling entirely new to her. 'You mean, you went round asking questions? Trying to find out that Tony slept with people and where he did it?'

She was attacking him now, but her blows were like those of a child. They didn't move him from his position or hurt him in the least. He smiled at her complacently, knowing, as he always did, that he was in the right. Sooner or later she would have to agree with him.

'I didn't just *try* to find out when Tony slept with people. I succeeded.'

'What for? Whatever *for*?' She was looking at him, not only angry but amazed, as though he were a creature from outer space.

'So you'd be free of him.'

It was a shock, of course, he understood. She'd come to terms with it. Sooner or later.

'Free?'

'All right,' he admitted. 'So we'd both be free. I did it for both of us.'

'You did it for me? I don't understand.'

'I'm sure you will.' Now he sounded like a doctor, promising her that if she took the medicine she'd get better quite soon. 'You will when you think about it. I'll leave you in peace, if you like. We can talk in the morning.'

'In peace? How can I be in peace now?'

'I'll sleep next door. I think you'll find the worst is over.'

He left her then, like a man conscious of a job well done.

Something was over, but what was it? Certainly not the worst, probably the best. Had Tony died at last, killed effectively by Leslie Titmuss? Was her marriage to Leslie over, to be only another memory, ending in a disaster more final than death? Had she a friend she could trust? Jenny stood alone in the middle of the bedroom floor, turned and saw herself in the dressing-table mirror, a pale figure who seemed as far from her as the smiling image on the television screen had been remote from her husband.

She would have liked, above all, to get into bed, to pull the pillow round her ears and try to forget everything Leslie had told her. That would have been to follow her instinct, not to meet trouble half-way but to take refuge from it, in silence, in a refusal to argue, in sleep. But she had to get away from Leslie. She couldn't lie down in his bed, in his house where he might come to her in the night, get in beside her and, failing to understand the enormity of what he had done, attempt to make love to her. She had to go. This need was stronger than her usual passion for avoiding trouble, so she began to dress quickly, to pull on jeans and a sweater, to find her bag, her keys and her money, and then she went down the big staircase, seeing no light under the spare bedroom door. She moved quietly, as though she were leaving a child who, after a great deal of trouble, seems at last to have fallen asleep. She crossed the marble-paved hall and then, still trying her best to make no sound, unbolted and slid open the heavy front door. When she stepped out into the darkness it was as though she were breathing clean and un-polluted air at last.

She took off the handbrake of her car and let it roll down a gravel slope silently before she started the engine. Then she switched on the headlights and saw the trees, the hedges just starting to turn green, the walls of thorn and twigs, all speed past her, lit for a second. At the head of the valley she looked out towards dark fields and woods and remembered that they were now to be obliterated in a tidal wave which her husband had not been able to control. But that, she told herself, was the least of the troubles of that night. The road was empty so she drove fast towards the lights on the motorway and the signs for London.

When she got to the flat she was surprised that it was not yet one in the morning. Leslie's revelations which seemed to have gone on forever must have been over by eleven and she had broken all records on her journey to London. Now she longed to avoid meeting Sue and had no idea how she could put the questions that had to be asked. Her heart sank when she saw the lights on in what had been their sitting-room, and when she rang the bell Sue came down to open the door almost at once. She looked suddenly older and much less pretty than Jenny had pictured her when she thought of the scene to come. Sue was wearing glasses, as she only did when she was reading or watching television on her own, and a dressing-gown which looked as if it were ready for the cleaners.

'Jenny! What is it? You look terrible!'

'Are you alone?'

'Worse luck. Come in. It's wonderful to see you.'

And when she was inside and Sue had closed the door Jenny, who could believe she looked terrible, said, 'Not so wonderful, I'm afraid. Not now.'

'What's happened?'

'Happened? Everything seems to have happened.'

'My poor Jenny. I can imagine. Has Mr Titmuss turned out awful? You'll stay here, won't you? What else can I do to help?'

'I suppose' – and now Jenny realized that she was asking for the last thing she really wanted – 'you can tell me the truth.'

CHAPTER TWENTY-SIX

Kev the Rev. thought an all-night vigil outside the Rapstone Nature Area would be the best way of dealing with the matter. He saw a great crowd of protesters holding up candles and singing together.

'We'd never get hold of enough candles.' Daphne Jones was practical. 'They've even given up selling them in Worsfield supermarkets.'

'They've got those curly, coloured things people buy for dinner parties in the Hartscombe Hostess shop,' Mrs Vee remembered. 'But they'd be terribly expensive.'

'Not much good getting a crowd assembled together at night,' the herbalist said. 'That's not going to cause much inconvenience to traffic.'

'We could get a good few people together,' Mrs Vee thought. 'Our phone's never stopped ringing. But night time wouldn't be much use to television. What are your views, Chairman?' It was an emergency meeting of S.O.V. committee members, a solemn occasion after they had read the news in their copies of the *Fortress*.

What Fred thought was that he was back in his youth again, in the time of protest marches and all-night vigils. As the Reverend Kevin Bulstrode spoke he seemed to hear a more shrill, less elegant version of his father's voice. How many times had Simeon Simcox coughed the night away in draughty churches, or led singers down country lanes to put an end to apartheid or the Bomb – and these things were still obstinately there when the guitars had been put away and the churches emptied. All the same, Fred would have liked to tell them that Fallowfield Country Town would vanish into the mists of legend if only they could exorcize it with candles and protest songs. He said, 'It's up to Leslie Titmuss. He could still stop Fallowfield.'

'Absolutely,' Mrs Vee agreed. 'That's why we need to demonstrate. To show Titmuss we mean business.'

'Of course, he has said he'll stick by the inquiry's decision.' Mrs Wilcox was pessimistic.

'Then it's up to us,' Mrs Vee said cheerfully, 'to persuade him to change his mind.'

Fred remembered his father, in a rare moment of insight, saying that protests and marches might not do much for a cause but they certainly made the people who took part in them feel better. He also wished that Jenny had managed to preserve her loyalty to the group and they could have talked, stood together under the trees, held candles, sung songs or done whatever else came into their minds. These thoughts he immediately recognized as fantasies and did his best to dismiss them.

It hadn't taken Jenny long to learn all she needed, and far more than she wanted, to know from her friend, Sue Bramble. Sue might have been capable of years of silent deception but she couldn't lie when asked a direct question by her friend.

'Oh, damn!' she said. 'I suppose it's true. Would it be pointless to say I'm sorry?'

'Yes,' Jenny told her. 'Quite pointless.'

'You were always special to Tony. Absolutely special,' Sue said after a long and hopeless silence. 'I'm sure it didn't make any difference to his feeling for you.'

'I don't know.' Jenny felt she was in a dream from which there was still, perhaps, some hope of waking up. 'I don't know what difference it made. But I do know' – here she was certain – 'something's changed. Changed forever.'

'It's useless to say I'm sorry.'

'Yes.'

'But I'm truly sorry you had to find out.'

Jenny thought that if it hadn't happened, it wouldn't have been there for her to find out. But that wasn't the point either.

'What're you going to do now?'

'I don't know. I don't know at all.'

'But you can't go back to Leslie?'

'No. I suppose not.'

'Not to a man who sets on detectives.'

The detectives were the worst part about it. It was the thought of detectives, shadowy men in macs, Jenny imagined, lying in wait for her, thumbing through her past and Tony's, which had turned a quarrel into a nightmare.

'You'll stay here tonight, anyway?'

'No.' Jenny looked at her friend. 'No, I don't think I can.'

'Because you can't forgive me?'

'I don't feel I can do anything yet.'

'Then I'll move out somewhere. You can stay here on your own.'

'No. I'll go now, honestly. I need to think.'

'Can't you think here?'

Jenny looked round the flat and thought of all it had meant in their long friendship.

'No,' she said. 'I don't think I can.'

When Jenny left Sue Bramble, she couldn't make up her mind about anything, even where to go next. She thought of going to a hotel, and then decided against turning up without luggage at almost two in the morning. During her time with Leslie she had lost touch with London and there was no friendly front doorbell she felt she could ring. She stayed in the car because it was warm, because its familiar shell protected her and because driving was, after all, some sort of occupation. She travelled at random, taking turnings without thinking, until she found herself by the river. She drove along it and saw Big Ben and the Houses of

Parliament, which made her think of Leslie and then she accelerated, wanting to put him out of her mind.

Then she was in the City, finding herself among tall banks and office buildings, places where her previous life had never taken her. The streets were silent and deserted, as in a town that has been evacuated in time of war, but the area was so strange to her that she was lost immediately and took turnings which brought her back, after a long detour, to the river again, so she was driving in aimless circles. At last she turned northwards, through streets which were still alive with drunks and minicabs waiting outside all-night discos and couples quarrelling, and, somewhere in Kilburn, two gangs of teenagers chasing each other across a wide road. She saw bottles thrown and heard glass breaking. Later it was quiet again, among rows of sleeping houses with cars parked in front of small, trim gardens, decorated with plaster lions and sundials. She turned by a sign to a motorway, not caring particularly where it led her.

Jenny drove in the slow lane and container lorries surged up behind her, flashed their lights angrily and lurched past. After a while she pulled into a service area, parked and sat for a long time before she felt she dared get out of the car.

The café was still open, filled with muzak and the smell of frying. In the passage outside it a few tired men were playing with the Space Invader machines which squeaked and gibbered complainingly. Jenny sat in a corner, among empty tables. In the distance a Sikh family, the men in anoraks and turbans, the women with plastic macs over their saris, the children falling asleep among plates of egg and chips, were resting, on some endless journey. Nearer to her a grey-haired man and a girl who looked very young were talking in low voices and holding hands. Was it a father recovering his runaway daughter or two apparently ill-suited lovers escaping? Jenny knew she wasn't the only one with troubles, a thought which seemed to clear her mind a little.

She thought a lot about her grandmother Paget and the house

in St Leonards where the sea muttered all night and the doors and windows rattled in the wind. With so much of her faith shattered and still needing someone she could trust, the small woman in the floppy shower-hat who plunged into the waves on Boxing Day seemed the only person capable of filling the role. Granny Paget had, like Tony Sidonia, been dead for a long time and the house in St Leonards-on-Sea had been sold, or Jenny might have turned her car southwards. She would have liked, more than anything now, to be battling against the wind with her grandmother along the prom. As she thought of it, she could feel her mind clearing further. She would have told the old lady the whole story. It would have been received, no doubt, without any particular surprise, and over the 'slap-up tea' in the sitting-room afterwards, when the fire was lit and the circulation starting to return to her toes and fingers, she would have got her answer.

But what would the answer have been? She remembered Granny Paget's contempt for lies and 'fairy tales' and the brusque way in which she had dismissed her mother's failure to understand 'the importance of sticking to things'. She could also imagine what her grandmother would have had to say about men who imported detectives into their married lives. Jenny sat for a long time in front of half a cup of cold coffee thinking about these things. When she left the motorway café it was already light. She now drove with some idea, at least, of where she was going.

When she got to the Rapstone Valley there was a mist on the ground from which low hills and clumps of woodland emerged into the pink light of a landscape as in a Chinese painting. As she approached the road past the Nature Area, she heard an eerie sound which might have seemed, to a nervous ear, to be the lamentation of souls in torment. When she turned the corner she saw a surprisingly large crowd of people, some still holding candles which flickered in the daylight, surrounded by vans, cars and television cameras. Their banners and placards, fluttering in the breeze, read SAVE OUR VALLEY, SAY NO TO FALLOWFIELD and LISTEN TO US, TITMUSS. Blocked from going further, she stopped and rolled down her window. A man approached her, carrying pamphlets.

'We haven't all been here all night,' Fred told her. 'But they did a piece about us on the news and it's extraordinary the number who've come. Students from Worsfield, Hartscombe people on their way to work. Almost everyone who lives in the valley. Are you sure you're all right? You look exhausted.'

'I look terrible.' She remembered what Sue Bramble had told her. 'As a matter of fact *I've* been up all night.'

When he had put his head through her car window, Fred had smiled at her and invited her to breakfast. With the window open she realized how hungry she was and how cold. There was no reason why she couldn't stay a little and let more time cushion her from a final decision. She let him direct her into a lay-by and when she was parked he took her to a place where the landlord of the Baptist's Head had brought out urns of tea and coffee, bacon rolls and piles of sandwiches. Now they had moved a little away from the crowd and she was warming her hands on a plastic cup.

'If you were up all night,' he said, 'you should have joined us. You'd've had a marvellous time, singing "We Shall Overcome" with your teeth chattering. Oh, I forgot. You're not allowed to do that sort of thing, are you?'

'I don't know.' She looked down into her coffee cup. 'God knows what I'll be able to do now.'

She had said too much, out of tiredness and loneliness, and a longing to speak to someone who was alive and would listen. Fred felt a sudden and irrational hope.

'Why *now*?' he asked. 'Has something happened?'

'Something, I suppose.'

'With you and Leslie?'

She was too tired to be careful. 'Yes,' she said. 'With me and Leslie. Last night.'

'Is it serious?'

'I don't know. I suppose if anything's serious this is. I'll drink my coffee and go. I don't want to bore you.'

'Of course you won't bore me. Anyway, you can talk to me. People tell me things. I'm a doctor.'

She looked up at him hopefully. He knew she wanted to tell him her story. But no longer as a friend, still less, he was afraid, in spite of all his fantasies, as a potential lover. He had put a professional distance between them. If she confided in him now it would be for medicinal purposes only.

'I might want to tell you, sometime,' she said. 'I suppose.'

'Please do.' Now he thought the best thing he could do for her was to entertain her. 'I've become a bit of an expert on marriage guidance.'

'Marriage guidance?' She repeated his words in wonder.

'Oh, yes. I've discovered it's a most powerful aphrodisiac. I had a patient. I can't tell you who it was but . . .' Like many doctors and lawyers, those to whom confidences are given, Fred found it hard to keep a secret. He started to tell Jenny about Evie and Len Bigwell.

Leslie Titmuss had got up early as usual and found Jenny's car gone and although he went all over the silent house looking, he discovered no note, no message, nothing. He stood for a moment, uncertain, and then he told himself that she would be back. Of course she would. Where else, after all, had she to go? He went through the scene of the night before and saw nothing unreasonable or untrue in what he had told her. He had, he thought, scored a notable victory and freed her from an old deception. Of course she would return and they would be closer to each other because he would now have no rival. This is what he told himself as he waited for his driver. By the time he got into his car and started for London he was convinced that he was right.

On the road past the Nature Area he met the crowd of protesters. Their candles were out and they had stopped singing.

The Hartscombe herbalist thumped the black bonnet of the
Rover as it slowed to get past and there were a few shouts.
Someone called, 'Don't be the valley vandal!' and he gave them a
pale smile and an almost royal wave of the hand. The demonstrators were too polite, or too much in awe of him, to stop
the car, which accelerated past the last banner and a platoon of
Curdles, who were cheering ironically.

He was now travelling too fast to notice the couple drinking
coffee under the shadows of the trees. Had he done so he might
have been perturbed to see his wife with Fred Simcox. For the
first time during that long night Jenny was laughing. By making
her laugh Fred had given her courage for what she knew she
must do next.

CHAPTER TWENTY-SEVEN

INTERVIEWER: Mr Titmuss. You've announced that you're prepared to give planning permission for a new town called Fallowfield to be built near Hartscombe, where you have a home?

LESLIE: Yes. I said I'd leave the decision to the inquiry. That's the democratic way we do things in this country.

INTERVIEWER: It's going to cause a bit of an upheaval for you, isn't it? The town's going to be built all over your back garden.

LESLIE: You might say I'm used to upheavals. We caused a bit of an upheaval when we came to power, didn't we? Anyway, what do you want me to do? Change our free enterprise policies just because they might cause me a bit of personal inconvenience?

INTERVIEWER: Well, no. Of course not. But –

LESLIE: That was the old Socialist way, wasn't it? Preaching one thing and practising the other. Wonderful old clergyman I used to do odd jobs for when I was a boy –

INTERVIEWER [who knows this bit by heart]: Cutting nettles –

LESLIE: Cutting nettles was the easiest part of it! Cutting nettles was a holiday task compared with the other jobs that I had to do. Anyway, he never stopped his sermons about equality and the evils of capitalism. He could afford to do that on the private income he got from shares in the local brewery. Let me tell you this, my lad. Scrape a Socialist and you'll find a member of the privileged elite.

INTERVIEWER: Will you and your wife be moving, perhaps to somewhere more rural?

LESLIE: And you can say what you like about the present government. We're not a collection of hypocrites. We don't vote one way and live the other. No, I don't suppose I'll be moving. My roots are in that part of England. That's where my father was born, and my old mother of course. I expect I'll stick with it and see it dragged into the twenty-first century. There's a lot of wonderful opportunities ahead of us, you know.

INTERVIEWER: Does that go for your wife also?

LESLIE: I think you've had your interview now, haven't you?

At which the Secretary of State stood up, not before the tactful director had switched back to the presenter. Leslie, frowning and dangerous, marched out of the studio ignoring his interviewer's stumbling apology and inquiries from an anxious girl about his waiting car. Once safe in the back of the official Rover and on his way home, he realized his mistake. They had no reason to know of the quarrel and Jenny's disappearance. He had been foolish to get angry, and all he had done was to make an innocent question look damaging. 'I expect, my lad, she'll go where I go. That's what she usually does.' If he'd said that with the well-loved Titmuss chauvinism it would have stopped all rumours. In fact, at the mention of his wife, he had felt a rising panic. Suppose he had been wrong. Suppose Jenny had been foolish enough to refuse the challenge of adjusting herself to the truth about Sidonia. Suppose she had simply run away somewhere to hide from him and the uncomfortable facts he had been forced to tell her. Suppose that Jenny, unfairly and unjustifiably, was lost and gone from him forever, just as Sidonia was lost and gone from her? As he peered into a bleak and lonely future, Leslie felt something which was unusual for him. His hands were sweating and he was afraid.

So, when he reached his gates and saw, at the other end of the avenue of lime trees and in front of the green-grey walls of the house, Jenny's small, shining Fiat, a huge weight of anxiety seemed to be lifted. As had happened so often in his life he had taken a risk and the gamble had paid off. He had refused to compromise or keep silent. He had taken the positive – he would like to have said, the bold and dangerous – action and he had been rewarded. Jenny had come back. No part of her, he was now sure, would have to be shared with the dissolute and deceiving Tony Sidonia.

He dismissed his driver and went into the house. It was very quiet but the doors and windows were open. There was a fresh wind blowing through it as though someone had been trying to air the rooms after a long illness or a death. He called in all the downstairs rooms but got no answer. He went up the stairs. Perhaps she was asleep and hadn't heard him. He opened the bedroom door gently but he needn't have troubled. The room was empty. Then he crossed to the window and looked down on to a patch of lawn sheltered by tall yew hedges. And there she lay on her back, her arms and legs stretched out as though she had just fallen from the sky. He turned quickly and ran down the stairs to find her.

Jenny had slept for a while where she lay on the damp grass, grateful for the silence. She heard him call her name and she sat up blinking. He thought how pale she looked and how exhausted. 'I thought you'd be back,' he said.

'Yes. I came back. There's no point in not forgiving.'

'Forgiving?' He couldn't believe it. 'You don't mean you've forgiven Sidonia?'

'That's not important. I mean forgiving you. I was going to make some tea. Do you want some?'

She got up quickly and left him. He stood still for a while, trying to make sense of what she had said. When he knew that he was angry he followed her.

She was in the kitchen when he said, 'What the hell have you got to forgive me for?'

She had her back turned towards him, filling a kettle. 'What you did to me. I don't suppose you could've thought of anything much worse. I don't want to talk about it any more.'

'Well, I do!' He was sure of himself, of course, and sure he was in the right. 'I suppose you kidded yourself I was all wrong about your late husband. You think I've slandered his blessed memory!'

'No. Not that. I went to see Sue.'

'And I suppose she lied to you?'

'No. I'm afraid she told me the truth.'

'So. What am I supposed to have done wrong?'

'I don't see that there's any point in talking about it.' She put the kettle on the hotplate of the Aga, where it began to spit and rattle. She tried not to hear him shouting, '*I* see the point! I've a right to know what you've got against me!' She felt him grip her wrist to hold her, so she couldn't escape. She thought he might free her if she told him. 'I had a life,' she said. 'It was mine until I met you. I was in love with a man. He might have tricked me. I don't know why he should have but I suppose he did. Anyway, I loved him. He's dead now. So there's nothing to be done about it. But to pay someone money to pry and peer into everything that happened to me! Behind my back . . .'

'Sidonia did things behind your back, remember.'

'Perhaps for love.'

'Why do you think I did it?'

'How can I tell? I don't understand you.'

'Because it was my right, that's why. I always came second.'

'You came afterwards. Did that give you a right to spy on me?'

'Not on you. On him!'

'On someone dead?'

'Not dead to you. That's what I told you. I'm not ashamed of what I did. Why should I be?' He looked at her, as though for reassurance, but she gave him none. Instead she pulled away from him and he let her go.

'All right,' she said. 'I'll have to be ashamed for you.' She found the teapot, warmed it and put two spoonfuls of tea in carefully, as though these small actions deserved her full attention. Then she started, as calmly as she could, to explain. 'I've thought about it all as much as I can –'

'And talked to your friend Sue Bramble, who cheated you?'

His voice was full of contempt and at once Jenny felt as protective of Sue as she had been of Tony. Blazing with unusual anger, she heard her voice, from what seemed a long way off, shouting, 'I think you did something awful. So awful that I still can't believe it. No one had the right to do that to me. No one! But I took a risk when I married you. A deliberate risk. I didn't really know what you'd be like. You've turned out to be like this. It's who you are.' She was quiet again now. 'All right. We'll try and forget this happened. Perhaps we can.'

'You want to forget about Sidonia?'

'About what you've done. If we're going to live together.'

He looked at her for what seemed a long time in silence. Then, 'You want to live with me?' He said it like a challenge.

'I want to stay with whatever we've got left. I don't want to run away.' The kettle was boiling and she made the tea, pouring it out through a strainer. 'It's important to stick to things. Not like my mother. I don't want to be like her.'

'You want to forgive me.'

'Please' – she had never felt so tired, she thought, in all her life – 'there's nothing else to say.'

'Did you go to the Doctor?'

'What?'

'Did you tell Fred Simcox your troubles?'

'Perhaps . . . I started to.'

'Oh, yes.' Leslie looked suddenly triumphant, as though he had found out something else unpleasant. 'And did he tell you to forgive me?'

'No.'

'Just the sort of bloody patronizing thing he would do. Tell him that when you next see him. I don't want to be forgiven.'

'I won't tell him. No one else has got anything to do with it.'

'Not by you. Not by him. Not by anyone. You understand?'

'Perhaps forgiven's the wrong word.' His fury seemed, she thought, to come from suffering and she wanted, now that they were to stay together, to console him.

'What's the right word? Overlook? Make allowances because I don't know any better? Maybe my feelings aren't quite as delicate as yours and your friends'. Oh, Leslie Titmuss, he wears the wrong tie and the wrong suit, but you've got to make excuses. He was tactless enough to tell the truth in a common sort of way. The poor bastard doesn't know any better, so we'll have to forgive him. You think I want to spend the rest of my life being forgiven by you? Do you think I'm going to sit here being *tolerated*?'

'You won't be,' she promised. 'We won't ever talk about it.'

'No,' he said. 'We won't talk about it because we won't be together. We can't be now.'

'Why not?' She was almost too tired to ask him.

'Because I'm not prepared to forgive you for forgiving me. That's why. For God's sake, can't you understand?'

He opened his hand then and, quite deliberately, dropped the cup and saucer he was holding. He moved to the table and sat, apparently calm. Jenny said nothing but fetched a dustpan and brush and swept the pieces up from the stone floor, grieving for the china that was broken.

'There's going to be a new town,' he told her. 'That's decided. You won't like it. Your friend the Doctor's going to hate it. I can't be sure I'll like it much myself. I tried to stop it for you, but in the end I couldn't. Perhaps that's the best that can happen. Things can't stand still, can they? It's no good being in love with the past all your life. That's what we're in power to tell people.'

She emptied the dustpan into the bin and put it away in the cupboard. She no longer wanted to hear about his power.

'So at least it'll be something different. You won't want to live

664

here any more, will you? Not when it's surrounded with super-markets and multi-storey car parks and all the things that you lot wish people didn't want nowadays.'

'And you?' she asked. 'Where'll you want to live?'

'In the future,' he told her. 'After all, I made it happen.'

CHAPTER TWENTY-EIGHT

There followed days of extraordinary stillness. The sun shone and there was almost no wind or cloud to be chased across the sky. The valley was silent and deserted as though preparing itself, in a period of withdrawal, for the onslaught of the bulldozers. Driving between the hedges, Jenny had an unusual sighting of a hare. Knowing what was to happen she found she no longer wanted to look at the landscape that had become a home to her. If everything had to change, it was time for her to go.

'Are you sure it's what you want?' She and Leslie had been sleeping apart and when they met at breakfast they treated each other with the politeness of strangers.

'You haven't left me any choice,' he told her.

'I think I have.' His unfairness had a sort of daring about it which took her breath away.

'Either to be forgiven or forgotten? I'd best be forgotten.'

'I shan't forget you,' she said. 'I promise you that.' He stood up then to leave for the airport. He was on his way to another European meeting, this time in Luxemburg. He stood, tall and pale in his dark clothes, and she wanted, for a moment, to comfort him. But he looked at her in a way that gave her no encouragement. Then he turned from her and left the house.

Alone and because, in spite of all that had happened, it had become such a habit with her, Jenny telephoned Sue Bramble.

'It's Jenny.'

'Jenny! How are you?' Sue sounded nervous and falsely cheerful.

'All right, I suppose. Leslie's gone. It's all over.'

'What's all over?'

'Us.'

'I see.' And then, 'I'm only surprised it lasted so long.'

'That's not the only thing. This place seems to be over as well.'

'Your house?'

'Yes. They're going to build a new town all round it.'

'Oh, of course. I read about that.' Sue sounded as if she couldn't believe they were talking as though they were still friends.

'I'm coming up to London.'

'To the flat?'

'Yes. I've got to live somewhere.'

'Of course you have. I told you I'd move out. I'll go today. Oh, and I'll get it all cleaned up for you . . .'

There was a silence and then Jenny said, 'No need to do that.'

'No need to get it cleaned up?'

'No need for you to go.'

'Oh.'

'I don't really want to be alone. Not for a while. Please stay if you think it'll be all right.'

'What do you mean, if it'll be all right?'

'After that awful business of me finding out.'

'How on earth was that your fault?' Sue was incredulous.

'Well, I suppose none of it would have happened. If I hadn't taken on Leslie Titmuss.' Jenny's voice was very quiet, as though at the start of tears.

'Come up to the flat,' Sue Bramble said. 'I'll do my best to look after you.'

'Congratulations, Ken.' The Minister looked up from his seat in the first-class compartment of the B.A. plane into the smiling face of his Secretary of State. 'You've done very well out of all this, haven't you?'

'You mean out of the new town? I think you've done well, Leslie. Your reputation for selflessness is higher than ever.' Ken Cracken, in his general disappointment at the turn events had taken, allowed himself a touch of irony.

'Oh, I don't mean the new town.' Leslie settled himself down and fastened his seat-belt. 'That's all ancient history. I mean the reshuffle. Your new job, Ken.' He smiled again. 'Your great opportunity.'

'Opportunity?'

'Oh, yes. You're the new generation, after all. The young lad with the future before him. As for me, well, I've thought things over. Perhaps it's time I made a nuisance of myself on the back benches. Then I can have a real go at you lot in the Government whenever I think you deserve it.'

'You're going to retire?' Overcome with amazement and hope Ken Cracken could do little more than repeat his leader's words.

'I made a mistake, it seems. I'd better be moving on, before I make any more.' If what he said was a confession of failure, Leslie Titmuss's smile showed no sign of it. What was the mistake? his number two wondered. Did he know he'd been outmanoeuvred over Fallowfield? All such speculation was drowned in the rising tide of his ambition.

'I suppose that *will* mean a reshuffle.' It was all going exactly as Ken had planned, with the ever-present help of his political adviser. Titmuss had been defeated over the country town and was retiring hurt, leaving a post for which his Minister of State was the obvious successor.

'I hope you'll enjoy your new job, Ken.'

'Thank you. I'm sure I will.'

'I had a word about you. In the appropriate quarter.'

'That was very generous of you.'

'I thought so. I pointed out your special talents. You do have special talents, don't you, Ken?'

'Well. I'm not sure which ones you're talking about.' Ken Cracken did his best to sound modest.

'Strategic, tactical talents. "Young Cracken," I said, "is a genius at guerrilla warfare. He lives and dreams ambushes and surprise-attacks. In his briefcase he carries a Para lieutenant's swagger-stick. He'll do well somewhere where the fighting is certain to go on forever." So you've got it, Kenneth.'

'Minister of Defence?' Ken was puzzled.

'Something that'll suit you much better than that. This is really active service. You're going to be number two at the Northern Ireland Office. Now, what time do we get back tomorrow? I've got an extremely important dinner date.'

'Oh, yes?' Ken Cracken spoke in the tones of a man who has just seen himself bound for oblivion. 'Who with? Someone beautiful?'

'Someone extremely beautiful.' Leslie got out his briefing papers and prepared to conceal his feelings for the rest of the journey. 'My mother!'

'I know. I promised you'd never have to move from here.'

'You did, Leslie. You promised me faithfully.'

'And I'm going to keep my promise to you, Mother.' Leslie Titmuss was being cooked dinner by Elsie in 'The Spruces' in what must have been one of the most dust-free environments in the world. Even the glazed crust of the steak and kidney pie looked as though it had been done over with Mansion polish. He paused to eat, deciding on how to put the matter in the most politically advantageous fashion. 'There is this business,' he said carefully, 'about the new country town.'

'Can't that be stopped?'

'I don't see how it can. I gave my word, you see.'

'You gave your word to me as well, Leslie,' Elsie Titmuss said with one of her sweetest smiles, and scored a hit.

'Of course, these things take years to build. Ten years at least.' Leslie Titmuss came back at her with an even more powerful smile.

'That's all right then. This place will see me out.'

'It might see me out too. I'm going to sell the Manor. No good rattling about that old mausoleum now, is it?'

'But Leslie. It was to be your home.'

'Not my sort of home, really. The sort of place where the old-school farts hang their tweed hats in the hall and sit for hours reading *Country Life* in the lavatories. That's never been my style at all. You know that, Mother.'

There was silence as they ate. Then Elsie said, 'Are you sure you have to be on your own, Leslie?'

'Yes, Mother. Quite sure.'

'That Jenny seemed such a nice girl.'

Leslie didn't answer.

'Not a ban-the-bomber, was she?'

'No, Mother. She wasn't one of those.'

'I suppose you're not going to tell me what was wrong then, exactly.'

'What was wrong?' He looked at his mother very seriously. 'She couldn't make a steak and kidney to touch yours, Mother.'

'Would you have another helping now, with the crust on it?'

'It's very more-ish.' She helped him to another slice of pie and he took a potato with butter and parsley. In the brightly shining room the clock on the mantelpiece ticked like a bomb and the china ornaments gleamed behind the glass door of the display cabinet. Elsie gave herself a minute second helping just, as she said, to keep her son company. She wanted to console him, even if he didn't want to be consoled. 'There wasn't somebody else, was there?'

'I suppose you could say that.'

'Another man?' She breathed in sharply.

Leslie's mouth was full so he nodded and then looked down at his plate.

'She didn't seem at all that sort of girl to me,' his mother told him. 'Appearances are deceptive.'

'Yes. I'll tell you what we'll do. If they do build this new town while we're both around, Mother . . .'

670

'*You* will be, Leslie. You surely will be.'

'And you, most probably. We'll make them put in a new house, just where this one is. A new "Spruces". You'd like that, wouldn't you? And it'll be in the middle of town, you see. Handy for the shops.'

Elsie thought about it and then repeated, 'This'll see me out, Leslie.'

'Well, we'll have to see. There's a long time to go yet.'

'Perhaps you could live in it, Leslie. If you have to sell the Manor. I'd like to think of you settled.'

'Live in it? In Fallowfield Country Town?' There was something about the idea that seemed to amuse him. 'Well, yes. Perhaps I could.'

'I'm sorry,' Elsie said after another silence. 'About that other man.'

'Don't worry,' he told her. 'I think I've seen him off. I shan't be lonely. Not so long as I can keep working. Oh, and have dinner with you here, when I feel like home-cooking.'

'I don't know how Jenny could do that.' Elsie Titmuss pursed her lips in wonder and outrage. 'Not when she had you, Leslie.' Then she looked again at her son's plate and saw that he was down to his last mouthful. She lifted the spoon over the pie dish hopefully. 'Won't you take pity on this last little bit?'

'No, thank you very much. I couldn't fit it.' Leslie pushed his now empty plate away from him and said, as his father had before him, 'That was very tasty, Mother. Very tasty indeed.'

And Ever Afterwards

Then wilt thou not be loth
To leave this Paradise, but shalt possess
A Paradise within thee, happier far.

Paradise Lost
John Milton

CHAPTER TWENTY-NINE

Just over a decade later, the world had got considerably warmer. The sea rose, sloshing over many Pacific islands and flooding expensive houses on the coast of Australia. Ice-caps in the north began to thaw, leaving polar bears stranded, alone and hungry, on floating rafts of diminishing ice. The increasing temperature produced plagues of locusts and the ladybirds became intolerable. The biological clocks of many tortoises were put considerably out of time and the world's ornithologists sought in vain for Ketland's warbler or the burrowing owl.

Defeated on local issues, the Vees turned their attention to wider matters and the remnants of S.O.V. still met in their house for buffet suppers and talks on the ending of the world. One speaker broke the news to them that the ice was being melted not, as was popularly supposed, by the fumes of ever-increasing traffic; the damage was done, so he said, by myriads of termites, set at large by the destruction of the rain forests, breaking wind. 'Is this the way the world ends?' Fred asked with attempted solemnity. 'Not with a bang but a termite's fart?'

'Honestly, Dr Fred,' Mrs Vee rebuked him. 'Can't you ever take the universe seriously?'

Despite Fred's scepticism, the global changes affected Harts-combe. The punts tethered at the riverside rose and were known, in certain weathers, to float into the road. In what was left of the countryside, the harvest mouse was an exotic rarity, the nightingales had been decimated and the adonis blue butterfly was totally extinct. And, as inevitably as the Pacific Ocean advanced to kill the crops and displace the islanders, Fallowfield Country Town flooded the Rapstone Valley.

The change had started slowly. It was noticed that the narrow lanes became full of traffic. Then cars often had to back up to allow the passage of heavy lorries and building machinery. Then bulldozers came to tear up the hedges and flatten the fields for urban construction. These beginnings were greeted by a final flurry of S.O.V. demonstrations from which the Curdles were notably absent, for as the tide of Fallowfield advanced this family was washed to a new height of prosperity.

What had happened was this. With his new-found authority as Chairman and Managing Director of the family business, Len Bigwell had consulted Jackson Cantellow on the question of the lease of the rabbit hacienda from one of the farmers who was about to turn his arable land into car parks and supermarkets and high-priced housing estates. When he saw the lease, Jackson Cantellow pursed his lips and couldn't resist humming a triumphant bar or two of Haydn's *Creation*. What Dot Curdle seemed to have obtained, more by luck than legal cunning, from a farmer whose mind was clearly on other matters, was a tenancy protected by the Agricultural Holdings Act. 'And they can't shift you,' Jackson Cantellow rumbled in his most resonant bass. 'Except with untold gold.' So that was how the Curdles became converted to the 'country town conception' and could afford to buy the freehold of Rapstone Manor when the Right Honourable Leslie Titmuss put it on the market.

So the house remained unaltered, on the very outskirts of the town. The garden was given over to a high-density development of rabbit hutches, mainly containing angoras. The food-producing animals were left to the many subsidiary farms and freezer-packing facilities the Curdles had acquired in various other parts of Southern England. From their headquarters in the Manor the family branched out into other businesses, including double-glazing, patio doors, loft conversions and the covering of ceilings with whirling patterns of raised plaster – a form of folk art which had become enormously popular with the inhabitants of Fallowfield Country Town. The Bigwells had now produced three healthy children and Len, who had been elected to the town council in the Conservative interest, would become one of Fallowfield's early mayors. Grandmother Dot had retired from business and sat for much of the day dozing in the conservatory and dreaming of past lovers. Billy, her youngest child, having grown out of his period of juvenile delinquency, now ran the Cordon Bleu Lapin Frozen Dinners export department. He had fallen wonderfully in love with Sharon Wellings, the daughter of a Fallowfield dentist, who was still in her last year at school. They had met at an old-time Barry Manilow concert in the Fallowfield Arts and Leisure Centre and they carried on their affair secretly, it having been expressly forbidden by Mr and Mrs Wellings who disapproved of Billy Curdle as an older man with a criminal record and as such unsuitable company for young Sharon.

Rapstone Manor remained unchanged and isolated amid the ocean of new building, and so did the Rapstone Nature Area which had been privatized and become the property of Greener Than Green Ltd (Chairman and Managing Director Sir Christopher Kempenflatt), a concern which owned a number of other nature areas as well as maximum security prisons, mental hospitals and remand centres. Hector Bolitho Jones, ten years older and ten years more lonely, was still in charge and ran his kingdom in accordance with the strict rules laid down by Greener Than Green Ltd. The new regime was entirely to his taste as it was designed to make public access to the area brief and patrons were encouraged to spend as much time as possible in the café, the hall of animal waxworks and the gift shop at the area gates. Children, of course, were allowed to enter the area, but only at specified times, in supervised parties and if they followed the clearly marked Instructional Nature Trails. Their grandparents could also visit at certain times, but they were confined to Senior

Citizen Rambles. Young people were allowed in only in accredited groups and had to show their identity cards at the turnstile in accordance with recent legislation designed to stamp out Nature Area hooliganism. No one of any age was permitted to stray from the designated paths, sit or lie down, carve their initials on trees, sing, dance, picnic, drink alcohol, smoke or play any sort of musical instrument. As he looked over his domain at night, under a sky turned orange by the lights of Fallowfield, Hector Bolitho Jones was profoundly grateful that in his small world plants and animals reigned supreme. Men, women and children were second-class citizens.

Walking home one evening from having locked the turnstile, Hector saw an unwelcome scrap of litter on one of the trails. He stooped and felt sickened by the sight of a small packet which had once contained what his ex-wife Daphne, in a way which had distressed him, had called 'rubber johnnies', but which he preferred to give their proper medical title. The appearance of a condom here revolted him as a piece of obscene graffiti on a cathedral column might have outraged a Bishop. He went indoors to burn the offending object and in doing so forgot to repair a small gap in the fencing down by the stream, a job he had postponed once before. From that time he didn't merely dislike the human beings who polluted his Nature Area, he hated them passionately.

It cannot be said that Fallowfield Country Town, when it was complete, was quite the bright and shining monument to the success of Titmuss's England that its developers had promised. To pay back the loans raised from Jumbo Plumstead and other bankers, Kempenflatts charged the Fallowfield shopkeepers heavily. Those who had opened in high hopes in the glistening, mock-Georgian shopping malls, setting out their health foods and designer knitwear, their Country Craft table mats and their large selections of sentimental or suggestive greetings cards, found their sales inadequate to meet the soaring rents and soon went bankrupt. The big chain stores moved in. But they also found that the amounts they were required to contribute to Jumbo's interest charges made their businesses unprofitable. Many shops closed and remained empty. Some pedestrian precincts became deserted, being used as public urinals by those made pugnacious or nauseated by Fortissimo lager.

In the most expensive areas of the country town the roads had been privatized and the householders who lived behind locked gates had men from security firms always on the beat. 'The Spruces' didn't occupy such an area. The old house had stood for a long time at the end of a row of shops in Babcock-Syme Boulevard and, while she lived, Elsie Titmuss had worked doubly hard to keep it clear of dust from the construction work going on around it. Elsie died before the house was finally pulled down to be rebuilt according to the architects' specification for that part of Fallowfield.

During the period of rebuilding, Leslie Titmuss travelled a good deal, going to America, Canada and Australia, partly to promote his book of memoirs which he had called, summing up his childhood labours and what he still felt to be the daring and radical nature of his political career, *Grasping the Nettle.* He never saw Jenny and although his solicitors had offered her a large settlement she refused it. When he moved into the newly built 'Spruces', he was photographed crossing the threshold with a smile which might have been ironical.

Jenny and Sue Bramble shared the flat again and lived together almost as they had in the days before Leslie Titmuss sent his gift of the orchid. Jenny, wishing to find a reason for forgiving her friend, came to the conclusion that she wouldn't have known the truth if it hadn't been for Leslie's unacceptable way of finding it out, and facts unearthed in that manner were far better buried again. For a while Sue's guilt made her treat Jenny with exaggerated politeness and consideration, as though she were suffering from a fatal disease. At last Jenny told her to come off it and be in a bad mood if she felt like it, and their lives returned to normal. Sue went on working for Mark Vanberry at the art gallery and Mark, through the good offices of the lover of one of his ex-wives, found Jenny a job as a picture researcher. She advised publishers and magazines on illustrations and she found a good deal of satisfaction in tracking down paintings and drawings with some meaning to them, leaving the Abstract painters to Sue, who almost never rested her eyes on their work.

For Jenny, the past seemed to have vanished. Remembering Tony, her first husband, had for long been her main occupation. Now he had left her because she no longer knew quite what to think of him. Her time with Leslie seemed insubstantial also, a dream which began with their first dinner and ended when he awoke her with the truth about Tony. So, in her new existence, she spent very little time remembering things.

When Sue announced she was going to marry Mark Vanberry, Jenny was, at first, appalled. 'How can you? He'll get you muddled up with all those girlfriends and the wives who're always hitting him and making scenes and, honestly, Mark of all people! He's just got no talent for marriage.'

'Oh, dear, do you really think so?' Sue looked as though she might be dissuaded. 'I used to say exactly the same sort of thing about your Mr Titmuss.'

'Well, yes,' Jenny said. 'Exactly!' However, she knew that Sue wouldn't take her advice and, in point of fact, it didn't turn out badly at all. Sue was pregnant and Mark, as is the way with fathers in their fifties, became besotted with the baby. During the next four years she presented him with two other children, of whom he was also intensely proud. Mark began to look younger and less haunted. He was determined to stay alive in order to see as much of them as possible. He also put himself on an unusual diet of marital fidelity.

So the Vanberrys became Jenny's family. She stayed in their house and looked after the children when they went out or at times when Mark took Sue to America in search of more

Abstract art. Jenny remembered the children's birthdays, worried when they were ill and took them on expeditions into what was left of the countryside. On such trips she never went near the Rapstone Valley and she had no idea what Fallowfield Country Town looked like.

It would be wrong to say that Jenny was unhappy but, although she had one or two discreet affairs, she never fell in love again. Like Fred Simcox she had loved two people in her life, and that was as much as she could manage.

Fred thought that he had found a great value in Fallowfield; it reconciled him to death.

A benevolent providence, he thought, or told himself he would have thought if he had believed in such a thing, mercifully allowed everything to deteriorate during one man's lifetime. The summers got worse, the music noisier and more senseless, the buildings uglier, the roads more congested, the trains slower and dirtier, governments sillier and the news more depressing. Good things, glow-worms, barn owls, farmland, fish shops and girls who enjoyed being called beautiful, were slowly withdrawn. The process was no doubt a merciful one because, when he came to the end of his allotted span in a world so remote from the one he had grown up in, the average citizen was quite glad to go.

When he thought like this Fred realized what had happened. Titmuss and his colleagues had done what he would never have believed possible. They had made him a conservative.

He thought about this for a while and then told himself to stop indulging in such thoughts. Fallowfield Country Town was there and the Rapstone Valley was gone forever. People in Fallowfield would continue to fall in love, give birth, play with their children, lie in bed together on Sunday mornings, make up quarrels, come home singing from the pubs and enjoy occasional happiness. Sometimes, seeing its familiar glow in the sky as they crawled home along the eight-lane motorway, they would think of Fallowfield as home and perhaps find it beautiful. He told himself all this, but was not entirely convinced.

'Just as well they make these changes or no one would ever want to die.' Fred was explaining his ideas to his old friend Agnes, who had cooked him dinner in her flat in London. It was a pleasantly untidy room which smelt of her perpetual French cigarettes. It was the only place Fred knew that smelled as France did when he was young, Calais now being as odourless as Fallowfield Country Town. In this room Agnes lived, cooked, wrote letters, and often, after going out to prepare a directors' lunch or a Hampstead dinner party, stretched herself out on the hearthrug and fell asleep. 'My God,' she said, 'you really are cheerful tonight.'

'Although Leslie Titmuss lives bang in the middle of the Country Town, he seems to enjoy it. He doesn't give any sign of wanting to die.'

'And Mrs Titmuss?'

'Nothing more's been seen of her. Nothing.'

'You still think about her?'

'Not as much as I think about you,' Fred assured Agnes. 'I mean, I have so much more to think about when it comes to us. But sometimes she does cross my mind. Mainly, I suppose, because of the mystery.'

'What mystery?'

'Why she ever took up with Leslie. And why she left him. I don't know how he did it, but he had a few years of her life.'

'Does that make you jealous?'

'It gives him more of her to think about. That is, if he ever thinks about her at all.' He had no idea of what went on in the mind of the old back-bench M.P. who had once again become his patient. But then Fred had never entirely understood Leslie Titmuss. Even in Leslie's comparatively harmless old age the Doctor could only look on the politician as some sort of natural disaster, at which people would always shake their heads and wonder.

*

Of course Leslie Titmuss thought about Jenny.

When he told Ken Cracken, long before, on an aeroplane bound for Luxemburg, that he had been mistaken, he didn't only mean that he'd been mistaken about Fallowfield Country Town, although it was his defeat in that particular battle which had made him decide that the time had come for him to fire at his colleagues from the back benches. He meant that he had been, more deeply and importantly, mistaken about Jenny. He had thought that, bound together by the accident of their love, he had found an ally, a supporter, someone he could rely on for loyalty; but she had done the one thing which, if she had thought about it for a moment, she must have known would make their lives together impossible.

He was prepared for almost any other reaction to his fair and necessary destruction of the Sidonia legend. He expected her to be hurt, for a while. He thought she might be angry, again for a little while. She might have been desolated at the destruction of her past, until their lives together, starting again on a realistic basis, more than made up for anything she might have lost. But when she turned on him and forgave him, as though all the damage had been done by him and not Sidonia, he realized that she was, like Christopher Kempenflatt and his friends who, in their arrogance, had pushed him into the river, one of the enemy. As such she could never be trusted again.

But of course he thought about her and memories of her, seductive and appealing as she had been, flitted across his mind. He was defended from them, as an anchorite might be by his vows of chastity, by his perfect certainty that he had been in the right. And perhaps, although he had resented Ken Cracken teaching him the lesson, he had been right about Fallowfield when he made his speech, so long ago, to the building trade. No doubt it was just that the green welly brigade, the complacent and comfortable country-dwellers, should be defeated. He had always believed in the future, provided it was built on competition, free enterprise and consumer choice, and if the consumers chose Fallowfield, who was he to set himself up as a superior being with purer tastes than all those good people queuing at the supermarket check-outs who, at regular intervals, obliged him by voting Titmuss? So he often left his elderly housekeeper at home and did the shopping himself, pushing his wire wheelbarrow and comparing the prices carefully before he committed himself to an investment in frozen vegetables or washing powder. He was widely recognized and people would stop and ask him his views about all the problems that beset the world. He was never at a loss for an answer.

His health remained excellent. This fact didn't stop him calling in Fred from time to time, mainly for the purposes of argument. He also enjoyed making the Doctor drive out to the end of Babcock-Syme Boulevard and would always apologize for the pain it must cause a nicely brought up member of a wealthy Socialist family to see how the other half lives. Leslie Titmuss became white-haired and seemed, as the years passed, to have found a way of life that suited him. His blood pressure remained constant, although his teeth gradually deserted him. During his years without a wife he managed to recover his son.

Nick wrote soon after his father's resignation from the Cabinet. It seemed that he felt he could make contact again once Leslie was free of the embarrassment of power and there was no danger of him helping the librarian in his career. Leslie went to visit his son and Nick came to stay in 'The Spruces' for part of his holidays. On one such visit he brought a solid girl in spectacles called Margaret, a devout Christian whom Leslie enjoyed shocking by recommending that village churches should be leased out as bingo halls and leisure areas when not needed for divine service. Nick married Margaret and she gave birth to two extremely aggressive small boys in whom Leslie found traces of the characteristics of his distant self, in the years before he started cutting down nettles. Fred, to whom these infants were shown proudly when he visited, felt his worst fears confirmed.

There would be a long line of Titmusses, stretching out to the crack of doom.

Billy Curdle and Sharon Wellings found it difficult to know exactly where to go. Her home was forbidden to him and although Dot Curdle welcomed all lovers enthusiastically at the Manor, Sharon dreaded the old woman's eagerness to discuss the details of each encounter. She also disliked being taken to the Mine Host Motel on the big roundabout outside Fallowfield, the place of assignation for many of Billy's former girlfriends. Sharon, except at the high point of love-making, embarrassed easily and one of the girls who operated the computer at the motel reception desk had been in the form above her.

'Where do you want to go then?' Billy asked her one night, anxious to get the matter settled.

'I don't know really. Couldn't we drive out to the country?'

'The country's here!' Billy told her in what he thought to be a moment of inspiration. 'No need to drive out. I'll show you where I used to go when I was a kid and watch the old badgers.' He didn't tell her that he used to capture them with terrier dogs and organize badger fights on the rabbit hacienda, as he had put that part of his life far behind him. So Sharon finished up her lager and lime and they walked together, past the huge computer sales and insurance company offices, down the shopping malls and through a middle-range housing estate to the road which ran round the Nature Area. They found a gap in the fence beside the stream where, it was rumoured, kingfishers used to nest.

Avoiding the official Nature Trails and Senior Citizen Rambles, they climbed in the moonlight across the chalk grassland which was still, in that carefully preserved environment, the home of gentians, several varieties of orchid and many unusual snails. They moved, hand in hand, up towards the beech wood which was murmuring in a small wind. Billy led his girlfriend to the place where he remembered the badger setts used to be, but soon their interest in wildlife dwindled.

They lay on a soft bed of decaying leaves and began to undress each other.

On that night Hector Bolitho Jones had also been out to look for the remaining badgers, but these retiring animals stayed aloof. He was armed, as always, with his father's old shot-gun. He had never used this weapon; he hadn't troubled to renew the shot-gun certificate when his father died, and not even his wife had known of its existence. Now he walked quietly, carrying it in the crook of his arm, a man living in a small prison of countryside, who had almost forgotten his wife and daughter and who certainly had no friends. His eyes shone out over his beard in alarm, as though he feared that the surrounding buildings would close in on him.

Walking through the woods he heard a sudden sobbing cry which he knew came from no bird or small animal. It was a sound he remembered his wife had made, in their distant days of love-making. Standing still and looking through the trees, he saw something which filled him with cold rage and grim determination. He slid in two of the cartridges he carried, raised the shot-gun and he had, in his father's sights, two gently moving white bodies who were breaking all the rules and regulations of the Nature Area.

What became known as the Fallowfield Double Murder was never solved. The Warden gave the police every assistance but they never found where the shot-gun was buried. Most of the newspapers blamed local lager louts, of unknown identity, on the rampage. Others thought it the work of a sex murderer who might strike again. It was generally agreed that the Nature Area had become a health hazard and a place far too open to crime. Sir Christopher Kempenflatt, acting on behalf of his company Greener Than Green Ltd, received planning permission to turn it into a Space Age theme park. Hector Bolitho Jones still presides over it with his beard trimmed and wearing moon boots and a suit of silvery clothing. No one has been caught making love there again.

FOR THE BEST IN PAPERBACKS, LOOK FOR THE 🐧

In every corner of the world, on every subject under the sun, Penguin represents quality and variety – the very best in publishing today.

For complete information about books available from Penguin – including Puffins, Penguin Classics and Arkana – and how to order them, write to us at the appropriate address below. Please note that for copyright reasons the selection of books varies from country to country.

In the United Kingdom: Please write to *Dept JC, Penguin Books Ltd, FREEPOST, West Drayton, Middlesex, UB7 0BR.*

If you have any difficulty in obtaining a title, please send your order with the correct money, plus ten per cent for postage and packaging, to *PO Box No 11, West Drayton, Middlesex*

In the United States: Please write to *Dept BA, Penguin, 299 Murray Hill Parkway, East Rutherford, New Jersey 07073*

In Canada: Please write to *Penguin Books Canada Ltd, 2801 John Street, Markham, Ontario L3R 1B4*

In Australia: Please write to the *Marketing Department, Penguin Books Australia Ltd, P.O. Box 257, Ringwood, Victoria 3134*

In New Zealand: Please write to the *Marketing Department, Penguin Books (NZ) Ltd, Private Bag, Takapuna, Auckland 9*

In India: Please write to *Penguin Overseas Ltd, 706 Eros Apartments, 56 Nehru Place, New Delhi, 110019*

In the Netherlands: Please write to *Penguin Books Netherlands B.V., Postbus 3507, NL–1001 AH, Amsterdam*

In West Germany: Please write to *Penguin Books Ltd, Friedrichstrasse 10–12, D–6000 Frankfurt/Main 1*

In Spain: Please write to *Alhambra Longman S.A., Fernandez de la Hoz 9, E–28010 Madrid*

In Italy: Please write to *Penguin Italia s.r.l., Via Como 4, I-20096 Pioltello (Milano)*

In France: Please write to *Penguin France S.A., 17 rue Lejeune, F-31000 Toulouse*

In Japan: Please write to *Longman Penguin Japan Co Ltd, Yamaguchi Building, 2–12–9 Kanda Jimbocho, Chiyoda-Ku, Tokyo 101*

BY THE SAME AUTHOR

The Rumpole Books

'One of the great comic creations of modern times' – Christopher Matthew in the *Evening Standard*

Rumpole of the Bailey
The Trials of Rumpole
Rumpole's Return
Rumpole for the Defence
Rumpole and the Golden Thread

Rumpole's Last Case
Rumpole and the Age of Miracles
Rumpole à la Carte
The First Rumpole Omnibus
The Second Rumpole Omnibus

Plays

A Voyage Round My Father and Other Plays
Edwin and Other Plays

Interviews

In Character
Character Parts

Autobiography

Clinging to the Wreckage

Fiction

The Narrowing Stream
'Energy, wit and sheer professionalism' – *Guardian*

Summer's Lease
'Amusing, entertaining ... the writing is smooth, the dialogue splendid and it's a cracking good read' – *Sunday Express*

Charade
'Wonderful comedy ... an almost Firbankian melancholy ... John Mortimer's hero is helplessly English' – *Punch*

and

Like Men Betrayed